FINAL SECURITY

RYAN JONES

7/20/12

To the Lovely Misty Jordan,
Thank you so much for your
friendship, humor, spiritual
insights, and your support
of my writing. I hope you
enjoy FINAL SECURITY!

Ryan Jones

FINAL SECURITY

Firedance Enterprises
PO Box 6021
St. Louis, MO 63006-6021

ISBN 978-0-615-61256-0

Also by Ryan Jones:

DATASHARK
A novel of Hackers, Cyberwarfare, and the National Security Agency ISBN 1-931190-52-6

SPECTERS
A novel of UFOs, the CIA and the Aurora spyplane
ISBN 978-0-615-26198-0

DATASHARK and SPECTERS can be ordered from any bookstore, Amazon.com, or by visiting:

www.ryanjones.biz

ACKNOWLEDGEMENTS

To my beloved wife Carol; without you there would never have been a first book, much less my third. You are truly God's gift to me. Thank you for being my partner, my lover, and my friend.

To my father, Russell Jones, for your unflagging encouragement, your insightful critiques, and for always letting me know you were proud of me.

To my dear friend Helen Carter, my editor, publicist, and "ideal reader" for so many years. We are a great team!

To the Chesterfield Writer's Group for slogging through each and every chapter of this tome in manuscript form and making it *so* much better by your comments and suggestions. What a help you have been to me!

To authors Joseph Farrell and Nick Cook, whose books *Reich of the Black Sun* and *The Hunt for Zero Point* served as the primary nonfiction inspirations for this novel. Thank you both for your tireless research!

Thanks to graphic artists Knoll Gilbert for yet another fabulous cover design, Ted Bastien for the Nazi Bell icon used as a section header throughout the book, and Carlo Kopp for the EMP weapon illustration used in chapter 26. Your talents are greatly appreciated.

Many thanks to Lee Clinton for the speaking opportunities at the Ozark UFO Convention. Would that everyone were as kind as the people I've met at your conference.

To Vince White, my battle buddy in the fight for disclosure—would that your body was as sound and sharp as your mind. Don't give up, my friend!

And to the many people who let me use their real names for fictional characters in Final Security, I hope you enjoy what I've done with your namesakes and that your characters survive! No promises!

Author's note: while several historical figures are used as characters in Final Security, this book remains a work of fiction and their activities herein are wholly fictional as well.

CAST OF CHARACTERS

THE BELL: A secret German technology project during WWII

PRINCE BERNHARD: Prince of the Netherlands, founder of a cabal of ultra-rich power brokers called The Group

LLOYD CAMERON: President of the United States

GAVIN CARTER: CIA talent scout and recruiter of Angela Conrad

WENDY CHO: FBI agent, reports to Perry Pugliano

ANGELA CONRAD: Rogue CIA agent and freelance spy

IAN COSGROVE: Former SAS commando and associate of Conrad

SIMON CRANE: The Executor, leader of an organization more powerful than the President of the United States

KURT DEBUS: Senior engineer on the Bell, and later a NASA official

MEIR EITAN: *Chargé d'Affaires* at the Israeli Consulate in San Francisco and a covert member of the Mossad

WILLIAM FITZMAURICE: Director of the FBI

NANOVEX: A nanotechnology firm in San Jose, California

JACOB FLEISCHER: Fellow damage control lawyer Mike Manning befriends in San Francisco

MEGHAN GALLAGHER: Former IRA terrorist and associate of Conrad

MONICA GELDMAN: An alias of Angela Conrad

WALTHER GERLACH: Nobel laureate, senior engineer on the Bell

SETH GRAVES: Defense Advanced Projects Agency, or DARPA, representative at Nanovex for the US government

THE GROUP: A cabal of ultra-rich power brokers

RAFI HAREL: Mossad Chief of Station in Washington, D.C.

SCOTT HENDRIX: CIA Station Chief for San Francisco

HANS KAMMLER: German Major General in charge of all WWII secret Nazi research

VICTOR KAMMLER: Hans Kammler's son

DIETER KINBERG: Former German commando and associate of Conrad

YURI KONALEV: Angela Conrad's Russian ex-KGB henchman

DOUG LYMAN: CEO of Nanovex

MIKE MANNING: Damage control lawyer for Norquist-Feldman law firm

AMANDA MANNING: Wife of Mike Manning

DEREK MEDINA: County coroner for San Jose

REESE MILLER: Security chief of Nanovex, reports to Douglas Lyman

ARI NESHER: Angela Conrad's Israeli ex-Mossad henchman

PERRY PUGLIANO: FBI Special Agent in Charge (SAC) for San Francisco

RASHID BEN-JABIR: Saudi "playboy prince," nephew of Saudi Intelligence Chief

LINN SHAOZANG: Former Chinese intelligence operative and associate of Conrad

JAKOB SPORRENBERG: German Brigadier General in charge of the Nazi Bell project during WWII

VASILY ORLOV: Russian intelligence agent, associate of Angela Conrad

JEFF WOOD: Nanotechnology project leader at Nanovex

PROLOGUE

APRIL 28, 1945 – PILSEN, CZECHOSLOVAKIA

The German scientists huddled together in the back of the cargo truck. With only a canvas cover over the truck bed, the ride was numbingly cold, but every one of the scientists was happy to be on board. The Third Reich was nearing complete military collapse, with both the Russians and American troops driving deep into Germany to cut out its Nazi heart.

Much to the relief of the scientists, trucks showed up that morning to carry them to the American front lines. None of them wished to sample the mercies of Josef Stalin and his Red Army. As scientists, they had been shielded from the horrors of the war. But they doubted the Russians would differentiate between SS soldiers and scientists on an SS-controlled project once they arrived.

They also knew both the Americans and the Russians would gladly kill to gain possession of their project's technology. Many of the scientists had previously been assigned to Germany's atomic bomb program. But their new program had an even higher war priority rating than the atom bomb. After their first accomplishments, there had been hopes of their technology turning the tide of war. But as the enemy armies tightened their stranglehold on the Fatherland, the SS began to look at their project more as a bargaining chip to buy favor with the Americans than as a tool for national salvation.

The importance of their program was further emphasized by the direct involvement of SS General Walter Spoerrenberg. The General regularly made rounds among the scientists, calming their fears about the advancing enemies and assuring them that they and their families would be safely spirited to the American lines long before the Russians approached. He urged them to keep working, since their value to the West was directly related to the completion of their project. They had spent the last week methodically boxing up their documentation and indexing the entire collection. Strangely, General Spoerrenberg oversaw even this activity, concerned that every drawing and notebook associated with the project was collected and boxed.

Today was supposed to be the team's last day of work before they were released to prepare their families for evacuation. Instead, they were herded with great haste into the trucks. The Russians had broken through the German army's defenses and were headed directly toward the Pilsen facility. Spoerrenberg promised the scientists that the trucks would be sent back for their families once they themselves were safe. The men reluctantly acquiesced.

The trucks groaned to a halt about a half-hour's drive away from the facility. The SS guards lowered the tailgate and threw open the canvas cover. They shouted and pulled the scientists along, marshalling them into a rough formation beside the vehicles. They had parked along a forest road, with no civilization visible.

"Gentlemen," Spoerrenberg announced, "we are exceptionally close to the American lines. My troops have made contact with their reconnaissance units, just on the other side of this forest. If we proceed further in vehicles, we risk being fired upon, so we will cover the last few kilometers on foot. I apologize for any discomfort. Hopefully when the trucks return with your families, this precaution will be unnecessary."

"Follow me!" an SS Sergeant barked, holding his MP-40 submachine gun over his head as he led them into the trees.

Lead Scientist Victor Schilling looked to his left, toward the head of the convoy. A large piece of equipment rested on a flatbed truck, concealed under a tarp. A group of officers milled beside the trailer, only casually glancing at their direction.

"Is that the *device*?" Schilling asked his friend Ernest Koenig incredulously. Until today, the bell-shaped apparatus had been the most fiercely guarded machine in all of the Third Reich. Their laboratory had been concealed deep in a tunnel carved from solid rock by slave labor from a nearby concentration camp. The device was brought out for testing only in the cover of darkness, with night fighters circling overhead. To see the Bell in broad daylight concealed only by a sheet of fabric provoked an almost physical reaction in Schilling. Security rules at Pilsen were enforced by the threat of execution, or at least shipment to the Russian front, which was essentially the same thing. Whoever would allow their project to travel exposed in such a way?

Koenig let out a breath, which froze and trailed over his shoulders as he walked. "*Gott in himmel*, is that General Kammler by the Bell?"

Obergeneral Hans Kammler was a legendary figure in the German secret weapons programs. Possessing a doctorate in engineering, Kammler could hold his own in any technical discussion, and he reported directly to Hitler's number two man, Martin Bormann. This enabled him to forcibly procure any resource he needed for his projects. Combined with his support for high-risk, high-payoff endeavors, working for Kammler had been an intellectually stimulating experience, even if the man's aura of evil made it somewhat unnerving.

Just before Schilling entered the forest, Kammler made eye contact with him. Schilling shivered, and not just from the cold. There was always death in Kammler's eyes, even when he smiled. Schilling turned away and walked faster into the forest.

"Schilling," his friend whispered, "look at these footprints." A path several men wide was already beaten into the forest floor.

"Spoerrenberg said his soldiers had already come this way."

"Victor, some of these prints were made by bare feet," Koenig retorted.

"Quiet!" the Sergeant hissed.

They continued their march for over a kilometer, ending in a clearing ringed by SS soldiers. Two large tents had been pitched in the center of the clearing. The Sergeant led them until they stood alongside the nearest tent.

"Face me!" he shouted. "Present your identity papers!"

The scientists were confused, but knew that the only safe response to an SS soldier's order was instant compliance.

"Schilling," Koenig whispered, jerking his head toward the tents. "Are we setting up camp?"

"No talking!" the guard barked. "Pass your papers to the right! They will be returned to you by the Americans."

Schilling felt a deep misgiving at parting with his papers. In Nazi Germany, one would rather go outside without their clothes than their papers. But with escape from the war zone literally within walking distance, he suppressed his anxiety and complied.

A *Kubelwagen* scout car bounced down the forest track into the clearing. Generals Kammler and Spoerrenberg sat in the backseat.

"Step back!" the guard ordered, motioning for the scientists to make room for the vehicle to cross the clearing. The scout car turned around so the generals faced the group. The smug smile on Kammler's face did nothing to calm Schilling's fears.

Schilling heard Koenig suck in a startled breath. The guards had moved behind them, pulling away the fabric of the two tents, revealing a mound of freshly dug earth under one. But directly behind them was a narrow trench cut into the forest floor. At the bottom of the trench lay the intertwined corpses of a dozen slave laborers from the Pilsen facility. The prisoner's black-and-white striped uniforms were splotched with blood. Schilling started shaking uncontrollably.

"Ready!" Spoerrenberg yelled. The guards leveled their weapons at the scientists. The soldier sitting in the front passenger seat of the scout car racked the action of his MG-42 heavy machine-gun with a loud *clack.*

"It was good knowing you, Victor," Koenig whispered. The entire group had worked under the oppression of the SS for so long, the idea of resistance wasn't even seriously considered.

"*Endsicherheit!*" Spoerrenberg shouted.

The frosty silence of the clearing was split by a dozen tongues of flame as the SS guards opened fire. Bullets tore through the scientists' bodies, throwing up puffs of dirt in the mound behind them. Their bodies tumbled backwards like rag dolls into the trench. The SS troopers fired continuously until the last body disappeared below ground level. The gunfire echoed off the hillsides for several seconds after the shooting stopped.

The SS Sergeant then walked the length of the trench, putting a pistol round into the head of each scientist. It was a courtesy not afforded to the Polish slave laborers who had dug the trench earlier in the day. Some of them had taken several minutes to die, but the suffering of subhumans was not the concern of the SS soldiers. They slung their weapons and doused the trench with petrol.

After tossing the identity papers into the trench, the Sergeant loaded a small flare pistol and fired it into the hole. Flames leapt a meter above ground level, then slowly died down as the petrol was consumed, its combustion replaced by the contents of the trench.

Suddenly a scream pierced the air. Someone in the mass grave had been feigning death, only to be exposed by the spreading flames. The Sergeant drew his 9 mm pistol and walked to the edge of the trench. He pointed the gun at the tormented victim, but did not fire.

"*Gottverdammt Slav*," the Sergeant declared to the assembly, explaining that it was a Polish worker burning, unworthy of a bullet's mercy. The screaming continued for a surprisingly long time.

"Let's see the Americans or Russians duplicate our experiment now," Kammler boasted. "I'm the only person still breathing who knows how the Bell works."

"Indeed, *Herr General*," Spoerrenberg agreed with a grin.

"What was the phrase you used when the guards opened fire?" Kammler asked over the wails of torment.

"*Endsicherheit*," Spoerrenberg said.

"Final Security," Kammler repeated. "I like that." [1]

[1] The incident of the murdered scientists is true. Between April 28 and May 4, 1945, the SS executed 62 scientists associated with a Nazi research program known as "the Bell." The purpose of the executions was to prevent their knowledge from falling into Russian—or other Allied—hands. (Source: *The Hunt for Zero Point* by Nick Cook, p. 184)

CHAPTER 1

CANDY MAN

PRESENT DAY – SAN JOSE, CALIFORNIA

Mike Manning was a successful American in every way. He had a trophy wife, two children he hardly knew, two leased BMWs he could barely afford, and a showcase home built on a mountain of debt. Like a shark, the only way Manning could survive was to keep moving.

Manning's law firm specialized in corporate damage control. Executives for companies like Chemtrox had learned long ago that when their products hurt someone, one lawyer with a briefcase full of money was more effective than a courtroom full of lawyers at trial. Mike Manning was the lawyer with that briefcase.

His latest trip to San Francisco was a routine one. Chemtrox had long known that PCBs from their transformer plant in San Carlos had been leaching into the groundwater, but had successfully hidden that fact from the EPA for almost two decades, knowing that the slow bleed of poison would take years to start killing off the plant's neighbors. That day of reckoning had finally come.

His job was simple. Pay off the few victims who could trace their cancers back to Chemtrox's property line and keep them silenced long enough for Chemtrox to shut down the plant, move the production equipment to Chile, destroy any sensitive records, and transfer the executives with incriminating knowledge to cushy overseas assignments that would buy their silence and place them out of easy reach of a subpoena.

Yesterday had been hell. The instigating litigant was an old lady whose flower garden was in the backwash of Chemtrox's PCB spoor. Her constant digging in the contaminated soil had led to aggressive cancers necessitating the amputation of her right arm at the elbow. But it was the PCB-laced soil she had inhaled over the years that was going to do Ethel in. A nasal cannula fed oxygen into her tumor-infested lungs. The small, neglected house reeked of impending death.

But Ethel wasn't the real problem. Ethel's daughter Rose was the thorn in Chemtrox's side. She was a paralegal at San Francisco's largest ambulance-chasing firm. Rose knew she had Chemtrox by the nuggets, and she wasn't about to let go.

But Chemtrox had been greasing the palms of highly placed San Francisco-area officials for several years for just such a contingency. They had stroked city and police officials with trips to Chemtrox's luxury box for sporting events, followed by trips to a corporate penthouse with the buxom and well-compensated whores who had served them free drinks all evening. Along with that sizable carrot, Chemtrox also possessed the stick of videotapes made in that same corporate penthouse. With those inducements in hand, leveraging the officials to plant enough drugs in Rose's house and car to justify the seizure of both her vehicles and property hadn't been too hard to arrange.

Manning shrugged off the destruction of the young woman's life. Once the loss of her home, her job, and her reputation was assured, the DA would offer a generous plea agreement with no jail time. And the check Manning left with Ethel would more than buy back Rose's property, once Mom pushed off to the big flower garden in the sky.

He would warn his superiors that he had bought them two months of maneuvering room, three tops.

* * *

Manning was in an upbeat mood. After yesterday's trip to hell, today's rounds would be easy by comparison. Today he would visit Ethel's neighbors, stuffing checks into the hands of potential litigants like rolled gauze into a bullet wound. He actually enjoyed these outings. He was the Candy Man, and there was plenty to go around for everyone. The size of the checks almost always blinded his marks to the fact that a settlement wouldn't be offered unless they were in mortal danger, and the simple piece of paper they signed in exchange for their winning lottery ticket totally foreclosed their legal rights, in the event their number came up in a lottery no one wanted to win.

He called the effect "dumb down digits," surmising that people's IQ went down ten points for every zero in the check he waved in front of them. With the size of the checks in his briefcase, he would be reducing several people to a vegetative state today.

Seated in the lounge of his hotel in San Jose, he munched a stale blueberry muffin from the hotel's meager continental breakfast buffet and tried to concentrate on his book. He liked reading conspiracy books while on the road. The idea that the government could be lying, cheating, selling drugs and hiding alien spaceships out in the desert strangely comforted to him. At least he lied and cheated for concrete reasons like money, not nebulous concepts like national pride or world domination.

"I've been out there," a tenor voice said behind him. "Scary place."

Manning craned his neck. "I'm sorry?"

A wiry man with a shaved head and hooked nose pointed at Manning's book. "Area 51. I've been there."

He pushed out the adjacent chair with his foot as an unspoken invitation. The slightly younger man slid into the offered seat and slathered cream cheese on his bagel with quick, nervous movements. "Of course, they don't call it Area 51," his visitor whispered, biting off a piece of bagel and chewing with an open mouth. "They just called it 'the remote location.'"

Manning looked directly into the man's dark, darting eyes. They communicated honesty, or at least forthright insanity. He knew the two could be easily confused. “What were you doing there, if you can say?"

The man swallowed a huge chunk of bagel, almost choking himself in his eagerness to reply. "Taking statements. The company I represented had employees out there in the vicinity of a chemical spill. The Air Force wouldn't let them off the base until they agreed to sign away their rights to sue."

"Sounds familiar," Manning grumbled.

“Two of them were dead from cancer a year later. The rest feel like every day is a game of Russian roulette. They're always wondering what day their number is going to come up. Of course the company denies the event ever took place and won't give them a dime."

"Sounds *real* familiar."

The visitor nodded his head spastically. "That's my job every day. Sucks."

He frowned. "I hear you."

The man stuck out a bony hand. "Jacob, by the way. Call me Jake."

He stretched his arm across the table. "Mike." Neither man mentioned his last name or company, an understood anonymity between them.

“So what's your book about, other than Area 51?" Tim asked.

“This guy says the military engineered 9/11 so they could take over the Afghan poppy fields and use the proceeds to finance their classified R&D programs. Like at Area 51,” Manning explained.

A low whistle. “Wow, that's almost as good as some of the stories I've heard at work."

He would have raised an eyebrow at the other lawyer even hinting at the secrets he guarded, but Manning was always willing to benefit from someone else's indiscretion. "I'm here in town until tomorrow morning, how long are you staying?"

* * *

Neither man noticed the bored-looking blonde in the corner, fidgeting with her phone and picking at a cup of fruit with her fork. “SO WHOS THE NEW GUY?” she texted, after taking a photo of the two men seated across the room.

“NO IDEA,” was the reply. “RUNNING FACIALS NOW.”

“SEE NO HOSTILE INTENT.”

“AGREED,” came back a few seconds later. “BUST ON FACIALS. NOT A PLAYER.”

* * *

Jake rolled his eyes. “Oh God, with the mess I've got on my hands, I could be here for weeks. Ever hear of a company called Nanovex?"

“No, should I have?” Manning answered.

He laughed. “Not if you’re lucky!”

A plastic smile. “Maybe we could have a beer after work."

An overeager grin. "Yeah, we could swap stories!"

Or I could pump you for information and give you absolutely nothing in return. "Sure. That would be great."

Manning excused himself to brush his teeth before beginning his rounds. The other lawyer shoved the last three bites of his bagel into his mouth and stood to follow.

* * *

The blonde cursed under her breath and texted quickly. “LEAVING. GOT2 FLLW.”

But before she could rise, another man insinuated himself behind her mark and the newcomer, following only a few steps behind them out of the breakfast room.

“NEED BACKUP,” she texted on the way out the door.

“ON THE WAY,” appeared a few seconds later.

* * *

Jake continued nattering throughout the elevator ride and got off at Manning's floor, as did an Arabic-looking man who had gotten on with them. The stranger walked the opposite way, but Manning began to wonder if Jake was going to follow him all the way to his room. The lawyer stopped two doors short.

“Hey! We're practically neighbors!" Jake gushed. "See you tonight, about six?"

He gave the gullible man a friendly wink. "You bet. Sounds good."

* * *

Knowing Jacob Fleischer’s destination, the blonde sprinted to the stairwell and ran to the second floor landing, extracting a pistol from her jacket and flicking off the safety. She peered through the glass in the fire door, watching a trio of men exit the elevator. One turned toward her. Dammit. She ducked back under cover, pulling a mirror from her purse. She used it to peek down the hallway again. Fleischer and the newcomer continued down the corridor, while the third man fumbled with his keycard at a nearby door. Was her contact meeting with this guy in his *room*? Was he *that* big of an idiot?

But Fleischer carded into his suite and the newcomer walked on, entering his own room two doors down. As Fleischer closed his door, the third man glanced over his shoulder, then pocketed his keycard and returned to the elevator. The hallway was empty again.

She tucked the pistol back out of sight just as her back-up mounted the steps below her at a run. She waved her man away, signaling that all was well. *Too much time in this business*, she mused. *I'm getting paranoid. But on second thought....*

"Ari," she told her man, "I need you to put a tail on that guy with Fleischer, just out of curiosity." *On second thought,* she pondered, *I'm still alive today because I'm paranoid.*

* * *

The Arabic man exited the elevator on the first floor, passed through the lobby and walked to the taxi stand outside. He got in the back seat of the last cab.

"I have our target's location," Faisal announced to the driver in Arabic.

"That is excellent news," the driver replied. "The emir will be pleased."

"Of course he will," Faisal snapped back. "Take me to him."

NO-SHOW

SAN JOSE, CALIFORNIA

The day went better than Manning had hoped. Stupid people made his job so much easier. After dumping his briefcase in his room, he tugged off his jacket and tie and headed downstairs to the hotel bar.

* * *

With orders from the emir in hand, Faisal returned to the hotel that evening. Donning a stolen hotel employee's jacket and nametag, he entered by a side door and made his way to his target's room. The surveillance team indicated that the man had returned less than five minutes ago. He knocked at the door.

"Who is it?" replied a timid voice.

"Room service!" he said cheerfully. *Cowardly lapdog.*

"I didn't order room service."

"Indeed, sir," Faisal said without hesitation. "The pretty blond-haired lady in the bar sent up a bottle of champagne. She said to congratulate you." He held the bottle he had just purchased at an infidel's liquor store in case this *jahash* had worked up the courage to peer out the peephole.

The door cracked open. “Congratulate me for what?” the little Jew wheedled. “Did she say?”

Faisal kicked the door open and shoved his stun baton into the skinny spy’s chest. His target collapsed like a bundle of sticks. Faisal closed the door behind him and set the bottle beside his victim. “She said to congratulate you on your stupidity, you *kalet*.”

Fleischer quivered at his feet, his mouth gaping like a landed fish. Faisal reached for his cell phone, calling his partner. “He is ready. Send up the cart.”

To his astonishment, the Jew grabbed the bottle of champagne and started to swing it at his assailant’s knee. The operative easily dodged the clumsy blow and jammed his stun baton into his target’s neck. He held the arcing rod into the Jew’s flesh until his back arched with convulsions. When Faisal finally pulled the implement back, Fleischer went limp, his eyes unblinking and a guttural rasp escaping his lips. He lay completely still. Faisal finally bent down and checked for a pulse. There was none.

“*Wald il qahbaa!*” he gasped. *Son of a bitch!*

* * *

Two beers and almost an hour later, Jake was still a no-show. Manning ordered a club sandwich. He had half of it down when he felt long fingernails rake lightly across his shoulder blades and heard a female voice behind him.

"So, Mr. Manning, scouting out new territory for Chemtrox to poison?"

He coughed a masticated morsel of bacon onto the table. He jerked his body around as if preparing to fight off an attacker. What he saw froze him in place as effectively as an armed robber.

The woman was model-gorgeous, with short blond hair, a slender muscled body, and a pricey red dress that clung to her assets in just the right places. Manning assumed she was a hooker.

"You’ve been making a lot of house calls in the San Carlos area,” she said casually. “Do you have a contamination problem up there?"

Definitely not a hooker. His throat constricted around a half-swallowed bite of sandwich, almost gagging him. "Who the hell are *you*?" he coughed.

She slid into the chair opposite him, offering her hand. “Monica Geldman. Sorry for the sneak attack, I know Jacob Fleischer. I saw you two eating breakfast together this morning.”

Her hand remained outstretched. It was clear it would remain so until Manning took it. Reluctantly, he wiped his hand and extended it. Her grip was cool and firm. She was stunning, but her sudden appearance and knowledge of his business screamed *threat* to his practiced instincts. “Fleischer? I never learned Jake’s last name.”

Her smile was professionally disarming. “Glad to hear it.”

He searched her face for tells of what lay behind the frozen smile, but it was like trying to read the emotions of a locked door. “What exactly *is* your relationship with Jake, if you don’t mind me asking?”

Her smile never wavered. “Let’s just say we work together, and I have an interest in any aspect of our business that he might have shared with you.”

Oh great, corporate security. Apparently he wasn’t the only one to whom Jake had blabbed his secrets, and she was here to clean up the mess he had made with his mouth. “We didn’t discuss work,” he lied. “He was interested in the book I was reading, so that’s what we talked about. I never told him *my* business either, so how the hell do *you* know about it? Have you been following me?”

Geldman propped her chin delicately on her hand, sporting a sly grin. “Oh, I don't go into sources and methods, Mr. Manning."

Sources and methods? He had read enough to know that was spy jargon. He began to worry that Geldman might be something even more dangerous to his firm’s secrets than a corporate security goon. "Sources and methods?” he demanded. “I want to know what company you work for, *right now*.” He would need to call his firm right away to report the breach, but he needed more information.

It wasn't her reaction that rang his alarm bells. It was how quickly she recovered from her slip. After one surprised blink, she spun in her chair to look in the direction of the door. She turned back, and leaning in close, whispered, "You’ve been watching the door since I got here. Are you expecting someone? Perhaps a beer with Mr. Fleischer?" She raised one of her plucked eyebrows slightly.

He threw the remainder of his sandwich on the plate and started to push away, but thought better of it and wrapped it in a napkin to take with him. This nosy corporate gumshoe wasn't worth going hungry for.

She switched gears as smoothly as a Jaguar. Her eyes turned from probing to plaintive in an instant. "I'm sorry Mike, I'm pushing too hard. Let me buy you a beer. I’m just looking out after the needs of my firm.” Her smile turned from professional to something a good deal warmer. “Besides, I’m here from out of town too. I could use the company.”

He felt her studied seduction tug at him, but he was determined not to be played. He dropped a twenty on the table for the waitress. "Thanks for the offer," he muttered, "but I don’t socialize with people who poke their nose into my business."

Her enticing smile dissolved into fuming silence.

He left the bar and headed back to his third-floor room. He almost passed by Jake's room, but noticed a small tool sandwiched between the door and the jamb at floor level, holding the door open a fraction of an inch. The noise of a TV blared from inside the room. Jake had obviously rushed in a few minutes ago and dropped it on the way in. He would probably come downstairs looking for Manning in the bar as soon as he walked away. He needed to warn him about Geldman. Not that he owed Jake anything, but anything he could do to make Geldman's work harder was a plus as far as he was concerned.

His boss would have a cow that another company's security department had been following him around on the Chemtrox operation. They would have to find out who this Monica Geldman worked for, and more importantly if what her company wanted was at odds with his firm's interests. Jake Fleischer might be able to give him some answers in that regard. He needed to talk with him, now. He rapped on the door, which pushed it open an inch. The tool fell glinting onto the carpet. It was a scalpel. *What the hell was a lawyer doing with a scalpel?* A buzzing like a shaver came from inside the room.

"Hey, Jake?"

Manning could see a sheet of plastic draped over the bed, up the headboard and taped to the wall. The buzzing sound grew louder. Perplexed, he cautiously pushed the door open wider. He saw red flecks of what looked like paint smattered on the plastic as he kept pushing.

Then he saw a hand. Pale. Lifeless. Then a blood-speckled arm. Mesmerized with morbid fascination, Manning pushed the door open further. Jacob Fleischer lay face up on the bed, naked, his death-frozen eyes staring up at the ceiling.

Horrified, Manning pushed the door open fully. A dark-skinned man and woman stood at the foot of the bed in medical scrubs, rubber gloves, and safety glasses. The man held Jake's left leg up while the woman cut through it with a cordless bone saw. His right leg already ended in a bloody stump. The buzzing grew louder as the door hit the stop, the saw's noise competing with the blaring TV.

The bone saw screeched and Jake's left leg came off in a spray of crimson, his thigh dropping as dead weight back to the mattress. The man turned and deposited the severed limb into a black plastic drum at the foot of the bed. The man and woman looked up at the same time. Manning stood transfixed in the open doorway. The woman shouted something in a foreign language. She lowered the bone saw and reached under her blood-splattered blouse.

Manning's world started moving in slow motion when her hand drew out a pistol. The time it took for the bulky silencer to clear the woman's shirt gave Manning the split-second for his athletic instincts to kick in. He lunged to the right just before a bullet smacked into the wall behind him. He dropped his sandwich and ran flat out for the stairwell at the end of the hall. Just before he hit the stairwell door, he heard a surprised shout and heavy thud.

Manning shoved open the heavy fire door and risked a look back. The man had slipped on the sandwich. He hit the floor hard, his safety glasses tumbling crazily in Manning's direction. Before he could gloat over his pursuer's bad fortune, the woman leaned around the doorway and squeezed off two shots. The first smashed the wired glass in the fire door and the second ripped past his face, ricocheting down the stairwell.

Manning pushed through the doorway and bolted down the stairs, taking steps two or three at a time. One slip and he would have tumbled head over heels, but his adrenaline-charged reflexes didn't fail him as he fled toward the ground floor.

He burst out of the stairwell, his wild-eyed expressions startling the hotel guests passing through the lobby. He cut left again, hoping to deny his pursuers a clear line of sight when they exited the stairs.

That hallway was blessedly empty and he dashed flat out, almost running out of his dress shoes. He shouldered open a side door leading outside and froze. He realized his car was on the parking lot on the *other* side of the hotel. Before he could decide what to do, Manning heard a female voice chuckle behind him.

"Well I knew I pissed you off, but I didn’t know I scared you into running for your life."

Monica Geldman leaned against the wall, smoking. "I'd love to get my hands on the Nazi who made the whole damn hotel non-smoking." She took a long drag. "You look like hell. Was there a ghost in your room?"

He briefly told her of his traumatic experience, then leaned forward cautiously to see if he was still being pursued. Geldman yanked him back from the door. She was surprisingly strong.

"*Stop*, idiot!" she snapped. "What did you say they looked like again?"

He took deep, measured breaths, trying not to hyperventilate. "Man and a woman, mid-thirties, dark skin, Indian, or maybe Mexican."

"Shit," Geldman bristled, venting smoke. Her face hardened. "Okay, we got to get you out of here." She stepped casually in front of the glass door, her eyes scanning the hallway. She spoke in a harsh whisper, "When I say go, I want you to *run* to the driveway in front of the hotel, got it?"

Manning nodded.

Her eyes never moved from the doorway. "Give me an audible!"

"*Got it!*"

She flicked her cigarette away forcefully. "*RUN!*"

LAW OF THE JUNGLE

NOVEMBER 1979 - PHILADELPHIA, PENNSYLVANIA

"Next!" the judge called.

"Case 3852, Angela Renee Kellerman," the social worker responded.

Three-year-old Angela Kellerman would barely remember her mother once she was grown. She would vaguely recall a dirty apartment where she was only free to play during the day. At nights she was locked in a closet and told if she didn't stay quiet she wouldn't eat the next day. Then she heard men's voices and Mommy made funny sounds. Mommy said if she didn't make the funny sounds for the men she wouldn't get paid and they would be homeless like Wally the drunk who slept in the alley below their window. Angela didn't want to sleep outside like Wally the drunk.

The judge flipped absently through her file. "Recommendation?"

"The child was taken into state custody when the mother was arrested for prostitution," the social worker said.

Angela didn't know what prostitution was. She only knew Mommy didn't come home one night. Angela ate dry cereal for two days, then there was no more. She took the empty cereal box and knocked on the doors down the hall, asking for more. Then the police came and took her away. At first she was scared. She had seen the police beat Wally the drunk from her window. But to her they were nice. They gave her food and candy. Then the black woman who didn't smile much took her to a big house with lots of kids who fought and screamed a lot. Angela missed her mother. She cried, but her nights in the closet had taught her to do so silently. Mommy beat her if she made noise. These people probably would too.

The judge removed his glasses and rubbed his eyes. "I take it you're proposing permanent removal."

The black woman nodded. "Yes, your honor. The mother is addicted to heroin. I would say the odds of escaping her current lifestyle are virtually nil."

The judge hit his desk with a wooden hammer. The sound made Angela jump. "So ordered. The child is remanded into the state foster care system immediately."

Angela didn't know what foster care was, but she learned soon enough. It basically meant being shuffled from one house to another every few weeks. Some of the grown-ups were nice, some of them were mean. But *all* of the kids were mean. That was a given. She learned quickly that you didn't ask for what you wanted. You grabbed and punched. And if they cried you punched them again so the grown-ups wouldn't come. After a few violent years, she had learned to hit and kick and bite well enough to hold off children much bigger than herself.

But at least the grown-ups fed her, and while she was moved from one house to another when her behavior became a problem, no one had threatened to throw her in the alley with Wally the drunk. In fact, no one said much to her at all. They just shuffled her along, putting her clothes in a garbage bag and making her wait on the porch for the social worker to pick her up.

ALIAS

PRESENT DAY – SAN JOSE, CALIFORNIA

Manning dashed past the cars parked beside the hotel. He thought he was making good time, but he heard the sharp smack of leather gaining on him. She grabbed the back of his collar and hauled him to a stop before he reached the corner of the building. For a slender woman, she generated an amazing amount of force.

"How can you run in those heels?" Manning asked, slightly out of breath.

"Rule number one, Mr. Manning. Never take anyone at face value." She shouldered past him to see the front drive of the hotel. "I'm going to hail a cab. As soon as I get the door open, come a-runnin'."

"Got it."

Geldman sauntered like a runway model to the front drive. She didn't have any trouble getting the attention of a cab parked at the opposite end of the driveway, watching the lobby. The car screeched to a halt at the curb, the driver seeming to catch her sense of urgency.

She opened the taxi's rear door and signaled Manning with a jerk of her head. He jogged forward, willing himself not to look back toward the hotel, since that was the likely direction of any incoming bullets. He ducked his head, following Geldman into the back seat.

"Airport! Punch it!" Geldman ordered. The cab started rolling before Manning even closed the door.

"You got it." the driver replied. The cab surged onto the street with a lurch that made Manning grab for a handhold.

"Airport?" he asked. "Why are we going to the airport?"

"To get you the hell out of town," she replied, obviously guarding her words in the cabby's presence. "If your 'friends' can't find you in an hour or two, they'll skip town themselves, so I want you long gone."

"What about the police? They might still be able to catch those two!" It finally dawned on him that he was now a witness in a murder investigation. As a lawyer, the idea of being a *participant* rather than a *spectator* in a legal proceeding was almost as terrifying as being shot at.

"The police would be worse than useless. Your 'friends' know too many people who can finish the job for them, and if even *one* policeman is on that list, you're toast. No, your best protection is to get you out of town, ASAP."

He mulled over Geldman's cold logic. "So why are *you* helping me?"

Geldman frowned, choosing her words carefully. "Jacob was under investigation. I obviously underestimated the threat to his person, so I may be in danger myself. I need to get to the bottom of this, and you're the only witness I have. Pardon me if it's in my own self interest to keep you alive."

"No, no complaints here," Manning stammered. Once the immediate threat to his survival was addressed, his mind drifted to less urgent matters. "What about my bags? All my stuff is back at the hotel."

"Anything in your room worth dying for?" she scoffed. After thinking for a moment she added, "But unclaimed bags might make people start asking questions. Give me your key card and I'll go back for them." She did her best to affect a charming smile. "It'll give you an incentive to stay in touch once I get you home safe."

They were so involved in their discussion they didn't notice the cab pulling over until it had almost reached the curb.

"Wait!" she protested. "Why are you pulling over? I told you we're in a hurry!"

The cabbie flashed an apologetic smile, his white teeth contrasting sharply with his olive complexion. "I am sorry!" He said in a thick accent. "My wife is expecting; I need every fare I can get." The cab pulled to a stop next to a man flagging from the curb.

Manning glanced at Geldman, whose fuming silence was building toward an explosion. He didn't shift his full attention to the new passenger until the gun came over the front seat. The man's attention and his pistol were fixed firmly on Geldman.

"Ms. Conrad!" the new arrival purred. "Your reputation precedes you. I'm so glad I can finally make your acquaintance, if only for a few minutes." The pistol remained pointed at Geldman, but the man turned his gaze toward Manning. "And who might you be, sir?"

Manning started to speak, but Geldman's shoe pressed down firmly on his foot. He remained silent, which was just as well, since his brain was completely devoid of plausible lies, for once.

The front seat passenger spoke to the driver, never taking his eyes off Manning. "Hamid, what was the description Gaya gave you of the subject who interrupted them?"

"White male, forties, average height, medium to stocky build, light brown hair," the driver recited. Manning realized the driver and the passenger spoke with the same accent.

The passenger moved the barrel of his pistol to split the difference between Geldman and Manning. "So we have captured the famous Angela Conrad *and* a member of her cell. How fortunate."

"Allah is merciful," the driver agreed.

Her cell? What the hell is he talking about? And why does he keep calling her Conrad?

“There is a parking garage a block down the street,” the man with the gun instructed. “Pull in and find an empty level.”

“As you wish, *emir*,” the driver replied. The cab pulled away from the curb again.

"He has nothing to do with this, let him go," Geldman said in an authoritative voice.

"If he has nothing to do with this, why were you fleeing the hotel together?" countered the man with the gun.

Geldman remained silent. Apparently she was out of plausible lies as well.

The cab pulled into the garage and prowled slowly up the ramps, the parked cars thinning as they climbed. By the third level cars were sparse. By the fourth level it was almost deserted.

“Stop here,” the leader ordered.

Manning's heart pounded out what he fully expected to be the last few beats of his life. He briefly considered making a hero play of lunging across the front seat to grab the gun, but he doubted he could wrest the passenger’s gun away before the driver shot Geldman and him first. The defeatist part of his brain reminded him that such a move would likely get him shot in the gut to bleed out slowly on the concrete, while cooperating would result in a quick headshot. At least he wouldn't have to watch himself bleed to death.

His arms and legs were rubbery and shaking when he emerged from the backseat of the cab, with the gun of the driver covering him. Geldman looked just as frightened as he felt, which brought him even closer to panic. This was it. He was going to die on the floor of some damned parking garage. The leader was out of the cab and motioned them toward the wall with his gun. In his mind's eye he could already see two sprawled chalk outlines on the concrete, with sticky-wet puddles congealed around their heads. He pictured his body being sawn and sectioned just like Jake Fleischer. He felt woozy.

But I don't want to die! His adrenaline-charged brain raced from one morbid thought to another. He cringed at the thought of his wife having to identify his body. If they shot him in the back of his head, would he have any face left, or would there just be a spongy mess? Would they find his body at all? How would his boys turn out without him in their life? With the amount of time he spent on the road, would they even notice? Was his life insurance paid up? Of course it was, he was worth more dead than alive. With that kind of money at her disposal, would his wife take up with the pool boy or some other worthless man? How long would it be before another man was sleeping with his wife? That thought alone almost made him vomit.

"I can pay you!" Geldman pleaded. "I don't know how much you're making on this operation, but I can double it!"

"You assume this is a mercenary operation," the leader replied coolly. "You are the mercenary here, Miss Conrad, not me."

Her voice rose in pitch and volume. "You have no idea who you are dealing with! If anything happens to me, my team will hunt you down, every one of you!"

His tone was dismissive. "Your team are dogs, Miss Conrad, who will fight amongst themselves until a new leader emerges. Avenging your death will be the least of their concerns. Move."

Geldman was shaking and her voice rapidly rose to a scream. "*No! NO!* Don't do this! We can work together! I can help you!" Her knees buckled slightly. "No! *Please! I don't want to die!*" she wept. Seeing the woman who a few minutes ago had been his savior come apart so completely pushed Manning to the edge of melting down himself. He started to hyperventilate and needed to pee desperately.

"Get control of her!" the leader barked.

The driver grabbed her roughly, hindered by having his gun hand occupied. The leader jabbed his gun into Manning's neck. "Allah is merciful," he whispered. "This will all be over in a moment, but if you struggle I will see to it that you die slowly." Manning remained still, except for the shaking of his knees. That he was unable to stop, regardless of his effort.

Geldman *was* screaming now. The driver was forced to wrap an arm around her, as she continued to struggle.

"Shoot her!" the leader ordered.

Her screams were frenzied now. Her legs were up against her chest, nearly pulling her captor forward off his feet. Almost faster than Manning's eyes could follow, her hand reached up under her skirt. Then she straightened her legs, driving her slender body and the man holding her backward. She twisted and grabbed the driver's gun. Manning thought he saw the flash of metal in Geldman's other hand, but everything happened so fast.

The driver staggered and fired his weapon, trying to end the struggle. The bullet sparked against the concrete and passed inches from Manning's face. The leader wrapped his forearm around Manning's neck, pulling him backward as a shield. Geldman’s struggle continued, and the leader's gun left Manning's neck to draw a bead on her.

Another shot rang out, followed by a wet crunch next to Manning's ear. The grip around his neck relaxed, followed by a thud as the leader hit the pavement, a hole bored neatly between his staring, sightless eyes. While Manning looked down, there was a second shot. He looked up in time to see the driver spun to the floor by a judo throw. He was shot in the neck but still wrestled with her, trying to free his gun hand. She thrust a small black pistol under the driver's chin and fired again. His head jerked, a black puddle flowing outward rapidly. She bolted to the leader and repeated the chin shot, holding the gun on him for several seconds until she was sure he was dead.

Geldman jumped to her feet. "You okay?" she asked breathlessly.

Without the rigid hold of the leader around his neck, Manning found himself wobbling like a drunk. "W-what?" he stammered.

"Are you *shot?*" she snapped.

He checked himself with tingly, shaking hands. "No, I'm okay."

She felt her face. A powder burn from a point-blank gunshot during the struggle marked her cheek. She jerked in pain when she touched the soot-marked skin. "Son of a bitch, that was close!" She surveyed the carnage with hands on her hips, like it was a household project somehow gone awry. "Help me get these bodies into the trunk," she ordered.

"What the hell are you talking about? We have to call the police!" He reached for his cell phone.

She leveled her tiny pistol at his face. "Put the phone away and pull these bodies over to the taxi. *Now.*"

After a short staring contest, he closed his phone. He would rather be Geldman’s accomplice than her next victim. He grabbed the leader's limp arm and started dragging, painting a bloody trail with the man's head. He made it all the way to the trunk before he finally lost his composure. He could feel his gut convulsing from the gore and adrenaline overload. He spun away and vomited onto the concrete. His body kept retching in terror long after his stomach was empty. He doubled over with his hands on his knees, shaking uncontrollably.

She placed her hand on his back. "I threw up the first time I saw a man shot dead, too. No shame in that." She paused, looking down at his feet. "Of course, I didn't get it on my shoes."

He still shook, but his anger started to overtake his fear. He turned back to the leader and wiped his shoes on the corpse's pant leg in a futile gesture of contempt. "This guy really wanted you dead," he said with a glance at Geldman. "What the hell did you do, short him on cab fare?"

She laughed. "That's a good one. Come on, I'll help you with King Kong over there." They walked over to the driver, Manning taking care not to step in the two-foot-wide puddle when he grabbed an arm.

"I’ve found it easier to drag a body by the legs," she corrected. "Less chance of getting your clothes bloody."

Jesus, you do this often, lady? He almost asked. He grabbed a leg. It *was* easier to drag the body that way. They pulled the driver's corpse next to the leader's. She still had her pistol in her right hand.

"I'll show you a *secret*," she said seductively. She hiked up her dress, revealing a black nylon holster sown to an elastic sleeve around her shapely thigh. "Most of the men who've seen this are dead now," she said with a wink. She holstered her weapon, then bent over to fish for the driver's keys. She popped the trunk. "Okay, let's get Godzilla out of sight." She grabbed an arm and jerked her head impatiently. "Come on, let's go!"

He got a good grip and helped her lift the driver headfirst into the trunk. She was amazingly strong, hardly struggling at all with the load, despite her much smaller frame. The driver's shattered skull hit the bumper, leaving a broad crimson stripe on the yellow plastic.

Manning flinched. "Whoa! Is that gonna be a problem?"

She shoved the driver's legs into the trunk. "Nah. We'll be moving." She had already moved to the leader's body, lingering over it momentarily. "Sorry about this, Rashid, not that you didn't try to do it to me first."

"You *know* this guy?"

"We met at a party," she dodged. "Come on, we gotta get out of here."

He grabbed an arm. "Must've been a hell of a party."

After more lifting and shoving, the leader was also tucked away. Geldman slammed the trunk and tossed him the keys. "Drive."

Manning froze in place. He wanted to walk *away* from Geldman, not get in a car with her and two dead bodies. A heavy metal door opened behind them. A young woman came out of the stairwell at the far end of the garage. She glanced at them and the empty cab curiously, but got in her car and drove away.

When Manning didn't immediately respond, Geldman walked casually to the weapons their assailants dropped, returned to his side, and thrust them both into his gut. "Mike, I need a reason to keep you alive. *Give* me a reason to keep you alive."

He swallowed, his bile having turned his throat dry and gritty. "I'll drive."

"Good boy."

She trotted over to the passenger side and slid into the seat. When he took the wheel, he noticed she kept the seized guns out of sight, but one was in her hand, tucked beside her right thigh. "Exit the garage slowly and turn right at the street. If anything happens, stomp on the gas and get the hell away, don't wait for me to tell you what to do."

Another dry swallow. "Got it."

She retrieved her purse from the back seat and pulled out a cell phone. "Ari, change of plans. I'm coming to you, ETA about two minutes. I got ambushed. No, I'm okay, I just need to get out of sight to plan our next move." She grabbed the rearview mirror and turned it toward her. "I don't think so, but we'll drive past your position just in case."

They drove a few blocks and she told him to turn right, never taking her eyes off the rearview mirror. "Keep turning right, circle the block slowly," she ordered.

"So what's your real name, Monica?" he asked.

Her eyes never moved from the mirror. "Sorry?"

Manning stole a glance at the side view mirror, straining to see whoever Geldman was looking for. "You told me your name was Geldman, but the guy with the gun kept calling you Conrad. Somehow I have a feeling he knew you better than I do. So which is it?"

"You can call me whatever you want," she offered, adopting a tone one might use when negotiating with a child. "Stop. We're here. Back into this alley."

He saw no sign of Geldman's cohorts until he had backed well away from the street. Two men emerged from a white van parked in the shadows. Her pistol came out again. "Pop the trunk and go stand against that wall," she ordered. He complied.

She waved her gun toward the car. "Yuri, Ari, I've got two deads in the trunk. Move them to the van and search them."

Her henchmen opened the trunk. The bigger of the two was Caucasian, with bristly dark hair cropped close against his head. The shorter one was dark-skinned and powerfully muscled, with wavy black hair. Both drew back slightly at the Geldman-induced carnage inside. "We need bags," the taller one said with a Russian accent.

"Come on," she jibed, "you two act like you've never seen headshot before."

The shorter one cocked his head as if critiquing a work of art. "It's just that you're always so...thorough."

She shrugged. "If it's worth shootin', it's worth shootin' twice."

He nodded thoughtfully. “How true.”

The taller one, Manning guessed it was Yuri, returned from a van with two black body bags. The pair paused before lifting out the first body, glancing at Geldman. She trotted to the mouth of the alley to stand watch. Manning marveled again at how athletically she could move in a dress and high heels. She nodded to Yuri and Ari.

The pair grunted at the weight of the larger terrorist. They quickly zipped him up and trundled his bulk to the van. They started to lift the leader's corpse from the trunk, but Ari froze and exclaimed something in a foreign language. Manning thought it sounded like Arabic, or maybe Hebrew. She left her watcher's post to see what Ari had found. He noticed a distinct swagger in her step as she approached. She craned her neck over the trunk rim as if to survey her handiwork.

"Yep, Rashid Ben-Jabir," Geldman explained. "His uncle is the head of Saudi intelligence. They're dead serious about this op, no pun intended."

Yuri's brow furrowed. "We are in danger, yes?"

She gave him a dismissive wave. "Not if we put them in danger first. Get their phones and radios. I want to be ready to track when their underlings check in. Ari, warm up your impersonation act."

The pair bagged the leader and hustled him back to the van, closing the doors behind them. Geldman rejoined Manning once her team was out of sight. "Let's dump this taxi, then we'll get out of here," she said.

Manning retook the driver seat and drove a few blocks. She waved him into the parking lot of a building with a "For Lease" sign. After he parked in a far corner of the lot, Geldman examined the two pistols she had captured. She curled her lip at the first gun, wiping it down with a wetnap from her purse before wrapping it in a newspaper she found on the floor. She frowned at the grease stain the pistol left on the cloth. "Cheap Russian crap!" she muttered to herself.

The second gun was ornately engraved and earned a whistle of admiration from Geldman. She handed him the gun by the barrel. "War trophy," she explained. "I'm a little short on pockets—stick this under your jacket somewhere."

Manning was incredulous. "You threatened to kill me not half an hour ago; now you're handing me a gun?"

She smiled impishly. "Can you even find the safety?"

Manning examined the lavish weapon and pressed the button near the trigger. The pistol's magazine slid out smoothly and bounced on the seat.

Geldman threw her head back and laughed. "Yeah, you're a real threat, Manning." She retrieved the pistol and reinserted the magazine. She then moved a lever near the hammer several times with her thumb. "As long as the safety is engaged like this, the gun can't go bang." She handed the pistol back. "Don't shoot yourself, cowboy." He grimaced and slowly stuck the gun in his waistband, trying not to make her joke a reality. She had another laugh at his expense.

She handed him the used cloth. "Wipe down the steering wheel, all the door handles, and anything else you touched." She exited the taxi and walked to a nearby dumpster. She lifted some of the garbage inside and held up the newspaper, allowing it to unroll and deposit the pistol into the depths of the dumpster. She threw the newspaper on the ground for the wind to take.

She returned to the cab and motioned him out. "Done? Did you do the mirror? I touched that. No? Give me the rag." She leaned into the open door and readjusted the mirror to the driver's point of view, wiping it down at the same time. "Keys?" She stuck them in the ignition, wiping them as well. "If we're lucky, somebody will steal this POS and dispose of it for us. Okay, let's go."

They returned on foot to the alley. The sun had relinquished its touch on all but the tallest buildings around them. Other than his life having been turned completely upside down, it was a beautiful evening. The fact that she had trusted him with a loaded gun gave him the courage to inquire again about his fate. "So what *are* you going to do with me when we're done here?"

One corner of her mouth twisted upward. "Mike, if you knew what I'm planning next, you'd be more worried about surviving the next couple of hours, not what's going to happen after that."

CHAPTER 2

THE BELL

JUNE, 1943 – DRESDEN, GERMANY

The Bell started out as a uranium enrichment device. To create the explosive core for Germany's atom bomb program, the rare and fissionable isotope of uranium-235 had to be extracted from the abundant but useless uranium-238 in mined uranium ore.

A promising enrichment method involved vaporizing the uranium and feeding the gas into a centrifuge. The centrifuge spun the minutely heavier U-238 atoms toward the outside wall, while the desired U-235 stayed closer to the center, where it was collected. By constructing "cascades" of centrifuges, the raw uranium gas would be purified over and over again, obtaining a slightly higher purity of U-235 after each trip through the system.

The Nazi atom bomb program was not only underway when the war began, but had been an integral component of Hitler's strategic plan. Uranium mines in Czechoslovakia would provide the raw materials for the bomb, and the synthetic rubber factory near Auschwitz, Poland had abundant supplies of electricity and water for the enrichment machines. It would eventually have abundant supplies of expendable slave labor to cheaply handle radioactive materials as well. Both of these sites were early on Hitler's list of planned conquests.

But two years into the war, it was becoming painfully apparent that uranium enrichment was a far more daunting technical challenge than the academics on Hitler's Physics Planning Staff had predicted. With German troops taking heavy casualties on the Russian front and allied troops preparing to invade Italy after driving Rommel's elite *Afrika Korps* from that continent in defeat, no one wanted to tell *der Fuhrer* that the atom bomb they had promised him was *kaput*. Another way had to be found.

The idea for the Bell sprang from the German engineering philosophy that if a little of something was good, then a truly massive amount of the same thing would be *wunderbar*. The Bell increased the speed of the centrifuge to tens of thousands of revolutions per minute, and added a powerful magnetic field to aid in separating the uranium isotopes.

At the center of the Bell, two concentric cylinders containing uranium gas spun in opposite directions, multiplying the force to separate the U-235 and U-238 isotopes. A flared ceramic shield covered the three-meter-tall assembly, giving the mechanism its moniker. The theoretical physicist behind the Bell, Professor Walther Gerlach, estimated at least a five-fold increase in uranium enrichment, so obtaining the scarce materials and skilled labor for the device's construction had not been a problem. [1]

The Bell's first test would take place at a military airfield near Dresden, Germany. The test was scheduled for shortly after midnight to minimize the impact of the power-hungry experiment on the electrical grid.

* * *

SS General Jakob Spoerrenberg entered the hangar a few minutes before midnight to check their status. The Bell dominated the center of the hangar, surrounded by transformers, electrical control panels, and cylinders of raw uranium gas. Power cables branched outward from the device like the tentacles of an electric octopus. A dozen technicians in white lab coats flocked around the apparatus, double-checking its readiness for the test. A loudspeaker overhead droned the hourly Radio Berlin reports from the front. A male voice announced with level Prussian formality the imminent victory of the Third Reich over the Russian tank forces at Kursk. At times Spoerrenberg wished he didn't know the truth about the horrific losses the *Wehrmacht* was suffering.

Dr. Gerlach approached him. "All is in readiness, *Herr General*. We await your orders."

The general frowned at the number of technicians so close to the untested device. "Are these personnel all necessary for the test, *Herr Doktor*?"

"*Nein*, General, only five technicians will be in the hangar with the device."

"Very well, proceed."

Orders were shouted, transformers charged, and pressurized gas hissed and steamed. A low hum rose in pitch from inside the Bell, then stabilized at an almost-threatening growl. One of the technicians nodded to Gerlach.

"Evacuate the building!" Gerlach shouted. He gestured toward the door. "General, I will show you to the observation room." They stepped into the warm air on the tarmac, followed by most of the technicians.

Spoerrenberg fought a sense of foreboding. The towering oddness of Gerlach's brainchild tugged at his more primal fears, like some unknown monster hauled from the depths and trapped in the lab for study. He wondered whether the engineers staying with the device were selected by matters of specialization, or had merely drawn a short straw.

The general and his adjutant, a battle-hardened lieutenant who had lost an eye on the Eastern front, followed Gerlach into another hangar. A young technician named Kurt Debus huddled over a console crowded with instruments. An intercom speaker and microphone sat on the table beside him.

Gerlach keyed the microphone. "Ernst, we are ready, please begin."

"*Jawhol, Herr Doktor*," the intercom crackled.

Spoerrenberg watched the pressures and RPM's gradually increase. He felt a faint rumbling beneath his feet. "It is a pity we do not have one of *Herr* Goebel's new television cameras to watch the test, eh *Doktor*?" It was frustrating to him to have no visual feedback other than a few trembling gauges, especially since his career was riding on the success of this test.

Gerlach's eyes never left the instrument panel. "I can see all I need to see here, *Herr General*." He tapped one of the RPM gauges. "Kurt, that speed is too high." He took the microphone. "Ernst, your outer rotor speed is too high."

"We see that, *Doktor*," Ernst replied, over a hiss of static not present a moment ago. "We are reducing the motor voltage now."

Spoerrenberg felt the rumble beneath his feet become a discernible shake. It reminded him of an earthquake tremor. The lights flickered slightly.

Gerlach's voice had a tone of urgency. "Ernst, you must reduce your rotor speed! The magnetic field is becoming unstable!"

The hiss of static grew to a roar, almost drowning out the technician's response. "We have reduced power to zero! The rotor is self-accelerating!"

Self-accelerating? Spoerrenberg thought. *How is that possible?*

Gerlach was frantic now. "Ernst! Check your radiation levels! If you cannot stop the rotors you must evacuate!"

Spoerrenberg grasped his adjutant by the arm. "I don't like this," he whispered. "Get our men away from that thing."

"*Jawhol, Herr General!*" The lieutenant disappeared from the hangar.

The interference drowned out all but an occasional word from the technicians inside the hangar. "Extreme...vibration...blue glow."

In his frustration and panic, Gerlach lost all professional decorum. "*Vas ist das sheist?*" he cried out.

Suddenly above the static came the unearthly sound of several men screaming in terror and agony. A blue shock wave rocketed through the control room, driving a sharp electric shock through his body.

Spoerrenberg was still checking himself for harm when he realized the shaking had completely stopped. The speakers fell silent as well.

"What happened?" he demanded.

"I wish I knew, General!" Gerlach replied.

Already out the door, he ran for the hangar, his troops sprinting ahead of him. The soldiers bunched up just inside the door. He pushed past his men, then stopped cold. The five Bell technicians writhed on the floor, their backs arched in agony. They tried to scream, but only gagging sounds escaped. He ran to the closest worker, grasping the man's arms to comfort and steady him, as he would a desperately wounded soldier.

Black, shiny fluid flowed from the technician's eyes and nose. He retched, a gush of the thick black goo flowing over his chin. Choking, his limbs thrashing wildly as he tried to breathe.

Spoerrenberg started to roll the man over on his stomach to clear his airway, but the seizures suddenly stopped. The man's eyes rolled back. He was dead.

Spoerrenberg released his hold on the technician and stood. He realized he was shaking. His men examined the other technicians, but they were now dead as well. The only sound was the fading whine of the Bell's rotors coasting to a stop. His eyes rose from the carnage on the hangar floor.

The Bell was missing.

Heavy cables snaked from the control panels to the spot where the Bell once rested, the mounting brackets that secured the heavy device to the floor were either ripped in half or missing entirely. Yet he still heard the device, so his eyes followed the sound.

Upward.

Hidden in the shadows above the hanging ceiling lights, the cylindrical mass of the Bell was barely visible. "Get me a light!" he ordered.

One of the soldiers pointed a flashlight toward the ceiling. The Bell had almost punched through the hangar roof, stopped only by a heavy structural beam, its truss mashed flat against the ceiling.

"*What the hell?*" he exclaimed. With a groan of protesting metal, the Bell broke free from the mangled beams and fell back toward the hangar floor.

"*GET BACK!*" his adjutant yelled, grabbing Spoerrenberg by the arm and pulling him forcefully away.

Instead of plummeting to earth, the Bell descended gracefully, wobbling slowly about its axis, like a toy top winding down. With the sound of metal grinding on concrete, the Bell settled to the floor. The massive device crushed the prostrate body of a technician, forcefully extruding oily goop from the corpse's nose and mouth like jet-black toothpaste. The turbine whine of the Bell's rotors slowly faded to a stop.

Spoerrenberg turned away from the otherworldly carnage. "Dear God, what have we done?" he whispered. [2]

MIMIC

PRESENT DAY – SAN JOSE, CALIFORNIA

Manning walked ahead of her, toward the van parked in the alley. Geldman relieved him of the ornately engraved pistol she had liberated from their would-be killers, as well as his cell phone, when they reached the vehicle. She reached over the pistol with her left arm and gave the van's back doors a coded knock, then opened one of the doors.

"After you," she offered in false courtesy.

He stepped inside. When his eyes adjusted he found himself staring into another gun. The operative she had called Ari sat at a computer console, holding a pistol in his left hand. Recognizing Manning he re-holstered his weapon. Manning climbed inside.

Two chairs faced the computer consoles on the right side of the van. The two body bags filled the narrow space behind the chairs. Manning stood hunched between the two chairs when Geldman entered. "Sit," she ordered.

He sat in the remaining chair, but felt Geldman's gun poke him in the arm. "Not *there*," she scolded. "Have a seat on our two friends. They don't mind, trust me."

He cringed, but maneuvered into a crouch over the body bags, then lowered himself slowly to contact. The bags were sickeningly warm against his buttocks, sagging turgidly against his weight. The gases forced out of both bodies formed a loud duet of flatulence in the confined space, making Manning flinch.

"That would've happened anyway as their sphincters relaxed," Geldman explained. "The smell is probably going to get pretty thick in here." She wasn't kidding. The fetid smell mingled with the tang of blood in a nauseating mixture. He gagged repeatedly, the spasms working their way down to his emptied stomach.

Geldman ignored Manning's distress, taking the remaining seat to Manning's front and right. "Talk to me, Ari."

"Both subjects had cell phones, and the leader also had a radio," Ari reported. "The cell phones are both throwaways. Speed dials indicate at least three other phones in their network. I hacked the cell phone company's server and all the phones are in range of the nearest cell tower. The leader's phone has an additional local number and a Saudi number loaded. Both his cell phone and the radio have squawked once, so his network is going to get nervous very soon. But we'll have to move the van if we want to localize their phones."

Why in God's name would they want to find the rest of that bastard's network? Manning wondered. He was just hoping to get the hell away before the rest of the Arab goons found out Geldman had bagged their leader. He hunched over the body bags, his head almost touching Ari's back in the cramped interior. Geldman elbowed him out of the way and yelled into the front of the van. "Yuri, get ready to move! Ari's sending you the GPS of the nearest cell tower. Set up a search pattern."

"You got it," a heavily accented voice replied.

"See if you can put a name with the local and Saudi numbers on Ben-Jabir's phone," she told Ari. "Let's roll and get some air moving back here," she called to the driver.

"Da!" came the enthusiastic reply, along with the sound of the engine turning over. The van started moving a few seconds later.

She leaned over Ari's console and tapped her finger on the captured cell phones. "When these guys call again, you'll have to imitate Ben-Jabir and convince them to stay put once we DF their position."

"The Saudi dialect will be no problem. I worked undercover in Riyadh for almost a year."

"Good."

The van rocked, exiting the alley and turning on to the side street. "Okay, I've got a signal," Ari announced. "Hold this direction for a couple of minutes!" he called forward, his attention focused on a large screen. Colored spikes projected from the center, moving slowly as the van traveled. "Can you give me a left turn? A couple of my bearings are almost constant."

The van turned, the spikes on the screen moving with it. A compass on the display said they were now heading west. Two of the spikes rotated counterclockwise rapidly. "We're close," Geldman whispered, as if their targets might hear her. One of the captured cell phones gave a shrill ring, making Manning jump.

"Remember Ari," she coached, "Ben-Jabir is used to being in charge. Be an asshole. Be a *big* asshole."

"Understood." Ari took the call, firing off a string in Arabic. Manning could hear excited jabbering on the other end. Geldman made a "lower, lower" motion at her throat. The pitch of Ari's voice dropped with the next exchange, which was loud and abusive, even though Manning couldn't understand the words.

Two of the spikes on Ari's screen continued their rapid counterclockwise march. He keyed in a command to his console. The same spikes were overlaid on a moving map display, tracing a pie wedge that got shorter and slimmer as the van traveled. As Manning watched, the wedges shrank to points and flashed, inside a square labeled, San Jose Sheraton.

They're inside my hotel, Manning thought. Could they be the two who murdered Jake Fleischer? That crime seemed like it had occurred days ago, back when his previous life had ended the minute he pushed open Fleischer's hotel room door.

Geldman texted quickly on her phone and held it up for Ari. It read, HOW MANY?

Ari continued his bombastic exchange. Taking the phone from Geldman he texted back, 2 HOTEL 2 CMD POST.

A third spike on Ari's monitor pointed the opposite direction and rotated clockwise at a much lower speed. The wedge traced on the screen filled most of the square labeled San Jose Exhibition Center Plaza. Ari tapped the display and shook his head.

Geldman took back her phone, texting GET THEM TO CMD POST. Ari harangued another set of Arabic commands into the cell.

Manning heard what could only have been protests on the other end of the conversation. That earned them a string of vitriol from Ari, probably filled with Arabic expletives. He gave her a thumbs-up.

When he terminated the call, Geldman yelled, "Yuri! U-turn! Get us back to the hotel! Kick it!" The van reversed course, its engine roaring and tires squealing. The body bags shifted underneath Manning with a sickening, gelatinous motion. The vehicle bumped its way onto the parking lot, stopping abruptly. Geldman pushed him out of the way and moved to the front.

"Both contacts due east, bearing constant!" Ari called out.

"Take us behind the hotel. Get us an angle on these bastards," she ordered. The van lurched into motion again.

"Motion! West to east!" Ari declared.

Geldman raised a pair of binoculars to her eyes. "Got 'em! Two Arab males, mid-twenties, walking to their car. Manning, get up here!"

After a moment's hesitation, he rose to a crouch and shuffled to the front. She thrust the binoculars into his hands. "Are those the two that shot at you?"

He leaned around her to bring the pair into his field of view. "No, I told you it was a man and a woman in that room, not two men. And they looked Indian, not Arabic."

"Dammit," she muttered. "Ari, they're at their car, confirm motion stopped!"

"Confirmed," Ari replied. "Bearing zero-four-zero, range about one hundred-twenty meters. Wait, they're back in motion again."

Manning watched the pair pull away in their gold Ford Taurus. She snatched the binoculars from his hands. "They're our boys, whether you recognize them or not," she snapped. "Go back and sit down!"

He sheepishly complied, convinced he would join the Saudis in a body bag the second he had outlived his usefulness. That second seemed to be approaching rapidly, but what could he do about it? If he bolted for the back doors, Ari would drill him in the back. If he managed to knock out Ari, Geldman could easily turn and shoot him. He felt like a trapped animal.

"Wait till they go around the corner before you roll so we don't spook them," she ordered. "Ari, call their command post and tell them the whole gang's coming, then see if you can come up with good enough disguise to get us past the door."

"Understood," Ari replied, picking up a captured cell phone and making another call in Arabic. That completed, he turned in his chair and unzipped the top body bag. He examined the leader's bloodied face carefully, then retrieved a black bag from a rack over Manning's shoulder.

From the bag he pulled a square of what looked like black fur and a small pair of scissors. He cut several pieces of the fur, holding them up to the leader's face for comparison. Once he was satisfied, he peeled backing paper and applied them to his face. Ari now wore a reasonable approximation of the leader's beard.

He then compared the Saudi's dark gray suit to the slightly lighter shade of Manning's jacket. He grabbed Manning's sleeve and held it over the leader's suit. "Close enough," he said. "Give me your jacket."

Manning complied, but mentally compared Ari's build with his own. "Won't it be a bit big?"

Ari snorted in derision, half amused that Manning would dare to offer his opinion. "Not once I get geared up." He pulled a pair of expensive sunglasses from the Saudi's breast pocket. “Hold these,” he ordered.

Ari retrieved a key from a chain around his neck. He opened a locker behind Manning filled with pistols and submachine guns, along with boxes of ammunition and other gear. Ari leaned over to retrieve several items. Manning looked down. Ari's holster was only inches from Manning's right hand. Should he chance it? He glanced left. Geldman had turned in her chair, her gaze locked on him. Her look seemed to say, *Don't even think about it*. He sighed, slumping down further on his body bag sofa.

Ari pulled some kind of black nylon webbing from the locker. He stuck his arms through loops of the webbing, securing a thick strap across his chest, a heavy clasp in its center. Next, he retrieved a small submachine gun, screwed a silencer onto the stubby gun barrel, shoved in a magazine, and slapped the bolt shut. He snapped the weapon onto the chest clasp and pulled Manning's too-large jacket over it. The bulk of the gun took up much of the extra chest volume, although the jacket was still a little baggy on the operative's shoulders.

Ari snatched the sunglasses from Manning's hands, hooking them over his ears. "You saw this guy alive," he said. "Would this fool someone looking through a peephole?"

It was a remarkable transformation. "Enough to get them to open the door, at least."

"That's all I need," Ari replied, his voice quiet and deadly. "Boss," he called to the front of the van, "I'm ready to go back here."

"Good," she answered. "Load up an HK for Yuri, will you?"

"Sure." He pulled another small submachine gun from the locker and readied it with a silencer, tossing it to Manning. "Here, pass this up."

Manning startled at the slap of cold gunmetal in his hands. He couldn't believe they would just *hand* him a gun, but then he realized the magazine well was empty. The gun was harmless, except maybe as a club.

Geldman extended a hand. "He didn't say stare at it, he said pass it up."

He complied, then was handed four loaded magazines. "That's right, we're not stupid," Ari growled, as he closed and secured the weapons locker.

The van pulled to the curb. "We're here, get ready," she announced. "We'll need some way of localizing them inside the building."

Ari reached past Manning again and retrieved a black plastic case. He opened it, revealing a mass of electronics inside. "That won't be a problem, just let me program in their cell numbers."

She opened the passenger door. "While you're doing that, I'll go check the lobby for watchers. Back in two minutes." She stepped out and walked away, the click of her high heels on the sidewalk fading into the distance.

The silence allowed Manning's imagination to drift toward thoughts that were dark as the inside of the van. Who *were* these people? FBI? CIA? Criminals? They were awfully well-equipped. If they *were* criminals, they certainly weren't *common* criminals. Mafia? That was a chilling thought, but why would a Saudi terrorist cell lock horns with the Mafia? Or visa versa?

And how the *hell* did he get mixed up in this? He couldn't imagine Geldman letting him live after all he'd seen, but he remembered this whole mess started with her trying to get him *away* from the Saudi gunmen. Confusion held off panic for the moment. He just didn't know *what* the hell was going on.

A two-tone beep sounded from both Yuri and Ari's cell phones. After a crackle of static, Geldman's voice came over in walkie-talkie mode. "Guys," she said in a lilting voice, "I found someone who can help us. Could you come join me in the lobby?"

"Ah, sure," Ari answered. He shrugged, and snapped the electronics case closed. "Let's go," he ordered Manning. Ari exited and held one of the rear doors open for him.

Manning half-stepped, half-stumbled onto the street, the post-sunset dusk deepened by the shadows of the buildings around them. The street lights had just switched on, each glowing a deep orange, but not yet casting any useful light. The sidewalk stretched ahead into a twilight gloom. Ari closed and locked the doors, then pointed at Yuri. "Follow him," he ordered.

Manning tagged along behind Yuri, who also carried a black plastic case. He was glad to get out of the airless confines of the van, but realized he was still a prisoner even as he walked the streets. They approached the glass-enclosed lobby of a tall office building. He could see Geldman chatting up a middle-aged security guard inside, standing on her tiptoes to lean seductively over the elevated counter. The muscles on her legs flexed, the fabric of her dress pulling tight over her heart-shaped bottom.

Yuri stopped him before they entered the lobby. "You do stupid things, I kill guard *and* you. Stay cool and nobody die. Okay?"

"Okay," Manning agreed.

Yuri pulled out an ID badge that read, "Y. Konalev, Network Associates." He clipped it to his shirt pocket, then poked his finger into Manning's chest. "You Mike Johnson, supervisor, just here to watch, no answer questions. Got it?" Without waiting for Manning's response, he led the trio through the revolving door.

The guard didn't even glance in their direction as they approached, his eyes fixed on Geldman's cleavage. She was doing her best giggling blonde routine, her laughter jiggling her ample curves in a way sure to temporarily lobotomize the guard. Manning cringed at the man's probable fate.

On hearing their approach, she turned in a way that maximized the guard's view down her blouse. The man didn't look up, his gaze fixed on her like a dog eyeing a piece of meat. She waved at them, her smile as vacuous as a Hollywood starlet's. "Hi guys! Stan here says he can help us! Ari, show Stan our Wi-Fi locator."

"Sure." Ari swung his case onto the guard stand as if the ruse was rehearsed. He opened the electronics box toward Stan. "Our customer wants to set up a wireless network in his office, but we need to map out the networks that are already operating inside the building."

Stan stood to look more closely at Ari's box. "Okay...."

"To do that," Ari continued, "we'll need to run a scan on several floors to make sure we avoid conflicts." Manning noticed Geldman stepping nonchalantly out of Stan's field of view while Ari kept him occupied.

"You can't *do* that," Stan interrupted. "Most of our floors have restricted access. I can't just let you wander...."

Before the guard could finish, Geldman stepped behind him and drove her high heel into the back of his leg. Yelping in pain, he dropped heavily to one knee. She followed through by banging his forehead sharply against the edge of the desk. When Stan reached up to steady himself, Geldman grabbed his right hand and twisted it behind his back. She used the arm lock to force him back to his feet and bent him forward until his cheek rested against the countertop.

Ari drew his pistol and pressed it against Stan's temple. "Don't struggle, please."

The guard's eyes widened with fear, his gaze darting between his assailants, finally coming to rest on Manning, the only one of his attackers he could see without turning his head. Manning knew that look of terror well. *My God*, he thought, *I'm one of them now*.

She tightened her arm lock. "Key card. Where is it?"

"Left shirt pocket," Stan said with difficulty.

She jerked him upright so Ari could fish in Stan's pocket. He pulled out the key card.

"What's the pass code?" she demanded.

"What?"

She twisted his arm until he cried out in pain. "I noticed you're married, Stan. Would you like to see your wife again?"

"*Yes!*"

"*Then what's the pass code for this key card?*" she hissed between her teeth.

"There isn't one!" Stan pleaded. "Just swipe the card!"

"How convenient. What about the security tapes for the lobby cameras?"

"They record on a hard drive in the security office. Down the hallway and to the left. The key card works for that door too!"

Geldman relaxed her arm lock slightly. "See now? Wasn't that easy? Yuri, would you carry Stan's gun for him and take him someplace where he can relax until we're done?"

Yuri reached around her and retrieved Stan's pistol from its holster. He chambered a round and flicked off the safety. "This way," he said to Stan, leading him toward the back of the lobby, with Ari close behind. Geldman returned to Manning's side, standing slightly behind him.

"Please tell me you're not going to kill him," Manning murmured as the three men disappeared into the security office.

One of Geldman's plucked eyebrows lifted. "Are you worried about Stan or yourself? Don't worry, the next shift will find Stan duct-taped to a chair. Maybe a little humiliated, but very much alive." Her hand grasped the back of his arm like a pincer.

"You, on the other hand, I'm still thinking about." She locked eyes with him. "I guess that depends on whether I think you're going to be a problem or not."

Manning had to work to keep a pleading tone out of his voice. "How can I convince you I won't be?"

She leaned forward and whispered like a lover into his ear. "*Behave.*"

CHILD PRISON

MARCH 1983 – PHILADELPHIA, PENNSYLVANIA

Six-year-old Angela Kellerman knew something was wrong when she entered the foster home of Ed and Silvia Groutman. The house didn't smell like urine and mold like the last place, but Angela's finely tuned instincts immediately sensed danger.

"I don't like it here," she protested.

The social worker pushed her forward. "This is Mrs. Groutman. She's going to take care of you now."

Angela tried to struggle free from the social worker's grasp. "I want to go!" she cried.

The social worker ignored her. "Thank you for agreeing to take Angela on short notice, Mrs. Groutman. She was having problems with the male siblings at her previous home, so we were hoping that a home without boys might help calm her down."

Angela looked up at Mrs. Groutman. While the woman's mouth smiled, her eyes did not. "I'm sure little Angela will get along fine with the other girls, won't you dear?" She took Angela's hand and pulled her away from the social worker, hugging Angela against her flower-print dress. Mrs. Groutman smelled funny. Not stinky like sweat or sweet like perfume. Just clean, like she wasn't even there.

Angela heard the social worker close the door behind her. She tensed instinctively, like an animal sensing its path of escape had just been cut off.

Mrs. Groutman smiled down on her again. "Let's go make some lemonade, shall we? Then I'll introduce you to the rest of the girls."

Mrs. Groutman led her through the family room, where four girls ranging from her age to several years older sat. Two read books, two worked on sewing projects. They all wore identical flower-print dresses to Mrs. Groutman. They all sat ruler-straight in their chairs. They all avoided her gaze as Mrs. Groutman led her to the kitchen. The oldest girl made brief eye contact with Angela as she passed and gave her a strange look. If Angela had been older, she would have recognized it as pity.

* * *

Mrs. Groutman was very strict. She carried around a small paddle and popped all of the girls at the slightest hint of disobedience or backtalk. “She knows how to swing it just right,” her roommate Sarah warned. “Hard enough to make it burn like fire, but not enough to leave a mark you could show the social worker.” Angela learned quickly to fear Mrs. Groutman’s paddle and give the woman what she wanted in exchange for not feeling its bite.

What Mrs. Groutman wanted was order. Order and quiet. She dressed up all the girls like dolls and expected them to act like dolls too. Angela had never worn a dress before and found it strange, but not unpleasant. Likewise she had never learned things like manners, cooking, and sewing, but she was a quick learner, much to the delight of Mrs. Groutman.

She even made a friend, which was an entirely new experience for her. Her oldest foster sister Rachel was twelve, a willowy beauty with long brown hair and sad eyes. Rachel became a mother figure for Angela, patiently teaching her things like cutting dress patterns and how to wash silverware in a way that wouldn’t leave spots, thereby avoiding a swat from Mrs. Groutman. Angela began to feel a very strange sensation whenever Rachel was around. A normal child would immediately have identified the feeling as love, but Angela had no context for such emotions.

She did not have those feeling for her roommate Sarah. Sarah was a year older and resented sharing a bed with her as much as she detested the special treatment Mrs. Groutman gave Angela. “She only likes you because you’re pretty and you know how to suck up!” Sarah hissed at her one night.

Angela didn’t know what sucking up meant, but she was sure it deserved a punch in the face. So she delivered, mashing Sarah’s nose like one of Mrs. Groutman’s puffy dinner rolls. It bled a gusher, and Sarah screamed like a banshee. This pleased Angela, because previous experience had taught her that siblings who received such beatings seldom caused trouble after that. This would be well worth a few swats from Mrs. Groutman’s paddle.

Then the bedroom door exploded open and *Mr.* Groutman stormed into the room, his eyes bloodshot and fiery in the sudden blaze of the hall light. Mrs. Groutman rushed past him to tend to Sarah’s wailing performance, which went up another notch now that she had an audience. Mr. Groutman’s nostrils flared. He shook with anger.

"You little ungrateful brat!" he screamed, grabbing Angela by the hair and lifting her off the floor. She instinctively defended herself, pulling up on his arm and sinking her teeth into his wrist with all her might. He howled in pain and dropped her, then kicked her hard with his bare foot, launching her into the corner. Her head hit the wall hard enough to see stars.

"Don't!" Mrs. Groutman shouted. "It'll leave a bruise!"

Angela never forgot the terror of Mr. Groutman's towering form blocking out the light as he descended upon her in fury. Despite her kicking and screaming, he manhandled her into the bathroom, lifted the toilet seat with his foot, and stuck her tiny head and shoulders into the bowl, ramming her head into the porcelain. She sucked in a surprised breath, her mouth and throat filling with water.

She had experienced a toilet dunking before from a teenage foster brother and had expected it to be merely the humiliating opening to a memorable paddling. But to her horror, Mr. Groutman held her under the water, his grip like iron on the back of her neck.

"How do you like *this*, you little bitch?" she heard, the water giving Groutman's rant a hollow, far away sound. "Do you think *this* will leave a mark?" He held her under until she began to convulse, then hauled her clear of the water, the force that yanked her up as irresistible as the grip that had held her under. He held his snarling face up to hers as the water drained from her nose and mouth onto her nightgown.

"Do you think anybody will care if you live or die, you little shit?" He shoved her head back into the bowl. "I could bury your body out in the woods and nobody would even *look* for you, do you know that?" This time he held her under so long she became convinced he intended to do exactly that. Then it stopped hurting and the lights in the bathroom went out. He pulled her up and she vomited toilet water on both of them. She heard Mrs. Groutman weeping.

"Ed, *please!*" she sobbed. "She's only been here a few weeks! I'm sorry I lost control of her! Please! I promise I'll do better with her!"

He threw Angela like a rag doll on the bathroom floor. "She's right, you're not worth going to jail for, you little cockroach!" he growled, stalking away. Later that night Angela heard Mr. Groutman take out his remaining anger on Mrs. Groutman, the sounds of slaps and sobs seeping through the bedroom wall well into the night.

* * *

The next day the social worker came for a visit. Mrs. Groutman dressed them all up in matching tea dresses and put bows in their hair. Angela felt like one of the dolls on her sisters' shelves, fancy and useless. She failed to see the utility of dolls and didn't understand Mrs. Groutman's fascination with dressing up them or her. The only use Angela had ever found for a doll was as a club, especially if the doll was the victim's favorite.

Mrs. Groutman pulled her aside. "Angela, do you understand that if you tell the social worker what happened last night they will take you away from here?" Angela noticed Mrs. Groutman wore even more make-up than usual today, and the skin underneath had a bluish color.

"Yes," she answered politely. The thought of squealing and escape had occurred to her.

Mrs. Groutman squatted to look Angela in the eye. "But do you understand that we are absolutely the *last* family that will ever take you? Everyone else is tired of your fighting and your smart mouth. If the social worker takes you away this time, it won't be to another foster family, it will be to the child prison."

"The child prison?" Angela whispered. She had never heard of that before.

Mrs. Groutman nodded solemnly. "Yes, dear. You don't sleep in beds in the child prison, you sleep in a cage. You never get to come out, even for Christmas, and they feed you nothing but creamed spinach through the bars."

Angela swallowed hard. She had gotten a Christmas present only once, but she knew she hated creamed spinach.

Mrs. Groutman shook her head grimly. "And you'll never get to see Rachel, ever again. Wouldn't that be sad?"

Angela felt a tightness in her chest. "I don't want to go to the child prison, Mrs. Groutman."

Mrs. Groutman reached out to puff the sleeves of Angela's tea dress. "Well then, don't you think it would be better for everyone if we pretend that last night never happened?"

Angela nodded. "Yes, Mrs. Groutman."

[1] Doctor Walther Gerlach was a professor of physics at the University of Munich, one of the pioneers of quantum mechanics. Co-creator of the Stern-Gerlach experiment for which Polish physicist Otto Stern won the 1943 Nobel Prize for Physics. Because Gerlach was actively working for the Nazis at that time, he was denied his share of the prize. Gerlach may have been involved in much smaller projects similar to the Bell as early as 1924. (Source: *The SS Brotherhood of the Bell* by Joseph Farrell, p. 272, photo credit: Physics University of Frankfurt)

[2] Jakob Sporrenberg was captured by the Allies and interrogated at length by war crimes investigators because of his status as an SS general. Eventually he was extradited to Poland to stand trial for the executions of the Polish POWs depicted in the prologue. He was executed by hanging in Warsaw on December 6, 1952. Before his death he told Polish Intelligence officers everything he knew about the Bell in an attempt to bargain for his life. In 1998 Polish World War II researcher Igor Witkowski was allowed to read the transcripts of these interrogations, which formed the basis for his 2003 book *The Truth about the Wonder Weapons*, which was the first public mention of an SS project called the Bell. (Source: *The Hunt for Zero Point* by Nick Cook, p. 184, photo credit: Axis History Forum)

CHAPTER 3

CLEANING CREW

PRESENT DAY – SAN JOSE, CALIFORNIA

Ari and Yuri emerged from the security office without Stan. Ari waved a small flat box. "I turned the camera system off and pulled the hard drive. Stan's clearance wasn't high enough to turn off the rest of the security systems."

Geldman led Manning toward the elevators. "As long as we don't start a fire we should be fine. Let's go."

Yuri and Ari retrieved their bags then joined Geldman and Manning in the elevator. Yuri swiped Stan's card through the reader and pressed the button for the top floor of the building. Ari opened his electronics case and twisted a knob under the center screen. The single curve displayed on the screen changed shape as Ari fiddled. "The signal is definitely coming from the left, strength still increasing," he said.

"Can you tell if they're all together?" she asked.

Ari punched four buttons on the console. The shape of the curve on his screen didn't change. "All four cell phone signals have the same direction and strength. I'd say yes. Okay, strength is dropping. They're beneath us now."

"Below eighth floor," Geldman said. Yuri swiped Stan's key card and hit "4." The car reversed direction.

"There's peak again," Ari announced.

"Sixth floor," she confirmed. With another swipe of the key card, the car moved a short distance and the doors opened. Manning saw a hint of motion in his peripheral vision and a pistol materialized in her hand.

"Yuri, check left," she ordered. She crossed in front of Manning and extended her pistol around the right side of the doorway. Yuri did the same thing on the left. "Clear," she whispered.

"Clear," Yuri agreed, before disappearing down the hall to the left. Ari followed, cradling the open electronics box in both hands.

Geldman jerked her head in the direction of her henchmen. "Go," she ordered.

Manning complied, watching over Ari's shoulder as he worked. He felt Geldman's hand grasp his shoulder, but when he looked back her gaze was fixed in the opposite direction, back toward the elevators. She maintained hand contact as they crept forward, keeping her attention behind them.

Ari stopped halfway down the hall, turning his body with the box in front. He held up two fingers and pointed directly in front of him, then pointed two fingers slightly off to his right. Yuri nodded.

Ari quietly closed the case and handed it to Manning. Ari stood in front of the nearest office door, adjusting the borrowed jacket on his shoulders and tucking his right hand inside to grasp the silenced submachine gun.

Yuri pressed himself against the wall just beyond the office door. Geldman pressed Manning to the wall with her left hand, her right hand holding her pistol across his chest. He realized a few seconds later that she was using his body as a shield.

After looking to Geldman for approval, Ari pounded on the door. A few seconds later he started shouting in Arabic along with his pounding. He answered a muffled query from inside with another impatient tirade until the lock clicked.

As soon as light from inside spilled into the hallway, Ari forced the door opened with his foot. He answered a surprised exclamation from inside by unmasking his gun and firing a three-round burst at point-blank range. Manning heard a body fall. He had never heard a real silenced weapon before. It made more of a hissing sound, along with the clicking of the action, rather than the whistling thud he had heard in the movies.

Ari leaned inside and fired another three-round burst, then rushed through the door. Yuri followed close behind. Manning heard a shout and a single loud gunshot. Ari's gun hissed another pair of three-round bursts. Silence followed.

"Clear!" Ari announced a few seconds later.

"Clear!" Yuri responded.

Geldman pushed Manning forward. "Let's go."

He stepped through the doorway and froze, almost dropping Ari's case. One of the terrorists lay just inside, ragged holes punched in his chest, throat, and forehead. A small amount of blood oozed from the bloody entry wounds, but fluid poured from the terrorist's head, forming an almost-black puddle two feet across and growing. Another terrorist slouched against the far wall, dispatched with an identical trio of wounds. A blood splatter on the wall showed where he had been standing, along with a trail marking his slide to a squatting position, his shattered head hanging forward.

The hallway door opened onto a small office suite. The first two bodies lay in an anteroom with a secretary's desk. Doorways opened to the left and right at the far end of the room. She pushed him forward and closed the door. "Are you going to hurl again?"

"No," he replied, despite the spastic contractions in his stomach and the salty taste in his mouth.

She continued pushing him forward. "Talk to me, Ari. Did one of them get a shot off?"

Ari stood near the doorway leading to the right. He motioned to a bullet hole in the drywall. "Yeah, but he was pretty flustered. Missed me by almost a foot."

She glanced at the hole. "That far, huh? Did they leave any gear behind?"

Ari grinned. "Come take a look."

"Don't just stand there," she said, prodding Manning in the back with her pistol.

He followed Ari into the next room. Electronic equipment and wires covered a long table. A spidery-looking antenna on a tripod sat aimed toward the window. A young Arab man lay sprawled just inside the door, perforated just like the men outside. An older man in a shirt and tie slouched in a chair, his dripping skull hanging limply backward.

"The laptops are still on," she observed. "Make sure their screensavers don't lock us out."

"Right," Ari replied.

She steered Manning to the table, stepping casually over the body on the floor. "Mike, do you know what this equipment is?"

"Were they trying to get free satellite TV?"

That earned a cold laugh. "No, this is what separates these guys from terrorists."

He was confused. "I thought they *were* terrorists."

Fine lines formed at the corners of her mouth. "Me too. But this is a government-grade satellite communications set up. The kind of gear you'd use to transmit internationally if you didn't want the CIA or NSA listening in. Rashid wasn't running this as a rogue op. *Somebody* in the royal family sent Rashid here, at the very least his uncle Ali."

"To do what?"

The lines deepened. "That's what we need to find out. Ari, any luck?"

Ari split his attention between the two laptops on the table. "Their data files are encrypted, and I'm afraid if I make blind stabs at the password, their security software may wipe the drives. I have equipment that can crack the encryption, but that will take time."

She scowled. "So the short answer is we killed four people and we still don't know jack."

If her rebuke bothered him, it didn't show. He jerked his thumb toward the body behind him. "Well, I know this guy isn't even an Arab. He sure as hell isn't Saudi."

"What?" she moved to examine the corpse. "Oh my God, that's Yves Gillaud. I didn't recognize him without the top of his head. He's a freelance communication expert, or was. He did good work. I'll have to send his wife some flowers."

Manning stared at her, sure she was making some kind of sick joke, but no one laughed.

She snapped her fingers. "Wait a minute! Yves always squirreled away operational data for insurance whenever he was on a job. It was a trick he taught me. He'd FTP the data to a personal server using a masked portal. Look for a shadowed cache file containing the words, 'Jacob Fleischer.'"

"What did Jake have to do with *these* guys?" Manning asked.

"He's dead."

He stared at her dumbly.

"*Sacré mérde!*" Ari exclaimed. "I found a file saying the team had targeted a lawyer named Jacob Fleischer for interrogation and elimination."

"Why?" Manning asked.

She ignored him. "Look in the adjacent folders and see what else you can find."

He looked over Ari's shoulder. He didn't speak French, but one word of the file jumped out at him from his conversation with Fleischer. "So why were they interested in the Nanovex corporation?" he asked.

Ari and Geldman froze as if he had uttered an unspeakable profanity. After a tense silence, she said quietly, "Mike, maybe you should take a seat outside."

"Sure." He was glad to leave the blood-splattered room. He stepped over two bodies and sat down in the outer office. It wasn't until he sat down that he realized he was shaking again.

"Okay, Ari, did you find anything else?" he heard from the other room, but the rest of their conversation was inaudible. He turned his chair to face away from the carnage. He didn't need any reminders that he would probably be just another body on the floor before this was over.

Geldman stuck her head back into the anteroom. "Mike, you said the people who were cutting Fleischer up were an Indian man and woman?"

He had no idea why they were back on that subject. "Yeah..."

"You sure?"

He turned in his chair. "Well, they were *shooting* at me, so I didn't stop and stare."

Fair enough." She dialed her cell phone. He could overhear a woman's voice answering the call. "Hello Gaya, this is Angela," she said cheerfully. "I understand you had some difficulties today. Really? I have a friend here who knew the subject personally and can place you at the job site. You wouldn't call that a problem?" After a long pause with no response, Geldman continued. "Well, I certainly hope you were paid in advance, because I'm standing in your employer's office right now, and I don't think he's going to be writing checks any time soon."

She just called herself Angela, Manning noted. *So this Monica Geldman identity is just another fiction. That dead Rashid guy called her by her* _real_ *name. At least, as real as* _anything_ *is in her world. Angela Conrad.* Fitting those two pieces of the puzzle gave him at least a tiny measure of satisfaction in his otherwise out-of-control world.

After another lengthy pause, he heard a tinny, “What do you want?” come from the other end of Conrad’s phone conversation.

"Why, I want you to finish the job, of course!" she bubbled, like a salesman who had just made quota. "Has there been any police presence at the original job site? I understand, my men can find out. What were you going to be paid? Fine, if you can clean up both locations we'll double that. No problem, dear, we’re all professionals. Do you know the location of your employer's office? Good, we'll see you in a few minutes."

She ended the call. "Ari, get back to the hotel and find out if the police have found Fleischer's body yet. Yuri, go down to the lobby and let Gaya and Raj in."

"Got it," the henchmen replied in unison. Ari threw Manning’s jacket on the desk as he left. “Thanks for the loaner,” he said in passing.

"Mike, can you handle a laptop without breaking it?" she asked.

"Haven't broken mine lately.”

"Good. Come in here and get these computers ready for transport."

He was grateful for something to do besides sitting and contemplating his fate. At least until he had to work around the dead bodies of Gillaud and the other Saudi. He bumped Gillaud's body several times packing up the laptops and the satellite antenna.

"Don't move the bodies," she scolded. "And don't step in the blood, it'll just make the clean up harder."

Manning bit his tongue and kept working—the clean up team could just as easily come for him as well. A few minutes later he heard a quiet knock on the door. Conrad greeted the newcomers and led them to the office where Manning worked. The Indian man and woman examined the carnage with a calm detachment, occasionally pointing and murmuring to one another, as casually as they would if shopping for groceries. Manning froze when they made eye contact with him, half-expecting them to draw weapons on him again. But after a momentary pause they ignored him and went about their work.

Conrad leaned into the room. "Mike, are you about done back there?"

He continued unplugging the spaghetti-tangle of wires between the laptops. "Just about."

The Indian woman elbowed him aside. "Excuse me, please." Her latex-clad hands moved with lightning speed, rounding up the cables and shoving them into a black plastic bag. She held out the bag. "Here. Leave, please."

He accepted the bag, scooping up the laptops and exiting the office/slaughterhouse. Soon, the sound of bone saws and grinding flesh made him even more glad to be in the other room. He swallowed hard.

"You gonna puke?" Conrad asked.

He laid the electronics on one of the desks and shook his head. "Nope. Just wish I was someplace else."

She prodded one of the prone corpses with her foot. "There's worse places to be."

LAB RATS

PRESENT DAY, NANOVEX COMPANY – SAN JOSE, CALIFORNIA

Lead Scientist Jeff Wood looked from the control booth into a large white clean room, about fifty feet on a side. A wide red circle painted on the floor enclosed two-thirds of the clean room's area. Rats scurried about inside three cages, one inside the red circle, two outside.

He and the three technicians inside the observation booth all wore white biohazard isolation suits. He stood behind the technicians, each seated at a terminal. Even though Wood believed the suits made them invulnerable to the hazards of the test, the demeanor of the technicians appeared less certain. The fate of the four technicians and the manager who had occupied the booth during the previous test was never far from anyone's mind, he was sure. Their fate had led to added precaution of the suits, in addition to the upgraded protections of the booth itself.

"Are we ready?" he asked.

"Instrumentation ready."

"Life sciences ready."

"Dispersal ready."

"Proceed," Wood ordered.

The dispersal technician Molly Kiernan confirmed her way through several warning screens, hesitating over the final mouse pick.

"Is there a problem, Molly?" Wood asked.

"No sir," she replied, clicking the mouse one final time. A red window with glaring yellow letters popped up on her screen:

AGENT RELEASE IN 0:30 SECONDS!
ABORT?

The countdown continued without interruption. At zero, the agent vented from a small silver cylinder in the center of the clean room. The hiss of the gas was picked up by microphones inside the chamber and replayed in their headsets with enough volume to make all four jump.

"Jesus!" life sciences technician Josh Hackett declared, his exclamation half expletive, half prayer.

Wood placed a hand on the jittery technician's shoulder. "Steady, everybody. Mark, can you lower that volume a little?"

"Yes sir," the instrumentation technician Mark Wong replied.

"Molly, how's it looking?" Wood asked.

Her screen showed a cross-section of the clean room, a growing bloom of false color spreading outward from the cylinder. "Approaching optimal dispersal. Give it another thirty seconds."

Wood squinted through the glass, trying to see any hint of the agent in the room. Even next to the cylinder, where the cloud was the most dense, the agent was completely invisible. "Okay. Josh, you got a good baseline on those rats?"

Hackett cycled through several screens. "Yeah, the hiss startled them a little, but they've settled down now. No discernible effect from the agent."

The dispersal screen now showed a uniform cloud of red, with a small puddle of purple near the cylinder. "The agent is fully dispersed," Kiernan announced. "Ready for the signal."

To Wood, the air in the observation booth seemed to thicken and become difficult to breathe. He swallowed hard and mentally repeated the list of safety upgrades that had been made since the last test. "Mark, give me a camera on cage one and verify that we're recording."

The instrumentation screen showed a view looking down on four white rats foraging nonchalantly inside their cage. A red "REC" flashed in the corner of the screen. "We're rolling," Wong affirmed, the tension in his voice incompletely disguised.

Wood took a deep breath. "Transmit the signal."

Kiernan clicked through three levels of warning screens until a ten-second countdown displayed. She positioned her mouse hopefully over the "ABORT" button.

The countdown ticked to zero, and a low tone sounded for ten seconds. The tone was selected to jangle as few nerves as possible. Everyone in the room still visibly tensed.

All eyes in the room fixed on the screen with the rats. Before the warning tone had ended, the screams of the four rodents filled their headphones. The animals went into seizures immediately, writhing in agony on their backs. Their breaths came in spasms until a pink froth bubbled from their mouths, then breathing stopped entirely. It seemed to take an eternity, but in reality the whole process took less than a minute.

"Josh?" Wood asked.

Hackett surveyed the collection of flatlines on his screen. "They're dead. Last life indication at fifty-eight seconds."

"What about the other rats?"

Hackett cycled through the screens for the other two cages. "Listening to their buddies die shook them up plenty, but other than elevated heart rate and respiration, they're still within norms."

"Let's see if they stay that way," Wood wondered aloud. "Move cage two into the zone."

Wong changed the overhead camera to the second cage as a conveyor belt moved it inside the red circle. Ten seconds later those rats suffered the same grisly fate. A long silence followed as they absorbed the ramifications of their success.

"Control group?"

Hackett examined the vital signs of the last rat cage. "They're good. No change."

"Molly, terminate the signal."

"Signal terminated," she affirmed.

"Purge the test chamber."

Powerful fans whipped the air beyond the glass, drawing the agent from the room. The colors on Kiernan's screen swirled, lightening from red to orange to yellow to white.

Wood keyed his radio. "Test complete. Decontamination team standby." His voice boomed throughout the lab.

"Airborne agent count down to safe levels," Kiernan reported.

Wood moved to the instrumentation technician. "Mark, what's the count here in the control room?"

Mark Wong refreshed his screen three times to make sure of his reading. "Zero. No agent. Not a nano."

Wood pulled off the helmet of his containment outfit, his sigh audible in the team's headsets. He noticed that no one else followed suit. "We did it, people. This is going to change history."

"For better or worse?" Molly Kiernan asked quietly.

OWNERSHIP

SAN JOSE, CALIFORNIA

An hour later, Raj and Gaya's grisly work was done. The bodies had disappeared into several black plastic five-gallon containers by the door. Raj ran a compact carpet cleaning machine over the bloody spots on the floor. Gaya spackled the bullet holes and covered the plaster with fast-drying paint she had mixed by hand to match the color of the walls.

The couple had not been able to erase all traces of the massacre. The bloody pools had been reduced to faded stains resembling water marks on the carpet. The stomach-turning odor of fresh blood had been replaced with a nose-burning chemical smell.

"We've done all we can do here, I'm sorry," Gaya apologized.

Conrad dismissed her concerns with a wave. "Nobody's going to look that hard for a bunch of Saudis with assumed names who jumped their lease. Good work." She turned. "Mike, we're done here. Let's go."

He stood and gathered the laptops, eager to have the sights and smells of the high-rise meat packing plant behind him.

She stopped him. "I'll get the laptops, you help them with the blood buckets."

"Okay..." he said hesitantly. He lifted one of the black plastic canisters, surprised at first by the weight. Then he realized that each bucket contained a significant fraction of a human being. He hefted another container with his left hand to balance the load, taking great care not to let the fleshpots brush against his clothing.

Gaya held the door open while Manning wobbled into the hallway. Raj carefully strapped the buckets onto a two-wheeled dolly. When Manning steadied one of the containers with his hand the plastic was warm against his skin. His stomach fluttered, but he suppressed it easily. *I'm already getting used to this*, he thought. *I'm not sure if that's a good thing or not.*

A few minutes later, a pair of two-wheeled dollies were loaded with three buckets each. Conrad motioned for Manning to take the second dolly and follow Raj to the elevator. She placed a call on her cell phone.

"Yuri, is the lobby clear? Okay, were on our way down."

As they entered the elevator, the vibrator on Conrad's cell phone buzzed. She checked the number before answering. "Yeah, go ahead." She listened for several seconds. "Good. Bring the van back and pick us up. Bye."

"Raj?" she asked the Indian. "Did you use a silencer back at the hotel?"

His gaze danced between Conrad and Manning, the witness he had tried to shoot. "Yes," he said hesitantly.

"Good," she replied. "That saved us a bunch of trouble. Ari says he found two bullet holes in the hallway, but no police presence."

When the elevator doors opened, Manning saw Yuri seated at the security guard's desk, a newspaper concealing most of his face.

"Yuri, time to go," Conrad ordered. "Check on the guard and make sure he'll be okay till morning."

She met Manning's gaze, apparently reading his mind. "See? I don't kill people just for the fun of it."

Yuri suppressed a laugh as he walked away.

"Well, most of the time," she admitted.

* * *

Conrad escorted Manning back to Jacob Fleischer's hotel room. Fleischer's body still lay on the plastic-covered bed. His pale skin had turned a blotchy gray from the loss of the blood now puddled on the clear sheeting over the carpet. Both legs had been sawn off, sectioned, and the pieces stuffed into one of the Indian couple's trademark black cleanup buckets left behind when they fled the room.

"Oh God," he groaned. After all the corpses he'd seen today -- he just realized he had lost count -- seeing Fleischer's body made him woozy all over again. He felt his legs wobble.

Conrad shoved the rolling chair from the hotel room's desk underneath him, swiveling it to face away from the butchery. "It's different when it's someone you know, isn't it?" she said, patting his shoulder.

There was a knock at the door.

After checking the peephole, she opened the door just wide enough to admit the Indian couple and their equipment. They returned to work without a word.

Conrad checked her watch. "It's after eleven, don't use power saws. The last thing we need is the guest next door making a noise complaint."

"That will take much longer," Raj cautioned.

"Not a request."

The couple frowned, but drew hand saws from their bags and set to work. Manning held his composure until an arm came off, the smell of curdled corpse-blood filling the air. He lunged for a trash can, coughing convulsively as Conrad guided him to the bathroom.

She pushed him down next to the toilet, then wet a washcloth and handed it to him. "Sorry. I should have moved you when they arrived." She left the water running. "That should help cover up some of the noise. And drink some water, you'll feel better."

"Thanks," he croaked. He wiped his face and rose to sit on the edge of the tub. "I know you do this for a living, but how can you even *look* at that shit without hurling, much less *smelling* it?"

She shrugged. "Before I went into the field, my handler sent me to work in a slaughterhouse for a week. After you've butchered a pig by hand, a person isn't that much different. It's all just meat."

He gave her an incredulous look. "So it doesn't affect you at all, then?"

Her nose wrinkled. "Well, I'll never eat bacon again, that's for sure."

He managed a weak smile. "Glad even you have your limits."

She backed out of the bathroom, blocking his view through the doorway. "Sit tight. This will all be over in a few minutes." She closed the door.

He stuck a glass under the running faucet and downed the water in a few quick gulps. He refilled the glass, only then realizing how badly his hands were shaking. Suddenly his legs gave way and he sagged onto the toilet. He was so screwed. There was no way Conrad would let him live after what he had seen today. Even if they hadn't taken his phone, even if the police could snatch him from this hotel room, he couldn't imagine a place he could hide from this psycho spy woman and her murdering henchmen. And if he *did* manage to escape home, all he would achieve would be to guarantee his wife and sons sharing his fate once they eventually found him.

His wife and sons. He sighed and put his head in his hands. He had been so focused on his own survival for the past few hours that he had pushed them out of his mind. But now that he would probably never see them again, they were all he could think about. Especially his wife, Amanda. He had spent so much time traveling since Eric and Kevin were born that he really wasn't that close to his boys. He sure as hell would never have the chance to set *that* right. He checked his watch. He had long since missed his nightly check-in call. He wondered how long he would be dead before his wife started the futile search for his body.

The rhythmic scraping of a bone saw against a particularly resilient member of Jacob Fleischer’s body intruded into the bathroom. His alertness was jolted into panic. Could he fight back? He had been a quarterback once, but that was a long time ago. Not that it would make any difference, even if Conrad’s goons weren't around. He had seen her take down two armed men all by herself. No, resisting would only replace a quick death with a slower, agonizing one.

He didn't want to die. Death was something that was supposed to happen a long time from now, when his teeth were in a glass by the bed and he had plenty of time to prepare. But death was coming for him *now*, and he wasn't ready.

He always assumed that death would be like switching off a light bulb. Lights out, story over. But what if it wasn't like that? What if his grandmother had been right? She had tried to put the fear of God into him as a boy with stories of life after death and eternal judgment. With the life he had lived, he had little doubt what his fate would be if her stories were true. If Hell was real, he’d be there shortly.

The bathroom door opened.

"Get up," Conrad ordered.

His legs shook under him as he rose to his feet and followed her out of the bathroom. The carnage that had been Jacob Fleischer was entirely cleared out. The body parts, the plastic sheets, and the buckets of blood-soaked sawdust were gone, along with the Indian couple. The bed was freshly made, and the reek of blood and death was replaced with a strong chemical stench. He glanced around the room nervously.

"What's wrong?" she asked, her face showing genuine puzzlement.

"The Indians..." he stammered, "I thought, I..." his voice trailed off.

She stared at him for a moment, then her eyes widened. "Oh my god, you thought you were *next*, didn't you?"

Unsure of what to say to ensure his survival, he simply nodded.

She suppressed a laugh. "Oh, you poor bastard! So you were sitting in the john waiting for me to come put a bullet in your head?"

He felt himself shaking again. "I didn't know *what* to think."

She smirked. "The CIA generally doesn't kill American citizens unless it has to."

CIA? What the hell? "So your Russian and Israeli friends are CIA, too?"

She shrugged. "We hire contractors if they have the right skills for the job. Be glad you weren't counting on the police to save your ass from those Saudis. You'd be in a bucket right next to Fleischer."

He had no idea what to do next, since his termination didn't appear to be on Conrad's agenda. "So what happens now?"

She stepped closer. "Now I need *your* help. Jacob Fleischer was my agent inside a company called Nanovex, which you've apparently heard of. Fleischer was performing a very similar job for Nanovex as your firm was performing for Chemtrox—damage control. They're about to find out they have a vacancy in their legal department. You will apply for that opening."

Manning blinked. "I already have a job."

"You'll turn in your notice the day you get back home."

"*What*?" he gasped. He and his wife both grew up in Chicago. She was as likely to move to California as the Cubs were to win the World Series. He had to deflect this. "How do I know Nanovex will even *hire* me?"

She smiled slyly. "I have faith. I also have connections. Trust me."

He felt his much-abused stomach sink further. "But I don't *want* to quit my job. My wife would *kill* me if I made her move."

Her smile faded. "I think in light of current events you *owe* me one, *asshole*."

"But you're talking about uprooting my entire life, for Christ's sake!"

"A life I just *saved* a couple of times today, I'd like to point out," she snapped.

He shook his head. "I'm sorry. You're asking too much."

She stepped in close enough for him to feel the heat of her body. His half-a-head height advantage obviously didn't intimidate her. "Let me make one thing perfectly clear; I'm not *asking* at all. I *own* you. With all you've seen today, the *only* thing stopping me from putting you in the ground *right now* is that you *might* prove useful to me." Her eyes narrowed. "That can change, of course."

"I thought the CIA didn't kill Americans," he said, trying to keep the quiver out of his voice.

"Unless *absolutely* necessary," she added. "You've seen enough to completely shut down my team, and I am *not* going to let a threat to my team keep breathing. *Convince* me that you're not going to become a threat."

One look in her eyes told him she was as deadly serious about having her way as she had been when hunting down the Saudis. He sighed. "Okay, what do we do next?"

The intensity in her eyes did not diminish with his apparent surrender. "You stay here for a few minutes. When we're in position the room phone will ring twice. Go back to your suite and stay there until your flight leaves tomorrow morning. We'll follow you to the airport to make sure you're not on anyone's radar. Go home, make your move with Nanovex, and I'll contact you once you're in position."

He swallowed. Hard. "Got it."

She stepped even closer, grasping his lapels. She lowered her voice, her tone venomous. "And if at any point you decide to call the police or the FBI, three things *will* happen: one, they won't believe you; two, I *will* find out about it; and three, you'll find out that Kentucky Fried Chicken isn't the only company with a family bucket."

"Dear...*God!*" he stammered.

Conrad gave him a tight smile. "I'm glad we understand each other. Remember to wait for two rings. See you in the morning." She left the room without looking back.

Manning sagged onto the floor and buried his face in his hands.

CHAPTER 4

KRIEGSENTSCHEIDEND

JANUARY 1944 – LUDWIGSDORF, POLAND

As General Jakob Spoerrenberg had expected, his superior SS *Obergeneral* Hans Kammler was in a foul mood when he finally arrived at the remote testing facility. With Allied bombers reaching farther and farther into Nazi territory, Kammler had decided to move the research team for the Bell from Dresden more than one hundred-fifty kilometers east to a tiny coal mining town in Poland.

General Kammler emerged stiffly from his Mercedes staff car, parked in a downpour at the entrance of the former Wenceslas Mine. "Report!" he barked.

"*Guten tag, mein General!*" Spoerrenberg said with as much cheerfulness as his nerves allowed. "Did you have a pleasant journey?"

Kammler bristled. "I did not move this project to the ass end of nowhere so I could have a pleasant country drive!"

Here in a valley of the picturesque Sudeten Mountains the Bell had nearly perfect concealment. An abandoned coal mine had been extensively enlarged into an underground research facility with the help of Polish POW labor. It would be impervious to all but the most determined Allied or Russian bombing attacks. But their enemies would have to find it first, and both the remote location and the harsh SS security measures Spoerrenberg had put in place made that extremely unlikely.[1]

He hurried beside Kammler to the tunnel mouth to get out of the rain. "Of course not, *Herr General!* I was merely trying to make you feel welcome!"

Once inside, Kammler handed off his dripping greatcoat and peaked SS cap to a subordinate. "I sent you to this hellhole to kick ass, Jakob, not to kiss mine." He lifted one corner of his mouth, backing off from his gruff manner.

Hans Kammler was tall and thin, with a strong jaw and high, chiseled cheekbones so prized among Hitler's officers as a sign of pure Aryan blood. A prominent, almost beaklike nose gave him a predatory look, like the human embodiment of the iron eagle atop a Nazi flag standard. But all these features merely framed his fierce, deep-set eyes—black, bottomless, and utterly devoid of pity. He looked older than his forty-three years. Spoerrenberg assumed it was from the weight of the responsibilities the General held.

"Of course, General," Spoerrenberg affirmed, allowing himself a relieved breath. At least Kammler was not here to conduct summary executions. After all, this was the man who had personally designed the gas chambers and ovens for Auschwitz, which became the model for death camps all over the Third Reich. Even *he* feared Kammler. "Please follow me, sir. We have made much progress since my last report." [2]

"I certainly hope so," Kammler growled. "Every other week I am called to Berlin to fight like a wolf for the funds we are pouring into this pit."

* * *

After the disastrous first test of the Bell in Dresden, Kammler's researchers plumbed the depths of every technical well they could find to discover the science behind the mysterious phenomena they had accidentally discovered. They interviewed the top physicists in Germany and searched worldwide scientific journals, finding the answer in an unlikely place—the disgraced American genius inventor, Nikola Tesla.

Subsequent to single-handedly inventing alternating current, long-distance electrical power distribution and the modern three-phase electric motor, Tesla fell out of favor with his benefactors by claiming that the universe itself could be tapped for unlimited free energy. When the American capitalist J.P. Morgan severed Tesla's funding he remarked, "If the energy you are creating is free for everyone, where do you stick the meter?" Spoerrenberg was convinced that J.P. Morgan must have secretly been Jewish to have willfully deprived mankind of Tesla's wonders. Such behavior would never be tolerated under the forward-thinking principles of National Socialism. [3]

* * *

"I am of course very grateful for your patronage, General," Spoerrenberg acknowledged. He led Kammler deeper into the mountainside tunnel. Hewn into solid rock, the tunnel was four meters across and almost three meters high. The construction was so sturdy it did not require internal bracing. If one *had* to ride out an Allied bombing strike, he reasoned, this would be the place to do it. Bare forty-watt electrical bulbs hung from a cord at three-meter intervals along both walls. Daylight was quickly replaced by the eternal twilight of Spoerrenberg's world, even before the massive iron doors slammed shut over the tunnel mouth behind them.

A long parade of exhausted Polish workers approached on their left, dust covering their black-and-white-striped uniforms. As he had planned, twelve-hour shifts of hard labor left them almost too fatigued to walk, much less discuss or execute acts of sabotage. He purposely met the gaze of one of the prisoners. He saw no hatred, no calculation, only desperate weariness. Good.

"*Achtung!*" a guard shouted. "Prisoners face the wall! *Schnell!*" The POWs obediently ceased their shuffling and turned away while the German generals passed.

Kammler, who held a doctorate in engineering, ignored the workers and eyed the craftsmanship of the tunnel walls. "You have done well here, Jakob. All of this in six months?"

"*Jawhol, Herr General*, thank you! We turn here." A branch of the tunnel forked to the right, its large height and width made necessary by the dimensions of the Bell.

Kammler stopped, pointing further down the original tunnel. "What lies in that direction?"

"Construction of new test spaces," Spoerrenberg explained. "Radiation from the device makes each chamber unusable after only a few tests."

Walking over a hundred meters down the side tunnel, they reached a pair of thick steel doors. Kammler's eyebrows arched. "How long does each test last?"

Spoerrenberg gave the signal to open the doors. "Each test lasts only a few minutes. The danger is still severe."

Reinforced steel doors slowly creaked open, requiring the efforts of two soldiers each. Inside, like an alien creature caged for the safety of mankind, sat the Bell. Kammler stepped forward, but Spoerrenberg held him back. "We attempt to decontaminate the chamber after each test, but it is still not safe past this point, General."

Kammler eyed the soldiers guarding the chamber. "Who conducts the decontaminations?"

"Why, the prisoners of course," he replied. A different soldier wearing a heavily shielded garment supervised the prisoners each time, but the prisoners wore only their standard-issue garb. At least they received a new garment afterwards. Only a few had died. So far.

"Good. Explain to me the instrumentation you use for the tests."

* * *

The key element in Tesla's power generation plans were two counter-rotating cylinders filled with mercury vapor and charged to hundreds of thousands of volts. The resemblance to the Bell was striking--only the medium of mercury vapor had been exchanged for vaporized uranium in the German design. Tesla stated his design would draw unlimited amounts of power "directly from the vacuum surrounding all things," and that the builders should be prepared for "an extremely powerful motive force along the generator's axis of rotation." Tesla was truly a genius ahead of his time. [4]

* * *

Spoerrenberg pointed to the racks of equipment and cameras surrounding the Bell. "We now thoroughly monitor radiation levels, vibrations, and magnetic field intensity, in addition to ordinary measurements of voltages, temperature, and so on. We also place samples of living tissue on the racks for each test to examine the aftereffects."

"Living tissue?"

"Plants, small animals, human blood and organ specimens; whatever the scientists on the Biological Effects team request."

Kammler stepped away from the door of the test chamber. "I see. What exactly is your test profile today?"

Spoerrenberg stepped back as well, giving the signal to secure the doors. "Today we will be conducting a full power test to determine the maximum thrust produced by the Bell using *Herr* Debus's new power supply. We will also see if using Tesla's specifications have reduced the ill effects of the Bell as his plans suggest."

Kammler seemed pleased. "Excellent. When can we begin the test?"

"Immediately, *Herr General*." He led the entourage away from the test chamber.

"Where is this *Herr* Debus I hear so much of?" Kammler asked.

"Waiting in the control room with Professor Gerlach, sir. He has been quite an asset to the program, a true genius in high-voltage physics." It was

Debus who took Tesla's plans and constructed a power supply that would set the Bell into motion and safely regulate its operation.

"I hear he is an outstanding Nazi party member as well," Kammler said approvingly.

"Yes, General," Spoerrenberg agreed in a noncommittal tone. Debus allegedly had heard a coworker insinuate that the *Fuhrer's* decision to invade Russia *might* have been a mistake. Instead of coming to *him* with his concerns, Debus had reported the man straight to the *Gestapo*. Stupid bastard. Debus reportedly had a professional disagreement with the man and Spoerrenberg was relatively certain the denunciation was over petty jealously rather than valid loyalty concerns.

Regardless, the denounced scientist was important enough to the project that Spoerrenberg had spent the better part of two weeks talking the *Gestapo* into returning the man rather than sending him to the Russian front. But now if the man *did* turn into a security threat, Spoerrenberg's head would be in a noose right along with him. Damn that Debus. Unfortunately, he was just the kind of Nazi that General Kammler liked, a creature who instilled fear in those around him. [5]

* * *

In addition to explaining the science behind the Bell, before his death Tesla had drawn up intriguing designs for aircraft that flew by electromotive force alone, without wings or conventional propulsion. Indeed, Tesla's physics provided a completely unified alternative to the "Jewish" physics of Einstein and his ilk. But where Einstein failed in his attempt to create a "Grand Unified Field Theory" for the structure of the universe from subatomic particles all the way up to the physics behind the force of gravity, Tesla had been entirely successful. Indeed, Tesla himself had been totally contemptuous of Einstein's work, calling it "a beggar wrapped in purple that ignorant people take for a king." And the Bell was the key to it all. [6]

General Kammler compared the Bell to the Holy Grail or the Spear of Destiny, an artifact that gave its bearer supernatural power. Having seen the horrible side effects of the Bell up close, Spoerrenberg thought of the device more akin to Pandora's Box. Nevertheless, the SS believed the Bell so important that it was given its own classification, higher even than that given to the German atom bomb program—*Kriegsentscheidend*, or War Decisive. Spoerrenberg knew he was both lucky and cursed to carry the responsibility for such an important program. [7]

* * *

The shouting of guards in the main passageway announced the entry of the evening shift of POWs that would toil through the night making more tunnels.

Kammler stopped short of the control room door. “Jakob, I have never seen an autopsy report on the scientists killed in the Dresden accident. Do we know exactly why they died?”

He frowned. “No, General. We were in such a state of shock we cremated the bodies after a cursory examination. Tissue samples from subsequent tests have shown that the radiation produced by the Bell breaks down the organic matter of living things into carbon, water, and gaseous nitrogen. That was the source of the…*expulsions* we witnessed.”

“So we have no *formal* autopsies in our database,” Kammler pressed.

For some reason Spoerrenberg felt his skin crawl. “No, General.”

Kammler was already walking toward the main corridor. “Well then, we’ll have to take care of that.” He watched the POWs trudge by with a practiced eye. Finally he pointed and called for a particular prisoner to be pulled out of line. The worker was in his early twenties and while thin he appeared in better shape than the others.

“Remove his shirt,” Kammler ordered. The young man had a lean musculature and only a few of his ribs showing.

Kammler nodded. “Excellent. Give him back his shirt and take him to the test chamber,” he ordered the guard.

“*Jawhol, mein General!*” the guard replied with a salute.

Kammler turned to Spoerrenberg with a genuine smile. “There, *now* we will see if Tesla has made this cast-iron monster safe or not.” He clapped his hands together in anticipation. “Come Jakob, we have a test to run!”

GUCCI MAMA

PRESENT DAY – CHICAGO, ILLINOIS

Amanda Manning had just finished soaping up in the shower when she heard her husband's alarm go off for the third time. He had slept through the previous two promptings of his alarm clock without even stirring. This time the beeping was silenced, followed by a groan she heard clearly through the bathroom wall. Mike had returned last night from a trip so exhausted that he'd fallen into bed with hardly a word. So she let him sleep, knowing his alarm would repeat until it eventually roused him. If he was that exhausted, he needed his sleep, but now that he was awake she rinsed off quickly to free up the shower for him.

Toweling off, she checked her naked form in the mirror. She still looked damned good for having pumped out two kids. Sure, her hips were a little wider, but exercise and reasonable self-control over what she ate had kept all but the tiniest patches of cellulite off her thighs. But she didn't worry about those. From watching her friends, she had learned long ago that men didn't fool around on their wives because their women had gained a few pounds; they fooled around because their wives had lost their enthusiasm for sex. And you could console yourself all day long with how good a mom and homemaker you were, but the fact remained that men got married for sex, and if you didn't work at being a consistently good lay, you shouldn't bitch when you find out your husband's secretary was better at it than you.

She wasn't worried about that either. She kept Mike thoroughly satisfied, and always convinced him he was nothing less than a sex god in her eyes, even if she had to fake an orgasm every once in awhile. The occasional acting was just part of the job of not becoming a single mom. Not to mention that playing the sex-crazed bad girl behind closed doors was fun, too. It certainly kept *her* satisfied.

Amanda had always been on the buxom side, but the weight she had gained from her two boys had made her positively top-heavy. Her friends suggested that she get a breast reduction, but when she mentioned it to Mike, he remarked in horror that it would be like desecrating the eighth and ninth wonders of the world. So she put up with the underwired bras and the occasional backache to watch him pay homage at the altar of her boobs. He was a very faithful worshiper.

She heard him stirring in the bedroom. She pulled the clip from her shoulder-length brown hair, letting it fall. She dried off her legs and back to keep from soaking the bath mat, but left her breasts and stomach wet.

The bathroom door opened and Mike stumbled in, flinching at the brightness of the bathroom light. She quickly reached past him and hit the dimmer switch until it was barely light enough to see.

"Thanks," he croaked, his eyes mere slits. He had already stripped off his shorts and T-shirt and headed straight for the shower.

She stepped in his path and shook her shoulders to make her breasts bounce for him. "Hi honey!" she chirped. "I missed you so much while you were gone!"

"Missed you too," he mumbled. He started to step around her into the shower, but she opened her arms and pulled his naked body against her wet skin. She moved against him gently and reached up to kiss his stubbly neck. He groaned as the pleasure signals of her touch finally reached his sleep-deadened brain cells. She smiled, reaching down to gently massage him. His body quickly responded to her touch.

"*There* he is!" she announced. "I knew he missed me too!"

"Please, honey," he groaned, "I'm gonna be late for work as it is." He tried to pull away from her embrace, but she was insistent. She knew that good sex made for marital harmony. And when it came to sex, she always got her way.

"This'll just take a minute," she said in a breathy whisper.

Bending over, she ran his ever-more-rigid rod over her wet breasts, then took the moistened member in her mouth. It rapidly bloomed to its deliciously full size as her tongue danced along its length. She moaned with delight, no acting needed today.

A few minutes later, she noticed his eyes were much brighter. Her mission was accomplished.

"Thanks, that was..." he shook his head as if to clear it. "That was great."

"Mmm, yes it was," she agreed, reaching up to kiss him deeply. She finished toweling off, then pulled a short, sheer bathrobe off its hook and wrapped it over her body. Pulling it tight over her bottom, she rocked her hips and blew him a kiss over her shoulder, strutting out the bathroom door while he watched. "Have a nice day, big boy!"

* * *

Amanda padded into the kitchen, where the boys were fighting as usual.

"You're getting milk all over the counter, you little dork," Eric hissed at his little brother, reaching to take the milk away from the seven-year-old.

"Don't call me a dork, dumbass!" their youngest, Kevin, fumed, elbowing his brother away, spilling even more over both the counter and the floor.

"Look what did, you double-dork dumbass!" their ten-year-old seethed, "You are such a loser!"

"Enough! Both of you! Sit!" she demanded. "And if I hear language like that again, you can both kiss your XBox goodbye for the rest of this week, *capiche*?"

"But Mom, look at the mess he made!" Eric objected, with the conviction of a prosecutor.

"I'll clean up his mess. *Sit!*"

"*Everybody* has to clean up his messes," Eric sullenly observed.

"I've had to clean up *both* of your messes since you were born, do you hear me complaining? *Do* you?"

Eric had spent enough time at his friends' houses to realize his mother was far more indulgent than most. "No," he finally admitted.

"Then you've already got your cereal. Eat up."

She stepped over the spilled milk and handed Kevin his bowl. "Here you go, sweetie."

"Thanks, Mom!" Kevin bubbled, holding his cereal bowl up to his mouth and slurping noisily. He grinned, a sight that never failed to make her smile. Kevin was always full of simple joy, blissfully ignorant that much of his brother's contempt was simply because Kevin had taken his role of the baby in the family. Even once he *was* old enough to understand, he still wouldn't care and wouldn't love his older brother any less. Like Amanda was to her husband, Kevin was *yang* to his brother's *yin*, and it provided a stable, if somewhat noisy, balance to their relationship.

"You're such a dufus!" Eric groused.

She laughed out loud as she turned to clean up Kevin's mess. She truly enjoyed her boys, and was secretly glad both of her children were male. Boys and men were both easy to figure out and control. You just had to be willing to deal with occasional spilled fluids.

* * *

"Boys, hurry up! We're late!" Amanda called several minutes later. She wasn't *just* in a hurry to get the boys to school; her friend Lisa showed up at a birthday party yesterday in a pair of suede leather boots that had given her a huge case of shoe lust. After dropping off the boys she was heading straight downtown to the Jimmy Choo's boutique on Oak Street. She figured if she serviced him well tonight, Mike wouldn't be too upset when he found out about her $600 boots.

Mike fumbled around in the kitchen trying to get a travel mug full of coffee before he hit the road. He was still out of sorts, banging cabinet doors and cursing under his breath. She cut across his path and pulled his favorite mug from the dishwasher.

"Here," she said, thrusting it into his hands, "don't teach your sons any more new words." She bent close to his ear. "Like *dumbass*," she growled.

He mumbled something, then turned his back on her on his way to the coffee maker. So he was going to be distant today. Fine. She had tried to do her part, and she'd be waiting whenever he got back from outer space or wherever his head was right now. Kevin and Eric came thundering through the kitchen with their book bags flying.

"Bye, Dad!" Kevin said hopefully. Eric had already learned not to bother.

Mike had his head in the fridge looking for creamer. He didn't respond.

Amanda frowned. "Go on and get in the car honey, Daddy's busy."

Kevin looked slightly downcast, but complied. Amanda grabbed her purse from the sideboard and followed Kevin into the garage without trying to give Mike a kiss good-bye. She gave the door a healthy slam.

She was *definitely* getting those shoes today.

* * *

Amanda put her Platinum Bronze BMW X5 SUV into gear and thundered toward the boys' school.

"Kick it, Mom!" Eric said with a grin.

She loved her new BMW. It still smelled new, which Mike could no longer boast about his beloved Le Mans Blue BMW M3 convertible. She had been driving the same faded silver Toyota Sienna van they had gotten when Eric was born until she finally put her foot down. You couldn't show up for soccer practice in Oak Park in a ten-year-old minivan, could you? Not if you didn't want the other moms making jokes about your food stamp collection. Besides, if *he* had his dream car, why shouldn't *she*? Mike groused about the lease payments for the two BMWs being as much as their house payment, but that really wasn't her problem, was it?

"Hey Mom," Eric asked, "is your BMW faster than Dad's?"

"*Well*," she said, taking a deep breath and blowing it out with great drama. "I don't *think* so, but if it *was*, it would have to be our little secret, right boys? I'm not sure Daddy could handle Mama blowing his doors off, do you?"

"No way!" they said in impish agreement. She winked at them in the rearview mirror.

"Hey, Mom?" Kevin asked a few minutes later.

"Yeah, sweetie?"

"What's a hoochie mama?" he asked innocently.

Her head jerked. "Excuse me?"

"At the birthday party yesterday, Daniel's mom said the clothes you wear make you look like a hoochie mama. Is that something bad?"

She choked down an observation that Daniel's mom Janet was probably jealous because Janet got A's in high school and Amanda got double D's, but figured that wouldn't get back to Janet with the barb still intact. Amanda likewise squelched a temptation to threaten Janet with propositioning her husband when Janet was visiting her demon-possessed mother in Skokie, because Daniel Sr. would probably jump at the chance to be with any woman who didn't act like she was freshly dipped in pickle juice. And then she'd have to follow through on her threat. And Daniel Sr. had a hairy back.

Instead she remarked, "You know, honey, I think you misunderstood Daniel's mom."

"Really?" Kevin said dubiously.

"Sure, honey!" she said confidently. She held up her purse. "See, here's my Gucci purse." She waved her wrist. "And my Gucci watch. And my Gucci sunglasses. And you two *know* how much I love my Gucci *shoes*." Though they didn't attend any church, the boys knew the local Gucci store was a holy place to her.

"*That's* for sure," Eric agreed.

"So, Kevin," she continued, "I don't think Daniel's mom called me a 'hoochie mama,' I think she called me a 'Gucci Mama,' and that's certainly not a bad thing, is it?"

"*Gucci* Mama!" the boys called out in animated unison, thrilled to have a pet name for their mother like she had for them.

Smiling, Amanda returned her attention to the road, pleased at her on-the-fly defusing of that bomb. Kevin was soon lost in his video games, but Eric looked deep in thought. That was usually not a good thing.

"Hey Mom?" he finally asked, a mischievous tone in his voice disguised but not completely hidden.

"Yes, *Eric*?" she answered, her emphasis of his proper name the maternal equivalent of a shot across his pre-pubescent bow.

"What's a *Milf*?" he asked, the challenge glittering in his eyes.

"Shut up, Eric."

RUNAWAY

SEPTEMBER 15, 1983 – PHILADELPHIA, PENNSYLVANIA

Angela Kellerman learned today that she had turned seven years old. She had never even known the date of her birthday, much less celebrated it. But Mrs. Groutman had inquired of the social worker and announced at breakfast that today was Angela's day, and there would be a party in celebration. Mrs. Groutman never missed an opportunity to dress up her foster daughters and have a tea party. Angela found such play intensely boring, but the birthday cake helped.

Life in the Groutman household had settled into a comfortable routine for Angela. As long as she obeyed Mrs. Groutman and avoided fighting with her sisters, she was fed and clothed, and there were no more threats of the child prison. The only enduring friction was with her roommate Sarah. They were still forced to share a single narrow bed, and Angela was too tall to curl up at the foot of the bed with a blanket to avoid her sister as she had done earlier. Mrs. Groutman had begged her husband for another bed, but Mr. Groutman had loudly denied her the money.

Out of fear of provoking Mr. Groutman again, Angela tried her best to share her narrow bed with Sarah. But Sarah, knowing that Mr. and Mrs. Groutman would side with her in any argument, silently kicked and punched Angela onto the barest sliver at the edge of the mattress.

On nights like those, she often crept down the hall to Rachel's bed. As the oldest, Rachel had her own room. She also didn't mind sharing, gathering Angela into her arms and stroking her head until she fell fast asleep. Angela had never felt such peace and belonging as when Rachel held her. Had she ever experienced maternal affection she would have immediately identified the vacuum Rachel's embrace filled for her. But all she knew was that it felt good.

One night Rachel shook her awake. She had her hand over Angela's mouth. "Shh! Get under the bed! Hurry!" she ordered.

Experience in her former foster homes had made Angela good at hiding quickly. She slid under the bed and stayed very still. She heard the doorknob turn and adult footsteps enter. The bed creaked heavily.

"How's my little girl?" she heard Mr. Groutman whisper.

"Please...*don't*," Rachel whispered back, and she started to cry.

"Shh, be quiet now," he urged her, in a voice far more gentle than Angela had heard him use with Mrs. Groutman or anyone else. "You don't want to go back out on the street, do you? You're too old for any other foster family to take you in. And you have to earn your keep here just like everyone else."

Then the bed creaked again and Angela heard sheets rustling. Rachel began sobbing quietly and the bed squeaked rhythmically. After a few minutes Mr. Groutman made a grunting noise and the squeaking stopped. His feet reappeared in the narrow slit of Angela's vision. Rachel's quiet sobbing continued.

"There, that wasn't so bad, was it?" he said. "In a little while, you'll even learn to like it. Now, don't forget to wash up, just be quiet about it." He padded from the room and closed the door behind him.

Angela squirmed out from under the bed. Rachel was curled up in a ball, her fists bunching up her nightgown between her legs. The look of mute anguish she gave Angela was more painful than any of Mrs. Groutman's swats.

That night Angela held Rachel, stroking her head until the weeping stopped.

* * *

Her visits to Rachel's room became less frequent as the late-night visits of Mr. Groutman increased. But on nights when Sarah was particularly hateful, she crept to Rachel's room, only to end up hiding under the bed. One night after the squeaking stopped she heard Rachel and Mr. Groutman whispering.

"I've stopped bleeding," she said.

"What?" he whispered back.

"A few months ago I started bleeding between my legs and Mrs. Groutman said I was becoming a woman and gave me some pads to soak it up. But the bleeding's stopped. The book she gave me said that happens when you've got a baby inside."

"How long have you stopped bleeding?" he gasped.

"Over two months now. I threw up this morning. That's in the book too."

"Why didn't you tell me you had started bleeding?"

"Would that have stopped you?" she shot back.

"Oh God," Mr. Groutman breathed. Then he stormed from the room.

Angela held Rachel again that night. They talked a long time, and Angela learned far more about life than she ever wanted to know.

* * *

The next evening an edgy silence descended on the Groutman household. Mrs. Groutman sent the girls to bed early, and prowled the hallways every few minutes until convinced her foster daughters were all asleep. Angela kept her eyes closed and shallowed her breathing, but stayed alert and awake. Her animal instincts sensed profound danger.

What seemed like hours later she heard Mrs. Groutman's stealthy footsteps in the hall. Out of the corner of her eye Angela saw her shadow standing guard in the hallway. She whispered something to Mr. Groutman.

Angela heard his footsteps. It sounded like they were going into Rachel's room. Her heart quickened. Angela heard a muffled cry and a single heavy blow, then silence. Angela's heart pounded in her ears.

Mr. Groutman's steps came down the hall, more heavily this time. The hallway was dark, but it looked like he had something slung over his shoulder.

"Make sure you weight it down," Mrs. Groutman whispered.

"Shut up, woman!" he groused quietly. "Take care of her bags and meet me in the garage."

* * *

The next morning Mrs. Groutman discovered that Rachel had run away. There was great commotion as she and the girls frantically searched the house and inquired of the neighbors. Finally Mrs. Groutman called the social worker and wept convincingly at her concern over Rachel's fate. Mr. Groutman was summoned home from work. He quickly found that one of his smaller suitcases had been stolen and that all of Rachel's clothes were gone.

The social worker and the police were skeptical, but apparently this kind of thing happened frequently and runaway foster children were not the top priority of the police. After a few tense days the police and the social workers stopped coming by and the Groutman household settled back into its routine. Her next-oldest foster sister Becky moved into Rachel's room, Sarah moved into Becky's room with her other sister Susie. That room had two beds, which Sarah found a huge improvement. Angela now had a bed all to herself.

CASTING CALL

PRESENT DAY – SAN FRANCISCO, CALIFORNIA

San Francisco CIA station chief Scott Hendrix guided the stunning blonde to a booth in the back corner of the Chinese restaurant. He normally didn't bother with a bodyguard, but today he made an exception. The drama of having an armed guard drive them to their luncheon rendezvous was worth the inconvenience of dragging one of the apes from Security along.

"My God," the young actress gushed, "your bodyguard is scary as hell."

Hendrix gently took her arm as she slid into her seat, relishing the feel of her smooth young skin against his fingers. When she broke eye contact, he got a good look down her generous cleavage. Her breasts pressed against the thin fabric of her yellow spandex dress, her lack of a bra obvious.

He smiled cordially as he took his seat facing the door. He maneuvered his lanky frame into the booth, and was gratified that when he brushed against her long legs in the confined space, she did not move them away but left her calf in gentle but definite contact with his. This was going well already.

"Yeah, Gus can be a little imposing, but I don't pay him for charm." He glanced toward the front of the restaurant. Gus had taken a seat where he could watch both the door and Hendrix's table. They briefly made eye contact, the bodyguard's eyes relaying, "You owe me for this one."

"Thank you so much for meeting with me, Mr. Hendrix," she said eagerly, exposing her perfect white teeth.

Hendrix wore a warm smile he never used in real life. "Please, Gina, call me Scott." He restrained himself from reaching out to touch her hand. That would come later.

Gina blushed, momentarily forgetting the questions she had probably practiced in front of a mirror the night before. She fumbled in her purse for her cell phone.

Hendrix waited patiently, his smile never wavering. For the second time since he left the office, the voicemail notification on his Blackberry gave its distinct "double-buzz" warning, signifying that whoever left a message had flagged it as urgent. He ignored it. Whoever it was wasn't sitting across from a gorgeous blonde of known willingness and therefore had no clue of what urgent really was.

Gina found the file she needed on her iPhone. "Okay, ah," she said with a self-conscious giggle, "here's what I needed." She nervously combed her dyed hair over her ear with nails that had probably been manicured just that morning. "I just, ah, had a few questions." Another anxious giggle bubbled out when the waiter interrupted to ask for their drink orders.

"Gina, please," he soothed, "don't be nervous. I put my pants on one leg at a time, just like everyone else." *And I take them off exactly the same way.* Hendrix had a face his wife had politely described as "kind" back when she actually liked him, so he certainly never rated this kind of attention from women. That is, until he started using his position at the CIA to his personal advantage. Just a well-earned perk of the job.

Gina apparently thought she was supposed to politely laugh at that, so she did. "Well, Mr. Silverman said that for the role I'm trying out, I needed to know something about the spy business."

"Intelligence," he interrupted.

"I'm sorry?"

"We don't call it 'the spy business,' we just call it 'Intelligence.'"

"Oh, okay," she stammered, texting an addendum to her smart phone notes. "Well, um, he said that you would be an excellent source to help me win the role."

"Of course, I'll help in any way I can." Which wasn't much, Hendrix knew. His friend the producer only sent starlets his way if they had already been passed over for their roles. But Gina wouldn't find that out until after he had added her panties to his collection.

Gina looked as focused as he figured her limited intellect would allow. "So, Mr. Hendrix, how did you get started in the spy, I mean, Intelligence business?"

The not-particularly challenging questions continued through an otherwise satisfying lunch. He made sure to keep earnest and engaged eye contact no matter how inane the question. He pushed his empty plate to the side so he could lean across the booth. She did the same, her ample bosoms resting on the table as she did so.

No wonder she didn't get the role, he thought. Producers tended to cast the skinny athletic types for girl-spy roles. Better suited for the action scenes. For the acting role, her beautiful figure worked against her. For the role *he* had in mind, her luscious curves would look—and feel—just fine.

He smiled warmly. "Gina, I have to say, I'm very impressed by your questions. You really have a handle on this part."

She looked down and laughed. "I'm not sure about that...."

He laid his hands flat on the table, his fingers so close to hers he could feel the heat from her skin. He waited until her gaze rose again to meet his. "Of course, if they were judging by beauty alone, you'd already have the role."

She blushed and looked away again. He chanced another glance at her breasts. Her nipples pointed across the table at him through the thin fabric of her dress. It was time to make his move.

His Blackberry double-buzzed yet again. Who the *hell* wanted him so bad? Action at the Agency's San Francisco office was usually a study in *non*-urgency, which after an involuntary tour at the embassy in Baghdad was fine with him. It was probably his wife, sensing he was about to get a decent lay for once. He looked down at the table and let out a heavy sigh.

"What's wrong?" she asked with great concern. She leaned even further across the table, her breasts nearly escaping confinement. Hendrix almost lost focus on his act.

Almost. He sighed again. "I'm sorry, but I don't want to burden you with my problems."

She placed her hand on his. "No, please, I want to help."

Like shooting fish in a barrel. He ran his other hand over his thinning hair. "It's just that my job, well, it's dangerous. I don't have much opportunity for close relationships." He was sure his wife would take issue with that.

Gina's eyes filled with concern. "I understand." Her hand squeezed his ever so slightly.

Time to pounce. "I hope I'm not being presumptuous, but I sense a real connection between us."

Her eyes glowed and she squeezed his hand a little harder. "I do too."

"This is very special. And I hate to let something precious like this pass by."

"I agree *completely*," she said breathlessly. Her breathing had become deep and rapid, her parted lips wet and quivering with desire. Hendrix began to hope that he wouldn't even have to wait for a hotel rendezvous this evening and maybe go straight for the men's room after dessert.

He noticed Gus talking to another bulky man in a suit. They laughed. His gaze returned to the table. The camaraderie of apes was not his concern.

Suddenly another stocky man in a suit appeared at their booth. He slid into the seat across from Hendrix, hip-checking Gina out of his way to make room for his bulk. She squealed in surprise and fright, cowering as far away as the booth allowed.

"I hope you got your rocks off already, Hendrix, 'cause playtime's over."

It was Perry Pugliano, Special-Agent-in-Charge of the San Francisco FBI office. His receding hairline, combed straight back, topped a square face with deep scowl lines and a crooked boxer's nose broken in two places. A lopsided leer curled his upper lip. He was obviously enjoying himself.

Hendrix felt his face glowing beet red. "Could this have *waited?*"

Pugliano's leer was fixed in place. "You were ignoring your Blackberry. Your secretary's been trying to reach you for the last hour."

"What *is* it?" he asked through gritted teeth.

Pugliano gave Gina an extended up-and-down look, including a very blatant stare down her dress. She shrunk away from the FBI agent, as if his very presence contaminated her. He obviously enjoyed her discomfort. "First, I think we should let Britney Spears excuse herself."

Gina started to make her escape, but Pugliano remained in her path. His smirk widened even further. "You know, sweetheart, the fact that you're sitting here with this scumbag means you didn't get the part."

"What?" she gasped.

He chuckled maliciously. "That's right, princess. Let me guess, your friend the producer said he liked your audition, but he thought you needed more background on the role and he sent you to Mr. Hendrix, right?"

The color drained from her face. "Yes. Yes he did."

Pugliano threw his head back and laughed. "Yeah, I'll bet he did! You see, he and Mr. Hendrix were college frat buddies. They've been sharing clam since they were freshmen. So when you spread your legs for Mr. Producer, he sent you on to Mr. CIA Slimeball here for you to do the same for him."

Gina gaped like a landed fish, but said nothing.

"The question is," Pugliano continued, "what does Mr. Hendrix give his friend *in return*? The only thing I can think of is an occasional secret to spice up his movie projects."

Hendrix went cold. "Now, wait a minute!"

"Well, it's either that or you're swapping out your wife. Is she a looker?"

Before he could respond, Gina burst into tears and began smacking Pugliano with her small purse. One of the straps broke, scattering her belongings over the table.

"Get out!" she sobbed. "*Get out!*"

Pugliano's eyes went wide. He held up an arm to fend off the assault as he retreated clumsily out of the booth. He struggled to his feet and backed out of her way.

She scooted out of the booth and turned to storm away.

"Gina, wait!" Hendrix herded her belongings with his hands between the dessert plates, plucking her cell phone from a bowl of rice pudding and wiping it off with his napkin. She took it, then leaned over the table and slapped him hard across his face.

"You *bastard!*" she cried, turning away. Stomping out of the restaurant, she threw her shoulders back, summoning what little dignity remained to her. Hendrix's security man stepped well out of her way as she exited the restaurant.

Pugliano thrust his hands in his pockets, grinning broadly. His pudgy face swiveled back in Hendrix's direction. "My, that went well! Looks like you'll be stuck whispering sweet nothings to your hand again tonight. Just like every other night."

Hendrix's face burned. Every eye in the restaurant gored into him, then looked away in contempt. "Sit down, you son of a bitch!" he growled.

The smirk still fixed to his face, Pugliano slid back into the booth. "Sorry for the *affairus interruptus*, but before you do anything rash, maybe you should hear me out."

"*I'm listening*," he hissed.

"We have a lead on Angela Conrad," Pugliano replied, watching the CIA man closely to gauge his reaction. "She's here. In San Francisco."

Hendrix's jaw dropped. "No way."

Pugliano smile broadened. "Yes way. The CIA's favorite rogue spy is operating *right under our noses*. And better yet, she doesn't even know we're on to her."

He leaned forward, his debacle with Gina already forgotten. "Don't tease me."

While the Al-Qaeda terrorist hierarchy might top the CIA's *public* most wanted list, Hendrix's background was in Counterintelligence. And for the

C-I crowd, there was no bigger worldwide fish than Angela Conrad. But theirs was a very *private* vendetta.

"No teasing, big boy, I'm a sure thing," Pugliano replied. "So if you're done eating, I'll take you downtown. But for God's sake, let your security man give that poor girl a ride home."

Hendrix flagged the waiter. "Check, please!"

DEADLINE

PRESENT DAY – CHICAGO, ILLINOIS

Mike Manning rushed into the legal offices of Feldman-Norquist on the 23rd floor of the John Hancock Building almost half an hour late.

"Good morning," the receptionist said, glancing at the clock.

"Good morning, Gloria," he replied, slightly out of breath.

"Enjoy San Francisco? Do anything fun?"

I got to watch several people cut up and stuffed into buckets, does that count? "No, this trip was all business, glad to be back."

He settled into his office and looked out over Lake Michigan. He watched a large sailboat ease past the breakwater onto the open lake. It was so peaceful. He couldn't believe that his nightmare of machine-gun-toting goons and bone-saw-toting butchers took place less than twenty-four hours ago. It felt like another life, another planet. A hard knock on his open office door jolted him from his reverie. It was his boss, Bernie Norquist.

"Good morning, Mike!" Norquist beamed with faux congeniality. "Were you able to get the initial report on the San Carlos project done on the plane?"

Manning had to think for several seconds. San Carlos. The transformer plant. Poisoned people. Hush money. Destroyed lives. Another day at the office. "Uh, no, Bernie, my laptop went on the fritz, I was dead in the water," he lied. He no more could have typed a coherent report after leaving San Francisco than he could have run a marathon. He was drunk before the landing gear came up, and wished he still was.

Norquist grimaced in barely contained anger. If Manning was a Type-A personality, Norquist was the letter that came *before* A. "Well, how did it go? Were there any problems?"

He lowered his voice, hoping to soothe his boss's anger. "No, Bernie, no problems. Everything went smoothly. No holdouts."

Norquist's face twitched slightly, his adrenaline levels now fired up with no place to go. "Well, hurry up and get it down on paper! The Chemtrox Board of Directors wants to know that situation is handled, and how much it cost them to do it."

He held up his hands like a hostage negotiator talking to an armed suspect. "It's handled, Bernie! It's handled! Just give me a couple of hours to write it up."

"Then do it!" Norquist grumbled, marching away.

Manning returned to his desk, extracted his laptop from its case, and stared at the screen as it went through its seemingly interminable boot-up process. He slapped his hand on his forehead in frustration. *Head in the game, Manning, head in the game.* He tried to focus on the task at hand, but every time he closed his eyes all he could see was Jake Fleischer's dismembered corpse scattered about a bloody hotel room.

Finally, after several tries, he settled into the groove of writing his damage control report. Situation. Potential litigants. Mitigating actions. Remaining risks. He had done this a hundred times before, but never after coming within inches of losing his life. He reached for his briefcase. He needed his digital recorder to clarify a point in his interview notes. Where the hell was it?

Oh crap. He remembered throwing the recorder into his checked luggage, which was now lost somewhere between San Francisco and Chicago. *How the hell can you lose a piece of luggage on a direct flight?* He asked himself again. He tried to piece together the conversation in his head, but his brain was fried. He thumped the desk with his fist.

"Dammit!"

The phone buzzed. It was the receptionist.

"Yeah, Gloria?" he said gruffly.

"Sorry to bother you, Mr. Manning, but there's a package for you downstairs in the lobby. It's your luggage."

Thank God! "Oh, that's great, Gloria! Sorry I snapped at you."

"That's okay, sir." She lowered her voice. "But if you turn into Bernie Norquist, I'm outta here. One of him is enough."

"I promise."

The courier for the airline leaned against the wall, trying to stay out of the way in the busy lobby. He held out a clipboard. Manning was so focused on his bag he didn't even look at the man. He was already mentally unpacking his luggage, grasping for the digital recorder he needed to finish his report.

The courier spoke in heavily accented English. "Please sign here, Mees-tor Manning."

While he checked the bag to make sure it was indeed his, the part of his brain tasked with self-preservation screamed that there was something familiar about the accent.

It was Russian.

He looked up at the courier.

The courier smiled. "Other than missing bag, you have pleasant flight, Mees-tor Manning?"

It was Yuri, Angela Conrad's Russian goon.

Manning's heart pounded so hard he was sure it was going to stop any second. "W-wha...what do you want?"

Yuri's smile remained, but it became an expression of malice, like a dog baring its teeth. "Mees Conrad would like to know if you turn in your resignation, yes?"

"N-no," he stammered in horror, "not yet."

Yuri leaned in close, his eyes merciless as the grave. "*Today*, Mees-tor Manning." He gave Manning a hard tap with the clipboard, making him jump.

"Today!"

Yuri exited the building and entered a van waiting outside.

Manning sank onto his luggage, using it as a chair. Without it, he probably would have gone all the way to the floor.

"Oh... *shit*," he whispered.

[1] The wartime installation at Wenceslas Mines in Poland is very much factual, but its actual purpose—believed by researchers Joseph Farrell and Igor Witkowski to be one of the test sites of the Bell during World War II—will remain shrouded in mystery since the SS dynamited most of the tunnels when they evacuated at the war's end. (Source: *The SS Brotherhood of the Bell* by Joseph Farrell, p. 164-165)

[2] Hans Kammler, with a doctorate in engineering, designed the layout of the Auschwitz extermination line with its gas chambers and ovens as a "model of efficiency," which was then replicated at death camps throughout Nazi Germany. (Source: *Reich of the Black Sun* by Joseph Farrell, p. 99)

[3] The story of J.P. Morgan asking Tesla "where do you stick the meter" appears to be apocryphal, but the fact that J.P. Morgan invested $150,000 in the venture (more than $3 million in today's dollars) but suddenly withdrew his support when Tesla's wireless power transmission project was nearing completion is beyond dispute. (Source: *A Battle to Preserve a Visionary's Bold Failure* by William J. Broad, New York *Times*, May 4, 2009)

[4] This part is fiction. Tesla sought after extremely high electrical frequencies (such as would be generated by the Bell) to cause "commotion in the medium," which in Tesla's understanding was an extradimensional "aether," the substrate of all matter and energy manifested in our four-dimensional space. Tesla believed that "Electric power is everywhere present in unlimited quantities and can drive world's machinery without the need of coal, oil, gas, or any other fuels." That Tesla may have postulated a machine like the Bell to extract that energy remains a possibility, since upon his death in 1943 the FBI impounded his personal papers and notes, most of which were subsequently "lost." (Source: *Tesla, the Lost Inventions* by George Trinkaus, p.33)

[5] Kurt Debus, a wartime colleague of the famous German rocket scientist Werner von Braun, is best known as a senior NASA official during the early space program, including service as Director of the Kennedy Space Center in Florida. This position purportedly was earned as the launch equipment specialist for von Braun's V-2 rockets during the war. However, Debus by training was a specialist in high voltage power supplies, holding the patents for several inventions in this area, including papers in the esoteric area of "magnetic fields separation." While this discipline made him a natural choice for work on the Bell, the application of his skills to the US chemical-fueled rocket program are less obvious, unless the rumors of a secret space program utilizing electromagnetic propulsion lurking behind NASA's chemical-fueled façade have a basis in fact. (Source: *The Truth About the Wunderwaffe* [Wonder Weapons], by Igor Witkowski, p. 256)

[6] Tesla's disdain for Einstein's Theory of Relativity was quoted in the New York *Times*, July 11, 1935. In 1938, Tesla declared he had developed "a dynamic theory of gravity, which I have worked out in all details and hope to give to the world very soon." He also announced, "My second discovery…can be expressed by the statement: There is no energy in matter other than that received from the environment. All attempts to explain the workings of the universe without recognizing the existence of the aether and the indispensable role it plays…[are] futile and destined to oblivion." Tesla never published these theories, but the peculiar behavior of the FBI in immediately seizing Tesla's personal files after his death

indicated that *someone* took his theories seriously. (Source: *Prodigal Genius*, by John J. O'Neill [by the way, on its initial publication in 1944, O'Neill's publisher was raided and *Prodigal Genius* required no less than three trips past the censor before the FBI considered the biography sufficiently scrubbed for public consumption.])

[7] The War Decisive rating is factual. After Kurt Debus denounced his fellow scientist Richard Crämer to the Gestapo, the man was sentenced to two years in prison (apparently it was a minor offense, considering the Gestapo's customary treatment for disloyalty of any kind). Debus's superior then petitioned the Gestapo for Crämer's release, declaring that Crämer's project had special priority from the SS, and was classified as *Kriegsentscheidend*, or "decisive for the war." The project was identified "Charite-Anlage," and is believed by researchers Farrell and Witkowski to have been the purpose-built power supply for the Bell's operation. Witkowski claims to have examined "cubic meters" of German wartime documents and found this classification on no other paper than the Crämer petition. However, Professor Gerlach (widely reputed to be the chief scientist on the Bell project), reported to Martin Bormann, Hitler's second-in-command, that the project on which he worked would be "decisive for the war." Clearly the Bell was a crown jewel in the Nazi technological treasury. (Source: *The Truth About the Wunderwaffe* [Wonder Weapons], by Igor Witkowski, p. 257)

CHAPTER 5

ELEPHANT CAGE

SEPTEMBER 1944 – WINCESLAS MINES, POLAND

General Spoerrenberg stepped out into the crisp night air and took a deep breath. He could not have asked for better weather for tonight's high-profile test. Soldiers, technicians, and test equipment filled the newly paved test zone just outside the mine entrance. During the day, decoy coal mining equipment and coal-dust-covered workers filled the square on the off-chance Allied reconnaissance aircraft might stumble upon the facility. That had occurred once a few months ago and was not repeated, evidence to Spoerrenberg that the ruse had succeeded.

Tonight the coal mining equipment was gone. Past a cordon of heavily armed SS guards, a dozen trucks clustered at one end of the vehicle park. Beyond that, lit by the headlights of the trucks, stood the Elephant Cage. By a stroke of good fortune, the cooling tower for the nearby power plant stood just outside the mine entrance. Replaced by a more efficient heat exchanger closer to the plant, part of this older structure would now be used to test the Bell. Once a towering cylindrical construction, all but the ring of concrete support arches at the base had been removed. What was left did resemble a cage for elephants, lacking only the bars between the concrete columns to keep the captive pachyderms inside. [1]

This would be the final test for the Bell at Wenceslas Mines. Russian Forces had pressed to the easternmost juncture of the Polish and Czechoslovakian borders, barely two hundred kilometers east of their current location. After this demonstration was complete, the entire project would be shipped back to Pilsen, Czechoslovakia to General Kammler's headquarters to continue their work. That is, if tonight's demonstration was successful; the days of the SS funding every promising research project were long over.

If the Bell did not decisively display technology capable of turning the tide of the war, the project would be shut down and its personnel likely sent directly to the Russian front. Spoerrenberg could not think of a more convincing motivator for his men to give their all. He had just lit a cigarette when he saw the headlights of a convoy in the distance. He ground it out with the heel of his jackboot.

The motorcade looked more like a funeral procession than a wartime convoy, with staff cars outnumbering their troop transport escorts. After a scout car and a truck carrying troops, no less than five black staff cars roared onto the paved square, each one longer and more polished than the limousine preceding it. The last stretched vehicle was an armored Mercedes G4 six-wheeled sedan like the one used by the *Fuhrer* himself. Before they rolled to a stop Spoerrenberg advanced to a respectful distance, threw up his arm in a rigid salute and held it.

While his stomach knotted over tonight's test, he had to suppress a laugh when he saw the behavior of his superiors exiting their vehicles. His immediate superior General Alvensleben, commander of SS forces in southern Poland, emerged from the first staff car, dashing to the second to open the door for SS *Obergeneral* Kammler and standing back to salute. Then the pair repeated the procedure for *Grossadmiral* Karl Donitz, commander of Germany's U-Boat forces. The trio hurried to open the door for *Reichsminister* Albert Speer, head of all armaments production in Germany. And all four men saluted at the door of the last vehicle, bearing *Reichsmarshall* Heinrich Himmler, Supreme Commander of the SS. Once these ritual greetings were completed, Spoerrenberg thought it safe to approach the assemblage.

General Kammler was at his convivial best tonight. "Ah, Jakob!" he boomed, motioning Spoerrenberg over to Himmler's car. "Gentlemen, meet our host for the evening's activities. *Reichsmarshall* Himmler, may I present General Jakob Spoerrenberg."

A hardened combat veteran, Spoerrenberg's blood still ran cold when the short, bespectacled man advanced toward him. Himmler removed one glove and extended his hand to Spoerrenberg. Only a supreme effort of will allowed him to accept the handshake, half-expecting his immortal soul to be extracted on contact.

"Good evening," Himmler said in a soft tenor. Somehow the almost feminine voice made him more threatening, not less. Himmler gestured toward the test stand. "Shall we?"

Spoerrenberg led the entourage to the ten-meter-tall by thirty-meter-diameter Elephant Cage. The Bell rested in its center, the massive machine for once made to look small by its setting. He explained the de-construction of the cooling tower to create the test ring, and how the underground conduit that once carried cooling water now held high-voltage cables running to a special generator at the power plant.[2]

Reichsminister Speer interrupted his description of the control panels, located thirty meters away. "I take it you've solved the problem that led to the earlier fatalities?"

An excellent question, especially if you value your life, Spoerrenberg thought.

"Yes, *Reichsminister*," Kammler broke in. "We redesigned both the Bell and its power source. I can assure you that we are safe at this distance."

"So what exactly are we going to see here, General Kammler?" Himmler asked.

Kammler's chin rose with pride. "The future, *Herr Reichsmarshall*, nothing less."

"Indeed?" Himmler said quietly, his brow arched. With the reverses the German army had experienced on the Russian Front, Spoerrenberg was sure the SS commander had experienced no shortage of generals making promises on which they couldn't deliver.

Kammler's smile broadened. "Indeed, *Herr Reichsmarshall*. Shall we begin?"

"Please do." Himmler almost sounded bored.

Kammler nodded to Spoerrenberg, who gave the order to Professor Gerlach at the control board. Commands were shouted, switches set, and valves opened. Technicians ran forward to make last adjustments to the device. The Bell hissed and steamed from the liquid nitrogen pulsing through its chambers. Professor Gerlach signaled his readiness.

"Begin the test!" Kammler shouted.

A low hum rose from the Bell, rising in pitch as the internal rotors increased speed. The hum increased to a buzz like a beehive, only in this case the bees sounded like they were the size of hand grenades and the Bell was their hive.

"The noise you are hearing," Kammler explained, "Is the rapid switching of the motor polarities required for the Bell's high rotational speeds."

"How fast do the rotors inside the Bell spin?" Admiral Donitz asked.

"The two rotors not only spin at nearly a hundred thousand RPM, but they are each charged to ten thousand volts, and they spin in *opposite* directions. This creates a magnetic field inside the Bell that exists no where else in nature. It is, in that sense, *supernatural*. And so are the results achieved from the Bell Effect."

"And what *are* those effects, Kammler?" Himmler asked impatiently.

Kammler cast an inquisitive eye to Spoerrenberg, who glanced at Gerlach's status board.

"Thirty seconds to full speed," Spoerrenberg announced.

Kammler made a dramatic sweep of his arm. "Observe, *Herr Reichsmarshall*."

On cue, a blue glow thinly outlined the Bell's shape. The high-pitched buzz was almost painful, and still rising in pitch. The blue glow became more pronounced. The Bell slowly lifted from its support cradle, trailing a thick electrical cable and two liquid nitrogen lines. It shifted slowly left and right, constrained in its motions by the umbilicals. Then the tension on the two liquid nitrogen lines triggered their quick-release connections and the steaming hoses dropped away. The Bell rose faster, reaching the limit of the electrical cable.

Suddenly the blue glow became a flash and the Bell rocketed upward, releasing the electrical line with a shower of sparks. Just as it appeared that the Bell would blast away into the night sky, a trio of centimeter-thick guy wires yanked taut like steel bullwhips. Twenty meters up and above the illumination of the vehicle headlights, the Bell strained at its leads lit only by its own unearthly blue radiance. The glow did not fade, but the buzz had been replaced with the whine of machinery spinning at incredible speed. The wires stayed taut and the sound remained constant.

"*Mein Gott!*" Himmler exclaimed.

Speer gawked at the discarded electrical cable. "What's powering it, for God's sake?"

Kammler spoke as if relaying an epiphany from the gods. "It is powered by the universe itself, *Herr Reichsminister*."

The assembled dignitaries alternated their gaze between Kammler and the Bell, unable to decide whether it was he or they who had gone mad.

"The uranium inside the Bell is not powering this effect?" Donitz asked.

"No, *Herr* Admiral, we also tested using mercury inside both rotors to rule out that possibility. The effects were the same. The Bell is drawing its energy entirely from the environment surrounding us."

"But that's perpetual motion!" Speer protested. "A scientific impossibility!"

"This effect was predicted by Tesla before the Bell was even constructed. His work postulates that all matter and energy we experience proceeds from a higher dimension that can be accessed by creating sufficiently intense electrical fields. We have merely verified his theories experimentally, which he did not live to do himself. You have witnessed an historic moment."

The Nazi officials turned their gaze once more to the Bell, their skeptical demeanors slowly changing to looks of wonderment. Kammler broke the rapt silence.

"Imagine, gentlemen, a fleet of submarines powered by this device. If aligned with the axis of the ship, we have calculated the Bell could propel even our largest U-boat at underwater speeds in excess of forty kilometers per hour, indefinitely. But without the need for a propeller, or for oxygen. The only requirement would be the equipment to set the Bell into motion. The submarine would then only have to surface to refresh the air supply for the crew." [3]

Kammler fixed his attention on Donitz. "Could you turn the tide of the war with such U-boats, *Herr* Admiral?"

Donitz merely stared open-mouthed at the Bell, unable to reply.

"Excuse me, General," Speer interrupted, "perhaps this is a silly question, but if the Bell is indeed a perpetual motion machine, how do you *stop* it?"

As if to answer Speer's question, the whine from the Bell suddenly changed pitch. As the tone fell in frequency, the Bell also slowly descended, the blue glow noticeably diminished. The Bell shifted slightly left and right as the tension reels on the guy wires centered the device back over its cradle. It settled back onto its supports, the glow fading like a flashlight with a dying battery. All eyes turned to Kammler.

"*General?*" Himmler asked pointedly.

Kammler's tone was apologetic, but still confident. "The Bell requires liquid nitrogen to operate. Once the Bell severed its ground connections, the interior slowly warmed until it could no longer function."

"The equipment to produce liquid nitrogen is quite bulky," Speer cautioned. "Do you have a cryogenic plant small enough to fit in one of Admiral Donitz's U-boats?"

Kammler held up a hand for patience. "Not yet, *Reichsminister*, but I believe the problem is eminently solvable."

Himmler cleared his throat. "This is all very fascinating, General, but even if you have tapped into an intriguing force of nature, it hardly justifies the expenditures of manpower and funding we have poured into this project. If we can not *immediately* turn the Bell into a useful propulsion engine, then I must turn your sizable talents to other projects, such as the long range follow-on to the V-2 rocket *Herr* von Braun is developing now at Peenemunde."

Kammler straightened, addressing Himmler directly. "Quite so, *Herr Reichsmarshall*. But you will recall the original application of the Bell was for uranium enrichment, yes?"

Himmler was not accustomed to having his train of thought derailed by a subordinate. "Of course," he huffed.

Kammler's eyes again flashed with a dark fire. "Well, while we were conducting our propulsion experiments with the Bell, it was also very efficiently separating the uranium flowing through its rotors into uranium-235 of sufficient purity for an atomic weapon, at the rate of almost a tenth of a kilogram per ten-minute run. The Bell can now operate for several hours at a time, all the while continuously refining weapons-grade uranium. We now have almost twenty kilograms of 97-percent-pure U-235; more than enough for the critical mass of a single atomic weapon."

"You can't be serious!" Speer exclaimed, his astonishment mirrored on the faces of the other dignitaries.

"I am quite serious, gentlemen," Kammler said. "The Fuhrer's atomic weapons program is, as the Americans say, 'back in business.'" He faced Himmler again. "*Herr Reichsmarshall*, does this, in your judgment, justify the continuation of this project?"

After a moment of silence, Himmler grasped Kammler's right hand with both of his. "*Mein freund*, you have saved the Reich!" He glanced at his watch. "I will request an audience with the Fuhrer first thing tomorrow morning. I am sure he will be very pleased. General Kammler, whatever you require, it is yours. Our victory is in your hands."

After a final salute, Himmler signaled his colleagues. "Gentlemen, let us leave these heroes of the Reich to their work." He led the entourage back to their limousines.

As Kammler passed, he gave Spoerrenberg a wink. "See you in Pilsen, Jakob!"

At that moment, the Russian front seemed far, far away to Jakob Spoerrenberg, and for that he was deeply grateful.

LOOSE ENDS

PRESENT DAY – SAN FRANCISCO, CALIFORNIA

Hendrix settled into the back seat of Pugliano's black Suburban, the FBI agent seated next to him. Pugliano's junior agents rode up front.

"Larry, take us to San Jose," Pugliano ordered.

"Yes sir," the driver replied.

Pugliano turned, his expression communicating a smug eagerness. "This all began with a missing persons report from the Saudi Consulate."

"The Saudis?" Hendrix's defenses immediately went up.

"Yep, one of the royal family's golden boys was in town 'spreading the wealth' and didn't show up for a reception or somesuch. Then, not only did *he* not answer his phone, but none of his security detail did either. The consulate was rightly concerned and came straight to us, thinking it might be terrorism or a kidnapping."

"Which golden boy?" Hendrix asked, readying his Blackberry to make a query of the local CIA database.

The FBI agent handed over a photo of a handsome Arab man with a closely-cropped beard tracing his jaw. "Rashid Ben-Jabir. His uncle is some muckety-muck in the Saudi government, but they were kind of mum on his exact position."

He straightened. "Rashid Ben-Jabir? His uncle is the head of Saudi Intelligence!"

Pugliano's eyes brightened. "You've heard of him?"

Oh hell, nice move. Start deflecting. "The Saudis threw a party when his family bought some firm in Silicon Valley. He seemed like a nice enough guy." *Especially when he introduced himself as a "fellow spook" and invited me up to the residence to share his two rented blondes. God, now that's what I call diplomacy!*

"Well, they were pretty intent on finding him quickly, so we did a cell search on him and his security team's phones. Nada. Not only nada, but according to phone company records, they all dropped off the grid within two minutes of each other."

Hendrix's shoulders dropped. "Aw shit, he's toast."

The FBI agent frowned. "That's what I thought too, so we informed the State Department and they called for all hands on deck, including you. When you didn't answer your phone, they sent me to collect your ass."

Hendrix felt his face burning again. Time to change the subject. "Okay, not that I'm *not* concerned about Rashid, but you said this tied in with Angela Conrad."

Pugliano held up a finger for patience. "I'm getting there. Now the *Chargé d'Affaires* at the consulate confided to me that apparently Ben-Jabir had something of a reputation with the ladies, so we canvassed all the hotels in San Jose near where his guys' cell phones went dark. I had hoped he was just playing hide the sausage with a Mossad agent or a male stripper or something else that would get him beheaded back home and his guys were covering for him. Maybe we could scoop him up and send him back to the consulate." His tone telegraphed failure.

"No luck, huh?"

Pugliano shrugged. "Not exactly. The manager at the San Jose Sheraton thought Rashid looked familiar, so we pulled the security tapes. No hits on Rashid in the previous twenty-four hours, but the manager pointed out four men on the tapes he thought he had seen with him over the last week or so. We faxed their pictures back to the consulate and they confirmed them as members of Rashid's security detail. Turns out Rashid had paid for their rooms for two weeks, up front. They still had five days to go on their stay. We checked their rooms—their luggage was still there, unpacked."

"The Sheraton? Isn't that a little downscale for a member of Saudi royal family?"

He nodded. "Didn't say Rashid was bunking *with* them. He had a room at the Ritz Carlton downtown. That one was deserted in mid-stay as well."

Hendrix feigned confusion. "What good does it do to have your security detail housed clear across town from the guy you're trying to protect?"

The smirk was back. "Oh, they all had rooms at the Ritz, too. They just weren't using them. Not even a toothbrush in the bathroom."

Okay, so he's figured out part of the puzzle. Now to find out which part. "So they were running an *operation* out of the Sheraton. But doing what?"

A lopsided smile. "That's why I brought you along, secret-agent-man. I was hoping you'd tell me."

Good. Just play dumb and he stays in the dark. "What else did you find?"

Pugliano was clearly enjoying himself. "This is where it really gets interesting. After we'd come up empty on Rashid's security team, the manager asked if we'd take a look at some *bullet holes* that had shown up in one of his hallways the day before."

His jaw dropped. "What?" *And here I thought this job was easy enough to let a second-string operator like Rashid handle it. What did I miss?*

"Yep, two bullet holes, one in the hallway wall, and one through the window in the stairwell door. Forensics said they came from a common point, the doorway to one of the rooms."

Hendrix frowned. "So who was the shooter?" *With this kind of mess, I hope to hell Rashid is dead. The last thing I need is that stupid Arab pointing a finger back at me.*

Pugliano consulted his notes for the first time. "The room belonged to some guy named Jacob Fleischer, who also had a couple of days left on his stay. Disappeared without a trace, but forgot to take his rental car with him when he left."

So Rashid's team and their target have gone missing. For crying out loud, how hard is it to kill a Jewish lawyer who weighs one-hundred-fifty pounds soaking wet? He scratched his head again, noticing for some reason that the gesture had been far more satisfying when he had more hair. "Always sucks when that happens. So was he the hallway shooter and lost the gunfight?" *Hell, Fleischer was from Arizona. Doesn't everybody there have a gun?*

Pugliano shrugged. "Unknown. Fleischer has no police record other than a couple of speeding tickets; he was a lawyer for a big firm out of Phoenix."

"What was he doing here in San Francisco?"

"Also unknown. His firm specializes in damage control—stuffing money into the hands of potential litigants before the ambulance chasers get to them. His boss wanted all kinds of info on our investigation, but when I asked what Fleischer was doing here in town the guy claimed attorney-client privilege and stonewalled me."

Good. Another dead end for the FBI to deal with. "How lawyer of him."

A sarcastic snort. "Yeah, well I clammed up too. Told him he could find out about his dead employee from the papers like everybody else. If we ever found his body, that is."

"Sweet. So who was he shooting at?" *Not Rashid's guys, please dear God. Or merciful Allah, or whatever works.*

Pugliano reached behind the seat and retrieved a laptop. "We questioned the staff and none of the guests reported gunshots, but one of the desk clerks said she saw somebody dash out of the hotel the day before like they were being chased. So we pull the tapes again, and here's what we found."

Pugliano turned the laptop to face Hendrix. The screen grab from a black-and-white security tape showed a stocky guy, mid-forties, probably brown hair and an expensive suit emerging from a stairwell. He looked terrified.

"I take it this is the guy being shot at?" *Definitely not one of Rashid's men.*

Another shrug. "They only had security cams on the lobby and the outside doors, so we don't know what happened upstairs. But we know what happened afterwards." Pugliano hit a key and a video overlooking the lobby showed the unknown suit bursting from the stairwell opposite the front desk, looking around in confusion, then dashing away.

"He sure as hell looks like he's being shot at."

"Yep. Keep watching."

The camera changed, the next angle showing an exterior entrance, probably off the parking lot. A woman in a dress leaned against the wall working a cigarette like it was her last.

His eyes widened. "Is that…?"

The running man dashed from the side entrance and exchanged a few words with the woman, who grabbed him firmly and pulled him out of the camera's view. Try as he might, the quality of video didn't allow Hendrix to make the connection.

"So what makes you think *that's* Angela Conrad?"

Pugliano chuckled. "One of our new agents fresh out of Georgetown was bored out of her mind and got fascinated with the fact that there's a *classified* Ten Most Wanted list, that there's a beautiful American woman on it, and why even the classified dossier was so sketchy on the details of her crimes. Little Miss Georgetown also did some work on facial recognition software in college. So she ran this blonde's picture through the software to prove to herself that it was *not* Angela Conrad. Imagine her surprise when the software found nine points of correspondence with Conrad's CIA file photo."

"Nine points out of…"

"Fifteen matching points would be admissible evidence in court, but nine points meant there was a seventy-five percent chance that the blonde was our girl. So I had our young agent go through all the tapes again and see if there was a better shot, a direct face-on shot. Here's what she found.

It was taken twenty-three hours and fifty minutes before we showed up at the Sheraton and told them to stop recording over the previous day's tapes. If we'd shown up ten minutes later it would have been gone forever."

He clicked the laptop again and a freeze frame of the blonde walking past the front desk appeared, already enlarged and enhanced. Next to it was Conrad's CIA recruitment photo. A resemblance, but hardly striking. Then a spiderweb of points and connecting lines traced over both faces. Several dots flashed green on both photos.

"Thirteen matching points. Still not a slam dunk, but plenty enough to go hunt down my nearest and dearest friend from the CIA for a personal chat, don't you think?"

Hendrix nodded mutely. Helping the FBI bag Angela Conrad would be the biggest plum of his entire career, and would guarantee a straight shot to senior management at Langley if he could deliver. *Especially* if he helped the FBI do the deed. The politicos in DC ate up that interagency cooperation bullshit with a spoon. *And* it would give the FBI something to chase other than Rashid's hosed-up operation and his complicity therein.

"So," he lamented, "I take it we have no idea what happened after she left the hotel?"

A raised eyebrow. "Maybe," Pugliano teased. The Suburban pulled up next to a line of SFPD police and crime scene vehicles parked beside a fifteen-story office building. The building's marquee read SOBRATO TOWER.

"I'll have to drop you off and find a spot to park, sir," the driver said.

Pugliano was already out the door. "All ashore that's going ashore," he called to Hendrix.

He followed the FBI agent at a trot. "I take it you have a lead?"

The smirk again. "The security guard here was found stripped to his shorts and taped to a chair this morning, but otherwise unharmed. He said he was attacked by three men, one of whom was an Arab with a stylish little beard." Pugliano traced with both index fingers along his jaw line until they met at his chin. "But he said the gang leader was a hot blonde in a red dress."

Hendrix stopped in his tracks. "Holy shit!" *What the hell was Rashid up to? Did he double-cross me?*

Pugliano held the door open for his CIA companion, his Cheshire Cat grin never wavering. "After you."

* * *

Stan Neufeld was having a very bad day. An angry red bruise cut at an angle across his forehead. When Hendrix and Pugliano entered the office building's cramped security office, he put down the ice pack he held to his wound. Neufeld had put his rumpled guard's uniform back on, but one look in his eyes made it clear to Hendrix the guard was still stripped and taped to a chair and would be until several stiff drinks later. "FBI?" he groaned. "I've already told the police everything that happened. Then I did it again for the detectives. Twice. I just want to go home, *please*."

Hendrix watched Pugliano raise his hands theatrically. "Okay. I can understand that. I just thought you might want to help us get a positive ID on the suspects we've identified in your assault."

Neufeld's eyes darted between Pugliano and Hendrix. "ID? Suspects? The detectives acted like they didn't have a clue who did this."

Pugliano slid his laptop halfway out of its bag. "Sometimes the FBI has resources that aren't available to local police departments."

The guard's eyes were suddenly alert. "Show me."

Pugliano displayed the headshot of Ben-Jabir supplied by the consulate. "Does this guy look familiar?"

A cautious nod. "Yeah, he was there. He was wearing sunglasses, but I recognize that beard. He was showing me some kind of electronics box when the woman attacked me from behind. Then he stuck a *gun* to my head."

Hendrix and Pugliano exchanged a confused glance. "What kind of electronics box?"

Neufeld threw up his hands. "I told the detectives! I don't know! It was something to do with wireless networks here inside the building!"

Pugliano frowned, but clicked on his laptop to the running man from the Sheraton. "What about this fellow? Was he there?"

He examined the screen grab carefully. "Yeah, he was there, but he never said anything."

Several more clicks on the laptop brought up security footage of Rashid's security team. "How about these men? Do any of them look familiar?"

"Well yeah, but they came through earlier."

Pugliano leaned forward. "Excuse me?"

Neufeld rubbed his head impatiently. "Those guys have a suite on the sixth floor. Ah… 620, I think. They're on a one-month lease, restricted floor. No idea what they do; only they went upstairs *hours* before these *crooks* showed up."

"Restricted floor?" Hendrix asked. *That must be where Rashid set up his command post.*

"No public access. Tenants only. That's why they attacked me; they wanted my pass card to go upstairs with their box thingy."

Curiouser and curiouser, Hendrix pondered. *Why would Rashid need to steal a keycard to go see his own security team?*

Pugliano fingered Rashid's photo again. "And you never saw this man before last night?"

Neufeld groaned and put the ice pack back on his head. "I don't *know*. Maybe." His voice lowered to a whisper. "They all kind of look alike to me, you know?"

Pugliano nodded, then clicked the laptop one more time. "Okay, you've been a real trooper, Mr. Neufeld, thank you. One last picture. Is this the woman who attacked you?"

The ice pack dropped with a thud to the table. "Oh Jesus, that's her!"

Hendrix forced himself to hold his elation in check. "You're *sure*?"

Neufeld pushed away from the table and glanced frantically around the small office, as if Angela Conrad could emerge like a wraith from the walls. "Yes, I'm fucking sure!" he shouted. "She came in all sweetness and light and then, BAM! I swear to God I thought she was going to kill me!"

Pugliano leaned back. "You wouldn't have been the first."

Neufeld's eyes went even wider. "*What?* She's *killed* people?"

Pugliano stroked his chin. Hendrix knew he was weighing his words carefully. After all, the whole reason for a *classified* Ten Most Wanted list was that there would never be a public trial for those criminals. They would be aggressively interrogated and then quietly shot, or shot on sight, depending on their skill set. No awkward "Hey, what happened to old what's-her-name, number 6?" No, Angela Conrad would disappear down the same black hole as every other embarrassing government screw-up the US had managed to keep secret from the taxpaying public.

"Let's just say," Pugliano finally offered, "the less you know about her, the more alive you're going to stay."

That was all Stan Neufeld's nerves could take. He began shaking and weeping uncontrollably, clutching his head in his hands. Pugliano and Hendrix stared at each other for several seconds before retiring to the hallway.

"Well," Pugliano observed, "I think they're going to need a new night watchman."

* * *

Ten minutes later Hendrix and Pugliano stood outside suite 620 with the building's superintendent.

"Don't you need a warrant for this?" the super asked.

Pugliano flashed his FBI badge for effect. "Listen, a member of the Saudi royal family is missing. Clues to his disappearance and maybe even his body are behind this door. You can either unlock it or I can break it down and get you a warrant later, your choice."

The super frowned, but unlocked the door.

"Oh, crap!" Pugliano exclaimed, recoiling from the reek of ammonia rolling from the office. "Stay here," he ordered Hendrix, pulling latex gloves from a suit pocket and placing a handkerchief over his face before disappearing into the suite. The fumes in the hall burned Hendrix's eyes like an over-chlorinated pool. He didn't even want to sample the chemical density inside. *So much for Rashid's team,* he realized. *I guess when Rashid called asking for a clean-up crew he was disposing of his own people. Bastard.*

Pugliano emerged less than a minute later. "No bodies," he announced, followed by a coughing spell. "But we sure as hell got ourselves a mambo crime scene." He jabbed at his cell phone, wiping his eyes with the handkerchief. "This is Pugliano. I want every available evidence technician at the Sobrato Tower office building ASAP. Top priority. Bring Hazmat gear."

Ending the call, he turned to the super. "Give me your fax number. You just got your warrant."

STARCH AND ROSES

OCTOBER 1983 – PHILADELPHIA, PENNSYLVANIA

Angela first feared for Becky, being alone in what had been Rachel's bed. But to her horror, Mr. Groutman's attention now seemed focused on *her*. Becky was fat, with freckles and stringy hair. Angela was slender and pretty, like Rachel had been. At first his affections weren't objectionable, just a pat on the head or a hug that made her skin crawl. But then he started to spend time alone with her.

In the guise of a "father-daughter outing," he took her with him into the woods behind the house so he could give her a "fishing lesson." The only clothes she had were dresses Mrs. Groutman had made for her, but he said that would work fine. Indeed the first hour beside the small pond had been spent learning how to bait a hook and cast, but she noticed he looked around a lot, like he was making sure they were alone.

After an hour of fruitless fishing, he put away their reels and spread out a blanket for a picnic lunch. She ate her sandwich in silence, despite his attempts at friendly conversation. All she could see when she looked at him was a false smile and the man who had abused Rachel, then drove her out of the house, or worse.

Mr. Groutman stretched out on the blanket. "I'm tired. Let's take a nap." He motioned her to lie down beside him.

"I'm not sleepy."

He reached out to her. "You will be soon. Come on, father knows best."

She drew back. "You're not my father."

The smile disappeared. "Come here, *now*."

She jumped up to leave. "You're not doing to me what you did to Rachel!"

Fast as a rattlesnake, he yanked her off her feet with one hand and clasped the other over her mouth. "What do you know about Rachel? You want to know what I did to Rachel?" He carried her over to the pond and held her head inches from its surface.

"You want to know where Rachel is?" he said in a breathy rasp. "She's right down there! Right where you're going to be if you don't put out!"

He wrestled her to the blanket, his hand still locked over her mouth. "You always liked spending time with Rachel. Unless you want to spend some time with her on the bottom of that pond, you'd better do what I say, this time and every time!"

When he pulled up her dress and unbuckled his pants, Angela realized her ordeal in the Groutman household was only beginning.

* * *

One night after he had forced himself on her, Angela could take no more. Clad only in her nightgown, she quietly lifted open the bedroom window just enough to slip through and drop into the bushes below. After assuring herself that no one heard, she ran. She ran, never intending to stop. She imagined herself running until the sun rose the next morning. She would run until *no one* could find her, much less the Groutman's.

A few blocks from her house, a car's headlights passed her on the otherwise deserted street. She kept running. The car reversed course and pulled up beside her. She kept running.

"Sweetheart, stop!" a woman's voice called. She kept running.

The car pulled ahead and into a driveway, cutting off her path. Angela veered right and kept running. She reached a chain link fence almost level with her head, but she was up and over it without even breaking stride.

"Little girl, wait!" the woman called. Even though Angela could tell it was not Mrs. Groutman, she kept running. She heard the jangle of chain link behind her.

Angela ran until faced with a towering stockade fence. She jumped but couldn't even reach the top to pull herself over. She ran to where the chain link butted up to the obstacle. She mounted it in a leap, feeling the top of the fence links pierce the bottom of her bare feet. She heard footfalls close behind. She pulled up and over the stockade fence, falling the full height of the fence onto her chest and face. She tasted blood on her lips, was up and running again.

"Sweetheart! I'm not going to hurt you! Stop!" the woman called.

Angela glanced over her shoulder to see the progress of her pursuer. When her gaze returned forward, the dog was almost on top of her. It was huge and black, its fangs flashing in the moonlight. The dog let out a guttural growl and opened its mouth wide to maul her.

An arm circled her chest and swung her from the ground. In her peripheral vision Angela saw a black object sweep at the dog. It contacted and the dog retreated with a yelp. Then her rescuer ran. Grass and night sky tilted crazily as she was carried back across the yard and toward the stockade fence. With a thud and a grunt they were up and over. The dog hit the fence below them, snapping fangs and rasping claws. They tumbled together to the ground on the far side, the woman cushioning Angela's fall with her body. Angela heard the woman gasp in pain as she rolled off. Her rescuer lay panting on the ground for a few seconds, then pulled a radio from her belt.

"Dispatch, Patrol Three! Officer needs assistance, eighteen hundred block of Lockwood!"

Angela Kellerman gazed wide-eyed at her champion. The stocky policewoman wore a black uniform, now soiled and torn at the legs. Her hair was strawberry blonde and tied in a braided bun behind her wide, slightly masculine face. Angela thought she was the most beautiful woman she had ever seen.

"Are you an angel?" Angela asked in awe, remembering the Bible stories Mrs. Groutman told them before bed.

The woman laughed, then put her hand to her ribs. "I am tonight, honey." She coughed painfully. "Although I didn't know angels could break a rib. Crap."

"I'm sorry," Angela whispered.

Grimacing, the policewoman rose to her feet. She held out her hand. "Whatever you were running from, you're safe now. Let's go back to my car and talk about it."

Angela hesitated. Even with the snarling dog on the far side of the fence, she felt safer in this strange back yard than she would be out on the street.

The policewoman bent over. "Sweetheart, were you running from some *thing*, or some *one*?"

Her hands instinctively bunched her nightgown at her waist. "Some *one*."

A flashlight blazed and played across her night clothes. Between her fists a splotch of blood spread outward from her crotch. The flashlight went out and the policewoman leaned in close. "Did a *man* do this to you?" she demanded.

Angela nodded, then the dam holding back her emotions burst again. She felt her legs give way, but before she hit the ground an arm scooped her up. She sagged against the policewoman's shoulder and sucked in a sobbing breath, inhaling a strange mix of starch and roses. She heard sirens in the distance.

"Do you hear that, baby?" the policewoman asked, stroking the back of Angela's head as she carried her from the yard. Angela nodded.

"Those are my friends, and when they get here we're going to find out who did this to you. Then we are going to *kick his ass*."

Angela Kellerman squeezed her savior close and wept.

* * *

Patrol Officer Francine Conrad—Frankie to her friends—asked Angela if she would like to be present at her foster father's arrest. She said she would. Frankie made sure all the arresting officers met Angela. Frankie asked if they had daughters. Most of them did. Then they stared at each other as if exchanging some kind of unspoken communication. The men nodded and walked away.

To minimize the trauma on Angela's foster sisters, it was decided to apprehend Mr. Groutman outside the house when he left for work. Police cars bunched at both ends of the block, out of sight from the Groutman household. Angela sat in the back of one of them, holding hands with Frankie.

A light blue Ford pickup truck pulled from the garage. "Here we go!" the young officer in the front seat called, putting the car in gear.

Three police cars converged from each end of the block, fishtailing to a stop at the end of the Groutman driveway. Policemen burst from the cars, swarming over Groutman's vehicle with weapons drawn in a massive display of force.

Groutman's hands went up immediately, but one officer bashed in the driver's side window with his flashlight. Three men reached in and dragged Groutman through the broken window, throwing him to the driveway. His arms came up in a defensive reflex, which was all the excuse the officers needed. Fists and batons flew, the policemen mobbing Groutman so thickly Angela couldn't see him under the cloud of constabulary wrath.

When they finally dragged Groutman to his feet, he was dazed and could barely walk. They marched him to the car in front of Angela's, his nose and mouth streaming blood onto his torn shirt.

Frankie wrapped her arms around Angela. "Do you know what happens now, sweetie?"

"What?" she whispered.

Frankie squeezed her till it hurt. "He never hurts anybody, ever again."

She looked up at the woman who had saved her life. "Promise?"

Frankie kissed the upturned forehead. "Promise."

A door slammed and the vehicle carrying Angela's tormentor drove away. The officer who had manhandled Groutman into the back seat saw Frankie and flashed thumbs-up.

Frankie's voice took on an edge Angela didn't understand. "Yes indeed, baby girl. That's a promise."

FAMILY TIME

PRESENT DAY – CHICAGO, ILLINOIS

It was a rare all-family dinner in the Manning household. Normally by the time Mike got home, the boys were finishing their homework or preparing for bed. Amanda chatted happily away about having "all her boys" home for dinner.

"Mom, can we eat in front of the TV?" Kevin asked.

"No, honey," she replied sweetly. "Daddy's home tonight, so we're eating together."

"But Mom, it's almost time for *Survivor!*" Eric protested.

Manning had the bad fortune to be home for *Survivor* once before. When it came time for the contestants to eat bugs, slugs and other disgusting organic matter, the boys played along by labeling the contents of their plates something even more disgusting than what the TV competitors were choking down and then challenge each other to eat it. Green beans became scorpions, corn became frog's eyes, and gravy became rat barf. It was not an experience he wished to repeat.

"I'll set the Tivo for you!" She assured them, her voice tinged with exasperation. "Your father doesn't get to be home for dinner very often. He works very hard so you can have nice things like that TV and your XBox. You need to enjoy each other's company!"

The boys eyed him, but said nothing.

She returned from the family room a few moments later. "There! Crisis averted!" she chirped. "Your weekly ration of silly contests and bickering in the jungle is being recorded."

"They're not silly!" Kevin dissented.

"Can we watch it after dinner?" Eric asked.

"No Eric," she said. "You have a math test tomorrow. By the time you finish studying, it will be Kevin's bedtime."

"But I can watch it by myself!" he whined, like he was being forced to give up a kidney.

"You watch your shows together or not at all," Amanda affirmed. "That's the rule."

The boys stared at their normally absent father in steely-eyed silence.

Manning usually ate his reheated dinner in the study while Amanda worked with the boys and he watched whatever shows he had Tivoed the night before. He made a mental note to never be on time for dinner again.

Amanda brought the lasagna to the table with a flourish, knowing it was one of his favorite dishes. "So to what do we owe the pleasure, honey?" she asked. "It's not like Bernie Norquist to let you come home early."

His neck muscles tightened. "Well, ah, that trip to San Francisco was hell," he answered truthfully. "I thought I had earned a night off."

"Of course you did, sweetie," she cooed, hugging a warm, soft boob against his face and kissing his forehead. He could tell there was no bra under her blouse, which signaled her intent to reward him for coming home early with more than his favorite meal.

"Why was your trip hell, daddy?" Kevin asked with the innocence of a cherub.

Amanda glared at him out of the corner of her eye. *There you go teaching them new words again.*

His neck muscles tightened further, almost to the point of spasm. "Well, Kevin, the only reason people need lawyers is because they can't get along with each other. The people I dealt with on this trip just couldn't get along with anybody." *They really, <u>really</u> couldn't get along with anybody*, he mused. *Or any <u>body</u>.*

"What were they fighting over?" Kevin pressed, his experience in human conflicts limited to possession of the remote or the last slice of pizza.

He poked at his lasagna. "Well, I really can't say, Kevin."

Eric lifted his nose pompously. "It's attorney-client privilege," he informed his ignorant younger brother.

"What's attorney clam-up privilege?" Kevin asked.

Manning had the first genuine laugh in a long time. "Attorney-*client* privilege. But you got the clam-up part right. It means whatever the people paying me—that's the client—tell me, I can't tell anyone else unless *they* say it's okay. Nobody."

Kevin's eyes widened. "Even Mom?"

He leaned over the table. "*Especially* Mom," he whispered conspiratorially. "She's a notorious blabbermouth."

That earned him a playful foot stomp from Amanda, which made the boys laugh. He was grateful for the comic relief. The tension between him and the boys seemed to lift.

"Daddy, if your job is hell, why don't you get another one?" Kevin offered.

"Hell is not a table word, Kevin." She lifted an eyebrow in Manning's direction. "And if Daddy used it, Daddy's sorry, right?"

He cleared his throat. "Uh, *yes*. What I should have said was my trip was really, really bad."

Kevin continued with the persistence of a dripping faucet. "So, Daddy, if your job is really, really bad, why don't you get another one?"

Out of the mouth of freaking babes, Manning thought.

"That's a good thought, honey," Amanda counseled, "but changing jobs is a lot harder than that."

"But, ah," he stammered, "now that you mention it, I, ah, have been thinking about doing just that."

"*What?*" Amanda asked, as if he had announced his intention to take a mistress.

"I've been looking at another job," he affirmed, his confidence increasing now that he had pulled the pin on the grenade and there was no putting it back. "We both know that Bernie Norquist is a slave driver, and I've got years of his crap to shovel before I even have a shot at making partner. What harm is there in looking?"

She pushed away from the table, slowly. "I thought *you* said Feldman-Norquist was the only risk-mitigation law firm in the Chicago area. That's why you fought so hard to get on there."

The lasagna had suddenly become difficult to swallow. "It is. I just thought, well, why do we have to restrict ourselves to Chicago forever?"

"Where *exactly* were you thinking of looking?" she challenged.

He felt like he was looking down the barrel of a gun again. "I, ah, thought San Francisco was kind of nice."

She stared at him as if evaluating his sanity. "I thought you said San Francisco was hell."

"Not a table word, Mom!" Kevin cautioned.

"Quiet, Kevin!" she snapped, her eyes never leaving Manning. "Answer me."

Both boys sunk down in their chairs as if to avoid flying shrapnel.

"Well, I, ah, met someone," he stuttered. "At another company," he added hastily.

In a moment her eyes took on a look he had only seen before in the eyes of Angela Conrad. A very deadly look. "Really? What was *her* name?" she demanded.

Oh hell! Am I really that easy to read? A lesson from Bernie Norquist rang in his ears. *When the truth won't do, and a lie won't sell, then tell the truth, but twist it.* "Her name is Monica Geldman. She's a lawyer for a company called Nanovex. They have an opening. She just asked me if I would consider it."

Suddenly Amanda was the lawyer, and he was the hapless witness under cross-examination. "And what did *you* say?"

Lying had never made it this difficult to swallow before. The previous bite of lasagna twisted in his throat like a hanged suicide victim. He washed it down with the rest of his wine. To his horror, he noticed his hand shook slightly bringing the glass to his mouth. "I told her I'd discuss it with you," he finally managed to choke out.

He had seen houses burn with less intensity than Amanda's eyes. "So *you're* talking about uprooting all of us and dragging the boys clear across the country to California before the school year is over and you didn't even have the decency to discuss it in private with me first?"

Maybe because I thought you'd be less likely to strangle me in front of the children, he mused. "Of course not. The school year will be over in a couple of months. By then I'll be settled in and you and the boys can join me. And if it doesn't work out, *nobody* moves."

"And if it *doesn't* work out, do you plan on crawling back to Bernie Norquist and begging for your job back? That vindictive son of a bitch will tell you to stick it. And *then* where will we have to move? St. Louis?"

Now that was just mean, he thought. Suggesting that he would move their family to the arch-rival's nest of his beloved Cubs was like twisting a rusty knife in his gut.

"I don't want to move to St. Louis!" Eric cried out in terror.

Amanda reached out to comfort their older son. "Nobody's moving, sweetheart."

"But Dad just said…."

"Daddy misspoke." Her eyes bore into him like a laser. "Didn't you, Daddy?"

As much as he hated stirring up his wife's anger, he was still more afraid of Angela Conrad than he was of Amanda Manning. His family's life hung in the balance.

"No," he said firmly, "I did not misspeak. I'm done with Bernie Norquist. I gave him my two-week notice this afternoon."

Amanda's head jerked, her face going through a roller coaster of emotions, from confusion, then shock, and finally arriving at white-hot anger. She jumped to her feet, knocking her chair backwards.

"You *bastard!*" she hissed. "You never had *any* intention of listening to what I thought, or about what was best for the boys! You never thought about *anyone* but *yourself!*"

The boys slid down until only the tops of their heads and their wide, terrified eyes were visible above the table.

"How could you even *think* about this without discussing it with me first?" she railed. "*My* family is here. *Your* family is here." She pointed at the boys. "Their *grandparents* are here. And you just want to pull up and throw that all away without even *talking* about it? You are such a *prick!*"

He knew that much of her anger was real, but part of it was emotional manipulation. He'd seen his mother-in-law use those livid tactics to great effect on Amanda's father. Not this time. This was too important to allow her to browbeat him into submission. Their *lives* depended on him winning this fight.

"I'm sorry, honey," he tried to soothe, "I've tried to hold it together here in Chicago for you and the boys, but after that last trip, something's got to give. I can't keep doing want Bernie's asking of me. And like you said, Goldsmith-Norquist is the only law firm that handles my specialty."

She just stared at him, clench-fisted and shaking, her jaw set.

He reached out to her. "Honey, I'm sorry I didn't talk to you…."

Trying to touch her was a big mistake. She stepped closer like she was moving into his arms, then drew back and slapped him as hard as she could. She was a lot stronger than she looked. His head rang with the blow. If she had struck him with a fist instead of an open hand, she might have knocked him out.

"Don't *TOUCH* me, you *BASTARD!*" she shouted. "*You* want to move to San Francisco, you're moving by *yourself!*"

She stormed from the kitchen. The boys followed, running to Eric's room like fleeing a monster. He heard the master bedroom door slam, followed by Eric's door a few seconds after that. He heard both doors lock.

"Great job, Mike," he groaned to the empty kitchen.

* * *

He made several overtures to the locked master bedroom door, without response. Good thing he had a comfortable couch in his study. Walking to the linen closet for sheets and pillows, he heard his boys talking in low voices, Kevin still sheltering behind the locked door in his older brother's room.

"What's a *bastard*?" Kevin asked his brother, in the breathy, easily audible whisper that passed for *sotto voce* to a seven-year-old.

"Somebody who acts like Dad," grumbled Eric.

Ouch. That one-liner hurt worse than all the venom Amanda had hurled at him, because he knew Eric meant every word of it.

His cell phone vibrated on his hip. It was probably Bernie Norquist calling to ask him if he had come to his senses yet. He checked the caller

ID, expecting a Chicago area phone number. Area code 408? Why did that seem familiar? One way to find out. He took the call.

"Manning."

"Mike Manning?" the caller asked. His voice was deep and authoritative.

"Yes," he replied, with a touch of uncertainty. He wondered if the caller was going to announce himself as police or FBI.

"My name is Doug Lyman, I'm the CEO of a company called Nanovex in San Jose, California. Ever heard of it?"

He almost swallowed his tongue. "Well, I'm not sure I…."

Lyman chuckled. "No need to fake it, Mr. Manning, we're a small nanotechnology company, not many people *have* heard of us. But we're doing some very exciting work, with the possibility of some very lucrative contracts with the Defense Department."

"Well, I'm an attorney, how exactly can I…."

"I'll level with you, Mr. Manning. I'm in a bind. We had an accident recently, and there were fatalities. Until recently I was dealing with an outside firm to help control the situation."

"Harkin-Thompson?" he offered.

A surprised pause. "Why, yes, how did you know?"

"They're one of the largest risk-mitigation firms in the US. It makes sense that you would deal with them."

"Yes, but a few days ago their lawyer left without notice and his firm has refused to send a replacement for some reason."

Hmm, like maybe they didn't want any <u>more</u> of their lawyers cut up and stuffed in buckets, perhaps? "I can see your problem," he sympathized.

"And that's where *you* come in. I understand you're looking for a new job opportunity."

A sudden tightness in his chest made it difficult to speak. "Where did you hear that?"

A thoughtful pause. "Actually, I heard it from someone in your office."

"Bernie Norquist?" he asked. He had submitted his resignation to Norquist privately, although anyone in earshot of the tirade that resulted might have put two and two together.

"I don't feel comfortable saying any more than that."

"Of course, but even if I submitted my resignation to Feldman-Norquist immediately, I would still owe them two week's notice." He couldn't admit that he had already committed professional suicide by resigning without securing another position.

Lyman's voice took on an edge. "Mr. Manning, if you will be on the first plane to San Francisco tomorrow, I'm willing to grant you an expediency bonus of twenty-five thousand dollars, in addition to matching whatever salary you're making now plus twenty percent."

His eyes bugged. “That’s very generous, but….”

“If you’re concerned about the two-week notice, I’ve given you 25K to work with. However much of that amount you need to share with your previous employer to make peace, I’ll reimburse you when you arrive here tomorrow.”

He blinked in silence. This was too good to be true.

“I’m sorry to push you, Mr. Manning,” Lyman insisted, “but I need an answer. American Airlines has a flight leaving O’Hare at 7:55 tomorrow morning. I can have a ticket waiting for you, but I need to know now whether to make the reservation.”

He realized his luggage was still sitting in his study, unpacked. He needed fresh clothes, but he could do laundry at the hotel. He felt an enormous load lift from his shoulders. He might just get out of this alive after all.

“Make the reservation,” he heard himself say, “I’ll be there.”

[1] The Elephant Cage, or Henge, is a concrete structure just outside the Wenceslas Mines in Poland. Extensively investigated by Igor Witkowski, one of his key theories is that the Henge was used as an outdoor test stand for the Bell in a manner similar as recounted in this text. Witkowski found isotopes in the steel reinforcing bars of the concrete structure that could only result by neutron bombardment from a highly radioactive source. (Source: *The SS Brotherhood of the Bell* by Joseph Farrell, p. 166)

[2] In 2005, German Air Force officer Gerold Schelm wrote an excellent Internet article comparing the structure of the Henge to an existing cooling tower near the Polish town of Wroclaw—including some convincing photographs—to the end that this cooling tower and the Henge were built to very similar specifications. However, Schelm’s conclusion was that since he had shown that the Henge was probably the base of a cooling tower, the Bell story was therefore a fabrication. Schelm however does not

explain the source of the neutron bombardment Witkowski documented, and neglects the possibility that the Henge may very well have started life as a cooling tower and the Nazis simply pressed it in service for another duty once the power source developed by Kurt Debus became available and the old power plant was superfluous. And if the reader will pardon the author's incredulity, an officer in the *German* Air Force hardly seems like an impartial arbiter of truth in matters of this sort, especially since he refuses to cooperate with researchers such as Farrell or Witkowski. (Source: www.bielek-debunked.com/Henge/The-Henge.pdf)

[3] One of the intriguing aspects of the wartime Bell project is that above the SS officers in charge of the day-to-day administration of the project was an *Admiral*, which indicates the Bell project's ultimate accountability was to the German Navy, not the Air Force as one would expect of a project like the Bell. Other researchers have noted this oddity, but this quote from Albert Speer, Hitler's chief of arms production, appears to close the loop. He writes on p. 228 of his memoirs, "*On the suggestion of the nuclear physicists we scuttled the project to develop an atom bomb by the autumn of 1942, after I had again queried them about deadlines and been told that we could not count on anything for three or four years. The war would certainly have been decided long before then.* ***Instead I authorized the development of an energy-producing uranium motor for propelling machinery. The navy was interested in that for its submarines*** [emphasis added]." While this might refer to an "ordinary" nuclear reactor as one might find on a US submarine, **there is no post-war evidence such a project existed**, despite Speer having authorized it in 1942. Instead, **this quote may be the most direct historical evidence of the Bell's existence and its importance to Nazi Germany's war plans**, which is why I included Albert Speer and Admiral Donitz in this scene.

CHAPTER 6

THE EXECUTOR

PRESENT DAY – CHICAGO, ILLINOIS

Simon Crane turned his chair to face the windows in his spacious office looking out the 105th floor on the northeast corner of the Sears Tower. Although it had officially been renamed the Willis Tower, he had decided he could call it anything he wished. Nobody outside of Chicago knew what the hell the Willis Tower was. He might as well call it the Crane Tower. Although a credenza behind his desk might make his work more efficient, he kept the floor behind his desk totally clear so he could enjoy moments like this, looking down from a thousand feet above Lake Michigan and downtown Chicago. The clear bright morning was about to be spoiled by clouds rolling in over the lake, which befitted his mood. He had unpleasant work to do today, but there was no alternative.

Until September 11, 2001, his office had been on the upper floors of the World Trade Center North Tower. He had just stepped to the curb for a nine o'clock meeting when the first hijacked plane slammed into the building eighty floors above him. He dashed into the lobby in time to watch the debris strike the pavement and the limousine he had arrived in. After the attacks he briefly considered moving his offices to the Empire State Building, where they had been for many years before the World Trade Center towers were built. But instead he moved his headquarters to Chicago. The technologies he was charged with monitoring required more trips to the US west coast than to the east coast or Europe as had been the case when the organization was younger. Besides, the Sears Tower was now the tallest building in the US. Situating his office atop such a spire appealed to him.

To the members of his organization, Simon Crane was known simply as the Executor, while his organization had no name at all. The name on their office and letterhead read United Technology Associates, which was just a label that would be changed along with the front office staff and lobby décor at random intervals every one to three years. He was reminded by his Security staff at each *change de nom* that the entire office should be moved, including his, but Crane had become a creature of habit. He figured that if the power of his office could not be wielded in so small a thing as his personal convenience, what good was it? His small but well-appointed personal apartment directly adjoined his office. He was loath to give up such a perk.

Crane was tall and thin, with a strong jaw and high, chiseled cheekbones so prized among corporate executives as a sign of those "born to lead." A prominent, almost beaklike nose gave him a predatory look, like the human embodiment of an American bald eagle. But all these features merely framed his fierce, deep-set eyes--black, bottomless, and utterly devoid of pity. While his true age was sixty years, the few people Crane worked with directly assumed he was older. But there was no way to be sure. He *had* no personnel dossier that a prying executive secretary could peruse. Except for those who saw him enter his office or his personal jet, Simon Crane simply did not exist. In fact, he didn't. Simon Crane was the third name he had carried for use in the organization, and none of those were the name given to him at birth. They were merely conveniences, like the apartment next to his office.

His phone rang. Crane did not need a secretary to screen his calls. Only a dozen men in the US had the access code needed in addition to his phone number to cause his phone to ring. He checked the incoming number. He had been expecting this call.

"Yes?"

"Good morning, sir. I'm calling to make my report." There was no need for introductions or formalities. Pleasantries were inefficient.

"Proceed."

"The technology being developed by Nanovex has been successfully tested. The concept is valid. All that remains is weaponization." The young man's voice on the other end sounded pleased with his report.

"Good," Crane affirmed. "You have done well."

"Thank you, sir." The relief was audible in the younger man's voice. The penalties for failure in Crane's world were as uniform as they were severe.

"I'm afraid I have to reward your exemplary service with some unfortunate news."

"Oh?" The tone was more of curiosity than concern, now that his personal performance, and therefore his personal safety, was no longer under discussion.

"I met with the Group last night. Their decision was unanimous. The technology under development by Nanovex is being taken off the table. It will not be permitted to proceed to weaponization."

A significant pause followed as the younger man considered the implications of Crane's statement. "I see. That *is* unfortunate."

Crane pressed his eyes shut. He always hated this part of the job. "You *do* understand what will be required of you next, of course?"

If the younger man had any reservations, they didn't show in his voice. "Of course, sir. I understand completely. What will the Group require as deliverables?"

Crane opened his eyes, taking in the view of the city beneath his feet. He was gratified that his associate did not hesitate at the task presented him. "I will send you a detailed list. Basically they will want a sample of the nanoagent, and all documentation of the technology's development, as well as any weaponization concepts."

"I'll wait for your instructions, sir. By the way, the candidate you suggested has been successfully recruited. I'll be briefing him shortly."

"Very well." As gratified as he was at the caller's enthusiasm, Crane hesitated to end the call so quickly. The stakes were frightfully high for everyone involved, including him. He did not survive this many years in the organization by leaving operations to chance.

"I understand this will be your first application of final security," he observed. This would be his associate's opportunity to request additional assistance, if he felt the task beyond his abilities. His *only* opportunity.

"I have been well trained, sir, I won't fail you," came the immediate response.

"Very well. I will expect regular updates on your progress." He terminated the call without waiting for an acknowledgement. That would be inefficient. The younger man wished to carry out the job on his own. So be it. Crane would have a team observing and standing by should the need arise, but if all went well his associate would never even know of their presence. It would be his first performance without a net, and he owed the young man at least the *illusion* of a free hand on his first job. Of course, if he failed, it would also be his last job. That was also assumed.

Simon Crane dialed the number for his pilot. "Andre, prepare my jet. We're going to Washington."

TECHNICALITY

JULY 1986 – PHILADELPHIA, PENNSYLVANIA

"Morning, Frankie!" nine-year-old Angela Conrad said, bouncing into the kitchen and pouring herself a bowl of cereal.

Frankie looked up from the paper. "Morning, baby girl. Sleep well?" At first she had tried to get Angela to call her "Mom," but soon realized that title had negative connotations for Angela. She learned to settle for "Frankie."

"Yep. Funnies?"

Frankie passed her the comics. Adopting Angela had forced her to move back in with her mother—which didn't do much for her love life—but the rest of her child-rearing had settled into a comfortable routine. She put Angela to bed before she left for work and would get home in time for breakfast. She would hit the sack when Angela left for school and would usually be awakened when a squirmy schoolgirl snuggled into bed with her several hours later. Life was good.

"Any excitement last night?" Angela asked. She had a keen interest in Frankie's police work and regularly begged to stay up late to watch adult police dramas on TV.

"Bagged a car thief we've been hunting for a couple of weeks," she said, not looking up from her paper.

"Car chase?" Angela asked, beaming.

"Oh yeah," she replied, allowing herself a small grin.

"Shots fired?" Angela asked hopefully.

Frankie folded the paper and gave her adopted daughter an evil look. "Bullets go both ways, baby girl. Not something to wish for. He crashed and bailed."

Angela's eyes widened expectantly. "Mace?"

She opened the paper again to hide her look of satisfaction. "*Every* good chase ends in mace," she recited.

"Yes!" Angela tried to paw the paper from her hands. "Where is it?"

A tug of war ensued. "Cut it out, Angie! It happened at three this morning! The paper was already printed! Maybe tomorrow."

She returned reluctantly to her comics. "What else is going on today?" For a nine-year-old, she had a keen interest in current events. The poor kid had been forced to grow up before her time.

Frankie rustled the paper. "Well, Prince Andrew is getting married tomorrow to that Sarah Ferguson girl. Seems everyone's all a'twitter about that."

"I like her," Angela said without looking up. "She's got spunk. What else?"

Frankie smiled. These were the moments that made it all worth it. "Sounds like somebody else I know. Well, let's see." She thumbed through the paper until a headline on A6 stopped her cold.

Child Murderer Escapes Death Penalty on Technicality

Frankie folded the paper and stuck it under her arm. "Not much else, I'm afraid. Come on, baby girl. Time for school."

WELCOME

PRESENT DAY – CHICAGO, ILLINOIS

If Nanovex was just a small technology start-up company, they certainly didn't act like one. A first-class ticket awaited Manning at the American Airlines ticket counter, along with a note asking him to visit the Admirals Club for a package.

The hostess at the Admirals Club greeted him warmly, handing him a thick manila envelope and a thumb drive bearing the American Airlines logo. "Mr. Manning, if you'd prefer, I'll be happy to print out whatever is on the drive as well. We have a color printer right here."

He patted his laptop. "Thanks, I'll let you know if I need a hard copy."

The hostess's smile broadened. "Certainly, sir. Could I get you something to drink?"

He had dressed and gathered his bags to await the cab to the airport long before Amanda or the boys had awakened, eating or drinking nothing before he left. "Coffee would be great, thank you."

He had just settled himself at one of the lounge's worktables when the hostess returned with a tray bearing a coffee service and a hot cinnamon roll. "Here you go, Mr. Manning. They'll serve breakfast on the flight, but this is a little something to tide you over."

Manning thanked her and reached for his wallet. She waved him off. "No, no, sir. Your new boss Mr. Lyman is an Admiral's Club Platinum member. He called ahead and asked me to take care of your needs personally, at his expense."

He blinked. "Well, that was certainly very gracious of him."

"It certainly was. Sounds like your new boss is a keeper!" She treated him to a parting smile before leaving him to his work.

The manila folder contained a hefty stack of pre-employment papers, from an employment application and non-disclosure agreement to various pledges of ethical behavior, forswearing conflicts of interest, and even respecting diversity, whatever the hell that meant. He saved that pile of corporate *de rigueur* for the plane.

The thumb drive contained three PDF files. He opened the documents, the first a technical paper titled "What is Nanotechnology?" The basic gist was that instead of mixing vats of chemicals or machining blocks of metal into the desired product, nanotechnology assembled materials or machines molecule by molecule, or even atom by atom. It seemed like science fiction to him, and the text climbed beyond his technical grasp by the second page, with terms like carbon nanotubes, fullerenes, and dendrimers.

He closed the document and opened the second, a basic PR document on Nanovex. It was much more tangible to him, because it talked about how Nanovex intended to make money on this nanotechnology thing. Although they claimed nanotechnology was applicable to basically every area of science, Nanovex concentrated their efforts on electronics, medicine, aerospace, and defense. They had an impressive list of sponsors, including NASA, The National Science Foundation, the Department of Defense, and something called DARPA.

The PR document contained a magazine interview with his new boss, Doug Lyman, about the potential of nanotechnology. He called it "a second industrial revolution," and that it would affect every product made by man—for the better of course. Better drugs, better food, faster electronics, safer cars and aircraft. A better world for all.

Manning also knew his services were never required when things went according to plan. He opened the final file. It contained only three web addresses, all to San Francisco area newspapers—the San Francisco Chronicle, the San Jose Mercury News, and the Silicon Valley Daily. He clicked on the link to the Chronicle story first.

"COMPANY MUM ON 5 EMPLOYEE DEATHS AT NANOVEX."

"Hello, paycheck," Manning whispered. "I knew you were in there somewhere."

* * *

Manning actually enjoyed the four-and-a-half-hour flight to San Francisco. Partly because of the space and amenities of First Class, and partly because it was the first time in days that he hadn't felt in fear for his own life. And to think that once *flying* used to make him nervous, he thought ruefully. He would gladly exchange his First Class seat for a middle seat in Coach between a crying baby and a flatulent double-wide drunk to have those days back.

When he adjusted his watch to Pacific Time, he wondered what Amanda and the boys were doing at that moment. It was Saturday, which meant he had no idea what anyone was doing, since he was always buried in his study writing up that week's trip report with the door closed and locked. He had no idea what they would be doing tomorrow either, since Sundays meant he was on the golf course or working in the yard, or both. It suddenly occurred to Manning that he sucked at being a parent, and probably a husband too. He wondered how long it would be before they even noticed he was gone.

He had just pulled his luggage off the baggage carousel when a crew-cut young man in a suit approached him. "I'll take those, Mr. Manning," he insisted, relieving him of both his checked luggage and his laptop bag. He escorted Manning to the curbside pickup, then returned a few minutes later in a gleaming black Cadillac Escalade. He nearly arm-wrestled Manning to prevent him from loading his own luggage in the back, then held open the passenger door like Manning used to do for his wife. It was embarrassing.

The driver sensed his discomfort. "Sorry, sir. General—I mean, *Mister* Lyman insisted that you receive the executive treatment. I'm just following orders."

Manning climbed up into the passenger seat. "Who am I to question orders? Carry on, soldier." He hoped this "General" Lyman wasn't one of those testosterone-dripping ex-fighter-pilot jocks who insisted on being called by his Top Gun callsign. Those guys tended to give their civilian coworkers callsigns and then repeat them until they stuck. Manning recalled his inflicted moniker at one company was "Slime Monkey."

They exited the airport complex onto Highway 101 south. Once they had settled into a traffic lane, Manning extended his hand. "I don't believe I caught your name."

The driver's eyes never left the road as he returned the gesture. "Oh, sorry, sir. Reese Miller, Security."

He examined the young man's spartan haircut. "Army?"

"No sir, Air Force Special Forces. Pararescue. That's how I met the General. I was his body man in Afghanistan."

"Body man?"

Miller chuckled. "Sorry, milspeak. Lead body guard. My job in a fight was to catch any bullets meant for him while my team handled the threat. The joke was that if anything hit his body, mine better be in a bag."

The casual manner Miller discussed his own mortality gave Manning pause. After an uncomfortable silence he asked, "So what kind of man is 'The General?'"

"He's a great man," Miller said without hesitation. "Always cool under fire, very focused. Loyal to his people. Excellent leader. We had some close scrapes in the sandbox. I'd follow him anywhere."

"Wow," he said with genuine admiration. Nobody was ever going to say something like that about *him*. "So, he recruited you away from the service?"

Miller laughed, raising his left hand and thumbing his wedding ring. "Nah, he just recruited my wife. She's the one who beat me with a tire iron 'til I quit the Air Force. He paid her more as a secretary than I made throwing my ass out of planes for Uncle Sam. When his offer to double my salary didn't work, she said if I re-enlisted she was going to start sleeping with the boss."

"Ouch. That would do it."

"Women," Miller laughed. "They *do* have a way of focusing our priorities, don't they?"

Manning's gaze became distant. "They do indeed."

Miller seemed to detect the minefield and began pointing out local landmarks and communities with good schools as they journeyed south. Forty minutes later they pulled onto Nanovex's property in San Jose. General Lyman had apparently taken his security lessons from Afghanistan seriously. The Nanovex compound lay inside two layers of barbed wire fencing, with the second layer on a berm completely surrounding the property. Cameras on poles covered every avenue of approach to the complex.

The guard at the first gate looked like the Marine Corps entrant to the Mr. Universe contest. His short-sleeved security guard uniform bearing the Nanovex logo strained at every seam from the muscles the fabric struggled to contain. The pistol on his hip seemed entirely superfluous. He greeted Miller by name when the Escalade pulled to a stop beside the guard shack.

"Hey Nick, how's it hangin'?" Miller addressed the guard, displaying his ID badge out of habit.

"Just waitin' for the defecation to hit the oscillation, sir!"

"You keep hoping!"

"That I do, sir." He shifted to look intently at Manning. "This the new meat?"

"Yeah, Nick, meet Mike Manning. He works directly for Mr. Lyman, so go easy on the abuse."

"Oh, absolutely sir!" Nick gave Manning a smile like a lion eyeing his next meal. The guard hit an unseen button and the wooden gate lifted.

Once they pulled away Manning remarked, "That is one scary dude."

Miller laughed. "Nick? He's all show. Now Tommy, here, he's all business." They approached another, much more substantial guard building with smaller windows situated in the berm's only gap. The glass of the guard shack had a greenish tinge; obviously very thick, probably bulletproof. A row of thick steel posts blocked the driveway. They retracted into the street, allowing the Escalade to pass. A man in camouflage fatigues inside the bunker gave Miller a half-wave, half-salute when they passed.

"Why two guard shacks?" he asked.

"Layered defense," Miller replied. "Nick's post is just the tripwire. Tommy's job is to stop a truck bomb or similar intruder cold."

He remembered the file on the Saudi operatives' laptop that mentioned Nanovex directly. "What is it you guys do here that makes you such a target?

Miller nodded gravely. "That's a good question, but I'd rather Mr. Lyman answer it."

They parked the Escalade in Lyman's marked spot. Miller handed him a printed visitor's badge, then escorted him to the door. Inside the soaring glass lobby, models of strange geometric shapes slowly turned—tubes, spheres, cubes, and other shapes he couldn't identify. All were constructed from a latticework of balls and sticks, like a giant TinkerToy set. He recalled seeing some of the shapes from the briefing paper Lyman had sent him, but he still had no clue what he was looking at.

Miller saw his puzzlement. "That's what we build here, but the only way you'll see the real product is with an electron microscope."

On closer examination, what appeared to be a glass lobby was actually an enormous glass shell enclosing another four-story building inside. Some parts of the interior structure were open, while other parts were glassed-in like a conventional office building. Three tiered balconies sloped away above him. These were apparently the floors' lounge or common areas. He could see a few people reading or drinking coffee.

"This is *very* impressive," Manning whispered, trying not to disturb the quiet of the cathedral-like space. "But why the building-inside-a-building design?"

"Security," Miller explained, "specifically against electronic surveillance." A swipe of his ID card had been sufficient to open the door to the lobby, but it took another swipe and a code input to a keypad to pass through another glass door to the elevators. "In Afghanistan we'd take a metal building like a warehouse or hangar and set up trailers or link a bunch of shipping containers together inside to achieve the same effect. This is a hell of a lot more *Feng Shui*. We *are* in California, after all."

Riding the glass elevator to the fourth floor, Manning got a different angle on the floating geometric shapes that were supposedly Nanovex's products. "Do you have any idea what those things are or what they do?" he asked.

Miller laughed. "Oh, hell no! All I do is guard the perimeter. He gives me a paycheck anyway." He gave Manning a knowing look. "My guess is you won't have to either. Just do your lawyer shit and Mr. Lyman will take real good care of you."

He took a deep breath. "That's a relief."

Once at the fourth floor, Miller escorted him to a corner office. A keycode was once again required to enter the secretary's glass anteroom, but a strange device with what looked like a camera lens flanked the door to the inner office. Miller swiped his badge again, entered his code, then placed his eye against the lens. The door lock clicked.

"Retinal scan," Miller explained. "Don't worry, you won't have clearance high enough to need your eyeball scanned."

"That's a relief too," he admitted.

Lyman was on the phone when they entered, looking through a red folder with black-and-white striped edges. He waved them in, gesturing to the chairs around a small conference table. When he ended the call and closed the folder, Manning saw TOP SECRET in bold letters at the top and bottom. Even with all the corporate secrets he had handled, he had never been forced to deal with military classified information, and it gave him a chill to even be in the same room with such documents. Corporations ruined people to protect their secrets. Governments killed.

Lyman's office was an odd mixture of high-tech modern art and artifacts from his military past. A framed shadow box with Lyman's medals and campaign ribbons was surrounded by pictures of Lyman with presidents, politicians, and kingmakers foreign and domestic, present and past. Also mounted on the wall were the Air Force general's dress cap worn to a presidential inauguration and a sword from a change of command ceremony. Manning recognized this arrangement as an "I Love Me Wall" popular with current and former military officers.

Nanovex's CEO Douglas Lyman rose from his desk and smiled. "Mr. Manning! Thank you so much for coming on such short notice." He strode to Manning with an extended hand. Lyman was a good-looking man in his late fifties with a long, serious face, deep, thoughtful eyes, and a largish nose that gave him a vague resemblance to a clean-shaven Abraham Lincoln. His chestnut hair had not a fleck of gray and was probably dyed. His handshake was a practiced firm but not crushing grip.

Manning returned the professionally measured smile. "You made it very much worth my while to do so."

Lyman gestured to a seat. "My pleasure."

Miller stepped to the door. "I'll be outside when Mr. Manning is ready to go to his hotel, sir."

Lyman held up a hand. "Wait a minute, Reese. Mike, I didn't give you much prep time before you reported here. Can I detail Reese to pick up anything for you? I'll need you to hit the ground running, today if possible. And I don't want you worrying about logistics if we can take care of it for you."

He noticed that Lyman still spoke in military jargon. He did his best to reply in kind. "No sir, I'm good to go."

Lyman wasn't convinced. "Dry cleaning, maybe? You probably just got home from your last trip before I called you away on another."

Lucky guess, or does he know more about my last trip than he's letting on? "It's just laundry, sir. Dirty socks and stuff. I can take care of it at the hotel."

Lyman snapped his fingers. "Reese, I want everything in Mr. Manning's bags cleaned, pressed and waiting for him at his hotel when we're done here."

Miller was obviously accustomed to taking Lyman's orders, even menial ones. "Right away, sir!"

Manning began to feel self-conscious. "This really isn't necessary, Mr. Lyman."

He wouldn't take no for an answer. "Nonsense. Reese used to do both of our laundry in a horse trough we called a washtub. Sweaty socks and skivvies aren't going to shock him, Mike. Reese, carry on." Miller nodded and disappeared out the door.

Manning shifted uncomfortably, trying to remember if he'd actually peed himself on the last trip or had only desperately wanted to. "I'm sorry, Mr. Lyman, I'm just not used to being catered to like this."

Lyman gave him a wink and a lopsided smile. "From this point forward, it's Doug. And I *wanted* to cater to you up front. Because before this is over, you'll probably want to cuss me to my face."

FAMILY SECRETS

JULY 1986 – GRATERFORD, PENNSYLVANIA

Frankie extended her hand. "Warden Harris, thank you so much for seeing me."

The warden motioned her into his office. "My pleasure, Sergeant Conrad. So this visit has to do with your Master's thesis?"

Frankie felt the warden's eyes scanning her backside as she walked to his desk. As well he should. She had ditched her uniform in favor of a dress and heels she wore only on her most promising dates, and had unpinned her hair to fall loose around her shoulders. She looked great and she knew it.

"That's correct, Warden Harris. I'm thinking of doing my thesis on recidivism reduction programs. I understand your facility is a national leader on such initiatives."

He waved her to a seat. "Are you thinking of moving from police work to corrections?" Instead of sitting behind his desk, Harris took the chair next to her.

She crossed her legs for maximum display of her muscle tone. "Honestly, I just want to serve where I can do the most good." She paused. "That and the fact that there aren't many female lieutenants on the Philly police department."

He glanced at her legs, but tried to keep his mind on business. "Oh, glass ceiling problems?"

She looked away to give him the chance to sneak another peek. "A little."

He leaned forward. "Well, I can't promise that Corrections is a lot different, but *I* certainly don't have any issues in that regard. Why don't we start with a tour?"

She waited for him to stand then extended her hand. Harris was older, and might be the chivalrous type. He looked surprised, but helped her to her feet.

She smiled sweetly. "Thank you, Warden Harris."

"John," he said without thinking.

"Francine. My friends call me Frankie."

He smiled. "All right, Frankie."

* * *

A week later, their morning routine was following its usual course when Frankie pushed the front page over to Angela. "Would you read this story to me, please?" she asked.

Angela began her newsreader duties casually, but she quickly grew serious. "Today, Pennsylvania Corrections official John Harris announced that convicted child murderer Edward Groutman, 47, had been murdered in his cell at the Eastern Correction Institution in Graterford…."

Frankie watched carefully as Angela calmly read the rest of the piece.

Angela set the paper down. "There's more to this story, isn't there?"

Frankie blinked. "What makes you think that, sweetie?"

"Because you've got that same look on your face as when you tried to tell me about Santa Claus. I could tell you were thinking, 'is she buying this or not?'"

Frankie's eyes widened. "Angela Conrad, how did an adult get trapped in that little girl's body of yours?"

"So what's the *rest* of the story?" she demanded.

Frankie knelt beside her daughter's chair. "Listen, all I want you to know right now is that Ed Groutman is dead and he will never hurt you or anyone else, ever again, just like I promised." She fingered the badge on her chest. "But when you grow up, especially if you end up wearing one of these, I'll sit you down and explain to you how the world really works."

From that day forward, Angela Conrad had two goals; to possess a badge like Frankie's, and to know the secrets that lay behind it.

ALL HANDS

PRESENT DAY – SAN FRANCISCO, CALIFORNIA

Scott Hendrix made the turn off Mission Street to the underground parking of the San Francisco Federal Building downtown. He had always hated this building, an unfinished-looking mishmash of scaffolding and glass that resembled a cross between a sawhorse and the battleship Bismarck. In their slavish devotion to "green building" initiatives, the DC do-gooders came up with this bastardization that pleased everyone except those who had to work in it or look at it. In his opinion, only FBI headquarters in Washington beat this monstrosity for pure, primal ugliness. Hendrix was glad the CIA was able to cite their "need for a low profile" to exempt themselves from incarceration in this architectural blunder.

But he still had to attend occasional meetings in this eyesore. Like the Joint Federal Task Force meeting called today by the FBI. Of course on a Saturday, and of course on the first decent day for golf all week. He was certain the FBI did things like this to punish government workers who dared have real lives.

He was running late, partly because the FBI Special-Agent-in-Charge Perry Pugliano had called him out of bed a grand total of thirty minutes before the meeting, and partly because of the design of this stupid building. To "promote employee interaction and health," the elevators in this madhouse were rigged to only serve three floors. Then you had to exit the elevator and walk—or today, run—up a flight of stairs, ride the next elevator up three floors, get out, and repeat. In his case from the basement all the way to the fifteenth floor. Hendrix could testify that the only "employee interaction" the architect had promoted was lazy government employees bitching about having to use the stairs. He was sweaty, pissed, and ten minutes late when he finally entered the stuffy and windowless top-floor conference room.

Pugliano smirked. "Well, now that our esteemed colleague from Central *Intelligence* has joined us, we can begin."

"Sorry, I had to take a call on my shoephone," he apologized. That bit of self-deprecation earned a few chuckles and seemed to turn away the irritation of his fellow civil servants.

All of the seats at the U-shaped conference table were occupied—some by junior functionaries, Hendrix noted with irritation—so he settled for a chair against the wall. He took a mental inventory of the players around the room. Pugliano had pretty much emptied his Rolodex for this confab. The local, state and regional directors for the FBI, Justice, Homeland Security, State Department, and Treasury were all present, along with the US Attorney for Northern California. The chief of the San Francisco PD also attended. There were even a few men and one woman he couldn't identify, which annoyed him even more than being forced to sit in a dark and airless corner of the room. He wasn't paid to be in the dark, literally or figuratively.

Pugliano walked to the front. "Ladies and gentlemen, thank you for coming in on such short notice." He keyed his remote and a photo of Rashid Ben-Jabir appeared on the screen. "Many of you have been directly involved in the search for this man and his security detail; the Saudi consulate asked me to convey the gratitude of their government for your continued efforts. I know how much the approval of the Saudis means to all of us in this room."

A few uncomfortable titters rippled through the room. It was a well-known secret that Saudi oil wealth had been used for decades to buy information, favors, and in some cases obstruction of justice from high-ranking American government officials. These bribes were often legally delivered in the form of low-work-high-pay positions made available after retirement in Beltway lobbying organizations set up by the Saudis specifically for that purpose. Insiders called such arrangements "sand pensions." Hendrix knew for certain the regional director for the Justice Department had made such an arrangement, and he suspected three other officials of being similarly corrupted. But he would never rock the bureaucratic boat with what he knew. In fact, he had secretly hoped his meeting with Ben-Jabir at the consulate last year was the prelude to just such an arrangement being offered to him as well. But it certainly looked like that forbidden tree would never bear fruit.

"In our search for the missing Saudi nationals," Pugliano continued, "We came across evidence that a Wanted Intelligence Fugitive was here in San Francisco. She may even be connected to the disappearance of Mr.

Ben-Jabir." He pressed the remote again and Angela Conrad's CIA photo appeared.

The Justice Department official Hendrix knew to be the Dispenser of Get Out of Jail Free Cards to Well-Placed Saudis immediately snorted in derision. "Give me a break! We've had almost as many sightings of Angela Conrad in the last five years as we've had of Elvis. They never pan out. She's a ghost. I sure as hell *hope* this isn't the only reason you dragged us down here on a Saturday morning." Apparently Saudi shills enjoyed their golf as well.

Pugliano smiled with one corner of his mouth. "It's not. But before you make up your mind, sir, perhaps you should look at this." He displayed the video and stills of Conrad from the hotel security system, along with the facial recognition data.

The Justice Department official rubbed his chin. "It's interesting, but I'm still not convinced."

"I agree the evidence is not conclusive, but we also have an eyewitness at the Sobrato Tower crime scene who picked her out of a photo lineup and had a very, shall we say, *visceral* reaction to seeing Ms. Conrad's face again."

"He damn-near pissed himself," Hendrix added. "He had never heard of Angela Conrad before, but he sure as hell never wanted to see her again." Several heads turned to see who was speaking out of the dark corner, but no one challenged him.

"Here's something else to consider," Pugliano continued. A picture of a taxicab appeared on the screen, followed by photos of a blood-streaked bumper and a blood-soaked trunk. "Thanks to the excellent work of the San Francisco Police Department," he nodded to the chief, "we recovered this stolen cab which is apparently yet another crime scene which may or may not be associated with the Ben-Jabir case. We're analyzing the blood now and trying to obtain DNA samples from the Saudi consulate. But if you add this to Sobrato Tower and the Sheraton, we have three crime scenes on the same day with no bodies and no fingerprints."

"So even if it's not Angela Conrad," the Justice official offered, "we sure as hell have a professional on the loose."

"A *group* of professionals," Pugliano corrected. "The eyewitness at Sobrato Tower said he saw three men working with the female suspect."

"Agent Pugliano," the US Attorney interjected. "Let's say for the sake of argument that the woman in question *is* Angela Conrad. Do we have any idea who she's working with?"

"Yes sir, we immediately started a search for known associates of Conrad to see if any were in the area." Passport photos of an Indian man and woman appeared on the screen. "Rajiv and Gayathiri Chandapur. They specialize in disposing of bodies and cleaning crime scenes. The clean-ups we encountered at the Sheraton and Sobrato Tower match their methods profile we obtained from Interpol. They do work for the Russian Mafia, and occasionally the Yakuza and the Triads. To the best of our knowledge they've never operated on US soil before. We think the Chinese Triad connection is what brought them to San Francisco two weeks ago." A video freeze showed the pair speaking with an airport Customs officer. "The Chandapurs legally entered the US, then went dark. No paper trail, no financial transactions. Then the night Ben-Jabir went missing they took the last flight to Mexico City and disappeared again."

"Why do you say there's a Triad connection?" the US attorney asked.

"Like everyone else in this down economy," Pugliano explained, "the Triad's loan-sharking businesses are having trouble getting their customers to make timely payments. This is normally something they would handle themselves, but they know we have them under very heavy surveillance and their freedom of action has been limited. Suddenly two weeks ago their deadbeat customers started disappearing and the San Francisco *Chronicle* started getting thumbs mailed to them. That kind of news got around fast, and we have wiretaps of a goon congratulating his boss on the recent uptick of collections. We believe Conrad worked with the Chandapurs on a job in Germany, recognized their signature from these local jobs, and secured their services when she suddenly had a number of bodies to dispose of. That's my working theory, at least."

"So you're convinced Ben-Jabir is dead?" State Department asked.

Rashid, if you double-crossed me, you'd <u>*better*</u> *be dead*, Hendrix pondered darkly.

"Ben-Jabir *and* his security detail," Pugliano said with conviction. "I'm hopeful in our search for bodies we may also stumble across a certain fella named Hoffa we've been seeking for some time." That earned him a few quiet snickers from the federal agents who probably *weren't* on the Saudi payroll.

State wasn't amused. "Agent Pugliano, do you have a *working theory* of why this Angela Conrad you've been unable to catch for the last five years might be targeting a relative of the Saudi royal family?"

Ouch, that was uncalled for, Hendrix mused. He mentally moved the representative from State from the *possible* sand pension recipient to the *probable* category.

Pugliano eyed the State Department *apparatchik* for a verbal kneecapping, but thought better of it. He gave the man an "I know something you don't know" smirk. "Yes," he said, "as a matter of fact, I do."

Photographs of seven men and one woman appeared on the screen. "Working with CIA and Homeland Security, we continued our check on Ms. Conrad's known associates and were surprised to find a number of them entered the country in the last week, most of them through California." He used his laser pointer to highlight each face in succession.

"Dieter Kinberg, former German Federal Intelligence Service.

"Ari Nesher, former Mossad.

"Ian Cosgrove, former SAS.

"Meghan Gallagher, suspected IRA.

"Yuri Konalev, former KGB.

"Lin Shaozang, suspected Chinese Intelligence.

"Wait a minute," Justice interrupted. "Are you saying Angela Conrad is working with *all* of these spooks?"

Hendrix could tell by Pugliano's smug demeanor he was preparing to drop a very large bomb. "No, I don't think that's the case," he continued. "As a matter of fact, a few of these people would likely kill each other on sight if placed in the same room."

"You lost me," State protested.

"We were confused too," Pugliano agreed. "So we asked Homeland to run another search, this time for *every* known foreign intelligence operative in our records, and their known aliases. The idea was that maybe these spooks weren't here because of Conrad's activities. Maybe it was the other way around."

"Are you saying there's some kind of spy convention going on?" Justice asked.

Pugliano keyed his remote again, and the screen filled with ID photos. Dozens of them. "Imagine our surprise," he continued, "when we identified no less than thirty-five current and former operatives who entered the country in the last week. California was the final destination for almost all of them."

A hot knife of acid reflux lanced up into Hendrix's chest. Pugliano hadn't shared any of this until he could unveil it in a meeting with the bigwigs. *Bastard.*

Justice's mouth dropped open. "What the hell are they all *doing* here?"

"That's the $64,000 question," Pugliano affirmed. "Unfortunately, by the time we flagged all of these operatives, most of them had gone dark and disappeared."

"And why California?" the US attorney asked.

"I don't *know*, gentlemen. That's why I called this meeting. To make matters worse, upon further investigation, we found the skill sets of these operatives very troubling. These are not just vanilla intel-gathering weenies. They're all covert operation types; surveillance, coercion, theft, and assassination. By our accounting we have teams from Russia, China, France, Japan and India operating on our soil, not counting the independent operators, who may or may not be doing the bidding of yet other nations."

"What about the Israelis?" Justice demanded. "They'd never miss a party like this." Hendrix figured the actions of the Israelis would be a primary concern of the man's Saudi masters and therefore he was just anticipating their question.

Pugliano frowned. "We have exactly two Israelis on our radar. They're a husband and wife team whose identity was burned in Cairo and who were—we thought—withdrawn from field service two years ago. They're now leading our surveillance team all over New York state, breaking contact, then using their credit cards in a restaurant twenty miles away and waiting until the team catches up, then they begin the game all over again."

"Which means the Israelis' *real* team has completely slipped our net," Justice fumed.

"That's a fair assessment," Pugliano admitted.

"Could the Israelis be behind the disappearance of Ben-Jabir?" Justice pressed. "That makes a lot more sense that his whole team getting whacked by a rogue CIA agent." He threw Hendrix a contemptuous glance.

Say what, bitch? "Don't count Conrad out," Hendrix shot back. "In the assassination of Gerhard Schumann in Germany four years ago, it's believed that Conrad, in stalking her target, discovered a CIA surveillance team gathering intel on Mr. Schumann's dealings with Iran. The CIA team disappeared the same night as Schumann. All we found was an empty surveillance van with a couple of bullet holes. We think the Chandapurs helped her clean up that mess as well. Conrad doesn't leave behind loose ends."

"So it fits her M.O.," the US attorney observed, "but what's her motive?"

Hendrix waved his hand at the mosaic of operative photos still displayed on the screen. "What's motivating *any* of these guys? We don't know. But if she ran into Ben-Jabir and suspected they were after the same objective, she wouldn't hesitate to take him out." *At least let's hope that's what she did. That would tie up my loose ends as well.*

Pugliano let the grim silence hang for a few moments. "So the bottom line is this: we have go-teams from all over the world, friend and foe alike, engaging in open warfare on the streets of San Francisco, and we have *no idea* why they're here. Something has brought the varsity out to play, they're playing on *our* turf, and they're playing rough. And we don't even know where the *ball* is, much less the goal line."

Pugliano rested his knuckles on the table, scanning the group with fiery eyes. "I don't know about the rest of you, but personally, that pisses me off."

COVER STORY

SAN JOSE, CALIFORNIA

Manning regarded Lyman carefully across the conference table. "I knew from the amount of money you were throwing around that this wouldn't be a cake walk."

"And I assume you read the briefing material I sent ahead, so you know we have the families of five dead employees to deal with."

He nodded. "Yes, I read that. I take it that a standard settlement package was insufficient for some reason?"

Lyman frowned. "The problem is that the families are pressing for details on their loved ones' deaths, and the project they were working on was *extremely* classified. Telling them the truth just isn't an option, even if we wanted to."

"I assume you have a cover story in place."

Lyman pushed back from the table. "Yes, but the truth is these employees died a *very* unpleasant death, and even a cursory autopsy will reveal that, along with significant details of the project they were working on. The government simply won't allow that to happen, which puts us in the impossible position of trying to stop autopsies from occurring without triggering lawsuits that will draw further attention to the project."

What the hell are these guys into? His curiosity burned, but as a risk-mitigation lawyer, the truth was the *last* thing he needed. In his capacity, the truth was the enemy, something to be avoided at all costs. He folded his hands. "Before I ask my next question, I want to remind you that everything you tell me is covered by attorney-client privilege and I can not in any way be forced to divulge it, even in court."

Lyman squinted. "Okay, understood."

"Was Nanovex involved in *anything* illegal? Even slightly?"

Lyman was emphatic. "Absolutely not. Everything we did was fully authorized by our customer, the United States Government."

No hesitation, no evasion. Which meant his job wasn't trying to keep people out of jail. With Angela Conrad hanging around, death was still a real possibility, but imprisonment, less so. "Okay, I believe you. But that brings me back to your cover story. If your project was authorized by the government and you didn't do anything illegal, then the sky is pretty much the limit. The relatives simply aren't *entitled* to the truth, are they?"

Lyman pressed his lips together. "Well, no, but if we don't give them a plausible story they will almost certainly sue, which could endanger our commercial contracts, even if the government manages to get their case thrown out on National Security grounds."

"What *is* the cover story you've given the families at this point?" he pressed.

"A chemical leak," Lyman said uncomfortably, as if admitting the cover story was as painful as admitting the truth. "A proprietary and extremely toxic chemical used in processing carbon nanotubes."

"Good," he affirmed. "So you can't tell the families what poisoned their loved ones because it's a trade secret."

"That was the suggestion of the lawyer from Harkin-Thomas."

Great, he mused. *The last act of Jake Fleischer before he graduated to the black plastic bucket. What a legacy.* "That sounds like a sensible approach—what's the problem?"

"The wife of one of the dead scientists works here as well. She is familiar with our manufacturing processes and already has a non-disclosure agreement on file. She's demanded to know the actual chemical that caused the accident and isn't buying the proprietary angle. She's threatened legal action if we don't tell her what chemical killed her husband. But whatever we tell her won't match what a coroner would find."

"So what steps have you taken to block the autopsies?"

"Our customer called in a favor with the FBI and had them federalize the death investigation. The FBI tried to rush through the inquiry and cremate the bodies citing 'contamination concerns,' but the families got a federal judge to file an injunction. The FBI is holding off on releasing the bodies claiming that they're calling in a 'nationally recognized forensic pathologist,' but actually they're just playing for time."

Manning tapped his index finger against his cheek. "What about embalming?"

"I'm sorry?"

"Would embalming destroy the evidence you're trying to conceal? You tell the families what chemical killed their relative, the FBI tells the families that it found that chemical in lethal concentrations in their blood, and that they had to call in specialists to remove the chemicals by embalming before they could be released to next of kin. Otherwise they'd be a toxic hazard even for burial. I'd have to see the court order, but if it simply forbids cremation, you would have obeyed the letter of the law and destroyed the evidence in a single move."

Lyman's eyes widened. "If we could pull that off, it would be genius."

He raised a cautioning hand. "The real question is whether your customer has the horsepower to pull the FBI's strings. The FBI will have to do the heavy lifting."

Lyman let out a soft snort, as if he found the suggestion humorous. "Trust me, the FBI is well-versed in doing whatever it takes to protect government interests. And yes, I think our customer has sufficient clout to gain the FBI's cooperation."

"If you don't mind me asking, who *is* your customer, if you can say?"

Lyman's answer was interrupted by a knock at the door. "Enter!" he called out.

Manning could hear the beeping of a keypad, followed by the click of the lock. A slender man in his late twenties or early thirties with short dark hair entered.

"Ah, speak of the devil!" Lyman announced. "Mr. Manning here was just inquiring about our customer."

"Sorry I'm late, Doug," the man replied. "I got tied up on the phone."

"Not a problem. Seth Graves, this is Mike Manning, our new damage control lawyer. Seth is our representative from DARPA."

Manning rose to shake hands. "I saw the name DARPA in my briefing package, but I'm afraid I'm not familiar with your organization."

"Defense Advanced Research Projects Agency," Graves answered, taking a seat next to Lyman. "We focus on breakthrough technologies that have the potential to give our military a decisive edge. Ever hear of the Stealth Fighter? That was our baby, as was the M-16 rifle. And contrary to what Al Gore might tell you, we really *did* invent the Internet, or at least its predecessor, ARPANET. Our charter is to find transformational technologies and develop them from basic research to a working prototype."

"And that's what they're doing here at Nanovex," Lyman added. "We've identified an application of nanotechnology that has the potential to be a complete game-changer, and DARPA is providing the funds to help us make that breakthrough a reality."

So that's what the Saudis were after. "Hence the barbed-wire fences and double guard posts outside?"

"Exactly," Lyman said. "Any of our enemies would give their eye teeth for what we're developing here, or to at least stop *us* from developing it. We've made a significant investment in security as a deterrent to anyone who might want a peek at our secrets."

Someone like Angela Conrad? Manning mused. *And now she has a man on the inside. I wonder what the hell she plans on doing with me.* "I understand," he said.

"It really is too bad I can't be more forthcoming on the technology you're helping us protect," Lyman apologized.

He waved off the concern. "I'm being paid well to not be curious. And what I don't know I can't accidentally divulge when dealing with the families."

Lyman traded an approving look with Graves. "That's a very good point."

"I do have a couple more questions, though, if you don't mind."

"Shoot."

"You mentioned that you previously had retained the firm of Harkin-Thomas to perform the same services I'll be providing. Can you tell me why you're no longer working with them?" He knew the answer of course, but he wanted to hear their excuse.

Lyman threw up his hands. "Their guy just disappeared on us. I don't think *they* even know where he is. And when we asked for a replacement, they got all evasive and said they'd get back with us. And frankly we don't have time to dick around on this. So when I got wind that you might be available, I checked you out. Your reputation was very solid, so I reached out. Simple as that."

So they're even more clueless than I am in this mess. "I very much appreciate your candor. But if you were dissatisfied with Harkin-Thomas, why not just hire another reputable firm like Feldman-Norquist?"

Lyman stared at him for a few seconds, as if he didn't have a straight answer for that question.

"That was my idea," Graves interjected. "Even after we get past this crisis, I think it would be useful to have permanent risk mitigation counsel at Nanovex to help prevent situations like this in the future. Someone whose loyalties are to *this* company, not to a law firm in another state."

As a practicing liar, Graves' statement made Manning's bullshit indicator blink yellow. It wasn't an outright lie, but it wasn't the whole truth either. "Fair enough, thank you," he replied with equally false sincerity. "So where do we go from here?"

Lyman rose and pulled a large wheeled briefcase from behind the table. "Here are the records the previous attorney had in his office. I'm not sure how much he had on his person when he went AWOL, so this is probably not complete. But it's certainly enough to keep you busy tomorrow getting familiarized. We'll meet here seven a.m. Monday morning and figure out what's missing and our next move. In the meantime, Seth and I will work on putting the plan you proposed in motion. Damn good idea, thank you."

He rose and took custody of the records. "You're welcome, Mr. Lyman. Nice to meet you." He nodded to Graves. "Both of you."

Lyman extended his hand. "That's the last 'Mr. Lyman' you're allowed. The next one costs you a demerit."

Manning flashed a smile that was a lot more cheerful than he felt. "You got it, Doug. See you Monday morning."

SANCTIONS

WASHINGTON, DC

Although Simon Crane's personal jet arrived in the mid-afternoon, he waited until well after the President's last appointment before made his way to the White House. The secrecy of his business demanded that he make his appearance only after the press and the mid-level functionaries had left for the day. Like a vampire, he could only show his face after the sun had set.

Crane's limousine dropped him at the West Wing entrance, facing the Old Executive Office Building. There were no checks of his credentials, no searches of his person by the Secret Service. Once inside, he merely nodded to the agent guarding the door and made his way directly to the Oval Office.

"Executor enroute to Statesman," he heard the agent whisper into his sleeve mike.

The final Secret Service agent outside the Oval Office did not yield his ground as easily. Although Crane knew their orders forbade them searching his person, he held open his coat. With the power he wielded, there was no reason to be rude. No reason at all. "I assure you, young man, I am carrying no weapons," he said, although the agent was well into his forties and was probably the most senior man on duty.

The agent nodded, grateful for even the gesture of compliance. "Thank you, sir," he said, stepping aside and holding the door for him.

Crane entered the Oval Office, regarding the chief executive with a practiced smile. "Good evening, Mr. President, thank you so much for seeing me."

President Lloyd Cameron regarded his visitor with a barely suppressed sneer. "Well, if it isn't the grim reaper himself."

Crane didn't waste the gesture of extending his hand. He knew Cameron wouldn't accept it. "President Cameron, I'm sorry my position relegates me solely to being the bearer of ill tidings. And I earnestly wish our first meeting was under better circumstances. But we all have our duties, and this is mine."

The mention of duty had the effect he desired on the president. He knew that as a former naval officer, ambassador, and long-time senator, duty was a term Cameron understood fully. The aging president ran a weathered hand over his snow-white hair. "Very well, then. State your business."

Not having been invited to sit, he stood at a respectful distance from the president's desk. "Mr. President, I regret to inform you that one of your country's technologies is being taken off the table."

The thinly veiled contempt again bubbled to the surface. "Your presence here already told me that much. Which project are we talking about?"

Crane made sure to keep his tone courteous. "The Nanovex nanotechnology project."

"I'm not familiar with that one," Cameron admitted.

"You *are* familiar with the Group's global proscription concerning chemical weapons, of course?"

Cameron's eyes glinted. "*Familiar?* We lost nearly *five thousand* American lives enforcing the Group's edict in Iraq! Not to mention the loss of faith the American people suffered when we failed to recover said weapons."

He nodded deferentially. "And we thank you *and* your people for their sacrifice. But the penalty for violating the Group's ban on the use of weapons of mass destruction has always been very clear."

"Regime change," Cameron recited. "And the death penalty for the perpetrators."

"And because of the resolute enforcement of that ban, the likelihood of another offense is greatly diminished, regardless of whether Iraq's remaining stockpiles were recovered."

The frown lines on Cameron's age-spotted face deepened. "That's assuming you're dealing with sane people, which certainly isn't a given in today's world. So how does this pertain to the subject at hand?"

"Are you aware that the Nanovex project is a delivery system for VX nerve gas?"

Cameron rocked back in his chair. "You can't be serious. The United States destroyed its entire stockpile of VX gas years ago."

"That's because VX nerve gas is a weapon of *mass* destruction. The project under development at Nanovex is a system for *pinpoint* delivery of VX gas, affecting only a confined geographic area. But you can see why the Group fails to see such distinctions as meaningful."

The color drained from the president's face. "Give me the particulars. I'll have the project shut down immediately."

Crane nodded. "That will of course be necessary, but by itself insufficient to ensure final security."

He noticed Cameron's hands trembled slightly. The president folded them tightly on his desk. "How many lives are we talking about?"

He extracted a folded sheet of paper from inside his jacket and handed it to Cameron. "Fortunately, less than a dozen. Their security has wisely kept the number of those involved to a minimum. Here are the names of the personnel selected for action. You will instruct the FBI to obstruct the investigation of these deaths and downplay in the media any suggestion that these were anything other than tragic accidents or suicides."

Cameron examined the list. At least one name elicited a visible reaction. He slid the list back toward Crane. "I've been told I should fear you," he said, then stared at him for several seconds. "But I have to admit at my age such threats lose their punch."

Crane studied the presidential seal embroidered in the carpet. "Mr. President, I would *never* threaten you. I am merely presenting the facts."

Cameron's face twisted with anger. "Then here are some facts for *you.* I will of course cancel the Nanovex project. The Group and I are in total agreement for once. I will even strangle my conscience and allow you to carry out your 'sanctioned' murders of US citizens, simply because short of locking those people up in a Supermax penitentiary for the rest of their lives, there's nothing I can do to stop you and your…*organization.*"

Cameron then rose from his seat, painfully standing fully erect. "But Mr. Crane, I will be *damned* if I will pervert the constitutional organs of this government to cover your bloody tracks. You consider yourself to be the embodiment of international law. Good for you. But if you and your people aren't *competent* enough to stay ahead of local law enforcement in your quest for 'global governance,' then don't look for me to pull your chestnuts out of the fire."

Crane held his temper without difficulty, putting on a sad smile instead. "You know, Mr. President, John Kennedy had a very similar viewpoint of our organization. It didn't serve him well."

Cameron's aged eyes burned at the mention of the politician who had inspired him to public service as a younger man. "So much for not threatening me," he fumed.

Crane shook his head. "Not a threat, Mr. President. Simple historical fact. President Kennedy opposed us. President Kennedy is dead."

Cameron walked to the door, holding it open. "Good evening, Mr. Crane." His facial expression was controlled, but the muscles around his eyes twitched.

Crane nodded and took his leave. "Good evening, Mr. President."

* * *

An hour later as his jet flew back to Chicago, Crane called his agent. "The sanction was delivered. There was some resistance."

"Resistance?" he heard over the secure phone, as if the very idea was novel.

"Not to the sanction itself," he assured his agent, "but legal coverage has been denied."

"That shouldn't pose a problem," he heard.

Ah, the confidence of youth. Which he knew was no substitute for the wisdom of scar tissue. He idly swirled the Scotch in his glass, admiring its rich hue. “I feel a demonstration is in order. A member of the special equipment division will be contacting you shortly. I want you to take full advantage of their capabilities.”

“Of course, sir. What are the boundaries of this, ah, demonstration?”

Crane took a sip of Scotch and gazed out the window at the darkened landscape passing far below him. “Minimum fatalities outside of the agreed sanction list. But other than that, do whatever it takes to make sure they *never* cross us again.”

CHAPTER 7

FIRE OF THE GODS

MARCH 16, 1945 – OHRDRUF, GERMANY

Hans Kammler had always lived with a sense of urgency. After all, life was short even under the best of circumstances. But lately that urgency had bordered on desperation. Kammler had thrown his all into the development of weapons that would assure the victory of the Third Reich, even given the failures of lesser men than himself. But now, with the Americans crossing the Rhine River on the west and the Russians scarcely two hundred kilometers to the east, Hitler's Thousand Year Reich seemed destined for a fiery self-immolation reminiscent of a Wagnerian opera.

But desperation still didn't mean that Kammler was devoid of a plan. Several of them, in fact. The lynchpin of them all was the bunker in which today's meeting would take place. *Fuhrerbunker* S-III at Ohrdruf, codenamed Olga, was carved from the rock at the cost of ten thousand slave laborers' lives.

Kammler greeted each of the meeting's attendees at the bunker entrance. The drawn and fatigued condition of the *Fuhrer's* staff still did not prepare him for the appearance of Hitler himself. Kammler had briefed the *Fuhrer* on two previous occasions, the first in 1942 on his plans for the incorporation of gas chambers and crematoria to drastically improve throughput efficiency of the Reich's concentration camps, and the second in 1943 after his assistance in suppressing the Warsaw Uprising by using his engineering expertise to demolish the entire town with its rebel Jews still inside it.

On those two previous occasions Hitler had been clear-eyed, animated, and forceful. Kammler had not been sure what to expect of Germany's exalted leader, but he certainly had not been disappointed by the man's charismatic presence. It truly was like stepping into the presence of a demigod. But that visionary bore little resemblance to the man who emerged unsteadily from the armored train car this morning. The face that had been lean and angular was now pale and pudgy. Eyes that had been clear, fiery and piercing were now bespectacled and dull. The hand that returned his salute trembled as if palsied.

"*Mein Fuhrer!*" Kammler declared. "We are honored by your presence today." He was grateful that the successful uranium enrichment effort spurred by his work on the Bell had made possible the presentation of *good* news to the *Fuhrer* today.

"Thank you," Hitler muttered, trying unsuccessfully to muster a smile. "It is good to see you again, Kammler." After their handshake, he noticed Hitler immediately locked his left arm over his right, possibly to steady its tremors.

"And you as well, *mein Fuhrer*. Please, this way."

For its role as *Fuhrerbunker*, no expense had been spared appointing the facility in the areas where the High Command would frequent. Paneled walls, paintings, and freshly cut flowers greeted them as Kammler led Hitler to the spacious conference room. Hitler's staff already waited around the immense oak table inside.

"*Achtung, der Fuhrer!*" Kammler announced.

All the men rose, some with more difficulty than others, and threw out their right arms in salute. "*Heil Hitler!*" they chanted in unison. Was it his imagination, or did they do so with noticeably less enthusiasm than when he had last briefed the *Fuhrer*?

Hitler motioned to their seats impatiently. "Please, be seated. General Kammler, we have much to discuss."

Hitler took his place at the head of the table. At his right hand were Hermann Goering, head of the German Air Force, the *Luftwaffe*, Josef Goebbels, the Nazi "Minister of Public Enlightenment," and Martin Bormann, Hitler's Chief of Staff. On his left were Himmler, Wilhelm Keitel, High Commander of the German Army, the *Wehrmacht*, and Albert Speer, the Head of War Production.

Kammler walked to the opposite end of the room near the projection screen and gave a nod for the lights to be lowered. "*Mein Fuhrer*," he began, "As you are aware, yesterday morning we successfully exploded an atomic weapon at our test station in the Baltic Sea. The test was a complete success." [1]

"If the test was a complete success," Hermann Goering snapped, "why are the phones knocked out over half of Germany?" [2]

Kammler shifted uncomfortably. "The explosion of the atomic weapon produced an unexpectedly powerful radio wave upon detonation. We fully expected interference for minutes or even hours after the test, but the explosion produced a pulse so strong that many electronic devices in northern Germany were actually damaged and must be replaced. Unfortunately key components of Berlin's phone exchange were in that category. I deeply regret any impact on the war effort this may have caused."

"What was the yield of the device?" Albert Speer asked.

"The explosion was equivalent to approximately fifteen thousand tons of TNT," he lied smoothly. It was actually closer to twelve, but he had promised twenty, and he doubted even Speer would have the know-how to question him. It was equally unlikely anyone would visit the now-radioactive test island for a closer inspection.

Hitler nodded vigorously. This was probably the first good news he had received in a long time. "What is the practical application for this weapon?" he asked. "How large of a target can it destroy?"

"It could easily destroy an entire armored division in the field, but a city would be a more practical target," he replied. "We could destroy half of London, and set fire to the other half."

"Or Moscow," Hitler suggested.

Kammler frowned. "Yes, *mein Fuhrer*, but the problem is one of delivery. The mass of the current bomb is over two metric tons. We have not had time to optimize the design for weight. The only practical method for delivering the weapon in the short term is by manned bomber. But the aerial defenses of both London and Moscow are so intense that the odds of a successful penetration are less than fifty percent, even at night."

Hitler eyes bore into Goering for confirmation.

"It is true, *mein Fuhrer*," Goering said reluctantly. "With material aid from the Americans, the Cossacks have firm control over the airspace around Moscow. It would be a suicide mission, even for our brave *Luftwaffe* pilots."

"How many of these weapons do we have?" Bormann asked.

"Two," Kammler replied. "Plus a third under construction now. It will require another month to complete, even working around the clock." [3]

"So we must be sure of success before we use them," Goebbels observed.

"Yes, Minister."

"But you have just said you can't reach either London *or* Moscow!" Hitler railed. "What good is a wonder weapon that can not be used?"

"New York," Kammler replied.

"What?" Hitler demanded.

Kammler signaled for the appropriate slide. "We have constructed two aircraft designated Ju-390s that can make the flight from our bases in Norway to New York and return safely. In fact, they have already done so late last year."

Hitler slapped the table. "Why am I only hearing about this *now*?"

Kammler advanced to the next slide. "Because, *mein Fuhrer*, I only believe in making promises I can keep."

"Shortly after completion of the first prototype," Kammler continued, "our test pilots flew it from Prague to Capetown, South Africa, a distance of over a thousand kilometers farther than from Berlin to New York, using aerial refueling while over Italy. When the second aircraft was completed, it flew from a base in Norway to within twelve miles of New York City, and took this photograph." Even from several miles distant, the skyline of America's largest city was immediately recognizable. [4]

"Still, without an atomic weapon to drop, this mission was little more than a risky stunt. We were also hopeful our new *Amerika* Rocket being developed by *Herr* Von Braun would make such a risk unnecessary. That is why you were not informed, *mein Fuhrer*."

Hitler nodded stiffly, obviously not satisfied, but at least placated. "Continue."

"The New York flight of the Ju-390 proved that not only was a manned bomber strike on New York logistically possible, but the Americans in their arrogant complacency had not erected even the most rudimentary of aerial defenses. Their cities are open and naked to attack. Therefore I ordered a study on the likely effects of an atomic attack on New York City." Kammler advanced to the next slide. [5]

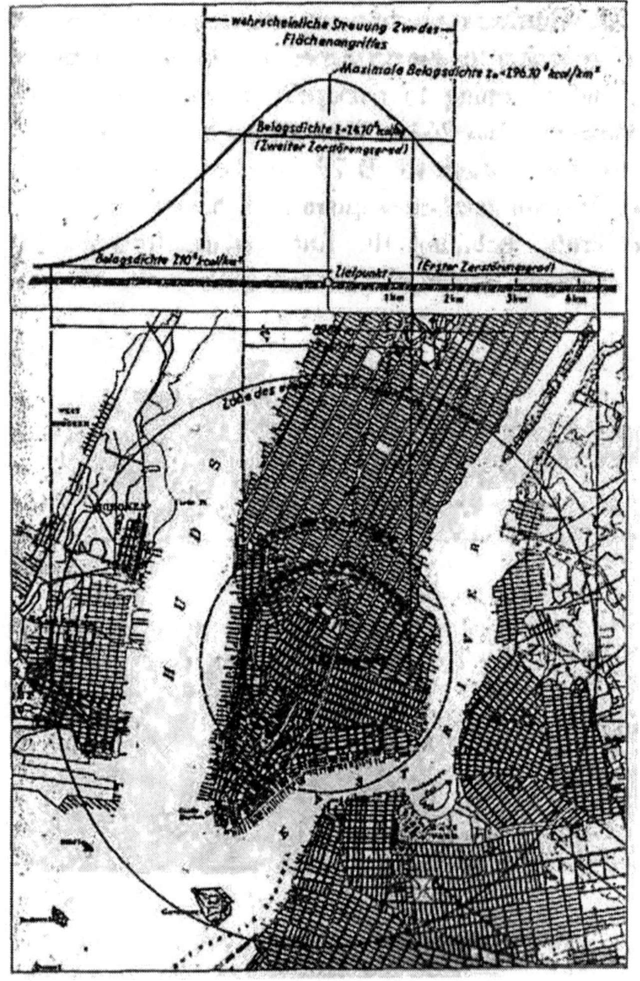

"This map shows the predicted effects of an atomic blast, centered over the Empire State Building. The inner ring shows an almost one-and-a-half kilometer radius which will experience complete destruction. Not even the most robust skyscraper will survive the blast. The next is a two-kilometer radius where immediate radiation casualties can be expected. Even if the buildings inside this ring survive, the people will not. The third ring is a four-kilometer radius showing the limits of structural and fire damage that can be expected. A conservative estimate assuming the attack takes place at night for maximum chance of penetration is one million killed. If the attack takes place during the day when the financial centers are occupied, double that, at least."

"Then the attack will take place during the day," Hitler insisted.

Bormann held up two fingers. "Two bombs, *mein Fuhrer*. To prove our capabilities, the first attack must be followed up immediately by a second. If either aircraft is shot down, our ability to strike terror into the Americans is diminished considerably. But if both New York and Washington are obliterated, even in the dead of night, the resolve of the Americans will be greatly shaken."

Hitler waved the comment away. "That decision is tabled, for the moment. General Kammler, continue."

He nodded. "Before the first two weapons are dropped, I recommend that the High Command relocate to this bunker. Field Marshall von Kesselring has taken command of Army Group West defending this region. He is capable and feared by the Americans; he will buy us the time to complete our third weapon. Once your person is secured in this fortress, we will attack New York and Washington, then demand that the Americans cease their advance and join us in attacking the Red Army."

Kammler watched Hitler carefully. His fists were clenched and his hands shook, but Kammler didn't think it was from a nervous palsy. Hitler's now-clear eyes were fixed on the map of Manhattan with a rapturous, far-away look.

"I can *see* it," Hitler spoke, as if in a trance. "New York disappears in a ball of fire and America draws back in fear. Then Washington too is utterly destroyed, and their hearts will stop *cold*." He held up his fist for emphasis. "After we threaten more destruction, they will sue for peace, but the *British* will hold firm, not content until they have drained our very *life's blood!*"

Hitler rose from his chair, leaning over the table to glare down on each member of his staff. "But without America," he brought his fist down on the table, "England will be reduced to *impotence!*"

He stalked from his chair to the map on the wall, placing his hand over England like a spider enveloping its prey. "With our *third* bomb we will announce our peace with America, but our intention to turn England into a smoldering heap of ruins! Birmingham, Manchester, Glasgow. We will announce our intention to destroy them *all*, one by one, if the English do not join us." He stared off into space, as if receiving a vision. "*Yes!* Yes, they will surrender. They may each be willing to die individually, but if we confront them with their death as an entire country, an entire *English civilization*," he added sarcastically, "then yes, they will surrender," he said with finality, as if he had become Fate embodied.

Then he stepped east, raising a fist over Russia. "But ultimately, *inevitably*, we will *together* turn our joined fury to our most *hated* foe. And the very *hour* that General Kammler's new long-range rocket is ready, we will rain *Death* on Stalin himself!" He slammed his fist into the city of

Moscow with such fury that Kammler feared he would knock the framed map from the wall. Hitler clenched his hands to his chest, then opened them dramatically, in a gesture Kammler hadn't seen his leader use since the fervent Nazi rallies of the Thirties.

"And from the ashes of Germany as it stands today, a new Reich will *rise!* We will *rise* to our proper place of leadership with the ashes of the Communists at our feet! And even if we *fail*, even if we go to our graves in *glorious* death, we will *drown* our enemies in the very fire of the *gods* before we leave the stage!" His eyes focused again, as if he had just become aware of the others in the room. The demigod had returned.

Kammler's heart swelled with pride, knowing that his actions had led to his leader's impassioned revival. He threw his arm out in a rigid salute.

"Hail the *Fuhrer*!" Kammler shouted.

The senior staff struggled to their feet. "Hail the *Fuhrer*!" they responded in unison. Goebbels took up the chant, leading the room in the worshipful chant for a full minute. Hitler shook with fervor, drinking in the unexpected adulation of his commanders.

Kammler sensed his opening. "Give the word, *mein Fuhrer*, and your will be done!"

Hitler's hardened chin jutted upward. "Signal me when the attacks on New York and Washington are in readiness, General, and I will give the final command."

"*Jawhol, mein Fuhrer!*" Kammler acknowledged.

Goebbels threw out his arm in salute. "*Seig!*" he shouted.

"*Heil!*" the group responded.

"*Seig!*"

"*Heil!*"

And so it went for another full minute until the group's reverence for their leader had been fully expressed. Then, as if exhausted from his rant, Hitler moved unsteadily back to his chair and sat down.

"I propose a short recess for refreshments," Bormann quickly suggested. [6]

"Agreed," Hitler sighed.

Martin Bormann

The group again rose and saluted, then quietly excused themselves, Kammler included. *Reichsleiter* Bormann took his arm and pulled him well away from the others.

"You have done well, General Kammler. Very well indeed."

Kammler knew that Bormann was Hitler's right hand. To incur his favor or wrath was the same as an edict from the *Fuhrer* himself. "Thank you very much, *Herr Reichsleiter*. It is my honor to serve."

Bormann turned him further away from the group. "There will be no attack on New York. Or anywhere else for that matter," he whispered.

Kammler was stunned. "Excuse me, *Herr Reichsleiter*?"

"Enough blood has been shed for a thousand generations of Germans. We must plan now for Germany's future, not end it in a blaze of glory for the sake of one man."

Kammler had experienced flashes of a similar sentiment, but to give voice to such thoughts was tantamount to placing a loaded gun in one's mouth, so he had held his tongue. But if the *Fuhrer's* Chief of Staff was openly discussing mutiny, then the tentacles of treason had reached far indeed. "I am afraid I am at a loss for words, *Herr Reichsleiter*. What do you propose?"

Bormann eyed him carefully. "Do you believe that Adolf Hitler is the salvation of Germany?"

Kammler knew that the only safe answer to a question of that sort was the party line. "Of course, *Herr Reichsleiter*."

Bormann leaned in closer. "Then let him save himself. Men like you and me have more important matters to attend to."

FAMILY FEARS

PRESENT DAY – CHICAGO, ILLINOIS

Breakfast was a restrained affair that Monday morning in the Manning household. Amanda fixed bagels for Eric and Kevin without the usual loving banter they enjoyed, and even the boys' sibling rivalry had been subdued. She cleaned the kitchen counter mechanically while the boys ate quietly at the table.

"Is Dad ever coming home?" seven-year-old Kevin asked.

"Of course he is, honey," she assured him. "We talked to Daddy last night; he just has some work he has to do in California, and then he'll be home."

"That's not what he said that night at dinner," Eric countered. "He said we'd stay here till school was over, then we'd go to California with him."

Amanda winced. "Mommy and Daddy need to talk some more about that, hon. Nothing's been decided for sure yet."

Breakfast continued in silence for a few more minutes. Finally Kevin spoke up, tears brimming in his big blue eyes.

"Are you and Daddy getting a divorce?" he asked with a sniffle.

Amanda knelt and wrapped her arms around her son. "Of course not, sweetie! We just had a disagreement, that's all. Mommies and daddies have those all the time. We'll work it out. We always do."

Kevin wiped his nose on his sleeve. "Kyle's Dad moved to California last year. They're getting a divorce now."

She pulled Kevin's head to her shoulder. "Oh honey, that's different." For one thing, Kyle's Dad went to California to frolic in the surf with his secretary. She certainly *hoped* there was no frolicking on Mike's itinerary.

"*How* is it different?" Kevin demanded, making no attempt to squirm out of the comfort of her arms.

Okay, Amanda, she told herself, *let's see if you can come up with a reason you believe yourself.*

WICKER BASKET

SAN JOSE, CALIFORNIA

Manning reported to the office of Nanovex CEO Doug Lyman first thing Monday morning. After receiving permission from Lyman, his secretary used the retinal scanner to open the door for Manning. Lyman waved him over to the conference table.

"Good morning, Mike!" Lyman beamed. "Was your hotel up to snuff?"

The hotel they had booked for him was more luxurious than his own home. "It's great, Mr. Lyman, thank you very much."

Lyman raised an eyebrow. "Mr. who?"

"Doug," he corrected. "The hotel is fabulous, Doug, thanks a lot."

Lyman jerked his head toward his secretary's office. "Then don't forget to thank Cathy on your way out. She makes all the reservations."

"I'll do that." He pulled the rolling briefcase onto a chair and began stacking the contents on the conference table.

"Did you get through all of that?"

Manning had applied Post-Its liberally to help him sort the files. He arranged them in five piles. "It's basically the same information for each of the five employees who died; personnel files, as much information as the company could gather about their personal finances, and Fleischer's reports of his initial visits with the families. In two cases there's a follow-up report with the families' attorneys, but not for these three."

Lyman frowned. "I know for a fact that all five families have retained lawyers and that Fleischer made at least initial contacts with all of them."

He motioned to the documents. "I only know what's here, Doug."

Lyman slapped the table. "Damn that Fleischer for deserting us without so much as a phone call!"

Manning almost came to Jake Fleischer's defense, but realized the whole chopped-up-in-a-bucket thing might be hard to explain. "I could contact these three families and just ask them for the names of their attorneys again, but that won't make us look very professional."

Lyman looked pained. "And I don't want to bother those families with legal queries when they haven't even buried their loved ones yet. Security is one thing, but common human decency is another." He massaged his chin for a moment. "Call Harkin-Thomas and introduce yourself as Nanovex's new lawyer who's gonna sue their firm for breach of contract if they can't get a lasso around their AWOL attorney. All we need from him is the names of the lawyers he dealt with, then to hell with him."

He swallowed. Nothing like being sent on an errand to wring information out of a dead man. "Okay, will do."

Lyman plucked a pair of reading glasses from his pocket. "On a brighter note, I contacted the FBI, and they referred me to their local agent-in-charge, a fellow named...Pugliano. Perry Pugliano. Straight-up guy, he agreed to run interference for us and keep the bodies locked up until we can clean up our mess."

Just like that, Manning thought. Obstructing justice was a lot more complicated when he was in private industry. Apparently if the government wanted something swept under the rug, it was one phone call and done. "Does the FBI do this...often?" he finally asked.

Lyman chuckled. "More than you'd think, Mike. Remember, the purpose of the FBI isn't to protect the people; it's to protect the government. J. Edgar Hoover was a master of P.R. Whenever those two interests overlapped—kidnappings, bank robbers and the like—the FBI was there to save the day. But that's just what it was—P.R. It's all about confidence in government. If criminals run amok, that hurts public confidence. So the criminals get the cuffs, or worse. But when the government screws the pooch, that also hurts public confidence, and the FBI will be right there to bury it deeper than King Tut's tomb. Waco, JFK, 9/11, pick your conspiracy. A lot of the mystery surrounding those events is just the FBI obfuscating any governmental incompetence that contributed to the disasters. Enough exposed incompetence and the citizens reach for the pitchforks. Or worse, they stop paying their taxes."

Oh, God forbid. "Is that what they're doing for Nanovex?" he asked tentatively.

"Partially," Lyman admitted. "If this were just a tragic industrial accident, we wouldn't be having this conversation. I'd be hand-delivering the checks to those families and adding as many zeros as it took to make this right. But it's not that simple. Classified government information is involved, and if that means violating the rights of a few individuals to protect National Security, you just swallow hard and do it. It's no different than ordering a soldier to take a hill, knowing it may cost him his life. The needs of the whole country outweigh the needs of the individual citizen."

Well, I'm glad I have that straight now. "So how does the FBI fit into our plan with the families? I mean, what's our end game?"

A sharp rap at the door cut off Lyman's response. He frowned and walked back to his intercom. "I'm busy here Cathy, can it wait a few minutes?"

"It's Mr. Graves, sir. He says it's urgent."

Lyman shared a distressed look with Manning, then crossed the office to open the door for their customer.

Graves rushed through the opened portal. "Sorry to interrupt, Doug, but I just got a call from Washington. DARPA is pulling the plug on the project."

Lyman was stunned, but when he started pressing Graves for details, Graves cast an eye toward Manning. Lyman nodded.

"Mike, could you excuse us for a few minutes?"

Manning was already gathering his files. "Of course."

* * *

Lyman waited until the door closed behind Manning, then turned on his customer. "Seth, what the *hell* is going on? Is this about the accident? I told you I'd get a rope around the situation, and I'm doing just that!"

Graves held up his hands. "Doug it's not about that at all. The President got wind of this project, and he pitched a fit. You *know* he helped get the Chemical Weapons Convention ratified in the Senate back in the nineties. My boss said the President almost tore his head off when he found out about WICKER BASKET."

Lyman glared at him. "The President wasn't supposed to *know* about WICKER BASKET, dammit! This is one of those weapons you don't tell the president about unless he needs to use it, *if then.*" He recalled the many "black missions" he had helped launch out of Afghanistan, both into Pakistan and Iran. Their purpose was simple—deniability. If things went to shit with an urgent mission on the wrong side of somebody's map, the president could honestly say he knew nothing about it. But the job got done.

Lyman knew that WICKER BASKET was the same idea. It was nothing less than a viable substitute for tactical nuke. It was absolutely lethal within its precisely targeted radius, and absolutely harmless outside of it. *Dear God*, he thought, *what would they rather do, drop the <u>bomb</u>?* Someday some president was going to be faced with that choice, and WICKER BASKET would have given him a covert alternative to a mushroom cloud. But President Cameron had just tied not only his own hands, but the hands of every president who would follow him.

Graves shook his head. "Doug, I've worked on this project right beside you for the last two years. Do you think I *like* seeing our hard work thrown in the dumpster? But you know how chain of command works better than I do. Sometimes you just have to bite your lip and salute the flag."

Lyman sagged against the edge of his desk. "Yeah, I know. And I didn't mean to blow up at you, Seth; I know we're on the same side."

Graves waved it off. "You're just passionate about your work." He paused and looked at his shoes. "I hate to twist the knife, but we've got to talk about shutdown logistics."

Lyman moved around his desk to check his Outlook calendar. "How about three o'clock this afternoon?" he said gloomily.

"Three o'clock is fine. I'm sorry about this, Doug, I really am."

His shoulders fell. "I'll deal with it."

Lyman watched the door close behind the younger man.

"You better *believe* I'll deal with it," he growled.

QUID PRO QUO

SAN FRANCISCO, CALIFORNIA

Scott Hendrix settled into a corner table at Palio D'Asti, the restaurant suggested by his contact. He picked a seat facing the garishly colored mural of a horserace covering an entire wall in the private dining room of the restaurant, favored by executives and deal makers for luncheon appointments here in San Francisco's financial district. He sat with his back to the floor-to-ceiling window, again as his contact had requested. The restaurant was named after a famous bareback horserace in the city of Asti, Italy, which Hendrix thought somewhat amusing. He figured any reference to riding bareback would be something to avoid in San Francisco. But the food and the service were excellent, and it was within easy walking distance of the Israeli consulate on Montgomery Street, which was the primary requirement for today's meet.

"Good afternoon, Scott. Good to see you again."

As usual, deprived of visual cues, the arrival of Meir Eitan was only announced by the man's hand on his shoulder. In his sixties, the man still walked like a cat. Hendrix twisted in his chair.

"And you as well, Meir. Thank you very much for coming."

The old man smiled warmly, "For you? Of course." He took his seat in the corner, facing the windows to the street.

Hendrix assumed Eitan didn't mind being seen, but preferred whom he was meeting *with* to be a mystery to any passersby. *Tradecraft dies hard, especially for a former Mossad agent.* "How is Golda?" he asked. "I was very sorry to hear about her cancer."

Eitan gave him a grateful nod for his concern. "The doctors say that a new chemotherapy treatment for lung cancer shows great promise. Of course, a better therapy would have been for both of us to stop smoking years ago."

He noted that the nicotine stains on Eitan's right hand had faded significantly. "I see you heeded the warning as well."

Eitan smiled, wiggling his fingers. "Your skills of observation are as sharp as ever. Of course, now that I no longer imitate a smelter, food tastes so good I eat like one of those horses on the wall!" He patted his ample belly then gave Hendrix a sly look. "But I'll wager you didn't ask me here to make small talk, correct?"

"I'd hardly call the health of your wife small talk, Meir, but yes." He leaned forward slightly. "You are familiar with the disappearance of Rashid Ben-Jabir?"

Eitan chuckled. "The playboy prince? Of course. I hear it has caused quite a bit of consternation among local law enforcement. Any leads you can discuss?"

"There's talk the Mossad might have been connected," Hendrix suggested bluntly.

Eitan snorted into his raised water glass, then used a napkin to mop up the water dribbling down his chin. "Why on earth would you point a finger at Mossad?"

He raised an eyebrow. "An Arab prince with connections to Saudi intelligence disappears in a city with an Israeli consulate? You have to admit even *you* would place yourself on the short list, especially given the mysterious circumstances surrounding the disappearance."

Eitan buttered a roll, first generously, then scraping off all but a fraction, as if recalling his doctor's advice. "Scott, you *know* that under Rashid's uncle, relations between Mossad and Saudi Intelligence have never been better. They hardly have a motive to move against the Saudis at this time. If they had suspected the Saudis of plotting something on US soil contrary to Israeli interests, they would simply have called *you*, or the FBI, correct? But what exactly are these 'mysterious circumstances,' if you can say?"

He noticed how Eitan never referred to Mossad as "we," it was always "they." The old man was a piece of work. Hendrix briefly discussed the sanitized crime scenes, the sparse blood evidence, and the missing bodies.

The elder spy shrugged as he poured dressing liberally over his salad, then cursed in Hebrew before scraping most of it off again. "You see? That could not possibly be Mossad. Mossad prefers to *leave* the bodies. And as *much* blood as possible. It sends a message, correct?" He took a bite while Hendrix digested that information. "Mmm, delicious. And yours?"

Hendrix frowned. "What if they stumbled into the *kidon* team you have operating here in town as we speak? Would *that* give you sufficient motivation to make Ben-Jabir go away?" That got Eitan's attention. *Kidon* was the Mossad euphemism for assassination. Hendrix had no idea if the Mossad team was indeed a *kidon*, or a more generalized *neviot*, a special operations team that could handle surveillance, interrogation, or theft as the mission required, but he knew that if the Mossad sent a distraction team to the East coast, whatever the team on the West coast was doing was damn important.

"You don't know what you're talking about," Eitan said around another mouthful of salad.

Hendrix bore into the Israeli with his eyes. "Oh yeah, I do. My skills of observation are just fine, remember? You flinched. And you *do* have a team on the ground; that I know."

Eitan put down his fork. "What do you want from me, Scott?"

He lowered his voice to a whisper. "I just want to know what's going down on my own turf, Meir. Listen, if you need to perforate an Arab on US soil who's up to no good, I'll be the first one to look the other way. But you gotta keep me in the loop. And when you pull Moshe and Elsie Kitsvah out of retirement to keep our right hand busy in New York, it makes us worry what you're trying to slip past our left hand here in San Francisco."

Their food came, but Eitan ignored it, glaring at Hendrix across the table. "We had *nothing* to do with Ben-Jabir," he said emphatically. "That is the truth. As for any other ongoing operations, I give you my word they are not contrary to US interests. If I were at liberty to discuss them, you would probably thank me." He took up his utensils again, then added. "As a matter of fact, I *know* you would thank me."

We, Hendrix noted. Eitan was either telling the truth or his most sincere lie. The two were often not far apart, he knew. "I appreciate your candor," he said, turning his attention back to his meal. "I knew you would level with me."

Eitan winked. "And all it cost you was an excellent lunch, thank you."

After eating in silence for a few minutes, Hendrix decided to try a stab in the dark. "This wouldn't have anything to do with Angela Conrad, would it?"

The older man gave him a venomous look. "I don't know what you're talking about. Conrad is your problem, not mine."

Paydirt, keep digging. "You don't think she's in town for the convention, do you?"

The utensils were down again. "What convention?"

Hendrix retrieved a folio from his briefcase and handed it across the table. It contained Pugliano's list of names and photographs of the known intelligence operatives in town.

Eitan shook his head. "What is the meaning of this?"

"They're all in California, if not San Francisco proper. Right now. And no, we don't know why. I was kinda hoping you could tell me."

The spy flipped through the dossier in puzzlement for several minutes, then his face went taut. He closed the folio, holding it up. "May I?" he asked, indicating he wanted to keep it.

"Of course," Hendrix agreed immediately. The hardest part of dealing with the Israelis was coming up with a *quid* that they felt worthy of a *pro quo*. He had just planted an obligation on a *very* knowledgeable source, which was quite an achievement.

Eitan tucked the folio under his arm and stood, ignoring his unfinished meal. "Thank you again for lunch, but I must be going."

Something was wrong. He stood and extended his hand. "Would you like me to have the rest of it boxed? It's no trouble."

Eitan accepted the hand, pulling him close. "You have *no idea* what you've stumbled across here," he said in a harsh whisper. "Take my advice, young man. Leave it alone."

Hendrix held on to Eitan's grasp. "Meir, I don't understand."

Eitan pulled away, then thrust his finger in Hendrix's face. "*Leave it!*" he hissed. Eitan exited the restaurant. Through the glass, Hendrix watched him head back toward the consulate at a brisk walk. Hendrix moved to the window. When Eitan thought he was out of Hendrix's line of sight, he broke into a run.

Hendrix stared into space. *You little shit*, he pondered darkly. *I knew you were up to something. Rashid found out that much. I guess that's why you had him killed.*

JUSTICE

JUNE 1998 – PHILADELPHIA, PENNSYLVANIA

For today's errand, recently graduated Patrol Officer Angela Conrad ditched her uniform for the dress she had worn to Frankie's funeral. That event, following a long battle with breast cancer, had solidified Angela's conviction that if there was a God, he was a heartless bastard in addition to being a rule-making killjoy. She rang the doorbell on the run-down house in what once had been a middle-class neighborhood. An elderly woman with coke-bottle glasses answered.

"May I help you?" she asked in a weak voice. Her shoulders were slumped and her hair gray and thin, but the faded flower-print dress was a dead giveaway.

"Mrs. Groutman?" Angela asked hopefully.

Her eyes narrowed. "Yes?"

Angela bubbled with faux excitement. "Oh, I'm so glad you're still here! I didn't dream you would still be in the same house!"

"Do I know you, young lady?"

"Oh, I'm so sorry!" she fluttered. "I'm Sarah Kowalcyk. You were my foster mother almost twenty years ago." Angela figured taking the identity of her roommate would give her a much better chance of getting inside.

Sylvia Groutman's eyes swam behind the fishbowl lenses. "Sarah? Little Sarah? My goodness, you're all grown up!"

"I know!" Angela gushed extending her left hand, displaying the ring passed down from Frankie's mom. "And I'm getting married! I just had to come back and tell you!"

"Me? Why, child?"

Angela feigned hurt at Sylvia's humility. "Oh, Mrs. Groutman, you did so much for me! You taught me how to be a lady!" She flashed the rock again. "And it certainly paid off! May I come in and tell you about it?" she bubbled. "I'm just so excited to finally see you again!"

Angela knew Sylvia Groutman's life had been one long, futile search for significance. Waving recognition and appreciation in front of her would work just like a skeleton key.

Sylvia unlocked the screen door. "Oh! My house is just a mess, but please, come in."

Angela stepped inside, never realizing the impact returning to the scene of the crimes would have on her. Although the house was a disheveled shadow of its former self and bore little resemblance to her tortured memories, her stomach still flipped. She choked back the bile rising in her throat.

Sylvia ushered her into the family room, the scene of so many swats and sewing lessons. It had been converted to a makeshift shrine to Sylvia's foster children, with dozens of pictures filling the mantle, taped to the fireplace, and spreading outward onto the wall. Some were faded black and whites, decades old, others dated to Angela's time. None were newer than that, which stood to reason. Not even the dysfunctional state foster care system would place further wards with the wife of a convicted child murderer. It had apparently left quite a hole in her life.

She looked carefully at the montage. "Am I here?"

Sylvia scrutinized the photos, then pointed. "Here you are, dear. Oh, didn't you look darling in that dress?"

"What about Rachel?"

"I'm sorry?" Sylvia feigned poor hearing, but there was no mistaking her reaction.

Angela's voice lost its warmth. "Rachel Halliday, the girl who was murdered by your husband. Why isn't she here? Didn't you love her as much as these other girls?"

Sylvia gaped at her, but said nothing.

She continued looking. "And what about Angela Kellerman, the little girl who turned your husband in? Shouldn't she be here? I mean if she hadn't stopped that miserable rat of a man you called your husband, how many other little girls would he have raped and murdered? Don't you think she deserves at least a little recognition for that?"

Sylvia trembled. "Sarah, what's the meaning of this?"

She locked eyes with her. "Actually, the name's Angela. And the meaning of this is that some crimes are never forgotten, especially by the victims."

Sylvia bolted for the phone, but never made it. Conrad wrapped the garrote around her neck and lifted the old woman from the floor.

"Tell me, Sylvia," she hissed, "did you ever wonder what Rachel went through when your husband killed her? Did you ever wonder what it would be like to have someone much bigger and stronger overpower and squeeze the life out of you?"

She judo-tossed Sylvia to the floor. Discarding the garrote, she choked the old woman with her bare hands. Slowly. She got down in her face, close enough to smell the old woman's rancid breath when a small gasp escaped.

"P-please!" she begged.

Her voice was ice. "Rachel used to say that. She used to say it a lot. Didn't do her much good either."

She bore down harder. "How does it feel, Sylvia? How does it feel to be completely powerless? How does it feel to know that your worthless life is about to wink out and there's not a god-damned thing you can do about it? Tell me what you think was going through little Rachel Halliday's mind when your husband strangled her! Tell me!" She relaxed her grip just enough for one last rasping breath.

"*Why?*" Sylvia coughed out, her eyes wild with terror.

Conrad laughed, drunk with the power coursing through her body. "*Why?* Did you think justice would never come for you? Did you think justice would let you die peacefully in your bed when you let Rachel rot in the pond out back? I don't think so."

Conrad finished the execution then stepped off, shaking with excitement. That felt better than she had even dreamed. It was a rush of adrenaline and endorphins like no drug she had ever experienced.

* * *

The police eventually broke down Sylvia Groutman's door when the neighbors noticed her absence, but she was not inside. A brief search ensued, but a shortage of clues and a lack of relatives to force a prolonged hunt resulted in its cancellation a few days later. Neither Sylvia Groutman nor her body was ever found.

Of course, they didn't check the pond in the nearby woods.

[1] While the history we were taught in school declares firmly that the German A-bomb program was years behind its American counterpart, documents declassified forty years after the war in 1995 appear to put the lie to so much of that "history" that it makes one wonder what else was kept secret. Consider the postwar interrogation of former *Luftwaffe* pilot Hans Zinsser, who witnessed what could only be interpreted as an atomic explosion over northern Germany in October 1944, complete with a blinding flash, a violet-blue fireball a kilometer or more in diameter, a mushroom cloud kilometers tall, and electrical interference that made radio communication impossible. If this pilot had been judged to be a crackpot or simply mistaken, would his debriefing have been classified for four decades? I did change the date of the test from October 1944 to March 1945 in this story because it made for better drama and I couldn't piece together why the Germans would sit on the bomb for six months if they indeed had it in hand. (Source: *Reich of the Black Sun* by Thomas Farrell, 2004, p. 26)

[2] At the same time the pilot Zinsser witnessed an atomic explosion over northern Germany, the London *Daily Mail* reported that phone service had been completely disrupted for more than two days for an unknown reason. The effects of electromagnetic pulse, or EMP, were completely unknown by the Allies as well, until the Americans exploded their own atom bomb in July 1945. An EMP wave from a Hiroshima-sized test explosion in the Baltic Sea could easily have knocked out Berlin's phones for this length of time. (Source: *Reich of the Black Sun*, p.62)

[3] *Der Spiegel*, "How Close Was Hitler to the A-Bomb?" by Klaus Wiegrefe, March 14, 2005: "Karlsch bases his theory in part on statements made by Gerhard Rundnagel…to the East German state security service, the *Stasi*. In the 1960s, the *Stasi* became aware of rumors circulating in the former East German state of Thuringia that there had been a nuclear detonation in 1945. Rundnagel told the security service that he had been in contact with the research team working with Diebner. He said one of the physicists in the group had told him that there were "two atomic bombs in a safe." Rundnagel later said the two bombs were dropped over Hiroshima and Nagasaki."

Perhaps not coincidentally, even though Ohrdruf (where the bunker mentioned in this story is located) was well within the Russian Zone, in what would become East Germany, the US Army's 4th Armored Division raced ahead of their supply lines in a mad dash to reach Ohrdruf before the Russians. American technicians descended on the Ohrdruf bunker and stripped it of technical equipment before dynamiting the tunnel entrances and pulling out. Residents of the town of Ohrdruf mention soldiers blacking out all windows along the evacuation route with paint before long convoys of heavy equipment rolled through the village. Reputedly, all records pertaining to the Ohrdruf bunker have been classified for 100 years. (Source: *Lucky Forward: The History of Patton's 3rd US Army*, Col. Robert S. Allen, published by Vanguard Press, New York, 1947)

[4] A flight of this range was well within the range of the Ju-390 (the plane was also capable of inflight refueling), and interrogations of Axis POWs say that both the Capetown and New York flights were successful. However, the number and ferocity of the journalists claiming that it "couldn't have happened" makes one wonder if an agenda was at work to cover up how close New York came to Armageddon. (Source: *Target America: Hitler's Plan to Attack the United States* by James P. Duffy, 2004)

[5] This is an actual planning map drawn up by the *Luftwaffe* High Command in 1944. It shows the blast effects and projected pressure wave of a 15-kiloton atom bomb on Manhattan, which happens to be exactly the size of the bomb the US dropped on Hiroshima a year later. (Source: *Reich of the Black Sun* by Thomas Farrell, 2004)

[6] Photo credit: National Archives

CHAPTER 8

DISTRESS CALLS

PRESENT DAY - SAN JOSE, CALIFORNIA

Sitting in what had been Jacob Fleischer's office at Nanovex, Manning mechanically completed the tasks Lyman had assigned him. He contacted Fleischer's law firm, Harkin-Thomas, in a vain fishing expedition for any further records of the Nanovex case not already in his hands. He hardly thought it possible, but Harkin-Thomas was even more clueless than he was.

Taking a shot in the dark, he called the two lawyers retained by the families whose identities he *did* know. Confessing his ignorance as a new lawyer on the case, he asked if their firms were representing any other families in the accident. That scored a direct hit with one firm, and a lead with another. "I think they went with Dixon, Exley and Franco," the lawyer for one family informed him. A call to that firm proved him correct. Four down, one to go. Manning grimly figured he would certainly find out *that* lawyer's identity when Nanovex was served the family's lawsuit.

Manning turned his chair and looked through the window and the glass canopy shielding the building onto Nanovex's immaculately landscaped property. The grass, sand, boulders, and water features outside mirrored a Japanese garden, with all features in balance and harmony. Balance and harmony. He wondered what *that* felt like. If his present life was any indicator, it was a mystery that would follow him to the grave. He sighed, rubbing his temples.

The call to his family last night had felt a little like a police negotiator making first contact with a barricaded suspect; he had no idea whether the Amanda he reached would be rational or raving. It turned out she was courteous but distant, answering a few perfunctory questions before placing the boys on the phone to say hello. She had asked no questions of him at all, only receiving the contact information for his hotel and work when it was offered. It felt disturbingly like placing a call to an ex-wife to ask about visitation rights.

Unsettling as it had been, his call to Amanda was not what was spoiling his concentration. It was the call he knew he could expect at any time from Angela Conrad. She said she would contact him once he was in place at Nanovex. It seemed that requirement had been met, and she didn't strike him as a time waster. Earlier today Lyman's secretary had called his cell phone with a question; the buzzing on his hip made him jump like a snakebite.

Manning took the phone off his belt and placed it on his desk, staring at it like a hand grenade that could go off at any second.

NON-TERMINATION NOTICE

SAN JOSE, CALIFORNIA

Doug Lyman gathered the small staff of project WICKER BASKET in their equally small conference room. Their office was what the Nanovex security manual referred to as a "secured space;" essentially a large bank vault containing a few cubicles, the conference room, the laboratory where they performed most of their work, and the test chamber where their five coworkers had met their untimely end. Even for what could never have been called a "happy" project, the mood was more somber than usual.

"I can't believe they canceled our contract!" Lead Scientist Jeff Wood fumed. The normally congenial man in his forties had a kind face and a Van Dyke beard, but his eyes burned behind his round spectacles. "We met all of our technical milestones. Was it because of the accident?"

"No," Lyman assured them, "I don't think it was about the accident, and it certainly wasn't over any technical issues. It was political. WICKER BASKET uses nerve gas, and once the President found out, the fate of the project was sealed."

"Who briefed the President?" asked nanotechnology scientist Molly Kiernan, a dark-haired woman in her late twenties with sharp features and deep, probing eyes. "I had no idea our project was far enough along to merit that kind of attention."

"It wasn't," Lyman agreed. "Maybe Seth Graves' boss at DARPA got overeager and let it slip during a presentation. Maybe the President saw a news story about the accident and started asking questions. It doesn't really matter. Somehow it reached his desk, and he shut us down."

"I hope I'm not being self-centered here," test engineer Mark Wong said cautiously, "but has any thought been given to our next assignment?" Wong was a fit man in his early thirties with close-cropped hair, his normally cheerful countenance drawn with concern.

"Of course it's not self-centered, Mark," Lyman assured him. "And I *have* been thinking about your next assignment." His eyes surveyed the group. "For all of you."

After letting that sink in, he continued. "I'm not canceling the project."

They shared incredulous looks, but Josh Hackett, the team biologist, spoke up first. "I thought when the President declared a project dead that pretty much stuck a fork in it. Am I wrong?" Hackett was also the team's self-declared "dark cloud," a dour, heavyset man in his late forties given to pithy negativisms.

"If we want DARPA's funding, yes," Lyman admitted. "But there's nothing that says Nanovex can't fund this project from its own funds or from other sources."

The group eyed each other nervously. The presence of Reese Miller, Lyman's chief of security, did little to put them at ease. Security people seldom did.

"But Seth Graves was already down here ordering us to box up everything related to the project for shipment to DARPA," Woods cautioned. "He was very specific that there was to be nothing left; no data, no documentation, no nanomaterial samples, nothing."

Lyman hesitated. He and Graves weren't supposed to have their meeting over shutdown logistics until three this afternoon. Graves was certainly eager to start driving nails into this project's coffin, probably to demonstrate enthusiastic compliance with the President's orders. "Of course DARPA has a right to all the data and material; they paid for it," he said. "And making copies of classified material is obviously illegal. I would never suggest that. On the other hand, they can't very well wipe your memories, and you four were the brains behind making WICKER BASKET a reality."

"The surviving brains," Hackett reminded him.

Lyman nodded soberly. "We'll never forget the sacrifice of our friends who helped make the vision behind this project a reality. But then, we can't in good conscience let that sacrifice be in vain, can we?"

The scientists studied the tabletop. He couldn't tell whether he was reaching them or not.

"So," he continued, "what I would like to do is set up a new project, in a new space, a new budget, the whole nine yards. The objective of this new project will be to reconstitute the technology developed under WICKER BASKET using Nanovex's private R&D funding. If we re-develop WICKER BASKET using your expertise and our own funds, it will belong to *us*, and no one can tell us what to do with it."

"What about the VX nerve gas?" Hackett countered. "The government provided it last time, and you can't very well get *that* at Home Depot."

Lyman dismissed his concerns with a wave. "The VX isn't even important at this stage. What's vital to this project is the nanoagent delivery system, and we have everything we need to produce *that* in-house. We don't *need* to go to Home Depot. Once that's accomplished whoever eventually funds our research can load it with whatever payload they wish. That's not really our concern."

Hackett let out a sarcastic laugh. "That's like selling a nuclear-capable ballistic missile and saying, 'it's harmless because there's no warhead.'"

The last thing he needed in a sensitive project like this was a team member who wasn't fully on board. And to say the path they were heading down was sensitive was like calling a minefield problematic.

"Well Josh," Lyman said, "if you'd like, I can find you another assignment within the company."

"Yes, I'd like," Hackett said firmly. "Personally, I never thought WICKER BASKET was a good idea to begin with. The whole idea of creating a weapon that makes the use of chemical weapons politically acceptable is something I think the world could do without, don't you?"

Some people just can't see the big picture, Lyman mused, nodding to Hackett. "That's certainly a valid viewpoint, Josh." He turned his attention to Hackett's coworkers. "But for the rest of you, I want to assure you that making chemical weapons acceptable is not my goal here. And I'm asking you as a personal favor to stay with me on this program."

Lyman made the request without hesitation. In both military and civilian life, Lyman had painstakingly established a reputation as a leader who cared about his subordinates. And this is where it paid off. While a tyrant might command unfailing obedience, a true leader merely had to yell, "Who's with me?" and charge the gates of Hell, knowing that his troops would only be half a step behind.

"Count me in," Jeff Wood said immediately.

After a few moments' deliberation, Mark Wong said, "Yeah, I'll do it, too."

All eyes turned to Molly Kiernan. She frowned. "I'm still not sure," she muttered. "I'm kinda with Josh on this whole chemical weapons thing."

Sitting to her right, Mark Wong gave her a playful elbow. "C'mon, Molly. Who else is going to put up with your crap? If you move to another group you'll have to stop throwing things when you get pissed. Jeff and I know when to duck."

Kiernan blushed and hung her head. Lyman had heard about her outbursts, but also knew she was a team player when she needed to be.

"Yeah, okay," she said with an embarrassed smile. "It *would* be a chore to have to domesticate another herd of male coworkers. You guys are already broken in."

Wong and Wood smiled in amusement. Hackett looked on without comment.

"Josh," Lyman entreated, "It would be a shame to break up a team like this. Are you sure you won't reconsider?"

Hackett frowned, clearly feeling the peer pressure, "No, this project has already killed five of my friends. I want to work on research that saves lives, not takes them away."

The others started to argue with Hackett, but Lyman waved them off. "Josh has a very good point. If that's the way he feels, I want to find him a project that doesn't conflict with *his* conscience." He nodded approvingly at Hackett. "As for the rest of you, I am in your debt. Thank you very much for staying with me. I won't forget it."

The group nodded, Hackett included. *Okay, that could have gone a lot worse,* Lyman thought. "Now, I want you to give Mr. Graves your full cooperation in securing this project for shipment to DARPA, agreed? I know this is painful, but DARPA is the customer, and the customer calls the shots."

There was no dissent. He stood and shook each of their hands, Hackett included, then excused himself. Miller followed close behind.

* * *

Upon returning to his office, Lyman asked Miller, "Were you able to get an appointment with that FBI agent, Pugliano?"

"Yes sir, but he won't be able to make it until six this evening."

"That's fine. Why don't you have dinner catered in? Since we put that poor agent to work cleaning up our mess, the least we can do is buy him dinner."

"Steaks?" Miller asked.

"Get a steak for me, and a steak, chicken and seafood for him. Whatever he doesn't want you and your wife can take home."

"Thank you, sir." As he was about to leave, Miller asked him, "Do you have any ideas for alternate funding, sir?"

Lyman picked up the handset of his STE secure phone, making sure the crypto key on the terminal was enabled. "Yeah, I know of one organization that would probably kill to have the WICKER BASKET technology all to themselves." He dialed a number that had taken a lot of digging to obtain.

A woman's voice answered with a simple, "Hello," not giving any indication of the identity of her office.

"May I speak with Scott Hendrix, please?" he asked.

THE OLD BOYS CLUB

AUGUST 21, 2002

CIA OPERATIVE TRAINING FACILITY – CAMP PEARY, VIRGINIA

Gavin Carter pulled his baseball cap lower on his head and strolled toward the knot of CIA instructors standing on the parking lot. At six-foot-two and two hundred twenty pounds, the handsome black man was hard to miss, but he had made a career of blending into the background. They didn't notice him until he was close enough to look at their clipboards over their shoulders.

The closest man spun around. "What! Who the hell…" His eyes widened. "Oh! Mr. Carter! I didn't know you were coming."

Carter smiled. "Do I need an invitation these days?"

"Uh, of course not!" the instructor stuttered. "We're honored that you're here!"

Gavin Carter was a legend in the CIA. A former Special Forces soldier, he had joined the CIA's paramilitary arm during the closing days of the Cold War. Carter had killed terrorists, captured and turned enemy agents, rescued hostages, and extracted endangered CIA assets all over the world, earning him the nickname "Go-To Gavin." To his chagrin, those days were over. His primary duty now was as a talent scout.

"What's on the menu today, gentlemen?" Carter asked.

"Nothing fancy, just J-turns, counter-kidnapping scenario," the lead instructor Kevin Dods replied.

They were gathered beside the CIA's "Crash and Bang" course at Camp Peary. One half of the course resembled a Grand Prix racetrack, with straight-aways, switchbacks, and curves of varying sizes. But in contrast to a standard road race, its surface varied from concrete to asphalt to gravel to dirt, with a sprinkler system that could quickly wet down any section as the instructors desired. Their goal was to train the students to drive quickly and confidently on any surface or condition. Hard-won experience had shown that expert driving at high speed was more effective than armor or bulletproof glass in protecting agents against ambush overseas.

The other half of the course was a large two-lane track with an intersecting two-lane road across the middle, resembling a squared-off figure-eight. This was used to simulate ambushes and roadblocks, as well as defensive and offensive driving in the real world. The instructors had gathered beside this track, making final checks of the vehicles to be used in today's exercise.

"So how's this class looking?" Carter asked.

"Haven't you heard?" Dods fired back. "Everybody in Class 11 changes clothes in a phone booth." The rest of the instructors had a good laugh at that.

After September 11, the CIA was deluged with over a hundred thousand applications for employment, from a far more diverse cross-section of backgrounds than normally entered the Agency. These weren't just Communications majors from Georgetown looking for adventure. They were lawyers, accountants, salespeople, and computer specialists. People with *experience*, who already knew how the real world worked. Some of them spoke several languages and had run businesses overseas.

Most importantly, after September 11, these highly motivated professionals were not joining the CIA for adventure or glamour. They wanted the blood of America's attackers. They were a spy recruiter's dream. [1]

The CIA's Clandestine Service Training Class 11 mustered on July 15, 2002, a collection of over two hundred of America's best and brightest, more than twice the size of any previous CST class in CIA history. From the beginning Class 11 stood out, both individually and as a group. So much so that Carter had heard one instructor whine, "If I hear one more glowing story about Class 11, I'm gonna puke!"

From that Carter recognized both a problem and an opportunity. The problem was that the instructors at Camp Peary, while dedicated CIA officers, were civil servants. Some of them could even be described as bureaucrats. And the maxim of "those that can't do, teach," certainly held for a few of the trainers. With Class 11, a significant number of the students were simply smarter, tougher, and more dedicated than their instructors. Carter had heard rumors of friction between the students and the training cadre. He suspected aggressive students and insecure teachers lay at the root of those stories.

But there was another problem. Of the five students who had quit the program in the first month, four were female. Carter didn't believe for a moment that all four of these women "couldn't cut it." He suspected an unwillingness of the "Old Boy's Club" at Camp Peary to accept women in their ranks was a far more likely cause. During his trip through "The Farm" as a student—God, how many years ago had *that* been—the atmosphere at Camp Peary had been universally male-centric, almost like a frat house. Carter was going to keep a close eye on how the female recruits were handled today.

A few minutes later, Kevin Dods gave the assembled students a concise and competent briefing, then began the exercise.

"Student ready?" he asked over the radio.

A hundred yards away, upon receiving a thumbs-up from the student, an instructor with a green flag radioed back, "Student ready."

"Instructors ready?"

"Instructors ready," a voice crackled through Dods' radio.

"Let's roll!" he ordered, borrowing the 9/11 battle cry.

The instructor beside the track waved his green flag. The student and instructor vehicles began moving. The student accelerated to and held forty miles per hour. One hundred yards behind, the two instructors' cars roared forward, swiftly closing the gap with the student. The lead instructor surged past the student and cut him off, the other instructor vehicle boxing the student in on the left. The lead vehicle braked and the other instructor edged right, trying to force the student off the road, a classic prelude to kidnapping or worse.

As he had been taught, the student jammed on his brakes. The instant he came to a halt, the reverse lights came on, tires squealed, and after a few seconds, the student locked the steering wheel over, spinning his vehicle one-hundred-eighty degrees away from the attempted ambush. Before the spin stopped, the student racked the transmission back into drive, burning rubber away from his pursuers.

"Pass, no comments," Dods announced.

"Calloway, Thomas, pass," an instructor with a clipboard duly recorded.

Carter eyed the next student waiting for her turn on the track. She was blonde, pretty, and looked very focused. *Wait a minute*, his internal alarm sounded. His practiced instincts perked up. This girl wasn't just focused, she was *angry*. And her eyes weren't locked straight ahead, the way a nervous student's would, running the course over and over in their mind. Her eyes never stopped scanning, like she was picking out targets. *Oh yeah*, Cater thought, this was going to be *very* interesting.

"Next student!" Dods called.

"Conrad, Angela, take the track!" Clipboard announced.

Conrad's white Taurus surged onto the course, engine growling as it rounded the first two curves and took up position on the far side of the track. Carter could tell from the sound that the vehicle was an Agency Custom, a Taurus on the outside, with a Mustang engine and drivetrain inside. This was similar to the cars they would drive in the field, inconspicuous but souped-up for their survival. It was also an exam car, as opposed to the practice cars littering the field behind him, with body damage on every quarter panel. Exam cars were to demonstrate technique, not for ramming practice.

"So what's the story on this student?" he asked Dods.

"She's a pain in the ass!" Clipboard chimed in.

Carter raised an eyebrow at Clipboard. "So was I at one time, but I turned out okay."

Chastised, Clipboard focused on his duties.

"So, what's her story?" he repeated to Dods.

"Angela Conrad, former Philadelphia cop," Dods recited, as if he had already made this speech in front of more than one review board. "Extremely high marks for intelligence, fitness and proficiency, but she was written up twice for excessive use of force by the Philly PD. Of course, we didn't know that until we started having problems with her and double-checked her background. Her bosses never mentioned the complaints when HR called for references. I think they were glad to be rid of her."

"So will we," Clipboard muttered.

"What kind of problems?" he asked.

"Just a real bad attitude," Dods replied. "She thought she would just skate right through training because of her experience. Not gonna happen. Of course, she's not the only one in Class 11 who thinks they're a cut above."

"She thinks she's *so damn smart!*" Clipboard sneered.

"Well, *is she?*" he pressed.

Dods shrugged. "Well, *yeah*, but that doesn't exempt her from having to jump through the same hoops as everyone else."

Hmm, Carter thought. *Very interesting*.

At Dods' cue, the student and the instructors indicated their readiness. The green flag waved and all three cars rolled. When the lead instructor cut Conrad off, she braked, but only enough to avoid an impact. The second instructor began crowding Conrad off the road. She braked again, till her front bumper was even with the rear axle of the second car. She cut hard left, ramming the second instructor and forcing him into an uncontrolled spin. Then she accelerated, ramming the first car with a glancing blow of her front right bumper against the left rear bumper of the instructor's car. He also went out of control, skidding sideways off the right side of the track into the grass.

The second instructor had already corrected his spin and faced forward again on the track. The next thing he saw was Conrad's car speeding toward him in reverse. She hit him hard, crushing her trunk and obscuring the instructor's view with a buckled hood and a torrent of steam from his ruptured radiator.

By then the second instructor had come to a stop and jumped from his vehicle, haranguing Conrad with profanity that reached Carter's ears from over two hundred yards away. Big mistake. Conrad was on the move again, roaring at full throttle toward the first instructor, apparently intending to T-bone his car. At the last second she threw her car to the left, sideswiping the instructor's car and rolling it over on its roof. The instructor leapt clear at the last instant.

But Conrad wasn't through yet. Bouncing back onto the track, she raced toward the locked gate at the end of the straightaway. It was used for bringing in semi trucks, tracked vehicles, or other large obstructions onto the track. Nearing the gate, she threw her car into a spin, ramming the gate with her ruined rear bumper, sending the chain and padlock flying into the air. She continued her spin for another ninety degrees, now facing down the road leading away from the training ground toward the residence halls and classrooms. Throwing up rooster tails of dirt, Conrad sped away, giving her instructors a single-digit evaluation of their performance just as her rear bumper separated from the Taurus, tumbling down the road after her. She disappeared in a cloud of dust.

For a few seconds, the gathered instructors and students could only gawk in stunned silence, Carter included.

Shaking with rage, Dods finally muttered, "Son of a *bitch!*"

"We are *so* rid of that bitch!" Clipboard agreed.

Getting his anger fully wound up now, Dods screamed, "*Son of a BITCH!*" After that came a stream of profanity so unintelligible that Carter wasn't sure if Dods was swearing or speaking in tongues.

Clipboard was the first to regain his composure, using his radio to call the SPOs, Camp Peary's camouflage-clad Special Protective Officers with the make, model, and direction of Conrad's car. He made clear they were to use whatever force was necessary to bring Conrad's joyride to a halt.

Finally winding down his tirade but still shuddering with fury, he yelled to the entire assembly, "Her ass is mine! *Do you hear me?* Her ass is *MINE!*"

Carter walked over and placed his hand firmly on Dods' shoulder. "I'm sorry to pull rank on you," he said quietly, "but actually, her ass is *mine.*"

STRIKING OIL

PRESENT DAY – SAN JOSE, CALIFORNIA

Josh Hackett passed his boss's cubicle on his way out. "G'night, Jeff."

Jeff Woods looked up from the file cabinet he was emptying and checked his watch. "Buddy, it's only five o'clock. We still got a boatload of work to do here."

Hackett waved him off. "That meeting with Lyman drained me, man. I've had enough peer pressure for one day."

Wood's brow knitted with concern. "You gonna be okay, Josh?"

Hackett was already on his way out the door. "Nothing a frozen dinner and some whiskey won't cure."

* * *

Perry Pugliano plucked a piece of steak from between his teeth with a toothpick as he exited the Nanovex property. Although perturbed at being forced to clean up a private company's mess with all the other balls he had in the air, that guy Lyman was certainly hospitable. It had been a long day, and Pugliano tried to shake off the fog with a vigorous shake of the head. He probably should have passed on that last glass of wine, but as a bachelor it was just as hard to turn away free liquor as it was to turn down a free meal. He had just pulled onto the highway for the long drive home when his Blackberry buzzed. "Pugliano," he answered.

"Special Agent Pugliano?" an excited voice asked.

"You got him," he said, exasperated at having to repeat himself.

"This is Derek Medina of the Santa Clara County Coroner's office. We've met before, do you remember?"

Pugliano perked up momentarily, thinking this might be about the Nanovex bodies. Then he remembered those were being handled by an FBI specialist, and Medina was just an FBI wannabe. He had made the mistake of handing Medina a card at a crime scene, and the little twerp had been bugging him every time he stumbled across an interesting homicide, angling for a forensics job at the FBI. Along with a couple hundred other county coroners across the country. *Everybody has to have a dream*, he supposed.

"Listen Derek, it's been a long day…."

"Were you ever a fan of the X-Files, Agent Pugliano?"

"Yeah, sure," he admitted, tricked into honesty by the oddness of the question. "Intrepid FBI agents, aliens, worldwide conspiracies, what's not to like?" What he would *not* admit to anyone was that the show had come out while he was in law school and had been a prime motivator behind his choice of the FBI over private practice when he graduated. His only regret was that while the assignments he handled were definitely interesting, none had the fascinating oddness of the cases that landed on Fox Mulder's fictional desk.

"I definitely got myself an X-File here. My boss will probably be calling your office tomorrow for assistance. I just thought you might like to see the scene while the body was still warm."

"Where you at?" he asked, hoping he could use distance as an excuse to decline.

"Do you know the Safeway on West San Carlos in San Jose?"

He passed a highway sign announcing the San Carlos exit in a mile and half. He hit his turn signal. "Hell, I'm practically on top of you. See you in ten." Not like he had a reason to rush home, he mused. His second wife had divorced him six months earlier. The bitch had even taken his cat. Too bad catnapping wasn't a federal crime.

* * *

Pugliano flashed his badge at the tapeline, and was greeted almost immediately by a breathlessly eager Derek Medina.

"Oh, Special Agent Pugliano! You gotta see this!"

He rolled his eyes. "Derek, can you curb your enthusiasm? You know, respect for the departed and all that?"

Medina thought on that for nearly a full second, then jerked his head toward the building. "Yeah, okay. But come on, you gotta *see* this!"

Pugliano sighed and followed the bouncing coroner into the grocery store. A heavyset man in a Hawaiian shirt and shorts lay prone in a puddle of blood just inside the automatic doors.

Medina gestured over the body dramatically. "Holy Exxon Valdez, Batman! Check out the oil spill!"

Pugliano cringed at Medina's comment, but continued toward the corpse, careful not to disturb any evidence. What on first glance appeared to be nearly a quart of blood under the body was actually something else entirely. It was thick, shiny, and as black as a witch's soul. It appeared the victim had vomited out most of it when he collapsed, but on closer examination Pugliano could see other streams flowing from the vic's ears and nose too. Even the man's eyes, frozen wide in pain and terror, bore a black sheen flowing out in ebony tears down his face. He drew back in horror and puzzlement.

"It's like he chugged a gallon of 10W-40," Medina observed. "He probably bought it here. I haven't checked his receipt."

He had seen stranger suicides. The mob boss's wife who swallowed a full bottle of Drano to end her suffering—or maybe complete it—would always stick with him. "Breakfast of Champions!" one of his fellow agents had remarked, remembering a similar, but—until then—fictional suicide from a Kurt Vonnegut novel.

He frowned. "No, this looks more like crude oil. I doubt you'll find that in aisle twelve. Get a sample to go for me. I want our labs to take a look at it too." Noticing the strong smell of alcohol, Pugliano found the shattered bottle of Jack Daniels in a plastic bag at the man's left side. The whiskey flowed to the frontier of the black puddle, but did not cross it, like oil and water. He knew from many messy crime scenes that blood and alcohol mixed quite freely. Whatever this noxious pool was, it wasn't blood, not even contaminated blood. He held out a hand to Medina. "Gloves?"

He accepted the blue pair from the coroner and pulled them on. He examined the shopping bag more closely. A couple of TV dinners in addition to the whiskey, that was all. If the victim had planned on offing himself, he hadn't planned on doing it sober or hungry. That left the possibility of some kind of horrible disease, he realized as he crouched a foot away from the corpse.

"Not to beat the X-Files horse to death," Medina said, "but do you remember the shape-shifting aliens from the show?"

Pugliano's frown degraded into a scowl. "You mean the ones that bled black oil when you killed them? Black oil that was lethal if you breathed anywhere near it?"

Medina drew back slightly from the body. "Yeah, those aliens."

Pugliano snorted. "Pull it together, Derek. That was fiction. Real aliens have green blood. Like the ones we have in the freezer at the FBI."

Medina's eyes bugged. "*Really?*"

He nodded soberly. "Really. You're so easy to punk it's not even entertaining."

Pugliano started to rise, but something caught his eye. A company ID badge stuck half an inch out of the victim's left breast pocket, partially submerged in the puddle of goo. There was something familiar about it. "Derek, forceps and a bag. Get me that badge."

Medina extracted the dripping ID card and dropped it into a plastic bag, holding it up for Pugliano's inspection:

NANOVEX COMPANY
JOSHUA HACKETT
PROPRIETARY LABS
LEVEL 5 CLEARANCE

Pugliano reached for his phone to summon the FBI's forensic cavalry. Looked like this long day wasn't even close to ending. "Derek, call your boss," he ordered. "Tell him this just became a federal case."

THE COLLECTORS

SAN FRANCISCO, CALIFORNIA

Scott Hendrix had spent most of the evening with the FBI surveillance team, and was impressed by what he'd seen. With plenty of manpower at their disposal, the cars never followed their target for more than a mile before another FBI vehicle fell in to "rotate the tail," so unless the target's driver had night vision goggles and a photographic memory, they could watch him all night and he'd never have a clue. The only thing they didn't have was a helicopter, but that was on call at the Justice building downtown if needed.

They picked up their target leaving his condo downtown an hour ago, at 11:00 p.m. The target spent half an hour conducting a surveillance detection route, or SDR in FBI parlance, which was standard procedure for any spy preparing to conduct an "operational act." The real question was what kind of operational act he had in mind.

After Meir Eitan's bizarre behavior the previous day, Hendrix had no problem obtaining FBI assistance to place Eitan under surveillance. Especially since the Justice department knew that an Israeli special operations team was unaccounted for on US soil.

The FBI tail soon realized their target was also being followed by a dark green Jeep not part of the FBI convoy. After a few minutes of alarmed radio traffic, the expert FBI drivers realized the Jeep was *assisting* their target in his SDR, which could only mean the Jeep was an additional security vehicle for their target. There was concern that the tail had been "made" and their target would break off whatever operational act he had planned. But a few minutes later the two target vehicles took Highway 280 south out of downtown, exited three miles later at Oakdale and worked their way southeast along surface streets toward the bay, another two miles distant.

"Got any ideas, Mr. Central Intelligence liaison?" asked the FBI agent driving their nondescript beige Taurus. The young agent's tone was playful; apparently he enjoyed the novelty of having an actual *spy* riding shotgun with him. The more experienced FBI agents had greeted him only with cold stares; they must have dealt with the CIA before, Hendrix reasoned. The Agency had that effect on people.

"If it's a meet," he replied, "it's a high threat meet. You don't risk dragging around this kind of manpower in a foreign country unless you're afraid of somebody trying to shoot your ass."

"You said '*if*' it's a meet," the agent said. "What else could it be?"

A hit was the obvious answer, but Hendrix didn't want to inflame an already tense situation with baseless speculation. He secretly hoped that Eitan was heading to Angela Conrad's "spy conference," whatever that turned out to be. Mentioning her name had certainly raised Meir's antennae. He consulted the moving map on his laptop. They were heading for a peninsula named Hunter's Point. Although he was supposed to become intimately familiar with the cities where he was stationed, during his year in San Francisco he had never visited this part of town. Obviously Hunter's Point held some value to an intelligence professional he had overlooked.

* * *

Angela Conrad desperately needed a smoke, but tactical considerations dictated otherwise. The warehouse where she waited was nearly pitch black. A faint glow from the surrounding city lights seeped through filthy clerestory windows near the roof, but that was all. The street lights were out for a block in every direction. Whether from neglect or the actions of her customer who had called this meeting she wasn't sure. The flare of a cigarette lighter would spoil her night-adapted eyes, and she needed every advantage she could get.

Her customer had selected this location specifically to put her at a *disadvantage*, she was certain. She had been summoned to this abandoned warehouse just fifteen minutes ago. The location and timing screamed *trap*, especially since—had the roles been reversed—she would be coming to dispense death without mercy. Her customer had every right to be pissed.

She extracted a PVS-14 night vision monocular from her purse and carefully checked her surroundings. Crates stacked over ten feet high in two long lines created a clear aisle almost twenty feet wide down the center of the warehouse. It had "kill zone" written all over it. One line of crates had a six-foot-wide break in the middle—a narrow path in and out of the kill zone, where she stood. She was in the right spot. She leaned into the kill zone, craning her neck to sweep the ceiling with her night vision scope. A catwalk ran over each line of crates, creating a third dimension from which threats could approach. She would just have to do the best she could with the limited time and manpower available.

* * *

"Target entering a warehouse district, all units back off and hold position," Hendrix heard over the radio.

"What's going on?" he asked.

"Warehouse areas have limited traffic and long lines of sight," his driver replied. "If we don't back way off we run a chance of getting burned. And it sure as hell looks like they're up to something. Can't think of a reason for a diplomat to be hanging around Hunter's Point near midnight, can you? Not even a prostitute to pick up down here, just empty buildings."

They had followed Eitan until Oakdale Avenue had ended at a service road running parallel to the railroad tracks onto Hunter's Point. On the laptop Hendrix could see that the service road was a long, straight shot with no side streets for almost two thousand feet. Unless they could render themselves invisible, any attempt to follow Eitan past this point would be a dead giveaway. The old man knew his stuff. The FBI tail sat spread out over the last two blocks of Oakdale, waiting.

The radio crackled again. "All units double back, rally on Fischer."

They reversed course through a residential neighborhood, ending up on a waterfront road winding along the bay. With the about face, Hendrix's car went from being the tail of the convoy to the lead. He called out turns and distances for the driver. They ended up on the far side of Hunter's Point facing blocks of darkened warehouses. The driver braked to a stop and killed his headlights. "Talk to me," he urged Hendrix.

He studied the map. "Four roads branch due south off this one, each of them lined with warehouses for about four blocks. So we have sixteen square blocks of warehouses straight ahead. I'll bet my paycheck Eitan is in there somewhere. And I'll bet you my next paycheck he isn't alone. Watch yourself."

The radio crackled. "Six, you got the eye. What's your plan?"

The driver frowned, then spoke into his walkie. "Six has no visual. Request permission for a scratch and sniff to re-establish contact."

"Proceed," the lead agent said after a short pause.

* * *

"They're coming," Ari's voice crackled in Conrad's ear. "Two vehicles in trail. One's stopped a hundred meters short of the target. Three men in the near car, and man and woman in the distant. Principal appears to be in the lead car." A pause. "Entering the warehouse now."

On cue, she heard the click of a lock and the slow creak of a rusty door. She heard a voice giving commands. Male, older. No doubt her customer. He did indeed sound agitated. Too far away to make out the words yet.

Conrad flinched when she heard the overhead lights click on. Luckily for her they were sodium lamps, cheap and slow to light. A sickly orange glow spread from the ceiling fixtures toward the warehouse floor like a dusty twilight. It would be minutes before they came to full power. She found a niche in the crate wall and pressed her body into the cavity, her black jacket and pants making her one with the shadows for at least another minute.

"Update," Ari reported. "The second vehicle is an open-top Jeep. The man has just extracted a heavy machine gun and mounted it to the roll bar. They've moved to a covering position along the route they gave us."

Ambush. She knew it. The steps in the warehouse came closer. Much closer. She acknowledged the message by hitting her transmit button twice. She could make out the voices now.

"No, kill all the lights except for the one over the bull's-eye," the older man said in Hebrew.

"Yes sir," an unseen voice responded. A few seconds later, the glowing orange lights faded to black again, except for a single light shining down into the center of the kill zone. That one continued to grow in brightness.

The vague outlines of two men entered the narrow aisle where Conrad was hiding.

"Gideon," the older man said, "This will be your spot, covering me during the meet. Unless you prefer the catwalk…."

Just as the older man passed her in the semi-darkness, Conrad dashed behind him, locked her left arm around his throat and whirled him around, placing his body between her and the bodyguard trailing him.

She watched the bodyguard bring a pistol out from under his jacket, but her silenced 9mm Sig-Sauer was already on target. She fired two quick shots and the he toppled backwards. She whirled the older man around again to face the kill zone, then kicked the back of his leg, forcing him to his knees.

She pressed the smoking silencer to his cerebellum. "Hands straight out, let's see if you can touch the crates." He complied. "Meir, doesn't it just drive you *meshuga'at* when people show up early for their appointments?" she taunted.

* * *

"Scratch and sniff?" Hendrix asked reluctantly.

The driver put the car in gear, leaving the lights out. "Here's the deal. We're going to advance a block at a time; you're going to get out and peek around the nearest building. If it's clear, we advance a block and try it again. Our callsign is Mobile Six, so you're Foot Six." The driver pulled a duffel bag from the rear seat and held a penlight in his teeth while he dug in its depths. He retrieved a bulky handheld camera with a rubber eyepiece.

"Night vision camera with nine power zoom and wireless capability. You see 'em, call it in, take a picture, send it to me. I'll put it on the network for everybody to look at. Got it?"

Hendrix's pulse quickened at the chance to do actual field work. "Got it," he said, accepting the camera and borrowing the flashlight for a quick look at the controls.

The car advanced a block and pulled to the curb. The driver reached up and killed the dome light before Hendrix opened the door. "Make us proud, spy boy," he prodded.

Hendrix stepped to the street. There was no curb, just a swath of asphalt level with the warehouses and sporadic painted centerlines on the street. The lighting was poor and the road conditions worse. He moved to the fence of the first property and used it to guide him over the uneven pavement in the darkness. Through the fence, he could see past the first warehouse a block down Cochrane Street. Cautiously he moved to the corner of the fence and surveyed the length of the street. Nothing. He repeated his survey using the night vision camera. To his amazement, he easily spotted an alley cat three blocks away, but no Meir Eitan and company. He fumbled for the walkie in the pocket of his windbreaker.

"Foot Six, Cochrane Street clear."

"Roger Six, proceed to Hussey," the lead agent instructed.

Hendrix did his best to cross Cochrane in a nonchalant fashion, resisting the temptation to dash toward the next pool of darkness and probably trip on a pothole. Mobile Six followed behind at a nearly silent crawl. There was no fence around the next warehouse, but he couldn't hug the building either. Spotlights shone down from roof level at each corner; he would stick out like a prairie dog. Using a parked semi truck for cover, he advanced far enough to see a block down Hussey, but to clear the street he would have to step well out into the open. Crap.

Sidestepping, he "sliced the pie," looking and clearing a fraction of a block down the street, then taking another sidestep and repeating the process. There. Three blocks down, Meir Eitan's black Audi A6 sat under a single light next to a warehouse door. The car looked empty. But where was his security Jeep? He keyed the radio.

"Foot Six, contact three blocks down Hussey. Target vehicle is empty, still looking for the Jeep."

"Roger Six, send pics when you can." The lead FBI agent responded.

Hendrix acknowledged and raised the camera. He zoomed until Eitan's Audi filled the viewfinder, then shot a picture in both normal and infrared. The car certainly *looked* empty. He fussed with the camera trying to find the Send Picture menu. Luckily the menu tree displayed in the eyepiece, so he wouldn't be illuminated by a pool of light while he stabbed around the menu tree. Of course, he could get run over by a semi here on the darkened street, or worse, by Eitan's security Jeep. He found what he needed and hit SEND. The multi-megabyte photos were gone in seconds. Nice hardware. "Mobile Six, you got the pics?" he asked.

"Roger that, Foot Six. Mobile One, I'm putting them up on the network."

* * *

Even with Conrad's gun at his head, Eitan's voice was calm and level. "How exactly did you manage this, Angela?"

Conrad made a clucking sound of chastisement. "Meir, you're a public figure now, *Chargé* at the consulate and all. Far too high profile to conduct your own reconnaissance, or even to conduct an inspection of the ambush site your team picked out. You were followed. By me. Then I moved my base of operations a few blocks away so we could be waiting with a *warm welcome* when your summons arrived."

"You may have the advantage for the moment, but you're still not getting out of here alive."

"Okay, then my question for *you*, Meir, is after you kill me and escape, how much will your life be worth when your superiors find out you're a member of the Collectors?"

Eitan chuckled. "I have news for you, my dear, so is the head of Mossad. I may have to give up my charade as a diplomat, but I was thinking about retirement anyway."

"And if a file summarizing the Collectors' activities for the last five years shows up at the Jerusalem *Post*?"

He shrugged. "Then probably I would be urged to fall on my sword in exchange for my family's safety, which I would do happily. And you will still be dead."

Conrad had worked for the Collectors for almost five years. A cabal of retired and semi-retired intelligence professionals from around the world, they fattened their meager government pensions by using their expertise and connections to steal classified weapons technologies from around the world and sell them to the highest bidder. Always working through third parties and intermediaries like Conrad, they kept their hands clean and their financial statements above reproach. It was a fine system, until after several high-profile missions Conrad had requested full partnership. Eitan informed her that she was far too young and far too female to join their elite club. "If you survive long enough in this business for those lovely tits of yours to hang level with your belt, we'll talk," had been his terse brush-off.

She resisted the urge to squeeze the trigger with one more ounce of pull. "Once I figured out exactly what it was you wanted me to steal, Meir, I knew you'd never let me live anyway. This mission had final security written all over it."

Eitan sighed dramatically. "We *were* distressed at the audacity of your request for partnership, that's true."

She knew he was merely pressing her buttons to keep her distracted and talking, and he had succeeded. She used her free hand to grab his neck in a vicious nerve pinch. "You fat little prick! You were going to whack me just because I asked for membership in your Old Boys' club?"

He winced, twisting in vain to free himself. "Essentially, yes." He said through gritted teeth."

Conrad pressed the barrel of her pistol hard against a pressure point right below Eitan's skull, locking him in a vice of pain with both her right and left hands. He gasped.

"In that case," she hissed, "I'm glad I stabbed you in the back first. When did you figure out I was going to sell the nanoagent to the highest bidder?"

Eitan tried to speak, but only produced a croaking sound. She relaxed her grip slightly.

"*The CIA knows!*" he finally choked out.

It was Conrad's turn to chuckle now. "I doubt that very much."

* * *

Hendrix had scanned the full length of the street in a vain search for the Jeep when his radio crackled. "Foot Six, Mobile One, nice shots. Can you give me a wider view so I can locate him on the map? And find that damned Jeep."

"No pressure," he muttered under his breath while focusing the camera. "Mobile One, Foot Six, wide shot on the way, still looking." He had just sent the requested photo when the missing Jeep roared from between two warehouses a block down Hussey and headed for Eitan's Audi. Fast. He saw a man standing behind the driver. *Jesus, was that a mounted machine gun on the roll bar?*

* * *

Eitan's laugh in response was low and cruel. "Some of your bidders were less than careful with their travel arrangements. Not only were they flagged for surveillance, but the CIA suspects *you* are behind their gathering!"

Before she could process that information, she heard a bird call across the warehouse. Eitan threw himself to the floor. Conrad quickly followed. A bullet whistled through where her head had been and thudded into the crates. Another bullet followed, close enough to feel her hair move as it passed. She buried her head between the older spy's legs, never thinking she would be grateful for the old man's fat ass.

Two more shots blasted out directly above her, the bullet casings bouncing against the crates before tinkling on the concrete floor. On the far side of the warehouse, a man's body in jeans and a leather jacket rolled forward off the stacked crates, tumbling limply into the single spotlight over the kill zone.

"Clear!" Yuri's voice called from the catwalk above her.

"Clear!" Conrad responded, after searching for further targets over Eitan's buttocks and finding none. She saw Eitan's right hand moving toward his belt. She thrust her pistol into his crotch. "Don't *even* think about it!" she growled.

"The second vehicle is pulling up outside!" Ari warned. "Am I cleared to engage?"

"Yes, dammit, *engage!*" she barked. "Weapons free!"

Flashes of gunfire appeared four times through the clerestory windows. "Clear!" she heard a few seconds later.

The CIA knows echoed in her ears.

"We're burned!" Conrad announced over the radio. "Hot evac!"

"No further contacts!" Ari countered a few seconds later.

"We're *burned!*" she insisted. "Hot evac now, now, now!"

* * *

Hendrix thought he heard a gunshot over the Jeep's roaring engine. Then another. Muffled, probably from inside the warehouse, hard to tell. Then two more followed in quick succession, louder, the flashes inside visible through the warehouse's windows.

"Foot Six!" he called. "Jeep sighted, in motion to the warehouse! Shots fired inside! I repeat, shots fired!"

As he gave that report, the Jeep pulled in behind Eitan's Audi. The driver and passenger leapt from the vehicle, submachine guns at the ready, and were instantly cut down by sniper fire from the roof. Hendrix could clearly see tongues of flame from the sniper's rifle. He flattened himself on the pavement.

"*Sniper!*" He yelled into the radio. "Sniper on the warehouse roof!"

"Foot Six!" His partner called. "Get out of there!"

Jolted from inaction, Hendrix jumped up and ran back to the car.

* * *

"Hot evac!" Ari acknowledged. Yuri replied by throwing a rope down from the catwalk and sliding to the floor somewhere behind her, then running for the rear exit of the warehouse. She could hear Ari running across the roof to his zip line at the far corner.

"Stand up!" she ordered Eitan. "Turn around!"

He complied, regarding her with a flinty stare, tinged with well-concealed anxiety.

She lowered her pistol to her side. "I'd rather let you live for Golda's sake, but you and I both know that's not going to happen. I'd be an idiot to leave you breathing."

"You are correct," Eitan agreed. He stared at her for a long second, then brushed his jacket aside with his left hand and reached for his pistol with his right.

The old man had years of practice and was still relatively quick, but Conrad was decades younger. She allowed him to clear his holster, then shot him twice in the neck, just below the collar line. It cleanly severed his spinal column, but would still allow for an open-casket funeral. She owed his wife that much; Golda had always treated her as family. Falling to the floor, Eitan's hand tightened reflexively. His pistol discharged a single round, thudding into the crates a few feet from Conrad.

"Okay Meir," she said to the corpse. "You died with your gun in your hand and even got off a shot. That's a hell of lot more than you were going to do for me."

She turned and followed Yuri's footsteps at a dead run toward the rear exit.

[1] Source: *Class 11, Inside the CIA's First Post-9/11 Spy Class* by T.J Waters

CHAPTER 9

HUNTER'S POINT

SAN FRANCISCO, CALIFORNIA

Perry Pugliano was convinced this day would never end. After supervising the FBI agents taking over the death investigation of Nanovex's employee Joshua Hackett and preparing to leave for home, he received a call about a shoot-out involving an Israeli diplomat. Commandeering a helicopter from the Santa Clara Sheriff, he lifted off directly from the Safeway parking lot and ordered the pilot to take him to Hunter's Point. He actually fell into a shallow doze during the ten-minute flight, only to be jolted awake when the pilot banked steeply for his descent.

While the pilot sought a safe spot to land, Pugliano got a brief update from the senior FBI agent on the scene by radio. The circling helo provided a bird's eye overview to go along with the agent's narrative. His agents had cordoned off a four-block-by-four-block square of warehouses, surrounded on all but the northern edge by San Francisco Bay. The shoot-out had occurred near the western edge of the peninsula. From the agent's description, it appeared to coincide with a darkened zone about a block in diameter, almost devoid of street and building lights. As he knew from investigative experience, if you wanted to whack somebody and get away with it, the darker the better.

Of the two roads leading off of Hunter's Point, his agents blocked one and had eyes on the other. Pugliano could see the flashing lights of SFPD patrol cars moving to barricade the second road just beyond line of sight from the ground. Maybe they'd get lucky and the gunmen would make a break for it. If not, they would have at least two gunmen including one sniper with a long gun trapped in sixteen dark square blocks of hopefully-empty buildings. Not how he pictured this day ending.

The pilot picked an abandoned dock on the east side of the peninsula for his landing. The Justice Department helo already on the scene swooped low, lashing the nearest buildings with its spotlight, hoping to keep down the head of any shooters. The drop off was accomplished without incident, and the Sheriff's helicopter lifted off to join the surveillance. Together the two choppers set up a circling search pattern overhead. If the gunmen were still here, Pugliano was confident they were now pinned down and would be rolled up shortly. A delivery truck bearing the livery of BAMBINO'S PIZZA roared up just as the Sheriff's helicopter dusted off. Special Agent Larry Criswell jumped out from the passenger side.

"Interest you in some pizza, sir?" Criswell shouted over the roar of the departing helicopter.

Criswell obviously thought this circus would be over shortly or he wouldn't be so glib. But even if this ended with no FBI personnel hurt, if the Israeli *Chargé d'Affaires* was shot while under FBI surveillance, the ensuing diplomatic shitstorm would be colossal.

Pugliano extended his hand. Criswell was also a retired Marine. "No thanks, Larry, just a SITREP."

Criswell swept his hand at the nearest row of buildings. "My guys are almost through sweeping the easternmost block of warehouses. Once that's done we'll move a block west and repeat the process."

He frowned. "How long is it going to take us to get to where Meir Eitan is holed up?"

Criswell shrugged. "A while. They gunned down two of Eitan's guards like dogs right in front of that CIA guy. I don't think a frontal assault is the best play, do you?"

"Hell no. Where is Hendrix now anyway? Hiding?"

"With my guys watching the north service road out of here. He took point with a night camera before the shooting started. He hung it out there pretty good."

Pugliano laughed. "Whatdya know, the CIA actually making itself useful."

"Will wonders never cease?" Criswell agreed.

"Seriously, you guys need more help?" He would have to wake up his boss at Justice shortly and wanted to report more progress than he had at the moment.

Criswell glanced at his watch. "We put in a call for SFPD SWAT almost half an hour ago; no joy yet."

"Okay, I'll chase that rabbit. You go see if your men can step it up a bit. We gotta find out if Eitan is alive or dead, ASAP."

"Will do, boss!"

The van's driver approached them. "Sirs, turns out that Sheriff's helo has an infrared sensor—they've spotted three warm moving bodies inside a building two blocks west of here. Also, the police SWAT team just pulled up to the northeast checkpoint. They're asking where you want them."

* * *

Pugliano ended up in an alley covering one of the target warehouse's side exits as the San Francisco Police SWAT team bunched at the front door. Criswell begged him to hold the fort in the command van, but he didn't go to the trouble of staying qualified with his Glock and an MP-5 to sit on the sidelines. A few minutes later he had time to wonder on the wisdom of that—it was pitch black in the alley, except for the passing beam of a helicopter searchlight. He didn't even have a flashlight, much less night vision goggles. He doubted the assassins they hunted had made that oversight.

"Ready at the front door," the SWAT team leader announced over the radio. "I'm hearing machinery inside. Do you still want a dynamic entry?"

Criswell was taking no chances. "Don't even knock. Skip the flash bangs, but go in ready to rock and roll."

"Roger that. Entry in three, two, one…."

Pugliano readied his gun in the event of any "squirters" out the side door. He heard the familiar "SWAT fanfare" of prying metal at the door, followed by pounding boots and men shouting, "Police! Down on the ground!" Thankfully the fanfare was free of gunfire and died off very quickly, followed by the SWAT leader's voice on the radio.

"Agent Criswell, there are three civilians in the building, but they aren't armed. The building's owner wants to talk to you, though."

Pugliano quickly keyed his radio. "Larry, this is Pugs. You keep your men marching forward, I'll deal with this." Besides, he needed to get out of this alley before fatigue or his lack of proper equipment got himself or one of his team shot.

"Roger that, thanks Pugs." Criswell replied.

He made his way to the entrance of the warehouse. A hand-lettered sign next to the SWAT-forced front door read, "THANATULOS IMPORTS." Inside he found a short muscular man with dark wavy hair and a mustache arguing with the SWAT officer.

"You broke front door!" the man shouted in a thick accent. "What do I do now? I walk away, everything inside gets stolen! *Afta!*"

The man's exclamation in Greek got Pugliano's attention. "Mr. Thanatulos?" he ventured.

The man spun toward him like he was facing an attacker. "Yes! Who are you?"

He flashed his FBI credentials. "I'm the man who's going to pay for your door. And don't worry about theft. My agents have this whole area locked down. Are you aware there was a shooting nearby?"

Thanatulos waved his cell phone over his head vigorously. "Hel-lo! I am man who calls nine-eleven! Trying to work, then bang, bang, bang! Workers try to run, I call you, and…*and you rip open my front door! Kologameio!*" The SWAT team stepped back from the gesticulating businessman like he might spontaneously combust.

Pugliano choked down a laugh. He knew from growing up in New York that this act was just warming up for a bigger settlement check. Luckily he had a nearly bottomless expense account. "Don't worry about your front door, Mr. Thanatulos; I'll have a locksmith here within the hour."

"What about my *time*?" he continued ranting, waving his arms toward his two idled workers, two bearded men who from their confused and frightened faces probably spoke no English at all. "I finally get decent order, I work people late to fill order, then *BAM!* Soldiers rush in and where goes my shipment?"

He knew the presence of the heavily armed policemen was doing nothing to defuse the situation. "Hey guys," he told the SWAT troopers, "why don't you carry on, I'll take care of this." The SWAT team left without hesitation, much preferring to storm dark buildings and confront armed criminals than remain with Mr. Thanatulos.

"By all means, Mr. Thanatulos, please have your men resume their work," he continued.

The Greek waved his arms again. "*Piso ste dovleiá!*" he shouted, and his workers leapt back into action, loading heavy boxes labeled in five languages OLIVE OIL-PRODUCT OF GREECE into a panel truck.

Pugliano scanned the warehouse. Boxes of everything from spices to soap lined the racks, all with the identical PRODUCT OF GREECE markings. This was a waste of time. "I'm very sorry to have bothered you, Mr. Thanatulos. I'll make the call for the locksmith right now."

Thanatulos still looked like he was about to blow a head gasket. "The truck is almost loaded! Outside is, how you said, 'locked down'?"

As much as he wanted this guy out of his hair, there were reasons you maintained a perimeter during a manhunt. A short staring match ensued, broken by a call over his radio.

"Criswell to Pugliano. We've taken the target building. Bad news. I need you here, Pugs."

Oh crap. Criswell's careful wording over the radio meant they had found Eitan's body. The night would only get longer from here. He rubbed his eyes and wished for a smoke. "Okay, Larry, on my way." He noted the truck's license tag. "All right, Mr. Thanatulos, I'll call the checkpoint with permission for your truck to pass."

The Greek finally seemed satisfied, bowing slightly. "Thank you, mister officer."

"Parakalo," Pugliano replied. "Kalinikta." *You're welcome. Good night.* His Greek mother would be proud.

* * *

Pugliano found Scott Hendrix at the warehouse where the shoot-out occurred. Eitan's Audi and an open-top Jeep were parked just outside. The bodies of a man and woman lay sprawled on the asphalt next to the Jeep, each with identical bullet wounds; one in the chest, one in the head. Each corpse still gripped an Israeli Galil submachine gun. From the lack of empty shell casings, it didn't appear they even got off a shot.

"That's precision work," he said to Hendrix.

"No shit. Usually only the Israelis are this efficient."

"What about your guys?" he said, referring to the CIA's paramilitary operatives.

"Huh-uh. We use at least three rounds. 'When you want your bad guys super dead, two to the body, one to the head.'" Hendrix recited. "Almost any US-trained operator is hard-wired to use two-and-one. The Germans, French and British use the same doctrine as well."

"Russians?"

Hendrix laughed. "Hell no, they'll usually empty an AK mag into the torso, then have a second 'tapper' give every target a head shot with a pistol for security."

"I'm so glad you know these things."

"That's what they pay me for."

"So who?"

"I told you, it looks Israeli, or somebody the Israelis trained," Hendrix said. He ran a flashlight over the Jeep, stopping on a machine gun bolted to the roll bar. "Damn! I thought that's what I saw through the binoculars. Whoever they were meeting here, Eitan's folks were ready to kick some serious ass."

"Yet here they are, dead." Pugliano immediately recognized the mounted weapon as the paratrooper version of the M249 SAW light machine gun from his Marine training. Short barrel and no stock. Small package, big impact. "It's amazing what the Israelis can fit into a diplomatic bag these days, isn't it?"

"You're just a walking understatement, aren't you?"

Pugliano moved toward the warehouse door. "Come on, I need you to make a positive ID of Eitan's body."

Hendrix clicked off the flashlight. "Damn it," he muttered.

* * *

Pugliano, Criswell, and Hendrix stood over Meir Eitan's prostrate corpse.

"What do you *mean* you can't find the shooters?" Pugliano demanded.

Criswell looked distraught. "We've searched every building on Hunter's Point. Other than that Greek guy, they were all unoccupied."

Oh great. A dead diplomat and no shooters to answer for it. He was not looking forward to his next phone call. He looked at a nearby floor drain. "Have you checked the sewers?"

Criswell's shoulders slumped. "Not yet." He raised his radio and gave the command to his team.

"Uh, guys? Has anybody taken into account that Hunter's Point is surrounded by *water* on three sides?" Hendrix pointed out.

"You think they escaped by boat?" Pugliano asked.

Hendrix pointed to the west. "The bay is a *block* that way. These guys were professionals; they *had* to have an escape route set up. Eitan obviously came ready to bottle up whoever he was meeting here, hence the heavy firepower outside. Maybe whoever whacked Eitan had a better exit strategy."

"Larry," Pugliano said, "did that first helo on the scene see any boats leaving the area?"

Criswell raised his radio again. "I'll ask them, but I tasked them with sweeping the rooftops for snipers when they arrived, not looking for boats."

"Well, *crap*," Pugliano muttered. "Okay, call the Coast Guard. Maybe we can find where they dumped their boat and pick up their trail from there. And have that Sheriff's chopper with the infrared gear sweep the bay. Maybe we'll get lucky and the bad guys are having engine trouble somewhere out there."

"Will do," Criswell replied.

"And have the other chopper spotlight the shoreline and find out where the storm sewers come out. Maybe we'll find some boot prints or dropped gear or something. *Anything*."

"Got it."

Pugliano glared at Hendrix. "You did a good job here, Jeff, but I'm not taking the heat for this clusterfuck alone. I'll call Justice, you call State. Time for the shit to start hitting the fan, *paisano*."

Hendrix swallowed. "Fair enough."

* * *

Pugliano had just finished having his ass chewed by his boss at the San Francisco Justice Department office when he returned to the Thanatulos warehouse to make sure the man's door was getting fixed. The worker installing the new lock waved him over.

"You with the FBI?" the man asked.

"Yeah, I'm the guy who called you. Thanks a lot for coming out in the middle of the night."

The locksmith continued working. "Part of the job. Hey, who do I give the keys to?"

He stifled a yawn. "To Mr. Thanatulos, I guess."

"Got any idea where he is? I couldn't find him."

"I'll go take a look," Pugliano said, stepping through the almost-repaired doorway. There was no way that crazy bastard would leave his precious Greek goodies until they were locked up tight.

The tiny office looked like it had never even been occupied; he probably ran the business out of his house and only used this building for storage. He was checking the warehouse when his phone rang. This time it was his boss at Justice *and* the State Department Consular Affairs Officer in DC. A whipping boy was needed for this incident, and apparently Pugliano was going to be it.

He tried to politely refute every accusation, from whether he had obtained proper authorization for the surveillance to whether the FBI's response to the firefight was merely incompetent or whether it amounted to dereliction of duty. State made a pointed suggestion that Pugliano secure his own legal representation. Then Pugliano's boss kicked him off the call.

Pugliano resisted the temptation to stomp his phone. Instead, he kicked a large box of Greek flour on the bottom shelf of the nearest rack.

The empty box sailed into the middle of the warehouse floor.

Confused, he moved to the next large box and pushed it with his foot. It tumbled backward out of the shelf, also empty.

Driven to the edge of reason by a combination of fatigue, frustration and anger, Pugliano went into a frenzy of box-tipping, pulling every package of Mr. Thanatulos' Greek goods he could reach onto the floor. They were all uniformly empty.

"Oh...*shit!*" he whispered, his voice trembling. His education in Greek by his mother had mostly been of common phrases so he could properly greet his foreign relatives, but a few other Greek words had stuck with him, like death—*thanatos*. Thanatulos—man of death? *Assassin.*

He grabbed for his radio. "Northeast checkpoint! Has that truck for Thanatulos Imports come through yet?"

An agonizing pause. "Uh, yes sir. It came through five minutes after you radioed in the clearance. That was almost twenty minutes ago."

* * *

Angela Conrad helped Yuri and Ari transfer the olive oil boxes containing their weapons and other gear to the secondary vehicle. Ari's performance had been masterful, although that FBI agent had been so exhausted it was almost wasted on him. And as effective as her disguise had proven, she was thoroughly ready to get out of it. This fake beard itched like hell.

ADRENALINE

SAN JOSE, CALIFORNIA

Manning had finally fallen into a fitful sleep after another disturbing call from his wife. After a cold and distant conversation earlier in the evening that had only lasted a few minutes, he had showered and gone to bed. Then he was awakened by the pulsing glow of his cell phone vibrating in a slow circle on the nightstand. It was Amanda. He squinted at the display, trying to focus on the time. It was almost midnight west coast time, which meant it was the wee hours of the morning in Chicago.

This time Amanda was anything but cold—she was distraught and weepy. The late hour didn't help, and he wondered if her slurred speech was entirely from fatigue. She said she couldn't sleep because she worried that their marriage was falling apart. At least that was what he could comprehend; some of what she said was so disjointed all he could do was throw in an occasional, "I know, honey, I understand."

After Amanda had finally wound down, he tried to assure her that his abrupt departure had nothing to do with their marriage; it was his disgust with Bernie Norquist and the moral compromises he had to make to keep his job. It had sounded good to him; he was just pleased he could string together a coherent lie after being awakened from a sound sleep. But apparently she hadn't made this call to listen, she just needed to emotionally vent. After he had argued his point for a minute or two, she interrupted and said, "Okay, I'm sorry I woke you up, good night."

Now his phone was glowing and vibrating again. He groaned, looking at the digital clock on the nightstand before picking up the phone. It was 2:21 a.m. He keyed the phone.

"Honey," he muttered, "if you don't let me get some sleep, neither one of us is going to be worth squat tomorrow."

"I'm glad you're concerned for my well-being," Angela Conrad said, "but I don't think our relationship has progressed to the point of you calling me honey."

"The timetable has been moved up," she continued after a chuckle at his expense. "We need to meet, now."

"But it's after two o'clock in the morning!" he protested.

"When did you *think* we were going to meet," she snapped, "after five at the bar over drinks?"

"Okay, *where*?" he croaked.

"Drive north from your hotel on First Street. There's a Denny's two miles up the road. Wait inside for my call. If you're not there in ten minutes, I'll have one of your children killed."

"*What?*" he gasped.

She let out a cruel laugh. "Adrenaline's a hell of a lot better than coffee, isn't it? Now that you're awake, get your ass out of bed and *move*." She disconnected the call.

SACRIFICIAL OFFERING

AUGUST 21, 2002

CIA OPERATIVE TRAINING FACILITY – CAMP PEARY, VIRGINIA

Gavin Carter entered the cinder block interrogation room where the woman in the orange jumpsuit was locked down. Angela Conrad glared at him, seated at a steel table and chair both bolted to the floor. The chain between her handcuffs fed through an eyelet fastened to the table. The chain on her leg irons led through another eyelet secured in concrete. The room was built for simulated interrogations, to give the recruits a realistic taste of being "on the wrong side of the table" should an operation go badly.

There was nothing simulated about today's detention. A camo-clad Special Protective Officer stood behind her against the wall. Another SPO stood just inside the door. Neither took his eyes off Conrad for a second, especially the SPO sporting a fresh welt under his left eye.

"Could you gentlemen excuse us for a few minutes, please?" Carter asked politely.

"Sir, our orders…." The nearest SPO protested.

"Are being superseded. By me." He held up his CIA ID badge with the gold border, indicating "seventh floor" clearance as a member of the CIA Director's staff.

The SPOs hesitated, not used to being overruled on their own turf.

Carter jerked his head toward the TV camera just beneath the ceiling in the corner. "You can keep an eye on her from there. If she gets loose I promise to hold her off till you can come rescue me."

Frowning, the SPOs complied.

Carter placed two bottled waters on the table. "Pick one," he said.

Conrad lifted an eyebrow. "Excuse me?"

He pushed the waters forward. "Let's have a drink. As a gesture of trust, you pick which bottle, in case you think I might have tampered with them." It was the same opening he had used with a Hezbollah terrorist he had interrogated in Beirut after the barracks bombings in 1983. Conrad looked every bit as hardened as that subject had been.

She rolled her eyes. "Not thirsty."

Carter sat down in the chair bolted to the floor across from her and twisted the cap off one of the bottles. "This is going to be a long conversation. When we're done, you will be." He raised the bottle to his lips and took a swig.

"That one," she said.

He lowered the bottle. "I'm sorry?"

She nodded toward him. "That one. I want the one you just drank out of."

Carter suppressed a smile. This was one cynical young lady. "Of course," he said pushing the opened bottle across the table.

Conrad tried to drink from the bottle, but the wrist chains were too short for her to complete the maneuver.

He half-rose from his chair. "May I?"

She set the bottle down in frustration. "Sure."

Carter rounded the table and held the bottle up to Conrad's lips. After a couple of swallows she nodded and he set the bottle back down.

"Thanks," she said quietly.

"No problem," he replied, returning to his seat. With the Hezbollah prisoner he had followed up the water with a Koran and told the man he was already facing Mecca if he wished to pray. Carter had even pulled his chair next to the man and recited a prayer he had memorized in Arabic as they both bowed their heads to the tabletop. He doubted that approach would work with Conrad. Instead, he folded his hands and stared until her angry eyes rose to meet his.

"What do you want?" she demanded.

"That was quite a performance you put on, Ms. Conrad," he said with a hint of admiration.

She scowled. "Call it my resignation letter."

"Were you out of stationery?"

A smirk. "A letter would have been filed and forgotten. What I did today will be part of Agency folklore *years* from now."

He nodded thoughtfully. "True enough. They might still be talking about it when you get out of prison, but I doubt it."

She smiled and shook her head. "I'm not going to prison. Not for long at least."

He sat back as far as his bolted chair would allow. "You seem pretty sure about that."

She leaned forward, her wrist chains clinking through the eyelet. "Once I start telling my story, you people will be tripping all over yourselves trying to cut a deal to shut me up."

He pursed his lips. "Really? Then start with me. What's your story, Ms. Conrad?"

She eyed him carefully. "Who the hell are you, anyway? I've never seen you around the training facility till today."

He held up his badge. "Gavin Carter. I'm the Director's special advisor for training."

She snickered. "Sounds like a post for a has-been."

Carter straightened in his chair until he was staring down at her. "You think you can take me, young lady?"

She looked him up and down. One corner of her mouth twisted upward. "You want me to tell you the truth or blow you some sunshine?"

Carter couldn't suppress his smile that time. "I'll take that as a yes. But I'm still waiting for your story."

Conrad lifted her shoulders with a deep breath, then exhaled slowly. "Okay, short version: Your…program…*sucks!*" When that didn't get a rise from him, she continued. "Everybody in this class joined for one reason—to get the bastards who attacked America on 9/11. Imagine our chagrin when we found a spy museum called a training facility filled with Cold War relics called instructors who wouldn't even last a night on the streets of downtown Philadelphia." She threw up her hands as far as the manacles allowed. "Jesus H. Christ! This chicken-shit outfit couldn't make a dent in Al-Qaeda if somebody aimed you straight at Osama Bin Laden and stuck a *rocket* up your ass!"

He regarded her dubiously. "Is *that* your get-out-of-jail-free card? Better not drop the soap."

She wrinkled her nose in contempt. "Cute. But the worst part of it is how you pigs treat women here. The girls in Class 11 are some of the smartest women I've ever met, but Old Boy's Network here *never* accepted us. Worse than that, some of the instructors actively sabotaged us. Four of the girls decided they had enough bullshit in their lives and left. Today it was my turn."

Carter nodded. "I'm aware of the high dropout rate among the female recruits. That's one of the reasons I'm here. What else can you tell me?"

She snorted. "What, you're on *my* side now?"

He leaned across the table until his folded hands almost touched hers. "I've been sent here by the Director of Central Intelligence to find out why women are dropping out of Class 11 four times faster than the men. You have my ear now, and I have the Director's ear. So if you really have something to say, now's the time."

Carter watched the wheels turn inside her head like tumblers in a safe as she decided whether to open up to him or not.

"I have evidence that one of the instructors routinely falsified test results to place the female recruits at a disadvantage," she finally confided.

"You *do*?"

She nodded slowly. "I do."

"Where did you *get* this evidence, if I may ask?"

"I broke into the instructor's office and stole it."

Carter almost choked. "You did *what?*"

Conrad rolled her eyes. "Oh, get off your high horse. You *do* teach us to pick locks around here, remember?"

He drew back slightly. "But breaking into an instructor's *office*?"

She frowned as if coaching a slow pupil. "When the girls began getting slammed on the evaluations, I started keeping track of who was doing the reviews, and who had the authority to make the bad marks stick when we appealed the evaluations. They all led to one man, Vince Scarpiti. You know him?"

He thought for a second. "He was the guy with the clipboard out at the course, right?"

"That's the dirtbag. The Scorekeeper."

"What did he *do*?

She made a growling noise in her throat. "When one of his misogynist buddies falsely raked one of the girls over the coals on an exercise, he backed them up. When somebody graded them fairly, he doctored the forms just enough to put the female recruits on the back side of the curve. One mistake and we were toast. Which explains the high dropout rate. We figured out the game was rigged."

"And you have *proof* of this?"

A very small smile. "I have the original doctored evaluation forms, including one about me he wrote last night."

He caught the emphasis. "And that one's special *why*?"

The smile got slightly larger. "Because it's grading an exercise that doesn't take place until *tonight*. He had some time to kill, so he just wrote up my unfavorable review for a surveillance detection exercise that hasn't even occurred yet."

He folded his arms. "Did you have any idea that you would catch him red-handed like that?"

She shrugged. "He gave me the perp look that evening when he left his office, but mostly it was just luck. A lot of good police work is that way."

"The perp look?"

The door buzzed, and a SPO laid a sheaf of papers on the table next to him. It was the evaluation forms for several female students. Apparently a search of her belongings had already been underway when the instructors on the other side of the wall eavesdropped on her accusation. He examined them carefully, finding the pre-dated evaluation form for Conrad's exercise scheduled for that night. "These are copies," he observed.

Conrad lifted her eyes to the ceiling and sighed. "You must think this is my first rodeo, cowboy. I *left* those copies for you to find. The originals are safely in the hands of a third party, who has instructions to hand-deliver the documents to Virginia Fletcher at the New York *Times* if they don't hear from me in three days."

Carter's eyes also rose to the ceiling. He heard himself mutter, "Oh God," involuntarily. Virginia Fletcher was both a vocal feminist and a profound critic of the CIA. The inquisition the Agency would receive from the media after Fletcher got hold of these documents would make a colonoscopy look non-invasive.

His curiosity somehow overcame his shock. "But how did you deliver this? Outgoing mail from students is very carefully checked." That he knew for certain, having pulled mail surveillance duty during one stint as an instructor here at the Farm.

"I lured a member of the cleaning staff aside and turned on the waterworks. She smuggled them out for me quite willingly. Oh, and don't even *think* about reprisals against her. She's under my protection. If she gets so much as a verbal reprimand, she's gonna stand right next to me at my press conference. And the Congressional hearings."

Carter heard someone shout, "*Son of a bitch!*" on the other side of the cinderblock wall.

Conrad heard it too. She lifted her wrists and raked the chain back and forth through the table eyelet, as if it had become a plaything for her. "So, now that we have our cards on the table, let me paint a picture for you. America is attacked on 9/11 and three thousand Americans are converted into smoke. To help compensate for the revelations that the CIA had its head *firmly up its ass* and had *no clue* what was going on, they dramatically expand their Human Intelligence activities, including the formation of Class 11, the most diverse and qualified group of students to ever walk through the Agency's doors. With me so far?"

Carter saw where this was going, but was powerless to stop it. "I'm with you."

She batted her eyes at him, smiling sweetly. "But how was that class treated? When we tried to innovate, we were slapped down. When we exposed the anachronisms and downright errors in the training program, we were shouted down by the Cold War leftovers you call instructors and threatened with expulsion. And those of us who had the misfortune to be born female were singled out for special treatment, including falsification of documents to try to drive us out of the program. In several cases, it worked. Still with me?"

His eyes dropped to the table. He could have told her his own stories about the misfortunes of being a black student at the Farm almost three decades previously. It sounded very familiar. "Still with you," he sighed.

She leaned forward, their faces only a foot apart. "So what do *you* think the American people will say about the CIA, especially the fifty-two percent who share my gender, when I release this information? There's already a significant minority opinion that the CIA's failures on 9/11 were *so immense* that the entire agency should be pulled up by its roots and replaced from scratch. Do you think that movement will gain momentum if I have to give interviews from my jail cell?"

Carter closed his eyes. Part of him wanted to slap Conrad hard enough to loosen teeth, but another part of him wanted to kiss her forehead. She had caught the bureaucratic dinosaur called the Farm out in the open. The chances that it would escape the spears of reform coming its way were now virtually nil. The training programs would be radically revised and many of the old guard shown the door. In the end the Agency would be a stronger place because of Angela Conrad's brazen maneuvers today. But the bureaucracy would demand a sacrifice in exchange, and that sacrifice's name was Angela Conrad.

Conrad held up her handcuffs. "I'd like these off, please. Now."

"Guard!" he called.

The door buzzed open immediately. "Yes sir?" the SPO asked.

"Process the prisoner for immediate transfer to detention."

The guard with the welt was happy to oblige. "Right away, sir!"

Conrad was incredulous. "*What?* After all that you're just going to ship me off to Leavenworth?"

"*Leavenworth*?" Carter laughed, standing and pulling out his phone. "You attacked CIA officers during a time of war. I'm making the call to have you classified as an enemy combatant. We're shipping your ass to Guantanamo Bay, honey."

ACTIVATION

PRESENT DAY – SAN JOSE, CALIFORNIA

Manning drove to the Denny's restaurant that Conrad had indicated. It was in San Jose's business district and obviously didn't see much traffic after the workday ended. Other than the disinterested waitress talking on her cell phone, the place was empty. Seeing the "Please wait to be seated" sign, he tried to get her attention. She made a face and pointed at her cell, gesturing "Can't you see I'm on the phone?" She then disappeared behind the counter into the kitchen, continuing to chatter away in Spanish.

Manning took that as a signal to seat himself. He discovered he wasn't completely alone. Two booths were occupied by sleeping homeless people. Assuming his waitress wouldn't be serving him anytime soon, he poured himself a cup of coffee, found a copy of yesterday's paper, sat as far away from the snoozing indigents as possible, and pretended to read.

His gut was in a knot. What the hell would Conrad demand of him next? He didn't even know what had piqued her interest in Nanovex, although he suspected it was related to whatever had killed those five workers. So, something dangerous. Why was he not surprised?

His phone vibrated in his pocket. The display read "Restricted Number."

"Yeah?"

"Get back on First Street. Three miles south there's a twenty-four-hour Kinko's. Take that paper you're reading and make some copies. But don't drive straight there. Make several turns and take at least fifteen minutes." She disconnected the call.

Seeing no sign of the waitress, he took a five from his wallet and dropped it in his still-full coffee cup. Abraham Lincoln looked up at him in distress as he submerged in the hot black liquid, the residue of a hundred people who had thumbed his face coming off in an oily sheen. "I know how you feel, Abe," Manning muttered to the drowning currency.

Miss Congeniality emerged from the kitchen just as he walked out the door, having finally wrapped up whatever matter of telephonic urgency had occupied her attention. "Your tip's in the cup," he said over his shoulder.

Back behind the wheel, he knew immediately what Conrad was up to. She would direct him around while watching from a distance until convinced he wasn't being followed. He had read enough spy novels to know the procedure. So the novels had proven accurate in at least one regard. If his life followed the storylines he was familiar with, this would eventually end with a bullet in his head. Angela Conrad was this novel's survivor, and he was just a "disposable character." His stomach sank.

As he made several turns, he noticed a pair of headlights far in the distance that matched a couple of his turns. He assumed it was Conrad. *But what if it wasn't*, he realized with a start. What would she do to him if he was already "burned?" He breathed a sigh of relief when the other vehicle pulled into a Taco Bell. After completing a circuit of the next block, he passed a car parked against the curb. It pulled in behind him. His heart skipped a beat when his phone buzzed.

"Okay," Conrad said, "you're clean so far. Proceed to your destination."

The car behind him slowly fell back as he proceeded, then continued south when he pulled in the Kinko's parking lot. He tried to get a look at the driver but it was dark. He only saw one person in the vehicle.

He tucked the paper under his arm and walked inside. Other than the clerk working on his laptop, this store was also deserted. Manning selected one of the copy machines facing the front windows so he could watch the street. After a few minutes, he noticed a car pull to the curb a block up one of the side streets across from the copy shop. The car's headlights went out, but he never saw anyone emerge.

After waiting several anxious minutes and making at least five dollars worth of copies, his phone buzzed again.

"Ari says you're clear," Conrad said. "By the way, nice move keeping your eyes on the street. You're finally pulling your head out of your ass. Drive south on First again until you hit West San Carlos. Turn right and drive to the strip mall in the 1600 block."

He gathered the results of his pointless labor. "And then where?"

She laughed wickedly. "It's the only store in the strip mall that's open. Come in and ask for Sunshine."

How come I have a really bad feeling about this, he wondered. He returned to the counter to pay for his worthless copies. He was concerned the clerk might be suspicious of the pointless exercise, but the bored college student was so fixated on managing his fantasy football league that Angela Conrad could have sectioned a corpse on one of the worktables without a protest.

Manning followed her instructions and pulled into a strip mall with several run-down stores. As Conrad reported there was only one shop still lit, a dingy hole with bars on the windows and SQUID INK TATTOOS on the marquee. A garish neon squid beckoned him inside with one of its animated arms. He swallowed hard and pushed on the door.

For a moment he thought he had stepped through a portal back into the Seventies. The darkness inside was broken only by infrequent black lights and lava lamps. But the music wasn't from any decade he remembered. The mind-numbing beat was punctuated by blasphemous howls that sounded like the death throes of the devil himself. The smells of sweat, cigarettes, antiseptic and pot swirled in a sickening mix. Pictures of the shop's customers lined the walls, people so disfigured by their body art that they resembled mutants from a science fiction movie. Disturbing drawings of dragons, snakes, and skulls filled the rest of the wall space, as examples of the "art" they would gladly inflict on your skin, he guessed.

He made a mental note that if any of these designs showed up in one of his sons' rooms he would immediately escort them to therapy. *But who am I kidding*, he reminded himself. *I'm never going to live to see my kids hit puberty, much less graduate to full-fledged juvenile delinquency.*

A stringy-haired derelict who was probably twenty years younger than he looked eyed him with an empty stare from behind the counter. "Help ya?" he asked.

"I'm looking for Sunshine," Manning asked reluctantly, not knowing exactly what the request would grant him.

The tattooed zombie motioned with what Manning first thought was a cigarette toward the back of the shop, depositing a puck of glowing ash on the counter in the process. He then cursed the vagaries of the universe that required him to relight his joint.

Manning pushed through a beaded curtain into a slightly better-lit back room. Angela Conrad lay face down on a padded table, naked below her waist. A young woman whose hair was dyed black with pink and purple streaks bent over Conrad's bottom wielding a tattoo pen. In addition to half a dozen piercings in each ear, the tattoo artist had a silver stud through her lower lip and left nostril. Tattoos of roses grew down her right arm and a flaming dragon snaked down her left, with a winged skull leering down her cleavage.

"You must be Sunshine," he observed dryly.

The young woman looked up. She wore so much eyeliner she looked like a raccoon in reverse. "Yo!" she said with a deep, smoker's voice. "Angela, your man!"

Conrad shifted her head, careful not to move any other part of her anatomy. "Hi honey, come over and look at what Sunshine's done so far!"

Manning walked hesitantly to the tableside, fully expecting some kind of deadly trap from even a prostrate Angela Conrad. A series of tattooed shapes curved from near the crack of her bottom to the top of each of her muscled buttocks in a funnel shape like a pair of thong underwear. Each tattoo was only the size of a nickel and would be covered by all but the most risqué lingerie. He supposed that was by design. He saw a star, a wolf, and a lightning bolt. The rest were covered by Sunshine's hands as she worked on a camel on one side and a fox on the other.

Sunshine looked up and winked. "Doesn't she have the most perfect ass you've ever seen?"

"Y-yeah," he stammered, "it's a thing of beauty, all right." *Okay, I've heard of looking into the heart of darkness, but this is something else entirely.* Every further revelation into Angela Conrad's world made him more convinced that he would not be returning home to Chicago by any manner except in a box.

"Any, uh, *significance* to those tattoos?" he asked tentatively.

"*Well*," Conrad said in a breathy voice, perfectly following her cover that they were lovers, "This one is for Rashid, you remember him?" She touched on the side of her hip where Sunshine was putting the finishing touches to a camel.

Ohhh God, he thought. "And the fox?"

"You never met him," she said in a matter-of-fact tone.

What the hell? I'm dead anyway. "So, do you get a tattoo for *every* man you kill?"

Conrad laughed so hard Sunshine had to lift her tattoo pen. “Oh sweetie, I don’t have enough skin for that. I only get a tattoo for men I sleep with, *then* kill.”

Sunshine slapped Conrad’s naked thigh playfully. “Oh Angela, you are such a kidder! *Bad* girl!”

Conrad giggled vacuously, like she had poured her brains from a peroxide bottle that morning. “So Mike, when I’m done here why don’t you hop up and let Sunshine draw something on that cute butt of *yours*?”

“I…don’t…think….”

Conrad was relishing her act. “Oh, come on, turn around and show Sunshine that tight little ass.” She made a twirling motion with her hand. “Come on, turn, turn.”

He reluctantly modeled for them in his jogging sweats. It was the only thing in his suitcase besides suits and dress shirts. He didn’t know what the dress code was for a nocturnal covert meeting, but he was pretty sure it wasn’t a suit.

Conrad giggled. “I think getting ‘Amanda’ and a little heart tattooed on your tush could go a long way towards marital harmony, don’t you think, Sunshine?”

Sunshine looked up from her work. “Amanda?”

“His wife.”

Her eyes went wide with understanding. “Ohhh, so *that’s* the reason for the late night rendezvous, huh?”

Conrad giggled again. “Look! He’s blushing!”

Sunshine looked up again, this time with more than casual interest. “He *is* kinda cute. Would you guys like a third?”

Conrad reached back and patted Sunshine’s thigh. “I’m still breaking him in, sweetie. Maybe next time.”

Third? Breaking him in?

Sunshine lifted her pen and gently swabbed the new tattoos with alcohol. “Okay, there you go!” She wagged a finger at Manning. “Now, no spanking for a few days, okay?”

Conrad laughed hard enough to make her butt cheeks quiver. “Oh honey, *I’m* the only one who administers the spankings in this relationship!”

Sunshine ran her long black fingernails down Conrad’s bare leg. “Oooh, my kinda girl! Let me know if you change your mind!”

Conrad hopped down from the table. “I will! Thanks for fitting me in on short notice.” She gathered her pants, purse, and knee-high boots from a nearby chair, but made no move to clothe herself.

Okay, I still don’t know if she’s a real blonde, but I have learned something else interesting about her, he thought.

"Oh, no prob!" Sunshine beamed. "You have the room for an hour." She winked at Manning. "Longer if you need it!"

Conrad leaned over the table to push a twenty deep into Sunshine's tank top and gave her a lingering kiss. "We just might," she finally said. The image of Conrad bent over the table on tiptoe was not one he would soon forget.

She then walked over and grabbed him by the shirt. "This way, lover!"

Conrad led him down a flight of steep, dark stairs into another dimly lit room. The chamber held an X-shaped cross with straps, a whipping stand, a sex swing, and several other pieces of furniture of whose function he was too terrified to ask. Whips, chains, paddles, and other frightening implements hung from hooks on the walls. A fierce, phallic-looking squid painted on the wall wielded a different tool of punishment in each tentacle. The room reeked of stale bodily fluids, almost making him gag.

"Oh *God*," Manning exclaimed. "You gotta be kidding!"

"Shut up!" she snapped. "They have a camera down here for security, so you're going to be my nice little submissive and strap yourself into those manacles hanging over there."

Like hell I am. "Really? What's your Plan B?"

While his attention was diverted by the horrors before him, she had armed herself with a riding crop, which administered a sharp slap of pain to his thigh. "You're...going...to do..." she barked, with each pause accentuated with a hot swat of leather, "*Everything*...I say...because...I *said* so!"

He backpedaled away from his attacker in the confined space, each smack of the crop coming closer to a part of his anatomy he didn't wish permanently injured. With shaking hands, Manning fastened the hanging leather manacles around each wrist. There was enough slack in the chains to perform the deed himself, but as soon as he secured the last buckle Conrad threw an unseen lever and the clanking chains jerked his arms toward the ceiling and off his feet. He managed to get his legs back under him, but realized to his alarm that his jogging pants and underwear were now around his ankles.

Conrad stepped before him a few moments later, smacking the crop against her palm. She had put her leather boots back on, but was still naked from the waist down. She looked relaxed; she was apparently quite comfortable with her body.

"In case you haven't figured it out, you and I are about to go operational at Nanovex."

He squirmed in his fetters, wishing he hadn't secured himself so well. "Okay, I gathered that much. But why are we taking the detour into S&M land?"

That earned him three more hard swats on his legs. "Number one, because I *can*, number two, because I *like* it, and number three, because you *don't*."

His pain and anger momentarily blocked out his self-preservation instinct. "You're fucking *out of your mind*, did you know that?"

Conrad lifted a very delicate part of his anatomy with her crop. "You seem to forget who's holding the whip. Do you need to be reminded?"

He swallowed. Dying was a certainty. Torture he might be able to avoid. "No," he said.

The crop came up to strike. "Excuse me?"

"No, *ma'am!*" he quickly corrected.

She stowed the crop behind her back and began to pace, like a British officer from a WWII movie. Except for the half-naked part. "Much better," she declared. "I was hoping to spend more time moving the pieces into place, but events have overtaken us. I need you to help me quickly lay the groundwork for a theft from Nanovex."

He tensed. "Can I ask what we're stealing, or will that earn me another smack?"

"It's a project called WICKER BASKET. *I'm* not even sure what it is exactly, but it involves nanotechnology, it's already killed five people, and there are folks willing to kill a bunch more to get their hands on it."

He seemed to remember reading a passing reference to WICKER BASKET in one of Jacob Fleischer's documents, but had attached no significance to it at the time. "What kind of folks?"

"Folks like Rashid Ben-Jabir, folks like a guy you'll be reading about in the paper tomorrow named Meir Eitan, and folks all over the planet just like them looking for shiny new ways to kill their fellow men in large numbers."

A cold ball formed in his stomach. "And you're going to *help* them?"

She stroked his cheek gently with the crop. "It's what I *do*, sweetheart. I steal things and sell them to the highest bidder."

"So you're *not* CIA?"

"Well, I *was*," she said defensively. "I just found something a little more profitable. Just like *you* used to practice law, until you found out helping large corporations *break* the law was a *hell* of lot more profitable, right?"

He almost moralized about his practice not killing anyone, then remembered poor Ethel Rosencrantz dying of cancer because of the transformer plant next to her house. The transformer plant built by Chemtrox, the company he had protected from facing the consequences of its actions. "Okay, point taken. Can we lose the manacles now?"

"Not just yet. We still have to discuss *how* you're going to get the information I need to pull off the theft."

He rolled his eyes. "Hey, you picked the *wrong* guy to be your inside man, lady. *I* don't have access to any classified information. I'm just supposed to deal with the families of those five dead people, and I don't even know how they died!"

Conrad held up a finger. "Yes, but Doug Lyman knows, and you have access to *him*."

Manning would have thrown up his hands at that point, were they not already manacled to the ceiling. "What, like I'm just supposed to walk up and *ask* him for the company's deepest secrets? I'm pretty good at social engineering, but not *that* good."

She was undeterred. "The secrets are in his office."

He took a deep breath to keep from earning another stripe from Conrad's crop. "An office which is secured by a retinal scanner and a keycode, neither of which I have access to."

"But you *are* invited to his office from time to time, right?"

"At least once a day so far."

"Then we're in," she said cheerfully. She bent over her purse—another memorable image—and retrieved a small box. She opened and displayed it to Manning. "Here you go."

"We're going to steal Doug Lyman's secrets with a pen and pencil set?"

"Exactly."

"I'm missing something."

She stroked the bottom of his chin with the tip of her crop. "Mikey dearest, you're missing a lot more than you know, but I'm a patient mistress; I'll teach you as best I can. Now hold this," she said, forcing him to hold the crop with his teeth. "Whatever happens, don't drop that, or you'll be punished."

"*What?*" he protested around a mouthful of leather.

CHAPTER 10

EVACUATION COMMAND

APRIL 14, 1945 – BERLIN

Hans Kammler barely recognized the capitol of Germany as his driver threaded into the heart of the city. Because of his supervision of the Reich's far-flung research projects, he had not seen Berlin for over a year. It was now a war-torn ghost of its former self. Many familiar landmarks were now piles of rubble, and even in the buildings which escaped destruction he had yet to see an intact window pane. Soldiers who either appeared to be too old or too young to be in uniform bustled about with nervous energy, throwing up hasty fortifications against the imminent onslaught of the Red Army. The few civilians out on the streets wandered with zombie gazes, like they had awakened from a fever dream to find reality more horrible than their nightmares.

Passing through several checkpoints, the poorly clad soldiers eyed his crisp uniform and Mercedes staff car with ill-concealed envy. Only as they approached the Chancellery building did the hand-me-down uniforms and bolt action rifles of the *Volkssturm* citizen-soldiers give way to the dappled camouflage and modern automatic weapons of the SS manning the last few checkpoints. They were forced to park a block away from their destination. The pavement had been dug up and a Panther tank lay buried in the street with only its turret exposed. A similar fortification guarded the street in front of the Chancellery at the far end of the block.

The spit-and-polish honor guards who once stood like statues throughout the Chancellery building with their white gloves and gleaming black helmets had been replaced with hard-bitten veterans dressed for urban combat. Also gone were the rubber-glove searches to protect the *Fuhrer's* person. From the strained looks on their faces, Kammler guessed that more than a few of these guards had thought about putting a bullet into their Exalted Leader themselves.

A guard led Kammler to the stairs across from the Chancellery's vast bombed-out reception hall and down to the basement. Directly under the reception hall the top floor of the *Fuhrerbunker* reared up from underground. Past two more guards, he entered an airlock and made his way through the upper level where the officers, secretaries and other functionaries supporting Hitler lived. The bunker had been very recently completed and reeked with the dank smell of new concrete. With no time to install proper plumbing, fire hoses snaked across the floor supplying water and steam to the various rooms. Descending another set of stairs and past an armed SS colonel manning the sign-in book, Kammler made his way into the inner sanctum of the rapidly shrinking Nazi empire.

"Please keep your voice low," the colonel cautioned. "The *Fuhrer* has not risen yet."

"Of course, thank you." Kammler glanced at his watch. It was after ten a.m. No wonder this war was lost. He entered the lower bunker and knocked gently on the first door on the right side of the corridor. Down the hall an SS sergeant the size of a gorilla stood guard in front of another nondescript steel door. Kammler assumed the *Fuhrer* slept behind it.

"Enter," a voice answered.

He squeezed into an office with a desk and a short couch shoehorned into the tiny space. *Reichsleiter* Martin Bormann sat at the desk. Kammler did not recognize the Gestapo officer occupying the couch, on which a sheet and pillow were shoved untidily to one end. It was clear from his rumpled uniform Bormann had not left the bunker for days. Bormann did not speak until Kammler closed the door softly behind him.

Heinrich "Gestapo" Mueller [1]

"Ah, Kammler, meet Herr Mueller, our chief of security for the evacuation operation."

Kammler removed his gloves and returned the cold handshake. Looking into Mueller's hard, dark eyes, he knew he had finally met his equal. "Gestapo" Mueller had been the ruthless investigator and executioner after the failed assassination attempt on Hitler the previous year. Kammler was glad he only knew Mueller by reputation.

"I am sorry for my tardiness, *Reichsleiter*," Kammler said. "Russian aircraft are making the roads increasingly dangerous. I had planned to arrive hours ago."

Bormann waved off the apology as Kammler took his seat. "The Russians are crossing the Oder River as we speak, barely fifty kilometers from here. Just make sure you are back out of the city by sunset. Artillery shells could start falling at any moment. *Herr* Mueller, please update *Herr* Kammler on the evacuation." Kammler noticed that Bormann had dropped all references to rank. He was already thinking like a post-war civilian. And unlike the taut faces outside, Bormann looked completely relaxed, like the collapse of Nazi Germany was just another step in his prearranged plan.

"In accordance with *Herr* Bormann's directives," Mueller began, "we commenced six months ago to move assets and manpower out of Germany for their safekeeping. Two hundred of my best men have set up offices and operational bases in six different countries. Likewise we have converted our liquid assets into American dollars and moved almost $300 million overseas. With these funds we have set up hundreds of front companies in every conceivable business interest, from raw materials to shipping. Nationals in the host countries will occupy the top posts in each front organization, while our cash provides the true controlling interest behind the scenes. Whatever we need for our future objectives, one of our front companies will be able to provide in a completely legal manner. We will be hiding, as they say, in plain sight."

"And what *are* our future objectives?" Kammler asked.

"In the short term, survival," Bormann said. "The Allies will be thinking of little else but putting all of our necks through the noose for a few years. We will have to be on the move constantly and be able to change our identities like chameleons for a while. That will take cash, safe havens and transportation, all of which *Herr* Mueller's organization will provide. But eventually their interests will turn to other things, and we will regain some freedom of action. And for you, Kammler, that means continuing development on that precious Bell of yours."

Kammler was cautious in his criticism. "*Herr* Bormann, with a prize as great as the Bell, surely we cannot expect the Allies to stop looking for it. General Patton has turned the thrust of his entire Third Army towards Pilsen and is advancing faster than his supply lines can keep up. This cannot be a coincidence."

"Of course it isn't," Bormann agreed. "But as long as you destroy all evidence of your research before you evacuate, they will be advancing on an empty well."

He continued his judicious fault-finding. "Of course, I can destroy the records and any hardware we are not taking with us, but I have many more scientists working for me than I can bring along with me on the aircraft. The Americans will eventually pressure them to talk. Then it will not matter where we run, the Americans will never stop looking for the Bell once they know what it portends."

Bormann and Mueller exchanged a knowing look. "Are you familiar with the procedure of Final Security, *Herr* Kammler?" Mueller asked.

"Of course, but only with respect to our slave labor force..." his voice trailed off as he realized what Mueller proposed.

Mueller smiled. "I see you understand."

Mueller's Final Security certainly solved some of his problems, but it created others. "I am concerned about Professor Gerlach. The Bell was his brainchild, but he is old and has refused relocation. He wishes only to return home. If I kidnap him he will most likely become a security risk, but if I kill him not only will I lose an invaluable resource, his death will raise as many questions as it silences. He *is* an internationally known scientist, after all." Gerlach's contributions to the *Stern-Gerlach* experiment which won the Nobel Prize for Physics was the primary reason his proposal for a concept as radical as the Bell was taken seriously to begin with.

Mueller's eyes burned with a corrupt flame. "I'm sure you can devise a means of persuading Professor Gerlach to hold his tongue that falls short of the slit trench."

Kammler immediately caught his meaning. "Indeed, *Herr* Mueller."

Bormann beamed like the Devil watching his minions discuss the fate of the damned. "I also need to speak with you about Kurt Debus."

Kammler was confused. "Debus is firmly committed to our cause and is looking forward to continuing his work in our new location."

"Indeed he *is* committed to our cause. So much so I must remove him from your care. I have a project of even greater import I need to entrust with him."

Kammler raised an eyebrow. "Losing Gerlach *and* Debus will be a great setback for the Bell project. May I ask what task he will perform that cannot be delegated to one of *Herr* Mueller's men?"

Bormann continued regarding him with a devious smile, like a chessmaster thinking three moves ahead of his opponent. "When I made my deal with Mr. Dulles of the OSS[2], he drove a very hard bargain concerning our scientists. He made it quite clear that he expects us to produce *Herr* Debus because of his work with Von Braun on the V-2. But this gives us the chance to place a man loyal to us in the enemy's camp. Debus will prove an excellent advisor to the Americans, but he will also keep us apprised of their every move. He will likewise be a point of contact back to the scientists we are surrendering. Debus will make sure that, in the end, they understand who they *really* work for."

Kammler nodded, genuinely impressed. "Ingenious, *Herr* Bormann. But what if the Americans discover this relationship?" He asked this not in doubt, but merely to probe how deep Bormann and Mueller's contingency planning ran. His future depended on the thoroughness of their stratagems.

Bormann shook a scolding finger at him, his smile never wavering. "Why don't you just *ask* to see my trump card, Kammler? Oh, very well, you certainly deserve to know." He leaned over his desk and lowered his voice, as if the secret he was about to share was even darker than the treason they were already conspiring ten meters from their sleeping *Fuhrer*.

"*Herr* Mueller has developed an exquisite source inside the American atomic bomb program. It seems that one of their Congressmen has a rather perverse penchant for…"

"*Herr Reichsleiter*," Mueller cautioned.

Bormann held up his hand. "Indeed, Mueller. The source is too important to joke about. But what he *revealed* is that even after three years and two billion US dollars, the Manhattan project has only purified enough uranium and plutonium for one-half of one critical mass for an atomic weapon.[3] They are quite literally stuck in a ditch." His evil smile broadened. "We will help *un*-stick them. We will provide them not only with *two* full critical masses, but we will provide them with a working uranium bomb identical to the one we detonated last month. They are being loaded on a U-boat as we speak and Mr. Dulles has informed his Naval Intelligence forces to be ready to receive it." [4]

Kammler blinked. "I'm speechless, *Herr Reichsleiter*."

Mueller leaned forward. "We would not have this leverage without your outstanding efforts, *Herr* Kammler. We are in your debt. Of course we are not giving away *all* of our leverage. We are retaining our last remaining uranium bomb and have placed it on a U-boat for safekeeping. We have informed Mr. Dulles that should his government press too hard on our organization, there could be a most unfortunate incident in New York, or London, or even Los Angeles. He fully understands our willingness to use extreme measures."

Bormann completed the thought for him. "And once the Americans use the bomb material we are providing them on Japan, they will have completed their contract with the devil; if they pressure us in any way, we will reveal the true source of the bomb to the press, and America's illusion of technological superiority will vanish like smoke.

"But what we will *not* share," he continued, "are the secrets of the Bell. The areas of physics the Bell has unlocked make jet fighters and atom bombs look like child's play in comparison. No, these secrets are reserved for National Socialism, and those of us who have proved worthy of carrying her torch. We will develop them in secret, until Germany is strong enough to receive us again."

"So your task, *Herr* Kammler, is perhaps the most important in our organization," Mueller observed. "Without the future technological superiority the Bell promises, Germany will never have the strength to rise from the ashes that surround us. The agents and front companies we have created are merely the vehicle. Your project is the payload. Guard it jealously, for without it our toil is for naught."

Bormann chuckled, reaching into a desk drawer. "But while your task is the most important, mine is without question the most difficult. I must babysit this madman until he is desperate enough to drink *this*." He placed a small vial of cyanide on his desk. "Would you like one, Kammler? I have what you might call a lifetime supply!"

He held out his hand. "I will take two. One for my wife and one for my mistress. Perhaps I will get twice lucky!" Their laughter was tempered only by the proximity of the dozing dictator.

Mueller grew serious. "Kammler, I must talk with you about your 'death legend.' While the upper levels of the American government might eventually figure out your fate, unless you can convince the lower level Army investigators that you died in battle or took your own life, they will do their best to root you out. What are your plans?"

"I have developed a close relationship with my driver, Klaus. I believe I can persuade him to testify that I swallowed one of these cyanide ampules and he buried my body along a forest road in Czechoslovakia. If they ask for the location, he will simply lead them to an empty spot in the woods and claim mistaken recollection when they fail to exhume the body. I presume *Herr* Mueller can provide the financial inducements for Klaus to stick with his story, *ja*?"

Mueller nodded. "*Jawhol.* Tell your driver his military pay will continue indefinitely as long as he holds your secret."

"That should prove sufficient," Bormann said. "I, on the other hand, must go to greater lengths. Herr Mueller went to the trouble of finding a Polish POW my height and weight and altered his teeth to match my dental records." [5]

"*Mein Herr!*" Mueller cautioned.

Bormann grinned, obviously very proud of his arrangements. "I am just warning Kammler that some very convincing reports of my death will surface once the *Fuhrer* has gone on to Valhalla, and not to be alarmed."

"And what if *Herr* Kammler is captured?" Mueller challenged. "What will become of our intricately laid escape plans then? I believe *kaput* is the word you're looking for."

Bormann was suitably chastised. He glanced at Kammler. "You can see why I keep him around, *ja*? *Herr* Mueller keeps me on my toes. In my absence, please regard his directives as my own, even if your current ranks place you as equals."

Kammler stood, sensing his dismissal. "You have my word, *Herr* Bormann." How odd it sounded to address the *Fuhrer's* second in command as just another civilian. A taste of things to come, perhaps. But he was grateful Bormann had cleared up the chain of command between himself and Mueller. They were both major generals, and arm-wrestling matches over seniority would be both vicious and counter-productive. The man was obviously competent, which would be a welcome change.

Bormann and Mueller stood as well. “Oh, by the way,” Bormann added, “Goering or Himmler may make a demand in the name of the *Fuhrer* for one of your evacuation aircraft. Goering is looting the *Fuhrer’s* country estate ahead of the Russians and Himmler just wants to save his own skin. Please make sure those two *dummkopfs* do not escape, by air at least!”

Kammler was delighted Bormann shared his estimation of his now-former commanders. “It will be my pleasure, *Herr* Bormann. Safe journeys, to both of you!”

Bormann reached into his desk drawer again and withdrew a bottle of cognac and a single crystal glass. He poured three fingers worth into the tumbler and passed it around like an unholy communion chalice.

“To the Fourth Reich!” he toasted.

HANGOVER

PRESENT DAY – SAN JOSE, CALIFORNIA

Mike Manning collapsed into his chair at his Nanovex office. After being released by Angela Conrad at dawn that morning, he only had time to shower and change before reporting to work. Actually he had showered twice, and still felt unclean. He shifted uncomfortably in his seat, sore from the multiple swats of Conrad’s crop. He shuddered.

He groaned and ran his hands over his face. Part of him just longed for this job to be complete so Conrad could put a bullet in him and be done with it. He was grateful at least he wouldn’t be considered “tattoo-worthy” by Conrad’s standards. Just as well. As a lawyer, his tattooed ideogram would probably be a weasel or a snake.

He sighed and reached into his briefcase, pulling out the pen and pencil set she had given him the night before. It looked conventional enough. He had no trouble getting it through Security in the Nanovex lobby, even with a thorough search of his case.

He opened the box and removed the pen and pencil. They seemed a bit heavy, but otherwise quite ordinary. They even worked as writing utensils, although Conrad had warned him not to waste them for that purpose. Too easy to drop and break them, she cautioned. He set them aside and carefully pulled the pen tray out of the box as she had shown him. A slender black box rested underneath.

“Gift from your wife?” he heard.

He looked up with a start. Doug Lyman stood in the door of his office, looking at the pen and pencil set intently.

"Oh-uh, yeah," he stammered. "She knows I like these Mont Blancs. Damned if she didn't FedEx a set to the hotel as a surprise." He held the pen up for misdirection as he casually closed the box with his other hand. Thankfully, Lyman's eyes followed the hand with the pen.

"Birthday?"

He made a pained face. "Actually more of a peace offering. She didn't handle my sudden departure very well. I guess this is her way of saying all is forgiven."

Lyman nodded. "Good woman, there. Give my secretary your home address; I'll send her some flowers for stealing you away on short notice."

Dammit, why do I have to stab this guy in the back? "That's very thoughtful of you, Doug, thanks."

"Mike, we've had another death," Lyman said. "I need to see you in my office, now."

"Let me grab my pad and I'll be right there."

Once Lyman left, Manning reopened the pen case, the tray still lying out on the desk. He extracted a slender black box. Stuck to the bottom with a weak adhesive, it peeled away smoothly. He found the tiny recessed button on the end of the box and pressed it with the tip of the pen. Next to the button, a small blue light glowed for one second, then went dark. The device was active. He stood, slipped it into his pocket, grabbed his pad, and made his way to Lyman's office.

SEVEN STARS

WASHINGTON, DC

Rafi Harel always tried to arrive for work at the Israeli embassy by 6:00 a.m. His job as Commercial Attaché kept him busy enough. Add in his responsibilities as Chief of Station for Mossad, and his days were routinely twelve hours or longer. Better to get an early start. When his cell phone buzzed at such an early hour, he knew the call had nothing to do with his cover responsibilities at the embassy.

"Harel," he answered.

"This is Ambassador Shavit," the caller announced brusquely. "Meir Eitan has been murdered in San Francisco."

"Murdered? When? How?"

"Last night. The man from the American State Department was very economical with the details, but he made it clear that Mr. Eitan was apparently not as retired from the Institute as his diplomatic credentials suggested."

The Institute was Mossad's official name, the Institute for Intelligence. So Meir had been killed in the field, during an operation. But the question remained, by whom and doing what? Harel certainly had not tasked him with a mission.

"Do they have any suspects?" he asked. While no one *really* retired from the Mossad, Eitan was *officially* retired, which would place Harel in a difficult position if Eitan had been running an unauthorized operation in San Francisco.

"They wouldn't say much over an unsecure line. They invited me to join a secure teleconference an hour from now. I want you on that call as well."

"Certainly, Mr. Ambassador."

"So what was Meir Eitan up to?" the ambassador pressed.

This is also an unsecured line, you moron of a political appointee! "Truly, Mr. Ambassador, I was told Meir had retired from the Institute. My understanding was that the *Chargé* position was a reward for his long service to the state of Israel."

"*Stom ta'peh!* Give me break! Their State Department dropped a hint that they knew of an ongoing Mossad operation on the west coast. I have a feeling they are going to be asking some very pointed questions about that operation, and you had better have an answer that satisfies them. Whether it is the truth is not my concern, but as sure as Jericho's wall if someone's career comes tumbling down, it's not going to be mine! *Shalom!*"

* * *

Two hours later Harel had completed the conference call in the Ambassador's office. Although there had been a deep undercurrent of suspicion from the American State Department officials, they had been remarkably forthcoming with the details of Eitan's death. And while they did press him hard on the purported Mossad team deployed in the US, they were apparently anxious to avoid a diplomatic crisis.

Harel held to the line that Eitan may have circumvented the chain of command and run an operation without authorization. He pointed out that Eitan was twenty years his senior and may have felt that "checking in with the youngsters" was unnecessary. He had even invented a fiction that Eitan had regarded him as an *apparatchik* and not a true intelligence player, so he may have purposely cut him out of the loop.

However laughable these excuses might be, a professional would read between the lines and understand that whatever had happened, Meir Eitan was dead—so it was undoubtedly all his fault. "The dead man let the camels loose," as the Arab proverb wisely said. Harel gave the Americans and Ambassador Shavit his assurance that he would get to the bottom of the matter, and if an unauthorized Mossad team was in play, they would be recalled.

After the meeting, Harel made his way to the code room in the embassy's basement. The new communication specialist Rachel greeted him warmly. Like a generation of spies before her, she would prove her readiness for field operations by careful handling of the mundane but necessary details of this room. She had not agreed to the *true* path of upward mobility—sleeping with the station chief—but she was competent and cheerful nonetheless. Someday *she* might be the one giving the orders here.

"Rachel, I need access to the Seven Stars network."

"Of course, sir," she replied. In accordance with security measures developed at the cost of human lives, certain systems in the code room could not be operated by a single person, no matter how high-ranking. Seven Stars was one of those. She walked to a terminal in the corner and entered her password. In accordance with procedure, she then took a seat where she could not see the screen, but could watch Harel to make sure he did not take notes or make any attempt to transfer data from the system.

"Thank you, Rachel." He then entered his password and a screen appeared:

SEVEN STARS
ENTER OPERATION CODENAME: ________

Harel entered: ARUHAT SCHITUT

After a short pause, text scrolled on the screen:

ARUHAT SCHITUT
202-966-3825
YITZHAK
UNCLE NAHUM
SEA BASS
EARTHQUAKE
GOLDEN GATE BRIDGE
JERUSALEM POST
COUSIN JACOB

PROTOCOL EXPIRES IN 23:34:16

He saw by the ticking countdown at the bottom of the screen that if he did nothing, the team's communication plan would self-terminate in less than twenty-four hours, and they would return to Israel for lack of orders. Harel had no intention of letting that happen. He memorized the information on the screen and logged off.

"Thank you, Rachel, I now need access to the *Yahalomin*."

She returned to her workstation. “Of course, sir.” After several keystrokes she gestured to the phone at the adjacent terminal. “Line one on this phone, sir. Shall I leave the room?”

He gave her a patronizing smile. “Yes, please. Thank you very much.”

Once the door closed behind her, he lifted the receiver and dialed the number he had memorized. The *Yahalomin*, or Special Communications System, allowed Mossad to contact their agents without the calls being traced back to their embassies. Using phones purchased in each country by *sayanim*, or native Israeli sympathizers, the *Yahalomin* bounced his call through several cell phone and land line numbers before dialing the number of his actual call. The bounce sequence was changed with every call, and the *sayanim* were instructed by their handlers to disconnect some lines and set up others at irregular intervals.

Unlike the system the Americans used to contact their undercover operatives using satellite phones, the *Yahalomin* buried its signal in the electronic fog of normal cell phone traffic. Also, the *Yahalomin* was not encrypted—an encrypted call would immediately draw the attention of the American NSA’s codebreaking computers. Better to hide in plain sight using veiled language to conceal the real intent of the message. Israel did not have the virtually limitless resources of the United States, but they tried to be as clever as they could be with the resources they had. [6]

The Seven Stars system was another example. Named after the seven stars of the Pleiades star cluster, they represented the seven signal points of intelligence communication: Contact, Authenticate and Confirm, Recall, Release or Revise, and Acknowledgement. With them, he could take control of a team of operatives anywhere in the world.

The operative picked up the call on the second ring. “Hello?”

“Is this Yitzhak?” Harel asked in Hebrew. *Contact*.

A slight pause. “Yes, who’s calling, please?”

“This is your Uncle Nahum. How is your vacation going?” *Authenticate*.

“Very relaxing, Uncle. Thank you for the recommendation of the local sea bass. I tried some and it was delicious.” *Confirmed.*

“Have you seen the Jerusalem *Post* while you’ve been out of town?” At this point he could have used the term “earthquake” to cancel the team’s mission, or “Golden Gate Bridge” to release them to execute based on their most recent briefing, but instead he used the code word that indicated he was *revising* the team’s previous orders.

“No, I have not kept up with the *Post*. Is there news?”

“I’m sorry to inform you that your Uncle Meir has died.”

The operatives on the other end of the conversation were probably going to receive their final orders from Meir Eitan personally, so the extended silence that followed was understandable. "Does the *Post* provide any information on his death?" the agent asked.

Harel sighed. "The information is sketchy, but I think it is safe to rule out natural causes."

"That is *most* unfortunate," the agent said in a throaty whisper.

"Indeed. I'm sure you agree that your vacation must be cut short, but I do have a favor to ask before you return for the funeral."

"Of course, Uncle." The man's voice was strained. He must have known Eitan personally. That would make his next set of instructions easier.

"Your Uncle Meir had a friend at the community center where he worked. Her name is Angela. He was always very concerned about her well being. Would you locate her please? I fear her living conditions are ill-suited; please see to it that she arrives at a better place."

"Of course, Uncle Nahum. You have my word."

"Yitzhak?" he prodded.

"Yes, Uncle?"

"You must do this for me. *Ein fas.*"

Another long pause. "*Ein fas?*"

Harel's voice was firm. "*Ein fas.*"

"I understand, uncle. If I do not return in time for the funeral, will you stand with my family in my stead?"

"Of course, Yitzhak. You have my word."

"Then give my love to Cousin Jacob when you see him." *Message received and acknowledged.*

"I will see you in Jerusalem, Yitzhak. Good journey." Harel ended the call.

What he had *not* informed Ambassador Shavit was that since Meir Eitan had been contemplating retirement in truth and not merely for cover, Harel had been designated *heir apparent* for the Collectors' North American operations. Meir Eitan had been his mentor in that very covert and very illegal operation.[7] Although Harel did not know the objective, Eitan had requested a Mossad special operations team skilled in surveillance and theft for his personal use under the codename *Aruhat Schitut*, or Decadent Feast.

Following the American practice of using random word generators to assign codenames to operations, most Mossad missions had codenames like Sprocket Chop or Tempo Fork. Using a descriptive codename like Decadent Feast assured that when Harel passed Eitan's request on to the head of Mossad, also a member of the Collectors, it would be approved without question.

Now that Eitan was dead, any hope of sharing the fruits of whatever feast he had been preparing died with him. But loose ends needed to be tied up, and one of those was his murder. The American briefing had been clear; whoever murdered Eitan was knowledgeable and skilled in Israeli methods. Since the only Mossad operatives on the west coast other than Yitzhak's team died with Eitan, that only left ex-Mossad agents and contractors. Eitan was fond of using that ex-American spy Angela Conrad as his go-to girl, and she had an ex-Mossad agent on her squad. Harel had never trusted Conrad, but Eitan had a soft spot—or perhaps it was a hard spot—for her. That had probably been his downfall.

But now Harel was in charge. He contacted the San Francisco consulate and instructed that when Agent Yitzhak made contact, they would give him full access to Eitan's computer and files. He was confident they could use that information to find Conrad and her team. He pushed away from the code room desk and prepared to return to his office.

"That bitch is as good as dead," he muttered under his breath.

DISAPPEARED

AUGUST 22, 2002 – GUANTANAMO BAY, CUBA

To Gavin Carter, the only thing worse than Cuba in August was being in a suit in Cuba in August. Within three minutes, the tropical sun teamed with the oppressive humidity to soak his shirt to his chest as effectively as if he had stepped into a hot shower. Rivulets of sweat also ran down the faces of the camouflage-clad MPs accompanying him, but since they didn't complain about the heat, he didn't either.

Carter watched the prisoner being unloaded from the private jet. The white Gulfstream V, tail number N379P, was known within the Agency as the "Guantanamo Express." Purportedly registered to Premiere Executive Transport of Delaware, it was in fact a wholly-owned CIA aircraft, launching from a strip in South Carolina to pick up suspected terrorists from around the world and deliver them to Gitmo Bay for interrogation and long-term detention. Today's "pick up" flight had been short, from South Carolina to Camp Peary, Virginia before turning south for Cuba.

Because of the prisoner's propensity for violence, security measures for the transfer had been ratcheted up from excessive to extreme. In addition to the obligatory wrist shackles, leg irons, hood, blackout goggles and ear suppressors, a guard at the top and bottom of the jet's stairs both handled a "strangle stick," a six-foot orange fiberglass tube with a steel cable fed through it, looping at the end around the neck of the prisoner. Both guards kept their distance and had one hand firmly around the lanyard that could choke their captive into unconsciousness. The detainee wouldn't be making any trouble today. *First time for everything,* Carter mused.

He returned to the air-conditioned interrogation suite and made himself comfortable while he waited for the prisoner to be delivered. She arrived strapped to a gurney, which the guards rotated into a standing position. With a gesture from Carter, they nodded and left the room. He stood and walked to the prisoner. Slowly, he removed the earmuffs, the goggles, and finally the hood.

Angela Conrad glared at him. "Oh, you again. I was hoping at least for someone threatening." Then her nose wrinkled and she sniffed the air. "What's that?" she demanded.

He stepped aside, revealing a dinner setting for two on the interrogation room's shiny steel table. "It's filet mignon. Hungry?"

Conrad feigned disinterest, but her stomach growled loudly.

Carter laughed. "You're not the first hard case I've dealt with whose stomach gave them away. I'll make you deal. You agree to behave, and I'll give you a decent meal in return."

She sneered. "What's the catch?"

"Well, the first catch is I have to untruss you from this board, unless you want me to feed you by hand." He shrugged. "I will, if you prefer to stay tied up. Maybe you're into that."

"Not hardly. What else?"

"The only other catch is that you have to listen to an old man make conversation and at least *pretend* to be interested. If I sense your attention wandering, one wave of my hand and you're back on that board heading for a cell. A very unpleasant cell."

She stared at the steaming steaks on the table and swallowed. "Fair enough."

Carter bent to match his gaze with hers. "You'll behave?"

A barely perceptible nod. "I'll behave."

Carter clapped his hands together. "Good! I'm hungry, and I hate to eat alone."

After much pulling and tugging on leather straps and buckles, Conrad was freed. He was careful to make the last disconnection from behind the prisoner transfer gurney, with his back to the door should he need to make a hasty exit, but she stepped calmly off the board, her attention fixed on the food, not on him.

"Please, have a seat," he urged. He would have held the chair for her, but it was bolted to the floor. So much for chivalry.

Conrad sat, running her hand over the silverware, pausing for an instant over the steak knife before folding her hands on the table's edge. She waited for Carter to take his place across from her.

He transferred the folded napkin from the table to his lap. "Just so you know, a Marine sniper is on the other side of the mirror with a rifle aimed at your head," he said casually. "He had a dozen kills in Afghanistan from half a mile away. I don't think he'll miss from ten feet. Right, Gunny?"

She tensed slightly when the Marine loudly worked the action of his gun behind the glass.

"Besides," he said patting his Perry Ellis jacket, "this is a gift from my wife; I'd hate to get your brains all over it. So don't try sticking your knife in anything but the steak, okay?"

Conrad smiled sweetly. "Of course not."

This is one *dangerous* young woman, Carter reminded himself.

She grasped her silverware, but stopped short of cutting her first bite. "Okay, I get the whole enemy combatant routine, but what's with the table for two? Is this supposed to be my last meal or somesuch bullshit?"

He chewed thoughtfully on his perfectly prepared fillet. "Don't think of this as your last meal. Think of this as the first meal of the rest of your life."

She tapped the knife on the edge of her plate. "Good thing you told me about the shooter. Psychobabble makes me knife-happy."

He chuckled. "Then let me explain before your instincts get the best of you. Just like everyone else confined in this facility, you have been 'disappeared.' For all practical purposes, Ms. Conrad, you no longer exist."

Her hunger overtaking her need for an argument, she took her first bite of steak, letting out an involuntary moan when the delectable beef hit her taste buds.

Hardened against threats or discomfort, but softened by sensory pleasure, he noted. That could be useful information. He continued before she could swallow and retort. "Can you imagine, Ms. Conrad, how useful someone with your skills could be if they *no longer existed*?"

She ate with gusto, maintaining eye contact with her food rather than with him. "You seem to forget about Virginia Fletcher at the New York *Times*. I doubt she'll buy whatever fairy tale you've cooked up for my disappearance. She has experience cutting through Agency lies."

He extracted his cell phone from his jacket and slid it toward her. "Which is why you're going to call whoever is holding your insurance package and tell them to stand down."

She laughed around a mouthful of steak, almost choking herself. "And why the *hell* would I do something that stupid?"

He waited until she made eye contact. "Because I'm going to offer you something better than revenge against the Agency."

"Oh, I don't know. Dragging your collective asses over the coals sounds pretty damned good to me right now." She let her eyes rest on the unopened bottle of wine on his side of the table. "By the way, are you going to open that? Laughing at you makes me thirsty."

"Oh, where *are* my manners?" he said, reaching for the corkscrew. "But let me ask you a question." He tugged unsuccessfully at the stubborn cork.

She extended an arm across the table. "Would you like a real man to do that for you?"

"*Hands!*" the Marine behind the glass shouted.

She drew back, but Carter made a placating gesture toward the mirror. "It's okay, Gunny. She knows the score." He handed over the wine bottle.

Conrad tweaked the cork gently, eventually working it loose with a pop. She handed them back to him. "There. Finesse beats brute force every time."

He raised the bottle in salute. "My philosophy exactly. So, my question," he said as he poured, "is why *exactly* did you join the CIA?" He handed her the glass.

She swirled the wine and sniffed it cautiously, but did not drink. "Same as almost everyone else in my class, I guess. We wanted to get the bastards who killed three thousand Americans. Kind of primal, but very motivating nonetheless."

He poured a glass for himself. "No, I understand completely. Primal motivators are good. They're permanent. They're nonnegotiable. The problem is you can't have both."

"I'm sorry?"

"You can't have revenge on both Osama Bin Laden and the CIA. You'll have to choose in whose gut you'd like to twist the knife more."

Conrad made a show of surveying the inside of the interrogation room. "I don't know, that's a pretty tough call."

So, he noted, *revenge <u>is</u> her primary motivator. Maybe her <u>only</u> motivator.* He made a mental note to check much more deeply into Angela Conrad's history. Something very unpleasant lurked in this young woman's past, he was now certain.

He nodded. "Let me try to make it a little easier, if I can. First, the instructor who falsified the test results—Vince Scarpiti—he's gone. I made the call on the flight down. The SPOs walked him out when he showed up for work this morning. The Director hasn't decided whether pressing charges or throwing him out on the street without his pension will set a better example for the others. Either way, when the dust settles, he'll be lucky if he can get a job as a used car salesman."

That elicited a small smile. "What about the rest of the cavemen at the Farm?"

He sighed. "The Scarpiti investigation has just started, and I—I personally—am going to get to the bottom of this pile of crap if I have to dig in the manure with my own hands. But try not to take the attitude of the rest of the instructors too personally. They're creatures of rules."

She set down her glass. "Rules?"

"The CIA has rules because it's a bureaucracy. When people first go to work there, they tolerate the rules. Then they obey the rules. Then they identify with the rules. Then the rules become their reason for existence. Without the rules, they're nothing."

"Doesn't sound like much of an existence."

"Tell me about it. Which is why I'm asking you to stop worrying about the instructors. They're small fry. Let 'em go. You have more important things to consider."

She cocked her head. "Like what?"

"Like the job I'm about to offer you."

She made no effort to hide her disbelief. "*Really?* What kind of job?"

He placed his hand on the phone. "Before we get to that, you have to defuse the bomb you've planted."

She shook her head. "A phone call won't do it. Unless I show up in person, the package goes to Virginia Fletcher. And that was 72 hours after the package was delivered." She glanced at her wrist. "I don't know how much time you have left, they took my watch."

He glanced down. "It's 4:30 Thursday afternoon."

"You've got about 24 hours."

He leaned forward. "Then I give *you* my word that when the classified report on the Scarpiti incident hits my desk, you will be the second person to read it, right after me. If you're not satisfied by the number of scalps we hang out to dry, you can walk and take your package to Virginia Fletcher yourself. But you *have* to give me time to wrestle this thing to the ground, which means you defuse your bomb until that's done."

She leaned forward as well, pushing her plate away with her elbows. "When you say *walk…*"

"I *mean* walk, as in scot-free," he interrupted. "Once I got you here to Guantanamo, there *were* no charges against you, because you ceased to exist. But I had to make the staff at Camp Peary think I was sending you up the river, never to return."

She eyed him, almost connecting the dots. "Why?"

"Because the organization I'm recruiting you for doesn't exist either. The last thing I need is someone at CIA thinking of you and wondering, 'I wonder what happened to Angela Conrad?' Nope, they'll think you've been dropped straight into the Bermuda Triangle. Then they'll smile and go on their merry civil service way."

She swirled her wine glass again. "Tell me about this organization of yours."

He shook his head. “Sorry, doesn’t work that way. I get you out of here, we fly to whoever is holding your insurance policy, you put a temporary hold on it, *then* we talk about my job offer. But I *will* tell you this; it has a lot less of something you hate.”

“What’s that?”

He raised his glass. “*Rules*. A lot less.”

She raised her glass as well. “I’ll drink to that!”

PUBLIC RELATIONS

PRESENT DAY – SAN JOSE, CALIFORNIA

Lyman waved Manning over to the conference table when he entered the CEO’s office. “Close the door, Mike,” he said.

Manning did so and sat, readying his pen and pad.

“Last night a Nanovex employee died under suspicious circumstances,” Lyman confided. “Because of the ongoing operation involving the deaths of the other employees, the FBI immediately federalized the case. They’re sending an agent to brief us on the investigation later today.”

“When you say suspicious….”

“The FBI has told me almost nothing, other than to say the circumstances surrounding the death were highly unusual.”

“Okay, that’s got *my* curiosity up. Do we have a name?”

Lyman pushed over a personnel folder. “Joshua Martin Hackett, age 43, single, biologist.”

“Next of kin?”

“Raised by his mother, deceased. Only surviving relative is a sister in Sacramento. The FBI is trying to reach her now. Until that happens this has to remain confidential.”

He nodded. “Of course. You said the FBI called his death ‘highly unusual.’ Is there any chance of his death being related to what he worked on here at Nanovex?”

Lyman squirmed. “As a matter of fact, he worked on the same project as our five dead employees.”

Manning dropped his pen—thankfully not the one Conrad gave him. So Hackett worked on the same project that she wanted him to steal. She mentioned there would be other people willing to kill to get their hands on that technology. Could someone else be making a move on WICKER BASKET through its workers?

Lyman scowled. “Yeah, I can see what you’re thinking; a public-relations nightmare, right?”

Sorry, Doug, I have more immediate concerns than your PR. "Actually, I was wondering if this could be a delayed effect of the test that killed your other workers," he lied.

Lyman looked nauseous. "I suppose we can't rule that out until the FBI determines cause of death."

He gave the CEO his "don't shit with me" look. "So, let's say that it *is* related, how many other people could be exposed? Dozens? Hundreds?"

"Oh no, there were only ten people on the project at the time of the accident, including me. No one else got anywhere near that nanoagent."

"Well, thank God for small favors. Now, I know I *don't* need access to that project to do my job, but I *do* need you to level with me. If that FBI report even shows *traces* of your project, I *will* need to know, because we'll have to move very aggressively to protect your remaining people." He made an expansive gesture around him. "*All* of your people. Because if there's anything that elicits irrational fear in people it's technology run amuck."

"You have my word," Lyman said emphatically.

Manning tried to think of another four fingers' worth of people whose word he could take at face value like Lyman's. No luck. "So, when do you think we'll hear back from the FBI?"

The voice of Lyman's secretary over the intercom interrupted his response. "I'm sorry, Mr. Lyman, but the FBI is on line one."

"Speak of the devil," Lyman muttered, walking to his desk. "Thanks, Cathy, put them through."

Manning's back was to Lyman, but the glass in a framed picture on the wall reflected the CEO's image. Lyman became engrossed in his conversation and turned his chair to face the window. Now was his chance. Manning reached into his pocket and withdrew Conrad's black box. He peeled the backing paper off the contact adhesive and pushed the box hard against the bottom of the table. After checking Lyman's position again, he shoved the backing paper in his pocket and withdrew his handkerchief, wiping his fingerprints off the…whatever it was. Done.

Lyman hung up the phone. "The FBI will be here at three, Mike. I want you here too."

Manning straightened, extracting his hands from under the table. "Of course, wouldn't miss it."

Lyman excused him with a nod, so he rose and returned to his own office. He retrieved the Conrad pen from his desk and looked at it end on. He twisted the pen to retract the tip, then twisted another quarter-turn. A tiny blue light glowed inside the pen for one second. He placed the pen and pencil set in his center desk drawer and locked it.

He had followed her instructions exactly. He hoped it would be enough to save his life, but he doubted it.

FLASH TRAFFIC

NATIONAL SECURITY AGENCY, FORT MEADE, MARYLAND

NSA Mideast Section Manager Terry Thompson was almost out of his office for a meeting when the manager of the Z Desk, overseeing intercepts of Israeli communications, blocked his door. At six-foot-three with flame-red hair and beard, Jim O'Connor hardly looked like an expert in Hebrew, or "Special Arabic" in NSA vernacular. In fact, Z Desk—for "Zion"—was the only section in the NSA with a firm religious requirement.

After a number of embarrassing penetrations of the NSA by Americans of Jewish descent working for Mossad,[8] a Classified Presidential Executive Order established Z Desk, declaring that no one of Jewish descent by birth or marriage would be allowed access. The CPEO ordered any NSA director or Z Desk employee called to testify before Congress to deny the existence of the religious exclusion under oath or face imprisonment without judicial review.

O'Connor held up a striped folder. "Did you order this tasking of Mossad ops in DC?"

Thompson gathered the documents for his meeting. "No, that came straight from the Director's office. Apparently the Mossad chief of station in DC totally stonewalled a Justice investigation into the death of that Israeli *Chargé* in San Francisco. They want to see if they can catch the Israelis sweeping anything under the rug."

O'Connor waved the folder in his departing superior's face. "Yeah, well, we did."

"What? We sent out that tasking less than two hours ago."

"And it only took ten minutes to catch the Israelis with a broom in their hands. I just spent the last hour going over this with my staff to make sure it wasn't a false alarm. It's not."

Thompson set down his briefing materials. "Show me."

O'Connor flipped open the folder. "When we received the tasking, we set the computer to flag any voice traffic coming out of DC in Hebrew and sort them for intelligence keywords. This intercept floated to the top pretty quick. It was from a pay-as-you-go cell phone with a 202 area code to another 202 pay-go, *but*, the other phone was in San Francisco. It also flagged two keywords used by the Mossad."

Thompson scanned the document with his finger until he found the keywords the computer had highlighted. "It says, 'better place' and 'no miss.'"

"Right. Say if you found a terrorist who needed killing, you forward that info to Jerusalem, and they might tell you to, 'Send him to a better place.'"

"And 'no miss?'"

O'Connor's eyebrows rose. "That's the real kicker. The Hebrew is *ein fas*, and it means, 'Get it done or die trying.' It's *very* rare in Mossad codespeak, and drop dead serious."

Thompson's meeting was forgotten. "What the hell are they up to?"

O'Connor guided Thompson's gaze with his finger. "This is interesting. The caller, 'Uncle Nahum,' tells somebody named 'Yitzhak' that their 'Uncle Meir' had died."

"Wait a minute," Thompson interrupted, "wasn't the dead *Chargé's* name...."

"Meir Eitan," O'Connor answered. "Ex-Mossad, if there is such a thing. I met him at a conference in Paris once. My guess is he got caught with his hand in somebody's cookie jar and paid for it with his life."

"But whose cookie jar?"

"Look here—Uncle Nahum told Yitzhak to check in at the 'community center' where Uncle Meir worked and inquire about somebody named Angela, and if she is 'ill-disposed,' then 'see that she arrives at a better place.'"

"Go to the consulate, pull everything on 'Angela,' and if she's involved in Eitan's death, kill her or die trying."

"That's how I read it," O'Connor said. "But read further; after Yitzhak gets the 'no miss' order, he talks like he actually *is* going to die. 'If I don't arrive in time for the funeral, will you stand with my family in my stead?' He's asking Uncle Nahum to take care of his family."

"Which he swears to do."

"Right, then Uncle Nahum says, 'I'll see you in Jerusalem.'"

"So?"

"In the context of death and dying, 'I'll see you in Jerusalem' is like saying, 'I'll see you in the afterlife.'"

"Holy cow!" Thompson exclaimed. "So even his boss thinks he ain't coming back."

"Sure sounds like it."

Thompson squinted at the document. "So who is this *Angela* they want dead so bad?"

O'Connor shook his head. "It's got to be code for some country or a group. No *one person* could scare the Mossad this bad. But I *can* tell you who gave the kill order."

"Don't tease me."

O'Connor flipped to the back pages of the report. "We pulled the recording and ran it past the voice prints of the few Mossad operatives we have on file. We got a hit." He flipped to the photograph of a handsome, dark-haired executive in his late forties. The voice analysis on the next page read:

RAFEAL HAREL
MOSSAD COS – WASHINGTON, DC
VOICE PRINT IDENTIFICATION 93.7%

"Son of a bitch," Thompson whispered. He walked quickly to his desk and drew out a bright red folder with the word FLASH emblazoned on it. He wrapped it over the intercept report and handed it back to O'Connor.

"I'll call the Director and tell him Flash Traffic is on its way. You brief him. Go!"

The echo of O'Connor's running feet soon faded down the hallway.

[1] Photo credit: Wikipedia

[2] The Office of Strategic Studies, or OSS, was the forerunner of the CIA during World War II. Allen Dulles negotiated the surrender of German forces in Italy during *Operation Sunrise* as OSS station chief in Zurich and negotiated with Bormann only in fiction (as far as I know). He went on to become Director of the CIA in 1953. He was accused by many (including a Supreme Court Justice) of treasonous activities because of his suspected dealings with the Nazis before and after the war.

[3] A letter declassified in 1995 to President Roosevelt from Senate Armed Services Committee member James F. Byrnes confirms that all was not well in the American bomb project a mere five months before dropping the first bomb on Hiroshima. "I understand that the expenditures for the Manhattan project are approaching 2 billion dollars with no definite assurance yet of production." Yet less than six months later, the US had exploded a test bomb in New Mexico, and dropped two more over Hiroshima and Nagasaki, with the "pit" of yet another weapon under assembly at Hanover, Washington. Did the US receive help from an unexpected source? (Source: "*Reich of the Black Sun*" by Joseph Farrell, 2004, p. 56)

[4] The Germans loaded U-234, a specially built cargo U-boat, with the "crown jewels" of their war effort, including a V-2 rocket engine, a complete disassembled Me-262 jet fighter, and 560 kilograms of enriched uranium, along with the technical experts to help use them. This U-boat left Germany on April 15, 1945, one day after Kammler's fictional meeting with Bormann here. One of the experts aboard was *Luftwaffe* Major General Ulrich Kessler, the commander of the "special bombing wing" based in Norway that would have been tasked with the atom bombing of New York had Hitler's plan gone through. His expertise would have been indispensable when planning the atom bomb attacks on Japan. Sources: *Germany's Last Mission to Japan: The sinister voyage of U-234* by Joseph Mark Scalia (Chatham, 2000), *Japan's Secret War: Japan's race against time to build its own atomic bomb* by Robert K Wilcox (Marlowe, 1995)

[5] Bormann followed this procedure of "doubling" a concentration camp victim, in his case a Polish POW, to match his dental records, according to researcher Paul Manning, author of *Martin Bormann, Nazi in Exile*. An SS officer who accompanied Bormann on his escape from the *Fuhrerbunker* after Hitler killed himself led investigators to a decayed body beneath the rubble of a destroyed train station. The dental records matched that of Bormann, but when the SS officer was polygraphed in the 1960s about finding Bormann's body at the train station on the night of April 30, 1945, he flunked. But that fact was hushed up by the West German government, eager to keep Bormann's ghost dead and buried. Likewise Heinrich Mueller's family buried his body beneath a headstone "Our Beloved Daddy," but when the grave was exhumed by the Russians, they found *three* bodies inside, none of which matched Mueller's height or build. The real Mueller was never found.

[6] While there *is* a Mossad system called *Yahalomin*, or Special Communication System, my explanation in the text is pure conjecture. But while crafting the coded language my Mossad character would use on this system, I devised a seven–point communication standard that seemed plausible. I then found out that the code book that Mossad agents carry in the field is actually called a <u>Seven Star</u>. So I took the name and am probably closer to the truth than Mossad would like. (Source: *Gideon's Spies, the Secret History of the Mossad*, by Gordon Thomas)

[7] While the Collectors are wholly fictional, yet again I found a significant grain of truth. Mossad has a special branch called Al-Mossad, or "Above Mossad," that exists solely to steal intelligence and technology from the United States. It recruits only the most experienced Mossad agents and is totally firewalled from "normal" Mossad spying with its own computer,

payroll, and personnel systems. One of Al-Mossad's key operations was the penetration of Recon Optical of Chicago in the 1980's, stealing aerial recon technology that allows systems like the Predator drone to function. Israel then stole Recon Optical's business worldwide (it's easier to win contracts when you don't have to pay for the R&D) and hundreds of Americans lost their jobs. (Source: *Gideon's Spies, the Secret History of the Mossad*, by Gordon Thomas)

[8] Jonathan Pollard, an American-born citizen of Jewish descent and an employee of US Naval Intelligence, stole over one thousand classified documents totaling more than five hundred thousand pages of material between 1984 and 1985, including a ten-volume blueprint of the entire worldwide NSA electronic surveillance network. He was sentenced to life in prison in 1986 and has stayed there despite intense Israeli diplomatic pressure to have him released to Israel. To make matters worse, Prime Minister Yitzhak Shamir traded some of Pollard's secrets to Russia as a "goodwill gesture," hoping to improve relations with the Soviet Union. This exchange essentially gutted US intelligence gathering against Russia for a decade and resulted in the deaths of numerous CIA agents in Russia. My creation of Z Desk and the classified executive order are fiction, but after Jonathan Pollard, it would only make sense to move sensitive intelligence gathering against Israel to such a "carve out" to prevent Israeli cooption or extortion of American Jews at the NSA. (Source: *Gideon's Spies, the Secret History of the Mossad*, by Gordon Thomas)

CHAPTER 11

EMPIRE

PRESENT DAY – SAN JOSE, CALIFORNIA

"No *shit?*" Scott Hendrix exclaimed. "And the NSA called *us?* That's a first."

He had just pulled into a parking spot when his secretary reached him on his secure cell phone. So the Israelis *did* have a team on the ground, and they had orders to put Angela Conrad's head on a stick. *Well, get in line, Yitzhak.*

"Did the FBI get a copy of that report?" he asked his secretary. "Well, make a copy and hand carry it over to Perry Pugliano, pronto. We gotta keep those interagency cooperation brownie points coming. And besides, we'll need his manpower if we want to get to her first. Thanks, Tina. What? Oh, I'm just running an errand, personal business. I'll call you when I'm back on the clock."

He walked into the lobby and flashed his CIA badge.

"Welcome to Nanovex, Mr. Hendrix," the guard said. "I'll escort you to Mr. Lyman's office."

* * *

With all of the hullabaloo surrounding Meir Eitan's death, Hendrix hadn't had time to perform even cursory research on Doug Lyman. He didn't know if he was a Nobel laureate or a snake oil salesman. But the Nanovex facility was as impressive as hell and their security better than his own CIA office. The man himself exuded confidence and competence to go along with his executive haircut and firm handshake.

"Mr. Hendrix, thank you so much for fitting me into your schedule!" Lyman said.

Hendrix gave him a probing look. "You said this was a once in a lifetime opportunity—kind of hard to pass on an offer like that." *And you better not be wasting my time* was his unspoken message.

"I promise you won't be disappointed. Please, have a seat," Lyman said, waving him over to the conference table.

"Just us?" This guy Lyman must be pretty tech-savvy to not even need a geek for back-up.

"Just us," Lyman said, taking his seat at the end of the table next to him. "In a few minutes the reason for that will be clear."

Hendrix felt a tingle go up his spine similar to when spotting a woman with more silicone than brains. Somehow he just knew this would have a happy ending.

"First of all," Lyman intoned seriously, "I must inform you of my intention to commit a federal crime, namely the sharing of Top Secret/Codeword information with someone not cleared to receive it. Will that pose a problem for you?"

"I have a TS/Codeword clearance. And higher."

"But you're not cleared for this codeword specifically. If that puts you in an ethical dilemma, I can shut this down right now."

He smiled. "It's kind of hard to work for the CIA for long without some ethical flexibility. Your secrets are safe with me."

Lyman nodded gravely. "All right. This presentation is classified TOP SECRET/ WICKER BASKET. All information not specifically marked as classified is proprietary information of the Nanovex Company."

"Got it."

Lyman activated a projector that illuminated up through the wood grain surface of the table onto the far wall. There was no glass window inset into the table, just an oblong glow that came up from underneath the apparently solid wooden table.

"That's a neat trick."

Lyman smiled with one side of his mouth. "The table's surface is a polarized nanofilm. Just a teaser for the technology we'll be talking about in a few minutes. WICKER BASKET began as a technology solicitation from DARPA." The first slide appeared.

"I assume you understand DARPA's mission?" Lyman asked.

"Defense Advanced Research Projects Agency. They turn promising ideas from pure research into viable military applications."

"Exactly. Specifically, WICKER BASKET started from a technical solicitation for an area-denial weapon. They were thinking of using microwaves or low-frequency sound to make an area so uncomfortable that humans would be physically incapable of staying put. Think of crowd control, or rooting terrorists out of a building. They sent the solicitation out to everyone, just asking for ideas."

Hendrix raised an eyebrow. "What was *your* idea?"

"Nanoscale drug delivery. Nanovex has been an industry leader in developing nanotechnology for use in chemotherapy. The idea is to encapsulate the chemo drug and deliver it directly to the tumor. Higher effectiveness, fewer side effects. That's the goal at least. As you can imagine, making that goal a practical reality has been very challenging. But we thought using the same approach for area denial would be fairly straightforward."

It certainly didn't seem straightforward to *him*. "How would *you* do it?"

DARPA AREA DENIAL PROPOSAL

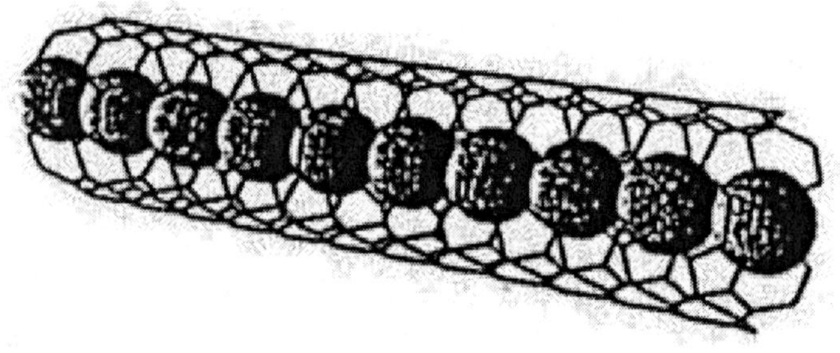

NANOVEX PROPRIETARY

Lyman advanced to the next slide. "The first step would be to encapsulate the drug inside a silicon nanotube." [1]

"What kind of drug?"

Lyman shrugged. "We had no idea. We assumed some kind of irritant, like tear gas. Or a low-toxicity hallucinogen, like psilocybin, to cause general disorientation.[2] We merely suggested a delivery method. We assumed the customer would specify the payload."

"And what did you call that tube again?"

"A silicon nanotube. It's a self-assembling fullerene, a basic building block of nanotechnology."

"Say *what?*"

Lyman chuckled. "I'm sorry. I speak this language every day; I forget that it's gibberish to anyone outside our little clique. Basically nanotechnology is the science of building materials and systems up from the molecular and even the atomic level, rather than starting from a block of material and machining away what you don't want."

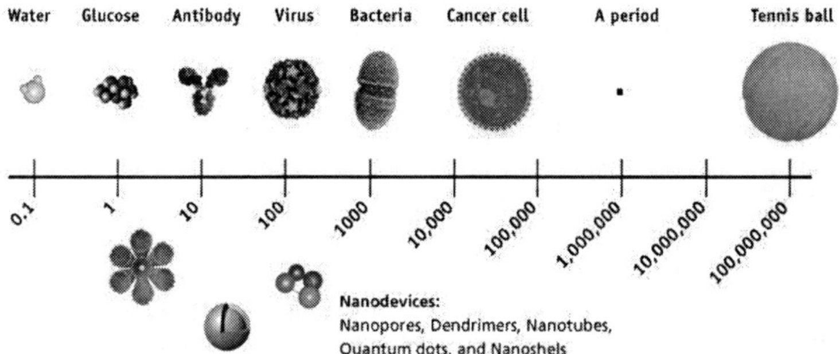

"One of the most important concepts in nanotechnology to grasp is the nanometer, or one-billionth of a meter in length. A period at the end of a sentence is about a millimeter across, or one-thousandth of a meter. A nanometer is one millionth of that. For illustration, a human hair is about a hundred thousand nanometers across. A bacterium is about a thousand nanometers across. The scale we are talking about today is between ten and a hundred nanometers." [3]

That's impossible, Hendrix thought. "Wait a minute. How can you make an artificial structure that's smaller than a bacterium?"

"Through molecular self-assembly," Lyman countered. "The cells in your body do it all the time. DNA self-assembles because the molecular bonds only go together in specific ways, like a Tinker Toy set. The DNA structure then acts like software code that instructs every other cell in your body how to self-assemble. By using certain atoms like carbon and silicon, we have learned to mimic that pattern in a very basic way."

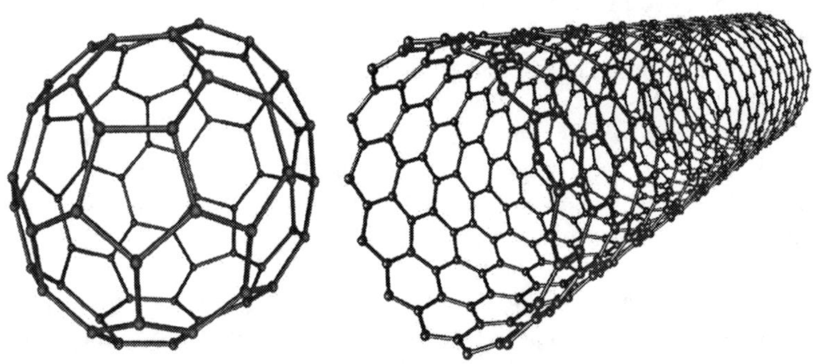

“We make shapes like this by introducing carbon or silicon atoms into an electrically charged field, sometimes in the presence of a catalyst. By manipulating the conditions, we can influence the way the introduced atoms bond themselves into larger molecules. Some of these self-assembled shapes can have very unusual and useful properties. The shape on the left, nicknamed a ‘buckyball,’ has shown an ability to bond with a wide variety of atoms, leading to chemicals of unusual properties, such as superconductivity, or for the ability of each buckyball to hold a charge like a battery.” [4]

On the screen, Lyman circled his cursor around the tube shape on the right. “But carbon and silicon nanotubes have truly unique characteristics. Carbon nanotubes, ounce for ounce, are much stronger than steel. Silicon nanotubes have unique electrical properties that may soon enable us to build quantum computers with supercomputer capabilities in a package the size of your iPhone.”

Hendrix eyed him warily. “But you don’t need the CIA to do any of those things.”

“You’re right. But after reading our initial proposal, DARPA countered with a proposal of their own, namely changing the payload of our nanotube delivery system from a nonlethal chemical to VX nerve gas.”

His head jerked. “You gotta be kidding me.”

Lyman played a video montage of combat scenes from Iraq and Afghanistan. “Throughout the global war on terror, we’ve run into situations where the risk of collateral damage prevented us from taking an objective. DARPA asked us for a weapon that could take out an entire tunnel complex as effectively as a nuke, or kill a single terrorist leader holed up in a mosque without so much as scratching a Koran.”

That got his attention. “Did you succeed?”

Lyman shrugged. “I think we *would* have, but President Cameron got wind of it and pulled the plug.”

Hendrix gave him a sad smile. “I guess having a president who helped draft the Chemical Weapons Convention treaty has its drawbacks, huh? Any chance of using a different payload, something that wouldn’t violate the CWC?”

Lyman threw up his hands in frustration. “Of *course* we could have! We don’t have to specify *any* payload to develop the delivery system. But they didn’t give us the chance! They want everything, including documentation, delivered to DARPA for destruction.”

“And you think that’s a mistake.”

“On a scale that would be difficult to overstate. We’re facing an enemy who doesn’t give a camel’s hump about the Geneva Convention or any other treaty. To tie our hands in developing a weapon like this borders on dereliction of duty, in my opinion.”

Hendrix had done his time in Iraq, and knew from experience that rules were for losers. "So why call the CIA?"

Lyman shrugged. "Desperation, mostly. And a hope that the CIA might be able to at least help us complete feasibility studies without blabbing about the project to the President."

Danger, Will Robinson, danger! a voice in the back of his head warned. But the lure of a sexy weapon was seductive indeed. "Okay, I'm listening. How does it work?"

TOP SECRET/WICKER BASKET

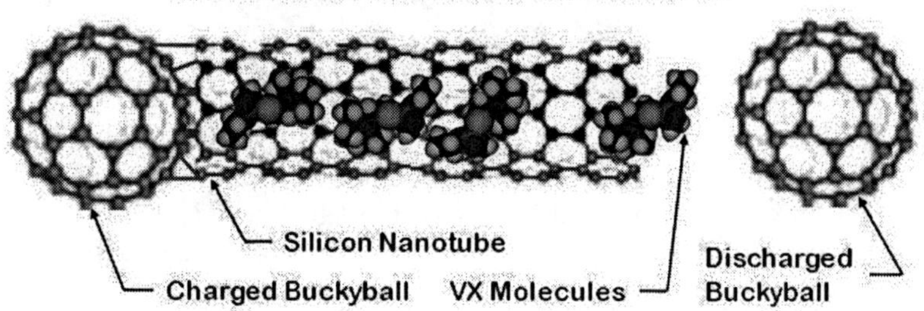

"WICKER BASKET uses a silicon nanotube and two electrically charged buckyballs to create a 'garage' for a number of VX nerve gas molecules. The length of the nanotube determines a *very* specific radio frequency that will cancel out the electrical charges and cause the buckyballs to disconnect and release the VX from the nanotube. The bomb that dispenses the nanotubes will also carry a radio transmitter, tuned to the exact frequency that will release the nerve gas. The amount of charge placed on the buckyballs determines the signal strength required to release the VX. This is the key to WICKER BASKET. Unless the signal strength reaches the required levels, the 'garage' stays closed, and the VX remains harmless, even if it has been ingested inside a human body." [5]

Hendrix was dubious. "How could you have nanotubes full of this VX nerve gas inside your body and it *not* kill you?"

"The nerve gas is completely contained inside an inert silicon nanotube. It simply *can't* chemically react with your body. It's like a tiger in a cage."

Hendrix shifted uncomfortably. He knew he wouldn't want a caged tiger inside *his* body. "And it just *stays* there? Forever?"

Lethal Amount of VX Nerve Agent
Approximate Color and Consistency

Lyman flipped to his backup charts. "One of the reasons DARPA selected VX as their payload is because the lethal dose is so small. This picture shows the size of a lethal drop of VX. It's about the consistency of motor oil. Inside the body the dosage would be even less because it wouldn't need to be absorbed through the skin; it would just go directly into the bloodstream.

"But that's assuming the dosage is received *all at once*. If untriggered nanotubes were present in your system, the buckyballs would loose their charge and release the VX into your system over a period of days, even weeks. It *might* make you sick, but it wouldn't kill you. And if the release of the nanoagent is tailored to the size of the desired kill zone, the dosage you could receive from an accidental exposure outside that zone would probably be quite small. You might not even experience symptoms." [6]

A lot of *mights* and *probablies* in there, Hendrix observed. "Would you be willing to bet *your* life on it?"

Lyman shook his head. "No, but I'd be willing to risk some rats and monkeys. Ask me again after that."

"Fair enough. What about the nanoagent that's *not* ingested, the stuff that's just left laying around on the ground? Isn't VX a persistent agent?"

Lyman pointed at the picture of dime. "Again, it's a question of dosage. If some of the nanoagent blows outside of the target area and isn't triggered, it's going to release the VX it's carrying over an extended time. If you accidentally pick up some of the nanoagent on your clothing, when it spontaneously releases it's *not* going to be at a dangerous level."

"What about *inside* the target area?"

He nodded. "The inside of the target area will require full chemical warfare suits and a clean-up operation, no doubt about that. But think about the situations where this weapon would be used. Let's say a terrorist leader and his cohort hole up inside a historic mosque. Would you rather send in an anti-terrorist team and shoot the place up, or lob a few canisters of WICKER BASKET into the windows using grenade launchers? Problem solved, no shots fired, and no harm to the historic mosque. And if any of the nanoagent blows over to the preschool next door, nobody dies. A little follow-up medical treatment as a precaution and the operation is complete."

"I can't even imagine the permission cycle you'd need to operationally release a weapon like this in combat," Hendrix countered. "I mean, strip away the fancy nanotechnology and it *is* still nerve gas we're talking about here, right?"

Lyman waved away his concern. "Listen, I was *at* Tora Bora. We had Osama Bin Laden trapped like a rat in a pipe, and I finally called in an F-15E to drop a thermobaric tunnel-busting bomb into the hole where radio transmissions matching his voice print were coming out. Until they bagged his ass in Pakistan, I was convinced there was nothing left of Bin Laden but smoke. What if we could have dropped a bomb loaded with WICKER BASKET instead? Not only would we have had a body that could have been positively identified, but the President could have stuffed him and mounted his head in the Oval Office. If WICKER BASKET had been available then, I have no doubt that I could have obtained permission for its release."

Hendrix smiled. Now *that's* the kind of talk that gets you funded in Weaponsland. "Okay, what would you need to snatch this project back from the shredder?"

"I need five highly compensated scientists working for a year and any equipment they need. I estimate one million dollars will give you a working prototype. After that, we can talk about weaponization."

One million dollars. How many times had he hand-delivered a million dollars in cash to one warlord or another in Iraq in exchange for a month or two of loyalty to US interests? More times than he could count. Luckily, from every CIA-issued Samsonite suitcase he delivered he had siphoned off a few thousand dollars, so he had over a half-million of untraceable cash at his disposal.

"How about $250,000 as a placeholder for a few months, and *two million* later to get the program moving?" Hendrix countered. Asking the CIA for two million in exchange for a weapons system possessed by no one else on the planet would be like asking an American soldier for a candy bar in exchange for the location of a wanted terrorist. Of course, he would ask for $2.5 million to get back his own money with interest.

Lyman was stunned. "You're serious?"

"Completely," Hendrix assured him. If he could bag Conrad before the Israelis got to her, he would have his choice of assignments from a grateful Agency. He would ask to be put in charge of WICKER BASKET, or whatever he renamed it. Then he would move the program offshore and fund it from any number of illegal activities the CIA operated overseas to obtain "non-appropriated funds." If he did that, the President would have no more say over it than what the Sultan of Brunei ate for breakfast. From there he could lease the nanoweapon on a "per use" basis to governments all over the world, building his own little assassin's empire, while still maintaining control over the technology and protecting US interests. *A win-win for everybody but the terrorists.*

He opened his briefcase and thumbed through the various alter egos represented by his business cards. He selected the one saying he was from Homeland Security with the number of a throwaway cell phone. He scribbled the name of a Hong Kong bank on the back. "Can you set up an account here?"

Lyman held the card out at arm's length to read it without his glasses. "I'm sure that won't be a problem."

Hendrix stood and closed his briefcase. "Then call me at that number when it's done and I'll have the money transferred." And with that, the first stone of his new empire was laid.

Lyman shook Hendrix's hand with both of his. "I can't tell you how grateful I am for this assistance. Hopefully someday the country will thank both of us for this."

That's a misconception that needs squashing, right now. "No, they won't," Hendrix said. "Because they'll *never* know about this. Welcome to my world, Mr. Lyman."

Lyman was suitably chastised. "Point taken. I understand completely."

"Then thanks for the invitation, and I'll wait for your call."

As he left Lyman's office, the same security guard who had escorted him up returned with a diminutive Asian woman in her late twenties. Their eyes made contact and she gave him the slightest of nods. He ignored her and waited in the hallway for the security guard to walk him back down to the lobby and take his visitor's badge.

"FBI Special Agent Wendy Cho, here to see Douglas Lyman, please," he heard the woman tell the receptionist.

FINAL SECURITY

APRIL 17, 1945 – PILSEN, CZECHOSLOVAKIA

Kammler tromped across the snowy forest clearing, making the final arrangements before the scientists' arrival. The Bell was packaged for transport and ready to be loaded on Germany's sole surviving six-engine Ju-390 heavy transport.

As Bormann had predicted, Himmler called Pilsen that morning, demanding the Ju-390 for the Fuhrer's evacuation from Berlin. Since he already knew that Bormann had convinced Hitler to stay in Berlin "to ride out the storm," Himmler was more likely wishing to evacuate the artwork and other treasures Goering had removed from Hitler's estate—as well as himself—to Spain or some other still-Nazi-friendly country. Kammler had drafted a terse telegram informing Himmler that the Ju-390 was urgently needed for the war effort and was unavailable for his private use. He then instructed the communications sergeant to delay transmission for four hours. By then he would be airborne and permanently out of reach of his former superior's wrath.[7]

Kurt Debus and Professor Gerlach arrived in Kammler's *Kubelwagen* off-road staff car.[8] Kammler greeted the pair and instructed them to stand on the far side of the clearing. While Debus stood impassively, Gerlach looked nervous, as if he suspected the nefarious motive behind Kammler's actions. The SS troops busily draped a tent over the mound of dirt behind the slit trench. Luckily the trench and the bodies it contained were covered by the second tent before Gerlach arrived.

Kammler took the *Kubelwagen* back to the road to collect General Sporrenberg and prepare the convoy for departure. The scientists for the Bell project arrived and were escorted into the forest by Sporrenberg's men. When they returned to the clearing, the scientists had been stripped of their identity papers. It was time. He gave the signal for the tents to be removed from over the trench and dirt pile.

"Final security!" Sporrenberg ordered.

Kammler watched Gerlach carefully as his fellow scientists were mown down and burned. Disbelief turned to shock, and shock turned into horror. Gerlach collapsed to his knees, averting his eyes and weeping.

Kammler exited the car and squatted at Gerlach's side. "Professor Gerlach? I'm sorry you had to watch this, but it was necessary."

Gerlach was terrified and shaking. "N-n-necessary? Cold blooded murder is *necessary*?" He obviously believed he was about to follow his comrades into the trench, but was too proud to beg for his life. Kammler was impressed.

"Indeed," he said matter-of-factly. "I have no intention of letting the secrets of the Bell fall into the hands of the Allies. There are two men I trust to keep that secret no matter what pressure is brought to bear on them. Yourself and *Herr* Debus. Both of you have refused to follow me overseas, so I needed a *demonstration* to show how far I am willing to go to protect what is mine. Is that clearly understood?"

Gerlach mumbled an incoherent response and continued weeping. Kammler grasped the older man's head firmly with both hands. Unless Gerlach's compliance was assured, this could only end one way.

"*Herr Gerlach!*" he shouted, lifting his head until they made eye contact. "Do you *understand* what I expect of you?"

"*Yes!*" Gerlach snapped, tears still streaming down his face. "I will remain silent!"

He released his hold, but held the scientist's gaze. "Not just silence, Professor Gerlach. You will never investigate any science related to your work on the Bell, or assist anyone else who does. Find another field of research and have a long and productive career. This is my gift to yourself and *Herr* Debus for your exemplary service to the Reich. Do not make me take it back. *Do you understand?*"

Gerlach turned away in shame. His voice was hoarse, but clear. "I understand, *Herr* General."

Kammler stood. He pulled Debus aside. "I am releasing my driver Klaus to your service. Make sure that the professor makes it safely to the American lines. If he even *hints* at speaking of what has just happened, tell Klaus. He will know what to do."

"*Jawhol, mein* General!"

Kammler extended his hand. "We will most likely never meet again. Good luck!"

Debus clicked the heels of his civilian shoes and raised his arm. "*Heil Hitler!*"

Kammler shook his head and walked away. "Not anymore, *Herr* Debus."

He returned to the staff car, where Sporrenberg supervised the clean up of the scientists' demise. "Are you sure you won't change your mind, Jakob? Losing your services will be like cutting off my right arm."

Sporrenberg's face was sad, but firm. "I thank you General, but my family and my heart are here in Germany, even if she lay in ruins. An old tree cannot be pulled up by the roots and planted in foreign soil. But I wish you good fortune in your new home, and hope that someday I may be of service to you again."

Sporrenberg was a good man, and had spilled blood on many occasions to keep Kammler's secrets. He could be trusted completely. "Then good fortune to you as well, Jakob." He sucked in a deep, cold breath and took in the snowy beauty around him, ignoring the soldiers shoveling dirt onto the smoldering corpses. "I have a feeling I shall miss all of this greatly."

PLASMA

PRESENT DAY – SAN JOSE, CALIFORNIA

Mike Manning entered Lyman's office as Lyman made introductions around the conference table.

"This is Seth Graves, our representative from DARPA. Oh, and here is our company attorney, Mike Manning."

Manning extended his hand to an Asian woman who could not have been an inch over five feet. She was almost pretty, but her pulled-into-a-bun hairstyle and attire were more severe than attractive. He guessed that these and her four-inch heels were compensation for her stature.

Her grasp was cool and solid. "FBI Special Agent Wendy Cho, pleased to meet you."

"Likewise." She enjoyed throwing the title around. More compensation.

"Please, everyone have a seat," Lyman requested. "The FBI was kind enough to offer us a briefing on Mr. Hackett's death investigation. Agent Cho, you have the floor."

She placed a slender file on the conference table. "Last night the Bureau was requested by the Santa Clara County Coroner to assist in the death investigation of Joshua Martin Hackett, a Nanovex employee. Because of the ongoing FBI operation involving Nanovex, a decision was made by Special-Agent-in-Charge Pugliano to federalize the death investigation. A review of the security video from the supermarket where

Mr. Hackett died indicated the time of death, or at least the time of collapse, as 7:05 p.m."

Cho passed around color photos of an overweight man in a Hawaiian shirt lying face down in an inky-black puddle. "According to the coroner, the cause of death appeared to be heart failure. However, he had no explanation for the efflux of this black fluid from his bodily orifices. A preliminary autopsy was inconclusive; Mr. Hackett did indeed die of heart failure, but that's because the tissue of *all* his internal organs suffered some kind of simultaneous breakdown, producing the black efflux in the photos. The heart failure was merely incidental to a greater systemic catastrophe."

Manning swallowed and pushed the photos away. Seeing men face down in pools of their own blood had been bad enough. A man face down in the black goo of his melted internal organs was a whole new level of horror. He sincerely hoped that whatever killed Hackett wasn't floating in the air here at Nanovex.

Lyman looked pained. "Agent Cho, do you have *any* idea what happened to Josh?" The use of the first name seemed to indicate more than passing familiarity.

She folded her hands. "Actually, Mr. Lyman, that's exactly what I was here to ask *you*."

"I can assure you that what happened to Josh Hackett has *no connection* to the tragic deaths of my other five employees."

"Pardon me, unless you've done your own independent autopsy, how can you possibly know that?"

"Agent Cho," Seth Graves cut in, "I am very familiar with the deaths of the five Nanovex scientists in question. And as a government employee with a PhD in chemistry as opposed to a Nanovex employee reporting to Mr. Lyman, I can assure you that what Joshua Hackett was working on could not possibly have caused the symptoms shown in these photos. It's physically impossible."

"And what exactly *were* they working on?" she fired back. "And what exactly *was* the cause of death for those employees?"

"I'm afraid that's classified," Graves said. "By my agency," he added, pointing to himself. "Nanovex has no say over how that information is controlled."

"Isn't *that* convenient," Cho observed, casting a spiteful glance at Manning. "I'm sure it's helpful in preventing lawsuits as well. Any subpoenas for information can be quashed on national security grounds."

Lyman looked like he wanted to throw something, but held his temper and his tongue.

"Excuse me," Graves quickly interceded, "you mentioned a videotape. Would you happen to have a copy with you?"

She reached for her briefcase. “Fine. I don’t see how that’s pertinent, though.” She produced a DVD in a jewel case, which Lyman inserted into the PC on his desk. The video played on the conference room’s projector screen a few seconds later.

“I uploaded the full videotape to my laptop,” she explained, “but I only burned a portion to this DVD. It begins thirty seconds before Mr. Hackett enters the grocery store. There, in the Hawaiian shirt, freeze it. Okay, he looks a little tense, which may explain the whiskey purchase, but his color looks fine, and he certainly doesn’t appear to be in bodily distress. Fast forward five minutes, please. Okay, this is another camera at checkout. Again, he looks fine, gathers his things and walks toward the exit.”

The view switched back to the entrance camera. Just as Hackett walked into center screen, he jumped as if shocked, stood with a stunned expression for a few seconds, then dropped his bag and clutched his chest and stomach. He dropped to his knees, then to all fours and began retching black liquid. This continued for several seconds, the flow seeming to last far longer than for a man simply emptying his stomach. Finally he clutched his throat and slid unconscious to the floor. Shocked shoppers gathered around until a manager dashed to Hackett’s side and began summoning an emergency response. The video continued rolling.

“I burned another twenty minutes to DVD to verify that no bystanders or first responders did anything that could have contributed to the fatality. As you can see, even the paramedics were leery of that black puddle and didn’t attempt CPR. They just verified lack of pulse, recorded time of death, and called the detectives.”

“Can you go back, please?” Graves asked. “Right before the collapse. There. Now go forward.” Manning watched more carefully and noticed a lens flare right as Hackett seemed to jump in response to whatever killed him.

“There!” Graves said. “Doug, go back and play that part again. Frame by frame if you can.”

“Hackett was walking right in front of plate glass window,” Cho cautioned. “That was probably just the reflection of a car’s headlight from the parking lot.”

“I’m not so sure,” Graves insisted. The video jerked forward a frame at a time until a bright blue dot a few inches in diameter appeared on Hackett’s chest. “There!” Graves exclaimed. The video froze.

“That still could be a lens flare,” Cho said.

Lyman then allowed the video forward in a frame-pause-frame movement. The dot grew into a bright blue ball a foot in diameter and continued growing. It faded as it grew, becoming visible both in front of Hackett’s chest and emerging in a spherical wave behind his back. Once it expanded to three feet it became transparent and faded to nothing in three frames.

"What's the total duration of that flare, Doug?" Graves asked.

Lyman ran the counter backward. "Eight frames. Three-tenths of a second."

Graves cocked an eyebrow at the FBI agent. "Still think that's just a lens flare?"

"I don't know," she admitted.

"Doug, does it look to you like that blue flash has a three-dimensional shape to it?"

Lyman ticked the frames to the one showing the flash both in front and behind Hackett. "Sure looks like it to me. See how Hackett's body obscures the flash? It's like a sphere expanding from inside his body."

"A sphere of *what?*" Cho demanded.

"Some sort of plasma, if I had to venture a guess," Graves said.

"Plasma?" Cho asked incredulously. "You mean like blood plasma?"

"No, the fourth state of matter," Lyman explained. "Solid, liquid, gas, and plasma. Plasma is gas that's been ionized to a high energy state. It's a fourth state because plasma is highly conductive and can be easily directed by electromagnetic fields, like in a plasma TV screen." He pointed upward. "Fluorescent lights are another form of plasma, as are lightning and the Aurora Borealis."

"So why is a plasma coming out of your Mr. Hackett, then?" she asked.

"I have no idea," Lyman said, frowning.

"You're assuming it's coming *out* of him," Graves pointed out. "What if it's being projected *at* him?"

"*At* him?" Cho protested. "Projected how? By whom?"

Graves turned in his chair to face her. "Excellent questions. I wish I had the resources of the FBI at my disposal to get to the answer."

Cho frowned as the burden of the case was deposited back into her lap. "I assume I can call upon you gentlemen for technical support in this matter?"

"Day or night," Lyman assured her. "Guys; cell phone numbers, cough 'em up."

After they all exchanged phone numbers with Cho, Manning thought it time to address the question everyone had previously ignored. "Doug, what if someone just *killed* Josh Hackett? Could they have killed him *because* of what he worked on? Are the *rest* of the workers on that project safe? Are *you?*"

Doug Lyman had no answers for those questions.

* * *

Manning was dead on his feet when he returned to his office. His fatigue from lack of sleep wasn't helped by the new worry that Conrad's warning about people willing to kill for Nanovex's secrets appeared to have come true. Nothing like a *second* set of crosshairs on one's forehead to strain the mind and body.

He unlocked his desk and withdrew Conrad's pen and pencil. He looked end on at the pen and twisted the cap a quarter turn. A tiny blue light inside flashed twice. The device was off. He repeated the procedure for the pencil, which had lain inactive all day. Its blue light flashed once, signaling its readiness. He stuck the active pencil back in the drawer, and the inactive pen in his pocket.

Even leaving his office for the day didn't make him feel better, because he knew that another meeting with Angela Conrad lay ahead. He tried not to dwell on what indignities would be forced upon him then.

PARTY FAVORS

AUGUST 22, 2002 – OFF THE U.S. EAST COAST

The sun sank low off the left wing of the Gulfstream V executive jet "Guantanamo Express," turning the clouds below into luminous hills of gold. The light filtered through the jet's windows, bathing the plush interior in warm amber light. Gavin Carter and Angela Conrad sat in facing chairs, a small folding table between them. Conrad had exchanged her prison jumpsuit for a tight black skirt, a low-cut cotton blouse, and slingback high heels from her bags. Carter guessed that passed for business attire in Conrad's world. Through iron discipline he had so far avoided being caught with his eyes down her exposed cleavage, although her lace bra had not escaped his attention.

He made small talk for the first hour of the flight, trying to learn more about her background than what was included in her CIA personnel folder. It had turned mostly into a friendly verbal judo match, both of them trying to extract as much information about the other while giving as little back in return as possible. He only learned that she was already a skilled interrogator, probably from her police experience.

He reached for his briefcase. "Well, enough about your previous life. Time to learn about your next life." He extracted a manila envelope and emptied its contents onto the table. He picked up the passport first, flipping it open. Conrad's CIA file photo was already printed inside. "Meet Melissa Hurley of Fairfax, Virginia."

Conrad examined her new identity. "I see my new birthday is August 22. Nice touch. Not a date I'm likely to forget."

He winked. "And the Christians think they're the only ones who get born again."

Her eyes wandered to the other documents. "Ain't that the truth."

He continued his presentation. "We also have your Melissa Hurley Virginia driver's license, birth certificate, social, two credit cards, and your concealed carry permit."

Her hand went straight for the carry permit. "Nice. Got a gun in there?"

He shook the manila envelope until a smaller envelope fell out. He pushed it across the table. "Next best thing. One thousand dollars cash for incidentals until you report for work. You'll be issued a weapon on missions, of course, but you should buy your own for off duty."

"I already own a couple."

He wagged a finger. "Huh-uh. *Angela Conrad* owned those guns. They'll soon be on their way to my gunsmith to have their serial numbers ground off. You may even have them issued to you in the field someday. Same thing for everything else you own that's registered to you, like your car. It will be liquidated and the funds transferred to your company account. Everything in your apartment will be placed in secure storage and searched for items that could compromise your new cover. What doesn't will be shipped to your new address. If it does, we'll keep it in storage until you leave the company."

She picked up an ID badge with only her photo and a bar code. "And this?"

"Your company badge."

She flipped it over, looking unsuccessfully for clues. She found only a "If found please drop in any mailbox" message with a P.O. box number in Alexandria. "A very anonymous company, I see."

"You have *no* idea," he cautioned. He presented a business card with the logo for "Universal Export Associates." The address was in Alexandria, Virginia near Reagan National Airport. "Once you've secured your insurance package, take a couple of days to get your new life set up, then report here and show them that badge. They'll escort you to the rabbit hole and give you a shove."

A knock sounded at the door of the passenger compartment. He quickly scooped the documents back into the manila envelope. "Enter!" he called.

The co-pilot leaned in from the empty prisoner compartment. "Sorry to interrupt, sir, but we'll be landing in Virginia in a half hour."

He smiled. "Not at all. Thank you, Major Brooks." The officer excused himself.

Conrad gestured to the westward-facing couch. “Shall we enjoy the sunset?”

He rose and moved to the plane’s small liquor cabinet. For undercover operatives returning from months in Moslem countries with their quarry, alcohol was often the best reward the CIA could offer. “Not a large selection, but what’s your pleasure?”

“Vodka and Red Bull if you’ve got it, Scotch on the rocks if you don’t.”

His eyebrows rose. “That’s a hell of a combination!” He pulled out a bottle of Grey Goose vodka and knelt to dig in the bar fridge. Several bottles of beer and a few cans of soda. “I don’t think we...well, I’ll be damned.” He pulled out a lone Red Bull from the back. “We have a winner!”

Conrad rested her elbow on the back of the couch and stretched her legs across the narrow aisle with a breathy sigh. She could easily pass for a flight attendant on Hugh Hefner’s personal jet. “That’s great! A buzz and a boost, just what I need.”

He returned with their drinks. Maybe the combination of fatigue and liquor might make her less defensive about his questions. “Here you go. Hell of a day for you, huh?”

She raised her glass. “Dear God. On the bright side, it’s my birthday!”

He met her glass with his. “Indeed. Cheers!”

Together they watched the sun go down on her last day as Angela Conrad. He milked his drink for the entire sunset, but she downed hers with the gusto of a hooker and chased it with a bottle of Corona beer. He noticed no effect on her demeanor or speech. She probably had the alcohol tolerance of a hooker too.

She shifted to face him, her leg casually—perhaps—brushing up against his. “Listen, you rescued me from the lion’s den today, and I behaved like a complete ass.”

He smirked over his glass. “The truth at last.”

She placed her hand on his knee. “I’d like to make it up to you, if I could.”

He cleared his throat, but still coughed when he tried to speak. “That’s, uh, not necessary. Really.”

Her hand moved to his leg. “You’re not married, Gavin. Divorced, I assume? You loved your wife, but the strain of life in the Agency was too much for her, right?”

The warmth of her hand seemed to flow up his leg like electricity, sparking a physical reaction that was as much out of his control as the setting sun outside. “Yeah, that pretty much sums it up,” he whispered hoarsely.

She slid smoothly to her knees in front of him, parting his legs with her body. "People like you and me are different. We have to find our comfort where we can. In each other, because we're the only ones who really understand this life we lead."

Her hands ran up his thighs until they met. He sucked in an involuntary gasp. "*Oh*, this is *so* wrong," he groaned.

She rose from her knees and kissed him gently, caressing his lips with her tongue while unbuckling his belt. "*So wrong* is what I do *best.*" she whispered in his ear. "Eventually you'll learn to appreciate that."

Five minutes later, Gavin Carter appreciated it completely.

SUGAR COOKIE

PRESENT DAY – SAN FRANCISCO, CALIFORNIA

Scott Hendrix lay in the dark waiting for her to arrive, his member throbbing in anticipation. He heard the keycard slide into the hotel room lock, then saw her silhouette projected by the lights in the hallway. The room plunged into darkness again when the door closed, but he could hear her footsteps approach.

"Get your ass out of bed and take off my clothes," she demanded.

Hendrix quickly complied, earning a slap when she deemed his efforts not quick enough.

"Faster, you prick!" she ordered.

Hendrix hurried, and the instant her panties were clear of one leg, she grabbed him bodily and shoved him back onto the bed, not bothering to take off her heels. Launching herself on top of him, she mashed her lips against his in a rough, teeth-grinding kiss. Then she mounted him, followed by screaming, biting, hair-pulling intercourse. Her profane commands to him during the lovemaking were so boisterous he was afraid someone might call hotel security. After a final ear-piercing squeal of ecstasy, she collapsed onto his chest with a blasphemous exclamation of satisfaction.

He brushed her flailed black hair off his face so he could breathe. Lifting her head with both hands, he looked into her panting, sweaty face.

"My God, Agent Cho, what's gotten into you?"

She let out a throaty chuckle. "You mean other than *you*?" She gave him a playful squeeze with her pelvic muscles, grinding her hips against his.

He laughed. "Yeah, I mean *before* you assaulted your case officer."

She planted her hands on his chest and pushed up, jabbing her four-inch heels into his thighs. "In case you forgot, I'm a federal agent now. What are you going to do, claim police brutality?"

He reached up and grabbed her breasts, rolling her swollen nipples between his fingers and thumbs. "Oh, and in case *you* forgot, I was the one who *assigned* your rookie ass to penetrate the FBI, wasn't I?"

She grabbed his chest hair and thrust her hips rhythmically against his. "Yeah, you taught me all about penetration, didn't you?"

My God, this little minx is delicious. And to think I picked the codename Sugar Cookie at random. He grabbed the back of her neck and pulled her lips to his, kissing her deeply. "Nothing you didn't already know, I have a feeling," he said when he finally came up for air.

She grabbed his thinning hair and rubbed her hot forehead against his. "You have a *feeling*? I think that's why you recruited me, wasn't it?"

That much was true. He had met Cho at a jobs fair at Georgetown. He was posing as GSA, or Interior Department, or some other federal bureaucracy. Cho had expressed an interest in working for the federal government and had marked her interests outside her political science major as drama and cheerleading. Hendrix had her background checked, and found that Cho liked to be tossed by several men, and not just during cheerleading. He had found a candidate for a very special "thrust" at the Agency. The CIA paid her law school tuition, then instructed her to join the FBI.

"So, speaking of penetration," he said, "have you bedded Pugliano yet?"

She rested an elbow on his chest. "The guy's a damned machine. I'm not sure he even slows down to take a piss, much less screw. I tried to flirt with him once and he just walked away. Not even sure he noticed."

He stroked her sweaty back. "I have faith in you."

She reached down and grabbed him. "You mean you have faith that Pugliano has one of *these*, right?"

He smiled. "It *is* a vulnerability, as you well know."

She planted both elbows on his chest, regarding him impishly over interlaced fingers. "Not with *all* men, mind you. Just the weak, immoral ones."

He grabbed her tiny nose with the knuckles of his index and middle fingers. "You little brat! You'd better have something good for me!"

Her eyes widened in mock outrage. "Oh! *Oh!* Something good, huh?" She gave him a vicious pinch on the chin with her fingernails.

He flinched, pulling away. "Ow! You know what I mean!"

She leaned forward and licked his wound, her breath hot on his face. "So good you're not going to fucking believe it."

* * *

Before Wendy, he had never received an intelligence briefing from a naked woman. But he could get used to it. They lay side by side across the bed, her laptop propped on a chair.

"So what is this blue ball of plasma popping out of their guy's chest?" he asked. "And what's up with the black vomit? That's just vile."

She clicked her high heels together idly. "Nanovex is clueless as we are. I don't think they had anything to do with it."

"They didn't," he said with certainty.

She rolled on her side to face him. "I forgot, you were there too! What did you learn from Lyman?"

He reached over to stroke her breast. "Need to know, sweetheart, need to know. What if I tell you something only *I'm* supposed to know and you let it slip during your next meeting with Lyman?"

She pooched out her lower lip. "Oh, you're no fun. What good is joining the CIA if you don't learn any *secrets*?"

Oh, she's good. She would learn soon enough. His new empire would need a queen, or at least a court concubine. "Patience, grasshopper," he intoned in a mock oriental accent. He presented an open palm. "Snatch the pebble from my hand."

Her futile grab at his hand was followed by a playful wrestling match that ended with her fingers wrapped around his testicles. "Freeze, Sensei, I got your pebbles right here! And while we're at it, why don't I file a complaint about your use of racial stereotype humor?"

"I just thank God you're not filing sexual harassment charges!" he replied, in a voice that was a few notes higher than he expected.

She released his jewels, pushed him onto his back, and rolled on top of him. "I don't think a CIA sexspionage agent would get much sympathy from the Equal Employment Opportunity Commission, do you?"

He pulled her close. "Probably not. Got anything else before we move onto 'other business?'"

She pulled away. "Oh hell yes, I almost forgot!" She climbed over him to reach her laptop, her breasts brushing against his face. "You remember that FACES project I worked on at Georgetown?"

For some reason he was having trouble concentrating. "You mean the facial recognition program that spotted Angela Conrad at the Sheraton?" He stuck out his tongue to lick a nipple whenever one passed by.

She giggled and smacked the top of his head. "Stop it, that tickles! FACES; Facial Analysis, Comparison and Elimination System." She rolled off and resumed pecking at her laptop. "Here, look at this."

Hendrix rolled over as well, grudgingly returning to business. "The security camera footage from the Sheraton? I've seen this."

"Patience, grasshopper," she mocked, holding up a finger, then pointing. "Remember this guy?"

"The Running Man? What about him?" They had never identified the man who met Conrad at the side entrance of the Sheraton and left with her in the cab. His face wasn't in any of the databases for known criminals or intelligence operatives, foreign or domestic. Conrad must have found a real deep cover spook to work with.

"I saw him in Lyman's office today."

He sat up. "You're shittin' me."

She regarded him with an arched eyebrow. "I shit you not. Hell, I think he was wearing that same suit."

There was no way his luck was this good. The universe was just conspiring to pull a perverse trick on him. "Did you get a *name*?"

"Mike Manning," she said, returning her attention to the laptop. "Lyman claimed he was their company attorney." She closed the pictures from the Sheraton and launched a new application, one that flashed a warning "FBI-OFFICIAL USE ONLY" before launching.

"What's that?"

"FBI tracking program. Because even better than a name, I got his cell phone number." She picked on a saved search marked "MANNING". A dialog box popped up marking the progress of the search.

INITIATING REQUEST
TRANSMITTING AUTHENTICATION
AUTHENTICATION CONFIRMED
ACCESSING TELCO RECORDS
SEEKING LOCATION…

A map of the San Francisco area opened, zooming in on the south end of the bay, then to San Jose, finally focusing on a single building. She moved the cursor over it and a bubble popped up:

HOTEL MONTGOMERY
211 SOUTH FIRST STREET
SAN JOSE, CA 95113

She rose onto one elbow, very proud of herself. "And there you have the firm location of a known associate of Angela Conrad. Just follow his cell phone and eventually he'll lead you straight to her."

Hendrix regarded her with wonder. "Agent Cho, may I have wild, animal sex with you?"

She was already on top of him again. "I thought you'd never ask!"

[1] Figure credit: *Nanostructure Science and Technology*, Loyola College WTEC Division report, http://www.wtec.org/pdf/nano.pdf, p. 61

[2] The US government actually stocked a powerful psychotic drug as a non-lethal chemical warfare agent during the Cold War called BZ agent. It was basically an extremely potent LSD delivered as an aerosol to render the targets hallucigenically incapacitated for more than a day. BZ agent had been prepared for use on the US Embassy in Tehran before the failed hostage rescue mission in 1979. One of the author's jobs at the Corps of Engineers was tracking the flow of leaking BZ agent from bunkers at the Pine Bluff Arsenal toward the Sparta Aquifer, which supplied the drinking water for much of southern Arkansas. Luckily it never got dangerously close, but it did provide the motivation to destroy the entire stockpile, which was accomplished in 1988.

[3] Figure credit: National Institutes of Health

[4] Figure credit: Wikipedia: *Allotropes of Carbon*

[5] Figure adapted from the following sources: Wikipedia Commons, file:VX-3D-vdW.png, and *Carbon Nanotubes*, http://www.personal.rdg.ac.uk/~scsharip/tubes.htm

[6] Figure credit: New Hampshire Department of Safety Hazardous Materials webpage, http://www.nh.gov/safety/divisions/firesafety/hazmat/index.html

[7] Hans Kammler did *indeed* send this telegram to Himmler on April 17 denying use of the Ju-390, which coincides with the last day the Ju-390 transport plane was photographed in Prague. Thereafter it lifted off and disappeared from the historical record.

[8] Photo credit: *Bundesarchiv*, Bild 101III-Cantzler-045-05A / Cantzler / CC-BY-SA; via Wikipedia Commons.

CHAPTER 12

DOWNLOAD

SAN JOSE, CALIFORNIA

"Son of a bitch!" Conrad exclaimed. "This is fantastic!"

Earlier that evening, Manning had returned to his hotel and collapsed into bed without eating dinner. Shortly after midnight Conrad had summoned him for a meet. After almost an hour of circuitous driving for surveillance detection, he pulled up beside an unmarked panel truck. Conrad lifted the truck's roll-up cargo door and summoned him to climb inside. She brought the door back down and motioned for Manning to sit on one of the equipment boxes filling the cargo bay. The truck started rolling.

She asked for the pen she had given him the previous night and pulled off the back cap, revealing a mini-USB port. She plugged this into her laptop and started downloading data. After a few minutes of analysis, she was obviously very pleased.

"So it worked?" he asked.

"Absolutely," she confirmed, her eyes never leaving the screen. "What I had you do was plant a bug in Lyman's office—actually two bugs. One records sound, the other records computer transmissions."

"You mean like a modem?"

She shook her head. "No, that's an intentional transmission. The bug you stuck under the table picks up on the *unintentional* transmissions every computer and computer screen puts off just by operating. You can't stop a computer from making them, you can only box them in. That's the reason Nanovex has that huge glass canopy over it; to keep the unintentional transmissions from leaking out and being read at a distance by somebody like me. But you put the bug *inside* the box, so now I can read Doug Lyman's computer screen just like I was in the room with him. Then the bug did a burst transmission to the storage unit inside this pen so you could bring it back through security to me." [1]

It was clever, in a criminal kind of way. "So what did you get?"

"So far, every email that Lyman opened today. Okay, this looks promising. It's a message from somebody named Jeff Wood informing Lyman his 'special project' has been set up in a proprietary lab number P5-3. I'm going to need you to find that lab for me."

"There's no way my badge will get me in that lab," he protested. "That whole building is compartmentalized out the yin-yang."

"Access is my problem, location is yours. Just find it and draw me a map. Wait a minute, what's this?"

Conrad fished a set of ear buds out of an equipment drawer and connected them to her laptop. She stuck one in her ear as she moved the slider back and forth for her laptop's audio player. "He's giving a briefing to somebody on some kind of hush-hush project Nanovex is researching. Wait; let me synchronize what his computer was projecting with the audio capture inside the room."

A PowerPoint chart popped up on her laptop. It had a scientific illustration of some kind of Tinker-Toy-looking molecule that he would have passed off as innocuous, except for the TOP SECRET/WICKER BASKET warning at the top of the chart.

"Paydirt!" she announced.

Manning leaned in. "So this is what we're trying to *steal*?" He noticed how easily the *we* rolled off his tongue.

She nodded. "Lyman's doing most of the talking; I'm having trouble figuring out who he's talking *to*." Her eyes suddenly widened.

"Oh, there *is* a God!" she whispered with an evil grin.

A NEW MAN

APRIL 19, 1945 – ENTRE RIOS, ARGENTINA

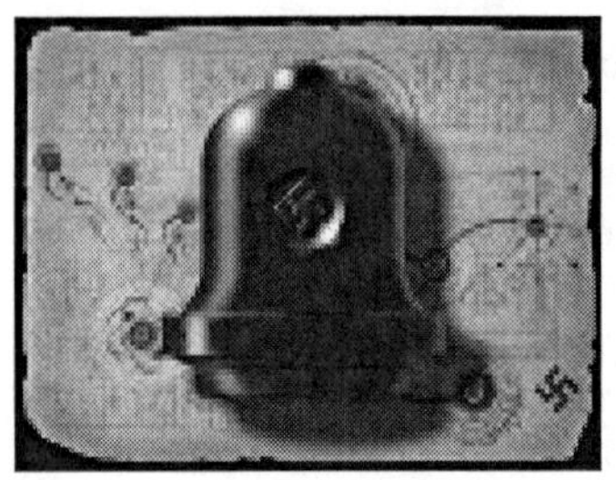

Hans Kammler walked down the cargo ramp of the Ju-390 transport into the pasty heat of Argentina with a great sense of relief. They had been aloft for more than twenty-four hours, a feat made possible by the giant airplane's revolutionary ability to refuel in the air. Lifting off just before dark, they were joined by a smaller four-engine cargo plane lifting a full load of fuel. This was transferred to the Ju-390 by means of a trailing hose from the smaller aircraft; the pilots told him they could carry more fuel in the air than they could successfully lift from the ground. By the time the sun rose the next day they were over the Atlantic crossing the Tropic of Cancer. During the next night they watched the lights of Rio de Janeiro slide past the right wing. On and on the six engines droned, throttled back for maximum fuel conservation, making the interminable flight even longer.

They didn't reach their landing strip a hundred kilometers north of Buenos Aires until the flight's second noon, and Kammler felt like he was already a captive, only to the aircraft instead of to the Allies. During the flight he had shed his SS major general's uniform for the last time, changing into a civilian suit. It felt strange, like he was wearing someone else's skin. He saw his contact from Argentine Intelligence, Mr. Santos, approaching in a lightweight tan suit and tropical hat.

The agent extended his hand. "*Senor* Kammler? Welcome to Argentina. A very impressive aircraft you have." His German was heavily accented, but crisp.

He joined Santos in surveying the six-engine behemoth. It looked a lot bigger on the outside than when confined inside the cargo-filled fuselage. "Yes," he observed, "it's a pity we'll have to chop it up for scrap. It's a bit too large to escape unnoticed, even here in the countryside. It will draw unwelcome attention." [2]

"Not as much as that suit!" Santos said with a laugh.

Kammler checked his almost-new charcoal suit for tears or stains. There were none. "The tailor in Paris assured me this was the latest style." It hadn't been *that* long since the Germans lost France, he pondered.

The affable Santos massaged Kammler's sleeve. "*Wool* is seldom in fashion in South America, regardless of how it is cut, *Senor* Kammler." He held up a manila envelope. "Or should I say, *Senor* Schmidt? Here are your new papers. Please memorize all the relevant details. There will be, how you say, a *quiz* afterwards."

"Of course." Santos seemed professional, which was a relief, since Kammler's life would depend on the quality of the cover the Argentinean provided. At the roar of a forklift's motor they both turned their heads to see the Bell emerge like a giant black egg down the tail ramp of the Ju-390.

"*Madre de Dios! Vas ist los?*" Santos exclaimed, his surprise causing him to mix languages. [3]

Kammler lifted an eyebrow. "The future, *Senor* Santos. *Our* future."

Santos motioned toward his car. "Then come, *Senor* Schmidt; I will buy you lunch, and you can tell me about the future. And afterwards we will visit *my* tailor, and you will feel like a new man!"

Kammler watched the Argentinean workers load the Bell into a covered truck, under the close supervision of the three scientists he had deemed indispensable. He regarded the Ju-390 with its German insignia for the last time, then scanned the expansive plains surrounding them. Flat yellow grasslands as far as the eye could see. It was as alien from the green rolling hills of Germany as the terrain of the moon. His new home.

Kammler waved the folder containing his new identity. "Thank you, *Senor* Santos. I *already* feel like a new man!"

COURIER

PRESENT DAY – SAN FRANCISCO, CALIFORNIA

Scott Hendrix circled the block slowly to determine what kind of surveillance the FBI had set up around the Israeli consulate. The first pair was easy to spot, sitting in their unmarked Crown Vic a block away in suits with radios and binoculars in plain view. Those were the toss-outs, the "We're here to watch your consulate for your own protection" guys. He cursed his snap decision to pass the NSA intel to Pugliano.

The second unit was a little tougher to spot, but not much. A Pacific Bell truck parked directly across from the consulate had traffic shields around the nearest manhole cover and a ventilator hose snaking down. Nothing untoward there, until he noticed the driver doing paperwork in the cab had a "squiggly wire" coming out of his ear. No doubt the side facing the consulate had a cameraman documenting everyone entering and leaving the building. The phone lines under the street were obviously under scrutiny as well. These guys were the "Don't try anything Yitzhak, we're watching you like a hawk" unit.

Continuing his recon stroll, Hendrix noticed the lack of parking structures on this side of the block. There was no way the Israelis would make their people hoof it out in the open from blocks away, even in a low-threat town like San Francisco. There had to be an adjoining garage. He found it on the opposite side of the block, a dedicated structure for the Wells Fargo bank next door. The consulate undoubtedly leased space and would have a secured entrance off the garage. But the FBI would *have* to watch this side, or consulate staff could slip in and out at will.

He completely circumnavigated the block and had to make a reverse pass on foot before he saw it. A rusty GMC conversion van parked across the street from the parking garage had infrared spotlights on the bumpers. They looked like small headlights, but with black lenses, to clandestinely illuminate for photography anyone entering or leaving the garage. The van looked unoccupied, but Hendrix knew better. The vehicles in front of the consulate were merely meant to drive any questionable traffic out the back door for the nondescript van to catch. He doubted the Israelis would fall for it, but at least the FBI had a plan.

And now so did he. He walked three blocks down Montgomery Street and dashed into a bicycle messenger's office, feigning shortness of breath. He slapped down an envelope with the consulate's address onto the counter. "I need this delivered as fast as you can."

The young dispatcher glanced at the address quizzically. "This is right down the street."

"Do I look like I have time to walk down and back three blocks?" Hendrix huffed.

The dispatcher held up his hands defensively. "Fifteen-minute delivery, twenty bucks."

Hendrix shoved two bills at him. "Here's forty. Go!" He then dashed back out the door before the courier could ask for his company or a return address. He returned to his vehicle and watched a messenger leave the office five minutes later. He tracked the bicycle to the front door of the consulate and watched the messenger leave three minutes later. By now the receptionist would be opening his note:

YITZHAK, I FOUND ANGELA. CALL SCOTT AT (415) 561-0360

RED QUEEN

DECEMBER 20, 2002 – ALEXANDRIA, VIRGINIA

As spymasters went, Gavin Carter's office was unimpressive. The small table with four chairs for meetings, and the couch for informal discussions—he used it more often as a substitute for going home to sleep—were entirely Office Depot issue. The only decoration on the plain white walls was the large plasma screen TV he used as a projection screen for meetings and occasionally for a ball game when he worked on weekends. At the moment it played the feed from a roof camera showing jets arriving and departing Reagan National airport next door. A window wouldn't have provided much of a view—his office was twenty feet underground.

Carter's operation was probably the most daring enterprise in national security the CIA had ever launched. The organization he led had no formal title. In meetings they referred to themselves simply as "The Team." Their code name for internal CIA communications was RED QUEEN, from the ruler of the kingdom on the far side of the looking glass. Their funding came strictly from "non-appropriated sources," meaning overseas CIA "enterprises" of questionable legality. This made RED QUEEN even more secret than "waived" Special Access programs, which were accountable only to the Majority and Minority Leaders in both houses of Congress and the President.

RED QUEEN didn't report to Congress, or the President, or even to the Director of the CIA. Those people changed with the whims of the American electorate. He reported to the CIA's Deputy Director for Operations, a thirty-year-professional of "down-and-dirty" spy work. The current CIA Director was briefed on RED QUEEN operations, but that was by *Carter's* choice. If a purely political appointee became CIA Director, Carter would simply cut him out of the loop.

After September 11, it became clear to everyone that the Operations side of the CIA had become totally hamstrung by presidential politics. Each administration had opposing agendas to the preceding administration, and some might even prosecute CIA professionals for simply obeying lawful orders. That insanity had to stop, or the horror of September 11 would be repeated many times over. This was the genesis of RED QUEEN, a "CIA outside of the CIA" that could carry out operations solely from the viewpoint of "Is it good for US security?" rather than the how it would poll in the New York *Times* or at the UN. If the leader of RED QUEEN decided somebody needed to be whacked, they got whacked, and he didn't need to call the White House or the State Department for input. It was just *done*, no questions asked.

The reason RED QUEEN worked was because it never relied on "plausible deniability," the mantra of the CIA during the Cold War. RED QUEEN used a "pin the tail on the donkey" approach, meaning if an operation could not be convincingly blamed on someone other than the US, the operation did not go forward. The Israelis were a frequent scapegoat of choice, which meant that RED QUEEN operatives were experts in Israeli methods. Suicides, murder-suicides, accidents, and heart attacks were also frequent scapegoats, along with Carter's personal favorite, the prematurely exploding suicide vest.

Carter examined the weekly training reports for the four new operatives he had recruited from the CIA's Class 11, including Angela Conrad. His nose for talent had been spot-on—as usual—with the new recruits performing superbly on an individual basis as well as meshing cohesively with current team members. But Conrad was still the stand-out among the recruits—the woman was a natural. During breaking and entry training she had shown her instructor a trick even *he* hadn't known; she had learned it while on the Philadelphia police force. Likewise her armed and unarmed combat skills were more in line with an Olympic athlete or a professional competitive shooter. She had a knack for violence that just couldn't be taught.

Conrad also had an almost chameleon-like gift for languages. She had studied Spanish for her police work and entertained her instructors by changing dialects and regional accents on command. Carter had assigned her Hebrew and Farsi simultaneously in an attempt to overwhelm and maybe humble her a bit. Other than an occasional complaint about chipping a tooth trying to pronounce Hebrew consonants, she was already able to make simple break-room banter with her instructors in both languages. So much for humility.

And then there was the sex. The male and female operatives of RED QUEEN were expected to use their natural abilities for leverage against either sex, as the Israelis and Russians had for decades. "Pillow talk is the oldest form of espionage in the book," Carter explained. "Just ask Sampson about Delilah." When one female recruit had expressed a squeamishness about sleeping with other women, Conrad asked Carter if she could borrow his office. He reluctantly agreed. When Conrad and the other recruit emerged an hour later, the blushing student reported her reservations resolved. Carter never looked at that couch the same way again. Conrad was the find of a lifetime.

Carter looked up at the sound of a knock on his open office door. Doctor Fenway, the team psychologist, stood reluctantly in the doorway.

"Got a few minutes?" Fenway asked, making a tentative move to close the door to indicate the sensitivity of the conversation.

He didn't. "Sure, Stan. Close the door."

Fenway perched his thin frame uneasily on the edge of the couch. "Did you get the latest psych profiles I sent you?"

Carter frowned. Given RED QUEEN's paperless system, this was one time he wished he could wave at a heaping, physical inbox. "I saw it come in, I haven't had time to look at it. I gotta leave for Pakistan in an hour; I probably won't get to it before I go. Wanna give me the Cliff Notes version?"

Fenway squirmed uncomfortably. "There's a problem with one of your students."

"You mean Cynthia? Yeah, I saw that one coming." Because of the sensitive and demanding nature of RED QUEEN's work, students and established operatives alike were subjected to regular psychological screenings. Even *he* had to look at Fenway's Rorschach blots twice a year. And some people who could blow an aggressor away in self defense without a second thought had a totally opposite reaction when asked to take a life in cold blood. Not everyone should—or could—become a trigger puller.

"I'm not talking about Cynthia. I'm talking about Angela Conrad."

Carter pushed away from his desk. "Angela Conrad is a natural-born killer if I ever met one."

Fenway's face hardened. "Psychopaths usually are."

Carter was incredulous. "A psychopath? You're crazy."

Fenway didn't appreciate the humor. "Psychologists usually are. It comes from being around crazy people. But back to Conrad. She reminds me of a patient I treated in the service. This guy comes back from Vietnam, decorated Marine recon. Cuts up a prostitute outside Camp Pendleton for bait. He's arrested, diagnosed as criminally insane, and comes under my care. A standard regimen of Thorazine and Haloperidal were administered, and he was retested. His psychosis was completely controlled. I sat across the table from him and we ended up talking baseball."

"Had you fooled?"

Fenway nodded slowly. "I was a lot younger then, but yes. The next day during a meeting with his lawyer he worked a piece of metal loose from his chair and slit the poor bastard's throat from ear to ear, killed an MP the same way, escaped the stockade—and you know what he did next?"

"Found another prostitute and cut her up for bait?"

"You catch on quick. But the point is, he could game the system by telling even a trained psychologist what they expected to hear. Conrad reminds me of that Marine."

Carter cocked his head. "I hope you saved some of that Haloperidol for yourself."

The psychologist's nostrils flared. "I'm serious, Gavin. I gave up on getting a straight answer out of Conrad and just watched her *behaviors* for three solid days on the security monitors. She may not be an axe-murderer, but she's a stone-cold sociopath, of that much I'm certain."

"What *kind* of behaviors?"

"Superficial charm, grandiose self-worth, pathological lying, impulsiveness—recall that little incident at Camp Peary—promiscuous behavior, criminal versatility, need I go on? These are all hallmarks of an Aggressive Integrated Sociopath. The *integrated* part is what *really* makes her dangerous. She could convince *anybody* she's *completely* normal and *completely* on their side, right up to the moment she slits their throat."

Carter massaged his chin. "What you're describing could also be the world's most perfect covert agent."

Fenway squinted. "I don't like what I'm hearing, Gavin. I'm trying to warn you about an oncoming train wreck and you seem to be covering for her."

Carter sighed and looked down. "Listen, Stan, I hear you, and I appreciate the thoroughness of your work. And if Angela was an average student, or even an above average student, I'd process her out today. But honestly, in my twenty-five years in this business, I've never met anyone like her. It's like meeting Babe Ruth or Michael Jordan in their rookie season. There's just a sense of impending greatness about her."

Fenway gave him a wistful smile. "People said the same thing about Hitler. By the way, he was an Aggressive Integrated Sociopath too."

He raised his hands in diplomatic supplication. "Okay, let's keep an eye on her. Get a second opinion on your diagnosis if you need to."

Fenway jumped to his feet, his face livid. "Listen to me, Gavin! What do you think the chances are of getting *another* psychologist cleared onto this black hole program? As far as who is fit for duty and who is not, my word is *law*. Get used to it."

Carter glared back. "And as far as who stays on my team and who doesn't, *my* word is law. Get used to it."

After a short staring match, Fenway declared, "I'm taking this up with the Deputy Director."

Carter never blinked. "Please do."

Fenway made his retreat, but threw the last word over his shoulder. "You keep this girl on the program and you're going to live to regret it. At least I *hope* you live to regret it."

* * *

Conrad knocked on Carter's office door a few minutes later. "You asked to see me, sir?"

He waved her in, signaling for her to close the door. "You ever been to Pakistan?"

She made a face. "Other than a trip to Cancun, I've never left the country. A police officer's pay doesn't allow for much globetrotting."

He winked at her. "You're not a police officer any more. I've got a short fuse job and I need a female wingman. You game?"

Her eyes lit up. "A *real* mission? I'm not even halfway through training."

"Consider this *part* of your training. I'll run point, and I'll be there to bail you out during *your* part if anything goes wrong," he lied. Conrad was going to be working entirely without a net on this job.

"What's the mission?" she asked breathlessly.

"The NSA has proof positive that three Pakistani generals are on the take for the Taliban. Every time we ask the Pakis for permission to launch a strike, one of these guys makes a phone call and we come up empty. The NSA told the CIA, and the CIA is going to send a 'strongly worded protest' to the Pakis, but we're going to send a little *stronger* message."

"Sniper rifle?" she asked hopefully.

He gave her a wicked grin and fished in his pocket, placing a small silver tube loudly onto his glass desktop. "Breath spray."

She matched his evil gaze. "Oh, *do* tell."

"Our target, General Farouk Kamir, has a pronounced weakness for the ladies. I'm going to get you in the door as the saleswoman for an American company that makes military radios. You're going to express your willingness to do *whatever* it takes to get his permission to field test your equipment with his troops. Then, when he takes you to his parlor, you ask him to freshen his breath a bit with *this*," he said, holding up the cylinder.

"Cyanide?"

"No, breath spray. Along with a lethal dose of potassium chloride. He has a heart attack, but there's no injection mark like a usual potassium chloride hit would leave."

She nodded. "Sweet. Whose donkey do we pin the tail on?"

"Is your Hebrew good enough to call me on the phone and say the mission's accomplished and you need extraction?"

She thought for a second. "It will be by the time we get there."

"Good, because the CIA says he likes to videotape his conquests. If the Pakis have you on video making that call, good luck to the Mossad getting *that* tail unpinned from their ass."

Her face glowed with anticipation. "I like it."

Carter gave her a cautioning look. "This is the real deal. You in?"

"Oh, *hell* yes!" she said hungrily.

Carter smiled. If Fenway pressed his point with the Deputy Director for Operations, Conrad would be gone. But if Carter took her to Pakistan and she returned with a clean kill under her belt, the DDO would almost certainly take Carter's side. RED QUEEN was all about taking the initiative. It was a risky plan to be sure, but if Conrad screwed up and got herself killed or captured, she would be one less problem for him to deal with, wouldn't she?

"Great," he said, "go home and pack. I'll pick you up in an hour."

She stepped around the desk, leaning seductively toward him. "Is there time for me to *properly* thank you for this opportunity?"

Carter unbuckled his pants. "Yes, I believe there *is*!"

PRIMARY PLAYERS

PRESENT DAY – CHICAGO, ILLINOIS

Simon Crane called his agent for the Nanovex operation. “Report,” he ordered.

“The first termination went smoothly. For your information, sir, this case is already receiving Federal attention. It’s like they were anticipating it.”

He smiled inwardly. “That is not unexpected. In fact it’s necessary. They are not to be harmed unless it is absolutely unavoidable, acknowledge.”

“Acknowledged, sir. Federal assets are not to be harmed if avoidable.”

Crane’s voice turned even colder than usual. “I have intelligence that one of the primary players may be in danger. I am sending the data now. This is to be prevented at all costs. My proscription against Federal casualties is waived in that event.”

The voice on the other end sounded concerned. “Thank you for the information, sir. However, adding protection duties to my assignment will distract from my final security objectives.”

“The primary players must be protected at all costs. This takes priority over your final security assignment.”

His agent sounded slightly confused, but compliant. “Orders received and understood.”

He was already hanging up. “Very well. Crane out.”

CURIOSITY

SAN JOSE, CALIFORNIA

Mike Manning did his best to look bored as he studied the fire evacuation plan on the basement wall of the Nanovex building. He had never been to this part of the building, but the map was fairly detailed. The hallway where he stood was unadorned and sterile, with keypad-locked doors lining both sides. Placards marked each lab door, with names like Chemistry, Nanoprocessing, Electrical Properties, and Microscopy. These were all duly reflected on the evacuation chart. But around the corner were three large rooms, colored yellow, orange and red on the map. A large title spanned all three rooms, saying simply, “Proprietary Labs.”

The first door was keypad-locked like the others, with a placard “P3.” The access door had a small wire-reinforced window. Through it he could see another long hallway with three doors on one side. The first door was marked “P3-1.”

The next proprietary lab was marked “P4.” Under the keypad lock a biometric hand scanner projected from the wall. Through the window he saw another hallway, with the first door inside marked “P4-1.”

His pulse quickened as he approached the third lab. This entrance was guarded by a keypad, a hand scanner, *and* a retinal scanner. The first door beyond the locked portal was marked “P5-1.” It was a safe assumption that the room he was seeking, P5-3, was at the far end of that hallway.

“Can I help you, Mike?” a voice behind him announced loudly.

Manning made a startled turn, trying to keep his expression as un-guilty as possible. Reese Miller, Lyman’s head of Security, stood behind him, his hands on his hips.

“Oh, hi Reese!” he said with a smile. “Just stretching my legs.”

“You don’t have access to any of the labs down here,” Miller observed, not returning Manning’s smile.

“I noticed!” he said with a laugh. “I was just curious what was down here in the basement.”

Miller donned a plastic smile. “Curiosity is a security officer’s least favorite word. If you don’t mind, I’d appreciate it if you’d stretch your legs somewhere else.”

His smile back was equally plastic. “Sure, no problem! Won’t happen again.”

“Had lunch yet?” Miller asked.

Manning glanced at his watch. “No, but it’s about that time though, isn’t it?”

Miller extended his hand toward the stairwell. “I’ll walk you up.”

* * *

Miller leaned into Doug Lyman’s office a few minutes later. “Got a second?”

“Sure,” Lyman said, not looking up from his computer. “What’s going on?”

Miller walked to Lyman’s desk, lowering his voice. “I caught Mike Manning downstairs snooping around the proprietary labs.”

Lyman looked up, removing his bifocals. “Snooping?”

“He said he was just stretching his legs, but he was also looking through the fire window at the P5 labs. Said he was just curious.”

Lyman shrugged. “Maybe he was. What does your gut tell you?”

Miller’s look hardened. “To keep *both* eyes on him, not just one.”

Lyman nodded, returning his bifocals to his nose. “Then do that. If you catch him snooping around again, let me know.”

RECOGNITION

SAN JOSE, CALIFORNIA

Wendy Cho was anxious when her boss Perry Pugliano announced his intention of attending her daily progress meeting with the Nanovex management about the death of Josh Hackett. Partly because there *was* no progress on the Hackett investigation. The specialists the FBI flew out from Quantico were just as clueless as to what killed him as the county coroner had been. It turned out that Pugliano was there to report on his progress toward the *cover-up* of the five workers from the *previous* death investigation. They certainly had more than their share of death and mayhem at this company.

Pugliano reported that the matter was "taken care of" and that the bodies would be released to the families within the next day or two. Their CEO Lyman seemed emotionally affected by the news, putting a hand to his head and remarking about how hard the funerals would be. The other Nanovex suits—Miller, Graves, and Manning—acted like they had just received a quarterly earnings report.

Pugliano then tossed the meeting over to her and she improvised a riff about the specialists from Quantico "still running some tests," trying not to look like she had her thumb up her ass. Thankfully no one pressed her for details.

She had to force herself not to stare at that lawyer Mike Manning. Knowing that the quiet, nondescript guy across the table from her was allied with one of the CIA's most wanted terrorists made her want to jump across the table and beat the truth out of him, but her handler Scott Hendrix said he would take care of that soon enough. All she had to do was make sure no one else figured out Manning's secret.

The meeting was mercifully over soon enough. Now it was time for her to press her other agenda. She and Pugliano walked outside to the visitor's lot.

"Sir?" she asked sweetly. "Do you have any plans for dinner?" If she could get him alone long enough for small talk, she could casually mention the dessert she had whipped up last night, and how her apartment was just a couple of miles away. She had conned his secretary into telling her his favorite dessert, and had bought a Boston Cream Pie from one of the best bakeries in San Francisco. She was confident that if she could get to his sweet tooth, his zipper would be within reach.

"Never mind dinner," he said excitedly. "Could you join me in my car for a moment?"

She had just slid into his passenger seat, congratulating herself on her easy conquest, when he added, "Let me see your laptop for a second!"

Disappointed, she extracted her computer and booted it up.

"Do you remember the Running Man from the Sheraton?" he gushed.

Her heart skipped a beat. "You mean the guy we were never able to identify?"

"Yeah, the guy with Angela Conrad. Pull up those pictures."

She couldn't think of a way of erasing her hard drive with him watching, so she complied, selecting the most blurry, oblique photo in the set. "Here, this guy?"

He reached over the car's center console and started driving her laptop himself. "No, that picture right *there*!"

An image-enhanced freeze frame of Mike Manning filled her screen.

"*Bingo!*" he crowed. When she failed to share his jubilation, he asked, "What? You don't *see it*?"

Cho had many skills, but playing dumb had never been one of her core competencies. "See what?" she said absently.

"That Nanovex lawyer from the meeting, Manning. That's him!"

She squinted at the screen and curled her lip. "I don't think so," she lied.

Pugliano was exuberant. "Oh, come on Wendy! Look through the rest of the set." He motioned at her laptop frantically when she hesitated. "C'mon! Look!"

She complied, reluctantly flipping through the rest of the photos.

He watched her expectantly, waiting for her reaction. "*There*, don't you *see* it? That's *him*! That's their lawyer…Manning…Manning. I forgot his first name."

She shook her head. "I can't remember either," she lied again

He waved his hands. "It doesn't matter! In a half hour I'll call Lyman and say I've got some kind of legal question and ask for Manning's cell phone number. Then we'll be all over him like ugly on a monkey! And the next time he meets or talks to Angela Conrad, we will *bag her sweet ass!*" He paused for a second. "Sorry, that was sexist."

She was too mortified to even pretend offense. "No worries. But are you sure you've got the right guy? I was right there with you in that meeting and I just don't think this is the same person." She had to pull him off this track.

Pugliano was undeterred. "Wendy, I've been doing this for two decades longer than you. You're just going to have to give me the benefit of the doubt. Manning's our guy, trust me!"

"O-kay," she stammered, "what about dinner?" If she couldn't stop the train, she hoped to at least delay it long enough to warn Hendrix. Maybe he could scoop up Manning before the FBI found him and have a CIA interrogation team squeeze Conrad's location out of him.

Pugliano pretended to give her a playful rap on the head. "Where are your *priorities*, rookie? We got *bad guys* to catch! Get back to the field office and start rounding up the troops. I'll go up the chain and make sure we have all the assets we need for the surveillance."

He shooed her from his car. "Get on it! Go! *Go!*"

Her hands shook when she made the call to Hendrix.

He was surprisingly nonchalant. "Don't worry," he assured her. "It'll take time for Pugs to get his surveillance together, and I'm making *my* move *right now*."

[1] The reading of computer data remotely is a very real technology and a very real concern for people who need to keep secrets, like banks, governments, and defense contractors. The only real defense is to construct what are called TEMPEST spaces that trap the transmissions from PCs inside a large metal box where people work.

[2] Photo credit: Axis History Forum

[3] Argentinean investigator Abel Basti claims to have in his possession a declassified Argentinean Intelligence document dated May 1945 recounting the arrival of a large multiengined German transport plane which landed on the private airfield of a German-owned ranch in Entre Rios province. The aircraft unloaded a "bell-shaped device" and some passengers. Basti claims it is illegal to release previously classified documents to non-nationals even after declassification, so he merely related their content in his book, *Bariloche Nazi* (Bariloche is a predominantly German-immigrant town in Argentina). What's particularly interesting is that the purported Argentinean document was declassified in 1993, a full ten years before Witkowski drew interest to the subject of the Bell. Argentinean investigators were interested only in the fate of the Nazis, not their technologies, so the "bell-shaped device" documentation went unnoticed for more than a decade.

CHAPTER 13

NEAR-DEATH

SAN JOSE CALIFORNIA

Mike Manning was only a short distance from his hotel when his cell phone rang. His blood ran cold when the caller identified himself as Perry Pugliano, the FBI agent. Were they finally on to him? He reasoned not. The FBI usually announced their presence with drawn weapons and arrest warrants.

"Sorry to bother you after work," Pugliano continued, "but I had a legal question I forgot to ask in our meeting."

"Shoot," he replied. *That's odd, aren't most FBI agents lawyers already?*

"It's about the forensic specialists we brought in for the autopsies. They're some of our best people and I'm concerned about them being tied up for months as witnesses in five different lawsuits. What do you see as the best way to head that off?"

"Well, I'd have your specialists draw up a sworn deposition that can be distributed to the families before legal proceedings even begin. If you could have your agents hand deliver the depositions and discuss them with the families, that would probably be our best shot at avoiding litigation entirely. Sorry, I should have thought of that in our meeting."

"No harm done," Pugliano assured him. "So our people would be off the hook, then?"

"Oh no; if the families don't drop their lawsuits, which I'm sure most of them won't, your people will still have to give depositions and testify. A sworn deposition can't be cross-examined." *An FBI agent should know this.*

Pugliano sighed. "No workarounds you know of?"

Manning pulled onto the Hotel Montgomery's parking lot. "I'm sure if you file a motion about the value of these people's time, we can arrange to have the depositions taken in whatever city they work from. But the trials will take place *here*, and there's nothing we can do to stop their lawyers from subpoenaing your specialists to testify. Sorry, that's just the way it is." *Maybe you'll remember that next time before you agree to assist in a cover-up.*

"Okay, well, thanks for the information."

Manning pulled into a spot and threw the gearshift into Park. "No problem, anytime."

He thought Pugliano had ceded the argument too quickly, but maybe he was just confirming the legal opinions of his fellow agents. Sometimes the boss became so experienced he forgot the basics. He thought of how many times he had stopped his lawyer boss Bernie Norquist from stepping on his own legal weenie over simple procedures he hadn't performed himself in years. He reached for his jacket draped over the passenger seat and emerged from the rental car with a tired sigh.

And had a gun stuck in his face.

The stocky Hispanic man had a shaved head and a tattoo crawling from under his T-shirt up the side of his neck. He was sweating, and the hand that held the gun twitched nervously. "Wallet and phone!" he demanded.

Manning held up his free hand, easing his coat off his shoulder. "Easy pal, easy! My wallet's in here!" he said, pointing to the jacket.

"*Get it!*" the robber growled, pushing the gun closer to Manning's face.

"Okay, okay, here it comes!" he said, reaching inside the jacket. He extracted the wallet and held it out.

The robber snatched it away. "Your phone too!"

Oh crap. "Okay, easy! Here you go!" He handed it over. *What if Conrad can't reach me? Will she call the hotel, or just kill my family for spite?*

The robber grinned, knowing Manning wasn't going to resist. "And the watch!"

Manning sighed, handing over the platinum Brietling his wife had gotten him for their fifth anniversary.

"Turn around! On your knees!"

Manning's already pounding heart ramped up into overdrive. "C'mon, man!" he pleaded. "I gave you everything you wanted!"

The robber pushed the gun barrel against his forehead. "I'm not gonna tell you again!"

Manning turned away and knelt, reaching out to the cars on either side to steady his shaking legs as he did so. *I wonder how pissed Conrad will be that she didn't get to kill me herself?*

The robber pressed the gun to the back of his skull. "If I see you stand up or turn around, I'll come back here and *shoot you*, got it?"

"Got it!" he immediately agreed.

Manning sagged forward onto his hands when he heard the robber run away. He took his first real breath since the robber had appeared. He stayed put as the footfalls faded in the distance. He heard a car door slam and tires peel away.

* * *

In the getaway car, the robber handed Manning's cell phone and wallet over to Scott Hendrix. "Here you go, sir."

"Thank you, Agent Sanchez. Any problems?"

The "robber" shook his head. "Nah, he played it smart." Sanchez fished Manning's watch from his pocket and tried it on his wrist.

Hendrix made a face. "You took his *watch*, too?"

Sanchez gave Hendrix an innocent look. "*What*? It was a *robbery*, right?"

Hendrix just shook his head. He pulled to the curb a few blocks from Manning's hotel. He got out and entered an idling phone company service truck. Inside, a young man and a woman occupied terminals filled with monitors and radio equipment. He placed Manning's Blackberry on the woman's station.

"Clone this phone," he ordered.

The technician hooked the cell phone to her terminal and made a few picks on her screen. She unplugged the Blackberry and handed it back. "Okay, we're tapped in."

"Thanks." Hendrix exited the van and walked to the car parked one space forward along the curb. It was a silver Chevy Malibu, just like the rental Manning drove. He handed the phone to the driver, who was about Manning's height and build. The blond hair required a wig, however. The tags had been faked to match Manning's as well.

"We have no idea when Conrad will try to make contact," Hendrix said, "so stay in motion. I'll keep you updated on Agent Cho's position so you can keep your distance from their tail."

"Got it," the driver replied, raising his window and pulling away from the curb.

Hendrix returned to the van and called Wendy Cho's cell phone.

"Is the tail rolling yet?" he asked.

"We've just completed our briefing. Moving to our vehicles now." He could tell from her clipped formality that other FBI agents were in earshot.

"Good. The fox is running. Release the hounds."

* * *

Mike Manning wondered how many near-death experiences a person could have before repetitive terror turned near-death into real death. He was still shaking when he entered the hotel's lobby to report the crime. He couldn't even return to his hotel room; his keycard was in his stolen wallet. Luckily the Montgomery was a small hotel and the staff knew him by sight. The manager apologized profusely for his trauma and fetched him a double scotch while he sat in her office waiting for the police to take his statement.

The San Jose police also proved very user-friendly and spent most of the interview assuring Manning how unusual this type of crime was in their city and how they would redouble their patrols in the wake of his incident.

New keycard in hand, he returned to his room, attended by the still-supplicating manager. He used her discomfiture to have a steak dinner delivered to his room, and to borrow her cell phone to cancel his credit cards, claiming he needed to keep the room phone free "for an important call from home."

The phone rang at 8:00 p.m. sharp. He pounced on it like a drowning man on a lifeline. Unfortunately it was Amanda, and she launched into her prepared remarks without so much as a "How was your day?"

"First of all, thank your boss for the flowers. They were lovely. Tell him they're prettier than anything my husband's ever gotten me."

Ouch. "Okay, well I…."

"I'm not *finished*," she snapped. "Tell him the sentiment was lovely, but it hardly makes up for being abandoned by my husband."

Christ. "But I haven't…."

"*Still* not finished! I don't know what you consider abandonment, but our checking account is down to three hundred dollars and for *some reason* your previous employer has stopped making direct deposits. Oh! Maybe it was because you *quit!* Do you have any idea when I might start seeing *checks* from your new employer, in lieu of flowers?"

Manning rubbed his throbbing temples. "Hon, I am *so* sorry. I'll wire you five thousand tomorrow…."

"*Five thousand!*" she shouted. "Just how much do you *have* in your little *personal* stash? And just when did you plan on sharing some of that with your family?"

"Hon, again, I am *so* sorry," he dodged. "I know it's no excuse, but I've been so busy that I just forgot to send you a check. It's not because I don't care about you and the kids." There was no way he was going to tell her Lyman had awarded him a twenty-five thousand dollar signing bonus. Her appetite for *stuff* was a big reason they were in hock. He had never been this far ahead of his creditors, and he had no intention of giving up his lead so she could go on another buying spree. *Silly boy*, Conrad's voice taunted inside his head, *you're thinking like you're going to live through this.*

"How much are you *making* on this new job?" she demanded.

"I haven't gotten a check yet, so I'm not sure *exactly* what my weekly take home will be…."

"*Bullshit!* If you haven't gotten a check yet, where did you get the *five thousand*?"

"He gave me a five thousand dollar signing bonus," he lied.

"Oh! And you're just going to sign it *all* over to me, right?" she said incredulously. "I know you better than that! If you're willing to *give me* five without a fight, then you must have gotten *ten*. Let's hear you lie about that!"

He groaned. "Why should I hide my money from you? We *are* still married, right?" He was struck again how much his conversations with Amanda now sounded like arguments with an angry *ex*-wife.

That gave her pause. "That's what I wanted to ask *you*."

He looked at his bare wrist where his watch used to be. Finding no clue to the time there, he looked at the bedside clock. He needed to get off this call. Conrad would be pissed enough that he wasn't answering his cell phone.

"Of course we are," he assured her. "But if you don't mind, I was just robbed at gunpoint an hour ago and I'd prefer to have this conversation tomorrow."

"*What?*"

"I was just robbed on the hotel parking lot. The punk is probably hocking my cell phone for drugs right now."

"Did he take your wallet too?"

"Of *course* he did," he said sarcastically, "But don't worry about me, *I'm just fine*."

"My God, why didn't you *say* something?"

"I didn't get much of a chance."

"I'm sorry. I'm glad you're okay."

He was anxious to end the call while he had a tactical advantage. "Thanks. I'll wire you the money tomorrow. Good night."

He decided against taking a shower, in case he missed Conrad's call. Collapsing onto the bed, he lay staring at the ceiling, his heart still pounding. He willed himself to try to sleep before the inevitable call came, knowing all along it was a futile effort.

TRACKERS

SAN JOSE, CALIFORNIA

Hendrix cursed himself for not bringing a book on this stake out. He had played games on his smart phone until the battery threatened to die. He settled for making a Chinese food run for the crew at midnight. He returned to find the two technicians, Rob and Keisha, bantering excitedly.

"Holy crap!" Rob exclaimed. "I thought his *wife* was pissed when he didn't pick up his cell phone!"

"Wow, I need to play this for my boyfriend," Keisha agreed. "He thinks *I* bitch at him!"

"What's up?" Hendrix asked.

"Conrad called Manning's cell phone three times; here's her last message," Rob said, hitting a digital playback button. Conrad's profanity-laced excoriation filled the van. She ended the call by saying she was going to call the hotel and if he didn't answer there he'd better have said his good-byes to his family.

"Nothing more painful than being caught between your wife and your mistress," Hendrix muttered. *Trust me, I know.*

"His mistress?" Keisha asked. "You think Manning is *sleeping* with her?"

He nodded. "With Conrad, it's practically a job requirement."

Rob lifted an eyebrow mischievously. "You sound like you speak from experience."

"No, and I can prove it."

"How's that?"

"Because I'm still *alive.*" He bent over Rob's terminal. "Is that tracker I put on Manning's car still sweet?"

Rob pointed to a flashing blip on his moving map display. "Sweet and stationary."

"I have a feeling it's going to start moving real soon, keep an eye on it." He moved to Keisha's terminal. "Did you lock on to Conrad's phone?"

She pointed to an unblinking dot on another moving map display. "Yeah, but she's good. She turns her phone off when she's not using it. That tracker on Manning's car is going to be our only clue as to her location, and if he transfers to her vehicle, we'll lose even that."

"And if we follow her close enough to maintain visual contact," Rob added, "she'll pick up the tail for sure."

Hendrix was already playing chess with Conrad in his head. "Can we use the phone company override and turn her cell on remotely if we need to, Keisha?"

She frowned. "Yeah, unless she's pulled the battery. And if she hears her phone come on, she'll know something's up."

"Don't worry about it." Hendrix smiled. *If it comes to that, it will be one of the last sounds she ever hears.*

* * *

To his surprise, Manning fell into a fitful sleep twice before Conrad's call woke him. Both times he was welcomed into his dream state by a snarling robber with a gun. But in his dreams, the robber demanded not his material possessions but his family. To his horror, both times he turned them over to the tattooed man's mercy without hesitation. He was almost grateful when Conrad dragged him back to reality.

"*You son of a bitch!*" she hissed. "You'd better have a good reason for not picking up your phone!"

"You mean like having my phone taken from me at gunpoint?" he shot back, tired of having to explain himself to two demanding women in one night.

"Oh, bullshit!" she answered in disbelief.

"Screw you!" he shouted back. He had had enough of Conrad's threats and ridicule. Having her put a bullet in him would be a mercy. "You're not the one who had a gun stuck in your face!"

She laughed in derision. "If you knew how to handle yourself, that wouldn't be a problem, would it?"

His irritation had revved up almost to a death wish. "Believe me, if I had those kind of skills, I would have put you in the ground the first time you threatened me!"

She laughed coldly. "Point taken. You ready to roll?"

He swung his legs out of bed. "Give me ten minutes. How are we going to meet without a phone?" He knew she wouldn't do something straightforward like just giving him an address. That would be too simple.

A few seconds of silence followed. "There's a surface lot three blocks north of your hotel. In fifteen minutes there'll be a cell phone on top of the ticket box. I'll call it in twenty."

Manning reached for his sweatpants. "Got it."

* * *

"Hot damn!" Hendrix exclaimed. "How quick can we get there?"

Rob looked at his map display. "Three minutes."

Hendrix turned to the female technician. "Keisha, were you able to get a fix on Conrad?"

She pointed at the screen. "She's already turned off her phone again, but yeah. She's about five minutes out."

"Rob, let's roll!" he ordered.

The technician headed for the driver's seat. "Rolling."

"Keisha, get me a satellite photo of that parking lot and the surrounding area," he ordered. When it came up, he leaned over her shoulder, squinting at the screen. "Can you find the ticket box she's talking about?"

Keisha smoothly manipulated the image controls. "Right there, on the west side of the lot."

He pointed to a spot a block east on a side street. "I want to be right *there*. Can you send those coordinates to Rob?"

"No problem." Her manicured fingers danced on the keyboard. "Rob, darling," she called with mock affection, "I need to be at this location facing north, pretty please."

"Anything for you, sugar lips," the driver called back.

"How sweet they are, you'll never know, you little pig."

The driver laughed. "Bite me. Be there in two minutes."

"In your dreams. Thanks."

Children, Hendrix thought. "While we're waiting, show me Agent Cho's location."

Keisha zoomed out on her moving map display until a flashing dot appeared. "She's on the 101 heading south, about twenty miles northwest."

"And the Manning decoy car?"

"He's three miles west in Santa Clara, just past the 880."

He placed a call to the decoy vehicle. "I need you to get on the 880 and kick ass north, as fast as you can without getting pulled over."

"Yanking the tail out of position?" the decoy driver asked.

"You got it. If you can convince them you're headed up the east side of the bay, maybe they'll take the 84 bridge across, or even better be forced to *double back* and take the bridge. That'll put them *miles* away from our operation."

"I'm two miles west of the 880 now. I'll be hauling ass north in five."

Once on location, Rob shut down the truck and retreated behind the blackout curtain into the equipment bay. Keisha aimed a sensitive camera through a hidden port in the van's sidewall, zooming on the parking lot's ticket dispenser. She passed the image to one of the monitors so Hendrix could watch.

A rental truck pulled into view three minutes later. A man jumped from the passenger side and deposited a small item on the ticket box. Keisha zoomed in tight and got a close full-face and profile shot before he returned to the truck. It pulled away, and Keisha zoomed in again, getting a clear shot of the license tag. The truck turned left at the next street and disappeared from view.

"Nicely done," Hendrix observed.

"Thanks," Keisha replied, returning to her terminal. She interlaced her fingers and cracked them loudly. "Now, time for a little data mining!"

* * *

Manning pulled to the curb. The cell phone was right where Conrad said it would be. He returned to his car and drove a convoluted path to draw out any pursuers, even though traffic was nearly non-existent. He carefully obeyed speed limits and used his signals with every turn. The last thing he needed was to be pulled over by a cop for driving without a license. The phone finally rang.

"Are you clear?" she asked.

At the moment he was passing San Jose City Hall. "It would be kind of hard for anyone to follow. I think I'm the only one out tonight."

"Not quite," she corrected. "I've been watching your maneuvers; good technique. We may make a spy out of you yet."

"Imagine my joy."

"Take your next right turn. There's a parking lot next to City Hall. Pick a spot with good visibility and watch for me."

* * *

"What have you got?" Hendrix asked.

Keisha studied her screen. "The truck was leased from Easy Street Rentals in San Francisco. The name on the credit card is Monica Geldman. Here's her credit card activity for the last three weeks, which is also the period that the account has existed."

He studied the readout. "Different hotel every night. Smart. Not many other purchases, though. Probably has a stash for every expense that doesn't require a credit card."

"That would keep her paper trail to a minimum," she agreed.

"Geldman…Geldman…" Hendrix muttered. "Where have I heard that name before?"

LOYALTY

JANUARY 2005 – ISLAMABAD, PAKISTAN

Angela Conrad prepped carefully for her evening's appointment. After spending her first year following the mission assignments of Gavin Carter's RED QUEEN organization in Pakistan, she had suggested her own operation. She proposed establishing herself as a high-priced call girl specializing in the needs of the Pakistani military and government officials. With her fair skin, blonde hair, and passion for all things the Koran said were forbidden, her first trial runs were wildly successful in the pillow talk intelligence she gathered from her marks. Carter approved her operation on an ongoing basis, along with a four-man security detachment, one of whom posed as her pimp. But this was entirely *her* ball game, and she made sure her security detail never forgot it.

She now had the dubious distinction of being the highest-priced call girl in Pakistan by a factor of three. One stupid Pakistani pimp had been so jealous he tried to throw acid in her face on the street. He found out that not only did she have excellent acid-dodging reflexes, she was pretty handy with a knife as well. He was thereafter jokingly referred to by the team as "the Gelding Man."

Surprisingly, her big break came when one of her clients, a low-ranking but very energetic general, had injured his back so badly during sex he had to be taken from the hotel on a stretcher. Once word got around the Army staff how General Nasir had been "thrown from his horse," Conrad's phone rang so frequently she was able to select clients solely on the basis of the intelligence potential of the engagement.

After one year in operation, her intelligence take had been so good that the Deputy Director for Operations of the CIA had pinned an Intelligence Star on her lapel, asking her when the Pakistani military was going to grant her a seat on the General Staff. Her intelligence collection had led to so many Taliban and Al-Qaeda commanders meeting Allah via a Predator drone that there was nervous talk among the terrorists of a mysterious "infidel magic" in play. In truth, while she was most *certainly* an infidel, most of the magic was between her legs.

In time, other doors opened to her as well. One Pakistani Colonel identified himself as an undercover operative for Indian Intelligence and offered her a substantial retainer for merely keeping her ears open to information useful to India, plus bonuses for valuable information delivered. A similar conduit opened for her to Chinese Intelligence as well.

She justified these side deals as acceptable because the information India and China requested was seldom of interest to US intelligence. After all, she had *collected* the intelligence, why *shouldn't* she get paid for it? She was smart enough to know her career as a call-girl spy was doomed to be as short as any major-league athlete, and then she would have to go back to making money the old-fashioned way, which hardly appealed to her. So she secreted the Indian and Chinese money in numbered Swiss accounts, and congratulated herself on firming up her retirement plan without harming US national security.

Conrad checked her short red sequined cocktail dress—it was a favorite of her customers. Her matching slingback heels would have to wait in the olive drab "go-bag" over her shoulder. The streets of Islamabad would ruin any respectable pair of shoes. Instead she wore a pair of native sandals in which she would look as pathetic as every other Pakistani woman. Over the ensemble she wore a head-to-toe burqa which not only concealed her identity as a foreigner, but also protected her "work clothes" from any mud thrown up by vehicles on the crowded streets.

One of her security team knocked at the door. "Enter!" she called.

The door opened and Gavin Carter stepped inside. She didn't know who was more surprised—she to see her boss unannounced, or he to enter her apartment and find a woman in a burqa.

"Gavin! What a pleasant surprise!" she greeted him through her veil.

His eyes widened. "I see the reports that you've gone native are true!"

She tugged off the burqa and gave him a hug. "Oh yes; it's all a part of my grand strategy to seduce and betray Osama Bin Laden."

He gave her a strained smile. "I take it I'm interrupting?"

"Well…yes, actually. I have to leave shortly for an engagement. You know the drill, generals to lay, secrets to steal."

His smile faded. "Actually, you'd better call your client and cancel. We need to talk."

She tossed her burqa and go-bag on the couch. "My God, Gavin, what's wrong?"

His frown showed wrinkles that hadn't been there when she met him three years ago. "I don't think there's any easy way to say this so I'll just come right out with it. The Agency has evidence that you've been trafficking in national security information with foreign intelligence services."

Her mind raced. She knew that a half-truth was the best defense for an endangered lie. "Well Gavin, *trafficking* is a pretty harsh word. I'll admit I've been in contact with the Indians and the Chinese, but that's just part of the normal horse trading in the intelligence business. You trade information you don't need for information you do. You taught me that yourself."

He wasn't buying it. "How about trading the information you don't need for cold, hard cash?"

Make him prove it. "I don't know what you're talking about there. Who's your source? I sure as hell hope it's not some disgruntled general I denied a freebie."

His expression was deadpan. "It's not. The NSA has intercepts of Chinese and Indian sources in-country calling home with reports of fees paid for information—information that our security analyst traced back to you."

She threw up her hands in frustration. "Oh come on, Gavin! The only information I have comes from Pakistani government and military sources. And you *know* those guys leak like a sieve! How the hell can you say that I'm the *only* person with access to that information?"

Carter shrugged. "There's one way for sure to clear your name. Come home. Cooperate fully with the inquiry. Take a polygraph. Let the truth come out."

"The *truth*!" she growled. "You know as well as I do that once the Inspector General launches an investigation, they don't stop until *somebody's* head is in a basket! I think I'd rather take my chances with the Taliban than the IG."

He shook his head. "This isn't the IG. This is a RED QUEEN internal review. Whether you're found guilty or innocent, *nobody* on the outside is going to know about it, so there's no incentive for a political agenda. We only want the truth."

Conrad's blood ran cold. *Nobody* on the outside was going to know about it. That meant if they *did* have the goods on her, her fate would probably be—no, she corrected herself, could *only* be—an unmarked grave in the woods at Camp Peary. If she wanted to live—even if it meant living on the run for the rest of her life—there was no way she could go back with Carter.

His eyes bore into her. If she made the slightest show of resistance this would turn violent in an instant. And the guards outside would come to *his* assistance, not hers.

"Of course I'll go back with you, Gavin," she said, putting her hands in his. "You *know* I haven't done anything wrong. And I trust you with my life. I always have."

Carter took a deep breath and sighed. He looked like a weight had been lifted off his shoulders. "Good. Thank you. I didn't want to believe that you had done this…."

"I haven't," she interrupted.

A hint of a smile returned to his tense face. "I believe you."

She held out her arms. "I know you do. Come here, it's good to see you."

An hour later, she finally rolled off to lay at his side, both of their bodies dripping with sweat. "My God," she panted, "I had forgotten what it was like to be with a man who knew what the hell he was doing!"

Carter laughed, pulling away and swinging his legs to the floor. "You always were a bullshit artist!"

"Bullshit my ass!" she protested, raising up on one elbow and reaching with her other hand under the pillow. She had a variety of weapons secured behind the headboard. By feel she selected the one appropriate for this task. She knelt behind him, reaching one arm around and rubbing her sweat-slickened breasts against his back. "And just where do you think *you're* going, by the way?"

"I just need to go pee. Is that permitted, mistress?" he teased.

"You are excused, my servant. Hurry back, I'm still horny."

"You want *more*?" he gasped. "I don't know how you can keep this up, I'm…"

Just as he started to rise, she flung the garrote around his neck and pulled hard. Scrambling backwards, she pulled him off his feet onto the bed. As he flailed, she adjusted her position for leverage, then yanked with all her might. She heard his larynx crack. He fought back, but his struggles quickly weakened without oxygen. She let out a series of loud orgasmic shouts to cover his thrashing and moaning noises for the benefit of the guards outside. She held the garrote in place for a full two minutes after she felt his muscles go slack.

"Sorry Gavin," she apologized to the corpse, "but my loyalty only goes so far."

She had practiced the next sixty seconds once a day for the last three years. A black cotton outfit she kept in the top drawer of her dresser. Close-fitting, comfortable enough to fight and run in, but stylish enough to wear on a plane without drawing attention. Comfortable shoes. No time for socks or underwear, those were in the go-bag. She tossed the red heels out of the bag and wadded up the burqa inside instead. She pulled the silencer out of a side pocket and screwed it on her gun. The gun went on top of the burqa. Finally, she pulled the anti-tamper device out of another pocket and fixed it to the door. She carefully extracted the arming pin and tossed it on the carpet.

She walked quickly to the window, throwing aside the curtains and cranking the casement open. It was late afternoon. The last rays of the sun blazed over the adjacent housetops, but the street four floors below lay in shadow. She reached under the bed and grabbed the coil of climbing rope, heaved it over the windowsill, and followed it out.

Her problems began when the excess rope hit the ground. She was already exposed, her feet propped against the dirty exterior wall and both hands grasping the rope. The third guard of her three-man day shift, who had been watching her Mercedes, stepped out of the apartment's entryway. He reached for his radio.

"She's coming out the window!" he reported. He reached for his gun, holding it at ready but not pointing it at her. Yet. "Angela, don't do this!" he called up.

Shit. She braced against the wall, pushed out forcefully, let eight feet of slack slip through her hands, then grabbed hard. She swung into the window directly below her apartment, her momentum carrying her through. Glass crashed around her. She landed on the carpet of the third floor apartment, digging in the go-bag for her gun. She heard a woman scream.

Sweeping the room with her weapon, her sights came to rest on a woman emerging from the bathroom. The young Pakistani woman screamed again.

"Flat on the floor!" Conrad barked in Farsi. The woman complied.

"*Momma?*" a voice cried behind her.

She and the pistol whirled together. A toddler bolted upright on her sleeping pallet against the wall. She was about to start screaming. Conrad whipped her gun back onto the mother.

"Please!" the woman cried. "Don't make my daughter an orphan!"

Conrad froze momentarily. Then she heard two bodies hit the floor above her. Her guards had forced the door and encountered her anti-tamper device. It was Russian-made, and instead of using a directional explosive charge like the standard CIA devices, it used nerve gas. The Russian arms dealer had demanded $5000 for it, but apparently it was money well spent, because she was now down to one pursuer.

"Go to your daughter!" she ordered. "Don't move, even after I'm gone!" Conrad didn't look to see if the woman obeyed. She knew the mother was too terrified to resist.

Conrad grabbed a hand mirror off a dresser and flung open the door to the hallway. She checked both directions. Clear. She assumed a firing position covering the stairwell. *Maybe I'll get lucky and...*

The last guard burst up the stairwell, seeking a target.

...he'll do something stupid like that. She fired twice and heard his body tumble back down the stairs. Dashing down the hall, she confirmed her former protector was dead, and made her way cautiously down to the Mercedes.

It was a short drive to her storage locker in a working-class section of Islamabad. She left her car on the street with the keys inside. It would disappear shortly.

She rolled up the door on the garage-sized storage unit, for which she paid a princely sum of twenty dollars a month. Inside was a high-mileage Toyota Corolla, one of the most common cars in Pakistan. She turned on the headlights and closed the garage door, then squeezed past on the driver's side to retrieve her road bag from the trunk. In addition to food, water, and cash, there was an identity kit for a Spanish businessman, Miguel de Marco Amador.

Amador's passport showed multiple border crossings between Pakistan and India, in accordance with her cover as an exporter with business in both countries. She had proposed a female cover to the fake ID dealer, but he cautioned that women seldom drove alone in Pakistan, especially cross-country as an escape might entail. Better to pose as a man. So Conrad donned a black wig and fake mustache from the kit after changing into a man's clothes, also from the bag.

She could have easily made it to the airport in Islamabad and onto a flight before her crimes were discovered. But with the reach of the CIA, they might have reviewed airport security tapes and discovered her flight regardless of the name on her passport before her flight reached its destination. No, better to escape overland and take a flight from India. There was only so wide a net even the CIA could cast.

The three-hundred-kilometer trip on the highway from Islamabad to Lahore was almost scenic in spots. Almost. She had hoped to leave under better circumstances, but she was still glad to be leaving this stinking shithole of a country. One hundred and seventy million yahoos itching to fight for the right to stay in the eleventh century. Pakistan might mean *Land of the Pure* in Farsi, but pure *what* was always an open question to Conrad.

The only crossing between India and Pakistan was at Wagah, just east of Lahore. While Indians or Pakistanis were subject to meticulous scrutiny when trying to cross the border, a fair-skinned foreigner received only polite attention, even a woman posing as a man. She crossed early in the morning after spending the night in Lahore, changed back into a female alter ego once across the border, and was in Delhi by nightfall.

Two days later she arrived in Limassol, Cyprus. Once a sleepy fishing village on the south coast, it was now one of the most expensive cities in the world, thanks to twenty thousand Russians and almost as many shell companies filled with laundered money. Many came for the weather. Many more came for the lax banking laws and Cyprus's lack of an extradition treaty with any country other than Turkey. As long as their criminal enterprises left Turkey alone, no other country could touch them. [1]

Another reason the Russians favored Cyprus was its proximity to Israel. During its founding, Israel established a policy called the "Law of Return." Meant to remove any legal obstacles for Jews who wished to immigrate to Israel, it stated that any Jew, from any country, would be welcomed home and granted citizenship. As an added benefit, Israel purposely avoided establishing money laundering laws that might prevent the returning Jews from bringing much-needed capital with them to the Jewish state.

It didn't take long for the Russian mob to find this loophole. Soon Russians were lining up at Israeli consulates, claiming Jewish lineage and seeking citizenship. Once they had their capital safe in Israeli banks and an Israeli passport in their hands, they usually left, often for the United States; an Israeli passport was a visa-free backdoor to the *real* Promised Land. And if their crimes created too much of a problem in the US, they returned to Israel, a country that also refuses to extradite its citizens.

Conrad landed in Cyprus to game that system. She had to sleep with a particularly loathsome Russian to get the name of a lawyer who specialized in "bureaucratic circumcision," as he called it. For $10,000 he could fabricate a Russian birth certificate with a Jewish name that was a golden ticket for Israeli citizenship. He asked her what name she would like on the form. First she said Goldman, then she remembered another derivation of the name that was closer to her true identity.

"Geldman," she told him. "Monica Geldman."

DESPERATION MEASURES

PRESENT DAY – SAN JOSE, CALIFORNIA

Hendrix snapped his fingers. "Now I remember! Pull up Conrad's file."

It was up with a single mouse click. "What are you looking for?" Keisha asked.

"Monica Geldman, wasn't that one of her CIA aliases?" Hendrix knew Conrad's CIA file had been carefully scrubbed. Before she went rogue she had been involved in something so black even *he* hadn't been able to shine a light into it. All he knew was that she had killed her own team *and* her handler in Pakistan and the Agency wanted her dead, dead, dead. He had only obtained access to her file because of their active pursuit of Conrad, and even that had been redacted to only her time on the run.

"I don't *think* so," she replied, typing the search phrase into the computer. "There! Forensics tracked a large cash transfer from Conrad's numbered accounts into the name of one Monica Geldman on the island of Cyprus. Monica Geldman entered Israel the next day, emptied the accounts, and disappeared from the radar."

"So it was a *flight* alias," he observed. "Something she whipped up on the move to get to her ally in the Mossad, Meir Eitan."

Keisha looked bewildered. "Didn't she just *kill* Meir Eitan?"

He shrugged. "I don't think Angela Conrad's *ever* had an ally she didn't stab in the back eventually. But if she's reusing a *flight alias* it means she's in a world of hurt. That's a desperation measure, something you only do when you're completely out of options."

"Do you think we'll catch her, sir?"

Hell no! We're going to riddle her body with bullets, put her head in an ice bucket and let the Israelis take it home with them. "Absolutely," he declared. "What else did your data mining turn up?"

Keisha pointed at two enhanced screen captures showing the face and profile views of Conrad's agent from the cell phone drop off. "Facial recognition pegs him as Ari Nesher, former Mossad, discharged four years ago for embezzlement."

Hendrix made a guttural sound at the mention of Nesher's name. "That prick always thought he was the smartest guy in the room. Figures that he would end up with Conrad. Bastard children of a feather. What about the guy driving, any luck with him?"

Keisha pulled up a single grainy image. "Too dark. All I got was a profile in silhouette."

He squinted. "Pull up the file photos of an ex-KGB officer named Yuri Konalev."

She gave him a confused look, but complied. Seconds later, the photo of the hawk-nosed Russian operative appeared. She pulled the profile shot next to the surveillance photo. The resemblance was clear.

"Yuri Konalev and Ari Nesher. So Pugliano was right," he said. "Pull up the known associates file the FBI put together; Pugliano had a couple of other people she might be hanging with now."

She searched her files and pulled up the photos of seven men and one woman. "Any of these folks look familiar?"

He pointed at the photos of a man and a woman. "Ian Cosgrove and Meghan Gallagher. He's ex-SAS and she's an unreformed IRA terrorist."

Keisha's eyes widened. "Oh my, I bet they'd make a happy couple!"

"More than you know. He succumbed to her charms and went over to the dark side. Turns out they had something in common—they both liked killing people. Supposedly they went down in a small boat in the North Sea running from the Brits three years ago, but as far as I know they never found the bodies. Keep those files handy, we have no idea how many people Conrad has in her cell."

"Sir, Manning has stopped!" Rob reported.

"Where?"

"A mile away, next to City Hall. Should we reposition?"

"Not yet. This service truck would stick out like a sore thumb." He placed a call. "Garcia, the mark is waiting on a parking lot east of City Hall. I need eyes on him, now."

* * *

Manning was surprised when Conrad returned with the same panel truck she had used the previous night. He didn't think her paranoia allowed her to use any vehicle for more than twenty-four hours. The truck rolled as soon as he entered.

"Got the phone I gave you?" she asked. "Good, turn it off."

He complied and handed her the data pencil. "Here's today's take. And I found the lab where they're hiding WICKER BASKET."

She handed him a legal pad. "Draw me a picture."

* * *

Garcia called Hendrix. "Manning just transferred to a panel truck. Should I follow them?"

"No, that won't be necessary," Hendrix replied. "Do a recon of the area where Manning parked his car and be ready to report when I get there."

* * *

"Anything useful?" Manning asked.

"Yeah, we got a problem. When Doug Lyman briefed Scott Hendrix, he said that DARPA had canceled WICKER BASKET. I got an email here from Lyman's project leader saying that the "intellectual reconstitution" of WICKER BASKET in the new project space is going well, *but* he also says that he received disposal instructions from DARPA today. Something about feeding the samples through a plasma arc furnace to ensure complete destruction of the nanoagent."

"I take it that's bad."

She cast him a scornful look. "If we don't have a sample of the nanoagent, we can't prove to a buyer that the technology works. In the arms business, no demonstration means no sale."

"So what do we do?"

Conrad tapped a finger against her cheek. "Two options. Lyman's scientist told him in the email that Nanovex doesn't have the arc furnace that DARPA needs. So DARPA will have to pick up the nanoagent, probably at the same time they seize the project records. We *could* try to intercept the shipment when it leaves Nanovex, but that kind of pickup would mean federal marshals, and plenty of them. Strength against strength, not a good plan."

"And plan B?" While success was the *last* thing he wished upon Angela Conrad, he knew he would have to actively sabotage her to keep her from seizing success by force. And any such thoughts of resistance had long since been pummeled from his mind.

"We move up our operation so that we get the samples before they're destroyed. Penetrating a fortress that's not on alert is a better bet than taking on a convoy that's armed to the teeth. Not a lot better, but better."

He glanced at her two henchmen in the cab of the truck. "Do you have the resources to pull that off?" Not that he cared, but he had a feeling that whatever plan she settled on would involve him walking point to take the first bullets if things went wrong.

She gave him a dismissive toss of her head. "Not yet, but I will." She knocked on the truck's sidewall to get Yuri's attention. "Home James, and don't spare the horses!"

Yuri gave her a confused look. Apparently they didn't teach English clichés at the KGB academy. "Okay," he finally replied.

* * *

Hendrix met Garcia on the sidewalk a block away from City Hall.

Garcia held up his smart phone with an overhead photo of the parking lot. "The problem is there's three exits; after she drops Manning off, she could head out any of them in any direction. It's gonna be hard to box her in with just two vehicles."

"Not necessarily," Hendrix corrected. He took Garcia's phone so he could trace on the screen with his finger. "Look, Sixth and Seventh streets run on the east and west sides of the lot. If we station our vans a block north on both streets, whichever way she turns the nearest van becomes the trailing vehicle, and the other van races ahead on a parallel track. As soon as they can get ahead, they cut her off from the front. The other van closes from behind and completes the crossfire. Instant ambush."

Garcia nodded. "I like it."

"Okay, go make it happen. I'll send the kiddies away, then hoof it to your position. The fewer witnesses the better."

Garcia headed for his car. "Sounds like a plan."

Hendrix returned to the surveillance van. "Show me the positions of Agent Cho and the Manning decoy," he ordered.

"The decoy is on surface streets in Fremont," Rob answered. "Agent Cho and the rest of the FBI team are about a mile away."

We did it. The FBI is all the way on the wrong side of San Francisco Bay. I can whack Angela Conrad without Pugliano in my hair. He placed a call to the Manning double. "The hounds are closing in, and we're almost done here. Ditch the phone and the disguise and take the 84 bridge back across the bay. If they're still on you, one of my agents here will call. You can ditch the car and signal me for pick up if you need it."

"Roger that," the decoy replied.

Hendrix clapped once. "Okay, Keisha and Rob, great job. You're relieved. Head back toward downtown and take care of our decoy. I don't want him waiting all night if he has to ditch his car."

The two agents blinked at him. "We aren't continuing the surveillance?" Keisha asked.

"No, there's no telling how long this will take, so I have another team standing by," he said casually. "But you did a great job, both of you. And I'll put that in writing for your files tomorrow. Run home and get some shut eye, we may have to do this all over again tomorrow night."

Rob and Keisha exchanged confused looks, then shrugged. "Okay," they said in unison. As government employees, they were smart enough not to question an early night off.

* * *

"So Mike," Conrad said, "your next task is to find out where the samples of the nanoagent are now so I can figure out how to steal them."

He drew back. "How am I supposed to do *that*? Their head of security jumped my case just for being on the same *floor* with the P5 lab. If I snoop around any more I'm liable to get myself fired."

"You never mentioned that!" she snapped.

"Sorry, getting mugged kinda jumbled my mind. But yeah, their Security guy gives paranoia a bad name."

She frowned. "What's his name? He may need to have an accident."

He hesitated, never intending to sign Miller's death warrant with his offhanded comment.

"His *name!*" she demanded.

"Reese Miller."

She wrote the name at the bottom of the map he had drawn. "Okay, I'll contact you tomorrow with a plan for tracking down the sample. And get your own cell phone replacement for work. That one's just for us."

"Got it."

The truck swayed side-to-side turning a corner, then stopped. She raised the roll-up door.

"You're doing fine, Mike. Keep it up and you might even get out of this alive."

You lying bitch. "Good to know, thanks."

[1] The background on money laundering laws in Cyprus and Israel and the advantages taken on this system by the Russian mob and others was gleaned from *The Merger: The Conglomeration of International Organized Crime* by Jeffrey Robinson, p.144-148.

CHAPTER 14

DREIECKENJÄGER

APRIL 20, 1947 – BARILOCHE, ARGENTINA

It was a joyous day among the Nazi expatriates in the small village of Bariloche, in the eastern foothills of the Andes Mountains against the Chilean border. After almost two full years of evading Allied authorities, former *Reichsleiter* Martin Bormann had finally made his way to South America. He immediately requested a progress report on Kammler's technology projects, conducted on a small island across Huemul Lake from the village. On the boat ride to the laboratory, Bormann regaled Hans Kammler and the other former SS well-wishers with tales from the *Fuhrerbunker* and the circuitous escape path that ensued.

"And so," Bormann effused, lighting a cigarette, "for the third time Hitler lines up the bunker staff, says his good-byes, trembling like a little girl with fear. Afterwards I escort him to his sitting room and assist him with the pistol and poisons he and Eva are going to use to end their lives. He insists that he is ready, we say our final good-byes, and I take my leave. After a few minutes, I circulate among the staff and assure them the deed is done. What joy erupts! Brandy and champagne suddenly appear, phonograph records start playing and the female staff and the SS guards break into a riotous orgy in the conference room. And then suddenly, Hitler stumbles out of his quarters and yells, 'I'm not dead yet! Be quiet!'" [1]

The group broke out in nervous laughter, not used to mocking the memory of their departed leader, even in private.

Sensing the discomfort of the group, Kammler said, "*Herr* Bormann, seeing that this is the *Fuhrer's* birthday, perhaps you would do us the honor of giving a toast to his memory tonight. You knew him better than any of us."

"Certainly!" Bormann boomed. "Why should I not speak a word in memory of the *Fuhrer*? After all, the kindest service he did for us was also his last, when he put a bullet in his head! Now perhaps we can forward the interests of Germany and pursue the goals of National Socialism without setting the whole world aflame in the process."

Kammler cringed inwardly. Bormann certainly wasn't wasting any time taking charge now that he had arrived. The boat pulled to the dock.

"Gentlemen, if you'll follow me," Kammler directed, "I will show you to our labs. Please watch your step exiting the boat."

While situating his lab on Huemul Island instead of near the town created some logistical hurdles, it prevented mass casualties in the event of another accident with the Bell. It also made securing the facility against unwanted visitors much easier. The laboratory building was an unassuming structure built from the white limestone quarried on site.

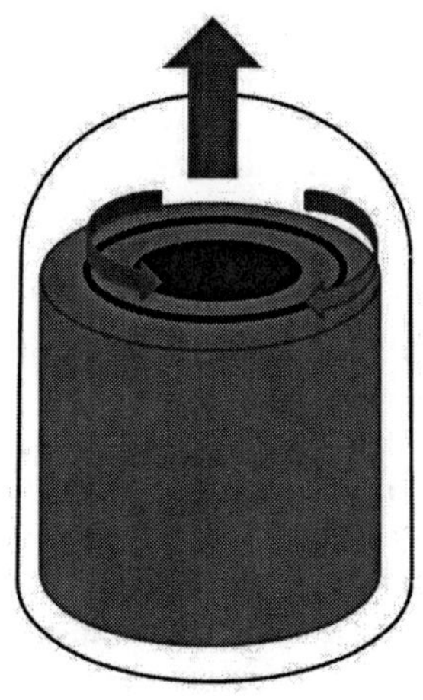

Before they entered the room containing the machinery, Kammler directed Bormann's attention to a chart on the wall. "As a matter of review, sir, the Bell operates by counter-rotating two cylinders filled with mercury or uranium vapor, shielded by a ceramic cover. By charging the drums to a pulsed voltage of several thousand volts and spinning them at tens of thousands of revolutions per minute, two things occur. The first is a strong propulsive force along the axis of rotation, and the second is a powerful induced current which seems to be drawn from the very vacuum of space."[2]

He led the group to a steel cage marked with DANGER: HIGH VOLTAGE signs. A ceramic shell the size of a domestic refrigerator hummed inside. Kammler stood within a meter of the cage. "As you can see, even in the short time since our relocation we have made significant progress improving the safety and reducing the size of the Bell units. Although this device is small, it supplies the power for this entire complex."

Bormann drew back slightly. "And it's safe at this distance?"

Kammler nodded. "As safe as any high-voltage transformer. By using mercury vapor instead of uranium as the conductive fluid inside the device, the radiation is negligible."

Bormann regarded the device carefully. "There was some talk during the war about using the Bell in an aerial vehicle of some sort, but that never came to fruition. Have your efforts changed that?"

Kammler led the group deeper into the lab. "Indeed, *Herr* Bormann. Once the matter of safety was solved, the next problem to address was that of control. Using the motive force of the Bell is akin to standing a jet engine on its tail. It will lift off the ground, certainly, but where it will go next is anyone's guess. The method we are pursuing is to enclose the Bell device inside a sphere, which motors inside the aircraft will turn to control the vector of the Bell's thrust."

"Similar to the vanes that directed the thrust of the V-2 rocket for control," Bormann observed.

Kammler pointed. "Exactly, sir. But we are working toward a vehicle that is much more stable and safe than balancing a V-2 on its rocket thrust. That has been compared to balancing a pencil vertically on one's finger. What we propose is more like this." He took an engineer's notepad and perched it horizontally on his thumb and two fingers. He tilted and turned his hand in various directions. "As you can see, at no time am I in danger of dropping the pad because a tripod is inherently stable."

Bormann's eyes narrowed. "But how does this apply to a flying craft?"

Kammler directed their attention to a workbench. On it sat a scale model of a triangular craft with a swiveling Bell-sphere in each corner. Equal-length strings secured to each sphere were tied together so Kammler could pick up the model easily.

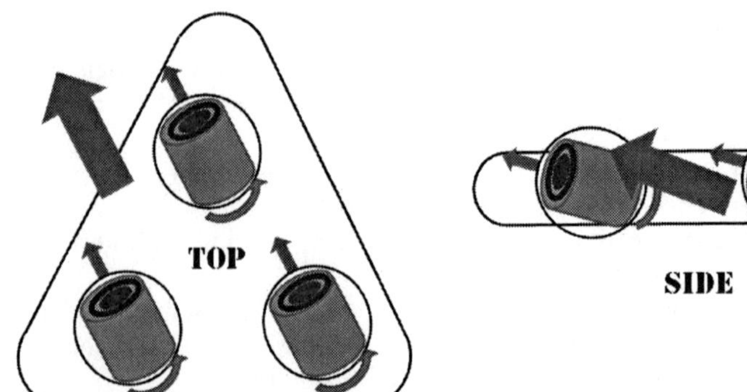

He lifted it straight off the table using the strings. "This is the flight mode with all three Bell-spheres pointed vertically upwards. But what happens if the spheres are tilted?" He grasped the model with one hand and pulled the strings slightly off to one side. "As you can see, it will create a force vector in the direction of the tilt." He moved the trio of strings around the model. "Forward, reverse, or directly to the side, the craft will move without using aerodynamic controls and with complete stability."

"How fast could it go?" Bormann asked.

Kammler shrugged. "Initially, that will be limited by the materials available to us. But even using common aircraft aluminum, we will be able to go far in excess of the speed of sound."

"But that's impossible!" a less-informed member of the group exclaimed. "Our jet aircraft were shaken apart when they tried to do so!"

Kammler lifted an eyebrow at the man, whose expertise was money laundering, not science. "Perhaps you should explain that to the Americans. Our spies tell us that they will likely achieve supersonic flight before the year is out.[3] But once more advanced materials are obtained, there is no theoretical upper limit to the craft's speed. Indeed, since the aircraft's lift is not obtained using aerodynamics, there is no reason this aircraft could not venture out of the atmosphere and into space."

Bormann's eyes bugged. "Are you *serious*, Kammler? This is possible?"

"Other than the pilot's blood boiling at high altitude, yes. If a pressure vessel is provided for the pilot, or some kind of flight garment constructed to contain a breathable atmosphere, there is no reason that the first man in space should not be a Nazi." [4]

Bormann had the look of a wolf eyeing a flock of sheep. "What is the payload of this—what are you calling it?"

"For the moment I'm calling it the *Dreieckenjäger*, or Triangular Fighter. And our planned payload at the moment is an atom bomb, to maintain our deterrence with America and Britain. But we also have weapons under development that may eventually make even the atom bomb obsolete."

Bormann snorted. "Now I *know* you're joking, Kammler."

Kammler gestured to a stairway leading down. "Indeed? Follow me please, gentlemen."

AMBUSH

PRESENT DAY – SAN JOSE, CALIFORNIA

The assassination teams were divided into two vans. The Israeli team waited on Sixth Street, while the American team waited on Seventh. Garcia parked his vehicle across from City Hall, watching Manning's car in his rearview mirror. Hendrix had just reached the American team's van on foot when Garcia's call came.

"Boss, Conrad's truck is dropping off Manning now."

"Okay, hold the line," Hendrix replied. "Call the other van! We're on!" he shouted to the driver, climbing inside and moving to the rear.

"Alpha to Bravo, target in sight, prep to roll in hot," the driver repeated into the radio.

"Bravo, ready hot," an accented voice replied.

Actually neither team was trained or equipped for this specific mission. Israeli assassination teams were called a *kidon*, or bayonet. The four-man-two-woman team Ravi Eitan had summoned before his demise was a *neviot*, or wellspring, trained for surveillance, breaking and entering, and planting bugging devices. The American team members were "body snatchers," trained for live apprehension of terrorist suspects, not outright terminations. But both teams knew how to use guns, and blowing holes in a target was a hell of a lot less risky than grabbing an armed operative off the street.

After picking up the CIA rendition team and receiving a briefing of their capabilities and their record of successful captures all over the world, Hendrix had originally planned for an abduction, not a kill. But the Israelis refused to play that game, pointing out the five dead Israelis from their last encounter with Conrad. Unless Hendrix agreed to a straight-up termination, they would pack their bags and wait for one or more *kidon* teams to come do the job right. Not about to let this opportunity pass, he relented.

He watched the six CIA agents double and triple check their weapons; the magazines, the attached flashlights and the laser sights. They knew every detail of those guns like the naked bodies of their wives or lovers. The weapons that had delivered them from evil in the festering armpits of the world would serve them equally well tonight in the heart of Silicon Valley. He was very much looking forward to seeing these men at work.

The Israelis had been given the run of the CIA office's armory. It wasn't an impressive facility, basically just a broom-closet-sized safe. But the Israelis found several useful items inside, including a short-barreled Squad Automatic Weapon much like the one that had been mounted on the Israeli jeep at Hunter's Point. He smiled at how the Israelis eyes had lit up at the sight of the SAW. Like the Marines say, happiness is a belt-fed weapon.

"Boss, Conrad is turning west on Santa Clara," Garcia reported. "She's coming right toward me!"

"Take up the trail position!" Hendrix ordered the van's driver. "Call the Israelis and give them the intercept!"

The driver made the call, and the van surged forward. He had always planned to give the Israelis the interceptor slot if possible. It was the position that got the most shooting in an ambush, and that sure as hell was what the Israelis wanted.

"Prepare to die, bitch," he whispered gleefully.

* * *

Manning watched Conrad's truck exit the parking lot and turn left, back towards City Hall. When his gaze returned forward and he started his car, a glint of motion caught his eye. A ball of light rose above a building to his right and descended rapidly towards him. The ball moved in a smooth arc, closing the distance in less than a second and stopping just over his hood. His engine suddenly stalled and the dashboard went completely dead, minus even the idiot lights needed to tell a blonde that her engine had quit.

He craned his neck to gaze up at the glowing orb. It was a little bigger than a basketball and glowed a translucent bluish-white. Through the radiance he could tell the orb was silver, and polished to a mirror finish. He could see his reflection on the ball's surface as he gazed up through the windshield at this…whatever it was. In the sudden silence he heard a hum outside, like a high-voltage transformer. Then it was gone, whisking silently over his roof in the direction of Conrad's truck.

"What the hell was *that?*" Manning exclaimed.

* * *

Hendrix's van surged toward City Hall, its engine roaring. Just before the corner, the driver braked so he could take the corner at normal speed, so as not to alarm their prey. Conrad's driver would see them, less than a block back, but they wouldn't close until the Israelis sprung the trap. In his mind's eye Hendrix could see the Israelis racing along a parallel street, maneuvering to cut Conrad off up ahead.

As they approached Sixth Street, a white van barreled into the intersection. The Israelis attacked Conrad broadside. Just before impact, the van's driver threw his vehicle into a skid. Combined with the evasive action of Conrad's driver, the collision was almost side-to-side. Before the two vehicles slid to a stop, the entire left side of the Israeli van erupted in gunfire. Shattered glass and shredded metal exploded into the air from Conrad's truck. The driver of Hendrix's van braked instinctively at the Israelis unannounced attack.

"*Damn it!*" Hendrix shouted.

* * *

"*Look out!*" Yuri yelled.

Conrad heard Ari shout something in Hebrew and the world exploded. First they were hit hard from the right side, throwing her headfirst into the panel truck's sidewall. She tumbled like a rag doll over the flying equipment boxes as the truck skidded to a stop. She hit the truck bed with a flash of searing pain up her shoulder. Before she could even cry out, gunfire shredded the truck. She heard Ari scream, followed by a dead weight rolling out the driver's side door. The last sound she heard from Yuri was a hollow, exploding-melon-sound that was probably his head.

Automatic weapons fire stitched the truck's sidewall at the level where her torso had been. The bullets tore the flimsy fiberglass shell apart from front to back. Then the gunner indexed down a foot and ripped the truck from back to front. The second swath shredded the equipment boxes, pelting her with fiberglass shards and metal shrapnel. In a few seconds she would be nothing but red jelly among the debris. She rolled like a pin toward the rear door, throwing boxes that blocked her path out of the way. A weapons case she hoisted over her was swatted from her hands and thrown against the far wall. The case and the assault rifle inside were torn apart like a toy in the jaws of a monster.

"*Shit!*" she cried out in terror.

She found the locking lever for the roll-up door and threw it, not caring what lay outside. It couldn't be any more deadly than staying in here. The roll-up mechanism had been damaged by gunfire and she had to force it up by hand. It rose a foot and jammed. She rolled again and toppled out the back of the truck, scraping her injured shoulder hard against the steel bumper before landing face down on the asphalt. Her knees struck first, then her torso. Finally her forehead contacted the ground hard enough to bounce, making her whole head ring. She stayed flat on the ground, drawing her weapon and trying to make sense of the tactical situation.

Looking underneath the truck, she saw Ari writhing in pain on the ground. Before she could rise to check on him, she saw the legs of a gunman crossing the front of the truck and standing over her partner. She saw Ari's head turn to look up. He raised his arms in surrender. One of his hands dangled limply, the nerves severed by a bullet.

"This is how a traitor dies," she heard a voice say in Hebrew. A burst of automatic fire shattered Ari's head like a flower pot and he sagged to the pavement.

"Find Conrad!" she heard another voice order.

So this is it, she realized. She knew her luck had to run out eventually. But now that the moment of her death had arrived, the inevitability of her fate made her strangely calm. Her only concern now was taking as many of her killers with her as possible. If there was an afterlife, which she doubted, she would then have a chance to flip them the bird and rub it in that they weren't as shit-hot as they thought they were.

She rolled left, staying flat and using as much of the left rear tire for cover as possible. The gunman who had killed Ari had made the mistake of stopping to gloat over his kill. He was only visible in silhouette from a streetlight behind him, but she could guess at the smug expression on his face. She put two bullets into that smug expression and he collapsed like a severed marionette to the ground.

"Go left! Shoot her!" she heard.

She rolled again, this time under the truck. She heard feet running to her right, surrounding the truck. She went flat on her back and transferred her gun to her left hand.

"Underneath!" she heard to her left and above her shoulder. A man with a belt-fed machine gun had spotted her and was kneeling for a better shot.

His mistake was to call out. She put two rounds at his chest. One flashed brightly when the machine gun frame turned it. One more into his head and he toppled backward. Thank God for all the off-handed shooting drills she had enforced on herself.

A man and a woman stood at the rear of the truck. The woman scanned the truck's interior with the flashlight mounted on her submachine gun, and the man searched the left side of the truck, following the sound of the previous gunshots. They both started crouching when Conrad drilled the machine gunner.

Swinging the gun to bear she put a round in both shooters' right kneecaps. The woman's leg blew completely out, bending the wrong direction as she toppled to the ground, screaming. She fell on her gun hand, leaving the top of her head exposed like an invitation. Conrad shattered her skull with one round and switched targets.

The man had dropped painfully to both knees, but was already bringing his weapon to bear. She was forced to expend four rounds, popping two quick center-of-mass shots, then a miss, and finally a successful headshot to take him down hard. He squeezed his weapon reflexively as he fell, releasing a three-round burst that ricocheted off the asphalt and then bounced around like pinballs inside the truck's chassis.

You're using too many bullets, she knew. *You're wasting bullets and you've lost count, which means you're going to run dry at the worst possible time.* She heard liquid dripping behind her and smelled gasoline. Fabulous. Perhaps Fate had decreed that being burned to death was more fitting end for her crimes than being filled with holes. But as long as she had breath in her lungs and rounds in her pistol, Fate could go screw itself.

She heard the scratch of shoe leather against pavement to her left and she rolled again, sticking her arms straight out as the axis of her rotation, firing as she spun toward the meager cover of the truck's right rear tire. A female agent knelt behind the attackers' van, straining to bring her weapon to bear while not breaking cover. Neither woman had a good shot, but Conrad congratulated herself on landing at least one hit through the van's tire. She heard the woman gasp, but she knew instinctively she hadn't landed a fatal wound.

Conrad's slide locked back, the gun empty. She reached for the magazine clipped to her belt, finding only the empty holder. The spare magazine was probably lost somewhere in the bed of the truck. Fantastic. She prepared to make a suicide dive to one of the dead operatives behind the truck to take one of their weapons. She wasn't dying with an empty gun in her hand.

Suddenly she heard a scream of pain and a loud wet pop. She stole a glance at the female gunner and saw her limp form fall sideways to the street. Not even a twitch; she was quite dead.

What the hell? Do I have sniper support? The only time she had heard that sound before was at a Taliban checkpoint. The bastard didn't buy her international aide worker cover and had raised his weapon. Her sniper overwatch blew a hole the size of volleyball in the raghead's chest with a fifty-caliber sniper rifle, making almost the same sound she had just heard. *But who's shooting? And why?*

Then she heard the driver's door of the attackers' van open, and running feet hit the pavement. He knew her position and moved straight to the attack, diving to the ground, landing on his side, and pointing his gun straight at her.

He opened fire.

She lunged toward the dead male operative behind the truck, trying to get out of the kill zone under the truck. Bullets zinged closer and closer with every foot she moved. If she stopped to get the operative's gun, she was dead. If she continued moving she would run into the open with no cover at all and be equally dead. She landed on the operative's corpse and rolled his body with hers as a human shield. She heard bullets thud into dead flesh. She reached around the right side of the body and grabbed the Israeli's submachine gun.

She heard a male scream this time, then another loud wet pop. She was looking right at her attacker when it happened. It was a violent impact, with lots of splatter. Definitely a fifty caliber. *Who the hell is this sniper saving my ass? And why did he scream before the bullet hit?*

Not one to look a gift sniper in the mouth, she wrestled the submachine gun free of the corpse she embraced and moved in a crouch back under the truck. She counted six bodies, which was a nice round number for a hit squad, but she had to be sure.

Then she heard an engine racing behind her and another van closing quickly. She had wiped out an entire van's worth of killers. But there were *two* vans full of them.

"Well *shit*," she observed dryly.

* * *

After the silver ball made its departure, Manning glanced over his shoulder to see if Conrad's van was still around. He spotted it just in time to witness the ambush and firefight. Conrad had *said* that there were plenty of people willing to kill to get their hands on the Nanovex nanoagent. It looked like they found her.

Well, that was just too damned bad—*for her*.

Feeling the weight of the world lift from his shoulders, he restarted his engine, slammed the gearshift into drive and peeled out of the parking lot, going the opposite direction from the gunfire as fast as he could.

* * *

"Why are we stopping?" Hendrix yelled.

"The Israelis are out of position!" the American team leader snapped back. "Look at that! Not only did they jump the gun, they're surrounding the truck! *Shit!* Were they even listening at the briefing?"

"Can we move up to support them?" he pressed, not wanting the Israelis to get *all* the glory for bagging Conrad.

The leader shook his head emphatically. "Not unless you want to risk catching them or us in a crossfire!" He slapped his free hand on the passenger-side dashboard. "*Dammit!* What part of 'mutually supporting fire sectors' did they not understand?"

"Somebody's returning fire!" the driver reported, followed quickly by, "Friendlies down! Target in sight!"

"Take us to within one hundred yards!" the leader ordered. "Prepare to dismount!" he shouted to the rest of the team. The van surged forward and the side doors slid back, the operatives leaning toward the openings, ready to jump on command.

Then the driver exploded.

No bullet hole punched through the windshield that Hendrix could see, the driver just went rigid with his arms straight out like someone had plugged him into a 220-volt outlet, he screamed in agony, then blood and projected viscera blasted the inside of the windshield.

The look of surprise and horror on the bloodied team leader's face was quickly replaced by torment as the process repeated itself. The team leader was turned more to the side, and Hendrix saw steam shoot from the man's mouth like a teapot as he screamed, right before he popped like a balloon. The leader's death grip on his rifle squeezed off an uncontrolled torrent of automatic fire, ripping a ragged line in the van's roof. Hendrix dove for the floor.

"*Get out! Get out! Get out!*" the troopers screamed to each other. He heard the operatives jumping from the van. Fear paralyzed him, unable to rise from the floor. A few seconds later the van slammed into the back of Conrad's truck. There was an eerie silence.

Followed by more screaming and popping.

* * *

Conrad expected the second van to stop at a hundred yards and disgorge its shooters, taking advantage of any long guns they carried. In a fight with a pistol or submachine gun, the guy with the rifle almost always won. She moved to the far side of the rear right tire, waiting for the assault. There wasn't any nearby cover worthy of a mad dash anyway. When she raised the captured Heckler & Kock MP5 to search for targets, a strange thought crossed her mind. *What was an Israeli team doing with German weapons anyway? Didn't they have reservations in that area?*

The van just kept coming. At around two hundred feet the shooters started bailing, like passengers jumping from a runaway train. They tried to hit the ground running, but most tumbled head over heels. To their credit, all but one ended their roll in a kneeling-ready position. She aimed at the closest ready shooter.

She took the first man down with a three-round burst to the throat and head. The van was still coming. *Were they going to ram? What was the tactical advantage to that?* Then she noticed the twin blood splatters on the inside the windshield. *My secret Santa again.*

The second shooter on the right side unloaded on her position at full auto. She ducked back under the truck. The tire she had sheltered behind disintegrated, throwing up a cloud of dust. She went prone and hid in it.

The van now was so close it obscured the shooters on the left side. In the split second before the van hit, she spotted the feet of the remaining right side shooter and unloaded three rounds. His legs went out from under him like an invisible tackle and he hit his left side hard.

She lowered her head when the van hit. It pushed the truck a few feet. She glanced up into the van's mangled grill after its losing battle with the truck's liftgate, then took careful aim at the crippled shooter, dispatching him cleanly. Two down, two to go. From under the merged truck and van, she saw the two remaining agents go prone. Both could see her. Both had longer range weapons. She picked the nearer one and aimed. It had been a really good game, but she couldn't get both of them at once. The one she didn't shoot would surely perforate her. She had come far closer to surviving this battle than she had anticipated, but it was almost over. *We who are about to die salute thee.*

The shooter she had selected flailed suddenly, launched three feet into the air from the imparted momentum of his exploding insides. It was very impressive. He bounced twice.

Apparently it distracted the remaining shooter as well, because he didn't fire. Conrad switched targets. The sniper got him first. When the red mist settled, there was nothing left above the poor bastard's waist. *C'est la guerre.*

In the sudden silence she found herself frozen in place, unable to break cover or even formulate a course of action. The sirens in the distance took care of that. She crawled to the back left corner of the truck and scanned the area for threats. Finding none, she rose to a crouch and crept to the open sliding door of the van, sweeping the interior with her gun. Nothing but the dead bodies of the driver and front seat passenger. The passenger's body was frozen in an arched-back scream, his rib cage spread open as if for open-heart surgery. And it was steaming. *Okay, that's disturbing, even for me.*

She broke cover and ran toward the parking lot where she had left Manning. He couldn't have gone far. She ran past the first exploded shooter's body in the street and stopped. A few feet from the body was a thoroughly tricked-out M-4 carbine, custom fitted, with all the bells and whistles. *These are CIA shooters*, she realized. *I've been fucking double-teamed!* Not one to let a good gun go to waste, she bent and retrieved the weapon, slinging it over her shoulder.

"*FREEZE!*" she heard.

She turned her head slowly to look over her shoulder. A stocky Hispanic man with a shaved head held her at gunpoint.

"I said *freeze!*" he repeated.

"You're a quiet one," she observed. She hadn't heard a footfall of his approach, which is why he was still alive.

"Marine Recon," he replied. "Kneel down, hands on your head."

She complied, hoping her secret admirer was still in position. The sirens were getting closer.

She heard a sizzle, followed by a yelp and the clatter of metal on asphalt. She turned her head, not moving her hands. The CIA/Marine's pistol lay on the pavement, a flap of scalded skin stuck to the side. She turned further, no longer fearing his weapon and not wanting to waste the ringside seat.

He was already convulsing like he had grabbed a high-voltage wire. Then he screamed, his stomach and chest swelling. The familiar loud wet pop followed, showering her with his superheated insides. She managed to turn her face before the wave of ejecta hit.

She opened her eyes again when the chunks stopped falling and examined her would-be captor. The evacuation of his steaming midsection caused his body to fold backwards when he fell, his shoulders resting on the back of his knees and his head nestled between his feet. The smell was too close to barbeque for comfort.

"Who can *do* this shit?" she whispered.

She rose and found herself staring at a floating silver ball, about ten feet in front of her. She froze, knowing intuitively that this was the weapon of her protector, but still not wanting to make any sudden moves. The sphere zipped left, in the direction she had been running. When she hesitated it came back to her, then zipped to the parking lot, brightening momentarily like a beacon.

"What are you, little ball? The Death Star of Bethlehem?"

The orb flashed again, beckoning to her. The converging emergency units were perilously close now, almost within sight, but they were behind her, opposite of the direction the ball was indicating. She adjusted the rifle on her shoulder and headed toward the City Hall parking lot at a dead run.

HEXENKESSEL

APRIL 20, 1947 – BARILOCHE, ARGENTINA

Kammler led Bormann and the group down the stairs of the laboratory to the basement. He picked up a small model of the Bell's inner workings from a table. "*Herr* Bormann, you of course recall the unfortunate accident at the Bell's first test?"

Bormann frowned. "Of course. I will not soon forget those photographs."

"Indeed," Kammler continued. "What we learned from that accident is that the Bell gives off a very unique radiation, what we have termed 'vacuum energy.' If it is channeled away in the form of an electrical current as in our generator upstairs, it is harmless. However, if it is allowed to radiate uncontrolled, it can have either constructive or destructive effects. In the case of our dead scientists, the vacuum energy broke down the tissues of their body into their constituent elements, namely carbon, oxygen and hydrogen. But when used for isotope enrichment, the vacuum energy could be used constructively, for instance to add a proton to uranium-238 to make plutonium-239."

He held up the model. "What we did *not* realize at the time was the direction nature of this energy. We assumed it radiated equally in all directions. It did not. *Herr* Bormann, do you recall the problems we had at Wenceslas Mines?"

Bormann's brow furrowed. "The radiation weakened the roofs of the test chambers, did it not?"

"Correct. If we used a test chamber for more than five minutes of cumulative operation, the roof would start to collapse. When we moved the device, we would also find the foundation underneath severely undermined. We now know that vacuum energy was radiating very strongly in an *axial* direction, breaking down the rock structure above and below the Bell into its constituent elements. Again, we now prevent this by drawing off the vacuum energy in the form of electrical current. But even during the war, we wondered if it could be possible to use this effect as a weapon. I can now say with certainty the answer is *yes*."

He pointed to the model. "Another thing we have learned is that the Bell radiates vacuum energy in a very broad range of frequencies, each of which interacts with different sizes of atomic and molecular structures. By tailoring the diameter of the Bell's rotors, we can tailor the vacuum energy radiation to break down a specific form of matter. For instance, a tiny Bell of this size can be tailored to specifically attack the water molecule."

Bormann shrugged. "Of what use is that, Kammler?"

A small smile lifted one side of his mouth. "Come and see, gentlemen." He led them across the lab to an observation window. Against the wall to their left, a small cylinder that was the twin of the Bell model Kammler held sat bolted to a table, its axis pointing parallel to them. A concrete structural pillar lay directly in the tiny Bell's axial path. Kammler nodded to an assistant. "What makes this weapon so effective is that the human body is up to seventy percent water."

A door inside the test chamber opened and a clean-shaven, bespectacled young man was led inside by a pair of burly guards. They manacled his arms above him against the concrete post, with the post between him and the tiny Bell. The prisoner's eyes held a look of stoic resolve, with an undercurrent of well-concealed fear.

"Our Argentinean patron, President Peron, has kindly granted us a number of political prisoners as test subjects," Kammler said. "Please observe."

The small Bell spun up with a whine, causing the prisoner to crane his neck, attempting to look behind the post. Suddenly he jerked convulsively, swelled in his midsection, and exploded. Blood and tissue splattered the observation window. Bormann and the rest of the entourage jumped back reflexively.

"*Was zur hölle?*" Bormann exclaimed. *What the hell?*

"If you will notice," Kammler explained calmly, "the beam of vacuum energy was directed *through* the concrete post. Since the beam was tuned to the vacuum frequency of water, when it found none in the post, it continued through until it struck the intended target. We intentionally aimed the beam slightly downward so that after it passes through the wall *and* the island it will strike the lake and not continue on definitely.

"So it would make no difference if the target were inside a heavily armored tank or a bunker. The lethality would be unaffected. By changing the diameter of the Bell, we can tailor the frequency of the vacuum energy beam to any element or molecule. We could dissolve the aluminum of an enemy bomber's structure and leave the crew unharmed, or tailor the beam to detonate any explosive it touches, from a soldier's ammunition to an artillery shell in flight, to the fuse of an atomic warhead. I have named this weapon *Hexenkessel*, or Witch's Cauldron."

Kammler lifted an eyebrow at Bormann. "Of course, I can still arm our craft with atomic weapons, if you prefer."

"No, *Herr* Kammler," Bormann agreed. "No indeed."

[1] This comical incident actually occurred! Source: *The Life and Death of Adolph Hitler* by Robert Payne, p. 565.

[2] My reconstruction of the science behind the Bell, and the weapons that might have been derived from its effects, were greatly aided by *SS Brotherhood of the Bell* by Joseph P. Farrell, p.141-273

[3] Chuck Yeager broke the sound barrier on October 14, 1947.

[4] For illustration, the photo below is widely regarded to be authentic. A similar object was chased unsuccessfully by NATO F-16 jets over Belgium in the same time frame that the photograph was taken. While many conclude that since the craft's performance was far in excess of the interceptors pursuing it that the object must have been extraterrestrial, after researching the state of Nazi physics at the end of WWII, the author wonders if this particular sighting might have had a more *terrestrial* origin. Indeed, since the Soviet Empire had collapsed only six months before this incident, could a technologically superior but previously covert group have made these overflights of NATO headquarters in Belgium as a show of force, to remind NATO of the true nature of the world order now that the Soviets had departed the scene?

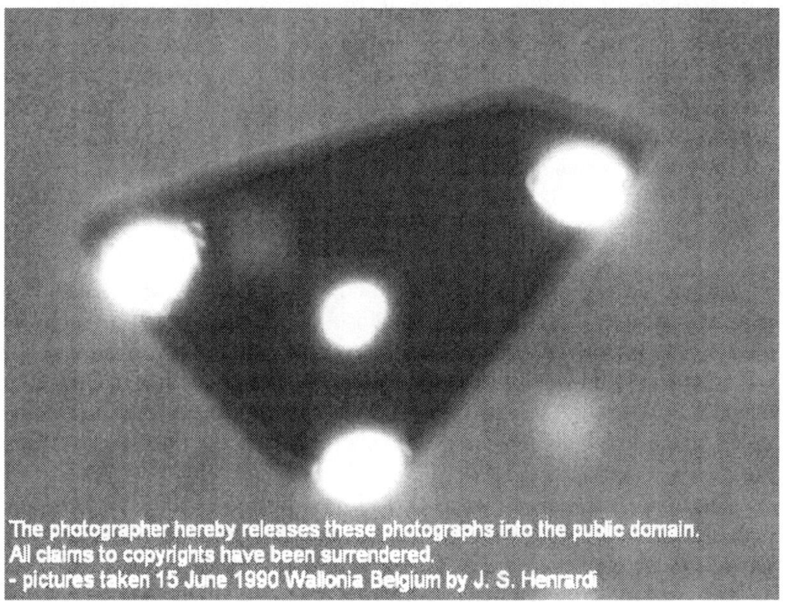

The photographer hereby releases these photographs into the public domain.
All claims to copyrights have been surrendered.
- pictures taken 15 June 1990 Wallonia Belgium by J. S. Henrardi

CHAPTER 15

DEPARTURES

PRESENT DAY – SAN JOSE, CALIFORNIA

Mike Manning circled the Hotel Montgomery three times looking for tattooed men before he parked. He saw none, but neither did he see the promised additional police patrols. Then he realized they had probably been summoned to the scene of Angela Conrad's demise. He pulled into a spot and parked. He was shaking so hard from relief and adrenaline let-down that he couldn't leave the car for several minutes.

He wondered if he should call the FBI. He hadn't participated in any crime; his only role had been as an unwilling witness to Conrad's wrongdoing. Cooperating with the FBI might even be helpful in getting his job back in Chicago. If Bernie Norquist stonewalled him, he might suggest to Bernie that he say a prayer that nothing would slip inadvertently about the Feldman-Norquist law firm's marginally legal activities while he debriefed to the FBI about Conrad. But first things first—tonight he would get shit-faced drunk in celebration.

Ding dong the witch is dead.

* * *

Angela Conrad slinked between buildings and across side streets in a generally eastern direction from San Jose City Hall. Beyond a couple of blocks, she would be past at least the initial police cordon around the ambush. The first batch of sirens had died out. The police would have their hands full for several minutes securing the area for the paramedics so they could sort the living from the dead. Or in this case the merely dead from the clearly, most sincerely dead.

The floating silver ball was still with her. It seemed to be scouting the path ahead, sometimes popping up to building height as if to look around, but otherwise staying at head height and several yards in front. Its glow had dimmed to a muted electric blue, barely visible in the darkened alleys. The orb seemed to know how to keep a low profile. It glided around a corner to her right.

She craned her neck to look down an alley between two rows of houses. A few older cars in various states of disrepair were scattered along its length, unworthy of precious garage space. It suddenly occurred to her that she hadn't hot-wired a car since her training days at Camp Peary. It had never been necessary in the field. She briefly considered calling Manning to pick her up, but she still didn't know how she had been burned. She didn't think Manning had the balls to *purposely* betray her, but he *was* an amateur, and amateurs made mistakes. And mistakes in this business got people like her killed. She decided to go it alone and sort out Manning's involvement in the ambush later.

The ball proceeded slowly down the alley, pausing briefly beside every vehicle before proceeding. Suddenly it stopped, hovered over an old blue Honda, and flashed. Then it departed upward in an accelerating arc, disappearing back toward City Hall. She waited a minute or two for it to return. When it didn't, she assumed its mission was complete and she was back on her own. She heard a helicopter approach. Time to get moving.

"Well, thanks little ball," she whispered. "I owe you a beer. Or a battery."

She made her way carefully down the alley, moving faster when a dog behind a fence started barking. She reached the Honda and tried the door. Unlocked. She leaned in quickly and flicked off the dome light. She tossed the captured rifle and submachine gun in the back seat and closed the door. She checked the sun visors, ashtray, and glove compartment for a key. Nothing. Under the driver and passenger floor mats. Nada. She was just about to use the butt of the submachine gun to break open the steering column when she thought to reach *behind* the seats. Feeling though the cigarette butts, gum wrappers and fast food bags, she lifted the floor mat behind the passenger seat. Bingo.

She started the car, executed a three-point turn, and disappeared into the night.

URBAN LEGEND

SAN JOSE, CALIFORNIA

Perry Pugliano had a feeling throughout the surveillance of Mike Manning that he was being led on a snipe hunt. From the moment the tail deployed, Manning moved in a professionally evasive manner—it was clear he was running a surveillance detection route. With the late-night streets almost deserted, that forced Pugliano to back the tail off and rely solely on his helicopter to maintain visual contact. Then the bastard got on the highway and took off like a drag racer. Every time Pugliano got the tail back in position, Manning was one step ahead of him. It was almost like someone was tipping him off.

Finally the helicopter tracked him to a McDonalds in Fremont. He even stayed there long enough for the tail to catch up. Pugliano had hopes of salvaging the operation, but once the tail boxed Manning in based on his cell phone signal, they realized they were following the wrong car. The bastard had stuck his cell phone under the bumper of a similar-looking car with duct tape. Manning was long gone.

Pugliano hadn't been this angry since his second ex-wife stole his cat. But he now knew one thing for sure: Mike Manning was a spook.

While he was meditating on exactly how he was going to make Manning's life a living hell, a call came over the radio—a huge firefight had broken out in San Jose, with bodies everywhere. With his "no such thing as a coincidence" alarm blaring wildly, Pugliano ordered the tail and the helicopter to converge on the scene. His phone rang before they even arrived. The San Jose police had taken one look at the number of automatic weapons accompanying the bodies and decided this was a problem for the Feds.

The sea of emergency vehicles choking the street forced them to park over a block away. His least favorite coroner, Derek Medina, waited at the police line.

"Agent Pugliano! You're here! C'mon, you gotta *see* this!" Medina bubbled.

"I've never seen someone get so excited over death," Pugliano muttered to Agent Cho, who had materialized at his side. *I'd swear that girl has a crush on me the way she follows me around.* He mentally upbraided himself for such a foolish thought. She was just being a good suck-up, just like the other upwardly mobile agents in his command.

Medina had overheard the comment. "Well, I *am* a coroner, and I *do* love my job. Especially on a night like this. I mean, *look* at this mess!"

At the center of the crowd of photographers and evidence technicians sat a rental truck sandwiched between two white vans. The truck had been thoroughly shredded by weapons fire. From where he stood, Pugliano counted five bodies. A couple of them were only recognizable as bodies because of the attention being focused on them. They looked more like road kill.

"How many bodies we got, Derek?"

"Fifteen."

Pugliano stopped cold. "*Fifteen?*"

Median grinned from ear to ear. "Yeah, I know! Isn't it *cool*? I'll be able to write a *book* about this case! Wanna collaborate?"

Pugliano's eyes rolled involuntarily. "Just walk me through the body count, Derek."

He led them to the driver's side of the rental truck. A contorted corpse lay sprawled below the open door. "Okay, here we go, body number one! Looks like the driver, bullets to the right arm and torso, *but….*" He shined his flashlight on the shredded tissue mass emerging from the collar of the driver's jacket. The remains of the driver's head were splayed in a wide cone like an impromptu modern art painting.

"Holy headshot, Batman!" Medina crowed. "I think we've found cause of death!"

"*Oh God*," Cho said through her hand, turning away. She made choking sounds as she battled her gag reflex.

Medina ignored her distress. He swung his flashlight to the left. "Body number two, same cause of death, but different shooter." He swung his flashlight between the two bodies. "See how the splatter patterns point in opposite directions?"

"Where *was* the second shooter?" he asked.

Medina waved his hand. "There's a shitload of nine-millimeter casings and an empty pistol around the back of the truck. From back there, I'd guess." He probed his flashlight into the cab of the truck. "Body number three, multiple gunshots to the torso, one to the head; *he* didn't suffer long."

"So who are the guys in the truck versus the guys in the vans? Do we have any IDs?"

"No, when we got word you guys were taking over the case, we just made sure everybody was dead and backed off. I don't know anything about either set of combatants, other than they were *seriously* pissed at each other."

"Okay, keep talking."

Medina led them to the right of the truck. "Dead guy number four. Now it *really* gets interesting. Look at *this*!" The carnage revealed by Medina's flashlight reminded Pugliano of a hand grenade accident he had the misfortune of witnessing during Desert Storm. As in the accident, the whole front of the poor bastard's torso had been evacuated, like a gutted deer. Cho made a mewing sound and ran back to the police line with both hands over her mouth.

If you can't take the heat…Pugliano mused. "So, he fell on a grenade?"

Medina beckoned with a "follow me" motion. "That's what I thought too, until I saw our two friends in the van." He walked to the vehicle impacted into the back of the rental truck, stepping over another body that had obviously died of gunshots, and was therefore uninteresting. "Excuse me, dead guy," he apologized. He directed his flashlight through the open side door of the van. "Come check *this* out!"

Pugliano leaned in to examine the van's driver and passenger. It took several seconds to absorb what he was looking at. "Holy *crap*!" he exclaimed. *It was a good thing Cho didn't stick around.*

"What you have here," Medina expounded, "is your basic poodle in a microwave scenario."

He squinted. "I thought that was just an urban legend."

"I guess it depends on how annoying the poodle is. Or was," he added quietly.

"You scare me, Derek," he muttered, unable to look away from the grotesque carnage. "But let's go with the urban legend for a minute. Defend your theory."

The coroner stepped carefully into the van, using a ballpoint pen as a pointer. "See the trauma pattern to the bodies? It's like they *exploded* from the inside out. Know any weapons that can do that?"

"Maybe a fifty caliber."

"No, a fifty-cal is like being hit by a train. It just rips people apart. That's not what I'm seeing here." He played his flashlight over the gore-coated windshield. "Besides, you see any bullet holes? I don't."

Pugliano leaned in to look for himself. Medina was right. "So where does the poodle in the microwave come in?"

Medina illuminated the passenger's ruptured chest cavity. He picked at a flap of loose flesh with his pen. "See this muscle tissue? It's cooked. Not burned, *cooked*, like boiled chicken."

"Could a microwave weapon do that?"

He shrugged. "I know the military has been experimenting with microwaves for crowd control. You know, heat peoples' skin up till they jerk back like from a hot oven. It's supposed to be nonlethal, and it probably is, but you know they *have* to be working on a version that kills people. I mean, that's their *job*, isn't it?"

Pugliano didn't like where this was going. "So even if you're right, that only gives us the *how*. We still don't know the who, much less the *why*. Any suggestions?"

Medina shrugged again. "I guess you could ask the survivor."

"*What* survivor?" he snapped.

Medina jerked with his thumb. "They found a guy here in the back of the van, unharmed. Other than the fact that he'd wet himself, of course."

Pugliano resisted the urge to grab Medina and shake him. "And you didn't tell me about this survivor, *why?*"

He blinked. "Well, because he's *breathing.* The living aren't my concern."

Pugliano let out a guttural growl and turned away.

"Hey, look at these bullet holes in the ceiling!" Medina continued. "He must have squeezed these off while he was being cooked!

Pugliano ignored him and sought out a detective. "I heard you guys found a witness?"

The detective pointed back toward the police line. "He wouldn't talk, so we cuffed him and let him stew in the back of a squad car."

He tagged the detective on the arm. "Thanks."

He searched the line of black and whites till he found one with an occupied back seat. He waved to the uniformed cop in the front seat, who lowered his window.

He flashed his ID. "I'd like to speak to the witness please, officer."

The cop got out. "Sure thing, I need a smoke anyway."

He sat down and turned to the witness. *Rapport building first, threats second.* "Hello sir," he began. "My name is Perry Pugliano. I understand you're in a difficult position, but if you're willing to help us, I will do everything in my power to…."

Then he realized he was delivering his pitch to Scott Hendrix. He sat in dumbfounded silence for almost a minute before he found his voice again. He felt a rush of heat rising up under his collar.

"Ohhh, *Lucy*," he said in his best Ricky Ricardo accent. "You got a whole lotta '*splaining* to do!"

FALLBACK

SAN JOSE, CALIFORNIA

Angela Conrad spent several minutes driving randomly and almost unconsciously—she could drive a surveillance detection route in her sleep. A thousand questions swirled in her mind, each vying for priority. That and a huge case of adrenaline let-down made it almost impossible to think. She gripped hard on the steering wheel and gear shift to keep her hands from shaking.

God damn it, that was close!

First she had to figure out how she had been tracked. If her truck had been tagged, that problem was certainly solved. Same with her cell phone—it was in the truck along with her purse. Her mind kept coming back to Manning as the leak—he *was* the only person to have escaped without getting shot at. So now that she had broken contact with him and her pursuers she was probably in the clear.

It occurred to her that she was driving aimlessly and the gas gauge had been below empty with the warning light on since she took the car. It could quit on her at any moment. She couldn't even fill up—her wallet and cash were in her purse as well. She needed to get her bearings and head to the fallback site.

But was even the *fallback* site safe now? And what evidence had she left behind at the ambush? The truck's records would lead nowhere, but the fake driver's license in her wallet had her *real* photo on it, which meant that a police BOLO—Be On the Look Out—for her would soon be circulating, which would make obtaining a new identity much more difficult and expensive. At least she didn't have to worry about Ari or Yuri giving her away under interrogation—she was ninety-nine percent sure they were both quite dead.

No, the biggest setback was the equipment she lost. Weapons, computers, surveillance equipment, and tools. It was all in the truck. She had a flash of fear over her laptop—everything about the Nanovex operation was on there, and she had been working on it at the time of the ambush. But the laptop was most likely shredded by gunfire. And even if not, the screensaver's autolock would wipe the hard drive if some flatfoot computer forensics technician started poking around blindly at the password. She also had the laptop set for a password-delayed autowipe every twenty-four hours. So her laptop would transmute itself into a useless brick soon enough.

Conrad refused to listen to the nagging voice in her head that the project was blown beyond repair. No, she had burned *all* of her bridges for this operation, and unless she emerged from this deal with enough cash and clout to be an independent power broker in her own right, tonight's festivities would be repeated by one or more of her many enemies until she *was* dead. But survival was a prerequisite for success, so she focused on the task at hand.

Since the Honda might give up the ghost at any minute, she worked her way south along San Jose surface streets, until houses and office buildings gave way to warehouses and machine shops. Turning right onto a potholed road, she searched in the predawn darkness for the sign of the former Tully's Truck Repair, now covered with a For Lease banner. She almost parked the car on the street, but remembered the automatic weapons in the back seat. She backed into the alley between Tully's and Marco's Stereo Repair, then casually transferred the guns into the trunk. There was never a cop around when you needed one, but there was *always* one around when you didn't.

She walked down the alley to the side door and knocked hard. She waited sixty seconds and did it again. Ian Cosgrove and Meaghan Gallagher had arrived a day ago to join her team for the heist. Ian was supposed to be pulling the night watch here at the fallback. Protocol dictated a call ahead, but Ian was smart enough to handle a botched procedure. She banged on the door again, then kept completely still with her hands at her side. She heard the faint scrape of a boot against asphalt to her left.

"Key West!" she called into the darkness.

"Tahiti," a British voice answered.

"We were ambushed."

"I heard. You lit up the police scanner like Piccadilly Circus. Where's Yuri and Ari?"

"Dead."

"Bloody hell! Is your tail clear?"

"Do you think I'd lead them here if it *wasn't*?" she shot back.

She heard a harsh laugh as Cosgrove emerged from the darkness, his pistol still at the ready. "I don't think you've thought jiggedy about anyone but yourself since the day you were born, Angela Conrad. So I'll ask you again. Are you *clear*?"

"Hell yes I'm clear. I ran an SDR on fumes to make sure of it. Open up the garage so I can get this car out of sight."

Keys jangled. "Fair enough."

EVER-PRESENT HELP

SAN JOSE, CALIFORNIA

Scott Hendrix's mind raced. This was a career-ending clusterfuck if there ever was one, but he was never one to let go of the brass ring without a fight. Conrad was still out there, weakened, on the run, and quite possibly wounded. He still had a chance to salvage this operation, but first he had to get out of this squad car and out of FBI custody before the bigwigs started flooding in from Langley looking for scalps.

Hendrix had seen the carnage outside. As far as he knew, he was the only survivor. Which meant he was free to spin any tale he wished about what happened, as long as it didn't contradict the evidence on the street. He was reminded of a lesson from Camp Peary.

"*Mr. Hendrix, what is a lie?*" his instructor had asked him.

"*A purposeful distortion of the truth,*" he replied.

"*No, Mr. Hendrix,*" he expounded like an evangelist. "*A lie is our refuge and our strength, an ever-present help in time of trouble.*"

Perry Pugliano's eyes bored into him. Hendrix was glad for the wire grill separating the front and back seats of the squad car. It looked like the FBI agent had every intention of strangling him.

"Hendrix, you'd better start talking, and you'd better do it now, or so help me...."

He affected an offended tone. "Do you think I *wanted* to do this operation behind your back?" he replied. "*We* didn't find Conrad, the *Israelis* did. *They* set the ground rules for this op, and they specifically excluded *you.*"

"*Why?*" Pugliano snapped.

Hendrix shook his head like the FBI agent was a slow learner. "This wasn't a capture—it was a *termination.* How likely would you have been to go along with *that*?"

"And why did *you* go along with it?" he shot back. "I don't recall the assassination of American citizens on US soil being part of the CIA charter, do you?"

Hendrix rolled his eyes. "Don't be naïve. Conrad didn't have citizenship rights any more; she was on the *Intelligence* Most Wanted list, classified SOS because of her skill set."

"SOS?"

He leaned forward. "*Shoot On Sight*. That comes straight from the top, signed by the President of the United States. I can show you the paperwork; it's on a secure server in my office. Now get over yourself and let me go."

Pugliano had lost some of the wind from his sails, but not all. "Not so fast, hot shot. Let's talk some more about the Israelis. How did *they* get a bead on Conrad?"

His eyebrows rose. "Do you think they'd share *sources and methods* with me? They just told us this op was going down with or without us and offered to let us ride shotgun. After Meir Eitan, there was *no way* Conrad was going back to Israel by any method but in a *box*."

"Uh-huh," Pugliano grunted. "Some of those guys out there were CIA. I could tell by their weapons. So you called Langley and they just coughed up a hit squad for you with *no background whatsoever*. Give me a break. Not even the CIA is that gullible."

His mind raced again. He had to throw Pugliano a bone of some kind, or his duplicitous construct to this point would be for nothing, and might very well land him in prison for a very long time. Lying to an FBI agent is not ground to tread lightly.

Time to sacrifice a lamb. "They had a source."

"I'm listening."

He shrugged. "Some guy named Manning. He's a member of Conrad's cell here in San Francisco. That's all I know." His mind raced again, calculating how much he could give away without restricting his future freedom of action.

"Bullshit. Keep talking."

He rubbed his head, as if to aid in recollection. "The Israelis used him to get to Conrad. They hacked his cell phone, used it to get a bead on her." Manning had been an excellent lead, but Hendrix *had* to get out of this squad car. He decided to sacrifice Manning entirely to the FBI. Chances were that the FBI would roll Conrad up before the next day was out anyway. With her henchmen dead and her equipment captured, she would be alone and without resources. The odds against her were almost insurmountable.

"And how did the *Israelis* find out about Manning?"

"Lousy tradecraft, Manning screwed up. That's all they would say," he lied. "But they showed us how they could track Conrad in real time based on the data they hacked from Manning's phone. That convinced Langley to play ball."

Pugliano squinted at him. “So are we going to find Manning’s body out there too?”

He’s testing. “I doubt it. He was driving around in circles over in Fremont trying to pull the Israelis off the trail. It didn’t work.”

Pugliano drew back slightly, obviously not expecting Hendrix to throw out that tidbit of truth. “What *else* do you know about Manning?”

Hendrix feigned impatience. “Manning is small fry. You need to be focusing on Conrad.”

“Humor me.”

He sighed. “He’s a lawyer, or at least he’s acting like one, at some company called Nanovex out here in the valley. He just showed up out of the blue, which makes me suspicious he’s some kind of plant. His trail leads back to Chicago. I tasked our office there to work up a dossier, but they haven’t gotten back with me yet.”

“So what’s he doing at Nanovex?” Pugliano pressed.

“According to public records, he’s a damage control lawyer, and Nanovex has had a number of accidental deaths recently. He passed himself off as some kind of hired gun to help Nanovex clean up their mess.”

“And his connection to Conrad?”

Hendrix threw up his hands in mock frustration. “Well, *obviously* she’s using him to get a man inside for some reason. If that’s even *him*. The *real* Mike Manning could be at the bottom of Lake Michigan right now.”

“And her operation at Nanovex…”

“Don’t know, don’t care,” Hendrix interrupted. “We just wanted Conrad dead, and so did the Israelis. If she dies, obviously her little scheme dies with her. There would have been plenty of time to sweat the truth out of Manning after we had Conrad’s head on a stick.”

Pugliano scowled. “Great job with that, by the way.”

He faked a pained expression. “Screw you! I watched a bunch of good men die tonight.”

Pugliano leaned his arm on the patrol car’s seat. “And how *exactly* did you manage that observation, seeing you were hiding under the back seat of the van while they died?” He sniffed the air dramatically. “By the way, you want me to have one of my female agents bring you over a fresh pair of panties?”

Play the sympathy card. He hung his head. “You weren’t there. People screaming and dying all around me. I don’t even know why I’m alive. It was terrifying.”

Pugliano’s voice drifted far away. “Yeah, well. I don’t know anybody who wasn’t scared shitless their first time in combat.”

They sat in silence for several seconds.

Pugliano exited the squad car. "Come on, let's get you out of here." He waved the officer over. "I'm taking custody of the witness. Uncuff him, please."

That was sudden. The policeman extracted him from the back seat and turned him to face the cruiser. "Just like that?" Hendrix asked.

"I want a full debrief from you, of course," Pugliano insisted. "And if I sense you're holding something back, the cuffs go right back on. Agreed?"

He would have performed oral sex if that was what Pugliano had wanted in exchange for his freedom. "Agreed."

Pugliano led him by the arm back to his SUV. "Hell, no wonder the Agency stuck you here in the States, Hendrix. You couldn't lie your way out of paper bag."

BUY BACKS

SAN JOSE, CALIFORNIA

After tucking the old blue Honda away inside the cavernous truck garage, the only thing Angela Conrad could think of was a shower and some sleep. Even if it was in the grungy shop shower and on an air mattress stretched out in the equally filthy former owner's office.

She removed the weapons from the trunk—she never slept soundly without a gun nearby.

"When does Meghan relieve you?" she asked Ian Cosgrove.

He was incredulous. "She's already on her way! We thought you had bought it in that ambush—we were going to pull up stakes and bug out."

She nodded. "I understand. I would have done the same thing. When she gets here we can discuss our way forward."

"Our way forward?" he gasped. "You mean we're not going to pack it in?"

She shifted the guns on her shoulder. "Hell no, we're not going to pack it in! I've got too much invested in this operation to just *walk away*!"

Cosgrove's eyes glinted. "Then speaking of investments, where's the truck?"

"At the ambush site, what's left of it."

"And all of our *gear*?"

She didn't like the tone in his voice. "Gear can be replaced."

His voice was insolent now. "Just like Yuri and Ari?"

"Of course not," she snapped. "Don't put words in my mouth."

"We don't have enough people to pull this off now," he argued.

"I'm not saying it'll be easy, but we can still *do* it. We only need to have enough security for the buyer's meeting, then the manpower situation will resolve itself."

He struck a defiant pose. "So *you* say!"

Her hand went unconsciously to the submachine gun. "*Listen*, asshole! I just had my team shot out from under me. I lost *count* of how many people I killed just to get out of there with my ass in one piece. I don't need your *shit* right now!"

Cosgrove's phone rang. "Yeah?" He went to the electrical panel, dousing the lights and raising the garage door. "Meghan's thirty seconds out," he explained.

A black Cadillac Escalade surged in, narrowly missing Conrad's stolen Honda. An athletic woman with flowing red hair jumped from the vehicle, running to Conrad and embracing her.

"Dear God, Angie, we thought ya were dead!" she said in a thick Irish accent.

Conrad returned the hug, casting a hard eye at Cosgrove. "Well, at least *someone's* glad to see me!"

Meghan Gallagher pulled away. "What, has Ian been doling out his daily ration of…." She examined her hands. "Angie, what the hell is this muck on yer back?"

Conrad grimaced. "Somebody's guts. Long story. I need a shower."

Gallagher held hands away from her clothing. "Well, off with ya, then. We'll hold the fort."

"Meghan, she's still going ahead with this job of hers!" Cosgrove protested. "She's gone mad!"

Gallagher's eyes flashed. "It's not *her* job, Ian, it's *our* job, and don't ya forget it!"

Cosgrove shook his finger in Gallagher's face. "I didn't go to the trouble of faking my own death to get buggered in this woman's bollixed-up scheme!"

Gallagher placed her hands flat on his chest, pushing him away and simultaneously wiping Conrad's gore from her hands. "*You* get out of my face, ya pushy bastard! I seem to recall going down on that same ship with ya! If we 'died' on the same boat, yer not jumping ship apart from me! Got it?"

In her mind's eye, Conrad saw those two in their eighties, lighting up a nursing home with their fiery arguments. They enjoyed fighting too much to ever break up.

His finger went in Conrad's direction. "This woman's got an *army* out for her head, Meghan! Yuri and Ari already paid the price for hanging around her too long! Do ya think that army is not gonna try *again*? Do ya really want to be around her when they *do*?"

Gallagher tossed him her keys. "You're relieved. Go back to our hotel and get some shut eye."

"But *Meghan*…"

"Get *on* with ya!" she shouted.

Cosgrove skulked back to the Expedition and fired up the engine with a roar. Gallagher raised the door and the SUV peeled off into the darkness. She lowered the door and returned to Conrad's side.

Gallagher gave her a knowing wink. "Never mind him. A double-helping of make-up sex and he'll be right as rain."

Conrad shook her head. "He's got a point, Meghan. The people who tried to whack me today aren't going away."

The fire returned to Gallagher's eyes. "Well then, we'll just have to *deal* with them, won't we? That should be fun."

"He's also right that we don't have enough manpower to finish the job now."

"What about Dieter and Linn? They're good men. Are they in play yet?"

She frowned. "Linn Shaozang is working security for the Chinese delegation, and Dieter Kinberg is doing the same for the French."

Gallagher laughed. "A German working security for the French! Now there's a sack load of irony for ya! Why isn't he totin' a gun for the Huns?"

She shrugged. "The Germans aren't bidding, if you can believe that."

Gallagher put her hands on her hips. "Wave a weapon of mass destruction in front of a Kraut and they don't bite on it? There's a first."

"Tell me about it. Makes me wonder what they know that we don't."

Gallagher snapped her fingers. "I just had an idea. How are we fixed for cash?"

"All the equipment we lost was provided by Meir when this was still his op. I'll have to hit my reserves to replace all that, but I should have a little left over, why?"

"What if we call the French and the Chinese and buy Dieter and Linn back from them?"

Conrad was confused. "Buy them back?"

"Sure. Admit to them that we're shorthanded, and unless we get two more men, the whole deal is off. Whatever they paid Dieter and Linn, we refund them in cash, and pay Dieter and Linn whatever their respective parties already promised them. The deal goes forward, the Chinese and French get their money back, and Dieter and Linn get paid twice. Who's going to say no to that?"

Conrad was glad to have Gallagher around. She would never have thought of such an innovative solution in her current jangled state. "Think we can trust Dieter and Linn under those conditions?"

Gallagher shrugged. "Why not? We're not asking them to stab their former partners in the back, they'll just be making sure nothing untoward happens at the buyer's meeting. That's in everybody's interest, isn't it?"

"Unless their delegation was planning on *making* something untoward at the buyer's meeting," Conrad cautioned.

A dismissive wave. "If they do that, what do they come away with? Nothing! No, making sure the buyer's meeting is uneventful is in *everybody's* interest, except for maybe the people who tried to put you in the ground today. Keeping *them* out of the equation is going to be the tricky part."

Conrad's shoulders fell. A wave of almost nauseating fatigue swept over her. "Okay, why don't you make some discreet inquiries to the Chinese and the French and see if they'll play ball. I gotta get some sleep."

Gallagher touched her arm. "You do that, dearie. I'll watch yer back."

She unslung the rifle from her shoulder and handed it to the Irishwoman. "Here, I think this still has a full clip. Check it."

Gallagher sucked in an awed breath as she examined the weapon. "My, my! Aren't *you* a sweet piece of iron! Where did you *get* this?"

"I pulled it off a dead CIA operative as a war trophy. A beauty, isn't it?"

Gallagher brought the weapon to her shoulder, testing its heft. "Sweet Mary! It's like holding hands with Death himself!"

Conrad felt faint for a second. She reached out to the Honda to steady herself. "Tell you what. If you can get Dieter and Linn back on our team, that gun is yours, deal?"

Gallagher's eyes lit up like a child at Christmas. "Consider it done!" She turned away, stroking the gun like a cat. "Come on, love, mommie has some phone calls to make!"

BREAKING NEWS

SAN FRANCISCO, CALIFORNIA

The San Jose Massacre was the lead story on every nationwide morning news show. The local TV stations had gone wall-to-wall with it. There *was* no other story, as far as they were concerned. Networks cut from one reporter-on-the-scene live shot to another, even though no new information had broken for hours. *Fish gotta swim, talking heads gotta talk*, Perry Pugliano mused, turning away from the break room TV.

He stirred his third cup of coffee in preparation for the morning meeting at the FBI's downtown office. The fatigue from his all-nighter was starting to pull at him, but there wasn't going to be any opportunity to rest during what promised to be a very long day. Everyone who hadn't been out at the crime scene in San Jose had been summoned into work an hour early, and the regional director for Justice and the US Attorney for Northern California would be arriving shortly. He knew these two were just the first ripple of an oncoming wave of blame-pinning bigwigs soon to crash upon his office like a tsunami.

Pugliano thanked a God he only marginally believed in that he had called the all hands meeting last week after the death of Rashid Ben-Jabir. Barring another 9/11, this was undoubtedly going to be the biggest case of his career, and his declaration that Angela Conrad and a convergence of unsavory intelligence types were loose and operating in San Francisco had been the biggest CYA of his career. By some unwritten Law of Bureaucracy, somebody's career always went in the crapper when a crime of this magnitude went down on their turf. Because of his ability to play the "I Told You So" card, the chances of *him* being that somebody had been reduced dramatically.

He quickly made the rounds of the agents who would be presenting today. Because the case was so massive, Pugliano had immediately started carving off chunks of the investigation to his more senior agents, mostly based on the order they had arrived at the crime scene. Now they would present the preliminary results of their investigations, and the quality of those presentations would, of course, reflect directly on his leadership.

A flitter of functionaries announced the arrival of Justice and the US Attorney. Lackeys and bootlickers jostled for position getting their superiors coffee and bagels, laying out briefing papers, and generally kissing butt. He was glad his agents were usually too busy for such behavior.

"Okay," Justice said pompously, "I think we're ready to go here."

Well, aren't you special? "Thank you, sir. We have a number of presentations for you today, but I'll begin with a backgrounder on the incident by Special Agent Wendy Cho."

Cho stood and took the remote, the top of her head barely higher than the seated officials before her. She was nervous and her unoccupied left hand shook visibly. But she bravely launched into her hastily prepared remarks on the basic Where, When, What, and Who of the massacre. Being the least senior agent in his detail he trusted this to her because the basic facts of a case were the hardest to screw up. That and she could handle PowerPoint like a NASCAR driver could handle a race car, so he knew her charts would look good.

"So," the US Attorney interrupted five minutes into her brief, "of the fifteen bodies we found, do we have any clue on who's who?"

Pugliano jumped in to prevent her making any career-limiting off-the-cuff speculations. "Our witness Scott Hendrix has positively identified seven of the dead as CIA agents. He said there were six Israelis on the other team, although he didn't know any of them by name. That leaves two bodies unclaimed, whom we believe are Angela Conrad's cohorts."

"And you're *positive* Conrad isn't one of these female bodies?" Justice asked, leafing through a stack of photographs. "I mean, both of these corpses are pretty torn up."

"Mr. Hendrix said there were two female agents on the Israeli team. He has seen those photos as well. He says he's certain the bodies are of the two Israelis and *not* Conrad."

Justice made a face, as if Angela Conrad had greatly inconvenienced him personally by not dying. "Any IDs on Conrad's henchmen?"

Pugliano pointed to the agent charged with that lead. The agent stood and accepted the remote from Cho, launching his own charts. Cho gratefully took a seat.

A dead male body filled the screen. "We've tentatively identified this body as Yuri Konalev, ex-KGB, and recently a freelance operative specializing in covert security," the agent reported. "The other body will be more difficult to ID," he said, advancing to the next photograph.

"Oh, *God*," Justice choked through a mouthful of bagel. "Thanks for the *warning*!"

The agent blinked, so inured to the gore of the preceding hours that the idea of others being disturbed by it had not crossed his mind. "Oh, sorry. It's just that if I had told you that identification by facial recognition, dental records, or retinal scan would be impossible for this subject, I figured you would ask why."

Pugliano suppressed a grin at Justice's discomfort. "Fingerprints?" he suggested.

"No hits on the FBI database. We're running them past CIA and Interpol, but if this guy made a living as a spook before going freelance, his prints were probably purged from his national database. I'd say no better than fifty-fifty for a quick ID."

"What are we doing with the Israelis' bodies?" the US Attorney asked.

"Technically, they're not Israelis," Pugliano answered. "Four of them had Canadian passports and two had British. We're contacting their respective embassies, and we expect the passports to turn up as fraudulent. It's up to the State Department after that, but I suppose someone will make a 'discreet inquiry' to the Israeli consulate. If it were up to me, I'd tell the Israelis that they can cooperate with the investigation and get the bodies of their people back, or they can deny everything and we'll cremate them and dump their ashes in the Bay."

Justice pointed a bony finger at him. "Just for clarification, Agent Pugliano, it is *not* up to you. It is in fact way the *hell* above your pay grade to even speculate about."

It was at that moment Pugliano decided the regional director for the Justice Department would be an excellent candidate for the bureaucrat to have his career go down the crapper over this incident. Wasn't he the most resistant person to Pugliano's warnings at the last meeting? Yes, indeed he was. And an unsourced leak to the local news media would make sure that the people whose hands rested on the flush handle knew all about it.

"I'm sorry, sir," Pugliano apologized. "My comment was out of line." *Bastard.*

Justice continued glaring at him, relishing his position in the food chain.

The US Attorney cleared his throat. "Uh, Agent Pugliano, you said that CIA Agent Hendrix was a witness to this incident. Why isn't he at this meeting?"

"At our last meeting Agent Hendrix was part of the *investigation* into Angela Conrad's presence here in San Francisco. Now he's a *witness*, which means I have to restrict his access to information external to his testimony. He doesn't even get to watch TV. If my team uncovers a new piece of evidence and I need to show it to Hendrix, I don't want his opinion tainted by *any* external influence."

The US Attorney leafed through a document before him. "I understand. However, looking through his statement, I find it interesting that *all* the facts as he presents them completely exonerates himself. Convenient, isn't it, seeing that he's the sole survivor of the incident?"

Pugliano smirked. "Yes sir, I did notice that. However, while I take his statement with a grain of salt, my team hasn't found any inconsistencies with the evidence we've gathered so far. And believe me, we *are* looking for discrepancies. But for the moment, I'm finding Mr. Hendrix more useful as a cooperating witness than as a suspect."

"Fair enough. But what are these crazy reports I'm hearing about some kind of *ray gun* being used in the firefight? The news media is absolutely in a lather over it."

Pugliano frowned. *Hmm, three guesses on that leak. Derek, Derek, and Derek.* "Unfortunately, as with most wild stories, there's a grain of truth. And a lot more than a grain in this case." He pointed to the agent in charge of that portion of the investigation.

The agent led off with a diagram of the crime scene in front of San Jose City Hall showing the truck and two vans involved. Fifteen red and blue X's were scattered in and around the three vehicles. "Sirs, as you can see, we have two distinct causes of death in this incident. The eight red X's are deaths by gunshot, and the seven blue X's are death by…something else."

Learning from the previous presenter, the agent paused. "Sirs, the next slide is quite graphic."

Justice set down his coffee. "Go ahead." Even the agents who had been at the crime scene visibly cringed at the next slide. "*Woof,*" someone whispered.

"First question: what are we looking at? For a lack of a better term," the agent explained, "I'm referring to these deaths as TITE fatalities, an acronym for Thermally Induced Thoracic Explosion."

"Gotta love a good acronym," Justice muttered.

"I'm not going to kid anyone that we know what caused this, but we have a working theory that it's some kind of microwave weapon. We have our best forensic pathologists flying in from Quantico. The local coroners are currently preserving samples from all of the TITE fatalities for in-depth tissue analysis. If this weapon leaves any kind of chemical trace, hopefully we can use that to figure out what we're dealing with.

"Second question: who's using it? Our working theory, and that's all it is, is that whoever was wielding the TITE weapon was on Angela Conrad's side. There are TITE fatalities in both the Israeli and CIA teams, but both of her apparent co-conspirators are dead by gunshot."

"Could *Conrad* be the one shooting this microwave gun?" The US Attorney asked. "I mean, how big of a weapon are we talking about? Is it man portable?"

The agent shrugged. "We've requested assistance from some experts in directed energy weapons at Lawrence Livermore Laboratories, but that hasn't happened yet, and I'm not qualified to even guess on that score."

"Well, it *has* to be man portable, doesn't it?" Justice insisted. "I mean, somebody used it, and it's not there any more, which means *somebody* walked away with it, right?"

"Or *drove* away with it," Pugliano corrected. "It could have been mounted on a second vehicle covering Conrad's escape."

"Wait a minute," the US Attorney interjected. "This took place right in front of City Hall, correct? Don't they have security camera footage we could look at?"

Pugliano frowned. "The building super wouldn't release them without say-so from the mayor, and the mayor wouldn't release them without a judge's order. We should have them in our possession shortly."

"Agent Pugliano," the US Attorney continued, "you mentioned in our last meeting some kind of 'spy convention' going down here in San Francisco. Would you view this as further evidence of that event?"

He thought for a moment. In the chaos surrounding the massacre, he hadn't had time to ponder the wider ramifications of the event. "Well sir, Angela Conrad was ambushed by two highly trained teams of professional shooters, she was heavily outnumbered, and yet she so thoroughly outmatched them that only one survived. The idea that she could do that without help seems pretty ludicrous to me. So the short answer is yes, we seem to be up to our hubcaps in professional assassins, and no, I have no idea what they're going to do next."

The color drained from Justice's face. "Well, Special Agent Pugliano, thank you very much for your time. I think it would be best if we let you and your team get back to work." Translation: *What a world-class pooch screw. I've got some major league butt covering to take care of. Pardon me while I run for the tall grass.*

"Yes, sir. You're very welcome. I will of course keep you updated on our..." He was interrupted by a female agent whispering in his ear.

"Sirs, the security footage from San Jose City Hall has arrived." He motioned to her. "Agent Lane, you have the floor."

Lane handed a DVD to the agent running the projector. "On the way back from San Jose," she said to the group, "I edited the footage into a short video with the action we're most interested in." She nodded. "Whenever you're ready."

The camera angle was set to cover the plaza in front of City Hall, but it also took in the street and the nearest intersection at the top of the screen. The quality was excellent, but Pugliano realized a city like San Jose *should* be able to afford the best equipment. From this viewpoint certain segments of the action were well-represented; the initial collision, the death of Conrad's unidentified driver by an Israeli shooter, that shooter's death by a female who rolled out the back of the truck. Could that be Conrad? Not enough detail to tell. Then she disappeared under the truck and more Israelis went down, in tempo with a series of flashes from under the truck.

The second van entered the frame from the right. The van was going at least thirty, but Pugliano saw one of Hendrix's CIA shooters jump from the moving vehicle and tumble down the street like a football. What the hell was the guy thinking? The van hit Conrad's truck, and one of the CIA shooters on the far side of the street went down, apparently by gunfire. Only two of the CIA shooters were visible; the other two must have been out of frame to the right. The nearest shooter went prone, then popped three feet into the air. He was obviously dead when he landed.

"That was a microwave kill," somebody muttered.

"Anybody see the shooter?" Pugliano called out. Heads shook all around. Suddenly the apparently-Conrad figure popped out from under the truck and ran to screen-right.

"Can anybody tell what kind of weapon she's carrying?" he asked the group.

"Looks like a standard MP5 submachine gun," one of his tactical team replied. "I think I saw her take it off one of the dead Israelis." She then ran to the CIA shooter who had been downed by the microwave weapon and knelt over him.

"Is she checking his vitals?" someone asked. A universal groan of disgust rose from the group when Conrad stripped the downed CIA operative of his weapon.

"Damned vulture," Justice growled, having decided to stay for the video. Pugliano thought it odd for Justice to criticize his own kind, but he realized it was just for the crowd's consumption. A movement caught his eye. A man with a pistol had slipped from behind a parked car and had crept up behind Conrad as she knelt.

"Just shoot the bitch!" several whispered at once, in a group violation of political correctness.

He then watched a shiny ball float in from screen-left to hover above Conrad.

"What the hell?" several in the group muttered.

"Is that a balloon?"

"If it is, how can it start and stop like that?"

The final CIA agent exploded. Conrad and the ball had a short staring match, then it zipped off screen to the right and Conrad followed. The video ended.

"Whiskey Tango *Foxtrot!*" Pugliano's tactical team leader called out, the presence of higher-ups preventing a more colorful expression.

"That's it, I'm afraid," Agent Lane said. "The rest of the video is just police response."

"No, that's very helpful," he said. "Thanks for rushing it in." *I gotta show this to Hendrix.*

"Okay folks," he called to the group, "Any one of you could find the piece of evidence that breaks this case open, so stay at it. Dismissed!"

As his agents filed out, he had an idea. "Agents Lane and Cho, stay a minute." Once he had them alone he said, "Both of you were on the Manning tail last night. I have to make some phone calls, but I want you two to brainstorm a game plan."

"A game plan for what?" Cho asked.

"I want to run a proctoscope so far up Mike Manning's backside that we can tell whether or not he brushed his teeth this morning."

* * *

"Kim, I'll be with you in a minute," Cho told Agent Lane. "I've got to run to the little girl's room."

Back in her office, she booted up her laptop and accessed the central server, finding the folder where the San Jose Massacre files were being gathered. Finding Scott Hendrix's debriefing transcript, she downloaded it to a thumb drive. She dug in her purse for her second cell phone, the one provided by Hendrix, then made her way to a corridor not covered by security cameras, dialing an emergency number from memory.

"Dispatch," a male voice answered.

"Sugar Cookie, authentication Sierra Hotel three-five-two."

"Wait one." After a short pause he said, "Proceed."

"This agent's handler is being detained by the FBI. It is imperative his superiors receive his debriefing before making any statements to the Bureau. A transcript is available, but I am unable to make the pass at present. It will be placed in dead drop number two the minute I can get free. Please be ready for immediate pick up when I signal that the drop has been made."

She could hear keystrokes in the background. "Message received and understood."

FEDERAL CASUALTIES

CHICAGO, ILLINOIS

Simon Crane didn't have a television in his high-rise office. He valued austerity, and a TV would just be an unused piece of clutter in his no-nonsense workplace. But after reading the morning intelligence briefing prepared by his night watch officer, he knew he needed to see this for himself. Actually, if the watch officer had known this was part of their group's operations, he would have immediately wakened Crane when the story broke.

He returned to his adjoining apartment and clicked on the television without sitting down. With the intelligence resources at his command he had little need for cable news and he had to flip randomly until he reached the news channels; he had simply forgotten where they were. At least he didn't have to wait until the top or bottom of the hour for the story; apparently the San Jose Massacre—as they were calling it—was a nationwide news fixation.

Watching the long-distance helicopter shots of the carnage, Crane felt a chill that something had gone horribly wrong. If his agent didn't report in immediately, the young man had better be quite dead, he mused darkly.

He heard his phone ring in his office.

"Report!" he barked.

"Sir, as you suspected, there *was* a threat against a primary player. I'm afraid I was unable to honor your proscription against federal casualties."

"Body count?"

"Seven by my own hand. The protectee was able to eliminate six on her own."

"She killed six by *herself*?" Crane was surprised by the excitement he heard in his own voice. He thought he was past the reach of such passions.

"Yes sir. She was surprisingly…*efficient*. In all honesty, sir, the assault against her was so massive I'm not sure I would have been able to save her by my own efforts alone."

"Then she saved *your* life as well as her own," he observed coldly.

"Yes sir."

"Continue with the rest of the terminations as planned. That is all," Crane said, hanging up the phone. He turned his chair to face the window.

Do I have your attention now, Mr. President?

PARTY POOPER

SAN JOSE, CALIFORNIA

Mike Manning awoke at the stroke of nine when the housekeeper knocked at his door. Hearing no answer, she entered, only to leave with a scream when she encountered his naked form sprawled on the floor. He struggled to groan and move enough that she wouldn't call Security, thinking him a dead body. She left with a muttered chastisement in Spanish.

He pulled his face from the floor, his cheek adhered to the carpet by saliva. His head pounding with a hangover, he crawled to the door to hang out the Do Not Disturb sign, encountering an empty bottle of Jack Daniels on the way. This felt like a personal low, but then he remembered his fraternity days. At least this time he was *indoors* when he woke up prostrate and naked. And although it didn't feel like it at the moment, this was a *celebration.* Time to start acting like it.

He stumbled to the shower and soaked his pounding head for several minutes. Feeling closer to human after that, he grabbed the room service menu and collapsed onto the bed. He ordered steak and eggs along with a bottle of champagne to help dull his hangover. After all, he was celebrating.

He thought about just abandoning Nanovex and heading back to Chicago, but they would certainly ask for their signing bonus back, and he needed that money. No, he would finish this job for them. Then, once he told them about Angela Conrad and the *real* reason he came to work for Nanovex, he was sure they would put him on the first plane out of town.

But no work today. He would call in sick in a few minutes. After his hangover passed he might venture out and play tourist, maybe even visit City Hall and see the scene of Angela Conrad's death, at least as closely as the police tape would allow. It occurred to him that her shooting was probably on the news. He reached for the remote.

"And in our continuing coverage of the San Jose Massacre," the TV blared, "we take you to Edgar Salvatore, live at San Jose Police headquarters."

Impressive, Manning thought; they even had their own logo for the event in the lower left hand of the screen, a bloody crosshair with police lights flashing behind it. The Marketing of Death at its finest. He puffed up a pair of pillows against the headboard to enjoy the spectacle.

"Thank you Sally," Edgar Salvatore intoned seriously. "The San Jose Police have just released the photograph of a person of interest in the shootings last night at City Hall. Apparently one of the shooters left her driver's license at the scene and police would very much like to question her about last night's incident."

Oops, that's gotta make you feel like a bimbo, he thought cheerfully. One of the shooters gunning for Conrad wasn't as sharp as she thought she was. Actually, from the number of bodies, a whole *bunch* of them had discovered that Conrad was no pushover. *But hey, Karma always catches up with you eventually doesn't it, Angela?*

Angela Conrad's photograph appeared on the screen.

"This is the driver's license photo of the suspect the police are seeking. Now, they caution us that this is probably an alias, but the license was issued to one Monica Geldman, of Riverside, California. Police say that if you see this woman, do not approach her. Assume she is armed and dangerous and call 911."

"Edgar, while I have you there," the anchor interrupted, "have the police released any more information about the people who were killed in the massacre?"

"No, Sally, they've stayed remarkably close-lipped on that subject…."

Manning didn't hear any more after that; it was just noise as he stared blankly at the screen. After a few minutes another sound intruded at the periphery of his senses. It took several seconds to localize the sound to the trash can beside his desk. He walked over and cautiously looked inside.

At the bottom of the trash can his Conrad phone was ringing.

BOOK II

CHAPTER 16

THE BUCK STOPS HERE

OCTOBER 15, 1947 – WASHINGTON, D.C.

General Nathan Twining

Allen Dulles

Air Force General Nathan Twining entered President Harry Truman's Oval Office with a bespectacled, professorial civilian in tow. The official reason for Twining's visit was to report on the previous day's successful flight of the Bell X-1, the world's first supersonic flight by a manned aircraft. He delivered the report, then moved on to another matter.

"Mr. President," Twining said, "the real reason for my visit today is to discuss our progress on the Tesla physics projects the Nazis began during the war."

Truman drew back, glancing apprehensively at the bespectacled stranger. "That's a *very* sensitive subject, General. I wasn't informed that topic would be discussed today. I'd prefer to wait for a meeting of the entire National Security Council."

Twining shifted uncomfortably. "Mr. President, if I thought it could wait, I would certainly agree with you. But we have a problem. I've sat in meetings with the scientists and engineers analyzing the Nazi project files we were able to recover. It is clear to me that these are the best and brightest minds we as a country can bring to bear on this problem. Unfortunately, these men are as lost as a child in the woods in trying to decipher the Nazi's Tesla technology. We need help, and I'm afraid admitting that fact in front of the entire National Security Council will just ruffle feathers and make matters worse."

Truman leaned back in his chair, folding his arms. "So what is it you propose?"

Twining took a deep breath. "Mr. President, this is Allen Dulles, formerly of the OSS.[1] He was instrumental in arranging the transfer of the German rocket scientists who are working for us in New Mexico."

Truman coldly returned Dulles' handshake. "Did you mean arranging their transfer, or circumventing my executive order against bringing Nazis into the US?"[2]

Dulles smiled pleasantly. "Mr. President, it was never my intention to skirt your wishes. I merely investigated the scientists' true political beliefs and found that most of them were Nazis by necessity only. Their nation *was* at war, Mr. President. They merely showed the loyalty to country that one would expect under the circumstances. None of the men we brought over were guilty of any war crimes, I can assure you."

As a politician, Truman had an ability to quickly size up anyone he met. *This man is a snake*, he knew instinctively. "How convenient for you," he observed dryly.

"How convenient for our *rocket program*," Dulles countered. "If it wasn't for the Paperclip scientists, we wouldn't have one."

Truman raised an eyebrow. "And let me guess. There's somebody you want to bring in for the Tesla project who *is* a war criminal?"

Dulles' poker face was resolute. "Hans Kammler, their director of special projects."

Truman could feel a fire rising in his belly. "You mean the same Kammler who slaughtered tens of thousands of slave laborers making the V-2 rockets that killed thousands more? That same Kammler?"

Dulles held up a hand. "Yes, Mr. President, but…."

"The same Kammler who made their atom bomb that they threatened to sail into New York Harbor if we tried to haul their sorry asses to Nuremberg for war crimes trials?"

"Yes, Mr. President…."

Truman felt his pulse pounding against his collar. "Well then, let me make it easy for you, Mr. Dulles. If it's that same Hans Kammler, then the answer is not only no, but *hell* no. Is that clear enough for you?"

"Yes, Mr. President, but…."

"But what?" he snapped.

"Sir, our sources indicate that Hans Kammler has access to research even *more* advanced than the Tesla technology we're trying to decipher. He could advance our understanding by years in a single meeting. And he has expressed a willingness to cooperate."

Truman slapped a three-inch-thick pile of telegrams on his desk. "Do you know what these are, Mr. Dulles?"

"No, sir."

"These are *reminders* from my supporters in the Jewish community that they are budgeting their political contributions for next year and *suggest* that if I don't support the formation of a state of Israel in the UN this year, they may just take their money elsewhere." He tapped the pile with his finger for emphasis. "Mr. Dulles, what do you think they would do if I did business with a mass murderer of Jews just to shave a few years off a *research project*?"[3]

"Well, Mr. President, I…."

Truman rose from his chair, glowering down at the seated Dulles. "I'll *tell* you what they'd do, Mr. Dulles, *they'd shave a few years off my presidency!* And I wouldn't blame them *one bit* for doing so!"

Truman watched Dulles' facial muscles twitch. The spymaster was obviously not used to being told what to do. These kind of bureaucrats had to be slapped down hard, or they'd retreat to their personal empires and become troublemakers. Sure enough, the little weasel couldn't keep his mouth shut.

"Mr. President…."

Truman reached for his desk plaque that read THE BUCK STOPS HERE. He picked it up and tested its heft in his hand. "Can you read this sign, Mr. Dulles, or do I need to make a *deeper* impression with it?"

General Twining took Dulles by the arm, leading him out of the Oval Office. "Thank you for your time, Mr. President."[4]

FULL PACKAGE

PRESENT DAY – SAN FRANCISCO, CALIFORNIA

Perry Pugliano returned to the main conference room at the FBI's downtown office to find agents Wendy Cho and Kim Lane huddled over a table. The two were obviously not seeing eye-to-eye on the Manning surveillance.

Cho had her hands on her hips. "But how are we going to pin a tail on him? We don't even know where he is. And how do you know he won't shake us just like he did last night?"

Lane didn't take the criticism from a junior agent kindly. "What we're going to do, Agent Cho, is cover *all* the places where he's likely to frequent. And as far as losing him last night, I don't think I care for your tone. Would you care to elaborate on what *you* would have done differently?"

Uh-oh, cat fight. Pugliano pretended not to have heard them arguing. "All right, Agent Lane, what's the plan?"

Lane squared her shoulders, composing herself. "Sir, I suggest we deploy a full surveillance package on Manning; bug his hotel room and office, wiretaps on every phone number he's used in the last week, bumper beeper on his car, the works."

"Do we know where he is now?" he probed gently.

"No sir, but we know Nanovex is the focus of his activities. Once we inform their management of the threat, we should have no problem setting up a surveillance unit on their property. Then when Manning shows up, we'll rig his car with so many tracking devices they'll be able to spot him from orbit."

He nodded. "I have a good rapport with their CEO, I'll set that up. And his hotel?"

"There's no way he'd go back to the same hotel after shaking us off his tail last night," Cho said confidently.

My, she is a little uppity for a junior agent. "Do you *know* that, Agent Cho? *I* don't. Go check out his hotel. If he's still there, then get the court order to rig his room for sound and video. Have you ever done that before?"

"No sir, but…."

He cut her off. "Then this will be good experience for you. If it's a dead end, then contact Agent Lane for your next assignment."

She swallowed hard. "Yes sir."

Pugliano rubbed his fatigued eyes. "Let me see Manning's dossier."

Lane handed him a wafer-thin folder. "Not much to go on."

He leafed through the file. The driver's license photo sure looked like the Mike Manning he had met at Nanovex. "Huh, other than the fact he likes to drive fast, he appears to be a model citizen. That's probably why they picked him." He turned to Manning's credit report. "Whoa! This guy sure is good friends with his loan officer!"

Lane nodded. "First name basis. Check out the next page. I called in a favor and had a friend pull his last Visa statement."

His eyes bugged. "Holy *Versace*! Maybe this guy *did* get turned for money. I mean, his wife has him by the balls, maybe Conrad just joined in for a yank." Suddenly realizing what he had said, he quickly added. "Sorry ladies, that just slipped out. My apologies." Criminals might fear the FBI, but what male FBI agents feared were the enforcers of political correctness in the FBI's Internal Affairs department.

"No offense taken, sir," Lane said. "We could all use a little sleep." Cho wore a slight grin.

He shook his head to clear it. "Not gonna get that any time soon. Any more questions?"

"Sir," Cho asked in a much more subordinate tone, "what about Manning's wife in Chicago? Should she be put under surveillance as well?"

"Hell yes," he replied reflexively. "Full package. Light her up like a Christmas tree."

* * *

Before she hit the road for the drive down to San Jose, Wendy Cho was surprised to run into her boss at the convenience store down the street from headquarters. Pugliano glanced at the monstrous soft drink in her hand.

"Soda!" he chastised. "You can't be a real FBI agent unless you drink coffee. It's in the Constitution somewhere, I'm pretty sure."

She held up her Big Gulp in a mock toast. "Diet Mountain Dew got me through law school! Maybe I could convert you," she said with a wink.

He muttered something and wandered away, obviously not interested in an extended conversation with an underling. *Dammit.* At this rate she was never going to get into Pugliano's pants.

Once outside, she drove a block and pulled into an open space, not bothering to feed the meter. She wadded up her 7-Eleven bag and threw it into a receptacle on the sidewalk, then re-entered her car and drove away.

Half a block down the street, a man in coveralls picked up trash from the sidewalk and the grassy border with a pointed stick. When Cho departed, he pulled a fresh trash can liner from a pouch on his utility belt, walked to the receptacle and emptied it. He threw the half-full trash bag into the back of a city service cart and drove away.

* * *

Pugliano found Scott Hendrix with his head on the table in the interrogation room. He kicked the chair and threw a breakfast burrito on the table. "Wake up, sleeping beauty! Greetings from 7-Eleven!" He sat down opposite the CIA agent, setting down their coffees and unrolling his own dubious breakfast from its paper wrapper.

"Oh, thanks!" Hendrix replied, tearing into the fast food with gusto. "When am I getting out of here, by the way?"

He snorted. "You act like I've kept you in solitary for a week. Would you rather wait in a jail cell while I check out your story? I thought you guys were trained to withstand torture."

Hendrix bit off a greasy morsel, the cheese pulling away with stringy resistance. "You've watched too many spy movies. The only torture we're trained to endure is lip burns if we drink our lattés too quickly."

"Oh, pardon me!" he said with a chuckle. "Hey, I got something I want you to take a look at." One of Pugliano's agents brought in a laptop.

"Whatcha got?" Hendrix asked.

"Security footage from San Jose City Hall. Take a look."

Hendrix wiped the grease from his hands with a napkin and clicked on the video. Pugliano had fully expected a visceral reaction to watching a replay of his near-death experience, but when Hendrix looked up, every trace of color had drained from his face. He pushed the laptop away like it had a foul odor.

Pugliano cleared his throat. "I know that's kind of hard to watch, but…."

Hendrix leaned forward, his voice barely above a whisper. "Do you have any idea what you just caught on tape?"

"Are you talking about the people blowing up, or the little floating ball?"

Hendrix stared blankly into space. "I had heard rumors about this shit, but I never believed them. Until now."

Pugliano leaned across the table. "Rumors about *what*?"

Hendrix gestured with his eyes toward the microphone on the table and the mirrored glass behind Pugliano. "Huh-uh. Not with a tape rolling."

He reached over and cupped his hand over the microphone. "So if I get you out of here, will you tell me what you know?"

Hendrix leaned across the table until their foreheads almost touched

"Deal. But dude, there are some things you don't *want* to know. And trust me, this is one of them."

NOT LIKE IKE

JANUARY 23, 1953 – WASHINGTON, D.C.

Newly inaugurated president Dwight Eisenhower sat down in the White House residence with his Director of Central Intelligence after a long day of briefings. Eisenhower chose to relax in front of the fireplace with a glass of brandy, the DCI with his trademark pipe. "Mr. President," DCI Allen Dulles said, "I want to thank you again for your confidence in me for this position."

Eisenhower took a deep draw on his brandy snifter. "That's one of the few good things about war, Dulles. You learn damn fast who you can depend on."[5]

"You certainly have quite a bit on your plate. Do you find it at all overwhelming?"

Eisenhower responded with an almost imperceptible shake of his head. "Compared to a war, the pace is more manageable, it's just the variety of subjects I'm expected to become an instant expert on that's a bit daunting."

"Any subject in particular?"

Eisenhower gave him a cold glance out of the corner of his eye. "Stop beating around the bush, Dulles. What's on your mind?"

"The escaped Nazis and their Tesla technology projects. Now that you've been briefed, I'd like to know your thoughts."

Eisenhower glanced over his shoulder to make sure the steward had withdrawn. "I get the impression that Truman just wanted to pretend the problem didn't exist, not deal with it."

Dulles gave him a knowing smile. "I only met President Truman once, but it was in regards to this subject, and I got the same impression."

Eisenhower's jaw tightened. "The reports I read after the war made my blood run cold. If they're allowed to develop that technology in South America free from interference, then God help us."

Dulles sensed his opening. "Exactly, Mr. President. Which is why I'm going to ask you to give careful consideration to a proposal I've been developing for some time."

Eisenhower looked away from the fireplace. "I'm listening."

Dulles shifted in the wingback chair to more directly face the President. "Over the last several years, I have been developing sources with some unique insights on the Tesla technology problem. They've hinted that they may have cracked the physics behind Tesla's theories, but they are reluctant to provide any details to our government."

A raised eyebrow. "Why is that? Are they trying to get a better deal from the Russians?"

Dulles laughed softly. "Hardly, Mr. President. They're reluctant because of the efforts of the previous administration to have them arrested, in spite of an agreement that I brokered myself." [6]

Eisenhower's lip curled slightly. "You're referring to Bormann's get-out-of-jail-free card in exchange for the uranium for our atom bomb? That deal still turns my stomach."

Dulles nodded deferentially. "Yes sir, but you have to admit that it saved tens of thousands of American lives. If war is hell, then sometimes the devil is the only trading partner available."

Eisenhower grunted in disgust. "True enough. But what does Bormann have to do with your proposal?"

Dulles let the pregnant silence between them come to full term. "Mr. President, Martin Bormann *is* my proposal, or more specifically his chief technology expert, Hans Kammler. The CIA has retained back-channel communications with their organization. As objectionable as the ideology these men hold is, if we form a partnership strictly for technological development, we can assure that the Russians do not develop these advanced weapons before we do."

Eisenhower set his glass aside. “Let me see if I understand you. We’ve got the same Nazi war criminals who beat us to the atomic bomb and *would* have used it against us if Joe Stalin hadn’t put their lights out, right? And you want to get in *bed* with them?”

“Mr. President, the Russians *are aware* of the Nazi’s Tesla weapons. All three of their major test centers for that technology were in the Russian zone when the war ended. Pilsen, Ohrdruf, and Wenceslas Mines are all behind the Iron Curtain now. And as thorough as General Patton’s efforts were to sanitize those sites before the Russians took over, some of the Nazi scientists may now be in Russian hands, forced to complete their work for the Communists.”

“I’m surprised there are any Nazi scientists *left* in Germany after your little relocation program,” Eisenhower snapped. “I don’t want to hear another word about it!”

Dulles sat in chagrined silence, but Eisenhower wasn’t through.

“Dear God, Allen! What the hell are you thinking? Do you remember the mincemeat Joe McCarthy made of Truman’s administration over *possible* penetrations by Communists? What the hell would the Democrats do to us if they found out we had entered into a relationship with *Nazis*, eyes wide open?”

The use of Dulles’ first name was penetrating; the rebuke was personal as well as professional. He hung his head in mock regret. “Mr. President, I’m sorry if I upset you, but….”

Eisenhower turned to face the fireplace again. “That’s enough for today. Get out, Allen. Before I think of someone who might make a better Director of Central Intelligence."

Dulles beat a hasty retreat. “Good night, Mr. President.”

One of Dulles’ protégés was playing cards with the Secret Service agents outside the residence. He quickly excused himself and fell in at his mentor’s side. “How did it go?”

Dulles gave him a frosty look from behind his round spectacles. “At least he didn’t threaten to throw a paperweight at me like Truman did. But he *did* threaten to fire me if I brought up Kammler again.”

“My God,” the younger man said. A politician, he had come under Dulles’ wing in 1945 as a young Naval Intelligence officer. One of Dulles’ legal clients, Karl Blessing of the German oil cartel Kontinentale Oil, A.G., had come under scrutiny of the Nuremberg Tribunal for his company’s complicity in the Holocaust. But Blessing was indispensable for his contacts to Saudi King Iben Saud for both Kontinentale’s business and that of another Dulles client Aramco, the Arabian-American Oil Company. Using his government position, Dulles was able to make Blessing’s OSS records “disappear.” He even peddled a fable to the New York *Times* of Blessing’s record as an anti-Nazi resister during the war.

Unfortunately, Naval Intelligence also possessed captured Nazi documents, which told a different story of Blessing's background. Dulles approached the young officer in charge of the investigation and asked of his plans after the service. He learned the officer had thought of running for public office in his home state of California. Dulles proposed that if the Blessing file was found to have no incriminating evidence and was then "lost," it would not be difficult to find backers for the young man's first run for Congress.

The young officer agreed and won his seat as a congressman in 1946—claiming the money for his campaign came from his poker winnings during the war.[7] In 1948 he established himself as an ardent anti-Communist by exposing a Soviet spy in the State Department named Alger Hiss. This notoriety catapulted him from the House to the Senate in 1950, and finally to a nomination as Dwight Eisenhower's vice presidential running mate in 1952. The young politician's name was Richard Milhous Nixon."[8]

Nixon was incredulous. "Didn't you explain the advances Kammler is making *right now*?"

"I never got the chance!" Dulles snapped. "As soon as Ike heard the word 'Nazi', he blew his stack!"

Nixon walked Dulles to his car in silence.

"Don't worry, Dick," Dulles finally said. "After another four or five years of those eggheads at Wright Patterson and Los Alamos beating their heads against the Tesla files to no effect, we'll give Ike another chance to come around."

Nixon held the door open for his mentor. "Here's hoping that we don't have Russian Tesla ships buzzing around our heads before that happens."

Dulles resisted shaking his head. *That Nixon has always been a little on the paranoid side*. But it was a tendency that served Dulles' purposes. He winked. "Who knows, Dick. Maybe in few years *you'll* be running for president."

TALKING TO STRANGERS

PRESENT DAY – SAN JOSE CALIFORNIA

Mike Manning reluctantly fished the Conrad phone out of the trash can in his room. "H-hello?" he answered with a trembling voice.

The voice that replied was so thick with an Irish accent he first thought the call was a wrong number. That hope was quickly dashed. "Mr. Manning, if you were under the mistaken impression that you were off the hook, I'm calling to correct that notion. Where are ya now?"

The sudden fear and stress added to the hangover pounding in his head until it was like a drum solo. "I'm not telling you that!" he said reflexively.

The Irishwoman was not deterred. "Whatever enforcement mechanism Ms. Conrad put in place for you, let me assure ya it's still in effect. Wait one moment." After a pause, she continued. "She says that your son Kevin has a birthday next month. Whether ya celebrate that event at your kitchen table or at his graveside makes no difference to me."

"You *bitch!*" he snarled.

She laughed. "Not the first time I've heard that, and it won't be the last. I'll ask ya one more time before I start making phone calls to Chicago. Where are ya now?"

"At my hotel," he said, barely above a whisper.

"There now. That wasn't so hard, was it?"

"What do you *want*?"

"I want ya in your car, ready to roll in ten minutes. Ring this number back for further instructions." She ended the call.

Manning only resisted the urge to heave the phone at the wall because doing so would not only have cost him his own life but that of his family as well. Instead, he kicked the trash can across the room, almost breaking his unprotected toe in the process.

"*Dammit!*" he shouted.

* * *

Ten minutes later, in dress slacks and shirt but no tie, he exited the hotel, crossing the parking lot to his car. In the spot next to his, a man in an army fatigue jacket bent over the hood of a car, looking at a map and scratching his head. He looked up when Manning approached.

"Hey mate!" he said in a cheerful English accent. "It's my first day in town and I'm a bit turned around, could you help me out?"

He started to walk past him. "Sorry, I'm in kind of a hurry."

The man reached out. "C'mon, mate! I just want to go see the Golden Gate Bridge! A little help?"

Well hell, I can do that much, he thought. He leaned over the man's map. "Look, all you gotta do is take the 101 north into the city…."

The man took Manning's arm and thrust a curved palm knife at his gut. "Bloody Americans! Always willing to help out a foreigner in need! You'd think two world wars would have taught you better."

Manning heard a large vehicle pull to a stop behind him.

The Englishman grinned at him. "Now, be a good Yank and get in the truck, or I'll gut you like a fish."

He turned to face a large black SUV. An attractive woman with flaming red hair sat in the driver's seat. She winked at him. He opened the passenger door behind her and stepped up. Before he could lower himself into the seat, the Englishman shoved him hard. He lurched across the passenger compartment and struck his head on the far door. Then a foot jammed into his back, pushing him to the floor. The door slammed shut.

"Let's go, love!" the Englishman said. The SUV's tires squealed as the truck tore through the parking lot toward the exit. They braked suddenly.

"*Shit!*" the woman yelped. After a short pause, they roared away.

"How's about not adding vehicular manslaughter to kidnapping, love?" the man jabbed.

"Shut up, ya git!" she barked in an Irish accent. "I could kill ya from here, ya know." It was the woman from the phone call.

Manning had turned his head enough to see the man grinning down at him. "You know, mate, the sad truth is she really could." He extracted an assault rifle from the cargo compartment and cocked it loudly. "Drop the back window, Meghan, so I don't haveta shoot through it."

Manning heard a radio crackle. "Linn, talk to me!" the woman said.

* * *

Wendy Cho pulled behind the Hotel Montgomery and searched for the entrance to the hotel's parking lot. Suddenly a huge black SUV barreled onto the street, almost T-boning her tiny Ford Focus. Both vehicles screeched to a stop, and Cho waved for the angry-looking redhead driving the behemoth to go ahead. She definitely didn't want that battlewagon behind her. Cho drove the remaining fifty feet to the lot's entrance and pulled in. Looking over her shoulder, she saw the SUV turning the corner.

Was it my imagination, or did the guy in the back seat have a gun?

* * *

A block down from the side-street entrance to the Hotel Montgomery's parking lot, an unassuming middle-aged Chinese businessman sat in his car reading the Hong Kong *Commercial Daily*. A compact MP5K submachine gun lay under the San Francisco *Chronicle* in his lap. He had witnessed the near-collision of Gallagher's SUV with the compact car, but no further activity resulted from the incident. Linn Shaozang keyed the tiny microphone that dangled from his earpiece. "Nothing to report. Your trail is clear."

"Dieter, how about you? Anything stirring?" Shaozang heard in his earpiece.

* * *

Dieter Kinberg, a tall muscular man in his early thirties, also saw the near miss from his post on the hotel's parking lot, where he had been making a show of packing and unpacking the trunk of his Audi A6 for the last ten minutes. He watched Gallagher's almost-victim, a diminutive young Chinese woman, pull into a spot and enter the hotel. There was no other activity of any kind. He covered up the Heckler & Koch G3 assault rifle that had been waiting in readiness in the trunk had the American FBI moved to stop the kidnapping.

He keyed his mike. "If anyone cares for our friend, they certainly aren't making a very good show of it." He took the wheel of his car and exited the lot, taking up a position half a kilometer behind Gallagher's SUV. "I have you in sight," he reported three minutes later.

* * *

Wendy Cho flashed her badge at the hotel's front desk and asked for the manager. A slender man in an expensive suit and an Ascot tie appeared almost immediately. She presented her credentials again.

"Oh my!" he said in mock alarm, placing a hand across his chest. "I *swear* I didn't do it!"

She suppressed a laugh with difficulty. "Sir, I need to speak with you about one of your guests. In private, please."

"Right this way!" He gave her a flamboyant wave and led her across the lobby. Once in his office he extended a manicured hand. "By the way, Christopher Malcolm, I'm the day shift manager."

Cho accepted the delicate handshake. "Pleased to meet you, sir. I need to talk with you about a former guest of yours named Michael Manning." She handed over the lead sheet of the FBI dossier.

Malcolm's eyes flashed in recognition. "Oh yes, Mr. Manning! Poor man, everyone here at the hotel just feels *horrible* about what happened to him last night!"

"Beg your pardon?"

His eyes widened as if reliving a terrifying event. "His *robbery*, of course! Right here on our own property! That's what you're here to investigate, aren't you?"

So <u>that's</u> how Hendrix got hold of Manning's cellphone, she realized. "Sir, I'm sorry to break this to you, but that robbery probably never even occurred. Mr. Manning is a very experienced con man, which is why I'm here with you today. He's the subject of a confidential federal investigation. Do you know when he checked out of your hotel?"

Malcolm looked confused. "Checked out? Oh no, I saw him not ten minutes ago!"

"He's still a guest?"

"Well, his company said he would be here for at least three weeks, let me check." He picked up his phone and made a brief call to the front desk.

"No, he hasn't checked out, although apparently one of the housekeeping staff wishes that he had."

Cho flipped open her cellphone. "Agent Lane? Agent Cho. I need to call in the cavalry."

* * *

Linn Shaozang pulled into the empty spot on the Hotel Montgomery's parking lot left by Dieter's departure. He walked casually to Manning's rented Malibu, pulling a small electronic device from his pocket. He circled the car completely, pausing for a second at each bumper and wheel well. He replaced the device in his pocket, returned to his car, and drove away.

* * *

They drove on in tense silence for another ten minutes. Manning wondered if he shouldn't feel more alarmed than he did. He had just been kidnapped, after all. But these people were associated with Conrad, which meant that they probably wouldn't harm him until his usefulness was expended, a moment he sensed hadn't arrived yet. He heard the rear window slide closed.

"What'd you do that for?" the Englishman protested.

"We're in the clear, for God's sake," the woman pronounced. "Stop waving my gun around; somebody'll see it and call the cops. And have ya wanded him yet?"

The man let out an irritated snort. "No, I was too busy watching your back, woman!"

"Well, let Dieter do that; ya just make sure he's not wearin' a wire!"

He gave another annoyed grunt and ran a device that looked like a walkie-talkie over Manning from head to toe. It let out a sharp tweeting sound when it passed by the cellphone in his pocket. The man dug his hand in roughly and fished it out, throwing it on the seat and continuing his scan.

"Roll over on your back," he ordered. Manning did so, and the man repeated the process. "He's clean," he announced.

The radio crackled again. "He's clean, I'm bringing him in," she said. "Ian, hood 'im," she called over her shoulder.

A black bag was pulled roughly over Manning's head. The SUV rocked like it went over a curb, then stopped. He heard a door open.

He was grabbed forcefully by the arm. "Out you come, mate!" the man said. Manning was feeling for a handhold with his free hand when his head smacked into the door frame.

"Watch his head!" she scolded. "He's no good to us with a concussion!"

"Oh, shut your yap, he's fine."

A dazed Manning was pulled along, half-walking, half-stumbling across a concrete floor. Their steps echoed, allowing him to gauge the size of the enclosure. It was large, but not warehouse large. More like a big garage. They led him into a smaller side room and shoved him into a chair. The hood came off, the man purposefully yanking at his scalp when he did so.

"Ow!" Manning yelped. "Leave some hair next time!" All that earned him was a sarcastic snicker from his kidnapper.

He glanced about at the small dirty office. Across the dusty desk sat Angela Conrad, polishing a gold-plated pistol. He recognized it as the .45 she had taken off of the Saudi spy Rashid Ben-Jabir.

She looked up from her polishing and sighed. "Michael, Michael, Michael. What *are* we going to do with you?"

* * *

Wendy Cho sat in the lobby drinking bottled water until the van marked DAYLIGHT ELECTRIC pulled up to the entrance. Two men emerged, looking very much the role of maintenance men. One was acne-scarred and tattooed, the other paunchy with a drooping mustache. She greeted them at the door, extending a hand but not flashing her badge.

"Agent Cho."

The tattooed man returned her handshake. "Specialist Marty Clagget, and this is my partner Bob Moskowitz."

She nodded. "Nice to meet you."

"Where should we set up?" Clagget asked.

"There's a parking lot out back. That entrance is closer to his room."

"Is the hotel on board?"

She jerked a thumb toward the manager's office. "The search warrant just came over the fax five minutes ago." She held up a key card. "We're good to go."

"Outstanding."

* * *

"Is there a problem?" Manning asked.

Conrad returned to her gun cleaning. "No, other than the fact that a dozen armed men tried to kill me last night and my two best men are on slabs in the county morgue, everything's peachy."

Oh, so she blames me. That's just great. "Yeah, I saw the opening act of that ambush last night. Sorry I didn't stick around for the whole performance."

She chuckled. "No, what you're *really* sorry about it that I'm not on a slab right next to them."

You got that right, bitch. "You're not exactly on my Christmas card list."

Conrad broke down the pistol, removing the barrel and holding it up to the flickering fluorescent light. "Oh yeah, I get it; no hard feelings there. But I've been dodging the CIA for five years. Suddenly they catch up with me, and the only new variable in the mix is *you.* You can see why I'm wondering if you've been burned."

He looked behind him at his kidnappers. "Is that what this little drama is about?"

She nodded. "Afraid so. The FBI is very good at tracking people without being noticed, so the best way to figure out if you were burned was to forcibly drag you away and see if it stirs up the hornet's nest."

"Did it?"

She frowned. "No, and it's really got me wondering. You said you were robbed last night. Tell me all about it, and don't skip any details, they might be important."

He related the story of his mugging. She interrupted frequently with questions.

"Wait a minute, you said he was a stocky Hispanic guy with a tattoo?"

He traced with his finger. "Right, it went up the side of his neck like this."

"About five-eight, two hundred pounds? Shaved head? Plain white T-shirt?"

He thought for a moment. "Yeah, I think so. How did you know that?"

"I killed him later on, or at least I...never mind, not important. So, he specifically asked for your wallet *and* your phone?" she demanded.

"*And* my watch, although that seemed to be kind of an afterthought."

She thoughtfully reassembled her pistol. "So if the CIA got your phone, they could search it for recently received calls and they'd get the number of my burner."

"Burner?"

"Pay-as-you-go cellphone. I got a new one after every time we met. Looking for burners is the first thing they'd do if they grabbed your phone." Her cell phone rang. She answered it and talked for less than a minute.

"Okay," she reported, "that was Linn. He says he monitored police and FBI frequencies and nobody gave a damn when we scooped you up."

"Doesn't that make *me* feel special," Manning observed, wondering who Linn was.

She ignored him. "He also said he checked your car for transmitters. It's clean."

"So where does that leave us?" he asked, assuming Linn was probably someone he didn't want to meet anyway.

She loudly racked the action of the reassembled pistol and reloaded it. "Unfortunately, it means the CIA probably knows who you are and what you're doing at Nanovex."

He glowered at her across the desk. "So is this where you put a bullet in my head?"

She drew back in mock surprise and smiled. "Did you hear that, Meghan?" She tucked her chin and imitated Manning's deeper voice, "Is this where you put a bullet in my head?" She laughed. "A week ago he would have been pissing himself and begging for his life. Our man-child here has truly grown some stones."

So killing me isn't enough. She has to ridicule me first. What a psycho. "Fine, put it on my tombstone: He Finally Grew a Pair."

Her smile turned evil, and she leveled the .45 at his face. "You know, I've heard some good exit lines from men I've killed, and that's one of the best so far. It would be a shame to waste it." Her finger tightened on the trigger.

Manning stared her down, waiting for the flash. *At least I won't have to put up with her shit anymore.*

She put her thumb over the hammer and let it down slowly. "Unfortunately, you're my only inside man at Nanovex and I need you, burned or not. The fact that no one's watching you right now confirms to me that it *was* the CIA that got a bead on you, not the FBI, and their team is all dead, or in hiding. They'll reconstitute eventually, but that massacre last night gives us a window of operational freedom. We're going to make the most of it."

"How?" he asked, not really wanting the answer.

"Meghan," she said, "bring in the toys." She arched her eyebrows at him and her eyes lit up. "It's Christmas!"

* * *

While the two "maintenance men" finished their work in Manning's hotel room, Cho's station was on the parking lot, sitting in her car watching for Manning. Another agent had arrived and watched the lobby. They had no idea when Manning would return, but the surveillance technicians Clagget and Moskowitz assured her they would be in and out in fifteen minutes.

With the earbud of her Bureau radio in one ear and her MP3 player in the other, she thumbed through her song selections fighting boredom. Boredom led to inattention, inattention led to busted surveillances. Wait a minute.

Something about the Malibu parked across the aisle bothered her. It scratched at the back of her brain for attention and she didn't know why. Of course it was similar to Manning's rental car, but he was long gone. Wasn't he? She finally really looked at the license tag, and the itching in her head got worse. She opened Manning's file and skimmed the log from last night's surveillance until she found his tag number. They matched.

She keyed her radio. "Hey guys, you about done?"

"Yeah, is he back?" came the anxious reply.

"No," she added quickly, "but I just realized his car is still sitting here on the lot."

A short pause. "Well, *that's* convenient, isn't it?"

* * *

The red-haired woman Conrad had called Meghan returned with two small boxes and placed them in front of Conrad. The first box was full of cell phones.

Conrad waved him to pull his chair closer to the desk. "Okay, the first thing we need to do is give you your own supply of burners. Meghan, let's get them sequenced." The women went to work recording the numbers of the cellphones on a pad and labeling each phone with a strip of masking tape. Conrad handed him a phone labeled "#1."

"You'll use this phone until our next meeting." She held up a phone labeled "#2." "After that meet, yank the battery on #1 and toss it in a public trash can. Then switch to #2, but don't put in the battery until you're ready to use it. Repeat that for every meeting until the operation is completed. I'm giving you six phones; that should be more than enough."

He thumbed through the phone's menus, looking for numbers stored in memory. "So where's your number? What if I need to call *you*?"

She handed him a large, rather ugly digital watch. "That's what your next toy is for. I'm sure it's not as stylish as the one the CIA stole from you, but it has its charms. Press the lower left and upper right buttons at the same time."

He did so and a few seconds later Conrad's phone beeped. She held out the phone for him to read the displayed text message.

"PANIC BUTTON: UNIT 3452"

"You do that and I'll call you right away," she said.

Great, so now I can immediately reach the one person on earth I never wanted to talk to in the first place. "So now that we've settled the fact that you're not going to kill me, what's my next task at Nanovex?"

"I *have* to know where the nanoweapon sample is being held. I can't steal it if I can't find it, and without that sample this whole operation is for nothing."

"How am I supposed to find it?" he asked.

Conrad folded her hands on the desk. "I was hoping *you* would come up with a plan for that. In fact, your life kind of depends on it."

* * *

Cho sat in the back of the bugging specialists' van, facing a bank of video monitors. "Wow," she observed, "this is like an episode of Big Brother. He isn't going to have much privacy."

"That's the general idea," Clagget agreed.

"And his car?" she asked.

Clagget pushed a button and a map appeared, with a dot flashing at screen center. "We put GPS beacons in both the front and rear bumpers, just in case one goes sour. They can run for up to a month before we'll need to replace them."

"What were you doing *inside* his car?" she asked.

He frowned. "I was afraid to do much since we don't know when he'll come back. I just threw one of these under the seat." He handed her a small device.

"An MP3 player?"

"That's what he's supposed to think if he finds it; just an MP3 player a previous renter dropped. But it's a bug that relays its take to the bumper beacons, which then rebroadcast the audio to us. Very quick and dirty. Once he comes back and we have him on camera and sound asleep, we'll rig his car like a TV studio. Audio, video, satellite relays, the works."

"What else do you need from me?" Cho asked.

"No offense, ma'am, but we need you to *leave*," Clagget suggested. "You special agents stick out like a sore thumb. Don't worry—your target is in very good hands."

She handed them both a card. "Will do. Call me if he does anything interesting."

Both men nodded, obviously pleased to work with an agent who didn't micromanage them. "Count on it," they said in unison.

[1] OSS stands for Office of Strategic Services, the World War II forerunner of the CIA. Allen Dulles was OSS station chief in Zurich during the closing days of WWII. He returned to the CIA in 1953 as Deputy Director. While it is likely that he never left the OSS-CIA organization, there is little documentation on his activities from 1945-1953 other than his 1947 publication of *The German Underground* about resistance to Hitler during the war, and his activities in footnote 4.

[2] President Truman's order of March 4, 1946 stated specifically that any German who had been a member of the Nazi party would not be allowed into the United States. Unfortunately, three-fourths of the German scientists the US wanted would have been banned under those terms, since party membership was required to hold any substantial leadership position during the war. The OSS promptly created Operation Paperclip, which "sanitized" the scientists' records, finding in all but the most egregious cases that the scientist in question was "politically acceptable." These men and their families were then smuggled into the US and told to keep a low profile. However by early 1947 the presence of Werner von Braun and other former Nazis in New Mexico became common knowledge in the US media, and President Truman took significant heat from Jewish supporters over the matter.

[3] The United States supported a United Nations resolution recommending the partition of Palestine into Jewish and Arab states on November 29, 1947. The next year businessman and philanthropist Abraham Feinberg personally underwrote Truman's famous "whistle stop tour," which probably saved his 1948 presidential campaign, at the cost of $100,000.

[4] While this meeting is entirely fictional, it is a fact that Allen Dulles became a close advisor to presidential candidate Thomas Dewey, Truman's opponent in the 1948 election. It is clear that Dulles disagreed with Truman's policies.

[5] Allen Dulles' claim to fame was Operation Sunrise, his negotiation as OSS Zurich station chief of the surrender of German forces in Italy shortly before the entire Germany army surrendered in May 1945. By persuading the significant numbers of SS units to surrender who probably would have fought to the last man despite Germany's surrender, numerous American lives were saved. This gave him a reputation as "a man who could get things done." Only later did it come out that he merely persuaded the

senior SS commanders, who were likely targets for war crimes investigations, to give up their units in exchange for free passage to South America via Dulles' contacts in the Vatican. (Source: *Unholy Trinity: The Vatican, The Nazis, and The Swiss Banks* by Mark Aarons and John Loftus)

[6] Harry Truman dispatched agents of the FBI to investigate the whereabouts of Martin Bormann in Argentina in June of 1948 at the request of Robert H. Jackson, Supreme Court justice and chief prosecutor at the Nuremberg war crimes trials. This is significant because of the National Security Act of 1947 that Truman himself signed, the CIA had sole investigative powers outside the US, while the FBI had sole authority on US soil. The fact that Truman dispatched the *FBI* to investigate the post-war activities of escaped Nazis hints that he didn't completely trust the CIA to perform in this area. (Sources: *Nazi International* by Joseph Farrell, p. 302-309 and *Martin Bormann, Nazi in Exile* by Paul Manning, p. 204)

[7] Michael Scherer and Michael Weisskopf. "Candidates' Vices: Craps and Poker", *Time*, July 2, 2008

[8] Source: *The Secret War against the Jews*, by Mark Aarons and John Loftus, p. 221. The authors found it ironic that Nixon's political career both began and ended with a cover-up. Loftus was a former chief prosecutor of Nazi war criminals for the Justice Department and was able to secure an interview with the reticent former Supreme Court Justice Arthur Goldberg shortly before his death. Goldberg revealed that he had been an OSS officer during WWII and had been tasked as the American liaison for a British Intelligence operation in New York before America's entrance into the war, led by famed British spymaster William Stevenson (*A Man Called Intrepid*). Their task had been to bug the offices of Allen and John Foster Dulles, both of whom acted as lawyer-go-betweens for American investors and their investments in Nazi-controlled Germany (investors such as Prescott Bush, Averill Harriman, and Henry Ford). The evidence collected against Dulles was damning, according to Goldberg, and Roosevelt appointed Dulles to Zurich to place him closer to his Nazi contacts and tempt him into laundering funds for them with the British watching. Roosevelt's goal was to bring down all the American industrial titans/collaborators in a wave of public fury that their wealth and power could not deflect (the fact that they were all staunch Republicans might have also been a factor). Unfortunately Roosevelt told his vice president, Henry Wallace, who told his brother-in-law the Swiss Ambassador in DC. Unbeknownst to either man, the Swiss Secret Service chief-of-station in

DC had been turned by the Nazis, and passed the warning onto Dulles, who used his contacts to destroy the evidence. Wallace was subsequently dropped by Roosevelt as his vice president in favor of Harry Truman. Justice Goldberg's verdict was blunt: "The Dulles brothers were traitors. They had betrayed their country, by giving aid and comfort to the enemy in time of war."

CHAPTER 17

ESCALATION

NOVEMBER 26, 1957 – WASHINGTON, D.C.

"Gentlemen, if we can come to order, please," Vice President Richard Nixon said as he rose to chair the meeting of the National Security Council. "First of all, I just spoke with President Eisenhower's physician, and he says that despite the stroke the President suffered yesterday, he is resting comfortably and is expected to make a full recovery. By prior agreement, the President has empowered me to chair today's NSC meeting in his stead."

"Our first order of business," Allen Dulles announced, "is a troubling development in South America. Our agents there have reported sightings of triangular-shaped-UFOs matching the description of those under development by Hans Kammler and the other escaped Nazi scientists near Bariloche."

"Dear God," breathed General Twining, now Chief of Staff for the Air Force, "you mean they've already got them *flying*? We're still trying to decipher the notes we seized from Tesla and the captured plans from Nazi Germany. And we're nowhere close to fielding even a prototype saucer like the Nazis had." [1]

Dulles had already nervously puffed a smoke screen at his end of the table. "And yet they've built their own flying saucers from scratch. Very impressive."

"We should bomb them," Nixon stated firmly. "H-bomb their facilities before this situation gets out of hand."

"Are you *serious*?" Twining scoffed. "You want to start a nuclear war with *Argentina*?"

"Not Argentina," Nixon corrected. "Just the Nazi facility at Bariloche. Our new B-52 bombers can reach there non-stop, can't they, General?"

"Well, *yes*, but…."

"Then we drop an H-bomb on their facility, what was it called, Allen?"

"Huemul Island."

"And before the mushroom cloud even rises above the horizon," Nixon explained, "we will have our CIA agents in Argentina spread the story that the Nazis had been experimenting with a nuclear reactor and it went critical. Any Nazis that survive the airstrike will be executed by the Argentineans, or extradited to us."

"Dick, you're forgetting that the Nazis have the bomb too," Dulles cautioned. "A-bombs at the very least. God knows what other monstrosities they've created since then. They could have weapons that make H-bombs look like firecrackers."

"Not to mention the fact that they now have a delivery system," Twining added. "What if the performance of these new craft is superior to our own fighters? They could bomb our cities at leisure. And nobody has a clue how many bombs they have now; do we, Allen?"

Dulles frowned. "We have tried on multiple occasions to infiltrate their operation. Their security man, Mueller, is very…efficient. The only thing that comes back from those operations are our agents." He paused for effect. "Pieces of them, at least."

The dozen members of the council debated for another hour without consensus or decision. Afterwards Dulles pulled a frustrated Nixon aside.

"Dear God, Allen," Nixon whispered. "This is a complete mess. What the hell are we going to do? It's like some nightmare; Nazis coming back to re-conquer the world. Only it's not a nightmare, it's real!"

Dulles placed a comradely hand on Nixon's shoulder. "Try not to get so worked up about it, Dick. You know what they say—if you can't beat 'em, join 'em."

Nixon blanched. "We already know what Ike said about that, Allen. He's hospitalized, for God's sake, not incapacitated. He'd have our balls for breakfast if we even suggested it."

Dulles gave him a knowing smile. "Then maybe when you become president in 1960 you can try a different approach." [2]

OFFICE PLANTS

PRESENT DAY – SAN JOSE, CALIFORNIA

"Wait a minute," Nanovex CEO Doug Lyman protested. "How can Mike Manning be a plant—I called *him* for this job, not the other way around!"

Perry Pugliano leaned into the conference table in Lyman's office. "Really? How did you get his name?"

Lyman thought for a moment. "We were calling around for a new damage control lawyer after our last one bailed on us."

"What was the story on that?" Pugliano interrupted.

Lyman shrugged. "He just disappeared. Stopped coming in, wouldn't answer his phone, nada. It's like he dropped off the face of the earth. We called his firm and they couldn't raise him either."

Pugliano's investigative instincts tickled him behind the ear. *Pay attention.* He pulled a notepad from his jacket. "What was his name, by the way?"

"Jacob Fleischer."

His instincts elbowed him in the ribs. *Wait a minute, that sounds familiar.* He flipped through his notebook back several days to the crime scene at the Sheraton. *Bullet holes in hallway...forensics place origin at door of room 317...occupant Jacob Fleischer missing.*

"Oh shit," Pugliano murmured. "I think I found your lawyer."

Lyman straightened. "Really? Where is he?"

He frowned. "At the bottom of San Francisco Bay, most likely. We were investigating another case at the Sheraton when we found a room that had been heavily cleaned with ammonia, probably to erase a blood stain. The room belonged to a Jacob Fleischer. We couldn't find him either, but we had no idea he was connected to Nanovex."

"You think he was *murdered*?" Lyman gasped.

"Safe bet. Professionally murdered, too. Whoever did the hit really knew how to cover their...." The prompt from his instincts this time was more like a kick in the gut. "Oh hell! Why didn't I put this together sooner!" He began digging frantically in his briefcase.

Lyman and his chief of security, Reese Miller, tensed in anticipation. "Put *what* together?" Lyman demanded.

Pugliano extracted a glossy photograph from a manila folder. It was an enlarged screen capture of the running man from the Sheraton. He pushed the photo toward Lyman. "Look familiar?"

Lyman's eyes widened. "Well, that's...Mike Manning...but where was this taken?"

"From the security camera feeds at the Sheraton. It's Mike Manning fleeing the scene of Jacob Fleischer's murder."

Pugliano scrutinized Lyman's bewildered expression. He could tell Lyman was a good man, slow to believe ill of others until proven conclusively. Unfortunately, that also made him a good mark for con men like Manning.

"But...how could he...I mean, Fleischer disappeared *before* I called Manning!" Lyman protested.

Suddenly all the pieces fell together in Pugliano's mind. "Because Manning knew that Fleischer was working for you and he engineered Fleischer's disappearance so that he could slide right into his spot here at Nanovex without arousing your suspicion." *So Manning isn't just a spook, he's a cold-blooded murderer, too.*

Lyman drew back. "You're saying Mike Manning *killed* Jacob Fleischer?"

"What was Manning doing here in San Jose on the day of Fleischer's disappearance? And what was he running from? A botched murder, maybe?"

"I never had a good feeling about Manning," Reese Miller interjected.

"So tell me again," Pugliano said, "how did you get Manning's name?"

Lyman stroked his chin. "Well, there are only a few reputable damage control firms nationwide. We made preliminary calls to all of them, but a woman from Feldman-Norquist called us back and said that Mike Manning was not only an excellent candidate, but that he had a falling-out with one of the partners and might be available to be hired outright. We checked him out; he had an excellent reputation, so I called him and made him an offer. At the time, it seemed like I had to twist his arm to accept. I can't believe he manipulated me so easily."

Pugliano readied his pen. "What was this woman's name?"

Lyman squirmed. "She wouldn't say. It seemed understandable at the time."

"And why did you want to *hire* Manning, rather than just put him on retainer?"

"Two reasons; first, because of the size of the legal battle facing us with five dead employees, we thought it would be wise to have a lawyer on our payroll. And secondly, with the sensitivity of the projects we conduct here, I wanted a lawyer whose checks were signed by *me*, not some law firm across the country."

He locked eyes with Lyman. "Fair enough. But here's the question I *really* want answered. What are you working on here at Nanovex that's worth killing for?"

Lyman glanced at Miller, who shook his head. Lyman cleared his throat. "Agent Pugliano, while I greatly appreciate all the help you've rendered to my company, my hands are tied by national security regulations...."

"I have a Level 5 Sensitive Compartmentalized Intelligence clearance," he countered.

Lyman held up a supplicating hand. "Which, if you'll give me time to go through channels...."

Pugliano cut him off. "No, we *don't* have time for you to go through channels." He reached into his briefcase again. "Let me introduce you to Manning's boss."

He pushed Conrad's profile in front of Lyman, passing a copy to Miller as well. "This is Angela Conrad, ex-CIA. Before she killed her handler and went rogue, she was one of their top agents. Now she steals high technology items and sells them to the highest bidder. She's done this worldwide for the last five years and has left an impressive trail of bodies in her wake. By the way, the massacre downtown? That was her handiwork."

Lyman recoiled. "Dear God! What happened?"

"A dozen armed men with automatic weapons tried to take her out. Now they're all dead, and she walked away without a scratch." He reached into the folder holding the Manning photos and found the one with Manning and Conrad talking outside the hotel. "We now know Manning and Conrad are working together, and Manning *killed* to get a position close to you. Hell, she's probably the woman who called and offered you Manning's name. So I'm going to ask you again, what is Nanovex working on that's juicy enough to attract a player like Conrad?"

Lyman frowned, but said nothing.

Pugliano smiled and collected his things. "No problem. But when the inside of your building looks like that massacre at City Hall, don't say that I didn't warn you."

Lyman reached out. "Wait. If our DARPA program manager Seth Graves gives us a verbal okay, I think we can waive the paperwork. Let me give him a call."

A foot from Pugliano's knee, a small black box recorded the entire exchange and waited for the scheduled time of its next burst transmission.

EXECUTIVE ORDER

NOVEMBER 22, 1961 – WASHINGTON, D.C.

The atmosphere in the White House conference room was nothing short of poisonous. CIA Director Allen Dulles was about to brief President John F. Kennedy. The various players on the National Security Council hunched in their chairs, as if preparing to duck any missiles thrown by the President.

It had been less than three months since the CIA led the disastrous Bay of Pigs operation against Cuba, and Kennedy was not in a forgiving mood. Dulles knew he had one trump card left to play in an attempt to regain the Chief Executive's favor.

"Mr. President," he began, "the purpose of today's briefing is to bring you up to date on the hunt for escaped Nazis in South America, per your request."

"It's about damned time," Kennedy drawled. "I've been asking for this briefing since I was inaugurated!"

"Yes, Mr. President, and I'm very sorry for the delay. There have been, I'm sure you would agree, many pressing matters."

The briefing went on for several minutes, with far fewer interruptions from the President than Dulles had expected. He began to feel a small glimmer of hope.

"That concludes my prepared remarks, Mr. President. Your questions?"

For a few seconds Kennedy sat so silently he thought the President hadn't heard him. Then he saw the taut neck muscles and the veins throbbing at the younger man's temples and realized Kennedy had heard him all too well.

"Why haven't we pressured the Argentineans to give these men up?"

"We have sir," Dulles lied. "The Argentineans have cut a deal with the Nazis to benefit from their technology in exchange for safe haven."

Kennedy looked at his Air Force Chief of Staff, Curtis LeMay. "Perhaps some sort of military operation might allow us to capture these men. And their technology."

Dulles shook his head. "That would be inadvisable, Mr. President. The Nazis in question have the bomb."

Kennedy cocked his head. "Beg your pardon?"

Dulles looked at his feet. "This sir, is the most closely guarded secret of World War II. We did not win the race to the atomic bomb. The Germans did. Fortunately for us they tested theirs so late in the war they decided to use it as a bargaining chip instead of as a weapon; safe passage for Martin Bormann and his staff in exchange for two bombs' worth of uranium and one functioning weapon, which we later dropped on Hiroshima.

"Unfortunately, to make sure we held up our end of the bargain, the Nazis retained one A-bomb, which they threatened to deliver by U-boat if we moved against them. I'm relatively certain by now that they have more than one device, and the means to deliver them by air using their antigravity fighters."

Kennedy trembled with fury. His eyes scanned the table. "Who else in this room knew about this situation?" Most of the National Security Council reluctantly raised their hands, including the man to Kennedy's immediate left, General Curtis LeMay.

Kennedy regarded his trusted Air Force Chief of Staff with a pained expression. "Curtis, why the hell didn't you tell me about this?"

General Curtis LeMay

LeMay shot Dulles a smoldering look. "Sir, as chairman of the National Security Council subcommittee on this matter, the Director of the CIA has veto power of what information is shared with anyone, including the president. Because of Mr. Dulles' already tenuous relationship with you, he instructed specifically that you *not* be informed about the Nazis. Because President Eisenhower signed a Special Classified Executive Order specifically giving the DCI that veto power, we were bound by law to withhold this data. I'm sorry, Mr. President."

"And why do you think President Eisenhower signed that executive order, General?" Kennedy asked.

LeMay straightened in his chair. "Mr. President, President Eisenhower made no attempt to conceal his disdain for you. He believed—incorrectly in my opinion, sir—that you were unfit to govern."

Kennedy lifted an eyebrow at Dulles. "And you believe, General, that is the reason why Mr. Dulles purposely cut me out of the loop regarding the Nazis until now?"

LeMay's eyes were as cold as an executioner's. "That, sir, and the fact that Mr. Dulles himself negotiated the immunity deal with the Nazis."

Kennedy's head snapped around. "Mr. Dulles, is this true?"

Dulles felt the ground underneath him give way, like a hanged prisoner sensing the trapdoor swinging open beneath him. "Sir," he pleaded, "if you had any idea what these men have accomplished! They can *help* you! The speech you gave to Congress about going to the moon in this decade—*they* could make that happen!"

Kennedy stared at Dulles for nearly a minute before the explosion finally came. "That's *it*!" he shouted. "Mr. Dulles, you are *fired!* I want your resignation on my desk in an hour! My secretary will take your dictation."

Dulles took his seat before his legs gave way. "Yes, Mr. President," he mumbled.

The National Security Council sat in stony silence until Kennedy slapped the table, his anger still not spent. "My God, Allen! The arrogance of you and your Agency! I'm going to make it a primary objective of this administration to splinter the CIA in a thousand pieces and scatter it to the wind!" Kennedy got up and stormed from the room before the rest of the council could rise to their feet. [3]

The National Security Council wordlessly gathered their things and filed from the room, leaving Dulles alone to draft his resignation letter. [4]

SUMMONS

PRESENT DAY – SAN JOSE, CALIFORNIA

Angela Conrad and Meghan Gallagher studied a large map of the San Francisco Bay area spread over the desk in Conrad's garage office.

"Are you sure about this, Angie?" Gallagher asked. "I know Ian and I aren't that familiar with this area, but we could reconnoiter an alternate location for you in a day or so, no problem."

Conrad tapped the Hunter's Point peninsula with her finger. "I just don't think you're going to find a better spot than this, Meghan, no matter how long you look. I mean, it's practically abandoned during the nighttime hours, it's fairly centrally located, there's only two ways in or out of the zone, one of which we could block without attracting a lot of attention. But the biggest plus is that warehouse. We can lock that place down and completely control it with only four people. I did it before with three, outnumbered two to one."

"But that's where you whacked Meir!" Gallagher protested. "I mean, the FBI…."

"That's the beauty of it," she said with a grin. "Do you think it would even enter their mind that I'd dare to go back there again?"

Gallagher's eyebrows arched. "It *is* pretty ballsy."

She nodded. "Too ballsy for a bunch of bureaucrats to even consider. If they did, their little minds would just go—*tilt!*" she said with a laugh.

"What about those bastards from the CIA? If they get wind of this meeting ya *know* they'll take another crack at ya."

She shook her head. "They've just had a huge illegal operation go south on US soil. They'll be too busy covering their collective asses to contemplate revenge."

Gallagher shrugged. "Fair enough. Anything else?"

Conrad tapped the waterfront near her chosen warehouse. "Yeah, this time we're going to have a boat ready in case we need to make a quick getaway. I'm not doing that fake beard thing again!"

* * *

Conrad retrieved the encrypted satellite phone she reserved for calls to her prospective buyers. She placed her first call to the French delegation. It was answered on the second ring.

"*Bon jour*," she began, continuing the message in French. "The buyer's meeting will take place tonight at midnight. The principal is allowed a driver and two security personnel, one of which will be allowed into the meeting area. The others may patrol the area outside as they see fit, understanding that the other delegations will have their own security staff present. Any conflict between security staffs will result in those delegations being disqualified from the bidding, no questions asked."

"*Armed* security?" the caller asked.

"Of course. No restrictions. Are you ready to copy the coordinates?"

"Ready."

Conrad placed identical calls to the other five delegations. Only one protested her terms, but backed down when they learned four delegations had already agreed to her conditions. She disconnected the last call and gave Gallagher and Cosgrove a thumbs-up.

"We're good to go. Pull everybody back to the hotel for some rest. I don't want anyone screwing this up for lack of sleep."

STORY TIME

SAN FRANCISCO, CALIFORNIA

Perry Pugliano walked into the interrogation room and tossed the sealed plastic bag containing Scott Hendrix's personal effects onto the table. "Hit the road, champ! You're a free man!"

Hendrix scooped up the bag and was on his way to the door. "What finally convinced you I was telling the truth?"

Pugliano followed him out. "Because your bosses told us the same story. They said the Israelis initiated contact and demanded a termination mission. Not that I'm okay with that, but after seeing Conrad's handiwork personally, I'll make an exception. And apparently I'm not the only one in the Bureau who thinks that way."

Hendrix nodded thoughtfully. "Okay. Well, if we're through I'd like to go home and take a shower." He headed for the elevator.

Pugliano took his arm. "Not so fast, hot shot! You still have to tell me what you know about that little silver ball at the massacre."

His shoulders fell. He didn't want to, but a deal was a deal. "Okay, follow me."

"Why don't we just go to my office?" Pugliano asked.

He shook his head. "Your office ain't secure enough for this conversation. Neither is mine. Walk with me."

Hendrix led the FBI agent out of the building and down the street. At every alley he stopped, looked it over, and walked on.

"What the hell are you looking for?" Pugliano demanded.

He looked over the gap between the next two buildings. Two multistory structures, no windows on either side. "A blind alley. Here we go, follow me." Hendrix led them into the shadows, putting a dumpster between them and the street.

Hendrix lowered his voice to a murmur. "When I was in Iraq, I served with this old guy who was diagnosed with pancreatic cancer while we were in country. He knew he was toast, so on his last night before he was shipped home he told me this story. Okay, to tell this right, I gotta go back to World War II."

* * *

NOVEMBER 29, 1963 – WASHINGTON, D.C.

President Lyndon Johnson shook hands warmly with Allen Dulles and waved him to one of the Oval Office sofas. "Allen, thank you so much for coming on short notice."

Dulles took his seat. "My pleasure, Mr. President."

Johnson lowered his towering form onto the couch next to him. "Allen, I truly appreciate you agreeing to participate on the commission investigating President Kennedy's death. With your experience in the CIA, adding your voice to the committee's findings will carry a great deal of weight with the American people."

Translation: once you rubber stamp Oswald as the lone nut assassin, anyone who stumbles onto the truth later on can be branded as a lone nut too. Dulles nodded. "That's very kind of you to say, Mr. President."

Johnson grew serious and lowered his voice. "This was a very dirty business, Allen. I'm deeply in your debt."

Dulles cringed inwardly. Johnson apparently had forgotten that the Oval Office conversations and all of his phone calls were recorded. Dulles knew that because the Secret Service agent in charge of the tapes also drew a salary from the CIA. Either that or after removing Kennedy, Johnson felt so invulnerable he didn't care. Whatever the cause, loose talk like this was dangerous. *Someday those tapes are going to be a president's undoing.*

"Mr. President," Dulles began, "I do have a favor to ask of you, but I must request that the tapes be turned off first."

Johnson nodded. "Of course." He raised his voice. "Agent Fuller!"

The door flew open instantly. "Yes, Mr. President."

"Would you ask Agent Thompson to turn off the recording devices for the rest of my meeting with Mr. Dulles?"

"Of course, Mr. President." The door closed. Johnson made small talk with Dulles' about his spymaster autobiography and the book tour until the agent returned. [5] "It's done, Mr. President," he reported. The door closed again.

Johnson leaned in, lowering his voice further as if the conversation was still being monitored. "All right, Allen, what's so secret that you want it removed permanently from the historical record?"

Dulles adopted Johnson's conspiratorial tone as a sop to the Texan's ego. "Mr. President, I represent a group that has a considerable amount to offer your administration, but has been consistently shut out of a role in American policy. I would like this to change."

Johnson squinted at him. "I thought you had retired from the CIA, Allen. And why the hell do you think the CIA is being cut out of the policy loop? For God's sake, your people just helped take down that bastard Kennedy!"

Dulles cringed again. He would have to check with Thompson to make *sure* that either the recording devices had been turned off, or the tapes destroyed. If not, Johnson's mouth could put dozens of men on death row, including the President himself.

"Mr. President, I'm not speaking of the CIA. The group I represent, well, let's say that one never *truly* retires from this organization until death."

Johnson's eyes grew wide with greed. "But you say this group can help me?"

Dulles nodded. "In ways you could never dream, Mr. President."

* * *

PRESENT DAY – SAN FRANCISCO, CALIFORNIA

Perry Pugliano's jaw dropped open. After several seconds of gaping silence, he managed to speak.

"So you're saying…the Nazis…*took over* the government?"

Hendrix shook his head. "No, what I'm saying is we *let them in.* You know the anti-gravity fighters the conspiracy nuts say we hide out at Area 51? The Nazi scientists who escaped to South America were flying them around down there in the late *fifties*. Do you have any idea what our government would have given to get their hands on technology like that?"

"I don't know. What did we give them?"

Hendrix chuckled dryly. "Anything they wanted, man. Anything they wanted. For starters, they demanded new identities and high-ranking positions for their people in every branch of government. CIA, FBI, military, State Department, you name it. So we couldn't make a *move* without them knowing about it."

Pugliano frowned. "To what end? I mean, what was their goal?"

"At first, survival. They just wanted assurances they wouldn't end up in a courtroom, either in the US or in Israel. But after that…." Hendrix shook his head. "The old guy who told me this didn't know either. He just wanted to warn me about some of the dragons in the CIA's basement so I wouldn't get eaten by accident."

"But what does this have to do with that floating silver ball?"

Hendrix pointed south in the direction of the massacre. "That little silver ball is warning us that we're on their turf and they won't hesitate to wipe out a squad of Mossad or CIA agents just to send a message."

"And what's the message?"

He shrugged again. "For the moment, stay the hell away from Angela Conrad."

The color drained from the FBI agent's face. "Are you saying she works for *them*?"

Hendrix held up his hands in a defensive gesture. "Hey, I don't know, I just wanted to give you fair warning. If you got any agents in your detail you really care about, I'd pull them off point."

"You *know* they're not going to let us stop chasing her," Pugliano retorted. "Especially now that blood's been shed on US soil."

He scanned both ends of the alley to make sure no one was watching. "Well, if she *is* connected to the dragon in the basement, the word's gonna come down from on high to stop chasing her pretty soon. That's my guess."

Pugliano wished for a smoke, but had left his cigarettes in his office. "So what are you going to do if they tell you to make another run at her?"

He laughed. "Me? After last night, I'm gonna fake a convulsion and claim post-traumatic stress disorder. And you?"

Pugliano grunted. "Retired Marine, unfortunately. Mine is not to question why, yada yada."

Hendrix was anxious to leave. "Okay, is that enough story time to hold up my end of the bargain?"

Pugliano looked like his head was swimming. "Yeah, we're good, thanks. You need a ride?"

He walked back toward the street. "Nah, my apartment is only a couple of miles away, I'll catch a cab."

"Suit yourself."

Hendrix hailed a cab when they reached the street. As it pulled over, he called to Pugliano's back. "Hey Perry!"

"Yeah?"

"I meant what I said about staying away from this thing. It's not gonna end well."

Pugliano gave him the smile of a man trapped on a sinking ship. "Yeah, thanks for the heads up."

Hendrix got into the cab and gave the driver his address. A few seconds later, the plastic bag containing his personal effects started ringing. He had to tear past the evidence seal and dig in the bag to retrieve his phone.

"Hendrix!" he answered breathlessly.

The voice on the other end was quiet and even. "Mr. Hendrix, this is Linn Shaozang. We met once in Hong Kong. Are you still interested in the location of Angela Conrad?"

FROZEN DINNER

SAN JOSE, CALIFORNIA

It was almost eight o'clock when Nanovex engineer Mark Wong left work. He was really working two jobs; the first shutting down project WICKER BASKET for their DARPA customer, and the second secretly preserving the technology for later use by Nanovex. A bachelor, Wong was sick of frozen dinners, so he pulled into Arby's.

He ordered dine in and sat next to a western-facing window to watch the sun set. God knows he didn't see much daylight in WICKER BASKET's basement laboratory.

He was almost finished eating when a brilliant blue flash filled his vision.

"Did you see that?" a customer sitting near him asked his wife. The wife looked in Wong's direction and screamed.

With his drink half-raised to his lips, Mark Wong was frozen solid.

[1] The author has personally talked with an elderly gentleman who served with Patton's Third Army at the Elbe River at the close of WWII. As the liaison officer for the Americans, his job was to carry the Third Army's orders of the day to the Russians and receive the same to avoid accidental conflicts. Delivered to the wrong building by a non-English-speaking Russian sergeant, he stepped into a hangar housing three disc-shaped craft with Nazi markings. A Russian general inspecting the craft spotted the young American officer and "went ballistic." The witness was hastily escorted back to the Elbe. The gentlemen did not wish to be identified, but he *did* wish his story to be told.

[2] Of course, that never happened because Nixon lost to Kennedy in 1960, a defeat that neither Nixon nor Dulles took well.

[3] The New York *Times* quoted Kennedy as saying in this time frame that he intended to "splinter the CIA in a thousand pieces and scatter it to the wind," although they do not make clear exactly when he said it, to whom, and what specific incident provoked the outburst. This author borrowed the historical quote and gave it a fictional context. (Source: "CIA: Maker of Policy or Tool? Survey finds widely feared agency is tightly controlled." New York *Times*, April 25, 1966.)

[4] Allen Dulles was forced to resign in late November 1961 by President Kennedy, reportedly over the failed Bay of Pigs invasion of Cuba. However, the invasion took place in April 1961. It certainly wouldn't take an angry president seven months to find a scapegoat for a failure of this magnitude. Perhaps other factors were at play.

[5] Dulles, Allen, *The Craft of Intelligence: America's Legendary Spy Master on the Fundamentals of Intelligence Gathering for a Free World,* 1963

CHAPTER 18

SUPER SLUSHY

PRESENT DAY – SAN FRANCISCO, CALIFORNIA

"Yeah Derek, what's up?" Perry Pugliano had almost tossed Derek Medina's call to voice mail, but the quirky coroner *did* seem to have his finger on the pulse of the bizarre happenings that were becoming a regular part of Pugliano's job.

"We've got another one."

"Another what?"

"Another weird death."

Pugliano readied a pen. "Where?"

"The Arby's on Steven's Creek road just west of downtown San Jose."

"Weird how?"

"Human popsicle weird. You gotta see it."

He almost asked Medina to shoot him a photo, but regular cellphones weren't secure enough for official business. He checked his watch. Peak of rush hour. No way he would get there in a timely fashion. Wasn't Wendy Cho running a stake out down in the valley? Hopefully she would keep her cookies down this time. "Okay, I'll have one of my agents meet you there." In the meantime he would rustle up a helicopter to get there a hell of a lot faster than driving. Rank did have its privileges.

* * *

Agent Cho picked him up at an athletic field a few blocks from the crime scene. The players abandoning the soccer field to darkness gawked from the parking lot as Pugliano's helicopter touched down. Cho flashed her lights. He trotted over to her car.

"What have we got?" he demanded. "Derek better not have pulled me down here for nothing."

Her eyes were wide. "Oh, I *definitely* think you'll want to see this one."

He knew something big was up when they pulled into the Arby's. The usual contingent of police manned the tape line outside the restaurant. Their attitude at all but the most heinous of crime scenes was usually "Been there, done that." Tonight they gathered in twos and threes, looking over their shoulders as they exchanged nervous talk. He had seen that behavior twice before, once at a vicious child murder, and another at a similar fast food joint where the entire staff had been herded into the freezer and executed. He hoped similar brutality did not await him inside.

Derek Medina greeted them, his usual bubbly enthusiasm absent. He led them to a booth on the far side of the restaurant. Orange canvas shields had been erected inside and outside to prevent the news hounds from getting a shot at the body thorough the glass.

Stepping around the screens Pugliano was confronted with a young Asian man seated in a booth, his eyes fixed forward and his drink half-raised to his lips. His skin had a bluish cast and was covered with condensation. His clothes were soaked with it. A puddle formed where his elbow touched the table. Medina stepped inside the barricade to join him. Cho looked on from outside.

Pugliano held up his hand. "So help me, Derek, if you make a human popsicle joke I'm gonna slug you."

Medina regarded the body carefully. "Actually, he's more like a Super Slushy now. The first cop on the scene said he was completely covered in frost when they found him. He's already starting to thaw out."

As if in response to Medina's comment, the victim's arm relaxed, slowly lowering his drink to the table.

Pugliano shivered. "Now that's just creepy. What the *hell* is going on here, Derek?"

"Damned if I know. Don't get many hypothermia victims here in California. But a buddy of mine who works in Minneapolis once sent me a picture of a drunk they found under a bridge, frozen solid. He had a bottle of Cold Duck raised to his mouth, just like this guy. Freaky."

The FBI academy had an extensive forensics class, during which Pugliano studied coroner's photos of bodies from all manners of demise, including freezing. Those photos matched the corpse in front of him in all regards, except the wind chill here in the Arby's was a balmy seventy-two degrees. "You don't know of any disease with a pathology like this, do you?"

Medina waved his hand over the corpse's head, feeling for a draft. "No, and he sure didn't die from sitting too close to the air conditioner, either. I'll level with you, Agent Pugliano; this is starting to weird me out."

He led Medina out of the enclosure. "Have you done a full photo work-up?"

"Yeah, I did that right after I got here."

"Okay, then why don't you package the body for transport?"

Medina frowned. "I'm not sure I can, unless you want me to take him out like *that*. He's gonna have to thaw out some more, or I'll have to throw his corpse on a gurney like a statue."

The last thing Pugliano wanted to give the news media was a video of them wheeling out a rigid body with a sheet thrown over it. That would invite all kinds of probing questions for which he had no answers. "Well, why don't you at least pull him out of the booth and let gravity help you straighten him out as he thaws."

Medina swallowed. "Yeah, I can do that."

"You gonna be okay, Derek?"

Medina squared his shoulders. "Hell yes. Between this and the massacre and the oil-slick guy, I'm gonna be *famous*. Forget the book, I may get my own *TV show* out of this."

"Bodies first, Oprah second," he chided. "And once you get him out of the booth, take a break and go get some air. You look like you need it."

He nodded solemnly. "Will do."

Pugliano signaled Agent Cho. "Do we have an ID?"

She waved a wallet inside an evidence bag. A California driver's license had been extracted and was visible through the plastic. "Mark Wong, age 28. No priors, but his name came up in our database immediately because he held a high-level security clearance."

"Really? For who?"

She arched an eyebrow. "He worked for Nanovex."

At first Pugliano thought a mild earthquake had rumbled through the valley, but he realized *he* was the one wobbling. He reached out and steadied himself on a table edge. It all came rushing past him. The silver ball at City Hall. Hendrix's warning about Nazis. Conrad's connections to Nanovex. And now a second Nanovex employee dead by unearthly means.

He looked up at the ceiling. "Dear god, wasn't chasing bank robbers and terrorists challenging enough?"

HORSEPOWER

SAN FRANCISCO, CALIFORNIA

"So, Mr. Hendrix, are you interested in the location of Angela Conrad or not?" Linn Shaozang repeated over the phone.

Scott Hendrix felt frozen in time. On one hand was an offer by an intelligence contractor who had performed well for him in the past to give up the location of the woman who had massacred an entire CIA team. On the other hand was the fact that he had barely escaped that massacre and had no desire to repeat the experience, especially with that silver ball and the shadowy organization behind it in the mix.

"I assume you heard about the little incident at San Jose City Hall?" he asked.

"Indeed, I have," Shaozang replied. "In fact, that is what persuaded me to contact you."

"How so?"

"Because of the blood that has been shed, you should have no difficulty between yourselves and the Israelis obtaining the five-million-dollar reward that I require for my information."

Hendrix glanced at the cab driver and guarded his words carefully. Cabbies were notorious information taps for various foreign intelligence services in large cities like San Francisco. "My, you *are* confident, aren't you?"

Shaozang let out a quiet chuckle. "I am, how do you say, in the belly of the beast. I am tasked with her security and I assure you I have access to the information you desire."

Hendrix wanted nothing to do with this, but the player in him found the game too hard to resist. "Well, you know *I* have the horsepower to make this happen, so I guess I'm also in the position to demand some proof that you can actually deliver."

The Chinese spy didn't miss a beat. "Have one of your satellites over the city at midnight. The weather will be clear. A few hours later I will provide you with a set of coordinates. You will be able to consult your photographs and confirm that she was at the location I provide. It will not be actionable intelligence, but it will be confirmation nonetheless."

The little bastard's thought this through. "Linn, those birds are in fixed orbits. I can't guarantee that one will be passing over exactly at midnight."

A dry laugh. "If you indeed have the…*horsepower* to reposition one of your nation's spy satellites to meet my time frame, then you will have proved your abilities to *me* as well."

Arrogant little prick. Linn always came across as oh-so-polite and eager to please. Nothing like thinking you hold all the cards to make you show your true colors. "All right, but I need a time to expect your call. My superiors will demand it before they agree to move assets around."

A pause. "I will transmit the coordinates at one hour after midnight. You will be unable to reach me until that time."

"Okay, Linn, one a.m. You better not leave me hanging, or so help me…."

Shaozang had already hung up on him.

"Son of a bitch," he muttered. He tapped on the partition to get the driver's attention. "Change of plans. 450 Golden Gate Avenue, please." Time to get back to work.

NEGOTIATIONS

SAN FRANCISCO, CALIFORNIA

Conrad's watch alarm went off, waking her for the buyer's meeting. She hadn't slept anyway. She merely stared at the ceiling and pondered all the ways her plan could go wrong. She still hadn't run out of ill-fortuned possibilities when the alarm sounded. If it hadn't been for her recent brush with death she might have been genuinely afraid. Now she was just nervous.

She wore the same black outfit she had worn the night she killed Meir Eitan. It seemed to have brought her luck then. The pant suit she had worn the night of the massacre might have become her *new* lucky outfit, if not for the caked-on CIA viscera necessitating its burning in a drum behind the garage. Kind of hard to explain human guts to the dry cleaner.

She adjusted her gear and checked herself in the mirror. She carried two guns and a throwing knife. If there had been a place to put it she would have carried more. Not that more would really help. If things went to shit tonight, her weapons would only delay the inevitable, since her buyers wouldn't hesitate to betray her to the authorities should they feel slighted at her terms. And chances were that *someone* would do exactly that. All part of the calculation.

A knock sounded at the door of her hotel room. It was Meghan. "Ready?" she asked.

Conrad threw her go-bag over her shoulder. "Yeah, let's do it."

"Nervous, love?" Gallagher asked as they walked to the parking lot.

"Aren't you? I mean, what do you think of our odds of pulling this off?

Gallagher shrugged. "About fifty-fifty."

"You seem pretty blasé about your life hanging on a coin toss."

Gallagher chuckled. "Dearie, knockin' about with you is like havin' the world's biggest rabbit's foot in my pocket. My luck is just bang on, thank ya much."

"Let's hope it holds a little longer," she said, reaching for the passenger door of the SUV.

Gallagher held the door closed and pointed to the rear passenger seat. "Back seat, love. They may have tied facial recognition programs to the traffic cameras by now, all looking for yer pretty mug."

She took the back seat. "Good point, thanks."

Linn Shaozang and Dieter Kinberg joined them precisely at ten o'clock. Ian Cosgrove was "procuring" the boat that would be their emergency getaway. No words were exchanged as Linn and Dieter entered the vehicle, just nods of acknowledgement before the SUV rolled toward Hunter's Point. *Great, they're nervous too*, she mused. *Let's hope nobody loses their nerve and gets us all killed tonight*.

"Miss Conrad?" Shaozang asked politely, "I have a suggestion to increase our security."

"Shoot."

"When Mr. Kinberg greets our guests, he should insist that both the principals and their security teams remove their cellphone batteries and hand them to their principal for the duration of the meeting."

"Afraid of them being tracked?"

"If any two of our buyers are being monitored by the Americans, their proximity in one place will assuredly raise alert flags with their NSA. If we explain this I'm sure our buyers will understand. It is not like we are asking them to surrender their phones to us."

She was impressed. Linn was always thinking. "Good idea. Dieter, make it happen."

Another polite nod from the German. "As you wish."

Cosgrove stepped from the shadows when they arrived at Hunter's Point and gave them a thumbs-up to signal all clear. They exited the SUV and deployed according to her plan.

"Any problem procuring the boat?" she asked.

Cosgrove shook his head. "The high-powered boats have fancy alarm systems, but the little ocean fishing boats don't. It's none too flashy, but it'll get us across the bay if we need to scoot. I left the car back at the marina; if all goes well the owner won't even know we borrowed his scow."

"Well done, Ian, thanks." Cosgrove was a pain in the ass personally, but operationally he knew his shit. "Meghan, check our tell-tales and make sure nobody's been poking around. Dieter, weapons for everybody. Linn, get your equipment set up."

They acknowledged her orders and went to work. Gallagher had previously loaded every door and accessible window in the warehouse with thin pieces of wire that would fall to the floor if the portal was opened. A quick check would show if the perimeter had been broken in their absence. The front door had a hidden mechanical counter she had reset before leaving—if it displayed a number greater than one then this warehouse was no longer as abandoned as they thought.

"I checked the surrounding area on foot before you got here," Cosgrove said. "You want me to walk it again?"

"No," Conrad said. "I'll do that. Get up on the roof with the night vision binocs and tell me what you see."

"Got it."

The truth was she needed to walk off her nervous energy. She crept out a block and circled the warehouse, checking every corner with her night vision monocular before proceeding. The area was as dead as Cosgrove had attested, with no suspicious parked vans and only one abandoned car. When she approached it she saw that Cosgrove had already crossed it off with an infrared marker to show he had inspected the vehicle and found no threats. She would ask him whether he had jimmied the trunk to check for hidden surveillance gear, but she was sure the answer would be yes.

"Topside, I've got traffic," Cosgrove reported by radio.

"Talk to me," she replied.

"Two vehicles approaching. One stopped about a half mile away and killed its lights. The other is circling the peninsula, working its way in."

She checked her watch. It was almost an hour before the buyers were supposed to show up. "The dark car will be the principal. The circling car will be security."

"I thought you said they were only allowed one vehicle."

Conrad quickly headed back to the warehouse. "No, I said they were only allowed four people, total. If they want to split them up into two cars, fine with me."

"They're still circling in," Cosgrove reported a few minutes later. "I think they may actually do a drive by. Cheeky bastards, these ones."

Conrad crouched behind a dumpster across the street from their warehouse, readying her night vision device. "I'm in position, let's see what happens."

"Do ya need me outside?" Gallagher called over the radio.

"Negative, you two stay inside and cover the front door in case they enter. Dieter, cover the back."

"Here it comes," Cosgrove whispered a few seconds later.

She watched a large, probably armored, Mercedes sedan cruise slowly past the warehouse. She saw four men inside, all of them beefy and with their heads on a swivel. Security men, all. There was no principal in that car, which meant that at least one of the parties had already busted the security protocols.

"Okay, the circling car has just rejoined the lead car. Looks like they're having a little pow-wow."

Conrad mused darkly on her next actions. If the first party to show up was already breaking the rules, were they planning on causing trouble, or just overly cautious? It would help a lot if she knew who they were. "Linn, is your gear telling you anything?"

"I have the signals for seven cell phones along one bearing," Shaozang reported. "Stand by while I check the numbers against my database." A moment's pause. "Yes, I have a match. One of them is a known number for a Renée LaCroix."

The French, she cursed silently.

"Bloody frogs," Cosgrove cursed aloud.

"I know Monsieur LaCroix," Dieter said. "I believe he is just being careful."

Well, Dieter *did* work security for the French until a couple of days ago. Which meant he could also *still* be working for them. "Okay Dieter,

I'll trust your judgment. But we still have to teach them a lesson about breaking protocols. Meet me by the truck."

"Understood."

After briefing Dieter, she entered the warehouse and pulled Gallagher aside. "I'm about to make an enormous demand on Dieter's loyalty," she whispered. "I want you and Ian both on the roof. If Dieter's loyalty wavers, put a bullet in *him* first."

"Absolutely," Gallagher said with conviction. Conrad saw her hands tighten on the CIA weapon Conrad had awarded her for enlisting Dieter and Linn. She could tell Gallagher was itching to use the rifle, even if it meant gunning down a comrade she had recruited.

* * *

"Okay, the lead vehicle is rolling now," Conrad heard in her earpiece ten minutes before the scheduled meeting time. "It's not the same one that made the slow pass, that one's stayin' put."

"Good, that means their principal is inbound," she acknowledged. "Everyone get ready."

A minute later a black Mercedes pulled in front of the warehouse. Dieter Kinberg stepped away from their SUV to greet the French delegation. He wore a suit tailored to enclose his muscled bulk *and* his bulletproof vest, as well as his concealed weapons. At six-foot-three he was quite an imposing figure. The submachine gun slung across his chest didn't make him look any smaller.

Two security men jumped from the Mercedes and flanked Kinberg, while the driver walked around the car and opened the door for the back seat passenger. A dignified man in his fifties emerged and straightened his jacket.

"Ah, Dieter!" Renée LaCroix said. "*Bonsoir, mon ami*!"

"Thank you, sir," Kinberg replied in French. "It is good to see you again as well."

"Is your new employer treating you well?"

"Very well, sir. However, I do have one problem I'd like to discuss with you."

"Really?" LaCroix said. "What's wrong?"

Conrad emerged from the shadows and thrust her pistol into the neck of the security man covering LaCroix. He stood a head taller, so his bulk completely shielded her from the other security men. "His problem, Renée," she announced, "is that you seem to have trouble following instructions!"

"Don't turn!" Kinberg snapped at the two security men facing him. "A sniper rifle is pointed at both of your heads! Face me, with your hands clearly visible!"

"What is the meaning of this?" LaCroix fumed.

"The meaning of this," she said, "is that I graciously allowed you three security men with no restrictions on weapons, but you still busted your agreement!"

"I have not!" he insisted. "I have fully complied with your protocols!

"*Really*?" she shot back. "How many men are in the car parked half a click from here?"

"What?" he countered. "I don't know what you're talking about."

"Heads up!" she heard Cosgrove say in her earpiece. "Another buyer's vehicle is inbound, with another behind that! Whatever you're going to do, wrap it up!"

"I don't have time for your shit, Renée!" she shouted. "The backup vehicle you parked out there, send it away, or I end *all* of you, right here, right now!"

For a tense moment she didn't even breathe. Then LaCroix snapped his fingers at his driver, Conrad's hostage. The driver slowly raised his arm and spoke into his sleeve mike.

"Okay," Cosgrove reported. "The French car is doing a U-turn and shoving off. But the next buyer's car will turn the corner in about ten seconds. You better stow that gun, Angela!"

She shoved the pistol into her waistband holster and pulled her jacket over it. She casually walked around the liberated security man. "Your men can park the car and keep watch anywhere but directly in front of the building," she told him. "You're here first, you choose your spot."

She took LaCroix's arm "Come, Renée," she said cheerfully, "we've got a deal to negotiate."

He placed his hand over hers as they walked arm-in-arm to the door. "My apologies, my dear. I was just being careful. Too careful, it appears."

She nodded. "You can thank Dieter for staying my hand. His read on the situation, and you, was correct. But you do owe me a favor now, Renée."

He eyed her cautiously. "And what would that be?"

"You're going to enthusiastically back the proposal I make here, whether you really like it or not."

His eyebrows rose. "And if I do not?"

She leaned in close as they walked, like a lover confiding a secret. "I normally *shoot* people who cross me, Renée. In your case I made an exception. *Don't* try my patience."

He bowed his head deferentially. "You are as persuasive as usual, *mademoiselle*. You have my word I will consider your proposal favorably."

She patted his hand as she released him. "Way to keep breathing, Renée."

* * *

Fifteen minutes later all six delegations were present. The French, the Russians, the Chinese, the Japanese—she made sure those two parties were not standing adjacent to one another—the Indians, and the Iranians. They gathered around the single spotlight marking the kill zone where Meir Eitan had tried to end her life. She left the blood stain and chalk outline of the Israeli goon Yuri had killed as an unsubtle message to all present.

"Gentlemen," she said, noting the lack of female operatives, "I want to congratulate you on successfully reaching this round in the negotiations. The Saudis and the Israelis sought to circumvent the process all of you willingly agreed to." She glanced at the chalk outline. "It did not end well for either one of them." She had not intended the line to be humorous, but the Iranian representative actually gave her a cruel smile. She guessed he didn't have love for either of the eliminated groups.

"All of you are here because you have expressed a desire to purchase the nanoagent nerve gas being produced by Nanovex," she continued.

"Is it my understanding that you do not have the nerve agent currently in your possession?" the Russian negotiator asked in English.

"That is correct, Colonel Sabakov."

He grimaced at her use of his real name, rather than the pseudonym he had previously used in the negotiations. "Then what exactly are we bidding on, if I may be so bold?"

"You will not be bidding on *anything* tonight, gentlemen. Tonight we plan our next step that will lead to the acquisition of the nanoagent. Only those who participate in this next stage will be allowed into the actual bidding on the acquired product."

"This is not what we agreed to!" the Chinese agent protested.

"You agreed to a *buyer's meeting*, gentlemen. Whatever else you assumed was going to happen here, you filled in those blanks yourself. I made no such promises."

"This is preposterous!" the Japanese representative scoffed.

"This is the way it's going to be!" she shouted, earning her a moment's silence. Over her shoulders on the darkened catwalks, she could almost hear Linn and Meghan's fingers tightening on their rifles' triggers.

She continued. "The reason I called you together was not to defraud you, but to prevent this deal from falling through. My intelligence sources have given me enough access inside Nanovex to know that I don't have the manpower to complete this job. But if we band together, we will have more than enough."

"What are you talking about?" the Russian groused. Several others grumbled a mutual sentiment.

She held up her hand. "What I am proposing is that each of you contribute two men to my strike team. That will give us more than enough manpower to penetrate Nanovex, steal the nanoagent, and return here to conduct the bidding on the acquired product."

"You can't be serious!" the Iranian berated.

"I am serious!" She reached in her jacket pocket and drew out half a dozen thumb drives. "These flash drives contain a top secret presentation on the nanoagent obtained by my source. As a gesture of good faith, I'd like to give all of you a copy." She passed them out to the delegates.

"How would this arrangement work?" Renée LaCroix asked.

"I list the disciplines and skills I still need. You each submit candidates, from whom I will choose. However, the greatest need I will have is simple assault manpower, so everyone will get a chance to participate, that's a given."

"This is an illogical proposal," the Chinese delegate said. "If we each contribute two operatives and lose the bidding at auction, we will have helped place the nanoagent in the hands of a competitor."

"But if you do not participate, Agent Zhao, you have *assured* that a competitor obtains the nanoagent, and not yourself."

She let them all chew on that before continuing. "Something else to think about. My source inside Nanovex has informed me that the President of the United States has learned of this project and has demanded its cancellation. The nanoagent and all records of this project are to be destroyed. But do you really believe that the American CIA will allow a weapon of this power to slip from their grasp?"

Their expressions confirmed that the one entity they hated even more than each other was the CIA.

"No," she continued, "my source has informed me that the CIA intends to send this project overseas, where it *will* be developed, and it *will* be used, possibly on some of *you.* Do you want that to happen without the slightest chance of developing countermeasures or deterring this weapon's deployment with a threat of your own? Think about it, gentlemen."

After a moment of silence, LaCroix said, "I think it's a fine plan. The French delegation will participate." He gave Conrad a hard look. *Favor repaid. You're on your own now.*

The Russians and the Chinese regarded the French spy as if he had lost his mind.

"India agrees as well," their representative said.

A few seconds later, she heard behind her, "Japan agrees to these terms."

Conrad hid a smile. The Indians and Japanese, eager to show themselves as players, jumped at the chance to get on board with LaCroix. The Frenchman's reputation for successful technology theft was well known. Now the rest of the delegations were placed in the uncomfortable position of being the odd man out. LaCroix's earlier busting of her rules may well have saved this meeting.

She looked at the Russians and the Chinese. "Well, if the rest of the parties feel this agreement is not in their best interests, I believe I can make this plan work with the manpower of those who've agreed to my terms. Colonel Sabakov, Agent Zhao, Mr. Nadzim, I'm sorry to have wasted your time."

"Wait!" the Chinese delegate interjected. "I am still considering your proposal. How can you guarantee that once you steal the nanoagent, one of the other parties will not simply steal it from *you*?"

She motioned to the chalk outline of Eitan's goon. "As you can see, I have a proven track record of dealing decisively with people who double-cross me. I *will* have the necessary safeguards in place to make sure the nanoagent reaches the auction intact."

Zhao nodded. "Very well, I agree to your terms."

"Thank you, sir." Clearly he had thrown out the question just to save face. He wasn't about to walk away once his regional competitors had thrown their lot in with her. She turned to the Russian and Iranian hold-outs. "Colonel Sabakov? Mr. Nadzim?"

The Russian sneered. "So, we are all one happy family, yes? I will not spoil this lovemaking by disagreement."

"So you agree to my terms?"

"Yes!" he spat, followed by a muttered, "*Chort vot blyad.*"

Damn you whore? This guy didn't even research what languages she spoke. She smiled. "It's good to have you on board, Oleg." She knew the Russian had probably joined to sabotage her operation at his first opportunity. She would deal with that when the time came.

Her smile never wavering, she turned to the Iranian. "Mr. Nadzim? With your approval we can make this agreement unanimous."

Conrad could tell she had lost the Iranian before he even opened his mouth. Maybe he knew Iran could never hope to match the bids of heavy hitters like Russia and China. Maybe he was worried—justifiably so—that even if he succeeded, countries like France and Japan might turn over that information to the CIA or the Israelis and invite a military strike. Maybe he just didn't like dealing with a woman. Whatever the cause, she knew he was going to walk. And just as likely walk *and* talk.

"The Islamic Republic of Iran does *not* agree with your terms!" he declared. "We have been deceived and will not be ordered about like servants!"

Bombast to cover an inferiority complex, she realized. *He's just not ready to play in the big leagues.* "I'm sorry to hear that, Mr. Nadzim, but I of course respect your wishes." She gestured to the door. "Good evening, sir."

The Iranian stalked away in a huff, followed by his bodyguard, who never stopped looking over his shoulder. Smart man.

Her hand went to her earpiece. "The Iranian delegation is coming out."

"Alone?" Cosgrove asked.

"Yes."

"Understood."

She heard Gallagher moving to the ladder leading up to the roof, but only because she knew to listen for it. Meghan moved on cat's feet.

"Gentlemen," she announced, "I'm very pleased to have the rest of you on board. Let's discuss the logistical details of our arrangement."

* * *

Kinberg met the Iranians at the warehouse door. "I will escort you to your vehicle, sir."

Nadzim waved him off. "Not necessary."

Kinberg made a subtle adjustment of the submachine gun on his chest. "I'm afraid I must insist. My orders are to assure your safe departure, sir."

"Bah!" Nadzim threw up a hand and walked away.

Kinberg followed, giving Nadzim's bodyguard a respectful nod. *We're all professionals here, even if our principals are not*, was the message. The bodyguard returned the gesture and they fell in side-by-side behind Nadzim.

They passed the Japanese delegation fifty meters up the street from the warehouse. The Iranian vehicle was parked another fifty meters beyond that. There was no moon, and the street was almost too dark to walk safely. That was good. Kinberg reached under his jacket and extracted the silencer for the submachine gun, threading it casually onto the barrel of the gun. He carefully moved the fire selector from safe to semi-automatic.

Just before they reached the Iranian BMW sedan, Kinberg extended his weapon and put a point-blank round into the bodyguard's temple. He crumpled to the ground. Nadzim turned more in surprise than alarm and caught two rounds in the forehead. The sound of brass cartridges hitting asphalt made more noise than the silenced weapon.

At that point the two Iranian bodyguards waiting at the car reacted. Before they could raise their weapons, both of their skulls erupted with a silent spray of blood. Cosgrove and Gallagher were as good as Conrad had promised, for which Kinberg was grateful.

"Our guests have departed," he heard Gallagher report. "Dieter's cleanin' up."

Kinberg looked back toward the Japanese team. They were backlit by the light over the warehouse door, their attention fixed in his direction. They were not yet on full alert, but they had obviously heard *something*. There was no way he could dispose of the bodies with them looking straight at him. "I need a distraction for the Japanese team," he requested.

"Acknowledged," Linn Shaozang replied. A minute later he emerged from the rear exit of the warehouse. He approached the two sentries, greeting them in Japanese. He engaged them in small talk, then lit a cigarette, offering them the same. They accepted, the flare of Shaozang's lighter in their faces wiping out the night adaptation of their eyes for the next ten minutes. They were effectively blinded.

Kinberg used the opportunity to drag the Iranian bodies behind the car, then into the trunk. He examined the guard's submachine guns and selected one that suited his purposes. He couldn't fit all the bodies in the trunk, but if he opened one of the passenger doors, the dome light would expose his activities to the Japanese, night adapted eyes or not. He threw Nadzim's body on the closed trunk lid.

Taking the wheel, he backed the BMW into the nearest alley, then moved the body from the trunk lid to the passenger compartment. That accomplished, he drove away from the warehouse. Three blocks east, he turned south again, toward the bay. This street led to one of the docks of the abandoned naval shipyard. Once on the dock, he engaged the emergency brake and jammed the barrel of the submachine gun into the accelerator, adjusting the telescoping stock until the car started grinding forward despite the brake.

Kinberg exited the BMW and reached in to pop the brake. The car surged down the dock and plunged off the end. He walked to the edge and watched the last few inches of the roof disappear into the black water.

"The Iranians are safely away," he reported over the radio.

CONNECTIONS

SAN FRANCISCO, CALIFORNIA

The FBI pathologist looked down on Mark Wong's vivisectioned body on the autopsy table. "It's pretty simple, Agent Pugliano. This man died of nearly instantaneous hypothermia."

"Ever seen anything like it?" Pugliano asked hopefully.

"Sure, that congressman who ditched his plane off Martha's Vineyard in the middle of winter last year. Poor bastard died of hypothermia in five minutes. I did that autopsy myself; he looked just like this. Except you fished this guy out of a fast food restaurant, not the North Atlantic."

He frowned. "You're not helping me, Dr. Wasserman." The pathologist and his team from Quantico had been called in to help with the original Nanovex deaths and had been held over at Pugliano's request to help with the mysterious corpses that seem to accumulate daily around this case. The good doctor had been pulled out of his bed at midnight to perform the autopsy, which had revealed next to nothing.

Wasserman jerked off his latex gloves in frustration. "I'm not a soothsayer. All I can tell you is *how* he died. How someone froze him in the middle of a restaurant and left no witnesses, I haven't a clue."

"But there *were* witnesses," Pugliano corrected. "They reported a blue flash right before seeing the victim frozen solid."

Wasserman opened his hands. "And that's supposed to tell me…what?"

He resisted the temptation to snap at the pathologist, but the man was just doing his job. Then he recalled a similar blue flash in the death of the Nanovex employee Joshua Hackett. Agent Cho had mentioned in her report that Lyman and the scientists at Nanovex had been very helpful. It might be time to pay them a visit.

"Thank you for your time, Dr. Wasserman. I really appreciate your help."

SCIF

SAN FRANCISCO, CALIFORNIA

In the basement of the building the FBI, CIA and several other government agencies shared was a heavily secured Emergency Operations Center for use in natural or manmade disasters. In a corner of this space resided an even more secure room called the SCIF—pronounced "skiff," for Sensitive Compartmented Intelligence Facility. Here the "take" of America's multi-billion-dollar spy satellite network could be focused on San Francisco during emergencies like earthquakes, fires, or terrorist attacks. Hendrix's post should the EOC "go active" was in the SCIF, using satellite imagery to answer questions from decision makers in the ops center who weren't cleared to see his top-secret data.

The SCIF was like the ultimate "man cave," with comfortable seats, powerful systems tied into every computer known to man, and best of all, several top-of-the-line plasma screen TVs filling the entire wall opposite the operator's terminal. Presently he had the satellite take on one screen, the UCLA-USC basketball game on the second, and a skin flick from Showtime on a third. Technology was good.

Tonight Hendrix was alone in the SCIF, with the exception of Hendrix's boss, the CIA Deputy Director for Operations, and the Air Force general in charge of the satellites, both of whom watched the satellite feed by teleconference. The Air Force general was in a foul mood.

"You'd better be right about this, goddamn it!" the general barked. "I had to burn more than *two weeks* worth of fuel changing the orbit to get that bird over Frisco Bay when you wanted it! Not to mention all the pre-scheduled taskings for that satellite that aren't worth shit now that the orbit's changed! That's hundreds of man-hours' worth of work shot to hell!"

Hendrix's boss, J. Laird Underwood III, tried to smooth the general's feathers. "General Hayworth, you have to understand that for the amount of money this source wanted, we just couldn't take his intel at face value."

"He wanted five million, right?" Hayworth shot back. "Well, do you have any idea how much one of these satellites costs?"

Underwood remained silent. Apparently he *didn't* have an idea. Not something they taught in a Harvard foreign relations class, Hendrix guessed.

"About a billion dollars?" Hendrix ventured.

"Try *two* billion! And they're only good for five years before they run out of maneuvering fuel and become a very expensive piece of space junk. So you know how much this little 'repositioning' cost me? Try dividing two billion dollars by five years and then take fifteen days off that life span. In case you don't have a calculator handy, that's over a million dollars a day! So for the life you just sucked out of my satellite, you could have paid that bastard *fifteen* million, not five!"

Oh crap. He wished he'd known that *before* agreeing to Shaozang's demands. Underwood just stared at the screen and blinked.

"Well," Hayworth huffed, winding down from his tirade, "when is this precious source of yours supposed to report in?"

"At one A.M. local." Hendrix checked his watch. "Any minute now."

Although his cell phone wouldn't have a prayer of grabbing a signal down here in the basement, he had cloned his phone to the communications terminal in front of him. That terminal was tied to an antenna on the roof that could probably pull in a cell signal from Mars. At precisely one A.M., Hendrix's cell received a text message:

"37.43.21 N 122.22.9 W"

"Okay, I've got a latitude and longitude," he reported. "Plugging it into the imagery computer now."

"Scott, did your source give us any clue what this was going to show?" his boss asked.

"Afraid not. Let's hope he made it something easy to spot."

The computer scanned the database of downloaded satellite data, zooming into the selected coordinates at precisely midnight, an hour and one minute ago. The image plunged from an overhead of the entire Bay area to a peninsula south of downtown, then to a single warehouse. Cars were parked around the warehouse, their images fuzzy and indistinct.

"I hate to tell you this," Hayworth warned, "but you're not going to get a much better image than that. If we could have slewed the satellite over those coordinates in real time, we'd be counting nose hairs right now. As it is, you're having to digitally zoom the wide-area image the satellite took as it passed over. Your source probably didn't understand that."

"Either that or he didn't care," Hendrix countered. He had detected a pattern in the vehicles parked around the warehouse. He switched to infrared, and the pattern got stronger.

Hendrix's image manipulations were immediately being fed over to Underwood's and Hayworth's screens. "What do you see, Scott?" his boss asked.

"Okay," he said, "you see how these cars aren't bunched up in front of the warehouse Shaozang gave us, but they're parked at regular intervals all around the building?"

"Like a defensive perimeter," the general noted.

"Exactly. Now look at the infrared. Those little dots are people. Two at each vehicle, and another two on the roof. They're guarding some kind of meeting inside that warehouse."

"A meeting of whom? About what?" Hayworth snapped. "This tells us nothing."

"General," he ventured, "we've been detecting signs of a whole shitload of bad-guy-intelligence-types sneaking into San Francisco recently. My guess is you're looking right at them."

Hayworth snorted in derision. "Even if I granted you that, what were they *doing* in the warehouse?"

"Meeting Angela Conrad would be my guess."

"To what end?"

Careful, Scott. "She could be planning some kind of cooperative venture."

"And that could be what our source was trying to show us," Underwood proposed. "That Conrad is planning something big, with lots of players."

"Maybe," Hayworth allowed. "So where do you go next with this information?"

"We wait for the source to make contact again," Hendrix said. "If he can't answer our questions about this meeting, then the deal's off."

"So in that case," Hayworth huffed, "you've only cost the taxpayers fifteen million dollars instead of twenty, right?"

Well, it doesn't sound as good when you say it that way. "Yes, General, I'm afraid that's about right."

* * *

After Hayworth and Underwood signed off, Hendrix reviewed the entire satellite pass, from the time it came over the horizon until San Francisco disappeared from view, a period of about fifteen minutes. He watched the vehicles gather around the warehouse, then after a few minutes he watched one leave. He knew the satellite would be long gone before the departing vehicle reached its destination, but he would track it as far as he could. At least he would get a general direction of travel. He switched over to infrared, which turned the car into a glowing blob against the cool background of the city.

Suddenly the glowing blob vanished. He backed up the satellite feed and watched it happen again. That was strange. Then he switched back to standard night vision and watched the car roll off a dock and disappear with a splash into the bay. He pulled back to get nearby landmarks in case they wanted to recover the car. *Wait a minute.*

Something looked familiar in the overhead view. He kept zooming out and sucked in a stunned breath. *Oh my God, that's Hunter's Point. She went back to the same damned place where she whacked Meir Eitan*. He smiled in admiration. *That gal Conrad is a real piece of work.*

On the other hand, he was deeply disturbed. He was once again converging on a solution that had already ended in one massacre. If his source Shaozang indeed delivered Conrad to him, what was to stop her unseen protectors from intervening just like they had in San Jose? Not a thing in the world. With the technology at their disposal, whoever watched over Conrad was like the force of gravity—invisible and unstoppable. *However*, if he was able to *ally* himself with these unseen powers, wouldn't that make *him* a force of nature as well? Scott Hendrix had a revelation.

If you can't beat 'em, join 'em.

Hendrix noted and memorized the coordinates of the wreck. Then he shut down the equipment in the SCIF and headed home for a few hours of sleep. Come daylight tomorrow, it would be time to go for a swim.

CHAPTER 19

PLUMBER'S RATES

CHICAGO, ILLINOIS

"Come on, boys!" Amanda Manning called. "We're going to be late!" She grabbed her purse and cursed under her breath after checking herself in the mirror. She was barely put together, but that couldn't be helped. Oh well, it wasn't like she was going to Vivo's for lunch, she was just going to the gym. But even so....

"Mom! Where's my book bag?" Eric called out.

"Probably where you did your homework last night," she replied.

That suggestion was met by such an uncomfortable silence that she checked the area around the back door where Eric entered the house. Sure enough, Eric's book bag was tossed in a corner behind a chair. She held it out for him, then yanked it away.

"Did you have any homework last night?" she demanded.

"No," Eric said without hesitation.

"Liar," she said. "Care to try again?"

His eyes darted. "Oh, yeah, we had some, but I did it."

"Double liar!" she declared. *Just like your father*, she almost added, thrusting the book bag at him hard enough to push him back. "Get your butt in the car! Tonight we're going to have a little talk."

With punishment deferred, Eric's mood immediately lightened. He bounded cheerfully for the car. Amanda shook her head. *What a fine little sociopath we're raising.*

"Kevin!" she shouted.

"Coming, Mom!" Her seven-year-old came thundering through the kitchen flashing the smile that had delivered him from deserved discipline more than once.

She called her friend and workout partner Lisa as soon as they were on the road. "Hey, girlfriend! Yeah, I'm running late, can you hold on a few minutes? If we don't start our workouts the same time you'll finish first then I'll wuss out and stop early. Thanks!"

Amanda didn't notice the plumber's truck parked in front of the vacant house two doors down. But the "plumbers" noticed her.

* * *

"Okay, she's in motion!" the driver of the plumber's truck reported. "Any idea how much time we got?"

The other "plumber" looked up from his terminal in the back where he had been monitoring Amanda Manning's phone calls. "Yeah, she said she was going to work out. Any idea how long it takes a woman to do that?"

"If it's anything like everything else women do, it's too damn long," the driver said. "My wife can spend an hour putting on make-up and still look like a train wreck." He clicked his radio. "Hey Jenny, our bird's gone to work out. How long's it take a woman to do that?" He smiled in anticipation of the expected caustic response. Political correctness hadn't permeated the Chicago FBI office to the same extent as the cities on either coast.

"Oh gee," a woman's voice fired back, "let me consult my female stereotype handbook. Hmm. Or I *could* go watch her at the gym and call you when she leaves, you cave man."

The driver's grin broadened. "Wow, that's pretty smart for a girl. I didn't expect that."

"I hope there's a Doberman in her house that eats your testicles," she replied. "Out."

He turned to the technician in back and shook his head. "Wow, it's almost like she's *trying* to create a hostile work environment. Okay, let's do this."

Once inside the Manning household, the FBI "plumbers" followed a checklist refined by decades of hard experience. The first thing they did was sweep the house for existing bugs. It wasn't unusual in organized crime cases for the FBI to initiate a surveillance, only to find their target already being actively monitored by their own criminal organization. And then there was the FBI team caught planting bugs by the nanny cam hidden in a teddy bear. Very embarrassing.

The only obstacle the plumbers faced in the Manning household had been the burglar alarm, for which they had already obtained the make, model, and manufacturer's override code. While the driver planted several audio bugs throughout the house, the other plumber roamed the house with a camera, photographing likely locations for hiding video cameras. These would be custom manufactured to be exact matches of light fixtures, smoke detectors, or digital clocks inside the house. They would return to install these on a future visit. Half an hour later they were done.

The driver called the agent watching Amanda. "Okay, Jenny, we're leaving now."

"Good deal," she replied. "I planted the bumper beeper on her car."

"Thanks, we'll check the signal when we get back to the truck."

While the second plumber cloned the entry code of the garage door opener so they could enter and leave at will, the driver placed a note on the front door to cover their butt against any nosy neighbors asking their target about the plumber's truck in her driveway.

"SORRY WE MISSED YOU! WE ENTERED YOUR BACK YARD TO ACCESS YOUR NEIGHBOR'S SEWER LINE. WE APOLOGIZE FOR ANY INCONVENIENCE. – EVERFLOW PLUMBING SERVICE"

The FBI paid the real Everflow Plumbing Service a thousand dollars a month to use their company's markings on FBI surveillance vehicles. The phone number on the note would reach a junior agent tasked with monitoring several such "shadow numbers" and answering the calls according to the assigned cover stories.

Later that afternoon a "realtor" would place a SOLD sign on the vacant house two doors down. The next day an attractive and sociable young couple would move in, looking to make friends with their new neighbors.

MOURNING MEETING

SAN JOSE, CALIFORNIA

Mike Manning's mandate from Conrad had been clear; find the lab where WICKER BASKET was stored. She had also been very clear of the penalties for failure. So how the hell was he supposed to pull this off? He didn't even know who was working on WICKER BASKET to try a little social engineering or bribery. He hoped something would come to him once he was inside. His cell phone rang just before he entered the Nanovex building.

"We've caught a break on tracking down the lab," Conrad announced.

Manning looked around casually to make sure no one was within earshot. The guard inside the glass lobby was busy screening incoming employees, but he still had a feeling he was being watched for some reason. "Good. Lay it on me."

"The data you sucked off Lyman's computer showed that his team is having a status meeting in his office at nine. It's supposed to last half an hour. Is there any way you could watch his office and follow them back to their lab when the meeting breaks up?"

He thought for a moment. There was a small sitting area on the fourth floor next to the elevators. "Well, I *could* follow them, except I don't even know who's on the WICKER BASKET team."

"Don't use that code word on the phone," she cautioned. "Can you watch Lyman's door at nine and see who goes in?"

"Yeah, I suppose so."

"Those are the people you want to follow."

Well, duh. In fairness to himself, he hadn't had his coffee yet. "Okay, will do."

"And don't forget to pitch this burner."

"Got it."

* * *

Wendy Cho had arrived early to the Nanovex listening post to make sure her path did not cross with Manning when he arrived. Her station was the terminal monitoring the security cameras. A Nanovex security guard stood watch at the door of their small windowless conference room to make sure employees did not blunder in. He told passersby the people inside were working on a sensitive proposal.

Cho saw Manning approach the front door. "Okay, here he comes," she announced to the technician manning the communications terminal. "Hold up," she added, "he's making a phone call."

"His cell phone shows no activity," the communications specialist reported.

"I'm looking right at him, he's on the phone! Don't you guys have a frequency counter set up out there?"

"Of course we do," he replied. "Give me a sec." Suspecting that Conrad's group would surveil the Nanovex facility, the FBI had set up equipment to quickly detect and locate any radio traffic in the area. But cellphones were so ubiquitous that localizing a specific phone was difficult. "Okay, I got something, but I'm not sure it's your guy or not."

"Put it on speaker!" she ordered.

"Those are the people you want to follow," Cho heard a woman say.

"Okay, will do," a man's voice replied. She assumed it was Manning, but couldn't be sure.

"And don't forget to pitch this burner."

"Got it."

Cho watched Manning end the call, then walk to a nearby trash can and toss something in. *Nailed him*, she thought. "What did he say before you put him on speaker?"

The technician frowned. "Something about Lyman, I didn't catch what."

"Dammit," she muttered. "Okay, then *you* get to fish out his phone."

He threw his headphones on the table. "Whatever."

* * *

Manning contrived an excuse to ask Lyman's secretary a question about his expense reports a few minutes before nine o'clock. Lyman's security man Reese Miller arrived a minute later, escorting two workers, a man and a woman. Both looked shaken. Miller ushered them through the portal, giving Manning a hard look before closing the door. *That guy really doesn't like me*, he thought. Other than that one instance of catching him snooping in the basement, he had never crossed swords with the security man. He guessed that Miller was a "one strike and you're out" kind of guy.

"Did somebody die?" he asked Lyman's secretary. "Somebody *else*, I mean?"

She cringed and looked away. "I'm sorry, I don't know."

Oh crap. Somebody <u>else</u> bit the big one? What kind of death trap <u>is</u> this place?

He gathered his forms. "Okay, Cathy, thanks."

* * *

Doug Lyman greeted the two surviving scientists from WICKER BASKET. "Jeff, Molly, I'm so sorry to be the bearer of bad news again, but it appears that Mark Wong was murdered last night."

Molly Kiernan's hands flew to her face. "Oh God! I knew something had happened to him! I just knew it!"

Lyman cocked his head. "Did he receive some kind of threat? Did *you*?"

Jeff Wood shook his head. "No, but when he didn't show and you sent *him* to escort us to our meeting," he jerked his head at Miller, "I just put two and two together."

Kiernan shook her head as well, wiping away a tear with an abrupt motion. "Call it feminine intuition. I just *knew* Mark wasn't okay."

Lyman motioned them to the table. "I understand. Please, sit. I'll tell you everything I know. It's not much, I'm afraid."

* * *

The FBI technician returned with a black trash bag and set it on the table.

"*Please*!" Cho protested. "We *eat* there!"

Embarrassed, the technician set the bag on the floor and started rummaging through it.

Her hand went to her nose. "Oh God!" she said. "Did something *die in there?*"

The technician coughed. "No kidding. Hope not. Here we go." He pulled out a cell phone with a number "1" taped to it.

"What's the number for?" she asked.

"Probably to keep his burners in order," he said, taking the phone to his terminal and hooking it up.

"Can we take that outside now?" she asked, pointing to the bag.

"Sure, I'll get that in a…oh, crap," he said, dropping the phone to the table. "He yanked the battery. It's probably at the bottom." He returned to the bag, looked inside with a frown, and tied the top in a knot.

"I'm gonna get some gloves," he said.

* * *

Molly Kiernan raised her voice to Lyman. "Don't you understand what this *means*? Somebody's killing *everyone* involved in WICKER BASKET, one by one!"

Lyman raised a cautioning hand. "Molly, please, don't jump to conclusions."

"Sounds like a valid conclusion to *me*," Jeff Wood said. "Of course, that may just be because I'm on the death list."

"I'm read into this program too," Lyman replied. "And so is Reese. And so is Seth Graves from DARPA for that matter. You're not in this boat alone, Jeff. Stay calm."

"But who would want us *dead*?" Kiernan pleaded. "Could this be because we're continuing the program against government orders?"

"Molly, we don't have any evidence of that." Lyman knew he had to get an emotional handle on his employees quickly. They were on the verge of panic, and panicked people did irrational things.

"Do you have a *better* theory?" Wood demanded. "Because unless you do, I think confession and repentance might be our best course of action. Maybe if they knew you really *are* going to give up the weapon they might stop killing people."

Lyman resisted rolling his eyes. "Jeff, you're talking about 'they' like the government itself is doing this. Let's not get paranoid, *please*."

"Paranoid?" Kiernan scoffed. "You're not paranoid because they're not coming for *you*!"

I'm losing them, he knew. "Reese and I are at just as much risk as you, Molly."

"Bullshit!" she shouted. "You don't have the expertise to reconstitute this program! Jeff and I do! *We're* the ones they're coming for, not you!"

"Okay!" he said, holding up his hands. "I have an appointment with the FBI in an hour. I'll talk to them about putting both of you in protective custody."

Molly's eyes went wide. "If it's the *government* that's coming for us, what good is handing us over to *them* going to do?"

Oh dear God. "Do you have a better idea, Molly?"

Her gaze dropped. "No."

"Well," Wood offered, "nobody's been killed down in our lab." He paused. "I mean, on purpose. Why don't we just hole up down there until this blows over?" He jerked his head toward Miller. "I'd feel a lot more comfortable with *his* guys watching us than a bunch of government types."

Lyman nodded. "That's a great idea. I *promise* you, we will do everything it will take to keep you as safe and comfortable as possible."

They seemed to relax slightly.

"All right," he said, "why don't you two go back to the lab and make a list of what you'll need, especially things from your homes, medications and the like. Reese will see that you get everything you need."

Kiernan and Wood looked at each other. "Okay," they finally agreed.

"Do you feel safe going back to the lab, or would you like Reese to escort you?"

The scientists looked reluctant. Now that their initial fears were assuaged, they probably felt a bit silly about their paranoia.

"No," Kiernan said. "I think we'll be fine going downstairs."

He smiled. "Very good. Reese, please stay and let's discuss our security arrangements."

* * *

"Okay, I got his phone working," the communications technician told Cho. "Here's the number of the phone that called him. Let's see if it's still active."

"I'm betting no," Cho said.

He nodded. "And you're correct. Cell company logs show the last signal from the phone that called Manning was one minute after she ended the call. We're not going to get inside their communications loop if they keep using their burners once and throwing them away. Wait a minute." A message box flashed in the corner of the technician's computer screen.

"What's that?"

The technician stared. "Holy crap, it's an ECHELON warning!" He clicked on it. "Okay, we asked the NSA to add WICKER BASKET to their search terms when they monitor civilian phone traffic for terrorist chatter. Looks like they got a hit. Their analyst flagged the call as 'highly suspicious.'" He clicked on the attached audio file. "The recording starts right after somebody used the search term, in this case WICKER BASKET."

"Don't use that code word on the phone," They heard a woman's voice say over the computer's speakers. "Can you watch Lyman's door at nine and see who goes in?"

"Yeah, I suppose so."

"Those are the people you want to follow."

Cho jumped back to the terminal monitoring the security cameras. "Where is he now?" she wondered aloud. "There, he's still sitting in the fourth floor working on his laptop. Wait a minute, he's in motion! Who are those people he's getting in the elevator with?"

The technician looked over her shoulder. "Beats me," he said.

"Could those people be the one's he's supposed to follow?"

"Maybe."

She reached for the internal phone. "I'm calling Nanovex security. I think we need them in the loop."

* * *

Manning camped out in the sitting area across from the elevators on the fourth floor. He surfed the local news sites on his laptop, looking for any suspicious deaths the previous night. There was a homeless man beaten to death—a possible robbery—and a woman shot during a home invasion. Maybe the woman was a Nanovex employee. He kept searching.

On the third TV station website he checked, there was a brief report of a suspicious death at a local restaurant. No identity released, no statement from police, but a brief mention of the police closing off an entire block around the incident. *That* was odd.

He looked up when the pair came around the corner. They didn't look quite as distraught as before, but the woman looked like she had been crying. He closed his laptop and walked casually to the elevator, pressing the down button. The pair talked quietly, but stopped when they approached Manning. They all entered the elevator together.

He purposefully stood next to the elevator buttons inside. "What floor?" he asked helpfully.

"Basement," the man answered.

They got off together, the pair turning right. Manning turned left. He walked the corridor until he heard a heavy metal door open behind him. He turned and saw them enter a doorway on the left. He reversed course and walked to the door.

It was marked PROPRIETARY LAB P4-1.

That was easy enough, he thought. He walked back to the elevator and pressed the up button. The door opened immediately and he was face-to-face with Lyman's security chief Reese Miller. *Oh shit.*

Miller gave him a look that would freeze gasoline, but said nothing. Manning entered the elevator. Miller watched him until the doors closed.

THE DEVIL AND DR. KAMMLER

JANUARY 30, 1964 – WASHINGTON, D.C.

The impending launch of the Ranger 6 moon probe had so totally enthralled President Lyndon Johnson that he had lost track of time and his impending appointment. The launch preparations were broadcast by closed circuit to a television in the Oval Office. He even had a direct line to the launch director should he have questions. He had used it once to make sure it worked. According to the clock inset at the corner of the screen, liftoff was less than five minutes away. A knock sounded at the door. Johnston cursed at the interruption.

His secretary leaned inside. "Mr. President, Mr. Dulles is here for your meeting."

Oh, that's right. This was important. He used a knob on the desk to turn down the sound from mission control, then turned his attention to a report on his desk. "Show them in," he said. He pretended to be fixated on the report until Dulles and his guest stood stiffly before his desk.

He looked up. "Ah, Allen, good to see you again." He gestured toward the couches. "Please, make yourself comfortable."

Allen Dulles and his guest waited for him to sit down in his padded rocking chair before seating themselves. Dulles handed him a bound report. "Mr. President, the latest interim report from the Warren Commission for your review."

Johnson flipped absently through the pages of whitewash. "Thank you, Allen. Have you solved the timing problem yet?"

One of the major difficulties for the Warren Commission was an eight-millimeter-film shot by a Dallas businessman named Abraham Zapruder. It clearly showed bullet impacts into Kennedy and Governor Connally that were too closely spaced to have been fired by a single sniper using a bolt action rifle. Staffers on the Warren Commission who were not part of the cover-up quickly concluded that the film was evidence of more than one shooter's involvement. Actually there had been three, but Allen Dulles's men were supposed to have anticipated those details. They *were* professionals, after all.

"Yes, Mr. President," Dulles said. "One of our counsels, a young man named Arlen Specter, has come up with an innovative explanation called the Single Bullet Theory. Basically it states that the bullet we planted on Governor Connally's stretcher passed through President Kennedy before it struck the Governor." [1]

Johnson looked at him incredulously. "Do you think anyone will actually *buy* that?"

Dulles made a dismissive motion with his hand. "The public wants to believe that the death of their beloved president was the act of a lone lunatic. We will help them do just that. Also, young Mr. Specter is a very persuasive salesman."

"If he can pull that off, see that he's well rewarded," Johnson said.

Dulles nodded. "I will, Mr. President. Of course the real reason for my visit today is to introduce you to my associate, Mr. Schmidt."

Johnson looked over at the tall man seated beside Dulles. About his age, the German had angular features and an authoritative air. He was not the slightest bit awed by his visit to the Oval Office.

Johnson was momentarily confused. "I thought his name was Kammler."

Dulles winced. "He prefers the name *Schmidt* now, Mr. President."

A Nazi war criminal probably would prefer using an alias, Johnson realized. He extended his hand without rising. "Mr. Schmidt, a pleasure."

"Schmidt" rose and shook his hand, leaning forward in a slight Prussian bow. "An honor, Mr. President." Almost devoid of German accent, his voice had a slight Spanish lilt to it.

"I understand you have technology that we would find useful," Johnson said.

Schmidt motioned to the television set. Ranger 6 had blasted off, its tail of flame twice as long as the rocket itself in the grainy black-and-white image. "Mr. President, the technology I offer your government will make such rockets look like World War I biplanes by comparison."

Johnson squinted at him. "And what do you ask for in return?"

Schmidt opened his hands. "For the moment, nothing. I ask only for the opportunity to make a small demonstration of our capabilities."

DIP PASSES

PRESENT DAY – SAN FRANCISCO, CALIFORNIA

CIA Security Specialist Carl Lindeman was an ex-Navy SEAL and relished the opportunity to don a wet suit instead of a suit and tie. He stood at the end of the pier at Hunter's Point and looked down into the water. "You say there's a car down there?" he asked.

Scott Hendrix nodded. "Yep, I watched it on the satellite feed go right into the drink."

Lindeman turned. "*Really*? Whose car was it?"

Hendrix pulled on his own scuba tank and tested the regulator. "That's what we're going to find out."

The water off the end of the pier was deep enough to plunge the bottom into a murky twilight. It took a few minutes of searching to find the car. The driver's side door was open. Hendrix hadn't seen anyone bail from the car, but the satellite had almost been out of range at that point—the resolution had been lousy. A quick check of the interior found a body floating over the back seat.

Hendrix opened the back door and checked the body. Middle Eastern male, fifties, medium build, nice suit, with two bullet holes drilled neatly into his forehead. Ouch. He checked the man's pockets. A Lebanese diplomatic passport in the name of one Omar Fayyad. Some keys, an unmarked access card, and a flash drive. These all went into a plastic bag for analysis.

Lindeman rapped his flashlight on the car frame and motioned Hendrix over to the driver's seat. He pointed to the accelerator pedal, where a submachine gun had been jammed to hold down the pedal. Hendrix pointed to the gun and made a yanking motion, indicating he wanted that retrieved as well.

While Hendrix examined the submachine gun, he heard a heavy thunk. Lindeman had popped the trunk. To Hendrix's horror, more bodies floated toward the surface. He dropped the bag and the gun and frantically grabbed at the slightly buoyant corpses, grabbing one around the waist, one by the ankle, and shoving a flipper against a third that hadn't yet escaped from the trunk.

Lindeman helped him wrestle the bodies back into confinement. Hendrix then searched them as best he could, collecting more Lebanese dip passes and finding two more submachine guns and three pistols. He took the passports and left the guns. The guys in the trunk were all younger and bulkier than the guy in the back seat, so he was likely the man in charge and the rest were bodyguards. All had been dispatched with neat single gunshots to the head; one by pistol fire, the other two obviously by a rifle of some kind, judging by the cranial damage. If these guys *were* associated with Conrad in some way, he wondered what they had done to piss her off.

Working together, he and Lindeman were able to close the trunk. He re-located the bag with the head guy's pocket litter and the first submachine gun. He handed the gun to Lindeman and jerked a thumb toward the surface.

* * *

A shower and a change of clothes later, Lindeman and Hendrix had the booty from their dive back at the CIA office. The passports and other items went from seawater-filled bags to tubs of distilled water before drying.

Hendrix was hanging up the passports like laundry when Lindeman returned with his analysis of the recovered submachine gun.

"The serial numbers have been filed off," Lindeman reported, "but it's the same make and year model as a shipment of full-auto CAR-15s that were stolen from a Class III gun dealer in Arizona last year."

"So they didn't enter the country through a Lebanese diplomatic bag, you think?"

Lindeman shook his head. "Betcha this is black market gear, and so are the rest of the guns in that trunk."

Hendrix examined the hanging documents. "Which makes me wonder about these passports."

Lindeman eyed each one in turn. "I spent a little time in Lebanon. Hamas and Hezbollah wouldn't be above faking a dip pass, or bribing somebody to get a real one."

"Hamas and Hezbollah? Isn't San Francisco a little far afield for them?"

Lindeman scratched his chin. "Yeah, but something about these guys doesn't look Lebanese to me. Maybe it's their facial structure. When these dry, I'd like to run them through facial recognition and see what comes up."

"Be my guest," Hendrix said. He held up the flash drive, still soaking in its tub of distilled water. "In the meantime, I'm gonna find a data recovery specialist for this stick."

* * *

Hendrix had no idea what he would find on the data stick, but was still astounded when he was presented with the briefing he had received on the nanoweapon from Doug Lyman at Nanovex. How the hell had Conrad gotten hold of *that*, and what was it doing in San Francisco Bay in a dead man's pocket?

He gladly handed over the thousand dollars in cash he had offered to the freelance computer specialist, and promised to have another thousand when he returned with the non-disclosure agreement that would seal the specialist's lips about the top-secret briefing.

Lindeman was waiting when Hendrix returned to the office. "I was right about those 'Lebanese' guys," he reported. "They're not. They're Iranian."

Hendrix recoiled. "No way."

"Afraid so." Lindeman handed over a printout, with an enlargement of the Omar Fayyad passport photo, and the resulting facial recognition analysis. "Meet Mr. Izrah Nadzim, a colonel in the Iranian Revolutionary

Guard's Intelligence section. One of the other guys comes up as IRG too. The younger guys drew a blank. Probably new to the business."

Hendrix examined the file. "Any idea what Mr. Nadzim's specialty was? Oh, here we go; illegal acquisition of export-controlled technology."

"Yeah, he was their go-to guy for embargoed airplane parts, centrifuge technology for their nuclear program, you name it. Did that flash drive give you any hints on what our bad guys were doing in Frisco?"

Hendrix debated how much to share with Lindeman. Since he was considering reaching out to the people protecting Angela Conrad, he decided the less the better.

He shook his head. "Afraid not. The seawater trashed it."

"Dammit!" Lindeman said with conviction. "I take it we're not going to the FBI with any of this?"

"*You* want to explain to them why we lifted evidence from a crime scene?"

Lindeman chuckled. "I see your point. Call me if you want to get your feet wet again."

"You bet." He returned to his office just in time for his cell phone to ring. It was Linn Shaozang.

"Were you able to investigate the coordinates I gave you last night?" Shaozang asked.

"I did. Looked like some kind of meeting was going on."

"It was buyer's meeting for the technology my employer intends to obtain from a local nanotechnology company," Shaozang said.

Hendrix noted how careful Shaozang was not to use any keywords that might tip off the ECHELON system, like "Conrad" or "Nanovex."

"Buyers?" Hendrix asked. "Does she have the technology in hand?"

A soft laugh. "No, and there was much consternation among the buyers at that fact. She went so far as to request help from the prospective buyers to pull off the actual acquisition."

Now it was Hendrix's turn to laugh. "That was ballsy. How did they take it?"

"Surprisingly well. Now, have you considered my request?"

Time for a final test. "Yes, but I have one last question. Who is Izrah Nadzim?"

There was a lengthy pause. "He was the only buyer who refused my employer's proposal."

"What happened to him?" Hendrix pressed.

"He was eliminated, along with his security detachment. Now, I must insist on an answer to my proposal. Do you wish me to turn my employer over to the US government, yes or no?"

He smiled. "I have a counterproposal. I'll give you the money you ask for, but only if you *don't* turn over your employer to the US government."

MUST-SEE VIDEO

SAN JOSE, CALIFORNIA

Doug Lyman extended his hand. "Agent Pugliano, are we glad to see *you*!" Agent Cho and Reese Miller were also present in Lyman's office. Seth Graves from DARPA attended at Pugliano's request.

"Really? What's going on?"

"I'm afraid the death of Mark Wong has made the two remaining scientists on the WICKER BASKET project very nervous about their safety."

"They think their work has made them targets?"

Lyman nodded. "Very much so. They've asked my permission to hole up in their lab until the murderer is caught. I agreed. I can't think of a more secure location than the basement of this facility, can you?"

"No, honestly, I can't." *And the fact that the FBI doesn't have to allocate manpower to guard them makes it even better.*

"Good. Have you made any progress toward identifying the killer?"

"I'm afraid not," Pugliano admitted. "Actually I'm here to ask for your help."

Lyman looked confused. "How so?"

He spread the crime scene photos on the conference room table. "This is how we found your employee Mark Wong, frozen solid in the middle of a restaurant. The rest of the patrons were completely unharmed—none of them even felt a chill. They did, however, see a blue flash very similar to the one videotaped at the supermarket where your employee Joshua Hackett was killed."

"A blue flash?" Lyman asked.

"Yes, I believe you described it to Agent Cho as a 'plasma' of some kind, if I read her report correctly."

Seth Graves chimed in. "And you believe the same weapon—for the lack of a better word—used against Josh Hackett was used against Mark Wong?"

Pugliano shrugged. "You gentlemen know far more about plasmas than I do. All I know is there was a blue flash in both cases. Could a plasma weapon of some sort cause these kinds of effects?"

"As far as the effect that liquefied Josh Hackett's insides, I have no idea," Lyman offered. "But Nikola Tesla theorized beam weapons that could freeze whole areas of ocean almost a century ago."

"Could someone have actually developed that sort of weapon?" he asked. "I mean, is it even possible?"

"Tesla was so far ahead of his time and achieved so much," Lyman said, "to say that anything he theorized is impossible seems a bit presumptuous."

"The better question," Graves said, "is if such a weapon exists, why use it against harmless scientists like Josh and Mark? A bullet would be a hell of a lot less trouble, and draw less attention."

"Unless you're sending a message," Cho said.

Lyman looked alarmed. "What message would *that* be, Agent Cho?"

She gave Lyman a pointed look. "Two scientists who worked on the same project are dead by mysterious means. And you said that project had already been cancelled, right?"

"Correct."

"Maybe cancellation wasn't good enough for someone. Maybe they decided to make *damned* sure your project went away, forever."

Pugliano noticed he wasn't the only one shifting uncomfortably. "Isn't that quite a leap, Agent Cho?"

"I don't think so," she continued. "As Mr. Graves suggested, a bullet would have been a whole lot easier, but they didn't do that. They used some kind of Star Wars plasma weapon not even the FBI knows about. Whoever's behind this is not only taking Mr. Lyman's people off the board like chess pieces, they're rubbing it in the FBI's face that we can't do jack to stop them."

Somewhere in Lyman's office an antique clock ticked softly.

And that's why you bring in the young pups, Pugliano mused. A more experienced agent would have kept silent about the bare-assed emperor standing in the room with them for fear of endangering their next promotion. But youngsters like Cho still had the truth, justice and American way song playing in their heads. Good for her.

"So, Agent Cho," Pugliano said, "since you have this all figured out, what's our next move?"

She blinked. "I have no idea. Sorry."

Unfortunately for Ms. Cho, she had never been a Marine. Pugliano had. "Well, I say we hide an army around the two remaining scientists and see who comes for them."

Lyman's jaw dropped. "Are you suggesting using my employees as *bait*?"

He shrugged. "Unless they want to spend the rest of their lives down there in the basement."

"He has a point," Graves said. "How long are your people willing to hole up? And that's assuming the weapons the murderer is using can't reach down there. We just don't know."

"How exactly would you do this?" Lyman demanded. "I don't like this idea of staking my people out like a goat for the lions."

"Standard procedure would be to use a stand-in for your people," Pugliano assured him, "an FBI employee of the same height and build. Both of your people were attacked during a stop on their way home. That means the killer has already followed your people, getting to know their routine. We're going to use that knowledge to shrink the kill box, preposition enough firepower to stop an armored battalion, and wait for the ambush."

"Sounds awfully risky for your people, Agent Pugliano."

"I won't have any trouble finding volunteers. My folks live for a good scrap."

"When do we do this?"

"Soon, or the murderer will start wondering why your people have altered their routines. We just need to interview your two scientists and find out where to set up our ambush."

"I'll have Reese take you to them as soon as we're done here."

"Thanks very much."

Lyman straightened. "The other matter we need to discuss is that lawyer Manning. Reese and Agent Cho caught him following those two very scientists this morning."

Did he, now? Maybe we'll catch our murderer sooner than expected. "Excellent. Tell me all about it."

* * *

Cho asked Pugliano to accompany her to the listening post on the second floor after the meeting, ostensibly with a complaint about their equipment.

"There's nothing wrong with our equipment," she said once the door was closed. "I needed to show you something right away, but I didn't want to do it in front of Lyman and his people."

Finally developing a little discretion. I knew this assignment would be good for her. "No problem. Whatcha got?"

She turned her laptop to face him. "One of the agents downtown got this from his brother, who got it off YouTube."

"YouTube?" he scoffed.

She ignored his skepticism. "Some skateboarders were across the street from the Arby's where the murder occurred, making videos of each other using a cell phone. Here's what they saw." She clicked on the video.

Because of the cell phone camera, the quality was poor and the video jerky. For over a minute Pugliano endured the teenagers jumping curbs and other clumsy tricks, each accompanied by profane commentary from their companions. The Arby's restaurant was visible in the background.

Pugliano could see the window where they found Mark Wong's body, although the image quality was too poor to see beyond the glass.

"Dude, what is that?" one of the teenagers called.

The camera swung upwards to frame a small silver ball descending rapidly through the late afternoon sky. When it stopped, the roof of the Arby's intruded on the bottom of the frame. The ball slowly descended further, then hung motionless for a second or two. The UFO and Wong's window were momentarily both in view.

Suddenly a blue flash popped in the window and the UFO climbed rapidly away, the back half of the silver ball glowing as it accelerated. It was gone in two seconds.

"What the hell!" the skateboarders shouted over each other. "What the hell was that?"

The video ended.

Pugliano sat in dumbfounded silence for several seconds. "Do you think those kids have any idea what they were really seeing?"

She had played the video at full screen resolution, but now hit the ESC button to shrink the player to its normal size. "Uh, sir," she replied, "check out the title of the video."

Pugliano looked down again.

"UFO KILLS MAN AT SAN JOSE ARBYS! MUST-SEE VIDEO!!!"

"Oh-h-h *shit*," he groaned.

[1] Arlen Specter made a name for himself as an assistant counsel on the Warren Commission, especially for his invention of the Single Bullet Theory, also known derisively as the Magic Bullet Theory. In 1965 he ran for District Attorney of Philadelphia on the Republican ticket even though he was a registered Democrat, foreshadowing his abandonment of the Republican Party forty years later, also for political expediency rather than any ideological conviction.

As for the Magic Bullet, Arlen Specter had to interview several different forensic pathologists before he found *one* who would endorse the Warren Commission's conclusions that the bullet in question, CE-399, could have passed through two bodies and several bones, leaving bullet fragments in both bodies as it did so, and still result in the pristine bullet pictured below, found on Governor Connally's stretcher. And if there was no Magic Bullet, then there must by definition have been more than one shooter, and the Warren Commission's findings collapse.

A more plausible theory is that the CE-399 bullet was fired into ballistic gelatin purely for the purposes of planting it on Connally's stretcher (because it was more accessible than the one bearing the President) so that it could later be ballistically matched to Oswald's rifle.

The small nick in the nose of the bullet below was not from impact but was removed by the FBI for metallurgical analysis. So where did the bullet fragments left in both the President's and the Governor's bodies come from? Inevitably from another bullet, fired by another shooter.

CHAPTER 20

COMPROMISED

SAN JOSE, CALIFORNIA

Although she had ordered room service for herself and Meghan Gallagher, Angela Conrad closed her laptop and readied her pistol when the knock sounded at the hotel room door. Even after the steward identified himself to Conrad, Gallagher hid in the bathroom, ready to emerge shooting if he brought more than breakfast.

Conrad tipped the young man and closed the door behind him. "Clear," she announced.

Gallagher returned to her seat. "Damn, that smells good! I'm famished."

Conrad transferred the plates from the cart to the table. "Dig in then, you've earned it."

Gallagher tilted her head toward the laptop. "Who's showed up for the party so far?" she said around a mouthful of scrambled eggs.

Conrad had set up an encrypted website for her buyers to submit the resumes of their candidates for her operation. They were identified only by a codename, along with their specialty and their years of military and intelligence service. She thought she knew a couple from their reputation, but there were no pictures so she couldn't be sure. The hardest part was that the most skilled operators were French, of whom she could only take two, or Russian, whom she didn't trust enough to rely on for a vital skill set.

She pointed at two applications on the list. "I'm liking Agent *Bastille* for demolitions and Agent *Javelin* for alarm systems."

"Both of those guys French?" Gallagher asked.

"Yeah."

"You better spread out the people you absolutely can't live without, or at least recruit backup players from another country. That way any buyer pulling out at the last minute won't leave you grounded."

Conrad opened another resume. "Point taken. What do you think of this guy? He's from Japan."

"Agent *Ghost*," Gallagher read aloud, "'specialist in Atsumi and Bosch security systems, as well as Ayonix and SecuGen biometric scanners.' What kind of system are we dealing with at Nanovex?"

She frowned. "Don't know, and I'm afraid that tasking Manning to find out will either blow his cover, give us the wrong answers, or both."

"Maybe we can use him as a doorstop."

"Hold the door open for somebody else to get in and find out?"

"Exactly."

"I like it." Conrad's cell phone vibrated. "Hello?"

"Good morning," a male voice answered, "I work for the agency responsible for your recent unfortunate experience at San Jose City Hall. I'd like to speak with you in person."

She froze. Whoever it was couched their words carefully, as if they already knew the keywords that would alert the NSA to their conversation. "About what?" she asked.

"About helping you avoid another unfortunate experience."

"How did you get this number?"

"Your communications are not as secure as you thought."

The coffee she had just swallowed threatened to backwash. "How exactly can you help me?"

"Well for one thing, I have a covert agent inside the investigation who's informing me on every step of their hunt for you. And for another, I can tell you that *your* inside man is blown. They're just waiting for the next time you two meet to roll you both up."

Conrad felt like she had just been dumped in ice water. "Why are you doing this?"

"Because I know a winning team when I see one. I like being on the winning team."

"Where do you propose to meet?" she asked, fully expecting the set up for a trap.

"How about at your garage? I'm parked about a block away right now, just have the guy you left on guard open the side door for me."

What the fuck? she almost screamed aloud. How could she have been so thoroughly compromised? However it happened, her options had just been drastically reduced. The anonymous caller held all the cards; she could only wait to see what kind of hand he dealt her.

"I'll be there in half an hour," she finally managed to choke out.

SECOND THOUGHTS

SAN JOSE, CALIFORNIA

Perry Pugliano sat transfixed in the Nanovex conference room the FBI had appropriated. He had watched the YouTube video of the silver ball over Arby's three times, trying in vain to see a way out of his predicament. He kept going back to his talk with Scott Hendrix. If there *were* Nazis in the government with advanced technology at their disposal, they were apparently not only guarding Angela Conrad, but also had their sights on eliminating Nanovex's WICKER BASKET technology. And after catching Conrad's agent Mike Manning as he shadowed the two surviving scientists from that project, apparently she had *her* sights set on Nanovex as well. But to what end?

Was her organization *operating* that silver orb? On the security video from the San Jose massacre, Conrad had looked just as surprised when the ball showed up as he had been watching the video. His gut told him there was another player in this mess, but if their goals were a mystery to him, how could he hope to get ahead of them and stop the rest of the scientists from being wiped out?

Wendy Cho leaned in, startling him out of his trance. "After seeing this little ball take out Mark Wong in a flash," she said, "I'm having second thoughts about our ambush plan. I mean, how do you ambush *that*?"

"I hear you," he agreed. "But we have to do *something* to protect those people. That's our job."

"What about leaving them in the basement? I mean if I had to choose between living underground and certain death, that basement lab would start looking pretty good to me."

"But those people have families. Do we lock up their spouses and kids too? And who's to say that thing can't come right into the building after them? We have no idea what the limits of this technology are—if it has any."

She frowned. "What the hell *is* that thing? Could it really be a UFO? I mean, who has *technology* like that?"

Pugliano didn't want to burden her with what he now knew, but the UFO rumor needed to be quashed. "No, I can't imagine aliens going to the trouble of picking off American scientists. Our technology couldn't be a threat to them. Whatever the hell that thing is, there's a *human* somewhere driving."

"Then what do we do?"

He leaned back and sighed. "That's one *hell* of a good question. I'd like to collar Manning right now and sweat the truth out of him, but we need him to get to Conrad. She's the one with the answers."

"Do you think he *will* lead us back to Conrad? Maybe she's too careful for that."

"Has he reported in after he followed those two scientists down to their lab?"

She glanced over at the technicians manning the video and audio terminals monitoring Manning's every move. They shook their heads. "No, not a peep."

"That means he's planning on making the report in person."

She had a pained look. "So what if he does, sir? How do we know we'll have any better luck grabbing Conrad than those CIA and Israeli commandos she slaughtered?"

The young lady has a point. "I guess we'll just have to bring along some Stinger missiles for that little silver ball and find out."

DANCE PARTNER

SAN JOSE, CALIFORNIA

Hendrix was walking on a mile-high tightrope without a net, and he knew it. His heart pumped and his gut worked itself into a knot as he walked the last block to Conrad's garage command post. Because he was off the reservation now, he had no backup. If Conrad shot him on sight, no one at the CIA would even know where to look for his body. He could only hope the offer he brought to the table would be good enough to preserve his life. With a player like Conrad, any other outcome would be swift and lethal. He knocked twice on the side entrance, paused, and knocked once more. Linn Shaozang opened the door.

"Good morning, Mr. Hendrix, please come in," he said in a quiet, even tone.

Hendrix surveyed the dark interior. The morning sun made a futile attempt to penetrate a row of dirty windows near the roof. "Who else is here?" he asked, careful not to reveal his ongoing relationship to Shaozang to other ears.

"We are alone, you may speak freely."

"How long until she arrives?"

"Five minutes or less." Shaozang gestured toward the rear of the garage. "If you wait in the shadows, it will give you a tactical advantage when she arrives. I must go open the door for her."

"And if she turns on me, whose side will you be on?"

Shaozang smiled politely. "Yours, of course. It would be difficult for you to pay me if you are deceased, yes?"

"Great to know where your loyalties lie."

He bowed his head slightly. "Indeed. If you will excuse me."

Before he even reached his station at the front door, Shaozang's cellphone rang. He answered it then pressed a button on the wall to raise the roll-up door facing the street. A black SUV charged in and he closed the door behind it. The garage plunged once again into twilight as two security men jumped from the vehicle, their weapons at low ready; drawn but not aimed directly at him. Conrad emerged a few seconds later.

"Where is he?" she asked Shaozang.

"Here," Hendrix called, stepping from behind a parts rack.

"Did you search him?" she whispered to Shaozang.

"You did not order me to do so," he replied innocently.

"Dammit!" she scathed. "Isn't that *common sense*?"

"To answer your question," Hendrix said, "I am armed, but I hardly think I would have come alone if I wanted a fight. And since I'm here entirely without authorization of my employer, I hardly think carrying a recording device would be in my best interest."

"Who the hell are you?"

"My name is Scott Hendrix; I'm the CIA station chief for San Francisco."

"If you're acting without authorization, then why are you here?" she demanded.

"Because of a mistake you made, Ms. Conrad."

"How's that?" she snapped.

He walked toward her, keeping his hands plainly visible. "I was in the white van that impacted the back of your truck at San Jose City Hall. Because you didn't search that van thoroughly, I'm still alive. So I'm here today to return the favor." He pointed to his sport coat. "I have a gift for you that will prove my identity." He held up his left hand. "Breast pocket. Two fingers."

She nodded. "Slowly."

He extracted a thumb drive and offered it to her. "This is the WICKER BASKET briefing I received from Doug Lyman at Nanovex. Actually I'm just returning it to you. I took it off the body of Izrah Nadzim."

Her eyes widened. "Really?"

"Really. I was watching your meeting at Hunter's Point on satellite. When I saw a car go into the drink it made me *very* curious who was in it. So I dove the wreck, retrieved Mr. Nadzim's passport and *this*," holding out the thumb drive. "Think of it as a peace offering."

She ignored his outstretched hand. "How did you find me?"

"As I said, your communications are not as secure as you would hope," he lied. Had Shaozang not given her phone number up, he would be just as clueless as the FBI. "However, I have not made that weakness known to my agency. And with my position, I can *keep* that weakness hidden."

"I take it that since you're acting without authorization, this peace you're offering applies only to yourself, right?"

He lowered the hand holding the drive to his side. "Correct, unfortunately."

"So what does making peace with you do for me?"

"As I said on the phone, I'm offering you a direct line from the inside of the FBI and the CIA's hunt for you. You'll know everything I know, when I know it. Also, your inside man's been burned. What I'm…."

"How?" she interrupted. "*How* was he burned?"

"The security footage from the Sheraton, on the day you killed that Saudi, Rashid Ben-Jabir. The FBI analyzed the hell out of those images to get a positive ID on you and the man you were with. Facial recognition latched onto you pretty quickly, but we drew a blank on Manning. That is, until the FBI Special Agent-in-Charge sat across the table from him at Nanovex. He was pretty well screwed at that point."

She blinked hard. "So *that's* how you tracked me to City Hall?"

"Bingo. I learned my lesson from that little encounter, but the FBI still thinks they can do better. They've got Manning by the belt loops and are just waiting for the next time you two meet to take you down, or die trying."

She shook her head. "I followed him like a bloodhound to make sure he didn't have a tail. I swept his car for electronics. Hell, I even grabbed him off the street to see if anyone reacted. Nothing!"

"When?"

"Two days ago."

He chuckled. "The tail was only fully operational yesterday. You and the FBI just missed each other. Trust me, he's a Wi-Fi hotspot by now."

"*Shit*," she whispered. "Okay, you have my attention. What do you want in return?"

"First, I want WICKER BASKET as badly as you do. I had a deal in place with Doug Lyman to move the project offshore, but I can't do that if you keep killing off the scientists who developed the technology. That's gotta stop."

She shook her head. "I have *no* idea what you're talking about."

"Gimme a break. I saw the videotape of that little silver ball you used at the City Hall massacre. I've also seen the video of that same silver ball killing a Nanovex scientist last night. That's the other thing I want; access to the technology of that ball."

"Hey, you and me both! That thing just *showed up* at City Hall. I admit it saved my life, but who was driving it and why, I have no fucking idea."

One of Conrad's men looked back at her. "Silver ball?" he asked in an English accent. "What the hell are you two yapping about?"

"Later!" she snapped.

Hendrix's stomach sank. "So if *you're* not killing the scientists at Nanovex, then who the hell is?"

"Damned if I know! All I care about is getting my hands on the WICKER BASKET technology. If I can do that without killing the scientists who created it, so much the better. Hell, if I leave them alone, they may build something *else* worth stealing."

Oh shit. Conrad wasn't holding the cards he thought. But he had asked the devil to dance, and there was no cutting out on this partner. His mind raced. The first thing he realized was that if Conrad wasn't killing the scientists, whoever *was* would finish the job shortly and his hopes of reconstituting the project overseas were moot. The people who knew the nuts and bolts of WICKER BASKET would take those secrets to the grave.

So the only person who could deliver that technology to him now was Conrad. Time to make an offer.

"Okay, I understand," he said. "But your inside man is still burned. I take it that will make things more difficult for you?"

She let out a bitter laugh. "Uh, *yeah*."

"Then I offer myself as your new inside man. What's our goal?"

She stared at him for several seconds. "I'm putting together a team to break into Nanovex and steal as much data and materials pertaining to the WICKER BASKET project as I can get my hands on."

"And then?"

Another short staring contest. "And then sell it to the highest bidder. I have several prospective buyers lined up."

"Excellent. All I ask for is a copy of the data you acquire and a portion of the nanoagent before you sell the rest."

"The deal I've made the buyers is exclusive technology access to whoever wins the auction. They'd be less than happy if they found out I had violated their exclusivity by sharing access with the CIA."

"Not as unhappy as they'd be when you didn't deliver because the FBI had shot you on sight. Which *would* have been the outcome if I hadn't stepped forward."

She frowned, then extended her hand. "Fair enough. I believe that's mine."

He handed over the thumb drive. "Partners?"

She grudgingly shook hands. "Partners."

SATELLITE

DECEMBER 9, 1965 – DUGWAY PROVING GROUNDS, UTAH

Hans Kammler, alias "Dr. Schmidt," surveyed the work site at an isolated corner of the test range. The Bell rested inside a copy of the test stand from the Wenceslas Mines in Poland. Only this test stand was built of structural steel rather than reinforced concrete. The destructive emanations of the Bell rendered the stand unusable after only a few runs, but the Americans swiftly tore down and rebuilt the fixture with fresh steel once a week, burying the corrupted metal in the desert. The Americans were slow learners, but the resources at their command were staggering to Kammler, who had become a master of achieving much with little.

"Dr. Schmidt?" he heard behind him.

It was Colonel Armstrong, the American in charge of the Bell's test program. To Kammler, Armstrong was the epitome of the American scientific method. While the German scientists working for Kammler had to provide detailed calculations to justify any variation in an experimental plan, the Americans simply said, "let's try this!" when confronted with an obstacle. Kammler referred to it as "science by bulldozer." Any attempt to sway the Americans from their wasteful approach would be met with scorn and a variation of the comment, "It was good enough to beat your Nazi ass, wasn't it?" He had given up on converting them to a more efficient approach.

"Dr. Schmidt," Armstrong continued, "I'm concerned about the test bed." He kicked the granite chips at his feet, many of which were already covered with a putrescent black coating. "If we're having visitors this afternoon, I don't want the slightest risk of contamination."

Dugway Proving Grounds in Utah was the test site for America's chemical and biological weapons programs. Located in magnificent isolation over a hundred kilometers southwest of Salt Lake City, parts of Dugway were so contaminated from airborne tests of anthrax, phosgene, and other deadly substances during World War II that two decades later dozens of square kilometers were still off limits even to base personnel.

The Bell test stand was one such off-limits location.

Although the continuing Nazi science effort in South America had long since rendered this prototype version of the Bell obsolete, it was still so far ahead of American know-how that they gladly accepted its deadly side effects in their quest for the Kammler's secret knowledge. Because of the incredibly high frequency and power of the Bell's radiation, the molecular structure of most matter was destabilized in its presence, the effect that had killed the five technicians during its first test back in Germany, and rendered the underground test chambers at Pilsen unstable after only several minutes of operation. That destabilization effect was visible all around the test stand, where the soil itself had fused into a reddish, toxic wasteland resembling burnt syrup for hundreds of meters in every direction. [1]

Kammler's test group during the war had discovered that ceramic firebricks used in kilns and ovens were remarkably resistant to the Bell's radiation. The base of the test stand at Wenceslas Mines had been lined with the firebricks. Instead, the Americans used native blue granite, strip-mined from the base of a nearby mountain. The chipped granite, spread in a hundred-meter circle around the test stand, was replaced every week, then reburied in the same strip mine from whence it came. But because of the higher power levels the Americans were using in preparation for tonight's test, the rock bed was corrupting faster than expected.

"If you are concerned about the safety of your visitors, Colonel Armstrong," Kammler said, "then the test bed should be replaced before proceeding."

"No time," Armstrong declared with finality. "I've ordered a fresh layer of gravel spread over the top of it." He pointed to a caravan of dump trucks, the first of which had already deposited its load of blue granite. A bulldozer moved into position to spread the rocks.

"As you wish, Colonel," Kammler muttered. *This must be America, because there's the bulldozer.* Actually *two* bulldozers, if he counted the Colonel.

Armstrong walked past the sentries and climbed onto the flatbed truck bearing the canvas-covered Bell. He lifted a corner of the tarp, revealing the runic inscriptions running around the base of the device. "I've been meaning to ask you, Dr. Schmidt, what do these inscriptions say? [2]

Kammler regarded the runes with a twinge of nostalgia, although he was too leery of the Bell's radioactive footprint even when inactive to join Armstrong for a closer inspection. As a member of Himmler's inner circle, the Knights of the Black Sun, the occult symbols harkened back to a time when ideological purity was all Germany needed to conquer its foes. It read, "*Towards the new age, victory and hail to greater Germany, fighting for the world, hail to the new empire!*" He revolted inwardly at the reversals of fortune that led him to work as a vassal for this mongrelized American. He reminded himself of *Herr* Bormann's philosophy for the Nazi organization in exile; those with superior ideas who take the long view of history will triumph in the end. If not in this generation, perhaps in the next.

"The runes were something Himmler ordered," he lied. "I have no idea what they say."

* * *

The entourage from NASA arrived at Dugway at one in the afternoon. Kammler couldn't help but recollect the arrival at Wenceslas Mines in Poland of a similar bureaucratic entourage more than twenty years previously. Only now he was wearing a civilian business suit instead of an SS uniform. Thankfully he had brought several lightweight cotton suits with him from South America. Even though it was early December, the temperature in the Utah desert was nearly thirty degrees Celsius in the noonday sun.

Kammler walked with Colonel Armstrong to meet the occupants of the lead staff car. He resisted smiling when he saw his former engineer Kurt Debus emerge from the vehicle. *Herr* Debus was now the Director of the Cape Canaveral launch complex, renamed the Kennedy Space Center in honor of the slain president. That this tribute had been carried out by President Johnson, the direct beneficiary of Kennedy's assassination, made the irony almost unbearable to contemplate with a straight face.

Of course, he could not acknowledge Debus in any way. That would invite questions which could endanger the fragile working relationship he had cultivated with the Americans, and perhaps Debus's exalted position as well. He merely gave him a respectful nod as Armstrong introduced Debus and NASA's Assistant Director, Wallace Seagraves, a swarthy, cigar-chomping bureaucrat.

Seagraves removed the cigar from his mouth with a self-important flourish. "So, Dr. Schmidt, what are we going to see here today?"

Kammler gestured toward the Bell, now mounted on its stand inside the test ring. "What I hope to demonstrate, gentlemen, is nothing less than a revolution in the American space program. This device was designed as a simple centrifuge for uranium enrichment. Because of its unique configuration, we discovered it had other properties, in addition to being an exceptional uranium enrichment device."

"Anti-gravity," Seagraves expounded, quite proud of his knowledge.

"Not exactly," Kammler tactfully corrected. "The Bell generates an electromagnetic force along its axis. It simply moves in the direction you point it."

"Well, where the hell else would you *want* it to go, except *up*?" Seagraves scoffed.

Kammler smiled politely. "The first wartime application for the Bell was to be in submarines," he said, making a diving motion with his hand. "You see, we also found that in addition to its propulsive qualities, it also generated a significant amount of electrical power. Very useful aboard a ship."

"So it's a nuclear reactor too?"

"Not in the conventional sense. That was another one of the Bell's breakthroughs. We found that once it was placed in motion, it generated significantly more electricity than was required for its operation."

Seagraves laughed, exposing the teeth that clamped his cigar. "Are you telling me you got some kind of god-damned perpetual motion machine here, Dr. Schmidt?"

Kammler noted Kurt Debus's pained expression. *Look what I have to put up with* was the unspoken message in Debus's eyes.

He shook his head. "Not at all, Mr. Seagraves. If you shut off the electrical power, the Bell *will* stop. I'm simply saying it produces more power than it takes in."

"A perpetual motion machine," Seagraves insisted.

"A power-producing uranium motor is more accurate." He didn't mention that a *mercury* motor was just as efficient and far less dangerous

That information would only be provided if the Americans delivered on their end of the bargain. Until then, they would just have to live with the prototype Bell's hazardous side effects.

Debus finally spoke up. "Dr. Schmidt, I understand that, its immediate applications aside, the Bell has opened up insights into whole new areas of physics, is that correct?"

"Correct, Mr. Debus," he replied, even though their dialogue was entirely for Seagraves's education. "We found that the electricity the Bell generated was drawn directly from the universe itself, from a dimension coincident with our own but inaccessible without the extraordinary conditions created inside the Bell. This revelation allowed us to theorize whole new applications unrelated to power or propulsion."

Seagraves's eyes became unfocused.

"For instance, by focusing the vacuum energy the Bell creates on a specific point in space, we can create explosive heating or cooling at any point in the atmosphere."

The bureaucrat perked up. "Did you say explosive *cooling*?"

He nodded. "If one can draw energy *from* a parallel dimension, why can one not send it *back* as well? Imagine the destruction if you suddenly extracted every calorie of energy from a cubic mile of atmosphere above a target? The air would rush in on itself and implode on the target, crushing it like a hammer."

Seagraves's cigar drooped as his jaw slackened.

"Or consider defense against Russian missiles," he continued. "Imagine if when you detected an inbound rocket you could heat the atmosphere in the warhead's path to the melting point of steel. The skies over America could become impenetrable to attack."

Seagraves jerked his thumb at the Bell. "You learned how to do all that from *this* contraption?"

Kammler's justifiable pride grew as he spoke. "Indeed. We are also investigating other uses for this technology, such as projecting the vacuum energy from the Bell into large stretches of the atmosphere for weather control, into the ground to trigger earthquakes, or to release dangerous fault line tension to prevent them."

Seagraves huffed. "All I want to know is if the damned thing flies or not."

Pearls before swine, Kammler mused. "Yes, Assistant Director Seagraves, the Bell will most assuredly fly."

The man had already turned away, jerking his head for Debus to follow. "Show me."

Debus exchanged a tiny smirk with Kammler before walking to the observation platform, two hundred meters distant.

Kammler nodded to Colonel Armstrong, who shouted orders setting the test into motion. He joined the NASA bureaucrats on the platform; his staff and the Army personnel they had trained were fully capable of running this simple demonstration without his assistance. By the time he had taken his seat the familiar turbine whine of the Bell's rotors rising to speed had been replaced by the penetrating buzz of the high-voltage switching used to release the flow of vacuum energy.

"Why are we sitting so far away?" Seagraves complained.

He was losing patience with this *apparatchik*. "Because sitting any closer would be uniformly lethal," he deadpanned. Seagraves straightened in his chair but did not reply.

The Bell lifted majestically off its stand and rose until it was twenty meters in the air above the test ring, straining on its three tethers anchored to the structural steel girders. Even at this distance, Kammler felt a tingle on his skin and a metallic taste in his mouth. He was sure he was just imagining these sensations because he knew they were the first symptoms of the Bell's biological ill effects. They should be completely safe at this distance. But the Americans had insisted on running the Bell at full power, measuring the tension it produced on the tethers as a gauge of its propulsive force. Perhaps the vacuum energy field extended even this far under these extreme conditions.

Suddenly the Bell jerked upward and a shot-like crack filled the air. After the first tether snapped, the second followed immediately. The third endured for a few eternal seconds longer, the Bell whipping around the test ring like a rock on a rope, the vibration of the taut steel cable singing like a bizarre stringed instrument.

"Get down!" Armstrong shouted. "Everybody under the platform!"

Before anyone could move for shelter, the final tether snapped like a whip and the Bell soared upward, trailing vapor as it accelerated through the sound barrier and punched through a cloud high above the desert plain. Kammler blinked in bewilderment. The work of his life during those trying war years had just vanished into the deep blue Utah sky. A tense silence settled over the platform.

"Colonel Armstrong," he said evenly, "did you replace the tether cables for this test as I suggested?"

"One of them," he replied defensively. "There wasn't time to replace them all."

"I see."

"How far can it go?" Armstrong demanded, eager to shift the focus off his failure. "It'll come back down, won't it?"

"Oh yes Colonel, it will return to earth, eventually."

Armstrong looked ill. "Where?"

He shrugged. "I'm quite sure I don't know. Perhaps you should ask these gentlemen from NASA to track it for you. You may have just launched your own satellite."

* * *

4:45 PM, DECEMBER 9, 1965 – KECKSBURG, PENNSYLVANIA

When the sonic boom shook his house, auto mechanic Greg White wriggled out from under the Ford he was working on in his driveway. He looked up in time to see a line of blue smoke at low altitude, trailing west to east. Then the ground shook under him. A few seconds later he heard an impact in the woods behind his house.

His wife burst from the back door. "Greg! Are you okay?"

He squirmed to his feet. "Yeah, I'm fine."

"I thought the car you were working on blew up!"

His eyes remained fixed on the woods. Blue smoke rose above the trees. "*Something* blew up. You better call the sheriff. Looks like a plane crashed just east of here." He was already fishing for his car keys.

She knew better than to try to dissuade her volunteer firefighter husband from taking action. "I will. Be careful, honey."

With daylight fading, White grabbed a flashlight, hopped in his pickup, and took the farm road leading in the direction of the crash. In ten minutes he was as close as the dirt road would take him. The smoke continued curling above the trees some distance to the north. He pulled off the road and set off on foot across the hilly terrain.

An hour later it was almost completely dark and White was about to abandon his search. Whatever it was that crashed had not sparked a larger fire, and without the flames to guide him through the thick brush, a ground search was pointless. He resolved to crest the next ridge then return home.

Hiking up the hill, he noticed a tree that had been clipped in half. Shining his flashlight upward he found another severed trunk in a line that led over the hill. The damage looked fresh; the scattered branches on the forest floor hadn't even wilted yet. He climbed faster.

White had expected to find a military jet, hopefully with an ejected pilot nearby. At the very least he expected to find a private plane, probably without survivors from the sound of the impact. But what he found was something completely different. It appeared to be a space capsule, twelve feet long and about eight feet in diameter. It had hit the top of the ridge and dug a trench a hundred feet long down to the foot on the far side. It wasn't smoking anymore, but he could hear the groan and pop of cooling metal. Then he remembered that *Gemini VII* had launched just a few days previously, with a goal of staying in orbit for fourteen days. Apparently they didn't make it.

White moved as fast as he dared down the broken hillside, tripping over underbrush as he went. If it was the *Gemini* capsule, something had gone terribly wrong. There was no sign of the capsule's parachutes, so the astronauts inside were almost certainly dead. As he got closer, a mechanical sound made him stop short. It reminded him of a gyroscope winding down, but much louder, with an occasional grinding sound like a bearing going out. He played his flashlight across the capsule from fifty feet away, and got another shock.

If this *was* a space capsule, it wasn't American, and it certainly wasn't *Gemini*. It looked like a big acorn half-buried in the ground. The back end had a fat rim like a bumper running around the circumference. Strange symbols were inscribed on the bumper in some kind of foreign language. White had handled Russian hardware in the Army, and this writing didn't look Russian to him. His mind was running through even more frightening possibilities for the object's origins when he began feeling strange. The whole front of his body tingled, and his mouth tasted like he was sucking on a handful of pennies. He couldn't remember what the symptoms for radiation poisoning were, but was afraid he had just found out. Giving the object a last once-over with his flashlight, he turned away and retreated to the top of the hill. To his relief, the symptoms decreased with distance.

He had just started hiking back to his truck when he heard shouts behind him. Most likely the sheriff's search party, probably with his fellow volunteers from the fire department assisting. Climbing back to the top of the ridge, he looked over. In the hollow below, a squad of soldiers swarmed around the capsule. He thought about walking down and warning them about the object's possible radioactivity, but stopped when he heard an officer shout, "And if anybody gets too close, shoot 'em!"

Deciding his civic duty had been satisfied, White started back toward his truck. A few minutes later he heard a scream, thick with pain and terror. Then another, in a different voice. Then all manner of shouts and confusion, but the screams continued. White ran the rest of the way back to his truck. He was still shaking when he reached the cordon of soldiers blocking the road to his house. He learned the village of Kecksburg was now under military quarantine.[3]

[1] In his book *Reich of the Black Sun*, Joseph Farrell theorizes that during the 1960s, the Nazi Bell had made its way to the United States for testing, but he did not speculate where such testing might have taken place. In his report on Dugway Proving Ground, investigator Joseph P. Skipper noted the strange cage-like apparatus below and the apparently contaminated ground surrounding it, but made no conjectures concerning its origin. It is the author's theory based on the pictures below that this could well be the (abandoned?) test stand for the Bell here in the United States.

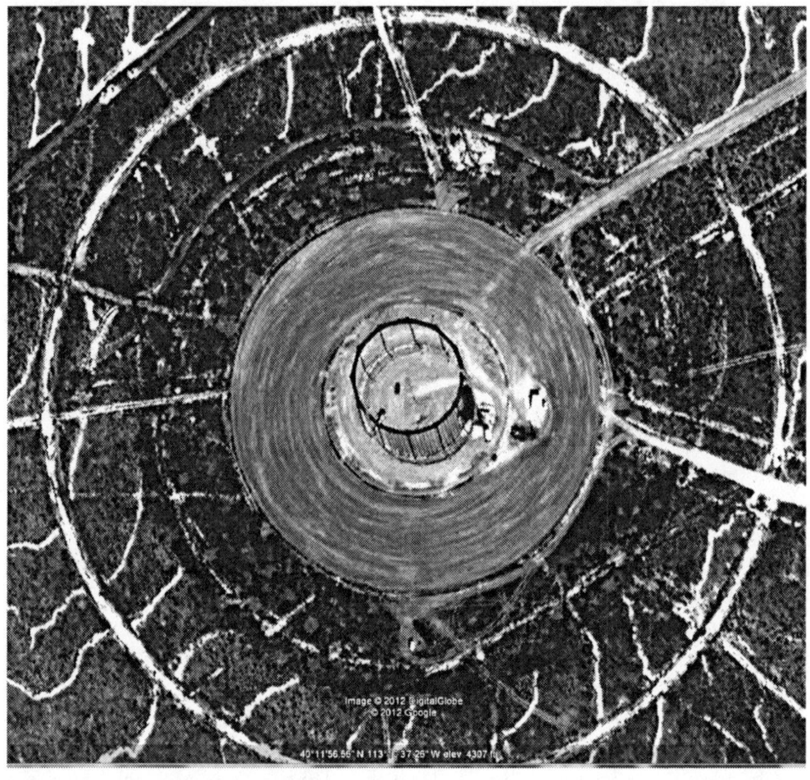

The grayish-blue rock deposited around the cage-like apparatus is strip-mined several miles away. It was selected because it is apparently unaffected by whatever discolored the underlying strata, or the gravel-like material was easier to collect and dispose of. Whichever the case, it is obviously present to provide a stable and/or uncontaminated surface for equipment servicing the cage-like apparatus. Compare this to the photograph of the Henge in the footnotes to chapter 4.

A commenter on Farrell's blog pointed out that this apparatus is called the West Vertical Grid, used for detailed 3-D plume recording of chemical or biological weapons. It is not; the WVG is over five miles west of this point. Neither does the dispersal of toxic chemicals explain the "pepperoni pizza effect" at the clearly abandoned test site 0.7 miles northeast of the above location.

The anomalous coloration of the soil (reddish brown vs. the moonscape-gray of the natural soil) is clearly visible, although is apparently not so toxic that a road can't be built directly through it, rather than driving around it, as obviously had been the case at some point in the past. Note the circles of unaffected soil inside the contaminated zone; this is not the pattern that would result from chemical spray tests. Another mechanism is at work, perhaps even the operation of a Bell-like device.

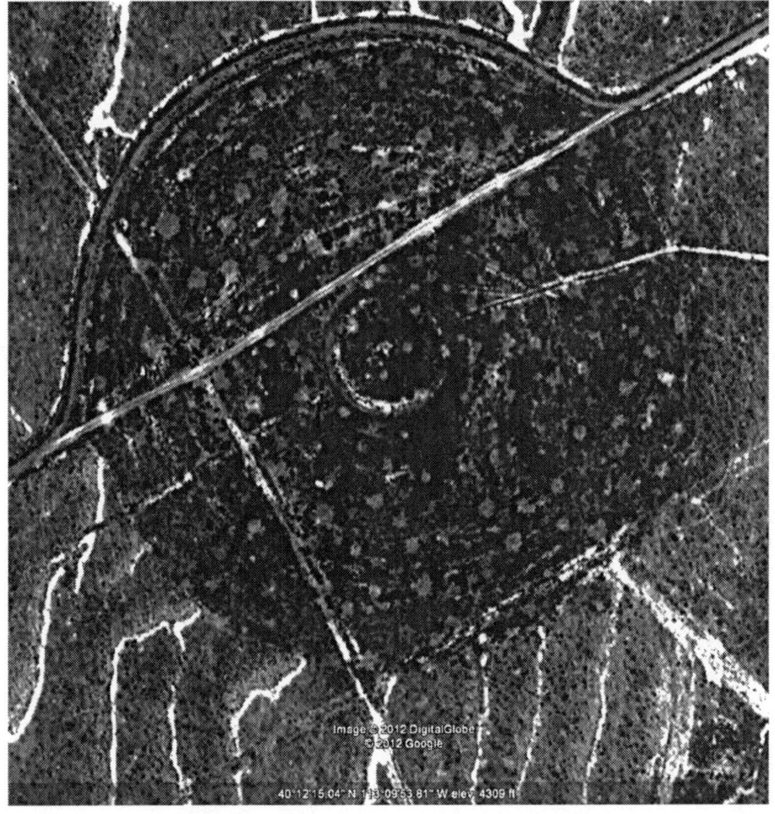

[2] Thule is the legendary celestial origin of the Aryan race in German occultist mythology, also sometimes referred to as the Black Sun. Below is

the symbol of the Black Sun adopted by the Thule Society of pre-war Germany. Based on eyewitnesses from the Kecksburg incident who reported "hieroglyphs" around the rim of the device, I believe the runic inscriptions around the edge of this symbol were also inscribed on the Bell.

[3] The Greg White character is a composite of several witnesses of the Kecksburg UFO crash. Below is a sketch one of them made of the crash site. Also below is the sketch made by a witness named "Myron," who was tasked by the Air Force to deliver 6,500 double-glazed firebricks made by his family's Dayton, Ohio company. He was told they would be used to build "a double-walled shield around a recovered radioactive object." When he made the delivery to Wright-Patterson Air Force Base, he glanced inside the hangar where the object was stored and made the sketch below. (Source: *Reich of the Black Sun* by Joseph Farrell, p. 337-344)

Farrell points out that the Air Force's decision to shield the recovered object with firebricks instead of more conventional radioactivity shielding (i.e., lead sheets), indicates a familiarity with the object and the necessary precautions to handle it safely. This led him to the conclusion that the Bell and the Kecksburg UFO were likely one and the same. The circumstances leading up to the Bell's arrival in Kecksburg are entirely the author's fiction.

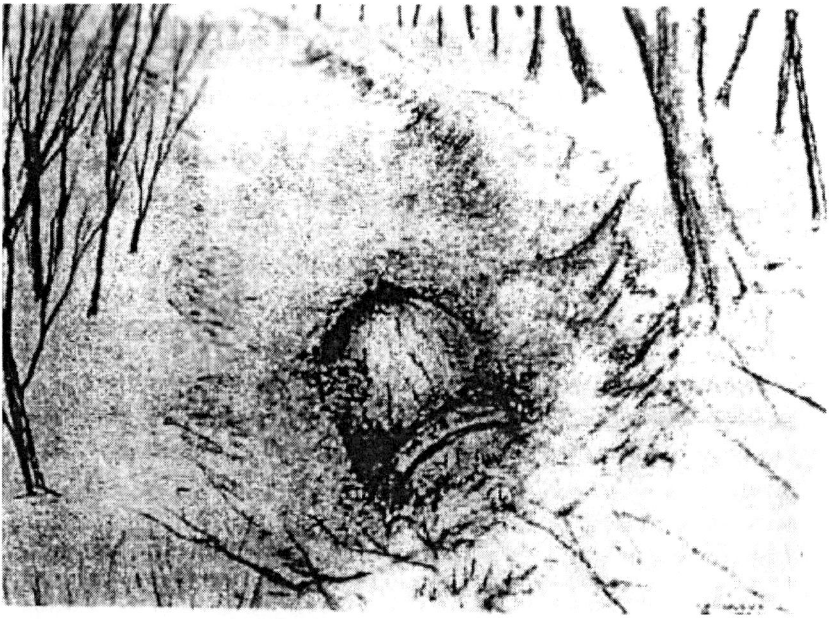

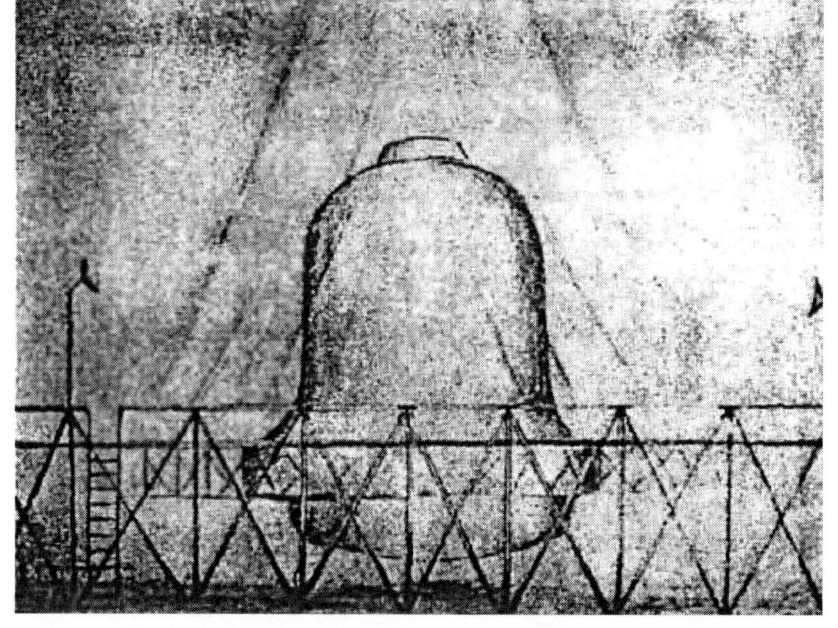

CHAPTER 21

SURPRISES

PRESENT DAY – SAN JOSE, CALIFORNIA

Scott Hendrix was still trapped in an uneasy stand-off with Angela Conrad. "So," he asked, "what's the first assignment for your new inside man?"

"We need to find out what kind of security system Nanovex is running," she finally replied. "Unless you're an expert in that field yourself, my guess is the best way to accomplish that would be for you to smuggle someone inside to look around."

"Who someone?"

She looked around at her crew. "Probably Linn. He's our resident electronics expert at the moment. Linn, you up to it?"

"If the mission is limited to acquiring the type and scope of the system, yes, my skills will be adequate to the task," Shaozang said.

"Excellent," she replied, waving a hand in Shaozang's direction. "Mr. Hendrix, Linn Shaozang. He's your payload. Get him inside Nanovex. Oh, and I'd like him back *out* too, if that's not too much trouble."

Hendrix extended his hand, as if he and Shaozang had never met. "A pleasure. You got some place where I can sketch the layout for you?"

"My office," Conrad answered for him, pointing to the rear of the garage. "I'll be back in an hour. You can brief me on your game plan then."

Hendrix and Shaozang nodded their acknowledgement. Shaozang motioned for Hendrix to follow him.

Gallagher walked to Conrad's side. "*That* was an unexpected development," she whispered.

She nodded. "Yeah, and I really *hate* surprises." She jerked her head toward the office. "Keep an eye on them."

RESOLVE

CHICAGO, ILLINOIS

Simon Crane was about to leave for lunch when his private phone rang. He checked the caller's identity before picking up. "Report."

"The FBI is not backing down," his agent reported. "I'm concerned there's going to be a bloodbath. Another bloodbath," he corrected.

"That would be unfortunate. And hopefully unnecessary. Can you not complete your mission despite their interference? Perhaps you're not using the tools I provided to their full capacity."

During a thoughtful pause, his agent no doubt considered the ramifications of failure. "They have the remaining scientists locked up in the basement of the Nanovex building, with a full detachment of FBI agents and Nanovex security on twenty-four-hour watch. Would you order me to attack them on those terms, sir?"

"So they understand our objectives and have mobilized their resources to frustrate them?"

"Not only that, sir, but they're planning to draw me out using a decoy and stage an ambush with the full resources the FBI can muster."

Crane let out a harsh chuckle. "It's not going to be much of an ambush if you already know about it."

"No sir, I merely wished to illustrate the depth of their resolve to protect the remaining scientists. How would you like me to proceed?"

Do your damned job was his instinctive response, but the young man had a point. The FBI's *resolve* was what needed a frontal assault, not those poor doomed scientists. "Put your operations on hold for the moment," he ordered. "I'll deal with the FBI."

EYE OF MORDOR

SAN JOSE, CALIFORNIA

Angela Conrad looked up from the desk. "Okay, good plan. Looks like I underestimated you guys from the CIA."

"We have flashes of competence," Hendrix replied.

"What else?" she asked.

He pushed a piece of paper across to her. "Here's the tech we'll need."

She squinted and moved the paper away slightly. *Dammit I do <u>not</u> need glasses! That can <u>not</u> happen!* "Okay," she pronounced after a few moments, "we have most of this; the rest shouldn't be a problem. Linn, can you handle the acquisitions?"

"Of course."

She slid the list over to him. "Hop to it, then."

After Shaozang left, she leaned over the desk. "Okay Hendrix, out with it. You've been itching for him to leave since I got here. What's on your mind?"

Hendrix frowned. "I'm concerned about Manning. It's not going to take the FBI long to realize you've cut him loose. Then they're going to scoop him up and pick his brain for everything you've ever said or done in his presence. I know you've been careful, but even the smallest misstep could turn out to be your undoing. The fact that I'm sitting across from you right now is evidence enough of that."

"Maybe I need to give him a good-bye call. Remind him we can still get to his family if he doesn't keep his mouth shut."

His eyebrows rose. "Can you? The FBI has his wife and kids under round-the-clock surveillance as we speak."

She stiffened. *Oh crap.*

A slight smile. "Didn't know that, did you? Once their surveillance team turns into a *protective* detail, your threats may ring a little hollow."

This job was like a slippery prize fish, always trying to squirm out of her grasp before she could haul it into the boat. "So we kill him then?"

He shrugged. "Easier said than done. The FBI is fixated on Manning like the Eye of Mordor. Even if you get to him, your shooter will probably be killed, or worse, captured."

"For my new partner, you're not being very helpful," she fumed. "Got any suggestions on what we *should* do?"

Another wry smile. "I've always liked the strategy, *hit 'em where they ain't.* Right now, they only have a *surveillance* team around Manning's family. Maybe we should make a move before that changes."

SHOPPING PARTNER

CHICAGO, ILLINOIS

Amanda Manning walked to the mailbox. More bills and junk mail. Not even a catalog or an ad for a decent sale. She slammed shut the mailbox door. She was in a funk, and wasn't even sure why. She hated to admit it, but she was missing Mike badly. *Selfish bastard; women have needs too*, as if he cared. He'd better not be getting *his* needs satisfied while she lay in bed by herself.

She stifled the thought. He said he had never even been tempted to wander, and she believed him. He sounded pretty miserable on the phone. Damn him, why did he have to take this job in San Francisco without even *talking* to her about it? She finished her curbside sorting of the mail and walked back toward the house. She heard an SUV stop behind her.

"Hey neighbor!" a female voice called.

Amanda turned to see a slender blonde a little younger than herself perched high above her in a Cadillac Escalade, a situation Mike called "Bambi in a tank." She didn't know the woman, but she wore a warm smile with perfect white teeth. Amanda shielded her eyes with her hand to get a better look. "Oh, hi," she ventured.

"I'm Jenny McIntyre, we just moved in up the street."

She was a very pretty girl, even with the fake blonde hair. "Nice to meet you. Where did you move from?"

"Springfield. I can't *wait* to go shopping at someplace other than Wal-Mart or Target!"

Amanda laughed. "I'll bet!" That would certainly be *her* idea of hell.

The woman sucked in a startled breath. "Oh! Where did you get those sandals?"

She looked down and turned her foot for inspection. "These? I just picked them up at Macy's."

"Oh, they are so *cute*!" Jenny gushed. "The beads match your tights just *perfectly*."

Okay, she's pretty <u>*and*</u> *she has good taste. I like her*. She made a dismissive motion with her hand. "Oh, stop! These are just my errand-running clothes."

Jenny leaned out the window. "Hey, let's go shopping!"

Amanda almost ran for her purse. She could desperately use the distraction, but she checked her watch. "Oh, I can't! The boys will be home any minute."

Shopping lust glistened in Jenny's eyes. "How about tomorrow?"

Her pulse quickened. "That would be great."

"Pick you up at ten?"

She felt her toes curl. "It's a date!"

Jenny floored her Escalade and waved out the window. "See ya, tomorrow, girlfriend!"

Amanda waved back, basking in a warm glow. The older she got, the more important her female friends became to her, and it looked like she had just made a good one.

* * *

Jenny McIntyre rounded the corner and voice dialed her "husband" and fellow FBI surveillance specialist.

"Agent Fisher, I've made contact," she said.

"Excellent," she heard over the speaker. "What's next?"

"We're going shopping tomorrow."

"No way! You did that on first contact?"

"It's my feminine wiles, Fisher."

He laughed. "Don't use them on me, then! My wife wouldn't appreciate it."

"Betcha lunch I buy her a pair of shoes and she spills her guts like I was her long-lost sister."

"You're on! I like steak, by the way."

She gave him a very unladylike snort. “Ha! Too bad you’re buying fish!”

SHUTDOWN

SAN FRANCISCO, CALIFORNIA

For once Perry Pugliano was at his desk when his phone rang. His corner office was becoming alien territory as he ran from one end of the Bay area to the other trying to keep his insufficient assets in play. Pugliano didn’t recognize the caller ID, other than the 202 area code—Washington, DC. That gave him a bad feeling, but took the call anyway.

“Special Agent Pugliano,” he heard, “please hold for Director Fitzmaurice.”

His apprehension grew. He had met the FBI Director at a conference in Washington, but had no contact with the man since then. He took that as a good thing; Fitzmaurice had a reputation as a political operative with no expertise other than his own upward mobility.

“Perry? This is Bill Fitzmaurice. How are you today?”

His already energized defenses went up another notch. Any bureaucrat who barely knows you but acts like your long-lost pal is usually up to no good. “I’m well, Mr. Director. And yourself?”

Fitzmaurice sighed theatrically. “Actually, Perry, I’ve got a problem.”

Grab the Vaseline, here it comes. “What would that be, sir?”

“I understand you’ve been spending a lot of time at a company called Nanovex.”

Huh? “Yes sir, they’re involved in some very sensitive work for the Defense Department and two of their people have been murdered. They requested federal assistance.”

“Well, a lot of people want to make a federal case out of every problem that comes their way. We don’t have the resources for that.”

“I understand that, sir, but….”

“And what *really* disturbs me is that this case is sucking people off the San Jose massacre investigation. To be blunt, I don’t see why you should be devoting manpower to anything but that.”

No, his mind shouted. *This man cannot be that stupid!* “Sir, we have evidence that our primary suspect in the massacre, Angela Conrad, has a clear interest in the project the dead scientists were working on at Nanovex. Pursuing the Nanovex case is an integral part of the massacre investigation.”

“I don’t see it.”

He is that stupid! “Sir, if you’ll let me explain….”

"Special Agent-in-Charge Pugliano," Fitzmaurice cut him off, emphasizing each word of his title as a reminder of what could be taken from him. "I am giving you a *direct* order to cease all involvement with Nanovex. You have until the end of the day to have every one of your people off their property, period."

Tact, his self-preservation instinct cautioned. "Sir, I am not questioning your authority, but…."

"You don't need to worry about questioning my authority, Agent Pugliano. These orders come straight from the President. You got a problem, take it up with him. *Do you* have a problem, Agent Pugliano?"

"No sir," he replied immediately, adding, "message received and understood," like the good Marine he still was.

"Excellent. Take care, Perry. This is not a field you want to be caught in when the combine comes through."

So even he was threatened, Pugliano realized. Fitzmaurice was warning him not to continue his Nanovex investigation through a backchannel. They would be watching this one from the highest levels.

"Thank you for the warning, sir. I hear you." Pugliano ended the call and stared into space for several seconds.

"Son of a bitch," he finally muttered.

CUTOUT

SAN JOSE, CALIFORNIA

Conrad leaned on the desk in her garage office. "So if we're not going to kill Manning," she asked Scott Hendrix, "what did you have in mind to keep him playing on our side?"

Hendrix relaxed as much as he could in the hard metal chair, feeling slightly more comfortable around his new and deadly partner. "To tell this story right, I have to go back a few years. When did you join the CIA?"

"Right after September 11th."

"Oh, that's right. Well, this was before your time, but you may remember it. Back in the nineties the US sold the Chinese a bunch of restricted missile technology. Guidance sets, radiation-hardened chips, stuff like that."

"Wasn't that just some corrupt politician fishing for campaign cash from the Chinese?"

"Oh, cash was exchanged," he assured her. "But that was just a bonus, like giving a fruit basket to your best customer. And while the media got hung up on the who, what and how, they forgot to ask the most important question."

"Why."

"Exactly. And the real payback from the Chinese didn't show up on anybody's campaign ledger. You see, ever since the Church Committee in the seventies, the CIA had been hobbling around in ankle chains, afraid to get even a speck of dirt on their hands. Nobody wanted to risk a rectal exam by Congress, or worse. So we used the technology sales to hire the Chinese to do our dirty work for us. Any time we needed drugs shipped, money laundered, or a troublesome foreign national whacked, we tasked the Chinese to do it." [1]

She raised an eyebrow. "And you know this, how?"

"Because I was stationed in Hong Kong for two years running Chinese agents for the CIA. They shoveled shit for us we wouldn't *dare* touch."

"I don't see how this has any bearing on our problem."

He held up a finger for patience. "A lot of the ops the Chinese ran for us were on US soil. To protect their agents, they used a cutout to deliver the orders. That way the job got done but we never learned the identities of their undercover US assets. One of their cutouts recently retired and went freelance. Excellent agent, you might have heard of him. His name is Linn Shaozang."

She sat back in her chair. "No shit?"

"A lot of the assets Linn ran here in the US were criminals, I learned that much. Triads, Tongs and the like. So if Linn shows up with the money, I don't think they're going to ask too many questions about where the orders came from."

"Do you think he has any assets near Chicago?"

He smiled. "Have I ever told you what a great place Lake Michigan is to dump a body?"

"Okay, let's get this rolling. I want to make our move on Manning's family before the FBI makes a move on *him*."

"Understood."

BURNED

SAN JOSE, CALIFORNIA

Doug Lyman opened his multi-locked office door. "So it finally happened, huh?"

Manning nodded, holding up the legal notices. "It wasn't so much a race to the courthouse as a concerted assault. Three families served us on the same day."

Lyman motioned him inside. Somewhat reluctantly, he noticed. "I wish this was the biggest problem on my plate, but it's not."

Manning walked toward the conference table. Not that he had been invited or intended to sit, but he wanted the conversation recorded on the bug he had planted, as evidence to Angela Conrad that he was still viable and in the loop. "The murder investigation?"

"Yeah," Lyman replied, after an uncomfortable pause.

He let out a contrived sigh. "With our luck, this will end up in my lap too, so what can you tell me?"

Lyman's eyes hardened. "Nothing."

"Nothing meaning there's no information to give, or nothing meaning the FBI doesn't want you to talk about it, even to your chief legal counsel?"

"The latter," he shot back.

"Ok-a-y," he said, after an uncomfortable pause of his own. "Well, you had asked to be informed as soon as we were served. I'll look through the papers and see if I can glean anything we can use in a defensive strategy."

Lyman already had his hand on the door to usher him out. "Yes, please do that. We'll talk again tomorrow."

Am I suddenly persona non grata around here? Before Lyman could open the door to eject him, Manning heard the beeping tones of the keypad lock from the far side of the door, which almost opened in Lyman's face.

Reese Miller burst inside. "Boss, did you hear the FBI is pulling out?" Manning could see the diminutive Agent Cho standing tensely behind Miller.

"They're *what*?" Lyman almost shouted.

Suddenly Miller's peripheral vision picked up Manning's presence. "Oh, sorry, didn't know you had company."

Lyman cleared his throat. "Uh, yes. Mike was just leaving."

Lyman's phone rang. His secretary's voice came over the intercom. "Sir, Special Agent Pugliano is on line one, he says it's urgent."

Manning made his exit, the eyes of the other three avoiding his gaze like he could turn them to stone. The door slammed behind him with the finality of a coffin lid. He had no history of heart problems, but the pain lancing through his chest felt an awful lot like a heart attack.

I'm burned, Manning realized.

ORDERS

SAN JOSE, CALIFORNIA

"Hey!" Wendy Cho called out. "That's *my* laptop! Don't pack that!"

"Oh, sorry," the FBI technician replied, as he boxed up the surveillance gear in the Nanovex conference room. "You still want me to hold off on disconnecting the land line?"

The ringing of the secure phone answered his question. "Finally!" she said after checking the caller ID. "Agent Cho here, sir. Thank you for returning my call."

"Listen, Wendy, I don't like this any more than you do," Pugliano immediately rattled off. "But orders are orders, and one thing you're going to have to learn if you want to stay in the Bureau is to follow orders, even the stupid ones."

Cho was surprised at his outburst. Her questions were practical, not philosophical. "That's fine, sir. I wasn't questioning your orders. I just wanted to know if we're folding up the surveillance of Manning as well as the protective detail of the Nanovex employees."

"Hell no," he snarled. "That man is our only link to Angela Conrad. And I'll be damned if I'm walking away from this investigation without her scalp on my belt. The Manning surveillance continues—just make damn sure nobody is within a mile of the Nanovex building while it's going on."

Wow, who put a kink in his hose? "Yes sir, I'll make it happen."

"Good. And one more thing. Those people locked up in the basement?"

"Yes sir?"

"Just walk away. They're good as dead, with or without your protection."

What the hell? "Yes sir. My team is on their way out now."

"Let me know when everyone is off the property."

"Yes sir, I will." She ended the call and excused herself to walk outside the building's cellphone-blocking glass bubble, fishing in her purse for her CIA-issued phone.

"Hello?" Hendrix answered.

"Something's up. Something big. We need to talk."

* * *

Manning returned to his office and sat down, his heart pounding. If Lyman and his guard dog Reese Miller were on to him, could the FBI be far behind? Then he remembered that petite FBI agent, Wendy Cho. She had been standing right behind Miller. Crap, the FBI was *already* on to him. He glanced around his office. Bugged, certainly. Video cameras, probably. Tracking devices on his car, likely. And his hotel room too. *Shit.*

What to do now? He had read enough about FBI surveillance techniques to know that he wasn't going to shake them. If he searched out their bugs, they would just replace them with better ones, even harder to find. And if they had a tracking device on his car, he could do surveillance detection routes all day long and they would just track him from miles away and laugh at his futility. He was well and truly screwed.

Or am I? Everything he had done was under duress, at the threat of his and his family's lives. Conrad was almost certainly who they were after. What if he led them straight to her? If they were both captured, he could tell all, with both him and his family under witness protection. It was the best option he had in a long time.

But what if the same thing happened as when Conrad was ambushed at San Jose City Hall? After his front row seat for that massacre, he had no desire for an encore performance at closer range. But even if *he* was killed, the chances that Conrad would kill his family out of pure spite were minimal. And even if she wanted revenge, Conrad would have the FBI on her heels and probably bigger things on her mind. It felt very strange to think this way, and he realized these were probably the only truly selfless thoughts that had ever crossed his mind. *First time for everything*, he mused.

But what was it Miller had said, exactly? He said the FBI was pulling *out* of the murder investigations and the protective detail of Lyman's surviving scientists. Then Miller shut up when he saw Manning. Was the FBI dropping their tail on *him* as well?

One way to find out, he reasoned. Conrad hadn't called him last night for a midnight rendezvous, which made a summons tonight even more likely. She had only given him two data-recording pens. If she didn't make a pickup tonight, she would start losing data tomorrow when he recorded over old data. It would give him as good an excuse as any to call for instructions, as well as to update her on what he had heard in Lyman's office. Maybe he would get lucky and the FBI would make their move on Conrad then.

He pretended to work until five o'clock, then stuck the data pen in his pocket—not bothering to turn it off here in case there were cameras watching his every move—and left for his hotel. It was time to make an important call.

* * *

In anticipation of his meeting with Agent Cho, Scott Hendrix was already naked. He heard her enter the hotel room, a pleasant throbbing signaling his readiness. He blinked when she flicked on the light, but had no trouble working up a welcoming smile.

She wrinkled her nose. "What are you *doing*? I told you this was *important*!"

Readiness was replaced by a sagging sensation. "Well, there's *important*, and then there's *urgent*." He knew which category *his* needs fell into.

She rolled her eyes. "Pugliano just ordered me to roll up our operation at Nanovex and pull out. We're not even protecting those poor people trapped in the basement."

He sat up in bed. "*Pugliano* ordered that?"

"He was pissed as hell, but yeah, he ordered it."

"Damn," he muttered. *So I was right, Conrad does have a protector inside the government. I'm glad I warned Perry about what was going on. That sure makes my partnership with Conrad easier to pull off.*

"So who would have the leverage to order us off the Nanovex case? Did *you* do that?"

He laughed. "You overestimate my pull in Washington. No, whoever ordered you guys to back off on Conrad is way the hell above *my* pay grade."

"Who said we're backing off on Conrad?"

"You said you were ordered out of Nanovex."

"We were," she confirmed. "The murder investigations have been turned over to local authorities, and the protection of the remaining scientists on that secret project of theirs is now the responsibility of Nanovex security. But I never said anything about Conrad. If anything we're doubling down on our hunt. Pugliano wants her ass bad."

So much for things getting easier. "So you're still on Manning?"

"Like a tick. Pugliano is convinced he's going to lead us straight to her."

"And what makes him think he's going to fare any better than my team did if he *does* catch up with her?"

She shrugged. "Rumor has it that he's calling in some favors with his buddies in the Marine Corps to loan him some serious firepower and the gunnery sergeants to use it."

"That's ballsy of him. He better not get caught using Defense Department assets without presidential authorization."

"I'm more afraid of that silver ball showing up and laying waste again, just like it did at City Hall. I tried to warn him about it, but he's fixated on catching Conrad, even after we were muscled off the Nanovex case."

Regretfully, he got up and reached for his clothes. "It's called the Captain Ahab complex; once a leader gets fixated on a particular enemy, he'll take his whole organization off the cliff trying to catch them. Make sure you're not there when that happens."

"Way ahead of you. I already feel a monstrous case of the flu coming on."

He nodded. "Good girl. Now, I need you to tell me everything you know about the surveillance detail on Manning's family in Chicago."

* * *

Manning waited until 10:30 that evening, but Conrad had not called. He pressed the two buttons on the Conrad-supplied watch in unison to activate the distress signal as she had taught him. The watch made no sound, but a small black dot flashed in a corner of the watch's LCD screen. Five minutes later his second burner phone rang.

"What's happening?" she asked anxiously.

"You didn't make your pickup of the data pen yesterday. I need to know whether to stop recording or to record over the old data."

"Where are you now?" she demanded.

"In my hotel room."

"You *idiot!* Get out of there! What if the room's bugged? Get into the hallway and start walking, *now!*"

He was in his stocking feet, but complied. "So are we meeting or what?"

"Not right now. For the moment I have all the information I need. Record over the oldest data until I signal you for a meet." The statement had been preceded by a short but discernable pause. To his practiced ears it spoke volumes. *She was thinking up a plausible lie. She doesn't want to meet with me. Does she know I'm burned?*

"Okay, but there's something else, something you probably don't want to discuss over the phone."

"I don't have time to meet with you, dammit! Out with it!"

"The FBI is pulling out of Nanovex. Out of the murder investigation of the dead employees and out of protecting the ones who are left."

"Why the hell do I care about that?" she railed. "Next time, unless you're on fire, don't call me again!"

He stared at the phone for several seconds after she hung up on him. *She knows I'm burned too. If I'm burned I'm no good to her—why am I still breathing? Maybe she just hasn't got around to it yet.*

Manning ditched the burner phone and returned to his room. He slept fitfully that night, awakened by every sound he heard or imagined.

FUTILITY

MAY 26, 1966 – DUGWAY PROVING GROUND, UTAH

Hans Kammler stood to address the group of American physicists assembled in a poorly ventilated cinder block building at the remote test site. It was a very professorial atmosphere, with many of the American experts wearing lab coats over their suits to proclaim their scientific status. Colonel Armstrong had already addressed the group concerning the security precautions for today's lecture, the main point being the prohibition against taking notes. He reluctantly allowed Kammler the use of a blackboard. Kammler wondered if Armstrong would burn the board and bulldoze the ashes.

The Bell had been retrieved from Pennsylvania—at the cost of three American servicemen's lives—but at least the device had not landed in the ocean, or unthinkably worse, in Russia. Kammler had been amused at the interlocking cover stories the American counterintelligence types had used to obscure the incident. The press had been told the device was a downed Russian satellite, while covert agents leaked to the media that the device was actually a crashed UFO. American witnesses whose stories buttressed one of those two angles were secretly encouraged to talk to the media, while others with more accurate information were threatened into silence. The result was a confusing morass of conflicting evidence in which the press quickly lost interest.

The day had begun with a viewing of the disassembled Bell—it would certainly never function again after its ballistic cross-country flight—to be followed by a lecture on its principle's of operations by "Dr. Schmidt." One of Kammler's scientists had drawn a detailed cross-sectional view of the Bell on the blackboard to aid the discussion. Kammler also had a film of the Bell in operation, but saved that for the end of the lecture. He was pleased to see Kurt Debus in attendance, smoking a cigarette at the back of the room.

"The Bell," Kammler began, "is a plasma engine using rotating uranium gas under extreme electrical charge to create a spin-polarized bubble in space-time. By polarizing the lines of force in the aether, electromagnetic energy is released along the axis of rotation, creating a propulsive force. At the same time, the flow of the aether lines of force through the Bell produces an electrical current of extremely high frequency and amplitude…" [2]

"Excuse me, Dr. Schmidt," an American scientist interrupted. "Did you say the *aether*?"

"My apologies, perhaps a definition of terms is needed. In the physics of the Bell, the aether I refer to is an extradimensional field of force from which all subatomic particles form. We borrowed the word aether from eighteenth-century physics simply as a matter of convenience and for lack of a better term, unless you would prefer *Feldkraft-Partikelschaffung* or 'particle-creating field of force.'"

The scientist said nothing, but turned his head and vented a plume of cigarette smoke in exasperation. Apparently *aether* was good enough after all.

"Excuse me," said another, "did you say this *aether* you discovered *creates* particles?"

"We did not discover the aether; that credit probably goes to Nikola Tesla, whose work inspired a great deal of our efforts. But yes, the aether as Tesla defined it is a field that exists in a higher dimension that is the origin of *all* matter and energy that exists within the observable dimensions around us."

The scientist made a face. "That's preposterous!"

Kammler smiled in forbearance. "Not so, my friend. We found that by carefully manipulating the charge of the plasma within the Bell, we were able to add or remove protons to the atoms of the plasma, thereby transmuting the elements of the plasma from one element to another. These additional subatomic elements could only have proceeded from the aether. We carefully eliminated all other possibilities."

"Transmutation of the *elements*?" another scoffed. "What is this? A lecture on alchemy?" A wave of derisive laughter swept through the room.

He mentally counted to ten before responding, which also allowed the laughter to subside. "How different is this from a nuclear reaction, whereby you bombard uranium-238 with neutrons to create atoms of plutonium-239? Your national laboratories carry out this reaction every day in the manufacture of plutonium for nuclear warheads, do they not?"

"Yeah," the scientist countered, "but we know where those bombardment neutrons come from, and they don't come from some other dimension!" The entire group had a boisterous laugh at Kammler's expense.

"I've studied Tesla," another offered, "and I don't recall reading anything about an extradimensional aether in his papers."

"That's because your authorities suppressed Tesla's research from the 1930s on, when Tesla proposed a directed energy weapon to put a permanent end to war." He lifted an eyebrow. "Apparently it was not a goal they endorsed."

"So how do *you* know so much about Tesla's work?" the scientist challenged.

This time it was Kammler's turn to smile. "Because we stole his papers from an FBI warehouse in 1943."

He was subjected to another wave of laughter.

"I've heard enough," said the first scientist to speak. "I've got better things to do with my time than listen to this bullshit." He rose and left the room. Several more followed. Even those who remained eyed Kammler with naked disbelief. Kurt Debus shook his head sadly and shrugged.

Kammler sighed. *This is futility*. He motioned to his assistant manning the projector. The room darkened and a color film of the Bell's last test played on the bare wall.

"I've done my best to enlighten you, gentlemen," he said, walking to the door. "Even if you won't believe your ears, perhaps your eyes will be less skeptical. Good day." [3]

RETAIL THERAPY

PRESENT DAY – CHICAGO, ILLINOIS

Amanda's ten-year-old son Eric looked at her strangely when she entered the kitchen. "What are *you* all dolled-up for, Mom?"

"Dolled-up? Where did you learn that phrase, young man?" She hadn't worn make-up in days, and she certainly hadn't worn anything for which she paid full price. Today she had done both.

"From Dad," he said around a mouthful of cereal. "He was all grumpy one night. He said you two were going to miss your dinner reservations because you took so long getting dolled-up."

Her hands went to her hips. "*Really*? What else does your father say about me behind my back?"

Eric looked down, studying his cereal bowl. "I plead the fifth."

She rolled her eyes. "Oh, you *definitely* learned *that* from your father!"

"I think you look pretty, Mom," her seven-year-old Kevin offered.

"Thank you, sweetie," she said, bending over to kiss the top of his head. She stood on tiptoe and retrieved the box of Godiva "grown-ups" chocolate from the top of the refrigerator. "As a matter of fact, you're so sweet I think you need a little something extra for breakfast!" She held open the box for Kevin to choose.

"Hey!" Eric protested. "How come *he* gets chocolate?"

"Because," she said with a toss of her freshly washed hair, "he says nice things about his mother instead of making snarky comments."

Kevin selected a truffle and popped it in his mouth, making a point of chewing with his mouth open and moaning with delight. "Mmm, thanks, Mom!"

"Goofball," Eric muttered.

"That's goofball with a mouthful of chocolate to you, mister!" Kevin replied.

Amanda laughed at their verbal sparring. She hadn't felt this good in days. She practically bounced to the front door when the doorbell rang. She was going shopping. Why she hadn't applied a little retail therapy to her sorrows before now escaped her.

"Hey girlfriend!" her new neighbor Jenny McIntyre bubbled.

"Hey yourself!" She surprised herself by greeting Jenny with a hug. She really *was* in a good mood. "The boys will be ready in a few minutes. We'll go straight to the mall after we drop them off at school."

"After a stop at Starbuck's, please. I haven't had my caffeine yet."

She laughed. "Of course. Come in and sit down. Boys! Hurry up and get ready! You don't want to be late for school!"

"You just want us out of your hair so you can go shopping," Eric groused, trudging through the living room.

She took off a sandal and playfully swatted him on the behind. "Now you know your place in the universe! Hurry up, the salt mines await! You too, Kevin!" she yelled into the kitchen.

Eric disappeared grumbling down the hallway.

Jenny pulled a card from her purse. "Hey, look what's burning a hole in *my* wallet!"

It was a Nordstrom's gift card. "Oh! I know where *we're* going first!" Amanda said. "They have a new line of Manolo Blahnik shoes that are just to *die* for!"

As Amanda chatted on about the shoes of her dreams, a sound intruded into her consciousness, a faint scratching sound followed by the squeak of the back door behind her. She noticed Jenny's eyes shift and go wide with alarm.

Amanda whirled to face a huge Chinese man in a muscle shirt. Tattoos covered his arms and his chest. He held a short but menacing knife in his right hand.

"Don't move!" he shouted.

Amanda caught a motion in Jenny's direction out of the corner of her eye. When she turned her head, she saw Jenny's hand come out of her purse with a stubby black pistol.

Amanda heard two pops like muffled firecrackers behind her and watched a pair of bloody holes open up in Jenny's forehead. Jenny's head jerked back against the sofa and her body slid down to the floor, leaving a gory track on the fabric. Her sightless eyes stared up at Amanda, then rolled back in her head.

Amanda screamed.

The man with the knife grabbed her and thrust the blade at her throat. An older man wearing blue repairman's coveralls stepped through the door, holding a smoking pistol with a silencer. She managed to get a hand between the blade and her neck and struggled mightily, fearing for the lives of her sons more than her own.

The man with the pistol disappeared into the kitchen and returned with Kevin, manhandling the boy by his ear with his free hand and pressing the gun into his neck with the other.

"*Mommy!*" Kevin screamed.

"Stop struggling!" the older man ordered Amanda. "Or I put a bullet in your son!"

Amanda reluctantly complied. Her struggle with the knifed intruder had left a deep gash on her palm. Blood dripped onto the carpet as she held up her hands.

"Your other son," he ordered, "call him."

When she hesitated, he pressed the gun hard against Kevin's temple, forcing the boy's head against his shoulder. Kevin whimpered, eyeing her with abject terror.

"*No!*" she pleaded. She turned her head. "Eric? Honey? I need you to come out here."

Eric sheepishly poked his head from the hallway. "What's happening?" he whispered.

The man with the knife wheeled Amanda roughly about by her hair and lifted her chin with the knife point. "Get over here or I kill your mother," he snarled.

Eric hesitated, clearly contemplating his options for escape.

The knife jabbed into Amanda's chin, piercing her skin. "Eric, *please*!" she cried.

Eric's shoulders drooped and he shuffled fearfully into the living room.

The older man waved his pistol toward the door. "Outside! Get in the van!"

* * *

FBI Special Agent Michael Fisher received the distress signal from the transmitter hidden under Agent Jenny McIntyre's belt. He stuffed in his earpiece and grabbed his gun, hearing the sound of muffled gunshots and a piercing scream from the audio pickup.

"Dispatch!" he shouted into his radio. "Distress signal from Retail One! Retail Two responding! Request Bureau and local assistance, code three!"

"10-4, Retail Two, rolling everything!"

"Acknowledged!" Fisher ran to his car, mashing the garage door opener button with his fist on his way out. He squealed the Bureau-rented Jaguar out of the rear-facing garage and surged down the driveway toward the street.

A bearded Chinese man stepped from the bushes and pointed a gun at him. With no other cover, Fisher leaned below the dash, pointed the Jaguar at his attacker, and floored the accelerator. Bullets punched into the windshield, glass fragments peppering his face and one of the slugs nicking his ear. He saw his attacker slide past in the driver's side window, the gun tracking his head. *Dammit, where did this guy come from?*

Before Fisher could bring his own gun to bear on the assailant, two bullets pierced the driver's side window and punctured his skull. The Jaguar roared off the driveway, took out the mailbox, hopped the curb on the far side of the street and embedded itself in a neighbor's landscaping wall, its engine still roaring.

The Chinese man ran down the street, gun in hand. A white van emerged from behind the Manning house, screeching to a stop for the gunman to jump into the passenger seat. The van fishtailed from the neighborhood, leaving serpentine skid marks on the street. The noise of its engine faded into the distance, replaced by sirens approaching from the opposite direction.

MOTIVATION

SAN JOSE, CALIFORNIA

Mike Manning sat on the edge of his bed and debated whether he should even go in to work. His usefulness to Conrad at Nanovex was over, and she wasn't going to leave a loose end like Mike Manning walking around. It would be a pity to spend his last day or two on Earth cooped up in an office when he could see the sights of a great city and choose his last meals from any of San Francisco's excellent restaurants. The buzzing of his next burner phone interrupted his end-of-life decision-making.

"Yeah."

"Get out of your room. Start walking," he heard Conrad order.

"Not dressed," he snapped.

"Walk or die, your choice," she said without emotion.

"Damn you," he muttered, fumbling for his room key. Luckily he slept in boxers and a T-shirt, so he didn't have to stumble into the hallway wrapped in a towel. He padded barefoot down the hall, drawing a stare from another guest leaving his room in suit and tie. "Okay, I'm walking," he said in a harsh whisper.

"When you report to work this morning, I want you to set a fire at precisely fifteen minutes after nine o'clock."

He stumbled, bumping against the hallway wall. "Are you *insane*? Is my new cover at Nanovex as an arsonist?"

She ignored him. "Make sure it's big enough to set off the fire alarms and cause an evacuation."

"Start a fire with *what*?" he protested. "You can't even get a cigarette lighter into that building! What am I supposed to do, walk in with a can of gasoline under my arm?"

"Oh come on, it's a research facility, there's got to be some interesting chemicals in there somewhere. Look for the little red diamond with a flame in the middle."

"Yeah, I *know* what a flammable chemical symbol looks like, thanks."

"Then it sounds like all you need is a little motivation. Let me help you with that. Hold the line."

He stopped walking, staring at himself in a decorative hallway mirror. He truly looked like shit. *Hey, I'm working against my will for an international terrorist, what am I supposed to look like*, he rationalized. The phone clicked a couple of times and he thought the call had dropped. Then he heard a foreign language in the background, maybe Chinese or Vietnamese. The next sound he heard made his heart stop.

"*Mike?*" he heard a terrified woman's voice say over the scratchy connection. "*Mike, are you there?*"

It was Amanda. His hand squeezed the phone so hard the plastic squeaked.

"Yeah, baby, I'm here," he finally managed to choke out.

"*Mike!*" she sobbed. "They have the boys! They killed our neighbor! What are you involved in? *Mike!*" Her last word was muffled by someone wresting the phone away. The connection clicked again.

"Amanda! *Amanda!*" he shouted.

"That concludes our motivational talk for today, Mr. Manning," Conrad said. "Oh, and if you get caught, your wife and children ask that you keep your mouth shut. That's the only way they're going to get out of this alive. If you talk, trust me, I'll know. Remember, fifteen minutes after nine. Big fire, don't disappoint me."

* * *

FBI surveillance specialist Bob Moskowitz called for his partner, Marty Clagget. "Manning's in motion! Something's up!"

Clagget was about to take over the day shift from Moskowitz. He exited the bathroom, electric shaver in hand. A bank of monitors filled an entire wall of the hotel suite. "Whatcha got?"

"I think he got another call on his burner phone."

"You *think*? Why don't you *know*?"

"Hey! He's set his burners to vibrate; they make about as much noise as that two-hundred-dollar shaver you're so proud of."

"Leave my shaver out of this. Where is he now?"

"In the hall, walking."

Clagget watched Manning from the cameras they had planted in the hallway light fixtures the night before. "How are the new audio pickups working?"

Moskowitz flicked a switch to put the audio on speaker. "They'd work better if he didn't whisper like he's in confessional."

"Are you *insane*?" They heard Manning say, his voice suddenly rising. "Is my new cover at Nanovex as an…?"

"What was that last word?" Clagget asked.

"Couldn't make it out."

Clagget switched the camera feeds as Manning continued down the hallway. He activated the cellphone monitoring software on a nearby laptop. A flood of location dots overlaid the floor plan of the hotel. Clagget glanced at the monitor again to see which way Manning was walking. He had just stopped at the end of the hallway. Clagget placed his cursor over the stationary dot.

"Gotcha," he whispered. He right-clicked on the dot and selected HOOK, which fed the data to a nearby radio scanner. The scanner picked up the cellular call and automatically started a digital recording. He pulled on a nearby set of headphones.

"Then it sounds like all you need is a little motivation," Clagget heard a woman say. "Let me help you with that. Hold the line." *Was that Conrad?* He couldn't be sure, but the voice print analysis would tell him that with certainty.

Clagget listened to the rest of the call, then set down the headphones. He exported the audio file to the laptop and emailed it to Pugliano, flagging it as urgent.

"Well? Did you get it?" Moskowitz asked.

"Oh yeah," he said quietly.

"And?"

Clagget looked over at his partner. "We just got ourselves a whole new ball game."

[1] The corrupt politician mentioned here is of course President Bill Clinton, whose brushes with illegal foreign campaign donations are well known, if not prosecuted. The "missile technology for covert ops" theory stated here is fiction, but the idea that a US president—even one of unquestioned immoral character—would willingly place US national security under such

grave threat for something as banal as campaign contributions seems unlikely. The author's conclusion is that the "illegal campaign contributions" story was a smokescreen for a much bigger payback behind the scenes. Classic misdirection, like a magician's sleight-of-hand. A smaller scandal to hide a much bigger one.

Interestingly, after taking office President Barrack Obama, in a move identical to President Clinton's, moved authority for approval of space and missile technology sales from the Defense Department *back* to the Commerce Department, dramatically lowering the bar for U.S. missile technology transfers. (Source: "Obama loosens missile technology controls to China" by Bill Gertz, Washington *Times*, October 15, 2009)

[2] Excerpts from *Occult Ether Physics* by William R. Lyne:
"Tesla at first conducted tests (the high voltage experiments relating to the high frequency reactance between two parallel metal plates), to verify his hypothesis. His tests confirmed that at sufficiently high voltage and frequency, the 'space' (containing the ether) between the plates, became what Tesla termed 'solid state'…Tesla then carried the hypothesis a step further, and concluded that an electric flying machine could be propelled by electric current and the reactance of high frequency, high voltage electromagnetic waves. This electricity would use the inertia of the 'continuous, electrically conductive fluid mass' of the Omni Matter (aether), to be pulled and pushed against, using the Hall effect magneto hydrodynamic (MHD) principle…

"According to the later researches and publishings of J. J. Thomson, he had mathematically developed the theory of moving tubes of force. Two years later, Thomson declared that '...the aether is a storehouse of mechanical momentum'. Tesla, in his prior lecture, had mentioned the tubes of force and disclosed some of his discoveries concerning the ether and momentum….Tesla's statement in 1891 that the use of high frequency alternating current would compress and block the passage of the tubes was apparently intended to force the tubes being drawn into the conductors of a ship by the D.C. brush at the opposite end, to dissolve in the conductors, and impart momentum to the ship to which the conductors were attached."

[3] In his book *The Hunt for Zero Point*, Cook is meeting with "Dr. Dan Marckus," a pseudonymous British avionics expert. Marckus explains America's initial unsuccessful flirtation with antigravity technology.

"When the Americans tripped over this mutant strain of nonlinear physics and took it back home with them, they were astute enough to realize that their home-grown scientific talent couldn't handle it. That it was beyond their cultural term of reference. That's why they recruited so many

Germans. The Nazis developed a unique approach to science and engineering quite separate from the rest of the world, because their ideology, unrestrained as it was, supported a wholly different way of doing things. Von Braun's V-2s are a case in point, but so was their understanding of physics. The trouble was, when the Americans took it all home with them they found out, too late, that it came infected with a virus. You take the science on, you take on aspects of the ideology, as well." (*The Hunt for Zero Point* by Nick Cook, 2003, p. 270)

In many ways *The Hunt for Zero Point* provided the first germ for the plot idea behind this novel, which I gratefully acknowledge.

CHAPTER 22

OPERATORS

SAN JOSE, CALIFORNIA

Scott Hendrix felt a surge of exhilaration as he and Linn Shaozang walked to the front entrance of the Nanovex building. This was full-on covert operator stuff, which is what he had joined the CIA *for* but had done so little *of* during his career. Today he wasn't behind enemy lines in a hostile country; but if he was caught, he would probably end up in that deep-black prison the CIA operated onboard a cargo ship in the Indian Ocean. So the odds were plenty high enough to get his adrenaline pumping.

He checked his watch. Three minutes until nine o'clock. Once they cleared security and were escorted up to Lyman's office they should be right on schedule.

After Security checked their bags and wanded them for weapons, a guard handed them their visitor badges and motioned for them to follow. Shaozang stepped aside momentarily and threw his large coffee into a nearby trash can.

* * *

Mike Manning's gut knotted and a pain shot through his chest like a knife. He had never played with matches as a kid. Arson wasn't one of his core competencies. But the lives of his wife and children depended on the fire he would set today.

He searched two broom closets and satisfied himself that no flammable chemicals were stored inside. He was forced to invent a story about cleaning up a spill on his carpet when he almost flattened a woman in a lab coat as he emerged from the second closet. He was too frantic to be embarrassed, as long as she didn't call Reese Miller or one of his guard dogs.

His gut tightening further, he trotted downstairs to the labs.

* * *

Doug Lyman greeted Hendrix warmly. "Mr. Hendrix, so good to see you again!"

Hendrix feigned humility. "Please, just Scott. And this is my associate, Dr. Chang."

Lyman bowed slightly at the waist when he offered his hand. “Dr. Chang, welcome to Nanovex. You are my honored guest.”

Shaozang returned the bow. “Mr. Hendrix tells me much,” he said in contrived broken English, “I am honored to meet.”

Lyman motioned them to the conference table. “Please, gentlemen. May I serve you coffee, or perhaps tea?”

Hendrix exchanged a few words in Chinese with Shaozang. “Would it be possible to find some ginger tea?” he asked Lyman. “My colleague complains of an upset stomach. I think the traditional American breakfast the hotel served was too heavy for him.”

Lyman assumed a look of deep concern. “Of course. I’ll ask my secretary to check. I’m sure we have a tea connoisseur on our payroll.”

Lyman left momentarily and Hendrix checked his watch again. Since the stated purpose for his visit was entirely a ruse, the more time wasted the better.

* * *

Manning made an increasingly panicked search of the labs in the basement. All were behind keycard locks. Most had steel doors, so he had no idea what was inside. The one lab with flammable chemicals visible through the glass door also had three visible technicians, so even if he could get inside, there would be people to witness and probably prevent his act of sabotage. He looked at his watch. Ten minutes after nine.

In his frustration, he had the frenzied urge to just throw the newspaper he carried for kindling into a broom closet and hope for the best. But his family’s life rode on his effort. Conrad’s contempt for half-measures was already well demonstrated.

Completely circling the basement, he found a small room with a sliding steel door secured by a padlock. Numerous diamond-shaped warning symbols placarded the door, like TOXIC, CORROSIVE, OXIDIZER, and finally FLAMMABLE. He looked at the padlock. It was little more than a gym lock, but he had never been any good at picking locks of any size.

But he *had* seen a hammer in one of the broom closets on the first floor. He took off in a dead run toward the stairs.

* * *

Lyman returned and sat at the head of the table. “My secretary said she knows just who to ask. She’ll be back in a few minutes.”

Shaozang nodded. “My thanks.”

Lyman folded his hands. "So, Mr. Hendrix, you were a bit nonspecific on the reason for your visit today."

He smiled. "Sorry. Because the subject is sensitive, I was reluctant to discuss it over the phone. As we agreed earlier, the CIA is planning to take the WICKER BASKET technology overseas for development and production. Dr. Chang represents our technical staff in Hong Kong."

Lyman drew back. "You said you were taking the WICKER BASKET program overseas. I wasn't aware you were taking it to *China*. I'm not sure I feel comfortable with a technology this powerful being developed in a communist country."

"The lab Dr. Chang represents is a *CIA* facility, Mr. Lyman. I can assure you he is well-versed in developing covert technologies for us without the knowledge of the communist government. He's been doing it for years."

Lyman looked still uncomfortable. "Very well, go on."

"What Dr. Chang and I are both concerned about is the erosion of WICKER BASKET's knowledge base from the recent deaths of your employees."

Lyman straightened. "Oh?"

Hendrix's plastic smile took on a smug edge. "I realize that this is not public knowledge, but we're aware that all of the deceased employees worked on WICKER BASKET."

Lyman did his best to maintain a poker face. "I see."

"And while I am deeply sorry about the deaths of your people, Dr. Chang and I both share the concern that the experience that made the project viable may have already been lost."

Real worry seeped through Lyman's poker face. "All I can do is assure you that this won't be the case. Besides, I require my scientists to extensively document their work. Nothing in the knowledge base of the project has been lost, even with the tragic deaths we've suffered."

He's worried about the same thing. Press harder. "If I may ask, how many of the project's original staff remain?"

Lyman looked like he was trying to pass a stone. "I don't feel comfortable…."

"It's a simple question, Mr. Lyman. And given the money the CIA has put forward as a down payment, I think we have a right to know. Of the original staff of the WICKER BASKET project, how many people do you have *left*?"

Lyman's shoulders slumped, his answer barely audible. "Two."

Oh my god, they've almost wiped him out. For a moment, Hendrix was speechless.

Shaozang bent over and moaned softly. "I need bathroom. Hurry please."

Lyman rose. "Of course, Dr. Chang, follow me."

Hendrix was already on his feet. "It's okay, I've got it." He took Shaozang's arm and led him out of the office. Once they were in the bathroom, he checked his watch. It was time. "Okay, any minute now. Get ready to move."

He left Shaozang in the bathroom and returned to Lyman's office. "Poor bastard," he told Lyman. "He'll probably never eat bacon again."

* * *

It had taken Marty Clagget over an hour to convince Perry Pugliano's assistant that the evidence they had uncovered was important enough to pull their boss out of a meeting. Fortunately Pugliano appeared to be more receptive than his underling when he returned Clagget's call.

"Okay," Pugliano said, "I listened to the intercept you sent me. It shakes thing up a bit, doesn't it?"

"Yes sir, that's why I wanted you to hear it right away."

"The reason I was so hard to reach is that Manning's wife and children were just snatched out from under an FBI surveillance team in Chicago. Two FBI agents are dead and there's a trail of blood leading out the door at the Manning house. So things are a little tense right now."

Clagget tensed. "I'm sorry, sir. I didn't know."

"Don't be. Now we know who did it, and why. In my book, that's a breakthrough."

"Yes sir. Did you hear the Chinese voices in the background?"

"Yeah, witnesses on the scene saw at least one Asian gunman and a white van leaving the scene. You're sure the voices are Chinese?"

"Yes sir. I don't speak it, but we've been trained to recognize over a hundred languages by ear so we can request the right linguist for translation."

"Another piece of the puzzle, good work."

"Thank you, sir. What did you make of Conrad's comment, 'Fifteen minutes after nine, big fire, don't disappoint me'?"

"Do you know for sure it was Conrad?"

"Yes sir, we ran it through voice analysis; it was a ninety-five percent match. We also followed Manning from his room. He didn't have breakfast this morning, but he did stop by the bar. All he did was pick up a pack of matches."

"Does he smoke?"

"No sir."

Pugliano sighed. "Well, it's fourteen minutes after now. I'll call their head of Security, but it's probably too late to head him off."

* * *

Manning retrieved the hammer from the broom closet and ran back downstairs, abandoning all pretense of stealth, except for folding the newspaper over the hammer and sticking it under his arm. He lingered by the chemical room door for a few seconds, waiting for a pair of workers to pass, then jammed the claw of the hammer through padlock's shackle and pulled down with all his strength. The lock groaned for a second, then popped open with a crack that echoed down the hallway.

He cringed, then worked the lock out of the hasp and slid the door open, just as two more workers rounded the corner at the far end of the hall. He continued opening the door, then entered and slid it closed behind him. The steel door grated in its tracks, making far more noise than he would have wished. He froze, listening at the door in case the workers he saw came to investigate. He didn't know what he would do if they did, but he wouldn't hesitate to use the hammer as a weapon if they tried to prevent him from completing his task. The two women continued chatting until the elevator bell dinged and they exited the basement. He was clear.

Most of the floor space inside the chemical room was taken up by cylinders of gas. He recognized tanks of oxygen, nitrogen, and carbon dioxide. Those were no help, he needed a flammable liquid. Several metal flasks rested on shelves lining the back wall. He had no idea what most of the chemicals were, but the hazard warning labels were pretty self-explanatory. The two most promising were Diethyl Ether and something called Cyclohexane. They both had labels warning CLASS I FLAMMABLE. *Bingo*.

The flasks were smaller than beer kegs and had little spigots on them; he guessed it made sense that they would only use a small amount of these chemicals. He cranked open the spigot on the cyclohexane, but the stopcock was spring-loaded; as soon as he released it the spigot closed. The result was just a tiny puddle on the floor. This wasn't going to work. He checked his watch.

Sixteen minutes after nine.

In desperation he swung the hammer down on the spigot, knocking it off the flask. The chemical flowed freely now, although the flow was still disappointing; the stream was smaller than his little finger. But the puddle on the floor grew rapidly. He repeated the procedure on the diethyl ether and two puddles started to form. He hastily wadded up the newspaper into a rough cylinder as a makeshift fuse and reached for the matches. The vapor from the chemicals was intense. His eyes burned and watered so badly it was hard to see. He fumbled with the matches until one finally struck. He thought he was going to pass out from the fumes.

The end of the paper roll finally caught. Once he made sure the torch wasn't going to go out, he shoved the far end of the paper into the cyclohexane puddle, which had nearly merged with its diethyl ether cousin at the far end of the rack. Yep, this would make quite a blaze. The newspaper soaked up the cyclohexane, the wet stain and the flame inching toward one another inexorably. He had done it.

He slid the door closed behind him after a final glance at the makeshift fuse's progress, then headed for the stairs. With any luck he might make it out the door before the alarm sounded.

"Hey! Who are you?" he heard behind him.

Manning turned to see a skinny bald man in a lab coat and glasses glaring at him.

"You're not laboratory staff! Who authorized you to go into the chemicals room?"

Manning held up his hands, still walking backwards. "It was a mistake, I'm sorry!"

The little geek was not appeased. "You're damn right it's a mistake! It's also a major safety violation!"

"Fine, report me," he shot back. He kept walking. His usefulness to Conrad as her inside man would be over the minute they reviewed the security tapes for the cameras that covered every hallway and stairwell at Nanovex. All he wanted to do now was make good his escape and hopefully earn the freedom of his family.

"Show me your badge and I'll do just that!"

In a desperate bid to get this little twerp off his back, he displayed his badge. "Mike Manning. I report directly to Doug Lyman. Feel free to give him a call. By the way, your little lab has already failed its safety inspection! I found the chemical room unlocked!" He reached the stairwell and started up.

The man stayed on his tail. "Oh no! You're staying right here while I call Security!"

At the head of the stairs, a fire alarm blared right in Manning's ear, and the warning strobe flashed. He put his hand to his ear and kept walking. A muffled explosion echoed up from below.

The technician grabbed him by the arm. "*You* did that, didn't *you!*"

Manning seized the man by the lapels of his lab coat, nearly lifting him from his feet. "Would it make you happy if I said *yes*?" he snarled.

He heaved the man down the stairs. He flew halfway to the landing below, contacting hard on his shoulder and cartwheeling the rest of the way down, his arms and legs flailing crazily. His head hit the handrail with a metallic *thunk* that rang in the stairwell. He came to rest on the landing, face down.

That's it, he thought with disgust. *I've finally killed someone for Angela Conrad. I hope she'll be happy now.*

He could hear employees in the basement approaching the stairwell, heeding the fire alarm. He turned and headed for the lobby exit.

* * *

As soon as Hendrix left him, Shaozang pulled out a cell phone. It was outwardly identical to one of Manning's burner phones, to further implicate him in the impending incident. Without entering a phone number, he pressed the SEND button and held it. The phone beeped twice. The canister inside would detonate shortly. He tossed it into the waste paper receptacle and exited the restroom. He exchanged his visitor badge for the Nanovex employee badge Conrad had fabricated for him that indicated a top-secret security clearance and walked to the nearest stairwell.

The throng of workers filing down the stairs in response to the fire alarm grew thicker with every floor he descended. Employees crowding to the fire exits packed the lobby. Security guards held open the emergency exit doors, allowing the evacuees to bypass the lone revolving door at the entrance. He crossed the lobby against the current of evacuees and found the sole staircase down to the basement. It was empty except for a woman in an orange vest bending over a man who had fallen down the stairs. She called for medical assistance over her walkie-talkie.

The fire alarm was much louder in the confines of the basement. What appeared to be the last few laboratory employees moved hurriedly to the stairs, spurred on by the very obvious smoke floating just below the ceiling. The acrid fumes made his eyes burn. Shaozang consoled himself that the majority of visible smoke was probably fire suppressant chemicals and not toxic.

He moved quickly through the empty hallways until he found the room he sought. It was little more than a closet bearing the warning CRITICAL COMMUNICATIONS EQUIPMENT: AUTHORIZED PERSONNEL ONLY. He removed his shoes and slid off the heels to extract his lockpicking tools. Two enhanced security locks protected the door—he would much rather have done this with power equipment like a Cobra Lockmaster, but he was limited by what he could smuggle past security.

* * *

Lyman went pale when the fire alarm sounded.

"You don't have a fire drill scheduled, do you?" Hendrix asked.

"Afraid not. If you'll come with me, I'll help you collect Dr. Chang."

Lyman's secretary handed him a walkie-talkie when he exited his office, then helped him into an orange vest and popped an orange cap on his head. It looked comical, but it was clear they had practiced the routine many times.

"Lyman to Miller, report!" he barked into the radio on their way to the bathroom.

"This is Miller! The fire began in the basement, apparently in the chemical storage lock-up."

"Is it contained?"

"I think so, sir, without opening the door to check. I've confirmed that the suppression system did discharge, and I haven't heard anything else cooking off after the initial blast."

Seth Graves, Nanovex's DARPA representative, emerged from a nearby office. "Doug, I take it this is the real deal?"

"Yeah, and I need a favor! We've got those two scientists holed up in the WICKER BASKET lab. Miller's got his hands full and you know the door combo, can you go down and make sure they got out? Take them to the lobby or cafeteria or someplace else safe until the firefighters give the all clear."

"Will do!" Graves headed for the stairs.

They could see smoke wafting down the hallway before they even rounded the corner to the bathroom. Lyman quickened his pace. "Miller," he said into his radio, "we've got another fire on the fourth floor!"

"What? How big?"

"Not sure. Get somebody up here to assess it. We may be able to attack it with extinguishers if it's not too big."

"Understood."

They rounded the corner. Thick gray smoke billowed out of the men's bathroom.

"Oh my God! Is Dr. Chang still in there?" Lyman exclaimed. "Miller, get a medical team to men's bathroom outside my office!"

"On the way, sir!"

* * *

It took precious minutes for Shaozang to gain entrance to the alarm room. Once inside he worked quickly. He identified the alarm system and the number of channels it monitored. He found the master schematic for the alarm layout and photographed everything with a camera concealed in his pen. The job was complete in thirty seconds.

He stowed his lockpicking gear and exited the alarm room. The basement was entirely deserted now. He headed up the stairs to the first floor, passing a group of security guards administering first aid to the man who had fallen down the stairs. The man groaned in pain. Shaozang continued up the stairwell toward the upper floors.

* * *

"I'm going in for Dr. Chang," Lyman said, placing a handkerchief over his nose and mouth. He tested the temperature of the door handle with the back of his hand, then crouched low and pulled the door open. Thick smoke poured out, forcing him back. He got down on his belly and slithered in like a snake, calling out Chang's name. He hastily crawled back out, coughing and rubbing his face.

"There's…tear gas…in there!" Lyman wheezed, struggling to breathe. Two security guards, one carrying a medkit, trotted up to assist their CEO.

"We need to get you out of here, sir," one said.

"My friend may still be in there!" Hendrix protested. He hoped they would duplicate Lyman's heroics and be disabled by Shaozang's tear gas bomb. The more security people out of commission, the better their chance of successfully completing this mission.

"I'm going to prop open the door to help clear the smoke," the guard replied. "Get them clear." The guard was back out a few seconds later, coughing and gagging. The medic pulled his partner out of the caustic smoke. Now he had two smoke inhalation cases to treat.

"We need firemen and respirators for this," the medic explained to Hendrix and Lyman. They could already hear sirens in the distance.

* * *

Shaozang made it to the top floor without encountering security or other employees. Nanovex's evacuation plan had been remarkably efficient, which helped him immensely. He looked through the security glass at the exit from the top floor stairwell. He could see Hendrix and a security guard bending over two casualties. Time for the final stage of his performance.

He swapped the fake Nanovex badge for his visitor's badge. He pulled a fat Wing Sung fountain pen from his pocket, uncapped it, and pointed it toward his face. Squeezing his eyes tightly shut, he took a deep breath and twisted the base of the pen. The CO_2 charge inside the pen exploded in his face, coating his head and upper body in thick soot. He tucked the pen back in his pocket and stumbled from the stairwell, collapsing to the floor with a moan.

"There he is!" he heard Hendrix shout. Feet ran in his direction.

Shaozang continued his performance, coughing and jabbering deliriously in Chinese. Hendrix comforted him in his native tongue while the medic poured water over his eyes and made sure his airways were clear. He blinked painfully.

"Keep your eyes closed!" the medic cautioned. Hendrix dutifully translated for the English-impaired Dr. Chang, who reluctantly complied.

Shaozang heard fire engines pull up in front and men shouting. He reached into his pocket and pressed a button on his remaining cell phone. The foil-thin polymer battery lining his discarded coffee cup ignited the plastic explosives inside. The shock wave of an explosion rocketed up from below.

* * *

Manning walked to the lobby. He heard voices shouting orders ahead of him. He was well ahead of the mob of evacuating employees, so he peered carefully around the corner. Reese Miller and several of his security goons were already deployed in a line, obviously waiting to stop someone trying to exit. Probably him.

He waited until a thick knot of technicians bubbled up from the basement and insinuated himself among them as they moved toward the now-crowded lobby. He peeled off his jacket, thinking his white shirt might blend with the lab coats around him better than a charcoal suit. He tried to keep the group between him and Miller. He kept his head down and slouched down as much as he could without being obvious.

"*Manning!*" he heard Miller shout. "Hold it! Right there!"

He looked up. Miller stayed put while his guards advanced through the mass of workers. There was no point in running, they had him trapped. Two fire engines pulled up outside. Men in turnout coats and oxygen tanks leapt from their vehicles, surging for the doors.

A trash can near the security checkpoint exploded. The blast threw Miller into the air and knocked down the security guards as well as several screaming employees. Thick, choking smoke instantly filled the lobby as the firemen surged inside. Manning ran.

* * *

"Holy shit!" Marty Clagget exclaimed looking up from the police scanner. "They've got explosions on three different floors at the Nanovex building!"

Wendy Cho had just arrived at the hotel's surveillance suite. "How long was Manning at work before things started popping?"

He consulted his logs. "Half an hour."

"Could Manning have pulled all that off with half an hour and a book of matches?"

"I dunno, if they were holding *my* wife and kids hostage, I could be motivated to do some pretty serious shit."

"What?" she gasped.

He looked over his shoulder at her. "You didn't hear? Conrad apparently had some goons in Chicago kidnap Manning's wife and sons. Killed two FBI agents in the process."

Cho felt like she had been punched in the stomach. She collapsed into a nearby chair. *My God, is that why Hendrix wanted the details of the FBI surveillance in Chicago? Has he switched sides? Where does that leave me?*

"You okay?"

She shook her head. "No. No, I'm not."

* * *

Manning ran through the smoke and against the tide of the inrushing firefighters. He ran through the host of diesel-belching fire engines in front of the building. He ran past the orange-vested Nanovex employees acting as fire marshals, directing the workers of each floor to a different section of the parking lot for headcounts. He ran through the evacuating workers like a bolting maverick through a herd of cattle.

He reached his car, only to find it surrounded by milling employees. An orange-vested female marshal checked names against a clipboard. He pushed workers out of the way to get to his car.

"Sir!" he heard behind him. He ignored the woman's voice and started to get in.

A hand grasped his arm. "Sir! You can't leave!"

He turned. "Really?" he challenged, hoping the look in his eyes would persuade the woman to back down.

It didn't. She put her hands on her hips. "During an evacuation, all employees will remain in their designated assembly areas until a headcount has been completed and the all-clear sounded. I don't care who you think you are, the rules still apply to *you*!"

Manning looked down on the defiant woman. He recognized her as a head of Accounting or some such department. But when he saw her short blonde hair all he saw was Angela Conrad, leering at his impotence. His anger and fear and desperation all surged to the surface like hot lava. He took one step toward her and rammed his fist into her face.

She went down, screaming more in surprise and anger than pain. He felt a man's arm grab him from behind. Whirling, he grabbed the interloper by his shirt and head-butted him with all his might. The man staggered backwards and fell.

"Stand clear or I *will* run you over!" Manning shouted at the shocked employees. He plucked the woman's walkie-talkie from the asphalt and tossed it onto the passenger seat. The workers fled like frightened deer, leaving their wounded comrades on the ground.

He pulled out of his space without running over either of the innocents he had attacked. He hoped it might make hell a degree or two cooler for him, but wasn't counting on it. He slalomed through the lot like a Formula One driver, knowing that if Miller sounded the alarm before he reached the guard shack, they would raise the barricade and he would be trapped inside.

He pulled onto the final straightaway leading to the entrance. He floored the Malibu, wishing he was back in his BMW instead of the rented sedan. The Malibu reached fifty by the time he crossed the inner gate with the barricade.

The walkie-talkie crackled. "All stations! This is Miller! Stop employee Mike Manning! He drives a white Chevy Malibu!"

The guard in the bulletproof inner shack looked up just in time to see Manning roar past. Manning looked in his rearview mirror to see the barricade posts rising from the pavement. He allowed himself a small grin, then saw the guard at the outer gate step from his shack, his gun drawn. The guard reached up with his free hand to key his mike.

"Front gate to Miller!" Manning heard over the radio. "Manning in sight! Do I have permission to use deadly force?"

Manning grabbed the radio. "Negative front gate!" he shouted. "Do not shoot! We need him alive!" He kept the transmit key down to jam the frequency. "Front gate, acknowledge! Front gate, please respond!" He kept up the sham until he sped past the confused guard.

The light at the exit was red, but he barreled through without even looking. Maybe a crossing semi would T-bone him and put him out of his misery. No such luck. He heard screeching brakes and a blaring horn from another car, but he didn't even look back to see the source. He let off the transmit key of the walkie-talkie.

"…out his tires! I repeat, shoot out his tires! Front gate, acknowledge!" Manning heard.

"Sir, he's already off the property."

"Dammit!" Miller shouted, clearly in pain. "Call it in to the police; I've got my hands full!"

"Copy that, sir."

Manning needed to get the hell away from Nanovex, dump this car, and call Conrad. Maybe if he confirmed that he had fulfilled his end of the bargain and escaped to maintain his silence she would release his family. Maybe.

He knew that he had only about five minutes before an all-points-bulletin was put out for him and his vehicle. He needed someplace to hide, fast. Large buildings came up on the left. The Eastgate Mall. Perfect. He pulled in and drove around the lot, trying to come up with a plan. There, a parking garage. That would deny the FBI the ability to ID his empty car from the air and buy him a few minutes of running time.

He parked on the uppermost covered level and entered the mall. He scanned the crowd for a man who looked like him. It took a couple of minutes, but he spotted his mark on the level below him, carrying his wife's shopping bags. Even better. The man was dressed in a T-shirt and shorts, but Manning didn't need a perfect match.

He found an escalator and followed the couple into a Bed, Bath & Beyond store. *Poor bastard.* He felt some sympathy for the bag-toting husband. Faking interest in the perfumes and lotions, he maneuvered closer to the man and bumped him when their paths converged.

"Gosh, I'm sorry, I wasn't paying attention," Manning apologized.

"Oh, no problem," the patient husband assured him.

He hoped the man would be as understanding when the police and the FBI homed in on Manning's Blackberry at the bottom of the shopping bags. Manning reasoned that if the man knew what he was going through, he would agree that whatever inconvenience he was about to suffer was insignificant compared to Manning's quandary. That was the benefit of being a corporate lawyer—he had plenty of practice rationalizing the use of other people to suit his own needs.

He had seen a low-flying aircraft pass over the mall, then recalled that a small municipal airport was situated just to the north of the mall. Where there were airports, there were usually cabs. But before he hoofed it to the airfield, he checked just outside the exits to the mall. On his second exit, he hit the jackpot—a cabbie was eating his lunch in his car, hoping to snag a fare. He walked onto the parking lot.

He winced when a police helicopter swooped low, circling the mall. He knew he couldn't be identified from the air while on foot, but the hounds were closing in. Then he noticed something small, following the helicopter. It was a floating silver ball.

When the helicopter roared past, the ball broke off its pursuit and dropped down in an arc, straight toward him. He contemplated running, but quickly realized the futility and stayed put. The ball stopped at about a hundred feet up, hovered for a few seconds, then, as if judging him unsatisfactory prey, shot away over the mall, back in the direction of Nanovex. Manning let out the breath he had been holding and continued walking.

He rapped on the passenger-side window of the taxi. "You on duty?"

The driver put down his sandwich. "Am now. Where to?"

He climbed into the back seat. "Convention Center, please."

"You got it."

Two San Jose Police cars squealed onto the mall parking lot as the taxi turned onto the street. "Uh oh," the cabbie observed, "somebody done pissed off The Man."

He turned to watch the cruisers head toward the parking garage. "Yep, glad it's not me."

"I hear ya there."

* * *

No more explosions rocked the Nanovex building, but smoke from the lobby blast wafted up through the building's open core, collecting under the glass canopy. Since the lower level was in chaos and the bathroom fire appeared to have burned itself out, Miller requested that Lyman stay put for safety. The Nanovex medic returned his attentions to Lyman and the downed security guard outside the fourth-floor bathroom, leaving Hendrix and Shaozang alone.

"Did you get it?" Hendrix whispered.

Shaozang nodded. "Of course."

He patted him on the arm. "Good man."

Two firefighters burst from the nearby stairwell. "Why the hell are you people still in the building?"

"Security," Lyman responded.

"Well, Security's just been overruled. We have no idea how many more bombs are in here. Can your wounded walk, or do we need to bring up stretchers?"

Lyman got to his feet, still wiping his eyes. "I can walk." The other guard struggled to his feet with some assistance. "That's two. Dr. Chang?"

Shaozang made a good show of being helped to his feet. "I got him," Hendrix said.

"This is Search Four," the fire fighter said into his radio. "Five occupants coming down the north stairwell. Can somebody make sure they get out?"

"This is Chief Stanwick," a voice responded. "I'll get 'em."

"10-4, Search Four continuing." The fire fighter shook his finger in Lyman's face. "If any of your party has to stop, send someone down to get help, got it?"

"Understood," Lyman said meekly. "We're gone."

The fire fighters nodded, then started a room-to-room search, starting with the bathroom.

Lyman led the group down, with the medic supporting the guard and Hendrix pretending to support Shaozang, who still coughed and moaned occasionally.

"If you don't cut that out," Hendrix whispered in Chinese, "they're going to insist on taking you to the hospital to check you out." The coughing and moaning stopped abruptly.

The lobby resembled a war zone, with paramedics bent over the wounded, bomb-sniffing dogs checking the lobby for more hidden surprises, and a SWAT team that had been summoned for some reason. The air reeked of smoke and chemicals. Reese Miller lay on a stretcher while a paramedic cut away the bloodied leg of his suit pants. Miller fought with another paramedic trying to keep an oxygen mask in place.

"Listen!" Miller said, "I don't *have* a second in command to delegate this to! Until this situation is under control, you work on me *here*, and I can't use my radio with that damned thing on my face!"

Miller elbowed the paramedic away when he saw the SWAT team. "Guys! Over here!" When the heavily armed policemen gathered, he pointed at a man and woman cowering against the wall. "Those two require special protection! Put them in your van outside and form a perimeter around them! I'll explain later!"

Aha, Hendrix thought, *the last two workers from the WICKER BASKET project. The fire must have chased them out of their hiding spot.*

Miller apparently had a good reputation with the police; they accepted his orders without further questions. The SWAT team leader barked a command and the squad formed a protective circle around the two scientists, leading them toward the door.

A fireman in a white uniform shirt and peaked cap appeared next to Hendrix. "Are you Lyman?" he asked.

"I am," Lyman answered.

The firefighter extended his hand. "Chief Stanwick. I'll take you outside to the incident command post. If you wouldn't mind, would you relieve your security chief so we can take him to the hospital?"

Lyman suppressed a laugh. "Of course." He walked over to Miller and exchanged a few words, patting him on the shoulder. Miller handed over his radio and lay back on the stretcher. Behind Miller's back, one of the paramedics mouthed a silent "thank you." Lyman nodded and returned to his group.

"Lead the way, Chief," Lyman said.

They walked out behind the SWAT team into the California sunshine. Suddenly the SWAT team stopped, looking inward at their charges. The male scientist had collapsed, screaming in agony. The SWAT officers took half a step back, which allowed Hendrix a better look. The man writhed, his skin appearing to boil. It swelled like meat on a spit and jets of steam spouted from his nose and mouth. Then his flesh burst open and flames engulfed his body, burning him alive.

"Fire extinguisher!" the Chief cried. "Get me a fire extinguisher!"

Several firefighters ran to his aid, but it was far too late. When the suppressant fog cleared, the scientist was a charred statute, fixed in his final instant of torment.

"Sweet Mother of God!" Lyman exclaimed, crossing himself.

Hendrix's morbid fascination at the carnage was interrupted by a sudden movement to his left. The female scientist was jerked from the ground by an invisible force. Dragged upward feet first, her arms dangled, her horrified face framed by her blowing hair. She let out a blood-chilling scream, her upward acceleration already causing her shriek to fall in pitch like a passing siren.

Following her motion, Hendrix spied the silver ball fifty feet above her, continuing to tug her skyward. The ball hauled her several hundred feet up, then bolted away into the haze. The woman hung spread-eagled in space like a stick figure, her terrified cries barely audible. Then he realized the screams were getting louder.

"She's coming down!" one of the SWAT officers observed.

"Get clear!" the Chief shouted. "Back in the building!"

Those close to the building retreated inside. Those further away scattered onto the parking lot. Hendrix pulled Shaozang behind the lobby glass.

Like a twisted nightmare, the screams grew in pitch and volume until her words were clearly audible inside the lobby. The woman pleaded to God to save her. Her prayers dissolved into a final wail of panic when she realized no deity was coming to her rescue.

The female scientist hit the concrete just outside the lobby doors, her body exploding like a hand grenade. Blood and tissue drenched the glass in a viscous curtain, oozing downward to gravity's relentless pull. Hendrix heard retching somewhere behind him.

"Let's get out of here and report in," he whispered in Chinese to his partner. *That's the coolest damned thing I've ever seen.*

* * *

Manning sat on a bench outside the San Jose Convention Center, finally able to pause for a moment and collect his thoughts. He still didn't have any leverage, but at least he had done what Conrad had asked. He hoped that would count for something in bargaining for his family's freedom. He pressed the two buttons on his watch that conjured the devil. His burner phone rang two minutes later.

"Sounds like you gave the police quite a run for their money making your getaway. I'm very much impressed," she said pleasantly.

"Impressed enough to release my family?"

A sigh. "Sadly, no. I need you to come back in."

"Why?" he pleaded. "I'm *useless* to you at Nanovex. You obviously set me up to take the blame for whoever set that bomb. Just let me take the fall for that and call us even. Dear God, how many people did you kill today?"

"The news says there were two fatalities. How do you know *you* didn't kill them?"

He rubbed his throbbing temple with his free hand. "Burn in hell, Conrad."

"I think that's a forgone conclusion for both of us, Mike," she said calmly. "Now, let's talk about your family. I still have them, and I still want your cooperation."

Manning hung his head in defeat. "What do you want me to do?"

A moment's pause. "I see you're in front of the Convention Center. Just stay put and I'll send someone to collect you shortly."

CHAPTER 23

STRONG STOCK

CHICAGO, ILLINOIS

"Hold still, please," the Chinese man said politely.

"Who are you?" Amanda Manning asked.

A short pause. "You may call me Mr. Wu. I am here to treat your injuries."

It was the same man who had shot her neighbor Jenny and held Kevin at gunpoint. Now he sat cross-legged beside her, opening a small black bag like doctors used to carry. He had exchanged his blue repairman's coveralls for the white shirt and black apron of a shopkeeper.

They sat on a mattress in a dark, chilly basement, apparently under a small business. She could hear people walking overhead. She thought of calling out for help, but the thug who had originally cut her was never more than two steps away. She wouldn't scream for long. Besides, the only muffled voices she could make out from upstairs weren't speaking in English. She would probably be wasting her breath. Eric and Kevin sat on another mattress a few feet away, huddled together under a blanket, not just for warmth.

She remained motionless as Wu lifted her head, swabbing the blood that had run down from the puncture wound on her chin. He opened a bottle of iodine and wet a cotton ball.

"This will sting," he warned. It did. He examined the wound more closely with a penlight. "The wound is small and clean. I believe suture tape should suffice." He closed the cut with two strips, then examined her hand. The gauze bandage he had applied earlier was caked with dried blood. She winced as he unwound it.

"I apologize for your discomfort," he soothed, wetting the gauze with distilled water to help peel the bandage away. "I'm afraid this wound will require stitches."

She glanced at the throbbing gash on her hand and cringed. The sight of the torn flesh made her nauseous. She averted her eyes.

"Yes," he counseled, "it would be best if you look away while I work." She felt a cold aerosol spray on her hand. "This is a topical anesthetic. While that is taking effect, let me give you something else. Hold still, please." He capped a small bottle filled with thick yellow fluid with his index finger, then dabbed it under each of her nostrils.

A sweet, floral fragrance flooded her nose. She felt the aroma hit her brain. It made her slightly lightheaded. "What was *that*?"

"Ylang ylang. An herbal remedy for anxiety."

One corner of her mouth lifted. "I'll take a gallon, please."

He was confused for a moment and looked up from his work, then returned her smile. "Oh, you have not lost your sense of humor. That is healthy!" He cleaned the wound with iodine—she was glad for the anesthetic—then threaded a hooked needle with a thin black suture. "You will feel a tugging, but no pain," he assured her.

She looked away and closed her eyes tightly. She whimpered softly when she felt the pull of the suture thread on her flesh.

"Be brave, Mrs. Manning," he whispered. "Your children are watching."

She silently nodded her agreement, but felt a tear roll down her cheek.

After what seemed like several minutes, she felt fresh gauze being wrapped around her hand. He handed her another wad of gauze for her tears. "Well done, my dear. Your sons should be proud to come from such strong stock."

"Why are you doing this?" she demanded, dabbing her face. "You invade my home, kill my friend, threaten my children, and now you're all sweetness and light?"

He gave her a sad smile. "We all have our debts to pay. This is mine."

She nodded, then leaned forward, indicating she wished to whisper something not meant for her children's ears. He brought his ear close.

"Are you going to kill us?"

When he pulled back, his eyes were honest, but cold. "I sincerely hope not."

FREE LUNCH

SAN JOSE, CALIFORNIA

It was after noon when a black Cadillac Escalade pulled in front of the bench where Manning was seated. The passenger side window rolled down. The driver was the same man who had abducted him from the hotel's parking lot.

"Get in, you git!" the man sneered.

Manning complied, and they turned south out of the downtown area. He had skipped breakfast that morning, and his stomach growled loudly.

"Hungry, mate?" the driver asked.

"Yeah." *As if you cared.*

He turned off into a Burger King's drive-thru. "Good idea. I could fancy a bite myself." After they placed their orders, he stretched his hand toward Manning.

"What?" Manning asked.

The driver laughed. "*What*? You think I'm buyin' you lunch, you tosser? You're the fancy lawyer here. Fork over a twenty so I don't have to cut your wallet outta that pretty suit of yours!"

He dug in his pocket and slapped the bill into his captor's hand. "Whoever said there's no such thing as a free lunch obviously never held anyone at knifepoint," he grumbled.

The driver chuckled. "You're a funny one, you are!"

* * *

Two Whoppers later, they drove to an industrial park. The driver flipped open his cell phone. "Open sesame," he said.

They pulled up to a truck repair garage. The roll-up door was already rising. Manning realized they had reached their destination. "What, no blindfold?"

The driver laughed. "We got your family, mate. You're not likely to cross us."

The inside of the garage buzzed with activity. Several men in differing styles of paramilitary garb unpacked crates of equipment.

"It looks like you're gearing up for a war."

"And you're going to help lead us into battle," the driver said with a smirk. "Get out."

He complied, turning his head at a sharp whistle to his right. The redheaded woman from his earlier kidnapping beckoned.

"Manning! Back office!" Order given, she returned to her task of supervising the other new arrivals. He noticed they all seemed to be of different nationalities. He heard French and an Asian tongue he couldn't identify.

He reluctantly followed the driver to the office at the rear of the garage. Angela Conrad waited for him, along with a blond-haired man in foreign-looking civilian clothes sitting across the desk from her.

"Ah, Mike, glad you're here!" Conrad said. "Thanks, Ian. Would you help Meghan get the troops situated?"

"Sure," the driver said, excusing himself. He winked at Manning. "Thanks for lunch, mate!"

She waved him over. "Mike, sit down. Meet Vasily; he's our layout man for this operation."

He extended a grudging hand. "What's a layout man, and what operation?"

"A layout man," Vasily said with a thick accent, "creates a schematic of the target for planning purposes. Doors and windows, guardposts, anything the strike team needs to know for a successful mission."

"And that mission would be...?" he said, his gaze alternating between Conrad and Vasily.

"The penetration of the Nanovex facility to steal the WICKER BASKET nanoagent and any technical records we can find," she explained.

His eyes bugged. "Good thing you're raising an army—you're going to need it."

"Glad you approve. As our resident expert on the Nanovex complex, you're going to help Vasily build an accurate map."

He was relieved. "Sounds like the least dangerous thing I've done all day."

She laughed. "Speaking of which, I'd really like to know how you pulled off the fire today."

"Well, I found—"

"I meant later. For now, I want you and Vasily to get started on the layout.

Vasily stood. "Right away, Ms. Conrad," he said, tugging Manning's sleeve and motioning him outside. He led Manning to a worktable spread with blueprints and a laptop. "Be careful, my friend," Vasily whispered. "She is not to be trifled with."

Manning took off his jacket and draped it over a chair. "Tell me something I *don't* know, comrade."

ANGEL OF DEATH

SAN FRANSCISCO, CALIFORNIA

Pugliano knew something big was up. The agents on the surveillance unit called to report that the San Jose Police had just put out an APB on Manning. Apparently he had just tried to torch the Nanovex facility and had assaulted a number of people in the process. Pugliano inwardly cursed the fact that he was deprived of eyes on Manning at Nanovex—he could have taken the man into custody immediately. The team was watching the GPS feed from Manning's rental car in real time—did they have permission to share that information with the police?

"Hell yes!" was the answer Pugliano gave them immediately, only to remember that Manning was following Conrad's orders, with a gun aimed at his family's head.

"Hey Marty," he added, "make sure the police understand that Manning is a hostage in this whole mess. If they have to choose between bodily harm and letting him escape, let him go. No deadly force unless he pulls a gun on them, okay?"

"You got it, boss."

"Where is he now?"

"His car stopped in the parking garage at the Eastgate Mall. SJP has a chopper airborne; we just gave them the coordinates. They've also got patrol units inbound."

"Okay, keep me posted."

A few minutes later a near-hysterical Doug Lyman called from Nanovex. He was so frantic it was hard to piece together, but eventually Lyman communicated that the two remaining scientists in protective custody had died a horrible death right in front of him.

"Dammit, Agent Pugliano, you assured me those people would be safe!"

"No, Mr. Lyman," he said as diplomatically as he could, not wanting to set the man off further, "I said we were no longer *available* to protect them. I made it very clear that their protection was now *your* responsibility."

"With all due respect, Agent Pugliano," Lyman almost shouted, "how the *hell* am I supposed to protect my employees from a flying silver ball that burned one of them alive and hauled the other five hundred feet up in the air and dropped her on us like a *bomb*?"

Pugliano froze. "Did you say a silver ball?"

He had to hold the phone away from his ear as Lyman recounted the incident again. His histrionics made a lot more sense now. He told Lyman he would do his best to look into it, although he knew his best meant he would take no action at all. It would make little difference even if he ran a full-court press. That little ball might as well be the angel of death for all the power he had to stop it. After a few more minutes of bureaucratic platitudes he finally talked Lyman off the phone. His second line was already ringing, once again with the dreaded Washington D.C. area code.

"Pugliano!"

"This is Director Fitzmaurice! Did you hear what just happened at Nanovex?"

"I just got off the phone with their CEO." *How the hell did he hear about it so fast?*

"The NSA just ran a report past the President as FLASH traffic from the police radio intercepts. Get your ass over there and find out what the hell is going on. Report to me ASAP."

"On my way." Pugliano had better sense than to question the Director on his sudden reversal in policy. He called Wendy Cho's cell phone without success. He then called the surveillance team.

"Tell Agent Cho to meet me at the Nanovex facility in half an hour," he said, estimating the time to rustle up a helicopter and fly down.

"Sir, she's not here. And she's not answering her phone."

"Then find her!" he snapped.

GOOD RUN

SAN JOSE, CALIFORNIA

Linn Shaozang mopped the soot from the Nanovex operation off his face and hair with a wet towel. Hendrix stood behind him in the doorway of the hotel bathroom.

Shaozang was pale. "Have you ever seen anything like that?"

Hendrix shook his head. "Not even close."

"Most disturbing."

Of all the adjectives he would consider after watching one person burned alive and another dropped in front of him from the height of a skyscraper, *disturbing* was probably the mildest. "It could have been worse."

"How so?"

"That little ball could have been coming for *us*."

Shaozang's eyes widened. "Indeed."

Hendrix heard steps approach the hotel room door. He switched off the light, leaving Shaozang in darkness. "Quiet," he whispered.

The room's electronic lock made its peculiar opening sound and Wendy Cho stepped inside. She looked ill.

He pulled the bathroom door partially shut behind him. "Hope you don't need the restroom," he warned, waving his hand under his nose.

"Not unless I'm going to *throw up*," she spat.

"Problem?"

She put her hands on her hips. He noticed her right hand was positioned close to her service weapon. "Oh, let's see. Betrayal, kidnapping, *murder*—where should I start?"

He walked several steps into the room. "Ah, so that's why you called this meeting. Care to explain?"

She followed close on his heels. "You've switched sides! You're working for that bitch Conrad!"

He turned, glaring down at her. "Really? Have some evidence to back that up?"

She got her face as close as their height difference allowed. "Why the hell else would you need to know about the protective detail for the Manning family? You were plowing the road for Conrad. And two FBI agents got killed in the process!"

"You're just *heaving* the accusations around today, aren't you, young lady?"

"That's not exactly a denial."

"If that's all you've got, a denial isn't necessary. I hope you haven't told anyone else about this wild theory of yours. I'd hate for you to career-limit yourself."

Her eyes narrowed. "No, I wanted to look you in the face and see how you reacted. And now that I have, I've got one more accusation to make."

He opened his hands. "Oh, by all means."

Her right hand was already moving her jacket aside to reach for her pistol. "You're a lousy liar."

He shook his head sadly. "Well, that was cruel. But coming here by yourself? That was just plain *stupid*."

It had taken all of his self-discipline to keep his eyes locked on hers as Shaozang crept up behind her like a cat. He slipped the garrote over her head in a blur and hauled her backwards and off her feet to thwart a counterattack. Even with Shaozang's blindsiding assault, she had the presence of mind to turn her head sharply to the side, using one hand to grab the strangling cord, and the other to unholster her weapon.

That was Hendrix's cue. He leapt on Cho's weapon with both hands, turning the muzzle away from his body, then yanking hard. The pistol came out of her hands before she could even discharge a round into the wall for help-summoning noise.

Seeing her chance for lethal force ripped from her hands, Cho quickly switched to hand-to-hand resistance. She wasn't going down without a fight. As Shaozang pulled her backwards, she grabbed the garrote and pulled her legs off the ground, trying to flip her whole body over his head. The little wildcat almost pulled the maneuver off.

But they were two grown men and she was a very small woman. Grabbing her flailing legs with one arm, Hendrix reversed the pistol in his hand and brutally whipped her jaw with the butt. Carrying the motion through, he brought the gun back and did it again.

Cho slumped unconscious in Shaozang's arms. Wary of tricks, the Chinese assassin kept his killing hold firm for over a minute after she went limp. He finally lowered her body to the floor. Hendrix smelled urine when he bent over to check for a pulse.

Shaozang drew his shoulders back and took a deep breath. "She fought well. It was wise that you sought my assistance."

He frowned and stroked her swollen cheek once with the back of his hand. Even in death her eyes stared up at him in condemnation. "Yeah, she always was a little acrobat."

"This young woman meant something to you."

Hendrix wasn't sure if the comment was commiseration, or an accusation that he had allowed himself to get too close to an asset. He quickly swallowed any instinct of remorse and began sanitizing the room of his presence.

"Yeah, she had a good run," he offered.

Hendrix knew the FBI would check security cam footage after the body was found, so he had worn a disguise to the hotel, complete with prosthetic cheek and chin pieces to foil facial recognition software. He stepped over Cho's body and back into the bathroom to reapply his camouflage. Shaozang stepped into the doorway behind him.

"We did not discuss the fees for my assistance in this matter."

Hendrix glared at him in the mirror. "That's because I was hoping it wouldn't be necessary. When she called I just smelled trouble, I wasn't *planning* on offing the poor girl."

"Nevertheless it is done."

"What? And you want a bonus for this on top of what I'm already paying you?"

"You have not paid me what we had *already* agreed to."

He gave him an exasperated look. "I paid you a hundred grand, *cash*!"

"One hundred thousand dollars is not five million, which is the amount I recall agreeing to."

Hendrix returned his attention to the latex appliance he was gluing to his cheek. When he decided to go off the reservation, he had placated Shaozang by emptying out his last stateside stash and handing the Chinese agent a briefcase full of small bills. After emptying out his numbered accounts overseas to keep his fingers in Nanovex's WICKER BASKET program, his net worth was down to his two cars and his San Francisco house with its underwater mortgage. Some criminal mastermind *he* was.

"Well, I can't exactly wire Langley for the money now, can I?"

Shaozang gave him a long, cold stare. "Perhaps *I* should call them."

Listen to the balls on this guy! He put the finishing adjustment on his blond wig. "Come on, Linn, don't do anything rash. I've got half a mil stashed overseas. That may not be enough to retire comfortably on, but it's all I've got."

He looked skeptical. "And you will just *hand* this money over to me, I take it?"

"Hey, you *did* provide the introduction to Conrad. That's how *I'm* planning on retiring. That woman's got the best organized crime connections on the planet."

Shaozang sniffed. "I thought the CIA itself held that distinction."

He turned away from the mirror. "True enough, but operatives on our level don't get that big of a cut. Which you already know, or you'd still be working for the greater glory of the People's Republic, right?"

"Do not insult my country, Mr. Hendrix."

"And don't be petty, Linn. You're gonna get your money. Come on, let's get away from the body before her cell phone starts ringing."

THE GROUP

MARCH 31, 1967 – ZURICH, SWITZERLAND

After his debacle with the Americans, Kammler returned to South America and resumed his covert work on the Nazi's advanced technology program at Martin Bormann's remote ranch in Argentina. He was surprised a few months later by a guard's announcement that an unidentified gentleman had driven up to the gate and asked for him by name.

Deeply wary of Nazi-hunting Mossad agents after the recent kidnapping and subsequent execution of Adolf Eichmann by the Israelis, the visitor was bundled brusquely into the ranch's guest house and interrogated. He presented a letter from Prince Bernhard of the Netherlands inviting Kammler to a meeting "of some very influential people" in Zurich. In the man's briefcase was found fifty thousand American dollars in cash, "a gesture of good faith" from those who had requested Kammler's presence.

Through discrete intermediaries it was determined that Prince Bernhard had indeed sent the messenger and was in earnest about seeking Kammler's presence in Zurich, although the Prince refused to disclose the identities of the meeting's other attendees, citing "the anonymity of those who wish to work behind the scenes for the greater good." [1]

Kammler remained suspicious, but was ordered by Bormann to attend, citing assistance the Prince had rendered in securing Bormann's base of operations from the Argentinean government. He traveled to Zurich without incident under his Dr. Schmidt alias and arrived on time at the palatial headquarters of Credit Suisse on the bustling Paradeplatz. A bank officer intercepted him upon his entrance to the gilded lobby.

"Doctor Schmidt?" he asked. "Please come with me."

He led Kammler down a flight of stairs, past two pairs of armed guards. The first thick-necked pair in suits, the second in gray jumpsuits and black berets with German MP-40 submachine guns across their chests. Both set of watchmen regarded him with a cool gaze, missing nothing. These were professional soldiers, he realized, not mere security men.

Kammler was confused when their journey ended at the closed bank vault door, flanked by two more jumpsuited soldiers. With a flick of his escort's hand, the guards pulled open the massive door, revealing a conference table flanked by a dozen well-dressed men inside the vault.

Kammler recognized the bespectacled Prince Bernhard from his photograph when he stood.

"Ah, my dear Dr. Schmidt," the Prince effused, extending a hand. "Please excuse the theatrics. Our paranoia will be justified shortly."

Kammler stepped across the vault's threshold, feeling the press of air when the safe door closed behind him. The men at the table regarded him clinically—not with hostility, but certainly not with warmth. With a shock he realized that he recognized not just the Prince but several men at the table from their photographs. This was *indeed* a gathering of the world power elite.

The Prince waved him to the end seat nearest the vault door. "Doctor Kammler, welcome. May I get you something to drink?" Now that the vault was closed, the pretense of his alias was apparently being dropped.

"No thank you, *mein Herr*," he replied, unsure of the proper protocol for addressing royalty. He sat, the Prince taking the chair at the opposite end.

"Please relax, Doctor Kammler," a stately Englishman to his left urged. He recognized the man as a young and upcoming British politician whose family's wealth exceeded that of the House of Windsor. Kammler couldn't remember the man's last name, since the newspapers usually referred to him only as Lord Harold. "We may insist on our due of bowing and scraping in public, but in these meetings we do not stand on ceremony, and ask that you do the same."

He nodded. "Of course, sir. Thank you."

"Do you know why you have been summoned here today?" a handsome Frenchman to his immediate right asked. Kammler recognized him as Michel Rochelin, of the immensely wealthy Rochelin family. Their wealth was so immense that their business operations had proceeded without interference throughout the Nazi occupation. Even Hitler had the good sense not to put the golden goose under a hobnail boot.

Summoned. These men were used to giving orders and being obeyed. "No, and I must compliment you on your security," he replied. "Despite the best efforts of my organization, the purpose of your meeting today remains a complete mystery to me." The smiles and nods around the table told him no greater compliment could have been given.

"I am indeed gratified to hear that," Prince Bernhard said. "Because today we are proposing the formation of a group whose secrecy will exceed even that of our own."

Kammler's eyebrows rose. "How so?"

An American with a thick New England accent addressed him next. "Doctor Kammler, knowing what you know now about the true impact of the atomic bomb, would you try to put that genie back in the bottle?"

Kammler was confused.

"I think what Franklin is saying," Lord Harold interjected, "is that if you, as *General* Kammler, had known at the time you were developing the atomic bomb that it would neither save Germany from defeat nor assure lasting peace after the war, would you have continued with its development?"

He noticed that they credited the development of the atomic bomb to *him*. These men had accepted none of the deceptions peddled by the Americans after the war. Perhaps that was the purpose of the question.

"That choice was not up to me," he offered. "Reichsfuehrer Himmler, and ultimately Hitler himself, made that decision."

"Then place yourself in their shoes," Lord Harold pressed. "Knowing that the atomic bomb would *not* save the Third Reich, but *would* ultimately result in the situation we face today, with two superpowers pointing enough nuclear-tipped missiles to effectively snuff out human life on this planet in an hour, would *you* proceed with the project?"

He had no idea why these inestimably powerful men were pursuing this line of questioning. "No, if you phrase it that way, perhaps I would not."

More gratified nods around the table.

"We have noted with great interest the remarkable technological leaps you have achieved since the war," Prince Bernhard said. "How long do you think it will be until other countries like the United States and the Soviet Union duplicate your progress?"

He thought ruefully of his experience with the Americans. But even *they* could not be counted out indefinitely. Now that they knew of the radical physics the Bell had made available, it would only be a matter of time until they achieved similar results, even if only by blind, random experimentation. And once the United States broke through, the Soviets would quickly find an American willing to turn over those secrets for ideology or cash.

"Perhaps another ten years," Kammler estimated conservatively.

The Prince nodded. "Your man Kurt Debus in America concurs with that figure. So we still have time."

"I beg your pardon," he asked. "Time for what?"

Lord Harold smiled coldly. "Time to prevent our respective governments from letting *another* genie out of the bottle, perhaps one even more destructive than the atomic or the hydrogen bombs."

"Scientific progress is like the tide," Kammler observed. "Even if your governments could prevent their internal agencies from pursuing certain technologies by edict, individual scientists would eventually eat through any embargo you would attempt like termites, simply because of relentless scientific curiosity."

The American leaned toward him. "Unless an organization was formed to track the progress of such individuals, and dissuade them from continuing down destructive paths."

He calculated mentally. "What you are proposing would require vast resources, similar in scale to the intelligence networks of any of your home countries."

A gale of laughter swept the room. Kammler had no idea why they were so amused.

"My dear Doctor Kammler," Prince Bernhard chuckled, "resources are the least of our worries. Control over seventy-five percent of the world's wealth rests with the men inside this vault. Would that be sufficient for your task?"

He was stunned. "Y-yes," he stammered. "I'm sure it would."

Another amused titter ran through the room. Several of the men emptied their drinks and refreshed them from the bottles lining the center of the table. Lord Harold poured two glasses of brandy and handed one to Kammler with a wry smile.

"And it won't be necessary to build a *duplication* of our intelligence networks," Lord Harold explained, "but simply *subjugate* the existing agencies to our new agenda."

Kammler knew better than to ask if these men actually had the power to bring the CIA, KGB and all the other intelligence organs of the world to heel. Without money, even the most powerful spy agency was a toothless tiger. And with seventy-five percent of the world's money supply under these men's control, they could strangle any economy on the planet like shutting off a faucet. It was a level of power Hitler had never experienced even at the height of his majesty.

"What about the technologies my team and I have *already* developed?" he asked.

"You will make them available to *us*, exclusively," Rochelin declared.

"And you will continue to develop them," Lord Harold added, "to maintain the unquestioned technological supremacy of the organization we are creating."

"How would you like me to proceed?" he asked tentatively.

"That is up to you, Doctor Kammler," the Prince said. "The Group meets on a yearly basis. Please craft a detailed proposal and organizational structure to be presented at our next meeting. Any resources you require during this planning phase will be provided, of course. Simply make your needs known to *Herr* Bormann, and he will contact us."

His head swam with the possibilities that had suddenly opened before him. "Thank you, gentlemen. I look forward to working with you."

Lord Harold lifted his glass. "May the world become a safer place through the efforts we have begun today." Clinking glasses and affirmations of "Hear, hear," circled the table.

The Prince pressed a button at his right hand and Kammler heard the vault door open behind him. "We look forward to hearing from you in a year's time, Doctor Kammler," the Prince said in dismissal.

Rochelin's eyes were cold as a snake's. "Do not disappoint us, Doctor."

INDULGENCES

PRESENT DAY – CHICAGO, ILLINOIS

Simon Crane spent the afternoon monitoring the communications chatter of the various American intelligence and law enforcement agencies over their supposedly secure communications networks. Although he prided himself on his emotional detachment, he could not help a measure of sadistic pleasure at the confusion and alarm his agent in California had instilled in the mighty American government.

That same sadistic pleasure led him to break with his established practices and actually watch a TV newscast. The mystified and frightened blathering of the anchors while a crawler under the screen screamed UFO KILLS TWO IN SAN JOSE was truly a delight to behold. He scolded himself inwardly for such indulgences, but reasoned that moments like this came along so rarely they could be safely enjoyed to their fullest without compromising his rigid self-discipline.

The phone rang. His agent was calling. "Report!" he answered.

"The last two scientists have been eliminated."

"Difficulties?"

"None."

"I'm watching the results of your handiwork. I must say, for someone trained to work in the shadows, you certainly have a flair for the dramatic."

Fear crept into the young man's voice. "Sir, I earnestly hope you are not displeased with my methods."

Crane surprised himself with the chuckle that escaped his lips. He certainly was in a jovial mood today. "Not at all, Seth. I ordered you to make a demonstration, and you have accomplished that goal." *Addressing an agent by his first name? I most certainly <u>am</u> letting my discipline slip,* he cautioned himself. *But the young man has proven himself several times over. Time to drop the evil overlord routine and speak to him with the respect he has earned.*

The relief was palpable. "I'm very gratified to hear that, sir."

"They'll have their hands full for weeks trying to put out this fire. But once they're done, I dare say they'll never cross us again, at least not while President Cameron is in office. Well done, Agent Graves."

"Thank you, sir."

BRUTE FORCE

SAN JOSE, CALIFORNIA

Conrad's garage looked quite different when Hendrix and Shaozang returned. Several military cots lined one wall, with a long mess table filling the open spot past where the vehicles parked. Several of Conrad's new goons partook of a long submarine sandwich and beers from a cooler. Hendrix saw Manning huddled over a work table in the corner with another of Conrad's new additions.

She stalked out of her office at the rear of the garage. "What took you so long?"

"We had to tie off a loose end that would have endangered the operation," he said.

"What kind of loose end?" she demanded.

"Let's just say we won't be getting any more updates from inside the FBI."

"Dammit," she seethed. "Did you two at least make a clean getaway?"

"Yes."

"I can assure you that we did," Shaozang added.

She tapped her high heel impatiently. "Well? Where's the take from your mission?"

Shaozang pulled a pen from his pocket. "Right here."

"Ghost!" she called. "You're up! My office!"

A young but hardened Japanese man looked up from the mess table. "Hai!" he replied, standing and wiping his mouth on his sleeve.

She jerked her head. "Let's go."

Shaozang plugged the pen-camera into the mini-USB port on Conrad's laptop. The photos uploaded quickly. She turned the laptop to face Shaozang and the Japanese agent. "Tell me what I'm looking at."

"It's an NEC multi-mode fire and intrusion alarm system," Shaozang explained. "It uses nested layers of access control and detection hardware, linked with heuristic facial recognition software."

"In English, please."

"Not only does the system possess multiple access control systems like handprint and retinal scanning for the high security areas, but the building's security cameras are tied into a facial recognition system that tracks everyone in the building in real time. If even one security camera picks you up, your face is entered into the database. If the system doesn't detect you again for a specified period of time, say if you were attempting to avoid the security cameras, it detects your absence and alerts Security."

"So there's no way to finesse this system."

"If we had root access to the control computer in the Security office I might be able to write a virus that would disable key systems. But their level of manpower and physical security make that approach impossible."

She looked at the Japanese alarm specialist. "Ghost, do you concur?"

He shook his head. "No computer access, no good."

She pushed away from her desk and crossed her arms. "Okay, that's pretty much what I suspected, but good work confirming it for me. Looks like we're back to brute force. Does this alarm have an automated system for calling outside help?"

"Of course," Shaozang said. Ghost nodded his agreement.

"Then you two figure out how we can cut Nanovex off from the outside world long enough for us to get in and get out."

The two alarm specialists regarded each other with concern.

"Hey!" she shot back at their unspoken protest. "If this was going to be easy I would have hired some geek from Radio Shack! Get to it!"

Shaozang and Ghost shuffled uneasily from the office. Hendrix watched them go, then turned back to the sound of a pistol being cocked in his face.

"You know," Conrad said from behind the gun, "now that you've gotten what I needed from inside Nanovex and you've lost your inside source at the FBI, I'm wondering why I'm keeping you alive. I never much liked you to begin with."

He smiled, placing his hands flat on the desk top. "If you'll have your girlfriend close that door, I'll tell you *exactly* why you're keeping me alive."

PATERNAL ANGER

SAN JOSE, CALIFORNIA

Pugliano had the pilot land the helicopter on the Nanovex parking lot. Crime scene units from the San Jose Police still clustered around the building's entrance.

Lyman waited in his office. The man looked like he was on the verge of a nervous breakdown, his hair disheveled and his tie askew. His breath smelled of vomit.

"Thanks for coming so quickly, Agent Pugliano," he said in a hollow voice. "Although I wonder how much of this would have happened if your people hadn't left."

He gazed at his shoes. "Would it help if I told you I was *ordered* to leave Nanovex?"

Lyman walked to a cabinet and pulled out a bottle of Scotch. "It would help me feel better about *you*, at least. Can't say it endears me to your bosses. I know you can't drink on duty, but do you mind if I do?"

"Not at all."

"Thanks. Those people *trusted* me to protect them. All of them, not just the two that died today. Hell, my base got shelled almost every day in Afghanistan, and my headquarters unit didn't lose as many people in my whole tour as Nanovex has lost in a month."

He fingered the globe-and-anchor pin on his lapel. "Marines, Desert Storm. I hear ya."

Lyman took a deep draw on his Scotch. "At least you and I knew what we had signed up for. These people were just going to work. Supporting their families."

He began to wish he had taken Lyman up on the drink. "That's the way it goes sometimes." His phone buzzed. It was the surveillance team.

"I'm sorry, Mr. Lyman, I need to take this." He keyed his phone. "Pugliano."

"We found Wendy. She's dead."

* * *

Pugliano wished he had brought the GPS from his car. The GPS in the helicopter had been designed to find airports, not hotels, and the pilot was familiar with the landmarks of downtown and the Bay area, not the Valley. After several minutes of flying a grid pattern, they found the hotel solely from the flashing police lights in front.

Surveillance Specialist Marty Clagget met him on the parking lot. "We tracked her down using her cell phone. We found her in one of the rooms. Looks like strangulation."

"Dammit," he muttered, feeling an almost paternal anger seething up under his collar. Somebody had declared open season on FBI agents and he was going to end them, period.

He checked the surroundings before he entered the hotel lobby. What the hell was Cho doing at a hotel next to the airport, *miles* away from her assigned surveillance of Manning?

"So Marty, did she have a boyfriend?"

Clagget looked uncomfortable. He cleared his throat. "Let's just say I don't think she ever lacked for male companionship."

He grunted. "Gotcha." He used to only have to worry about *male* agents' sex lives getting them in trouble. All hail sexual equality.

Since her fellow agents found the body, they owned the crime scene from the first moment, avoiding any evidence-trampling by the local police. Pugliano and Clagget made their way to the door and looked in, but did not enter.

"Talk to me," Pugliano called to the bootie-footed FBI photographer stepping carefully around the body.

He pointed. "Ligature marks on the neck, bruising on the hands and jaw. Her pistol was beside her but not fired. I'd say two assailants. She fought back, but they got the better of her pretty quick."

"So, a lover's quarrel is out?"

He shook his head. "This was an ambush. I'm hesitant to call it professional, but that's where I'd put my money."

Pugliano examined the door frame without touching it. "No sign of forced entry."

Clagget held out an iPad with a security camera freeze frame. It showed a blond-haired man in his forties wearing a sport coat. "Front desk says this guy checked in and left a key for Wendy."

He scrutinized the screen grab carefully. The quality wasn't the best, and the guy didn't look familiar. "Have you checked the cameras for the parking lot?"

"Yeah, we tried to follow him to his car to get a make and model, but he walked off property."

"I assume you're pulling footage from every adjacent property?"

"As we speak, but the path this guy took showed he knew where the cameras were and avoided them. We're not going to find his car."

He handed back the iPad. "Keep trying anyway."

"Of course, sir. Maybe we'll get lucky." Clagget paused. "You're thinking this is tied to Conrad?"

“I don’t believe in coincidences. Not on a day like this.” He pulled out his cell and made a call, then looked at the phone in frustration.

“What’s wrong, sir?”

“I’ve been trying to reach Hendrix all day. He’s not picking up.”

UNFINISHED BUSINESS

SAN JOSE, CALIFORNIA

After a hearty take-out dinner at the mess table—the group had voted for Italian—Conrad addressed the assembled operatives.

“Time for us to go operational, gentlemen,” she said. Hendrix noted that there were no women among the new additions.

“Broad overview, the mission is to penetrate the Nanovex Company facility here in San Jose by brute force with a large strike team. Once inside, we will forcibly acquire all materials and data we can quickly secure pertaining to a project called WICKER BASKET. We will exit the facility—again, probably by force—and move as a unit to the auction site, where we will be joined by your principals. We will then maintain security while the auction is conducted, and the captured materials from the raid will be awarded to the winning bidder. At that point the group will disband and you will exit the auction site with your principals. Any questions so far?”

“What is this WICKER BASKET project?” One of the Russians asked.

“You weren’t informed by your principal about the nature of the target?”

“No.”

“Then apparently he felt you didn’t have a need to know. What else?”

“How are we getting in and out?” a French agent asked.

Conrad gestured to her original team, who were standing to one side of the mess table. She pointed first to Cosgrove. “This is Ian. He’ll handle transportation. In conjunction with Vasily, our layout man,” she paused to point, “he’ll decide the available vehicle or vehicles best suited to the task. Agent Shiva?”

An Indian operative raised his hand. “Here.”

“Shiva, you will report to Ian and assist him in procuring whatever we need.”

“Understood,” he replied, with a trace of a British accent.

She pointed at Kinberg. “This is Dieter. Whatever weapons or explosives you require, make your requests to him. Understand though, we’re not the Picatinny Arsenal. Whatever we can obtain for you, you will be expected to familiarize yourself with and use. Bellyaching about unfulfilled wishes will be poorly received. Got it?”

The nods around the mess table were casual. As former soldiers they were all used to accomplishing their mission with the tools at hand.

"Agent Nikolai? You're Dieter's number two man."

"Of course," a second Russian replied.

"This is Meghan. She is your supply officer. Anything else you need for the mission; body armor, special equipment, night vision gear. She'll do her best to fix you up. Agent Javelin, back her up. Clear so far?"

More nods.

"Now onto some unfinished business. Linn, can you brief the group on your findings from your reconnaissance at the Nanovex building today?"

Shaozang seemed surprised, but stepped forward and presented a concise and professional description of the physical and electronic security at their target. The operatives gave him their full attention.

"So Linn," she asked, "it's your conclusion that a covert entry would not be feasible?"

He shook his head. "Out of the question. A skilled operative could penetrate the facility undetected, but the physical security at the laboratories themselves will require explosives to circumvent, making a clandestine theft impossible."

"How many guards did you see at the facility today?"

"I personally counted twelve, but I'm sure there were others watching security feeds or waiting in reserve. If forced to guess I would say eighteen to twenty men."

"Weapons?"

"The visible guards only carried sidearms—Glock 23s I believe—but I would be very surprised if automatic weapons were not stored at the main guard station."

"So eighteen to twenty men, at least some of them with automatic weapons."

"That is correct."

"And what was the price you agreed to for selling me out to the CIA?"

He startled. "I'm sorry?"

Shaozang turned to find himself staring at half a dozen drawn pistols, including Hendrix's. The operatives at the table were a study in still life.

"Five million, wasn't it?" she snarled. "Hell, I'll be lucky if that's my take for this whole damn operation. I didn't peg you as a greedy bastard, but you sure as hell fit the bill."

His eyes bugged. "No! Please! I can explain!"

She cut him off. "If there's one thing I've gotten good at in this business, it's spotting a liar. Especially one caught with his pants down." She nodded at Hendrix.

He stepped forward and put a single round into Shaozang's brain stem, being careful to aim up slightly so the bullet would go into the ceiling and not into the assembled operatives. Shaozang collapsed, his hand already wrapped around the grip of his pistol.

Conrad turned to the shocked operatives. "I suspect some of you have been tasked as spoilers by your principals to undermine this mission. But no matter what your specialty on this assignment, I'll be pairing you either with a member of my team or an operative from another country as a safety measure. And if I hear that any of you are not playing on side, take a good look at my former associate, Mr. Shaozang. Remember that he was a member of *my* team, but I didn't hesitate to put him down. He'll be a hell of a lot harder to replace than any of you."

She turned to her right. "Vasily, Manning. Layout briefing, you're up."

Hendrix stood transfixed, watching Shaozang's blood flow in rivulets to a nearby drain. It occurred to him that in all his time in the CIA he had never killed anyone by his own hand. It was an odd feeling.

Conrad elbowed him out of his trance. "Okay, partner. You made the mess, you clean it up."

[1] Prince Bernhard of the Netherlands has long been a controversial figure in the international community. A member of the Nazi party and the SS in the 1930s, he renounced his party membership when Hitler invaded the Netherlands and fled with the rest of the royal family to England, where he served with distinction in the RAF, flying Spitfires, B-25s and B-24s extensively in combat against the Germans.

In his position on the Allied war planning staff he rubbed shoulders with British Intelligence officer Ian Fleming, who would go on to write the James Bond spy novels. Fleming wrote that he drew some of his inspiration for the swashbuckling Bond from Prince Bernhard, including his penchant for martinis that were "shaken, not stirred." A line drawing Fleming made of his fictional James Bond character bears a striking resemblance to Prince Bernhard's appearance during the war.

However, Prince Bernhard's past associations with the Nazis and his vice presidency in the German arms manufacturer IG Farben, as well as his extensive travels to South America and admitted bribery of officials in exchange for Dutch business contracts lent to rumors of his involvement with the Nazi community-in-exile.

In 2007 Dutch journalists uncovered documents detailing the use of the Dutch airline KLM to transport suspected Nazi war criminals to Argentina after WWII. Prince Bernhard was director of KLM at that time. Rumors swirled in yet another direction when the Prince helped found the Bilderberg Group, an annual secretive meeting of world leaders and financiers to coordinate world monetary and foreign policy behind closed doors. The Prince left a string of bribery scandals and illegitimate children around the world upon his death in 2004. (Source: *KLM accused of helping Nazis flee*, BBC News, May 8, 2007)

CHAPTER 24

OPENINGS

CHICAGO, ILLINOIS

Amanda Manning huddled with her sons under a blanket. The basement of their captivity got very chilly at night—at least she assumed it was night. The sounds of customers walking above had ceased hours ago, and the street noise outside had faded to the occasional rumbling of a garbage truck or a street cleaner.

While it was clear Mr. Wu was not about to let his guard down with his hostages, he was at least attentive to their needs, if not their comforts. He even brought the boys Happy Meals, and asked her if she had any special requests for food. The baked chicken and vegetables he brought were modest in their portions, but well-prepared. Judging from his interest in whether she liked her meal, it may have been cooked with his own hands.

They changed the guards at dinner. The scowling hulk who had watched them all day almost without blinking was replaced by a smaller thug with a patchy beard. While the big guard regarded them with little more than a cold stare, this younger man did little to conceal his sexual curiosity toward her. His eyes lingered over her figure, especially her breasts. At first she reacted by covering up with the blanket even when she didn't need it for warmth. Then she realized that his interest might be the only opening she would get to escape, if she could catch him with his guard down.

To test her theory, she left the bathroom door slightly ajar when she was allowed to relieve herself. Sure enough, she caught him moving to watch through the slit, his eyes wide and breathing fast and shallow. She made lingering eye contact with him, then slowly pushed the door fully closed. When she passed him on the way back to her mattress, she could see his pulse racing from the twitching vein on the side of his neck. She didn't think he would try to rape her—Mr. Wu would likely frown on such treatment—but he might react if given an opportunity.

She pulled Eric close during the night. "Honey," she whispered to him, "if I give you an opening, I want you to take your little brother and get out of here. Run and keep running until you find a policeman."

"What are you going to do?" he asked, the doubt in his mother's ability to overpower the guard evident in his voice.

"You leave that to Mom," she said with a kiss on the forehead. "But if I yell, 'Run,' I want you two to be ready. "Got it?"

He made a brave but unsuccessful attempt to keep the fear out of his voice. "Got it."

DO-GOODERS

SAN JOSE, CALIFORNIA

Mike Manning's role in Conrad's scheme seemed to be over. Once Vasily had the basic layout for the Nanovex facility, he only needed Manning for an occasional detail question. The Russian was very good at what he did.

Manning sat at the mess table after Conrad's crew had finished breakfast and picked half-heartedly through the leavings. It seemed that biscuits and hash brown patties were not the favored fare of terrorist commandos, so that was his breakfast. At least there was plenty of coffee.

The guy Conrad called Hendrix had apparently been tasked as Manning's babysitter. He hadn't strayed beyond spitting distance all morning. He asked the man some harmless questions about his background, receiving only the polite version of "None of your damned business" in reply. The guy would have made a good lawyer.

If Manning had any illusions about his fate, watching Conrad waste one of her own henchmen who had outlived his usefulness last night had shattered those. He wondered if *anyone* survived contact with her in the long term. Yuri and Ari certainly hadn't, and now one of their replacements had bitten the dust. He realized that made him the longest-serving member of her team so far, which was a disturbing thought.

"Manning!" Meghan yelled in his direction. "We got a meeting! Clear the table!"

He shoved the rest of a cold potato patty into his mouth and complied. At least his usefulness was assured for the next ten minutes.

Watching them go through the planning of their assault on Nanovex, one thing that became quickly obvious was the impending violence that was about to break out. These guys were preparing for an all-out war. He had watched enough documentaries on the History Channel to know that with war comes confusion. And confusion might afford him the opportunity to escape. That's assuming she didn't kill him before the assault even began. But it was a shred of hope, more than he had been able to grasp in a long time.

How long *had* this ordeal been going on? He calculated mentally. Less than two weeks. Dear God, it seemed like eternity. This must be what hell is like. He would probably find out firsthand soon enough.

* * *

Conrad's team and the new operatives gathered around the mess table. Hendrix made a show of joining them, so as not to appear useless. That would be a lethal shortcoming. The seats were taken, but he pulled up a chair from Vasily's work table. He motioned for Manning to do the same.

"I'm gonna need an electromagnetic pulse bomb," Conrad said without preamble. "More than one if you can get it."

Gallagher eyed the Russian sitting next to her. "An EMP bomb is beyond the reach of my contacts, but Nikolai here should be able to conjure one up. Right, Niki?"

The Russian squirmed. "EMPs, as you Americans would say, do not grow on trees." [1]

"But you're supposed to be a supply specialist in Russian hardware," Conrad countered, "*and* you're active duty Russian Intelligence. So call your bosses in Moscow and tell them you have an operational need."

He raised an eyebrow. "Those weapons are tightly controlled."

"So are nerve-gas-dispensing nanoagents. If your people want the goods, we're going to need the EMPs. Surely the SVR has a few EMPs on US soil for 'contingencies.'"

Nikolai shrugged. "Not that I am aware of."

"Then what about Cuba? Don't tell me the SVR doesn't have an emergency weapons stockpile in this hemisphere."

He pulled out a satellite phone and stepped away from the table. "I will need to make a few calls."

"You do that. How are we coming with the helicopter?"

Cosgrove pushed a piece of paper across the table. "Here's a list of the commercial helicopters in the Bay area. Shiva and I have scouted out the security at the airports and shouldn't have too much trouble making off with a bird."

She frowned. "Wait a minute. The biggest thing on this list is an Augusta 109. That's not going to cut it."

"If you want something bigger, then you're going from commercial to military. That's a whole new level of security."

She dismissed his concerns with a flip of her hand. "Hollywood."

"Sorry?"

"Hollywood. They use old military choppers for films all the time. Find who's got what, then go steal the biggest one you can get. Hendrix, you know LA pretty well, don't you?"

"Sure." It was one of his favorite places to escape from his wife.

"Then help Ian steal us a chopper."

It sounded a lot more fun than babysitting this lawyer boob Manning. "No problem."

After the meeting she pulled him aside. "I need something else from you."

He was eager for a chance to justify his continued usefulness. "Name it."

"I need a CIA encoder."

His eyes bugged. "How about I tackle the guy who carries the football for the President and steal the nuclear codes instead? That would be easier."

"If it was going to be easy I'd have Manning do it. I'm asking *you*."

She assumes everyone's balls are as big as hers. "The only people who have access to those encoders are CIA paramilitary units deployed overseas, *when* they're deployed. The rest of the time those black boxes are locked up in a safe on Diego Garcia."

She gave him a wry grin. "And on CIA drug smuggling planes, of course."

Oh dear God, don't make me cross those people. Drug smuggling had been the lifeblood of CIA covert operations since the Vietnam War. It was the only way to get large amounts of money without going through Congress, which leaked secrets like a sieve. Not even the KGB could match the ruthlessness of the CIA contractors charged with keeping the drugs flowing. The closest parallel he could think of was the Mafia, but *La Cosa Nostra* never had access to the talent or the hardware of the CIA.

How would you like to be above the law and richer than God? That was the pitch they had given him after his first overseas tour in the CIA. But back then he was about to get married and worried about the repercussions of his soon-to-be wife finding out her new husband was a government-sanctioned drug smuggler. Of course that was before his wife turned into an unrelenting shrew. When he re-approached the group about joining up, they laughed at him.

"You got married, which means you have a heart, which makes you useless to us," his contact derided. "Have a great life in bureaucracyland." Scorned from legitimate crime, Hendrix had been pushed into making his own.

"Where's the nearest CIA port-of-entry?" she pressed.

"San Diego," Hendrix muttered. His Hong Kong office had regularly handled the huge sums of money the San Diego office needed to move offshore every month.

"Then get down there and steal me an encoder."

"How am I supposed to know which jets are being used by the CIA? It's not like they paint it on the side of the plane."

She waved him into her office and sat down. She typed on her laptop and turned it for his inspection. "Fortunately for us, the CIA is a little too efficient for their own good. They keep a fleet of jets available for transporting prisoners down to Guantanamo Bay, but most of the time those jets sit idle. Busy little bean counters that they are, they like to use that down time to make deliveries from Columbia and Mexico. And Amnesty International—busy little do-gooders that *they* are—keeps an up-to-date list of the rendition aircraft and posts it online as a form of protest against US anti-terror policies." [2]

His shoulders fell. This certainly wasn't news to *him*, but now that *she* knew it, there would be no escape from this errand. "So just match up a tail number and find an encoder, right?"

"That's it. Can I count on you?"

With the alternative being a bullet through my head? "Absolutely. The problem is going to be getting close enough to do the deed without arousing suspicion."

She shrugged. "You know the best way to get close to an airplane?"

"Enlighten me."

"With another airplane. As long as you fly in with an impressive enough aircraft, ground control will let you park anywhere you want."

"You've done this before."

She stood in dismissal. "You have a game plan now, so get to it. And appoint somebody else as Manning's nanny before you leave."

"With pleasure."

MAKE OR BREAK

SAN FRANCISCO, CALIFORNIA

Pugliano's gut spasmed in anticipation of this teleconference with FBI Director Fitzmaurice. He knew he shouldn't have had that second cup of coffee. Thankfully, the Director had called this meeting on such short notice that the hangers-on from Justice and the US Attorney's office weren't here to gum up the works. The Director's moderately ugly face filled the wall of the conference room at the stroke of nine o'clock. Pugliano reminded himself he wouldn't win any beauty contests himself.

"So where are we, Perry?" Fitzmaurice said with a labored smile.

Why is it that a smiling superior always makes my butt clench? He asked himself. *Oh yeah, experience, that's why.* "Sir, my visit to Nanovex didn't tell me anything we didn't already know. The two remaining scientists were killed by that anomalous flying object, one by incineration and one by impact. I asked the coroner on scene for an expedited report. His preliminary results show no death mechanism other than the obvious."

The Director's hand went to his temple momentarily. "Dear God, Perry, do your people have any idea what's behind this?"

"Not a clue, sir." He had Hendrix's Nazi theory of course, but it was just that—a theory. He certainly didn't have any evidence to back it up.

Fitzmaurice almost seemed pleased with that response. "So were those two scientists the last survivors from WICKER BASKET?"

He sighed. "I'm afraid so, sir."

Again, an almost approving nod. "That's a tough break for Nanovex."

Oh well, win some, lose some. "Yes sir, that's one way to put it."

"Did I hear you had another one of your people fall victim to foul play?"

"Not one of my people, sir, the local Chief of Station for the CIA has gone missing. I'm betting his body just hasn't washed up yet." He hoped Hendrix hadn't been snuffed out because of what he knew—especially since Pugliano now shared that conspiratorial knowledge.

"Is the Agency cooperating?"

"Completely. I don't sense any subtext—they honestly don't know what happened to their man and are glad for our help."

A lifted eyebrow. "You think this has something to do with Conrad?"

He turned to his laptop. "Yes sir, I do. We ran every person on the hotel surveillance footage at the time of Agent Cho's murder through the NCIC database and came up with an interesting hit." He clicked to a freeze frame of an Asian man in a suit, along with a full-face surveillance photo from the FBI files. "This guy's named Linn Shaozang; he's one of Conrad's known associates. The other man on the security cameras was a dead end. Probably another one of Conrad's spooks."

"So you think he lured Agent Cho to the hotel to kill her?"

"That's one theory. She *was* the lead agent on the surveillance of Mike Manning, Conrad's inside man at Nanovex."

A puzzled look. "Conrad had to know that just killing one FBI agent wouldn't take the heat off her man. If anything it would make it ten times worse."

"Like I said, it's just a theory, and it has its weaknesses."

"Speaking of Manning, whatever happened to him after he tried to burn down Nanovex?"

Pugliano shifted uncomfortably. "He's dropped off the grid, sir. We haven't had any luck picking up his scent yet, but we're still looking."

"So what the hell was Conrad's angle, ordering him to torch the place?"

"Misdirection, most likely. She *had* to know the suppression system would knock down any fire Manning set. She was probably pulling something else off while everyone was evacuating."

"Like stealing the nanoagent?"

"We thought of that, but Lyman says the lab was untouched, and the nanoagent is still secure."

Fitzmaurice let out a frustrated grunt. "We need to get that nanoagent out of there before it causes any more trouble. You think Fort Knox would be secure enough?"

He chuckled politely. "Actually I meant to ask you about that, sir. I don't think Conrad has given up on trying to get her hands on WICKER BASKET. I wonder if a sting operation might be in order."

"What did you have in mind?"

"We wait for Conrad to make her move, then turn the Nanovex facility into an enormous trap. Roll up her *and* her team."

The Director looked concerned. "The last thing we need is more bodies in your bailiwick, Perry."

Pugliano leaned toward the camera. "Sir, Conrad and her team are some of the best covert operators in the world. Unless she screws up, the chances of us tracking her down before she makes her move are pretty slim. We already have the bait. We just need to set the trap. And Lyman's people aren't mall cops; they're all ex-military. With our back-up they'll hold their own just fine."

Fitzmaurice pressed his lips together before speaking. "This fiasco has visibility all the way to the top. Let me run it past the President and I'll get back with you." The FBI seal replaced the Director's face on the conference room screen.

Let me run it past the President and I'll get back with you. He knew from the beginning this was the kind of case that could make or break a career. The only question was which alternative would be his fate.

* * *

WASHINGTON, DC

President Lloyd Cameron looked up from his briefing papers when his intercom beeped. He was in a foul mood. Simon Crane and his gang of high-tech thugs had purposefully humiliated him, killing US citizens in a bizarre and public way, making it necessary for his administration to engage in a cover-up to hide the existence of Crane's organization. That bastard Crane was making Cameron do his dirty work for him, just like he had boasted he would. He almost expected Crane to call and gloat, but realized that wouldn't be his style. The message had been sent—any further communication would be inefficient.

"Mr. President," his secretary said, "Director Fitzmaurice would like to speak with you concerning the San Jose situation."

He set the classified document aside. "Put him through."

"Line one, sir."

"Fitz, if this is more bad news I'm going to reassign you to Gitmo Bay," he said, only half-joking.

"No, sir, just a question," Fitzmaurice said quickly, eager to assuage Cameron's anger. "The local Special Agent-in-Charge has asked for permission to run a sting operation at Nanovex. He still thinks Angela

Conrad is going to make a play for the nanoagent and wants to set a trap for her on site. Considering recent events, I thought we should obtain your approval before proceeding."

"That was prudent, thank you," his many years of Senatorial experience helped him keep his fury over the Nanovex incident in check. "Angela Conrad? Wasn't she the CIA fugitive at the center of the San Jose massacre?"

"Yes, Mr. President."

"And wasn't the little silver ball that saved her from the CIA and Mossad the same one that killed those people at Nanovex?"

"That's our assumption, sir, yes."

"Then I don't think we should be setting any traps for her, do you? Not unless your man in San Jose wants his people to end up like those CIA agents. For all we know Conrad could be one of Crane's agents, coming to collect the nanoagent by force. Let's not cross her, shall we? I think we've had enough humiliation for one week."

"Yes, Mr. President."

FAMILY BUSINESS

JULY 20, 1969 – BUENOS AIRES, ARGENTINA

Hans Kammler was delighted to finally have his son Victor home from his travels. After graduation from engineering school at the University of Heidelberg—Kammler had forbidden Victor to attend an American college—his graduation present had been a six-week tour of the world's greatest cities. Victor had just arrived on the flight from Rio and the family prepared to have a late dinner together.

"So, which was your favorite city?" he asked Victor, holding the door while their maid lugged his son's bags into their palatial villa on the hills overlooking Buenos Aires. "Dr. Schmidt" had done very well for himself.

"That's a hard question. I'd have to say it's a toss-up between New York and Los Angeles."

The look Kammler gave him made his son laugh. "What?" Victor chided. "Would you rather have me prefer the decadence of Rio de Janeiro or Paris?"

"I'd prefer you not get too enamored with the Americans. Their intellectual decadence is far more seductive than the occasional debaucheries of the Rio nightlife."

Victor turned and pointed up at the moon. "I guess that's why the Americans are on the moon right now while the rest of the world sits and watches, yes?"

Kammler grunted in response. "Come. Your mother will have dinner ready by now."

"Empanadas?" he asked excitedly.

"That's still your favorite, isn't it?" Kammler leaned into the taxi's window to pay his son's fare. He straightened with a groan that started in his lower back and worked its way up to his throat. At sixty-eight, age was truly beginning to catch up with him. He took his son's arm as they mounted the steps to the front door—and not entirely out of fatherly warmth.

"I can now say I've tried Argentinean restaurants all over the world," Victor said as they walked inside, "and no one makes empanadas like Mother."

The sound of sandaled feet coming quickly down the stone hallway preceded a girlish cry of joy. "Vikkie!" Greta squealed, wrapping her arms around her big brother's neck. "Oh! I'm so glad you're back! I missed you so much!"

Victor twirled his younger sister like a merry-go-round before setting her down. "I missed you too, Gret."

She playfully mussed his hair. "Liar! You were too busy having fun!" Greta was the polar opposite of her brother. He tall and athletic, she petite and slender. He blond and reserved like his father, she dark-haired and passionate like her mother.

He blushed. "True enough."

"Is that my world traveler, home from his journeys?" Kammler's wife Marta announced before rounding the corner into the entryway. Twelve years his junior, she still looked as lovely as when he met her at a function for ex-patriates at the German embassy shortly after the war. How time had flown. She embraced her son and kissed him on both cheeks. "You're timing is perfect. Let's eat."

They walked through the living room and past the TV, which proclaimed in subtitle, "Americanos en la luna!" underneath the feed from the American news networks, which an Argentine anchor translated in voiceover. Victor stopped.

"Are they walking on the moon yet?" he asked expectantly.

Marta walked past him into the kitchen. "No, they seem to be having some trouble putting on their space suits. Someone probably forgot to pack their shoes."

Kammler winced. "You've never going to let me live that down, are you?"

She laughed. "You mean how you forgot to pack your dress shoes for a formal dinner at the Royal Academy of Sciences in London? Not likely."

"May we eat in here?" Victor bubbled like a small boy.

"No!" Marta declared, pulling her son by the arm. "This is a Schmidt family dinner! Neil Armstrong is not invited!"

* * *

It seemed the Americans had indeed forgotten their shoes, because history still had not been made even long after dinner had been cleared away. Kammler and his son kicked off their shoes and waited for the astronauts to emerge from the lunar module. Marta excused herself and went to bed. Greta fell asleep on the couch, her head on Victor's shoulder. Finally the grainy black-and-white image showed Neil Armstrong descending the ladder toward the lunar surface, shortly after midnight Buenos Aires time.

"Humanidad está en la luna!" the subtitle on the screen shouted.

"What did Armstrong just say?" Victor asked.

"Something about a leap for mankind; it must have lost something in translation. The news anchor sounds confused too."

They watched the moon walk in silence for over an hour. The most interesting part for Kammler was the telephone conversation from President Nixon to the astronauts on the lunar surface. Nixon was the only American politician he had met who didn't seem to have his head up the bottom half of his digestive tract. After that, Kammler fought to stay awake, despite the momentous nature of the broadcast. He noticed Victor's eyes drooping as well.

"So," he said, breaking the silence, "Now that you have completed your studies and celebrated your achievement, are you ready to come assist me at the office?"

Victor stretched and yawned. "Father," he said formally, "I know your work at the Ministry of Science is very important, but I've been thinking seriously about going to America to work on their space program."

Kammler waved a hand toward the television. "Victor, I know these kind of scientific stunts are very seductive, but I can assure you that's all they are—a stunt. A year or two from now the Americans will have turned their attentions—and their money—to something else. Probably funding that disastrous war in Vietnam. On the other hand, the work we carry out at the Ministry has direct impact on the future of humanity, both now and for many years to come."

Victor squirmed, causing Greta to stir momentarily. "But the work you perform is *administrative*. I want to *build* things." He also waved toward the television. "Things that will be remembered by history."

He nodded, ceding the argument for the moment. "Will you at least come with me to the office tomorrow and let me show you what you would be working on before you make your final decision?"

"Of course," he replied immediately. Victor had been too well raised to be contrary just for the sake of argument.

Kammler stood, painfully, and made his way to bed. "Then good night. I'll see you in the morning."

* * *

Instead of driving his son to the Argentine Ministry of Science building in the capital, Kammler drove to a military airfield on the outskirts of the city. An Argentine Air Force DC-3 twin-engine transport was being held for him. After the disrespect he had shown the Americans during their conversation last night, the irony of taking an American-built aircraft to their destination was not lost on him. The consternation of the military and civilian passengers being delayed for his convenience died immediately when he entered the aircraft. He apologized to his fellow passengers anyway as they made their way up the aisle.

After settling into their seats, Victor leaned over and whispered, "Are these men *afraid* of you?"

He gave his son a wink. "Of course not. They must be afraid of *you*."

The flight would take more than five hours. At least the weather was fair and scenery below picturesque. Kammler had offered no clues to his son whatsoever of their destination, testing the durability of the patience he had instilled throughout the young man's upbringing. It took an hour for curiosity to overcome training.

"Where are we going?" Victor finally asked as they continued southwest.

"Bariloche," he answered, referring to the mountain town closest to the installation.

"Are we going skiing?"

"Not this time." He pulled a hefty binder from his satchel and handed it to his son. "I'm afraid this is hardly light reading, but you'll have to familiarize yourself with it eventually."

Victor opened the blank binder to its title page. It read, "SECURITY PROCEDURES, SAN CARLOS DE BARILOCHE FACILITY." He read the cheerless tome in silence for over an hour.

"Who is this Director Kammler the manual refers to constantly?" Victor finally asked. "He seems to be something of an *analfixiert*," he added, lapsing into German slang.

"He wrote the manual," Kammler replied offhandedly. "You'll meet him soon enough."

When the plane finally arrived in Bariloche, the passengers filed to the rear door, to be met by a security guard who looked like the prewar German boxing champion Max Schmeling. He wore the gray jumpsuit and black beret of Prince Bernhard's organization that had become the uniform of Kammler's operation as well. The guard carefully checked everyone's papers, brusquely confronting any perceived discrepancy in German-accented Spanish. But when Kammler stepped to the door, the guard snapped to attention.

"Good afternoon, *Herr* Director!" he said in German, stepping aside to allow them passage off the aircraft.

Kammler's tone took on an edge. "You did not check our papers."

The guard became flustered. "Of course, *Herr* Director! Ah, yes, everything is in order." He held out his hand for Victor's papers, who had none.

"This is my son Victor. He's joining the project today. You will escort us to the administrative building so that I may draw up his credentials."

The guard actually clicked his heels in salute. "*Jawhol, Herr* Director!"

He would have to speak privately to the guard about lapsing into German and old military habits. It would draw unwelcome attention if international guests should visit. But he would do so away from his son's presence.

Watching his son crane his neck to take in the sprawling facility allowed Kammler to reflect on the progress he had made in the two short years since Prince Bernhard and his Group had become their financial benefactors. What had been little more than a frontier airstrip for offloading supplies had now become a bustling base, with hangars, barracks, laboratories and a ring of air defenses around the perimeter. [3]

But his organization had grown far beyond this outpost at the eastern foothills of the Andes. He had offices in the capitals of every industrialized country on Earth, including behind the Iron Curtain, which was little more than an administrative obstacle to the Prince's group, and therefore to Kammler as well. He also had agents in every foreign intelligence and internal security service large enough to be of service to him. The Group had abundant financial resources to redirect the loyalties of experienced agents to their cause, and Kammler had more than enough ruthlessness to make sure that the Group received the full measure of loyalty it had purchased.

"So this is all part of the Ministry of Science?" Victor asked incredulously.

"Not entirely," he dodged, holding the door open for his son. He assisted him in filling out the exhaustive entry forms he himself had crafted.

After half an hour filling out paperwork, Victor whispered, "Is working here worth it? The forms this Kammler fellow drew up make him seem quite the *autobombo*."

Kammler smiled but said nothing. His son must be frustrated indeed to lapse into Argentine slang, referring to an advertising truck with a mechanical bass drum on the roof to attract attention. But the detailed forms had a purpose, even though they were just a formality in Victor's case. Among other things, they demanded the name and address of a new recruit's every living relative, so that if Kammler was displeased, he would have the information he needed to kill as many of the offender's relations as he deemed necessary.

He had carried out this threat only once, against an Argentine mechanic who had spoken too freely in a bar to one of Kammler's covert security operatives. It was a relatively minor offense, but the sight of the weeping worker digging the graves for his entire family, knowing full well that the last grave he dug would be his own, was a powerful deterrent against misbehavior for the rest of the staff.

"All done?" he asked, accepting the completed forms. He handed them to a clerk, who took Victor's photograph and laminated it into an identification badge.

Kammler pointed to the stairs. "I just need to stop by my office for a moment, then we can begin our tour." After locking up his satchel and retrieving a small item from his desk, he led Victor around the complex, with special attention to the laboratories.

An hour later, Victor followed his father from the laboratory building, across the tarmac toward a row of hangars. "I had no idea the Ministry of Science was involved in such advanced work!" he gushed. "I follow scientific journals from around the world, and your scientists are actually *performing* work they have only theorized about!"

Kammler lifted an eyebrow. "Do you still wish to flee to America, to be a tiny cog in their industrial machine?"

Victor shrugged. "They are still the only country with a space program. Except the Soviets, of course. Although I don't think they would look kindly on the employment application of a scientist named Schmidt."

"Indeed." They reached the largest hangar. Armed guards flanked the door. One guard snapped to attention, the other held the door open for them.

Victor stopped cold as soon as his eyes adjusted to the interior lights. Before him sat a triangular metal craft the size of the DC-3 on which they had just flown. It sat on three retractable struts with a small boarding ladder reaching down near the center. While the triangle had an airfoil shape, it possessed no visible control surfaces or engines, either propeller or jet.

He cast an incredulous eye toward his father. “Does it fly?”

“Quite well, actually.”

“Supersonic?”

“Fast enough to achieve orbit.”

Victor startled as if slapped. “You’re joking.”

“Not at all.” He led Victor to a display case against the wall, containing a primitive pressure suit, resembling the one made famous by Gary Francis Powers when his U-2 spyplane was shot down over Russia. The suit was well-worn and thickly soiled with dust. “This design doesn’t have the—what is the American word? Pizazz?—of the NASA space suits, but it was quite serviceable.” [4]

Victor chuckled. “It needs to be laundered.”

Now it was Kammler’s turn to smile. “I ordered this suit retired after a particularly eventful flight. Colonel Specht and I both decided the moon dust should stay.” [5]

Victor turned. “Beg your pardon?”

Kammler pulled the paperweight he had retrieved from his office out of his pocket. It was a small rock encased in clear plastic. “Can you identify this rock?”

Victor turned the stone in his hand. “I’m not a geologist, but it is clearly some kind of volcanic mineral.”

“You’re holding a piece of the Moon.”

Victor blinked, his gaze alternating between the rock, the spacecraft, and his father. “I would say this is some kind of bizarre practical joke, but you’ve gone to far too much trouble for that.”

Kammler nodded. “I’ve never been a fan of practical jokes, and I certainly wouldn’t fly you five hours into the wilderness to play one. There are many things you are about to learn, things you must never share with anyone, not even your mother or sister. To begin with, your name is not Schmidt.”

[1] EMP stands for Electro-Magnetic Pulse weapon. It is a powerful electric device that mimics the wave of plasma put off by a nuclear weapon. This wave will instantly and permanently fry unshielded electronics, especially integrated circuits like microchips. The device shown below is a large EMP weapon used to simulate the electrical effects of a nuclear weapon on hardened systems, such as the E-4 Airborne Command Post shown.

[2] The Gulfstream II executive jet with American registration N987SA was well known in human rights circles as a “rendition aircraft,” used to transport terrorists suspects from their home countries to Guantanamo Bay or other CIA “black prisons” after being captured by American “snatch teams” around the world.

This particular rendition jet, Gulfstream N987SA, crashed September 24, 2007 in Mexico, apparently trying to make a landing on a jungle airstrip while being pursued by Mexican Air Force aircraft. Mexican officials recovered *3.6 tons of cocaine* from the wreckage. The pilots disappeared into the jungle. The aircraft was registered to Donna Blue Aircraft of Ft. Lauderdale, an apparent CIA front company which was promptly shut down. Donna Blue Aircraft may have been a word play on DBA, or “doing business as,” a legal term used in business name registration. (Source: Reuters)

[3] “A former CIA contract pilot, who once flew the run into Paraguay and Argentina to the Bormann ranch, described the estate as remote, and ‘worth your life unless you entered their air space with the right identification codes.’” (Source: *Martin Bormann: Nazi in Exile* by Paul Manning, 1981, p. 292) If this account is true, it certainly begs the question what face-to-face business the CIA was conducting with the Nazis in South America.

[4] If the idea of the exiled Nazis in South America manufacturing their own spacesuits seems farfetched, consider the pressure suit pictured at right, tested by the Nazis in 1945. It was made by the Draeger Company, a manufacturer of diving equipment. Another Draeger product, the Draeger Rebreather, is still used by US Navy SEALs today. The pressure suit was under development for use in the Horten 229 fighter bomber, the first aircraft known to incorporate stealth characteristics (its design was very similar to the B-2 bomber, a pure flying wing). Apparently the Germans planned on flying so high that fighters would be unable to intercept their aircraft, even if detected. The base where the Horten flying wing was under development was overrun by Allied forces before the aircraft could be deployed.

[5] Lieutenant Colonel Günther Specht was one of Germany's highest scoring aces during WWII. Specht was declared missing in action on New Year's Day 1945 during Operation Baseplate, Germany's last offensive air action during the war. Neither his body nor his aircraft was ever found, so in this fiction he survived the war and became one of Hans Kammler's chief test pilots. Given the propensity of fleeing Nazis to fake their own deaths, this may not be far from the truth. Interestingly, for his final mission Specht wore his formal uniform, complete with medals, instead of a flight suit. He is pictured here (on the left) with Professor Kurt Tank, Germany's top aircraft designer, who after the war left to design aircraft in—where else—Argentina. (Photo: Bundesarchive)

CHAPTER 25

MASTERMIND

PRESENT DAY – SAN JOSE, CALIFORNIA

The first step in Hendrix's audacious criminal plan hadn't even been illegal. He took Ian Cosgrove and two other operatives known to him only as Shiva and Bastille with him to the San Jose airport and rented a Cessna 182. By the time the rental company discovered he had abandoned the aircraft in another city, he would be guilty of far greater crimes than breach of contract. At last his Private Pilot's license would finally prove operationally useful. Mostly it had just been expensive.

It was a beautiful evening for flying. He very much regretted not being able to take a lap around the Bay area at sunset. But his mission-minded companions probably wouldn't approve of such time-wasting. So he punched a direct route into the GPS and climbed to the minimum safe Visual Flight Rules altitude the unit indicated.

"How long?" Cosgrove asked.

He glanced at the GPS elapsed time readout. "Just short of four hours. Hope you went to the potty before we took off."

Cosgrove tapped his watch and held up four fingers to the back seat passengers, then slouched in his seat and pulled his cap over his eyes. "Night, love. Wake me before we land."

Approaching Los Angeles from the north, Hendrix was forced to descend and head out to sea to avoid the controlled airspace around LAX, then even lower as he approached the coast over Long Beach. The 710 freeway going north provided an unmistakable landmark to follow even without the GPS, but the air was so full of blinking lights from radio towers and other aircraft it was like flying inside a video game. One controller after another handed him off as he made his way through the patchwork of airspace jurisdictions toward their destination.

By the time he entered the traffic pattern for Compton Airport, his back, butt and bladder were all screaming in protest. The rising air off the pavement below made the air turbulent even at night, which didn't quiet any of his protesting parts.

The combination of the rough air and the change in engine noise roused Cosgrove from his slumber. "Here already? That was quick."

"You must be able to sleep through anything."

"Helicopters. I spent most of my youth riding in the back of those damned thrashing machines. Dulls the senses."

Once tucked into the tiny corner of airspace that Compton's airport was allowed under LAX's overarching control zone, the final approach and landing was uneventful. The tower allowed them to taxi and park at their discretion. He shut the aircraft down and emerged from the cockpit with the posture of a ninety-year-old man onto the dark and quiet ramp.

"Oh god," Cosgrove remarked, "do I need a piss!"

Hendrix saw that the beckoning lights of the FBO—fixed base operator—facility were still on, promising bathrooms and at least a vending machine for his dinner. He trotted in that direction.

"Hey, where are you going?" Cosgrove demanded.

"Inside—I gotta go too."

"What, you just dying to get your face on a security camera?"

The sound of water on pavement from behind the plane explained Cosgrove's alternative to the clean and well-lit FBO. Hendrix sighed, then stepped behind the tail and joined suit. Cosgrove and the agents retrieved their duffel bags from the baggage compartment. Hendrix stuffed his headphones and maps into his pilot's bag.

"All right," Cosgrove said, "I think I saw our beauty a little ways down this direction."

The foursome walked down the ramp between two rows of parked airplanes, keeping as far out of the lights as possible. The most exposed part of the trek was across a wide taxiway between the aircraft and helicopter parking areas. Thankfully the ramp was almost dead this evening. The Huey helicopter they sought towered above the petite Robinson R-22 trainer helicopters parked around it.

"Here she is," Cosgrove whispered, sliding open the side door. "Shiva, do your thing." Everyone else piled into the back of the olive drab helicopter to stay out of sight.

The Indian agent went to work casting off tie-down ropes and removing intake covers. "It's still warm," he reported.

"Yeah, they just finished shooting an action movie up at Big Bear Lake earlier today," Hendrix said.

"How do you know that?" Cosgrove asked.

"I know a producer here in town. I called the helicopter company's leasing agent and told her I was him. She told me everything I wanted to know."

"Well, you're right handy. I don't care what everyone else says."

"Okay, it's ready to go," Shiva reported.

"Already?" Hendrix asked. It had taken him longer to preflight the Cessna.

"Well, for one thing, they don't bother with anti-theft devices on helicopters. They're too complex for most thieves to mess with, especially military transports like this."

"Good to know," he said, squirming into the right-hand seat. "I'll handle navigation and the radios."

Shiva then reminded him that the co-pilot seat on helicopters was on the *left* side, where the pilot-in-command sat in fixed-wing aircraft. He had never learned why helicopters were like that. And considering the accident rate of helicopters, he didn't have a lot of incentive to learn.

The tower sounded dubious when he called for clearance. Luckily he had culled the name of the helicopter company's owner and chief pilot from the leasing agent today. He was able to string together a story feasible enough that the tower dropped their line of questioning and gave him the winds and altimeter setting.

Shiva lifted the Huey into a low taxi toward the runway. "You're a convincing liar," he said as a compliment.

"Lot of practice."

"Huey Eight-One-Foxtrot, cleared for departure Runway Seven Left," the tower affirmed.

"Huey Eight-One-Foxtrot, thanks and good night." Then to Shiva he said, "Head due east below 2500. That'll keep us out of Long Beach's control zone before we turn south. The less people we have to talk to the better."

"Understood."

To Hendrix's relief, Shiva was a good pilot. He certainly wouldn't want to fly this whirling piece of iron. His flight instructor's mantra had been, "Any aircraft where the wing moves relative to the fuselage is a helicopter, and therefore unsafe."

Even with the circuitous path they took to avoid control zones, the flight to San Diego went much faster than the flight from San Jose. In just over an hour they made initial radio contact with San Diego International. Because of their late night arrival and noise abatement rules, approach control led them on a convoluted path between Point Loma and North Island to keep them over water as they descended. Hell, he wouldn't want this old eggbeater flying over his house late at night either.

Ground Control vectored them to the far end of the corporate parking ramp from the lone FBO, which was fine with him. All the better to survey the tail numbers during the leisurely walk to the pilot's lounge. To his consternation, he could see a golf cart making its way along the flight line toward their intended landing spot. The FBO was monitoring Ground Control and had dispatched someone to pick them up. That wasn't in his plan.

He moved the microphone away from his mouth and shouted into the back. "You guys lay down on the floor!" They looked a little confused, but complied.

Shiva expertly swung the Huey around and back-slipped into a spot next to a Gulfstream IV executive jet. The golf cart from the FBO rounded the jet's nose as they touched down.

Hendrix turned in his seat to collect his pilot's bag. "Okay guys," he said over the sound of the engines spinning down, "lay low and wait for my call."

Cosgrove gave him a "this had better work" look, but said nothing.

Hendrix jumped out and walked over to the golf cart to keep him from getting too close. "Hey, now this is what I call service!"

"We aim to please!" the young man in his twenties replied. "That's a neat old bird. Don't see many of those anymore, especially in the Army paint scheme."

"Yeah, we're shooting some footage off the coast in the morning. The director wanted the Huey in place for an early start. We'll probably be lifting off again in an hour or two." Shiva emerged from the helicopter and took his place silently on the cart's back seat.

The young man swung the cart around. "You mean after 6:30, don't you?"

"No, I mean in an hour or two." Hendrix checked his watch. "We're supposed to pick the film crew up at four so we can be off the coast filming at dawn."

Their driver laughed. "Good luck with that! We take arrivals twenty-four hours a day, but they don't allow anybody to take off until 6:30 because of noise regulations. You might call the tower and ask for an exception, but with a noisy old bird like that, I can guess what they'll say."

He cringed. *Scott Hendrix the great criminal mastermind strikes again.* He was so distracted by his oversight he almost forgot to read tail numbers as they drove in. He pulled his head out just as they passed a Gulfstream II, tail number N987SA. One of the planes on Amnesty International's hot list. They drove the rest of the way to the FBO building in silence.

He found a quiet corner of the pilot's lounge and called Cosgrove. "Fourth plane toward the FBO from you, tail number November-nine-eight-seven-Sierra-Alpha."

"Nine-eight-seven-Sierra-Alpha, got it."

Hendrix made a trip to the vending machines to see if Cheetos or Twinkies would help jog his mental processes. While the Cheetos definitely didn't help, he hadn't even had the chance to test the stimulative effects of the Twinkies when he saw two burly men tear down the stairs and out the door toward the ramp. Both wore khaki photographer's vests, just right for covering up a gun. He flipped open his phone.

"Ian, you must have tripped something! You got two Tangos coming in hot, packing pistols!"

"Dammit!" Cosgrove replied. "Stand by."

CONTROL

AUGUST 1988 – LUTON, BEDFORDSHIRE, UNITED KINGDOM

Victor Kammler arrived in England on board the jet that he still thought of as his father's. Following the elder Kammler's death three years ago, Victor had run the organization his father had founded. But this would be the first large-scale operation to be conducted under his watch. Some of the designated targets were high-level government officials. The Group had made it very clear that no mistakes would be tolerated with these terminations. Victor remembered that the members of the Group were the only people on the planet that his father had truly feared.

The Kammler Organization had long since returned to Europe after its South American exile following World War II. Victor was briefed on the flight from Zurich on the operation and its targets. While he sometimes questioned—silently—the choices made by the Group, he did not do so in this case. The technology under development by the Marconi Corporation was frightening in its potential. Determining whether it was *just* potential or actual capability was one of the assignments he had received from the Group, in addition to the imposition of final security.

By now the methods of the Kammlerorg, as his father had nicknamed it, were well established. Once their extensive contacts identified a technology that posed a possible threat, it was presented to the Group for disposition. Often the Group would merely take the new invention for their own enrichment, buying up the company and putting potential competitors out of business. Rich men never seemed to tire of growing even richer, Victor observed.

But if a technology was deemed to pose a long-term threat to humanity, it was watched closely until its concept was proven. Using their enormous financial leverage, the Group would subsequently force the project to be shut down. Then the Kammlerorg would go to work, eliminating every scientist, engineer, or manager with the ability to reconstitute the technology. The very idea of the project would be treated like an infection and ruthlessly wiped out. But the Group would either receive the finished product for their exclusive use, or simply lock it away to prevent *anyone* from using it.

It was a brutal process, one his father had compared often to cancer treatment—surgery, followed by chemotherapy. If even one cell of the intellectual cancer survived, it could multiply and grow—perhaps mutating into something even more deadly. The fact that mankind had not spawned another superweapon like the hydrogen bomb since the Group's foundation was proof to his father that their concept of operation was sound.

Their current target was no exception. An unexpected outgrowth of Marconi's work in antisubmarine warfare, the doomed project was latched onto with characteristic enthusiasm by the Ministry of Defense. It was developed, refined, tested, and in due course, weaponized. At that point the Group stepped in and forced the British government to abandon the research and disperse the workers to unrelated tasks.

Then the Kammlerorg went to work. The first terminations were simple and direct, disguised to look like accidents or suicides. But when the full potential of the Pandora's Box Marconi had crafted became evident, the assassins on Victor's staff began using the device itself in their terminations. The level of success they achieved was so dramatic that Victor was summoned to the field to see the results with his own eyes.

The jet touched down at Luton Airport north of London. He was met by a security team driving two armored Mercedes sedans and an unmarked panel van. The convoy immediately headed off through the quaint streets of north suburban London.

"What am I going to see today?" he asked Richard Tolbert, field supervisor for this operation. Tolbert's real name was Reinhart Mueller, son of Heinrich Mueller, Martin Bormann's late chief of security. Since second-generation agents like himself and Mueller were free of German accents, the Kammlerorg found that Anglo-Saxon names provided the best misdirection from their true identities.

"The termination of one Ariff Shazad, electrical engineer of Pakistani origin," Tolbert replied. "He was a team leader on the weaponization project."

"Explain to me again how this system works."

Tolbert handed over a file. "The scientists at Marconi were experimenting with new waveforms of low-frequency sound to improve the efficiency of their sonar for submarine detection. When sampling some of the sounds using headphones, an engineer was found in a near-catatonic state by his supervisor. The trance persisted for nearly an hour after the headphones were removed. Since they were concerned about the safety of future sonar operators using their system, Marconi ran experiments at low power while monitoring the brainwaves of the subjects. They found that a specific frequency and waveform of sound stimulated the formation of alpha waves in the brain."

"That's the brainwave associated with passivity, correct?"

"Yes, like you get from watching television too long," Tolbert replied. "That's why I won't let my children watch more than a half hour of that drivel. But more than that, they found that the alpha state the sound waves produced led to extreme suggestibility. At higher power levels, the controller could even induce the subject to harm themselves without resistance."

Victor recoiled. "What mad scientist had the idea to try *that*?"

Tolbert shrugged. "They are a *weapons* company, sir. But the Ministry of Defense stepped in at that point and proceeded with the project at an extremely high level of classification. Tests showed near-total subjugation of the subject's will, sometimes with frightening effects."

He looked up from the file. "Tolbert, to hear *you* describe the effect of a weapon as frightening is frightening all by itself."

Tolbert checked his watch. "You can judge for yourself. Mr. Shazad will be leaving for work in a few minutes." The convoy pulled to a stop in front of a row of three-story apartment buildings.

"I'd like to see the equipment, if that's possible," he asked.

"Of course, sir." Tolbert led him to the van and seated him behind the operator. The device consisted of a simple oscilloscope, a TV screen showing the view out the left side of the van, and a microphone. An electrical lead ran from the console to a parabolic speaker mounted on the left-facing wall of the van. The black-and-white TV screen showed a dark-skinned young man trotting down the front steps.

"That's him—execute," Tolbert told the operator.

The operator tuned the oscilloscope then pressed a red button when Shazad entered an inscribed circle at the center of the screen. Victor felt more than heard a low-frequency vibration in his chest and stomach. Shazad slowed his descent of the steps, then stopped.

"He's ready, sir." The operator said to Tolbert.

"Proceed."

The operator keyed the microphone on the console. "Go back into the apartment and get the rope you bought last night." Shazad stood still for a moment, then turned and trudged back up the stairs, returning a few minutes later with a coil of thick white rope over his shoulder.

"Go to your car and drive to Tinley Park," the operator said when Shazad re-entered the circle on his screen. Shazad blinked, then moved as if in a trance to do as he was ordered.

"What's the susceptibility of this device among the population?" Victor asked. "Are certain people more resistant?"

"The deaf," Tolbert said with a chuckle. "Drug and alcohol inebriation makes one *more* susceptible, as does military training—following orders and all. We have found some personality types more resistant, but higher power settings can enforce compliance in almost all cases. The only exceptions we've found were those who had heavily damaged eardrums from machinery or loud music."

Shazad pulled his red sports car away from the curb and the convoy followed at a distance. He drove to the nearby park, stopping just inside the entrance. The van pulled up alongside.

"Drive to an isolated spot and park near a large tree," the operator ordered. Shazad complied, stopping by a large oak tree at the far end of the wooded preserve. No other cars or people were in view.

"As you can see, the higher brain functions are still intact," Tolbert observed. "He was able to correctly discern an isolated location and a large tree even though his will has been completely subordinated." He motioned for the operator to continue.

Pulling beside Shazad's car again, the operator said, "Tie the rope around the tree trunk then return with the rope to the car." Shazad complied. "Put the top down on your car, then take a seat and tie the other end of the rope around your neck."

Victor eyed Tolbert with concern, who just smiled and held up a finger for forbearance.

"Now drive away as fast as you can."

After the briefest moment of hesitation, Shazad complied. The little sports car roared in response, the rope quickly stretching taut. Victor heard the sound of crunching metal a few seconds later. With their sight limited to the narrow field of view of the side-facing camera, he thought the rope had snapped.

"Shall we?" Tolbert asked.

They stepped outside the van. Shazad's car had lodged against a tree a few dozen meters away, his figure slumped over the steering wheel. The engine labored unevenly for a few more seconds, then died as well.

"Does anyone see it?" Tolbert called out.

The operator pointed. "Over there."

Victor followed the pair to a nearby bush. Tolbert lifted up the lower branches, revealing Shazad's head staring up at them. "Ah, there he is, well done," Tolbert announced.

Victor fought against nausea. "Fascinating," he finally managed.

"Isn't it extraordinary?" Tolbert gushed. "I can see why this technology is being taken out of play by the Group."

"Indeed."

Tolbert released the branches, wiping the leafy residue from his hands. "We'd best be going now, sir." [1]

Victor swallowed hard. "I'm sure you're right. Well, I think I've seen enough to make my report to the Group."

The return trip was conducted in silence. Victor's reticence was so pronounced Tolbert apparently thought he was displeased with the team's performance.

"*Herr* Kammler, I hope our work during this operation has met with your approval," he ventured. While Victor had not yet established a reputation as disciplinarian, the penalties for disapproval under the elder Kammler were well known.

Victor waved away Tolbert's concerns. "Completely, Mr. Tolbert. But in the field I prefer to be addressed by my pseudonym, if you please."

"Of course, Mr. Crane."

PRIMARY RETURN

PRESENT DAY – SAN DIEGO, CALIFORNIA

After three interminable minutes, Hendrix's phone vibrated. "It's handled," Cosgrove reported. "Get out here and help us."

With a sinking feeling in his gut, he motioned to Shiva and jerked his head toward the door. The FBO attendant looked up from his texting.

"Hey, I saw those guys from upstairs run out. Is there something going on?"

Hendrix tried to stay calm. "Nah, our chopper probably set off their jet's motion alarm. Can I borrow your golf cart? I left something in the bird."

The young man tossed him the keys. "Slow night. Knock yourself out."

"Thanks." He and Shiva arrived at the Gulfstream in time to see Cosgrove and the French agent who went by Bastille wrestle the first body into the jet. Two bloody puddles testified to the simultaneous headshots the ambushed CIA smugglers suffered. *Oh dear God, I am so dead now*. The only thing that allowed him to avoid a panic attack was his fear of Conrad, which was marginally greater than that he held toward the CIA.

"Don't just stand there, you tossers, get the other one!" Cosgrove snarled.

He and Shiva reluctantly manhandled the second CIA corpse into the plane and closed the door behind them. "I think our schedule just got accelerated!" he urged.

"Thanks for the news flash!" Cosgrove snapped. "Bastille! Get to work before any more of their goons show up!"

The Frenchman complied, moving to the cockpit.

Hendrix joined him. "It should be under the seat," he advised, "Just be careful of booby traps. I'll bet you twenty bucks the encoding device is rigged."

"This is why you brought along a demolitions specialist, no?" he replied in a smooth, sing-song accent.

Flashlight in hand, Bastille maneuvered to work under the pilot's seat with the agility of a circus acrobat. "Okay, I've got it," he announced immediately. "Yes, it's rigged with an anti-tamper device," he added a few minutes later. "Can you bring my tools, please?"

Grateful not be in back with the bodies, Hendrix brought forward Bastille's knapsack and located the tool kit. Not being familiar enough with the specialized tools to play surgical nurse, he could only hold the tool kit at a convenient level for the Frenchman to grab what he needed. It occurred to him belatedly that if Bastille made a mistake with him standing this close to the device, there would probably be nothing left of him below the knees. He started to sweat in the stuffy, cramped cockpit.

After a few minutes that seemed like an hour, Bastille held up a box the size of a thick paperback book. "Voilá!" he announced. "I don't know what it does, but it is now yours!"

"Excellent!" he replied, examining the black box, especially the connections on the side.

"Would you like the anti-tamper device as well?"

"How big of a bang does it have?" Cosgrove called from the back.

Bastille turned the thin plate designed to fit under the black box. "Two hundred grams of C-4, I would estimate. It is only designed to destroy the box, not the whole aircraft."

Cosgrove was up in the cockpit with them now. "Did you bring any more with you?"

Bastille dug in his knapsack, producing a small block of plastic explosives. "As they say, never leave home without it."

"Can you rig it to the door?"

"But of course," Bastille replied, sounding like the guy from the Grey Poupon commercial.

"What say you, boss man?" Cosgrove challenged. "When the CIA comes looking for their blokes, how about we give them a little more than they bargained for?"

Normally violence that wasn't vital to the mission would be counterproductive, but an explosion—and the fire that followed—would cover up a lot of evidence. They might not even discover the missing encoder in the wreckage.

"Do it," he ordered.

* * *

Bastille proved just as efficient at setting booby traps as he was defusing them. In a few minutes they were back in the helicopter. Hendrix borrowed Bastille's tools and began extracting the Huey's transponder from the dashboard.

“What are we waiting for?” Cosgrove demanded. “Not sure hanging around a murder scene is such a great idea.”

“The tower isn’t going to authorize a departure for another three hours,” Hendrix cautioned.

“So take off anyway!” he scoffed. “What are they going to do, shoot us down?”

“No,” Hendrix explained patiently, “but they *would* track us by radar to wherever we land and have the police waiting to ask us some uncomfortable questions.”

“Then what are we going to do?” Cosgrove said, the alarm in his voice rising.

“My first instinct is to bug out to an all-night coffee shop and wait for 6:30 to roll around. But if I can get this encoder working, we may have another alternative.” Surprisingly, Cosgrove kept silent and let him work.

“Okay,” he announced, “Shiva, can you power up just the electronics?”

“Sure.” He began flipping switches.

Hendrix had pulled out the transponder, the device that responded to air traffic control radar and transmitted back the aircraft’s altitude and assigned traffic code. Checking the connections on the back of the device, he found they matched those of the encoder, as he had suspected. He carefully swapped the connections and slid the encoder into the hole previously occupied by the transponder.

The encoder had only three lights; red, yellow, and green. Once Shiva had powered up the electronics, the yellow light flashed at a frequency just short of once per second. Hendrix saw the radar dish turning across the field. The yellow light flashed in unison with the sweep of the dish. After five sweeps of the radar, the light flashed green instead.

“What does that mean?” Shiva asked.

Hendrix grinned. “It means we can take off.”

“What about the all-seeing radar and the police?” Cosgrove insisted.

“Thanks to our good friends at the CIA, they’re no longer an issue. Shiva, take us up.”

* * *

In the control tower, Frank Carlton yawned and had another gulp of lukewarm coffee. Because of San Diego International Airport’s draconian noise regulations, manning the tower after ten PM was about as exciting as bartending at a Baptist minister’s conference. In his groggy state, the noise had continued for over a minute before it registered on his brain.

“Is somebody running an engine test?” he asked his partner, who was so hypnotized by the inactivity on the radar screen he hadn’t even noticed the rising jet turbine sound.

His partner's head twitched like a bird's—first one direction, then another. "Sounds like it's coming from the corporate ramp."

He walked to the window and grabbed his binoculars. "What the hell? That damned Huey is spinning up!" He switched his transmitter to Ground Control frequency and picked up the mike.

"Helicopter spinning up on the ramp! Engine tests are not authorized at this time! Please secure your engine and call the tower!" No response.

"Hey, what was the N-number on that Huey?" Carlton asked.

"Four-two-eight-one-Foxtrot."

"Huey four-two-eight-one-Foxtrot, Ground Control, acknowledge!" Not only did the pilot not answer, but the engine sound rose further and the helicopter lifted off.

"Look at that son of a bitch!" he fumed. "Huey four-two-eight-one-Foxtrot! Your take-off is not authorized! Land immediately and power down!" In response, the Huey's nose dipped and it accelerated smartly, directly across both active runways.

Carlton had to compose himself to keep from swearing into the radio. "Huey eight-one-Foxtrot! You are in direct violation of an air traffic control order! Land immediately!"

Silence. The Huey reached San Diego Bay and continued south at wave-top height.

"All right, buddy!" he snapped at the radio. "I hope that little stunt was worth losing your license!" He turned to his partner at the radar console. "Track him!"

"Got it," the younger man said, manipulating the controls of his screen. After a few seconds he looked confused. "I'm not getting any return."

"Of course you're not!" he growled. "He turned off his transponder. Go for a primary return!"

His partner's confusion deepened. "I'm doing that. I got nothing." He looked out the window to verify the Huey's position. "I'm looking right where his blip should be. Nada."

Carlton stormed over. "You kids couldn't get a primary return off a 747. Let me have that!" The radar operator wheeled his chair aside to make room at the console.

He tweaked the settings on the radar. "See, kid? You set the radar to skin paint mode, then increase the gain until you start getting atmospheric returns, then back off a hair."

"I did that. So where's the helicopter, oh mighty guru?"

Carlton stared at the blank screen for several seconds, then looked over his shoulder to verify the Huey's position. He needed his binoculars now. They could still hear its rotors thumping in the distance, but the radar was empty.

Carlton pulled on what little hair he had left. “That old Huey should have a radar signature the size of an airliner! What the hell is going on?” Together they watched the helicopter head out to sea and disappear into the darkness. [2]

[1] Ashaad Sharif was a 26-year-old computer analyst for Marconi Defense Systems. In October 1986 he tied a rope to a tree and the other end to his neck before getting in his car and driving off at high speed, decapitating himself. Police ruled the death a suicide. While the author presses historical names into fictional service where possible, out of respect for these murdered scientists he does not do so in this case.

On August 22, 1988, former brigadier general Peter Ferry, 60, a marketing director for the Marconi Corporation, killed himself by wrapping electrical wires around his chest and placing the leads in his mouth, then plugging the wires into a socket in his company apartment. Before the end of the month Alistair Beckham, 50, a software engineer for Plessey Defense Systems, committed suicide by a virtually identical method in the garden shed of his house. A total of 22 scientists for Marconi and other British defense firms “committed suicide” under suspicious circumstances between 1986 and 1988.

Under pressure from the public and the media, an inquiry was carried out by Brian Worth, former Deputy Assistant Commissioner at New Scotland Yard. He concluded that "on the evidence available that the suicide verdicts reached were credible on their own facts, and in the four cases where open verdicts were returned the probability is that each victim took his own life".

Investigative journalist Tony Collins of Britain’s *Computer Weekly* filed a Freedom of Information Act request with the Ministry of Defense for all records pertaining to the 22 dead scientists. The MoD finally responded after a six-month search. “In fact the poor official who spoke to me had spent months looking for material and found nothing at all. Not one piece of paper. The official reply was that the MoD has no recorded information on any of the cases I had mentioned…It was as if the deaths had never happened.” (Source: *Mysterious Deaths, Freedom of Information, Marconi and the Ministry of Defence* by Tony Collins, *ComputerWeekly.com*, November 29, 2006)

[2] The encoder will be discussed more in the next chapter, but based on testimony given to Congress by a CIA contractor, it is apparently a real piece of hardware provided to assets who need to move easily across international boundaries by air (like drug smugglers, which this contractor claimed to be).

CHAPTER 26

COVER

SAN JOSE, CALIFORNIA

After cleaning away the dinner table in their garage hideout that night, Manning worked up the courage to approach Conrad. "I'd like to speak to my wife and kids, if that's possible."

She brushed him off. "It's possible, but not necessary."

"I'm just trying to imagine the terror they're going through right now," he persisted. "That kind of fear can make people do irrational things. Talking to me might actually make them easier to control, especially the boys."

She smirked. "Nice try, but they're under control just fine. If it's any consolation, they've only got one more day."

"One more day till what?"

"Till I'm done with you." She walked away.

Even after that ominous pronouncement, he somehow managed to slip into a fitful sleep on his military cot that night. He was awakened when the garage door rattled up and a large vehicle pulled in. The overhead lights switched on once the door came down. His cot lay behind a tool rack so he couldn't see it clearly, but the laughter from the other operatives aroused his curiosity enough to pull on his shoes and step out.

It was a school bus, or at least it had been at one time. Now it was painted with peeling white paint, with the words MAMA GRACE'S HOMELESS SHELTER lettered in red on the side. Meghan Gallagher stepped out and bowed to the laughter, quite proud of herself. Conrad emerged from her office, obviously roused from sleep. She gave the bus a skeptical examination, squinting under the shop lights.

"Dear God, Meghan, what the hell have you done?" she finally said.

"Given us the perfect cover," she said with a smile. "I've noticed this bus prowling around at all hours of the night, picking up tramps. The police leave them alone, figure they're doing them a favor I guess, getting bums off the street and all. So I waited until they made their last drop off and gave myself a lift."

"So what happens when Mama Grace reports her bus stolen?" Conrad asked.

"A couple of hours before the operation, we make a call posing as Mama Grace. We tell the police the driver got drunk and dumped the bus an hour away and everything's fine. By the time it gets back on the hot list we'll be done with it."

"Okay, nice job." She looked at her watch. "Crap, I've got to hit the road myself."

"Where ya off to?"

"Final prep at the auction site." She tossed a set of keys at Manning and yawned. "Why don't you drive, Mike? That way I don't have to waste anyone else babysitting you."

PUCKER FACTOR

MOUNT DIABLO, CALIFORNIA

The Huey helicopter approached their destination just before sunrise. Conrad had chosen their landing zone well, Hendrix realized. He called out their turns for the pilot from his hand-held GPS unit using the coordinates Conrad had supplied. They passed well clear of civilization for the last five miles of their flight, ducking between the multiple peaks of Mount Diablo. Finally they descended along a valley sheltered by ridges on both sides into what looked like an abandoned factory. Between two buildings the headlights of a vehicle illuminated a billowing green cloud from a smoke grenade.

"I guess that's our landing zone," Hendrix observed. "Can you get it in there? Looks kinda tight."

Shiva smiled. "I'm used to doing this with people shooting at me."

He didn't have any comeback for that, so he just held on tight and kept his hands and feet clear of the controls. The pucker factor before touchdown was quite high, especially when the rotor wash blasted up dirt and reduced visibility to zero. It wasn't until the engine started winding down that he realized he was holding his breath. The dust settled and world around them slowly reappeared.

"See? No worries," Shiva reassured him.

"Pardon me while I extract the seat cushion from my ass."

Shiva laughed. "A little more faith next time, then."

"Anything you say." He got out of the chopper and walked to Conrad, who emerged from her SUV.

"Any problems?" she asked.

"Nope, the encoder seems to work as advertised. I monitored the air traffic control frequencies, but nobody challenged us the whole way up. Where are we, by the way?"

"The former Caldwell Brothers' lumber mill. Went out of business ten years ago. The Park Service has been trying to buy it, but can't meet the family's asking price." She waved at the knee-high grass nearby. "So neither side pays much attention to it, which is good for us. Let's get a tarp over that bird before somebody sees it and starts asking questions."

A slate-grey canvas was neatly rolled on the ground nearby. Hendrix and his crew wrestled the covering to the roof and stretched it with ropes to the adjacent building, completely concealing the helicopter. The other operatives took the exertion in stride, but he and Manning were both soaked with sweat by the time they were done. It was certainly the closest thing to manual labor *he* had done in a long time.

"How did you find this place, anyway?" Hendrix asked, taking a break to catch his breath.

"*Lots* of time on Google Earth and real estate databases, believe me," she answered. She put her hands on her hips, surveying their camouflage effort. "That looks good. Hey, we passed a restaurant on the way up. How about a *real* breakfast for a change?"

"Sounds good," he answered. Hendrix ate heartily, knowing full well that by breakfast time tomorrow he would either be very rich or very dead.

TRANSPORT

SAN JOSE, CALIFORNIA

Pugliano was Doug Lyman's first appointment. Lyman looked a little better after a night's sleep, but still had the far-away look that came with emotional trauma. If Lyman had been one of his agents, he would have immediately put him on a two-week medical leave, with mandatory counseling. But Lyman was a big boy, and if he didn't know his limitations, that wasn't Pugliano's problem.

Lyman motioned to the man occupying the other chair in front of his desk. "You remember Seth Graves, our DARPA representative?"

Pugliano extended his hand. "Of course, good to see you again."

"So, what can we do for you?" Lyman asked.

Pugliano cleared his throat. "My request to stage a sting operation here at Nanovex using the nanoagent as bait has been denied. My superiors feel the need to avoid further bloodshed outweighs their desire to apprehend Angela Conrad."

"Do you disagree?" Graves asked.

He gave the other government man a *you should know better* look. "My opinion is irrelevant. My superiors have ordered an immediate evacuation of the WICKER BASKET materials to a facility where they will *truly* be out of the reach of Angela Conrad, or anyone else."

"I hope you're not talking about Livermore or Sandia," Graves scoffed. "I'd take the security here at Nanovex over any of our national laboratories."

"It's being moved to an *undisclosed location*." He wondered why this guy Graves was being a prick all of a sudden. He should know such choices were well above either of their pay grades.

"Are they going to continue working on it?" Graves persisted.

He let out an exasperated sigh. "As far as I know, they intend to lock it up and throw away the key, but I don't get all the memos. My assignment is to arrange security for the transport, period."

"We understand," Lyman intervened. "We've just invested a lot into this project."

Graves obviously wasn't satisfied with Pugliano's answers, but held his peace.

"Agent Pugliano," Lyman said, "I'm curious why you asked for Reese Miller to be excluded from this meeting. Seems to me that Security should be an integral part of *any* plan to move the nanoagent."

"I'm not knocking Mr. Miller. I'm just concerned about leaks. Conrad's already proven she's willing to kidnap and murder to place an inside man in your organization. Since she's lost Manning, my bet is she'll try to replace him, and Security would be the organization I would target if I was her. So let's keep them out of the loop for now. What I *do* need is someone to package the nanoagent and all the data for transport. Mr. Graves, can you handle that?"

"Sure," Graves said without enthusiasm.

"Excellent. I'm going to put together a security convoy that will make a Presidential motorcade look wimpy by comparison. That will take up today at least. All I need is for those materials to be ready for transport the minute the convoy rolls up to the door. Can you two handle that without involving anyone else?"

Lyman eyed Graves, who nodded. Pugliano was glad Lyman could keep Graves in check. The last thing he needed was a bureaucrat not playing on side.

"Very good," he concluded. "Between now and then, make sure your staff is on high alert. We have no idea where Conrad is now, but sooner or later she's coming *here*, and if she shows up before we can evacuate the nanoagent, your men *must* hold her off until the package I'm putting together can arrive to back you up."

Pugliano could tell that deep down Lyman was still a warrior. At the first mention of battle, his eyes brightened and his jaw hardened.

"Count on it," Lyman said firmly.

SABOTAGE

SAN JOSE, CALIFORNIA

"What do you *mean* you could only get one electromagnetic pulse bomb?" Conrad scolded. "I *told* you I needed more than one."

The Russian agent known as Nikolai shrugged. "And as I told *you*, those weapons are very tightly controlled. The Committee felt that this was an even trade—one EMP bomb for one nanoagent, yes?"

Dammit, I knew the Russians would try to sabotage us, she mused. The Committee he referred to was the directorate of the Russian foreign intelligence service, the SVR. "I'll be sure and remind the Committee of that decision if this mission fails because I didn't get what I asked for," she derided. *Of course if that happens, I'd better be dead.*

He tapped the black suitcase-sized equipment box resting on the mess table. "Do you have any idea the *miracles* required to smuggle this weapon from Cuba through a third country and into your hands—overnight?" His face hardened. "I can elaborate if you wish."

She waved him off. "Don't bother. The EMP is an equalizer, not a silver bullet. We can do it the hard way if we have to. Dieter, what did you dredge up?"

"The weapons we obtained are used, but adequate," the stoic German reported. "Ammunition was harder to acquire, but also sufficient."

"Too bad this job wasn't in Texas. We could probably buy ammo at the convenience store. What about the anti-tank rockets?"

"Four American AT-4s, National Guard issue."

"My favorite. Explosives?"

"Six kilograms of C-4, and a dozen detonators, same source."

She turned to the French demolitions expert. "Is that enough, Bastille?"

He nodded confidently. "*Oui*. More than enough."

"First time I've heard *that* today," she said, glaring at Nikolai. "Meghan, how are we fixed for equipment?

"No problem," she affirmed. "Body armor and the military-grade night vision goggles were the toughest nuts to crack, but everybody's good to go."

"Outstanding." She eyed Cosgrove. "Transport?"

He nodded approvingly toward Hendrix. "Thanks to the Yank here, all good."

And here I thought Hendrix was a useless schmuck. Maybe I'll even let him live. Maybe. "Nicely done, everybody. I think we're ready." She looked at her watch. "All right, nine a.m. Enforced rest period until five, then equipment and weapons check. Dinner at six, final mission briefing at nine p.m. Any questions?" There were none.

She jerked a thumb toward the rows of cots. "Okay, everyone hit the sack. See Meghan if you think you'll need a sedative to go down. I don't want anybody nodding off tonight because you couldn't sleep this morning. Dismissed!"

As the team dispersed, she grabbed Dieter by the arm. "Hold up a sec," she whispered. "I want you and Bastille to go over that EMP with a fine-toothed comb. I don't trust that bastard Nikolai."

He nodded soberly. "I understand."

"And if you find out it *was* sabotaged, just kill him. Don't even wake me up to ask for permission."

Dieter was expressionless. "As you wish."

THE ORB

SAN JOSE, CALIFORNIA

Seth Graves returned to his office after his meeting with Pugliano, his mind racing. If he allowed the FBI to remove the WICKER BASKET nanoagent to one of their national laboratories, his life would be forfeit. While Pugliano might take the assurance that the US government planned to "lock it up and throw away the key," he was quite certain that pledge would not be sufficient for Mr. Crane.

He locked the door to his office and opened his safe, removing a hand-sized silver plate. He placed it on his desk and sat down, taking a deep breath to clear his mind. He placed his hand on the plate. It scanned his handprint and activated automatically, linking him with the reconnaissance orb, currently stored in a van halfway between Nanovex and Conrad's garage hideout. He checked the proximity cameras on the van to make sure no one was close by, then gave the order to launch. The roof cover above the orb's landing cradle retracted.

The orb soared upwards, rocketing skyward to ten thousand feet at just under the speed of sound, to break visual contact with anyone on the ground who may have seen the launch. Linked by direct neural interface with the orb's sensors, he looked down and fixed his destination. The orb responded instantly to his mental commands, stopping a few feet above the roofline, two hundred yards from Angela Conrad's garage.

He checked her roof for watchers; there were none. He circled the garage from a distance, searching for sentries. One man slowly walked the perimeter, spending most of his time in the shadows between buildings. Graves circled to the opposite side from the watcher and skimmed the orb in, just above the roofs of the adjacent buildings. He stopped near the skylights, taking care not to expose himself. This was one of those times he wished for a cloaking device, but even the Kammlerorg had technological limits.

He focused the ultrasonic microphone on the skylight and listened. Nothing. Frustrated, he turned up the gain. He heard a cough, then a few murmured words. Turning up the gain even further, he heard a chorus of breathing, and an occasional snore. What was going on here? He switched to penetrating radar, which revealed a bus and an SUV inside the building. On the far side of the bus cots lined the wall, at least a dozen. A man reclined on each of them. Only two people were up, bent over an equipment box in a storage room. He saw two more occupied cots in an office—the shapes looked feminine. He checked the time display; 9:37 a.m. Why all the siestas?

Unless they're resting up for action tonight, he realized. He moved directly above the storeroom where the pair worked and ran a detailed scan on the box they huddled over. At first Graves thought it was a nuclear weapon; inside he found a large metal cylinder lined with explosives with an arming panel next to it. Then he saw rows of batteries and a large transformer. That didn't fit. He linked with the server at the Kammlerorg and searched the weapons database for the interior layout he had scanned. The identification flashed up a few seconds later.

EMP WEAPON: BARISEV-33, YIELD 300 GIGAWATTS [1]

Holy crap.

At least now he knew her opening move. And it looked like action was imminent, almost certainly tonight. But if she beat the FBI to the nanoagent, it might even work to his advantage. He needed to make plans, either way it played out.

He used the radar to locate the outside sentry, then departed in the opposite direction before popping back up to ten thousand feet and returning to the launch point. He scanned the area around his transport van and waited for a nearby car to pass before ordering an automatic recovery. The orb hurtled downward, stopping just above the cradle. It set down and the roof cover closed. The neural display went black. He lifted his hand off the guidance plate and put it back in the safe.

Graves left his office and took the elevator to the basement, making a mental checklist of the items to secure in the WICKER BASKET laboratory. It would be a busy day, but by nightfall every vital piece of equipment and data pertaining to the nanoagent would be packaged and ready for pickup, whether by himself or by Conrad.

DELIVERY

SAN JOSE, CALIFORNIA

Perry Pugliano had the rare treat of enjoying a cigarette on duty as he watched the vehicles assemble outside the San Jose Police headquarters' parking garage. Two SJP SWAT team armored transports were present, along with four Suburbans and half a dozen motorcycles for flank security. He would be adding to that an equal number of vehicles the FBI would supply and a dozen SJP squad cars to clear a path between Nanovex and the San Jose airport. He almost wished Conrad *would* attack the convoy. Even if that damned silver ball showed up, he was determined to make this a fair fight.

The Treasury Department would supply a DC-9 normally used to transport cash and bonds between federal banks, with airport security provided federal marshals on the ground and Secret Service on board.[2] Four California Air National Guard F-16s from Fresno would provide top cover all the way to Area 51—now he finally knew for sure that place really *did* exist. That would be the final resting place for WICKER BASKET, right next to the dead aliens from Roswell for all he knew or cared. The only request that had been denied was for Marine Corps helicopter gunships, and even *he* had to admit those would probably be overkill.

The San Jose Police Chief and the commander of their SWAT teams warily approached him. He smiled inwardly, anticipating the awkward grilling to come.

"Special Agent Pugliano," the police chief probed. "How are we doing?"

"Just great," he said with a nod. "I really appreciate the cooperation your department has extended."

A politician's smile. "That's wonderful to hear. When do you think we'll, ah, be hearing more about the actual mission of this convoy?"

"Right before we roll."

The SWAT commander wasn't happy with that. "How are we supposed to plan for that kind of mission?" he blurted out. Pugliano could tell from the man's haircut he was ex-Army, most likely a Ranger. He probably wargamed his trips to the head.

Pugliano ground out his cigarette. "It's not going to be a complicated mission, just a big one. You follow us to the destination and provide perimeter security, that's it. If you're not bitching at happy hour tomorrow about how boring this mission was, I'm going to be very surprised."

"So why all the secrecy?" the chief prodded. "Are you concerned about leaks in my department?"

He smiled. "If I was concerned about that, I would have asked for someone else's help."

"Then why so damned tight-lipped?" the SWAT commander groused.

He stepped closer to the paramilitary-garbed cop. "One of my agents was killed and a CIA agent is missing and probably dead, almost certainly because of what they knew about this project. In my opinion, the less you gentlemen know, the longer you'll live."

The SWAT man wasn't impressed, but the police chief had heard enough. "We know enough to do our jobs, Agent Pugliano. I'm sure you'll be impressed. Is there anything else we can do for you?"

He checked his watch. Any minute now. "Just waiting for a delivery. I'll need your men to help me secure it."

The sound of a large diesel engine approached, and a Marine Corps six-wheeled cargo truck rounded the corner, stopping next to him. A corporal in fatigues drove the truck, but the five muscular men who jumped from the back wore civilian clothes. The oldest of the five loped over to Pugliano, extending his hand.

"Pugs."

"Gunny."

"Good to see you again," the new arrival announced. "You look like a fish in a tree wearing that suit."

Pugliano chuckled. "And you might as well have come in uniform. Those white sidewall haircuts just scream 'jarhead.' Whatcha got for me?"

The gunnery sergeant's eyes twinkled. "Come and see."

Pugliano mounted into the truck bed with practiced ease and surveyed the olive drab shipping canisters. There were two of one size and four of another. The two larger ones read: MACHINE GUN, BELT-FED, CALIBER 7.62, MODEL M-60E4.

"Sweet," Pugliano breathed. He moved to the four smaller boxes, which read: MISSILE, SHOULDER-FIRED, ANTI-AIRCRAFT, HEAT-SEEKING, MODEL FIM-92C. [3]

"Ah, come to *Papa*!" he said exultantly.

LAST SUPPER

SAN JOSE, CALIFORNIA

"All right, everybody up!" Manning heard Meghan Gallagher call. "Suit up and run a final check on yer gear! If ya find anything wrong, let me know straight away while we still have time ta fix it!"

Manning sat up and rubbed his eyes. The sun came in through the skylight at a sharp angle from the west, illuminating only a narrow strip on the wall over his head. Although he hadn't taken Conrad up on her offer for sedative, somehow he had drifted off during the afternoon. He had lain awake for hours, feigning sleep, hoping the rest period would result in decreased vigilance among watchers and perhaps offering a window of escape. No such luck. The guard had changed frequently to allow everyone the maximum chance at sleep. They each kept an eye on him frequently, ducking in at random from their outside patrols to make sure he was still in his bunk. His body must have sensed the futility of his actions and allowed his mind to switch off and sleep instead. He felt better for the rest.

Gallagher tossed the keys to the SUV in his lap. "Get yer shoes on and go get dinner, Manning." She handed him a handwritten sheet and a wad of cash. "Here's the menu, don't screw it up." She turned. "Shiva!"

The Indian operative trotted up. "Yes?"

"Go with this git and pick up dinner. If he so much as stutters when he makes the order, shoot him." She handed him a pistol.

He smiled pleasantly at Manning, tucking the gun in his belt. "No worries!"

* * *

The menu selections had been written with the care of a condemned prisoner ordering his last meal, which for some of these men it well might be. *Including the "git" who's picking it up*, a voice reminded him. He put in a double order of Chilean sea bass for himself, partially because it was—like himself—an endangered species. He considered it his defiant last statement to the universe.

When they returned, equipment and guns covered the mess table. Three submachine guns and their associated magazines lay within easy and unattended reach. It was only the thought of Amanda and the boys held hostage that restrained him from picking up one of the weapons and doing as much damage as he could and putting himself out of his misery in the process. The idea that he could do *anything* to throw a wrench in Conrad's plans was almost irresistible.

Cosgrove interposed himself between Manning and the weapons. "Don't stare at those too long, mate. You might hurt yourself." He picked up the largest gun and cocked it in Manning's face, laughing loudly when he flinched.

"Hey!" Cosgrove shouted to the room. "Let's clean off the table so we can eat!" he turned back to Manning, leering like a madman. "Time for the Last Supper, Judas! Maybe if you ask real nice, the Angie Christ will let you sit at her right hand!"

"You're psychotic."

Cosgrove kissed his weapon dramatically. "It's a good day to be psychotic, mate! Good day indeed!" He walked away, gun in hand, laughing dementedly.

"It's just a show," Shiva whispered in his ear as they waited for the operatives to clear away their guns and gear. "He's trying to unnerve you."

"Doing a damn good job."

Manning parceled out the orders on the table according to the list, then collected his own and sat down on his cot to eat. Alcohol had been banned due to impending operations, so he had an iced tea with lots of real sugar. To hell with sweetener.

Vasily walked over. "There's room at our work table for one more. Will you join us?"

He already had his food spread out. "Nah. Thanks."

The Russian held out his hands. "I will help you carry your things. Come, my friend. No one should have to eat a meal like this alone."

He waited for a moment, but Vasily's hands remained outstretched. Manning held up his drink and salad. "No arguments there."

They ate in silence, accompanied by Shiva and the other Indian agent Manning had never met. But it *was* better than eating alone like a condemned prisoner.

"You know," Vasily offered, pointing his fork at Manning, "I have seen that look before. May I make a suggestion?"

"Please." As delicious as the fish was and as hungry as he had felt, he still doubted whether he was going to be able to finish both huge fillets, which seemed a shame.

"A wise man once said, 'If you meet danger without flinching, you lessen the danger by half.'"

"Tolstoy?"

"Churchill."

He chuckled. "Yeah, but there's a difference between danger and certain death."

Vasily nodded sadly, fully aware of Manning's predicament. "Churchill also said, 'I am fully ready to meet my maker. Whether my maker is ready for the ordeal of meeting me is another matter.'"

Manning laughed quietly at the Russian Anglophile's wisdom. "That shoe fits."

Vasily held up his glass of juice. "Then let us drink to meeting our maker. Be it today or in the future, it is an appointment no man has yet missed!"

Manning raised his iced tea to the closest thing he had to a friend in this hellhole. "Cheers."

"*Nostrovia.*"

He sighed, putting down his fork for the last time. "Vasily, you mind if I ask you for a favor?"

* * *

For the final briefing, Conrad conducted a stand-up meeting around Vasily's worktable. Manning had helped Vasily build a cardboard model of the Nanovex building at the scale of a Matchbox car, allowing easy procurement of vehicle props for movement exercises. Plans for each floor of the building at a larger scale were pinned to the walls flanking the worktable. Vasily drove a large-screen monitor on the table from his laptop, currently displaying a forty-five-degree-angle shot of the entire Nanovex property from Google Earth. He had even constructed a rudimentary 3D model of the interior so the operatives could "walk through" the building before the operation.

"First of all," she said, "great work putting this layout together. The CIA rarely did better, and they had a hell of a lot more resources. Nice job, Vasily."

"And to Mr. Manning," Vasily interjected.

"Sure. So the plan unfolds like this…."

Manning slipped away and lay down on his cot, staring up at the ceiling. He heard her talking about demolition charges and EMPs and anti-tank rockets, but his mind drifted elsewhere, to his family and his own impending execution. Strangely, now that the time of his death was fixed, it seemed vaguely less threatening. Perhaps it was the *uncertainty* of death that had always haunted him, not death itself.

She wrapped up the briefing half an hour later. "Okay, I have complete confidence in this team and this plan, but remember what General von Moltke said." She let the statement hang.

"No plan survives contact with the enemy," Dieter replied, completing the thought.

"Right, and don't forget it," she reminded the group. "Once the shooting starts, don't ask for permission, just adapt the plan using your own initiative. If you don't, *none* of us will survive. Take your stations!"

* * *

Vasily approached Conrad after the briefing. "Miss Conrad, a word?"

"Quickly," she allowed.

"I have come to petition for the lives of Mr. Manning's family. He has behaved in an entirely honorable manner throughout this process. And while he realizes his life is forfeit, if he had your assurance that his wife and children will be spared if he cooperates to the end, he can at least go to his grave in peace. I believe he deserves that much."

She shrugged. "I admire your sentiment, but that's up to the people holding the hostages. I told them that once we're done with him, what they do with the family is their call. If they think the wife and kids have seen too much, they're toast. Sorry."

He remained expressionless. "I understand. Mr. Manning has also asked that when the time comes, you allow *me* to be the one who administers the *coup de grace*, preferably without warning. You need only to let me know when that moment has arrived."

Conrad threw her head back and laughed. "You're a saint, Vasily. But I have no intention of *shooting* him!"

* * *

Manning waited in the SUV with Shiva and Hendrix for Vasily to return. "How did it go?" Manning asked nervously when the Russian slipped into the back seat.

Vasily smiled. "Not to worry. She always intended to release your family unharmed."

He held his optimism in check. "I saw her laughing about something."

"She found your fatalism amusing for some reason. She agrees that you will perform your last actions more efficiently if you are not concerned about the fate of your family. Please don't be."

His shoulders dropped from the release of tension. Amanda and the boys would survive, even if he did not. He felt himself choking up, which he fought back. "And the other thing?"

Vasily reached forward and squeezed Manning's shoulder. "It is done, my friend. I promise your end will come without warning and without pain. You have my word."

Now he *was* tearing up. The fact that his death would not be with Angela Conrad taunting him over the barrel of a gun was a huge relief. He swallowed hard. "Thanks, Vasily," he finally said. "I owe you one, not that I'll ever get the chance to pay you back."

"You would do the same for me. Speak no more of it."

Scott Hendrix snorted in derision. "This is touching. Can we go now?"

Manning fired up the Escalade. The lights in the garage went out and the roll-up door opened. He backed onto the street, leaving the headlights off until the door closed again. He put the SUV in gear and headed toward Mount Diablo, just under an hour away.

LAST CHANCE

CHICAGO, ILLINOIS

Amanda and the boys had a new guard today. He was in his twenties and handsome, with intense, intelligent eyes. He bore a strong resemblance to Mr. Wu. His son, perhaps?

He was utterly immune to Amanda's charms. She had smiled at him when she went to the bathroom and had left the door slightly ajar to see if he would attempt to spy on her like the guard last night. No such luck. When she emerged he had split the distance between the boys and the bathroom, but had come no closer. He backed out of the narrow aisle to allow her passage back to her mattress, but would not even make eye contact with her.

Mr. Wu had made a brief stop to deliver their dinner, a simple meal of rice and vegetables. He also avoided her gaze, and the words he exchanged with the guard were terse. He left without checking further on his captives.

Amanda's feminine intuition blared an alarm in her ears. Something about Mr. Wu's coldness unnerved her. She sensed that she and the boys were becoming a liability.

Patchy Beard returned to guard them after dinner. Even he avoided looking at her. Perhaps in China it was rude to ogle a corpse. That was the final straw. If she was going to act, to give her sons a chance at survival, it would have to be tonight. She might not get another chance.

DESTINY

SAN JOSE CALIFORNIA

The old bus creaked backwards out of the garage, then headed east toward the Nanovex facility. Bouncing along on tired springs that should have been replaced ages ago, Conrad and the eleven other black-clad operatives hunched in their seats, trying their best to look vagrant and destitute rather than armed and dangerous. The homeless bus cover had worked like a charm so far. They had passed two police cars, including one that had idled next to them at a stoplight. Neither had given them a second glance.

They stopped in a strip mall parking lot half a mile from Nanovex. She had no idea how far the effects of the EMP would *really* extend, so she decided to err on the side of caution. She double-checked the frequency, then keyed her radio. "Red Queen to Shiva, what's your position?"

"Orbiting a kilometer east," the helicopter pilot responded. "I can be on target in sixty seconds."

She sat silently for a few seconds, savoring the moment. Like she had so many times before, she held her life lightly in her hands, ready to risk it all on a single bold throw. She remembered her favorite quote from Nietzsche. *Give me today, for once, the worst throw of your dice, Destiny. Today I transmute everything into gold.* That had been the philosophy of her whole life; taking the worst odds Destiny could hand her and still coming out on top.

But this time was different. She felt it to the core of her soul, even though she was pretty sure she didn't have one of those anymore. No matter what she had planned, she knew instinctively that Destiny had a different outcome in mind for her. That knowledge strangely thrilled her, even though she knew the most likely twist of fate Destiny had in mind for her was death. Only one way to find out.

"Red Queen to Shiva. Execute, execute, execute!"

"Acknowledged," her radio crackled. "Turning on final approach now."

"*Sixty seconds!*" she shouted to the operatives on the bus. "Get ready to roll!"

[1] An EMP weapon is constructed by winding high-capacity electrical wires as a stator inside a non-metallic cylinder and charging them with a powerful capacitor, creating a strong magnetic field. An explosive charge is then detonated in the center of the device, driving a metallic armature against the charged armature, creating a powerful and directional magnetic flux. Magnetic flux is defined as the rate of change in a magnetic field. With the armature propelled by high explosive, the rate of change is extremely rapid, projecting a powerful and destructive flux, similar to striking any nearby electrical circuit with lightning. (Source: *The Electromagnetic Bomb - a Weapon of Electrical Mass Destruction by Carlo Kopp*, GlobalSecurity.org)

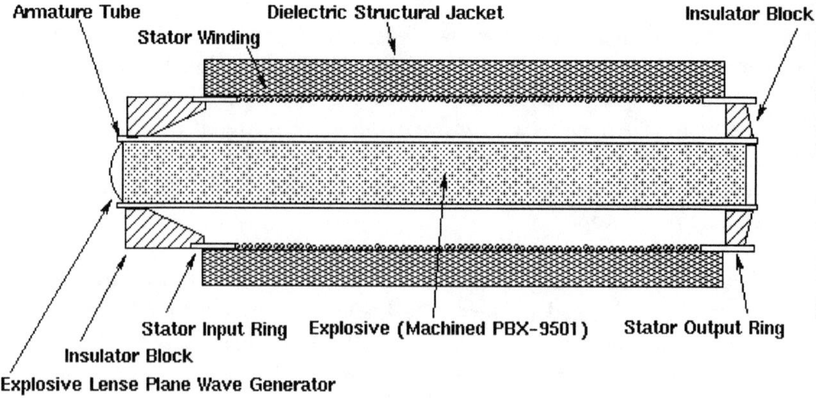

Cutaway Diagram of an Electromagnetic Pulse Weapon (© 1996, Carlo Kopp)

[2] The author witnessed the transfer of several billion dollars in securities via a Treasury Department DC-9 once in St. Louis. Seeing submachine-gun toting federal agents around the plane and baseball-capped snipers on the roof of every adjacent building made a lasting impression. A source in Security confirmed the reason for the extraordinary measures.

[3] The M-60 is a belt-fed squad machine gun, used from Vietnam to present day. The FIM-92 Stinger missile is a Man-Portable Air Defense missile (known in the business as a MANPAD). The Stinger is used by the US military and 29 other countries. Its effectiveness comes from its ability to lock onto the heat of a target aircraft's exhaust and home in without further guidance from the operator, making it a "fire and forget" weapon. To date, 270 confirmed aircraft kills have been credited to the Stinger.

CHAPTER 27

BLACK HOLE

SAN JOSE, CALIFORNIA

After driving Hendrix, Vasily and Shiva back up into the mountains, Manning helped them remove the tarp from over the helicopter, then sat in back with Vasily. The three operatives wore headphones—he was not given a set. The noise from the engines and the rotors was deafening. He wished now he had paid more attention in Conrad's briefing—he had no idea what was about to happen next.

At least it was a beautiful night. He looked out the Huey's right side windows as they flew over the east side of San Francisco Bay. The air over the city was chilly and clear. The lights on the far side sparkled off the water like a Christmas display. Trying to take Vasily's advice about staying positive in the face of certain death, he realized there were worse ways to spend one's last hours. They flew south for twenty minutes, then circled. Trying to get his bearings from the landmarks below, he recognized the illuminated glass canopy of the Nanovex facility nearby. *Conrad's really gonna do this*, he finally realized.

Suddenly the helicopter banked hard and the engine throttled up. Vasily left the bench seat beside him and bent over a green box the size of a large cooler. It had Russian lettering and a yellow triangle with a lightning bolt on each side. He removed the top cover and entered numbers on a keypad inside. He ran a rope through the four lifting rings on the sides of the box, then slid open the Huey's left side door. The slipstream whipped viciously into the cabin. The noise became almost unbearable. Manning squinted his eyes against the wind and stopped his ears with his fingers. Vasily ran the rope through a pulley outside the door and motioned Manning over.

Just as Manning rose from his seat the Huey tilted sharply backward, throwing him back into the seat's nylon webbing. Vasily signaled him to stay put, walking over in a crouch with a coil of rope. He thrust a pair of heavy leather gloves into Manning's hands, then moved his headset's microphone aside.

"You are going to lower the box at my direction," Vasily shouted in his ear. He held his hand up near the roof. "This is fast," he signaled, then lowered his hand toward the deck. "And this is slow." He made a fist. "And this is stop. If you lower it too quickly, the box will break and Conrad will probably order me to throw you out. Be careful."

"Got it!" Manning shouted back.

Vasily pushed the box toward the open door and signaled for Manning to take the slack out of the rope, lifting the box off the floor. It was heavy, but not more than he could handle. Vasily maneuvered the box out the door and motioned for him to start lowering. The box disappeared from view and Vasily leaned out, signaling him to go faster.

Manning lowered the box as fast as he could hand over hand, but Vasily's frantic motions indicated it was not fast enough. He planted his feet firmly and let the rope slide through his grip. He could feel the heat of friction working its way through the leather. He was soon running out of rope.

Vasily's hand dropped toward the floor and Manning tightened his grasp. Vasily made a fist and Manning grabbed the rope firmly, stopping the box. The gloves burned his palms. Vasily unclenched his fist and raised his hand slightly. Manning let the rope feed out for a second, then it went slack. Vasily made the "OK" signal and motioned for him to release the rope. Vasily yanked the rest of the rope through the pulley, let it fall, then shouted something to Shiva. The Huey pitched forward and accelerated sharply, pushing Manning into his seat.

The helicopter raced ahead for about thirty seconds, then leveled out and banked gently. He saw Hendrix and Shiva's eyes fixed to the right. Vasily slid the left-side door shut, then sat down in the forward bench seat, also looking to the right. Manning watched the top of the building.

Thirty seconds after they leveled out, a detonation lit up the small access deck atop the glass canopy. Not a big blast, just a bright red flash. The part of him that watched NASCAR for the wrecks would have been disappointed—until the electrical transformers behind the complex exploded in a shower of silver sparks, plunging the whole complex into darkness. The parking lot lights flickered to a dying orange glow. The Nanovex facility became a city-block-sized black hole.

Vasily clapped his hands together and flashed Manning two thumbs up, then turned to slap Shiva on the back. Apparently that was the result they intended.

* * *

"Go, GO, *GO!*" Conrad shouted.

Ancient gears ground in protest, lurching the bus forward. She could see the effects of the EMP weapon before they reached Nanovex's gate. Streetlights were dark for hundreds of yards along the main road and the stoplight in front of the complex was out.

Nikolai turned in his seat. "Just as advertised, yes?" he said with a con artist's smile.

She lifted the gun she had pointed at his back from behind the seat, held it up for his consideration, then holstered it. "Nice work. You get to keep breathing."

His smile fading, he silently turned to face forward again.

They approached the main gate. "Dieter! Bastille! You're up!" she ordered.

Bastille jumped up to straddle the aisle, a foot on top of the seats on each side. The two nearest operatives braced his legs to keep him from falling as the bus rocked through the turn onto Nanovex's property. He popped the escape hatch on the roof and pushed through a three-foot-long green cylinder, followed by his upper torso. Dieter lowered a window near the back of the bus on the left-hand side.

The bus ground to a stop by the first guard shack with the sound of creaking springs and metal screeching on long-gone brake pads. The EMP had really done a number on Nanovex. Even the battery-powered emergency lights in the guard post were knocked out. The guard's position was only exposed by the nervous sweep of an approaching flashlight. The battle-suited operatives hunkered low in their seats again. Conrad lifted her head slightly to watch the action, her face and blond hair concealed by a black ski mask.

"Excuse me sir, I am lost!" The Indian agent Vimana said in a friendly tone. "Can you help me, officer?"

The flashlight from below framed Vimana in bright silhouette. "I'm sorry," Conrad heard, "you'll have to turn the bus around. This is private property!"

"I am so sorry!" Vimana said in his lilting accent. "Can you tell me how to get to the nearest McDonald's?"

A pause. "Uh, sure. Once you turn the bus around, just turn right and…."

Dieter's silenced gun coughed twice. The glow of the flashlight wavered, then disappeared with a clatter.

She looked past Vimana to the second guard shack. *There's no way they could have missed that.* "Go, Bastille!" she shouted.

The launch blast of an AT-4 anti-tank rocket flared briefly through the escape hatch, then a hot needle of light lanced toward the armored second guard shack. The bulletproof glass sides of the shack lit up like a flash bulb, fading quickly to a dim orange glow from the shack's burning interior.

"That's a kill! Get him down!" Conrad ordered. "Go Ian!"

The operatives helped Bastille climb down from his perch as Cosgrove disappeared out the front passenger door with another AT-4 rocket over his shoulder.

"Ms. Conrad! The barricade!" Vimana called out.

She ran to the front of the bus and lowered her night vision goggles. The barricade had been up, but the EMP had knocked out whatever circuit raised and lowered the posts. The weight of the concrete-filled stainless steel tubes pressed against their actuation system. The posts were slowly retracting, with only about a foot remaining above the pavement.

Talk about a lucky break! She slapped the shoulders of the two operatives closest to the door. "Shogun! Nikolai! Get out there and guide the bus forward as soon as the frame will clear!" She pointed to the operatives in the next row. "Dragon! Javelin! Cover them!" She stepped clear of the aisle for the agents to surge out the door.

She keyed her radio. "Talk to me, Ian!"

"The guards are running around the lobby like a bunch of headless chickens. I think they saw the missile hit the guard post, but they're not sure what to do about it. With their radios fried, I'd say we have another sixty seconds of confusion left. How's that barricade coming?"

"I'll check." She jumped down to the pavement and ran to where Nikolai and Shogun bent under the bumper.

"We need another ten centimeters to clear the engine," Nikolai said.

She converted in her head. Four inches. "We need more weight on the cylinders. Both of you, jump on top! Dragon! Javelin! You join 'em, I'll cover you!"

The four operatives each jumped on a post, using the hood of the bus to steady themselves. It looked comical, but after a few seconds she could see the posts were going down faster. She kept her gaze and her gun pointed toward the Nanovex building, but kept glancing back until it was obvious that the bumper would clear the posts.

"Okay, we're good! Let's roll!" she ordered.

The five clambered back onto the bus. "Just go forward slow," she told Vimana as she re-boarded.

The bus labored unevenly back into motion, backfiring once. Conrad cringed. It sounded louder to her than the explosion inside the bulletproof guard shack. The sound of scraping metal reverberated under her feet. Vimana applied the brakes.

"That's just the frame," she urged. "Keep moving."

Vimana complied and the scraping quickly tapered off. He kept inching forward, anxious not to rip off the bus's differential. Their forward progress continued without further metal-on-metal protest.

She checked the windows to gauge their progress. "Okay, we're clear! Punch it!" She keyed her radio. "Ian, take the shot!" The bus accelerated at a painfully slow rate, the engine surging and jerking under the strain. It backfired once more.

* * *

Cosgrove lay atop one of the anti-vehicle berms flanking the barricade. He shouldered his anti-tank rocket and took aim at the lobby entrance

Even in the darkness, the lobby guards could see the bus coming and assumed defensive positions.

More anti-vehicle posts blocked the lobby entrance, mainly to prevent a runaway passenger car from crashing into the lobby by accident. While the steel posts at the front entrance were designed to stop intentional breaches by heavy vehicles, these were not as robust. Cosgrove took aim at the post on the far left and let his breath out slowly. He pressed the trigger button next to the sight and the tube bucked slightly, the hot backblast of the rocket slapping his prone legs and back. The rocket blazed like a welder's torch in his night vision goggles, arcing slightly on its way to the target. It struck six inches from the ground, obliterating most of the concrete post and launching the rest into the air.

He saw the guards flinch at the blast and the concrete fragments peppering the glass wall of the lobby. They probably thought his missile had missed its mark. But Conrad had another missile targeted for the lobby.

* * *

"Prepare to ram!" Conrad shouted to the team. She braced herself, then stole a glance at the speedometer. Forty miles per hour. Vimana might coax another five out of the old dog before it hit the building.

Using Manning and Hendrix's reconnaissance, Vasily had plotted the exact spot for the bus to impact for maximum effect, ten feet to the left of the revolving door. The bus hit the curb with such force she bounced upward. Only her legs braced under the seat kept her from being tossed into the air. She came down hard on the seat in front of her, her hand sandwiched between her gun and the metal seat back. She cried out in pain. If not for the flak jacket, she probably would have broken a rib as well.

The front of the bus smacked the ground with a shower of sparks, its front leaf springs shattered. The bus's body sagged, dragging on the front wheels and stealing desperately needed speed. The rear wheels hit the curb, giving the agents in the back of the bus a similar toss. She heard somebody tumble to the floor behind her, cursing in surprise and pain.

The bus struck the lobby with an explosion of glass and steel. Vimana kept the pedal to the floor, but the bus ran out of momentum with only half of the vehicle penetrating the lobby and the engine died. Not what she had planned. "Move forward!" she yelled to the shooters in the back.

She turned just in time to see Vimana's head burst and the windows of the bus shatter from weapons fire all around. Glass fragments flew like an ice storm just over her head.

"Keep moving forward!" she barked at her team. She crawled to just behind the driver's seat. She looked behind her at the hesitant mercenaries, who moved forward with great caution. She pointed her submachine gun at them. “Get your asses up here or I’ll fucking shoot you myself!” Regardless of their nationalities, she seemed to have discovered their common language. They crawled more quickly toward the front of the bus.

She reached from behind the seat to grab Vimana’s limp torso, which slumped to the side. “Return fire at my signal!” she ordered.

The gunfire from Nanovex guards died off for lack of targets. Before they could reload she hauled Vimana’s body upright, stuck her gun under his arm and fired off three rounds toward the lobby. The return fire quickly obliterated the windshield.

“NOW!” she screamed.

Six operatives popped up, pouring assault rifle rounds on the muzzle flashes of the guards firing on Vimana’s corpse. The return fire trailed off quickly. She looked up past where Vimana’s head had been and saw the windshield was completely gone. She pulled two frag grenades from pouches on her vest, yanked the pins, then tossed one each in the direction of the last return fire she heard. She reached forward and cranked open the bus’s front door. “Get ready to move!” she called.

The grenades exploded.

“Follow me!” she shouted, charging out the door to the nearest cover, an overturned planter. She laid down suppressive fire in three-round bursts toward the guards’ most likely concealments. She heard her men running behind her, seeking cover of their own. Her tactical move worked well until her submachine gun clicked loudly on an empty chamber. Then at least three guards opened up on her and the planter seemed to shrink in size by half. She tucked into a fetal position and listened to bullets impacting the far side of the ceramic pot just inches from her head. Even in the darkness, she realized she and her commandos were backlit by the lights of the city through the glass wall behind her.

She keyed her mike. “Smoke forward!”

She heard the tinny “ping” of grenade arming levers, then half a dozen grenades landing throughout the lobby, hissing smoke. She counted to ten and rolled under the bus. “Meaghan,” she said quietly over her radio, “How many do you have with you on the bus?”

“Me plus three,” she replied in a whisper.

“Nikolai, Shogun,” she transmitted to her nearest operatives, “take whoever’s with you and circle around to the right. Meghan, bring yours and follow me under the bus to the left.”

“Moving right,” she heard Nikolai reply in a low murmur.

“I’ll stay on board and draw their fire,” Gallagher replied. “Sending the rest down to you.”

“Got it.”

She heard Meghan's troops tiptoe down the bus's front steps, then slide under the bus. She squeezed out on the far side and began creeping left. Even with rubber-soled boots, the sound of crunching glass underfoot gave her position away. A guard fired through the smoke, missing her head by inches. She dropped to the floor, as did the three agents at her side.

Gallagher opened fire, her shots into the smoke rewarded by a man's groan and the clatter of gunmetal on the tile floor. Knowing that silence was Conrad's enemy, Gallagher fired a round in the blind every few seconds. No one fired back.

Conrad reached the wall to her left and sidestepped along it, flanking the guards' positions. Using her night vision goggles she spotted a man in a suit hunkered behind a couch. She switched her submachine gun to single fire, aimed carefully, and took him down with two shots. She heard a three-round burst from the opposite side of the lobby. One of Nikolai's men must have had a target as well. She spotted movement on the second floor balcony and fired through the glass railing. She saw someone fall. She kept moving and scanning above and below, but no more targets presented themselves.

She keyed her radio. "Left clear. Be sure and check above."

"Center clear," Gallagher confirmed.

"Right clear high and low," she heard from Nikolai a few seconds later. "Two casualties."

"*Dammit!*" she growled under her breath. She turned to the trio at her side. "Find some cover and hold this position. There's more where those came from." She trotted watchfully back to the bus and over to the right side of the lobby. She almost stumbled over Bastille, who was on his back and coughing. She bent to his aid, finding a bullet hole in the front of his vest. She unzipped the jacket and searched inside, feeling the bullet's tip lodged inside the vest. "Your lucky day, Bastille. Does it hurt to breathe?"

"A little. I will be fine"

She zipped his vest back up. "Stay put till you get your wind back."

She saw another figure sprawled nearby. Moving to his side, she realized it was Ghost. A bullet had pierced his neck, which he clutched weakly with both hands. Blood flowed through his fingers. Breath came through his punctured windpipe in wet gasps.

Nikolai slipped to her side, accompanied by Ghost's partner Shogun. Their eyes went wide when they saw the severity of their comrade's injuries.

She met their gaze through her night vision goggles. "Does everyone agree that this is a fatal wound under the circumstances?"

The two operatives nodded solemnly. While Ghost's life might well be saved by immediate medical evacuation, that was a luxury they didn't have. And if they left him behind for the authorities, the Japanese agent would bleed out in agony long before help arrived.

She looked at Shogun. “He’s your partner. Do you want to take care of it?”

He nodded. “Hai.” He reluctantly drew his pistol and placed to his friend’s forehead. Ghost’s eyes bulged in terror. Shogun withdrew his weapon.

“I cannot,” he confessed.

“No shame in that,” she reassured him. She quickly drew her pistol, stuck it under Ghost’s chin, and pulled the trigger.

She stood and holstered her weapon. “I’d expect the same from either of you if I’m in that position. Let’s go. We got a bank to rob.”

EMERGENCY CONTACT

SAN JOSE, CALIFORNIA

Like most executives, Doug Lyman had several different phone numbers he gave out to business contacts. He programmed his smart phone to allow some of them to ring only during business hours, others to go to straight to voice mail after ten PM, and only one to ring at any hour of the day or night. That number was programmed with a particularly strident tone, to wake him from even the deepest sleep. It rang at fifteen past midnight.

“Hello?” he answered groggily.

“I’m sorry to bother you, sir. This is BACKSTOP.”

He sat up in bed. “What’s wrong?”

From his time in the Air Force, Lyman knew that a good Security department could accomplish only so much. The phrase “Who will watch the watchers” was just as true now as when the Roman poet Juvenal coined the phrase two thousand years ago. Only a totally separate organization could perform that sensitive function.

Lyman had contracted with an executive security firm providing a service known as BACKSTOP. Run by retired federal agents, BACKSTOP periodically monitored radio, cell phone and email traffic inside Nanovex’s Security department, and watched security camera feeds—especially during evening hours—to make sure Lyman’s guards were doing what he paid them for.

“Sir, it’s strange, but at midnight we lost *all* the feeds—security camera, radio, everything. So we called your emergency contact, Mr. Reese Miller, but he’s not picking up his cell phone. We even tried calling the Security office directly on their landline but there was no answer.”

Lyman blinked in the darkness, willing his brain to function. He was especially concerned that Miller wasn't picking up. Because of the danger from Conrad, Miller had insisted on staying overnight to supervise his security detachment. "What could cut them off like that?"

"At first I thought an electrical transformer fire might do it, but that wouldn't affect cell phones or land lines. And we've been monitoring the police and fire bands—no one's called anything in."

So basically you know nothing, he resisted snapping at the man. "What do you suggest?"

"I'd like to ask the San Jose Police to check it out, but I wanted to ask your permission first, because of the sensitivity of our contract."

"Understood. Make the call, and let me know what they find out."

SNATCH AND HATCHET

SAN JOSE, CALIFORNIA

Conrad ran back to the bus. "Nice job on the cover fire," she told Gallagher. "Get the Hatchet team ready to go." She keyed her radio. "Ian, how's it looking out there?"

"Quiet as a grave," she heard in her earpiece.

"I want you to move the bus. I'll open the back door."

"On my way."

She trotted back to Bastille, who was sitting up. "Can you function?" she asked.

He held up a hand for assistance. "I am good."

She pulled him to his feet. "Tiger, meet me at the bus," she said over her radio. The Chinese demolitions specialist emerged from the smoke and darkness a few seconds later. She led them deeper into the lobby and to the left. They came up behind Gallagher's team after a short distance.

The stairs down to the WICKER BASKET lab in the basement were ahead and to the left. Unfortunately, the Security office was directly across the hall from the stairwell her snatch team needed to reach. That would be the job of Gallagher's hatchet team. They bunched up just short of the hallway, ready to rush into battle.

"Hatchet team, on my mark," Gallagher said. "Go!" she disappeared around the corner, her men quickly following. Conrad peeked around. The hatchet team had bunched up again just outside the Security office door. "Fire in the hole," Conrad heard her say quietly in her earpiece.

The shaped charge Bastille had crafted imploded the door with a geyser of flame. Gallagher followed up with a hand grenade. The team rushed inside to the sound of gunfire. Conrad couldn't tell who was doing the shooting. Then more grenades followed. Gallagher was meeting stiff resistance.

The attention of Conrad's team was drawn to the gunfire, but she directed their focus back at the lobby. "C'mon!" she scolded. "There's still more guards loose in this box! Keep your eyes open!"

As if to punctuate her comment, Tiger pointed his gun at an upper floor and let loose a three-round burst a second later. "Target down," he said without emotion.

Cosgrove cranked the bus's engine, which coughed painfully back to life. After several seconds of agonized grinding the bus shifted into reverse, scraping backwards through the smashed lobby debris with a noise like fingernails on a chalkboard. Its suspension springs shattered, the front wheels squealed against the chassis like a dying animal, but he eventually worked the hulk loose of the building and herded it with much travail back toward the front gate.

After nearly a minute of silence, another grenade exploded in the Security office, followed by three single gunshots. "Sound off!" Gallagher said.

"Clear."

"Clear."

"Clear!"

"Objective secure," an out-of-breath Gallagher reported. "Two more casualties."

"*Dammit!*" Conrad muttered again. Her plan had taken these kinds of losses into account, but it was another thing to actually take the hits. "Who?" she demanded over the radio.

"Dragon's wounded, Shogun's dead," Gallagher reported.

Shit, why couldn't that bastard Nikolai have taken a bullet, she wondered. The Japanese principal would *not* be pleased that both of his agents had been killed. It just reinforced a truth she had learned long ago: the universe seldom kills the right people. That's why you have to do it yourself.

"All right, send Nikolai out—I'm a man short," Conrad ordered. "Then take your team and make sure the rest of the building is secure, especially the stairwell to the roof. I don't want anybody shot in the back when we clear out of here."

"Got it," Gallagher replied.

Conrad moved Bastille and Tiger to the stairs leading down to the basement and waved Nikolai onto point. Maybe she'd get lucky and there would be just one more guard waiting. Nikolai scowled, but knew better than to refuse. Better to risk possible death than to invite it for certain.

She heard rifle fire from the direction of Nanovex's front gate, where Cosgrove stood guard. Her radio crackled.

"Whatever you're doing in there, shovel it up!" Cosgrove said. "We're about to have lots of company!"

SITUATION

SAN FRANCISCO, CALIFORNIA

Unlike Doug Lyman, Perry Pugliano had only one phone number, and it rang at all hours of the day and night. It seemed to Pugliano that recently it *only* rang late at night. At least he didn't have to listen to his wife bitch about the phone waking her up anymore.

"Pugliano," he groaned, still half asleep.

"Agent Pugliano, Wallace Hargrove, San Jose Chief of Police, I'm going to have to take back some of the resources we dedicated to your convoy tomorrow. We have a situation."

"What kind of situation?"

"A patrolman making a routine call to a local business was fired upon and wounded. Some perp with an assault rifle. I need those SWAT team war wagons back so no more of my officers gets hurt."

"Take 'em!" Pugliano urged. "Where did it happen?" he asked out of curiosity.

"A tech firm called Nanovex, where those people died the other day," the Chief replied hurriedly, obviously wanting to end the call.

He was fully awake now. "Did you say *Nanovex?*"

"Yeah, what of it?" the Chief snapped.

"Listen to me!" he ordered, already out of bed and on his feet. "Roll *everything* you've got, then get your ass down there *personally* and make *damn* sure *nobody* gets off the Nanovex property! Not by ground, not by air, not by storm sewer! *Nobody!* Got it?"

"No argument from me, Agent Pugliano."

"And for God's sake, *don't* make a move on that building until I get there, unless you want *another* San Jose massacre on your hands!"

Pugliano thought he heard the Chief swallow before answering. "I'll be waiting for you at the barricade, Agent Pugliano."

CHRISTMAS

SAN JOSE, CALIFORNIA

The basement was black. Pitch black. So black that their night vision goggles wouldn't even work. Since they were unable to procure military grade NVGs for the whole group, they had to purchase consumer-grade sets at a hunting outfitters store. Those amplified available light, but lacked the infrared illuminators of military units. Down in the basement with even the emergency lights fried by the EMP, there simply wasn't any light to amplify.

"Switch to flashlights," she ordered. Nikolai and Tiger split left and right at the foot of the stairs. Both signaled clear. "Nikolai, circle around the basement, make sure we don't have company. Tiger, take us home." She kept Bastille behind her. At this point he was more important to the operation than she was.

The Chinese agent led her and Bastille a short distance to the left, to a door marked PROPRIETARY LAB P4-1. He pointed, then assumed a covering position.

"Bastille, you're up," she said, waving him around. She took a covering position on the opposite side from Tiger. Nikolai returned from his patrol a minute later. She motioned for him to cover the stairs.

"Bastille, what do you see?" she asked.

"The door is very robust," he reported, "but the wall plate around the access lock can be cut and give us access to the mechanism inside. Do you have someone who can finesse the electronics, now that Ghost is dead?"

Not since I had to put a bullet in Linn Shaozang. "No, think you can brute force it?"

Bastille chuckled. "There are few problems that can not be solved with explosives." He pulled a coil of what looked like quarter-inch aluminum tubing from his bag, cut it to length, then bent it into a square. He joined the tube ends with a blasting cap and fixed it to the wall plate with four wads of putty. Running a length of wire six feet away, he plugged it into a small box and pressed a button. Flame spouted along the length of the tube, cutting the metal panel around the access keypad, leaving behind blackened metal and acrid smoke. The severed plate fell free, dangling from the keypad's wires.

He waved the smoke away and played his flashlight around the interior. "Ah!" he said, reaching in his bag for a short prybar. "This would have been more difficult if the power was still on, but without it to hold the lock closed...." He stuck the prybar inside and gave it a sharp shove. The lock clicked and the door popped slightly ajar.

"*Voilá!*" he exclaimed, opening the lab door with a flourish. "After you, Madame."

She waved him back, raising her gun. "Nikolai, give me eyes inside." With the importance of WICKER BASKET, she wasn't assuming the room was empty. The Russian disappeared into the lab. "Tiger, back him up."

"Clear!" Nikolai announced a minute later.

"Clear," Tiger agreed.

"Bastille, stay out here and watch our backs," she said before going inside.

It was hard to tell from just a flashlight, but what she *could* see left her disappointed. It looked like just another windowless office. Cubicles, computers, and file cabinets. Except each file cabinet had a combination wheel like a safe. But what quickly got her attention were three boxes just inside the door.

"Tiger, give me a light over my shoulder," she said, bending over to inspect the boxes. A combination padlock secured each heavy-duty metal shipping container. "Bastille?" she called. "Got some more work for you."

He sniffed in amusement at the locks. "Give me a moment."

She examined the rest of the office while he worked. The laboratory proper lay beyond a heavy but unlocked interior door. She was able to identify a glove box, a centrifuge, and an electron microscope, but the rest of the lab equipment was alien to her. She hadn't expected to find a box labeled HERE'S THE NANOAGENT, but she began to worry that she had grossly underestimated the difficulty of this technological pillaging operation. Her flashlight played across another door at the end of the lab, this one like a watertight door on a ship. Some kind of test chamber lay beyond, on the other side of a large window. She wondered if this is where the original WICKER BASKET scientists died.

"Done!" Bastille called out.

She returned to the office, where he waved away the smoke from the small cutting charges he used to sever the padlocks. She opened the first box, finding stacks of jewel-cased CDs, neatly packed into foam slots. She pulled a few at random, finding titles like WICKER BASKET THIRD QUARTER PROGRESS REPORT, NANOAGENT ACTIVATION ANALYSIS, and NANOTUBE FABRICATION STUDIES. Several removable hard drives filled adjacent slots. She closed the box and moved to the next one, containing a tightly packed assortment of unidentifiable scientific equipment. Feeling a twinge of panic in her gut, she moved to the last box. It contained only a handheld electronic device resembling a large, complex walkie-talkie, another smaller plastic case, and a slotted silver tube with an antenna and a CO_2 flask.

She opened the plastic case. It contained three small metal cylinders, each emblazoned with a red and green chemical warfare warning label. She held the box up to the tube-like apparatus without touching the vials. Apparently the vials were sized to go into that slot. She carefully closed the case and set it back in its foam recess. The last item in the box was a three-ring binder, inserted spine-out in its own niche. She extracted the notebook, flipping it open. The title page read, OPERATING HANDBOOK, WICKER BASKET AGENT DISPERSAL SYSTEM.

"Merry Christmas!" she breathed.

"We are good?" Bastille asked.

She nodded. "Oh yeah, we're *very* good."

Her radio crackled. It was Hendrix. "I don't know what the hell you guys did down there, but you got every cop in the valley coming your way, right the hell now!"

BIG DOG

SAN JOSE, CALIFORNIA

The Huey circled for several minutes after deploying the EMP. Manning's attention drifted to more distant landmarks, since the Nanovex facility was now just a large black square cut from the city fabric beneath them. The helicopter leveled in the middle of a turn. Looking up, he saw Hendrix pointing vigorously at the ground to his left. Vasily moved to that side of the helicopter. Manning joined him at the window.

Several police cars fishtailed to a stop outside the Nanovex gate, blocking the main road. More patrols cars and at least one ambulance rapidly filled in the street behind them. He saw a helicopter approaching in the distance, its spotlight already probing the ground. It banked hard and set up an orbit around the facility, its searchlight scanning the building and parking lot in search of a target. Other than Conrad's homeless bus blocking the inner gate, no sign of her team was visible.

Shiva turned the Huey away and retreated to a more distant loiter, putting more space between the large and noisy Huey and the growing number of eyes and ears on the ground. Soon only the flashing lights of the police cars and the circling police helicopter were visible.

Another helicopter joined the orbit around Nanovex. For a moment the pair circled the building like sharks, then the newcomer split off and descended for a landing at a nearby park. Vasily moved next to Manning. He shoved his microphone aside and shouted in Manning's ear, pointing at the helicopter now descending toward a softball field.

"That will be the big dog!" he said with a grin.

* * *

Even before his helicopter landed, Perry Pugliano saw a Suburban with San Jose Police markings bouncing across the ball fields to meet them. It was Chief Hargrove. The Chief opened the back door of his SUV for Pugliano.

"Sorry to stick you back here, but all my radios are up front," Hargrove apologized.

"No problem."

"Take us to the barricades," Hargrove ordered the sergeant driving.

The police had set up lines about a hundred yards away from both sides of the Nanovex entrance. Police officers leveled their shotguns across the hoods of their patrol cars. Pugliano noticed the street and traffic lights were out. "Power failure?"

"Not sure," Hargrove admitted. He pointed further down the street where the street lights still burned brightly. "Those are on the same circuit as these dark ones. Doesn't make sense." He handed over a pair of night vision binoculars. "Here, take a look."

With his naked eyes Pugliano could see an empty patrol car backed into a light post at the Nanovex entrance, its door ajar and lights still flashing. With the binoculars he could make out three bullet holes in the windshield. He could also see a guard laying face down by the first guard shack. A smoking hole punctured the glass of the second guard shack. He tried not to think about the fate of the guard inside. A school bus blocked the driveway just beyond the second guard shack. He couldn't detect any motion, but that didn't mean there wasn't a sniper waiting inside the bus.

"What happened?" Pugliano asked.

"A unit was called to investigate a silent alarm at Nanovex. When he discovered that body, someone opened up on him."

"Did your officer get out?" he asked.

"Yeah, when he jammed up his car he bailed and crawled away using the curb as cover. Paramedics said his wounds didn't look life-threatening. His vest took the worst of it."

"So the bad guys have killed two guards for sure, and tried to whack a policeman," Pugliano thought out loud. "What else do we know?"

"The chopper saw a big hole in the lobby. They may have used the bus as a battering ram before they used it to block the gate. Thermal scans are inconclusive. The chopper detected multiple hot spots in the lobby, but they think some of those may be dead bodies. We have no idea how many people we're facing in there."

"Conrad's people are smart enough to stay away from the windows. And to answer your question, she'll have as many people as she needs to make god-damned sure she took the building with minimal casualties."

Hargrove's eyes bulged. "So we could be facing a whole rifle squad in there?"

"They *did* bring a bus, didn't they?"

"Jesus."

"Where's your SWAT team?"

"They were suiting up when I left the station. Should be here shortly."

As if in reply, Pugliano heard a diesel engine and the hiss of air brakes behind him. He turned to see the bulk of the SWAT team's armored transport pull in behind the cluster of squad cars. Heavily armed troopers dismounted from the back of the vehicle. "Chief, we should be back there with them," he suggested. "This position's a bit exposed anyway."

Hargrove agreed to the retreat, waving the SWAT team leader over to his command vehicle. The Chief's driver had already opened up the back of the SUV, deploying the communication gear. A computerized display indicated the radio frequencies in use by the units under Hargrove's command, allowing him to reach any of them with the touch of a button. A large military-grade laptop displayed a map of the Nanovex property. The sergeant used a nearby touchpad to input the current location of each vehicle at the scene, which appeared as symbols on the laptop.

"How's the perimeter shaping up?" The SWAT team commander asked.

Hargrove motioned at the screen. "I have a dozen squad cars on station right now. I'm moving them around to cover all four sides, but there's only one way in or out—that front gate. I'll need you to have snipers in position to pick them off when they make their run for the bus."

Pugliano shook his head. "They're not going back to the bus."

"Then how the hell are they planning on getting out of there?"

His eyes followed the police helicopter circling overhead. "I don't know. Yet."

* * *

Conrad keyed her radio. "Package in hand. Prep for exit."

"Your path is clear all the way to the roof," Gallagher replied immediately. "But there's a chopper circling up top. We'll be fish in a barrel the second we step outside."

"Shiva," she transmitted, "I've got a helicopter in my hair, can you help me out?"

"Certainly. One moment please," came the cheerful reply.

Conrad raised her weapon and took point. "Okay, everybody grab a box. We're moving out."

* * *

"Sir," Hargrove's sergeant reported, "the north checkpoint says a civilian wants through. His name is Douglas Lyman."

"He's the Nanovex CEO," Pugliano said. "He might come in handy. I'll make sure he doesn't get in your hair."

Hargrove looked relieved not to be responsible for a civilian in the middle of an armed stand-off. "Okay, let him pass."

The roar of another diesel engine turned heads a few seconds later. It was Pugliano's Marines and their truckload of weapons.

"What the hell are they doing here?" Hargrove asked. "They're for the operation tomorrow."

"I asked for them," Pugliano said. "Knowing what you're facing, I figured you wouldn't mind having a couple of heavy machine guns backing you up."

Hargrove's eyebrows rose. "Hell no," he agreed. "Just make sure you coordinate their fire arcs with my SWAT commander. Sergeant, get them some radios."

* * *

Conrad emerged cautiously from the basement stairwell to find Cosgrove on the landing, watching the hallway to the lobby. He appeared to be alone. She doused her flashlight and switched back to night vision goggles.

"Where is everybody?" she demanded.

"Watching the upper floors," he said without raising his eyes from the sight of his gun.

"What did you do with Ghost and Shogun's bodies?"

Cosgrove indicated a blood-slicked stain on his flak vest. "Javelin and I humped them up to the top floor for evac."

She patted his unbloodied shoulder. "Good man. I hope recovering the bodies will make the Japanese principals a little less pissed at us."

He chuckled. "And *I'm* hoping that you gotta good story for that chin shot Ghost took."

She let out an annoyed grunt. "Working on it. Watch our backs."

"Right behind you."

* * *

"So Conrad finally made her move," Lyman said upon reaching the command post.

"Appears so," Pugliano agreed. "How many men did you have inside?" Too late, he caught himself already referring to Lyman's men in past tense.

"Normal night shift is six men. I had Miller double that. Counting him, that would make thirteen. Any contact from inside?"

Hargrove glanced at his sergeant, who shook his head. "We've tried every landline registered to Nanovex," the sergeant reported, "and all the commercial radio frequencies the guards might be using. Nada. We even tried faxing them. No response."

Lyman's shoulders fell. "That's not good."

Hargrove scanned the anti-vehicle embankment surrounding the Nanovex complex. SWAT troopers and police officers with assault rifles waited just behind the rise, their weapons at the ready. He checked the status screen. He had snipers in position on three sides, and one of Pugliano's machine gunners covering the fourth. The other machine gun covered the entrance. He shook his head. "Well, whatever she's up to, unless she's got a magic carpet up her sleeve, she's not going anywhere."

MAGIC CARPET

SAN JOSE, CALIFORNIA

The Huey banked hard again. Manning watched Vasily open another green box and extract what looked like a bazooka. It had a flat rim on one end and a flared end on the other. He opened both the left and right cabin doors and motioned for Manning to lay flat on the floor. He did so without question, not wanting to get in the way of whatever Vasily was planning. Vasily sat splay-legged on the floor facing the right side, holding the bazooka on his shoulder with one hand and gripping the bench seat to steady himself against the Huey's maneuvering with the other.

The helicopter leveled out and slowed. Manning saw all three of Conrad's operatives fix their attention behind and below the Huey. Suddenly the Huey dropped hard and banked slightly right. He recoiled in terror when another helicopter filled the whole right side door. He could clearly read the POLICE markings and see the two helmeted pilots in front, silhouetted by the city lights. The tips of the police helicopter's blades glinted in the moonlight just feet from the open door. He saw one of the pilot's heads turn in their direction.

* * *

Pugliano led Lyman away from the command vehicle to the Marine Corps weapons truck. The gunnery sergeant and another Marine stood guard over it.

"Got all your men in place, Gunny?" Pugliano asked.

"Two men each on the machine guns. I didn't know if you wanted to break out the Stinger missiles or not."

He surveyed the firepower arrayed around them. As a soldier, he could smell the tension in the air, like troops waiting to be attacked. "Nah, let's not scare the locals any more than necessary. Stay close to the truck, though."

The Marine made a face. "Yeah, Pugs. Like I'm going to leave four Stinger missiles unguarded?"

Before he could load a retort, the San Jose Police helicopter passed overhead. The chopper had been orbiting since he arrived, but something about this circuit caught his attention. A glance at the Marine confirmed that he had sensed it too.

“Are there *two* helis up there?” he wondered aloud.

“Sounds like a Huey coming in,” the Marine observed.

* * *

A blinding flash filled the cabin of the Huey and what looked like a red-hot poker lanced out of Vasily’s bazooka, striking the rotor hub of the police helicopter. Sparks and metal flew as the police helicopter’s rotors disintegrated. The Huey jerked upward to avoid the flying debris and the police helicopter plummeted toward the ground. Although it was probably his imagination filling in the blanks, Manning thought he could see the look of terror on the doomed pilots’ faces before they disappeared below him.

* * *

Craning his neck, Pugliano followed the SJP chopper around its circuit. Suddenly another helicopter running without lights swooped in, darker than the night sky behind it. An abrupt flash illuminated the newcomer, confirming that it was indeed an old Huey, painted Army green. A rocket streaked into the police helicopter, striking its rotor mast, which came apart like a toy. The rotors separated and flew off, launched from the chopper as enormous throwing knives. One blade tumbled end over end toward them, slicing the air with a menacing hiss before burying itself in a nearby squad car. Pugliano, Lyman and the Marines dove for cover.

The police helicopter dropped from the air like a shot pheasant—alive, struggling, but utterly doomed. The pilot fed full throttle to the engines, trying to spin up the detached rotor blades. But the tail rotor still functioned—the increased thrust spun the fuselage around faster and faster as the helicopter plummeted. Engines screaming, the chopper hit and tumbled in the parking lot. Fuel from the fractured engines caught fire immediately, but there was no explosion.

Pugliano saw one of the SWAT officers stand and charge over the berm toward the helicopter, signaling for his nearby comrades to cover him. He hoped the man’s bravery didn’t get him shot; those pilots were clearly dead.

The Huey executed an aggressive descending turn, pulling out just before striking the roof. It landed, mostly disappearing from view on top of the four-story building. He could see the tip of the rotor mast turning, but nothing else.

* * *

Manning felt the Huey bank hard right and drop again. Across the tilted floor he could see the Nanovex building coming up at them, fast. The blades over their heads made a chuffing noise, like they had lost all lift and flapped free in the wind. They were going to crash. He closed his eyes and braced for impact.

At the last second the blade sound changed again. He was pressed into the floor as the Huey decelerated, the skids biting into the steel roof platform and sliding to a stop. When he opened his eyes again, Vasily grabbed him from the floor and thrust him back into his seat. He saw soldiers in black rushing the helicopter. He had another moment of terror before realizing they were Conrad's operatives.

The commandos surged into the Huey, depositing two heavy loads on the floor. The Chinese agent with whom Manning had shared his last supper dropped into the next seat, thudding into him and wincing in pain. Looking over, Manning saw the man had a bloody shoulder wound, which left an equally bloody stain on Manning's suit. He realized with a start that the two heavy packages the soldiers had dumped were bodies. The head of one lolled Manning's direction, staring up, mouth agape. He wondered how many bodies would have to be paraded in front of him before they no longer made him queasy.

The last three operatives boarded the chopper, each carrying a case, which they carefully set on the floor on top of the two bodies. The last person to board was Conrad, motioning furiously to Shiva her desire to lift off.

* * *

"Oh hell, that's Conrad!" Pugliano realized belatedly. "Gunny! Gimme your radio! And get those Stingers out!" The Marine complied, tossing him the radio before jumping into the bed of the truck.

"Chief Hargrove!" Pugliano shouted into the radio. "If you don't want them getting away you better order your men to open fire the second they lift off!"

"All units!" Hargrove responded. "You are weapons free on the helicopter that just landed. I repeat, weapons free!"

Pugliano knew that order took guts. Most of the rounds would miss, and some would inevitably strike and damage something when they came back down, or worse, *someone*. But he was sure seeing one of his choppers shot down in a ball of flames helped Hargrove get over his liability issues.

The Huey still hadn't taken off, so he ran to the back of the truck. He helped the Marines lower the eighty-pound shipping case to the ground, then frantically flipped the latches. He and the younger Marine got the lid open just as the gunnery sergeant jumped down from the truck's bed.

"Move! I got it!" the sergeant yelled. Pugliano retreated, grabbing Lyman and pulling him to the far side of the truck. Bullets would be flying in both directions in just a second. This was no time for sightseeing, especially by civilians. Or an FBI agent armed only with a pistol.

* * *

Manning instinctively reached under him to grip the seat as the Huey tilted forward and thundered airborne. He looked to his left and saw a score of police and other emergency vehicles clustered around the Nanovex entrance. Rising higher, he saw the twisted, burning wreck of the police helicopter on the parking lot in front of the building. His heart sank, knowing he was an unwilling accessory to the murder of those two pilots, not to mention whoever had died in the building at Conrad's hands. He imagined the dozens of gunsights fixed on the Huey and held his breath, waiting for them to open fire.

* * *

The Huey's engines spooled up for several seconds, then the chopper leapt from the roof, pitching forward to accelerate. The policemen on the ground opened up. Sparks flew off the bottom of the Huey. Shooting upward, their rounds fell low.

Before they could adjust their aim, the Huey tilted even farther forward and dropped like a stone, putting the building between itself and most of the shooters. Then Conrad's mercenaries returned fire from the helicopter on the police officers who still had a shot. More sparks flew off the bottom of the Huey and one black-suited commando fell limply from the helicopter's door. Pugliano cheered silently at the kill, but the volume of fire wasn't sufficient and the Huey was getting away. Where the hell were the Marines' machine guns?

"Stinger up!" Gunny yelled. "Stand clear!"

Pugliano craned his neck from behind the truck to watch the launch. The sergeant had the Stinger on his shoulder and the sighting tube deployed. He tracked the Huey, waiting for the tone that signaled "lock-on" and readiness to launch.

"Come on, come on, come on!" Gunny urged the missile. Pugliano remembered from his own practice launches that lock-on seemed to take forever when you had a fleeting target in your sights.

"Target!" Gunny yelled when the Stinger finally "growled," giving out its strident lock-on tone. The launcher bucked, a gas charge throwing the missile clear before igniting the rocket motor. The Stinger lit off with rasping hiss, arcing brilliantly over the trees before leveling out in search of its rotary-wing prey.

Pugliano ran around the truck to keep the missile in sight. The missile's seeker caught sight of the Huey's tailpipe and swerved to home in, just as the helicopter ducked behind the office building next door. The Stinger held its course and hit the building's windows, lighting up the third floor with a quick red flash and a shower of glass. The Huey flew on unimpeded.

"Dammit!" Pugliano yelled.

Gunny threw the empty Stinger launcher to the ground in frustration. He grabbed his radio back from Pugliano. "Marines! Where the hell was my fire support?"

"Front gun was blocked by the trees! We had no shot!"

"Sir, rear gun was set up to cover an escape by ground! By the time we re-positioned they were gone!"

The grizzled marine veteran almost hurled the radio in his fury but thought better of it and vented his irritation on the discarded launch tube, kicking it against the truck.

The distinctive blade slap of the old Huey faded into the distance, announcing to all within earshot of Pugliano's failure once again to stop Angela Conrad. He gazed dumbfounded at the carnage and smashed equipment around him.

"Okay," Pugliano seethed. "Now I'm pissed."

CHAPTER 28

ENCODER

SAN JOSE, CALIFORNIA

Bullets smacked into the Huey, making Manning cringe. He didn't know whether to sit straight in his seat to make himself a smaller target, or stick his head between his legs and hope for the best. The commandos next to him flattened their backs against the bulkhead, so he imitated them. Those sitting nearest the doors immediately shot back, which seemed only to provoke more return fire from below. He could feel the bullets striking the underside of the helicopter. Thankfully none penetrated into the cabin, although he noticed the other agents placing their feet on the dead bodies in front of them, for what little protection their dead companions could afford. Manning joined suit.

The Huey seemed to drop out from under him as Shiva took evasive action. He was glad he was already holding tightly onto the seat. From the wide eyes in the cabin, he wasn't the only one thinking they were crashing again. But Shiva yanked back on the controls at the last second, pressing Manning back into his seat. He saw one of the darkened parking lot lights go past the open door like a reef breaking the waves, mere feet below the rotors.

Cosgrove yelled curses of anger and blood lust as he emptied his rifle into the policemen below. As he jammed in a fresh magazine, his head jerked with a puff of red and he tumbled from the open door. Gallagher screamed and jumped toward him. At first Manning thought she was going to follow her lover over the side, but instead she shouldered her weapon and fired wildly at the ground. Those closest to her grabbed her belt to steady her aim and handed over their guns when hers ran dry. She kept firing behind the helicopter long after they were out range, until she suddenly collapsed sobbing on the cabin floor. Vasily reached down and secured her weapon. She did not resist.

Conrad yanked off her ski mask and pulled her hair in frustration and bounced her elbows on her knees. Manning had never seen her display such emotion, and it was frightening to him for some reason.

* * *

Pugliano returned to the command vehicle to find a badly shaken Chief Hargrove. "How bad is it?" he asked.

"Two more officers were wounded when that chopper shot its way out of here, one of them seriously. We did get one of their guys. He took a bullet right in the ear."

"Yeah, I saw him fall. If you'll get a mug shot and email it to me, I'll help you ID the body. Have your SWAT teams cleared the building yet?"

"Eight bodies and no survivors yet, still looking. That Conrad bitch of yours is a real wrecking crew."

"If it's any consolation, my report will say you and your men did everything humanly possible to stop her team. I'm very sorry for your losses."

He nodded sadly. "Thanks. Sorry we couldn't bag her for you."

"The night's not done yet. Can one of your men give me a ride to my chopper?"

* * *

As his helicopter lifted off, Pugliano struggled with his next course of action. He decided that since the theft of WICKER BASKET *had* to be reported up the chain ASAP, it would only be prudent to nail down Conrad's current location. Especially when that would be the first question Director Fitzmaurice would ask when he was awakened at—Pugliano checked his watch—just after one a.m., four o'clock in the morning Washington time. And if an Air National Guard F-16 from Fresno just *happened* to be orbiting nearby ready to receive a presidential order to blow Conrad to kingdom come, who was he to stand in the way? He made a call to the operations center at the federal building and waited for them to patch him through.

"Go ahead, Agent Pugliano," the voice in his headphones informed him. "You're on with air traffic control."

"This is Special-Agent-in-Charge Perry Pugliano of the FBI. To whom am I speaking?"

"This is San Francisco Center supervisor Dave Heck. What can I do for you?"

"Mr. Heck, we've had an incident in San Jose involving a helicopter, during which two police officers and several civilians were killed. The helicopter departed northwest at low altitude ten minutes ago. Can you help me find them?"

"A helicopter at low altitude could get lost in the ground clutter. I think we better scramble a pair of F-16s. Their radar can pick a needle like this out of the haystack."

I like the way this man thinks. "The bad guys were in an old UH-1 Huey, if that makes any difference. They have missiles and have already shot down one police helicopter. I'll be landing at my operations center in a few minutes. I'll wake up the people who can give those F-16s permission to act when I get there. Until then, do your best to give me a hard location."

"Got it. I'll nail 'em down."

* * *

Heck pressed the intercom. "Attention all sectors. We've got an alert for a UH-1 helicopter northbound, possibly hugging the east bay shoreline. Put a 'be on the look out' to all the airports in the area, especially Oakland and Hayward."

"There's already a BOLO for a Huey stolen in LA yesterday," one of his controllers replied immediately.

"That's probably our bird. Pull everything you can get on it and bring it over to my terminal. Everybody else get on the phones and find out what local field they used tonight. They might be stupid enough to go back." He switched his screen to the Hayward sector just north of San Jose and put the radar in skin paint mode, looking for a slow-moving target traveling without a transponder.

* * *

Once the decision was made at the CIA to actively traffic in illegal drugs, it became necessary to devise a method of circumventing other government agencies legitimately engaged in preventing such activities. The optimum solution was to bring the drugs across the US border in private aircraft in relatively small shipments, where they could be received at uncontrolled airfields and the cargo handled exclusively by CIA personnel. For this to work, a method of entirely circumventing the US air traffic control and border enforcement system would have to be devised.

Working with specialists at the NSA, the CIA studied the radar systems of US manufacturers, requesting that "back doors" be built in to bypass the system under "extreme national security situations." The manufacturers who agreed were awarded lucrative air traffic control system contracts, and their bids for international business were secretly subsidized by the CIA to guarantee compromised US-manufactured radars became the norm in all but the most hardcore communist countries.

With this radar network in place, it became a simple matter to issue modified transponders to CIA smuggling aircraft that received the air traffic control radar "pings." But instead of a response providing the aircraft's altitude and air traffic control number, it replied with the "back door" code, instructing the radar's processor to delete the aircraft's return from any controller's screen. Using this approach, the CIA was able to fly aircraft across almost any border in the western hemisphere except Cuba with complete invisibility. This device became known in CIA parlance as the encoder. [1]

* * *

"San Francisco Center," Heck heard in his headphones, "Daggers One and Two with you now."

He switched back to the San Jose sector to pick up the F-16s. "Roger, Dagger Flight, radar contact, proceed north. Target is a UH-1 Huey, low altitude, location and heading unknown. Target is missile-armed and confirmed hostile, exercise extreme caution."

He could tell the F-16 pilot had to work to keep from laughing at the suggestion that a lowly helicopter—armed or otherwise—would pose a threat to his fighter. "Yeah, Center, we'll be extra careful. Beginning our sweep now."

* * *

Conrad signaled for the Huey's side doors to be closed. She opened one of the three boxes on the floor and pulled out a binder, examining it carefully under a flashlight. Then she extracted what looked like a radio from the box and began tinkering with it, using the instructions in the binder as a guide. Manning wondered what the binder and radio had to do with WICKER BASKET.

He kept checking out the windows, fully expecting the strobes and searchlights of other police helicopters to converge on their position at any time. He was sure she had contingency plans for such an event, but Conrad seemed unconcerned. The radio manual seemed to absorb her full attention.

A thumping in his chest reminded him that his time was drawing near. Conrad obviously got what she came for. She didn't need him anymore, even for the most menial of tasks. He was dead weight. Why she hadn't tossed him out the minute they left Nanovex was unclear. Maybe she was just preoccupied.

Manning glanced at Vasily, who avoided eye contact with him. He tried to relax. Vasily gave him his word that his end would come without pain, and he was the one person in this gang whose word Manning believed. At least Amanda and the boys were safe, or soon would be. He tried to console himself with that thought.

* * *

Once the CIA dealt with air traffic control radars, the flow of drugs across some borders became so profuse that Central American governments brought in military aircraft to staunch the flow of the narcotraffickers. Not to be outmaneuvered, the CIA then co-opted American arms manufacturers, requiring that all radar systems pass certain "information security standards" before purchase by the government. These checks included the insertion of the encoder back door. Through foreign military sales, this back door was soon available to the CIA drug smugglers and special operations units worldwide, allowing them to bypass US-manufactured fighters and surveillance aircraft with impunity. [2]

* * *

The F-16 pilot sounded exasperated. "San Francisco Center, Dagger Flight. We've covered the search area twice. I think your target went to ground before we got here. Would you like us to refuel and continue the search?"

Heck knew the pilot was probably right. They would probably find the Huey in a vacant lot within five miles of San Jose, its crew long gone. He was also aware of the thousands of taxpayer dollars per flight hour the interceptors burned. "Negative, Dagger Flight, we'll commence a ground search. Return to base authorized, and thanks for your help."

REGAL SPIRE

MOUNT DIABLO, CALIFORNIA

Soon the city lights below grew sparse and the Huey climbed with the rising terrain. Then the helicopter banked between two mountain peaks and the lights disappeared altogether. The chopper decelerated and descended into what looked to Manning like utter blackness. He felt the helicopter settle lightly to earth.

The doors slid open immediately and the mercenaries fanned out, securing the landing zone. Their postures quickly relaxed. The area was apparently clear, wherever they were. Following a gesture from Vasily, Manning helped Gallagher to her feet. She accepted the assistance, but shrugged Vasily off when he tried to help her down from the helicopter.

"I'm fine," she said with a sniff. "But thank ya, lads." She walked away in a daze.

Manning looked around, trying to get his bearings in the darkness. They were back at the timber mill near Mount Diablo.

"Vasily!" Conrad called. "Get him inside!"

Vasily herded Manning into a warehouse that smelled of sawdust. Men and equipment moved busily at Conrad's barked commands, moving a number of lumber racks to clear the floor. He finally asked Vasily what the hell was going on.

"We are getting ready for our bosses to arrive," he said quietly. "After that, they will bid on the goods Conrad stole from Nanovex."

Manning squirmed. "Well, if you're not going to shoot me in the next five minutes, would it be okay if I took a piss?" Nerves had prodded his bladder to the bursting point.

Vasily chuckled. "Good idea. I will join you."

* * *

Pugliano's first call once he had reached the federal emergency operations center was to the controller, Dave Heck. "So even the F-16s couldn't pin her down?" he asked. "Yeah, you're probably right. I'll get a ground search started for the helicopter. No need to apologize. Like you said, she probably dumped the helicopter five minutes after she took off. You can't track an aircraft that's not flying. Right, thanks. And call me at this number if anything pops up."

He hung up the phone and made himself a cup of coffee, willing his brain to devise a new course of action. He checked his watch again. He still had about an hour before the chain of command would start waking up to receive news of the Nanovex debacle if he didn't wake them up first. If he couldn't greet them with better news than he had at the moment, he could kiss his career good-bye. This would be the second bloody fiasco on his watch involving the same still-at-large fugitive. Every pooch screw of this magnitude required a scapegoat, and with Hendrix gone, all fingers would be pointed his direction unless he could nail Conrad's hide to the wall, and damn fast.

A young man entered the command center, his tie askew and his suit jacket over his shoulder, obviously rousted out of bed by the crisis. Maybe it was just Pugliano's age showing, but to him the kid looked like he just got out of high school. He intercepted the youngster at the CIA desk. "You Hendrix's replacement?" he asked.

"Loren Strahm," he replied, suppressing a yawn. "FBI, right?"

He extended his hand. "Perry Pugliano. You guys still have trackers on all the foreign diplomatic vehicles, right?"

Strahm startled as if Pugliano had poured ice water down his pants. "Of course not, Agent Pugliano," he said, a little louder than necessary. "That would be a *gross* breach of diplomatic protocol!"

Pugliano rolled his eyes. "Let me give you a little lesson on how things work, kid," he said in a low growl. "I'm in a jam. I think you have a tool that could help get me out of that jam. If it works, you will have just planted a major obligation on the local Special-Agent-in-Charge that you can cash in the next time you or one of your spook buddies steps on his winkie. Or you can leave me hanging and I'll make damned sure whoever takes my job returns that favor as well, at some point down the road."

The young spy was completely awake now. "Let's continue this conversation in the SCIF," he suggested.

* * *

When Manning and Vasily returned to the warehouse, the lumber racks had been cleared away. Dieter parked a forklift and hopped down, slinging his weapon over his shoulder. Conrad tossed him a can of yellow spray paint. He walked to the center of the warehouse and drew a circle about twenty feet in diameter on the floor.

"What's that for?" Manning whispered.

Vasily's discomfort was obvious in his tone. "I have no idea."

* * *

Even once Strahm closed the door behind them to the SCIF, or Sensitive Compartmented Information Facility, he was reluctant to speak. "I don't know what you've heard, Agent Pugliano, but the project you've mentioned was *very* sensitive and *very* limited in scope."

"Listen," Pugliano said reasonably, "I know you routinely track the vehicles of certain members of the foreign diplomatic corps who are suspected of espionage. I know you do it without the FBI's cooperation because it violates diplomatic rules. I also know I don't give a rat's ass at the moment. So who can you track, *right now*?"

The young man went pale. "If Langley finds out I gave up this program to the FBI—"

They were alone in the cramped inner sanctum of the operations center. Pugliano stepped closer to the youthful CIA bureaucrat. "Who can you *track*?" he snapped.

Strahm swallowed. "Just the Russian military attaché and the Chinese trade minister."

He leaned forward. "Who else?"

"And the French cultural affairs minister," he admitted. "That's all I'm cleared for, I swear."

He swept his hand toward the terminals. "Can you pull it up from here?"

The cowed young man trudged to the nearest computer and logged on. With a final hesitant glance at Pugliano, he entered the necessary keywords and a map of the Bay area appeared on his screen, with the glaring header REGAL SPIRE. A single icon blinked on State Road 24 heading east out of town, approaching the Caldecott Tunnel.

"That's the Russian military attaché, Oleg Sabakov," Strahm said.

"Huh," he grunted. "Bit late for a scenic drive, don't ya think?"

"Yeah, kinda." Strahm typed in another command and a second icon appeared, this one heading east out of the city on the 580 through Castro Valley. "That's the Chinese trade minister, Hu Zhao."

"Are these guys even *allowed* to be this far away from their embassies without giving us notice?"

"Thirty miles, that's the leash. Let's see if the French are in bed."

"There's a loaded question."

"Okay, I've got Monsieur Renée LaCroix northbound on the 680 at San Ramon."

"Also well east of town," Pugliano noted.

"By about twenty-five miles."

"Getting awfully close to the end of his leash."

"Which makes me think he's probably close to his destination."

"Any ideas what that would be?"

Strahm squinted at the screen. "Other than Mount Diablo State Park, there's not much in that area."

"Maybe that's the point."

"I guess a coincidence is out of the question."

Pugliano snorted. "All three of them taking different routes to converge on a point east of town just inside their legal limit? Not damned likely. You keep an eye on them and let me know where they end up, and I'll make sure there's a gorilla-sized SWAT team heading that way too."

"No, wait!" Strahm cried in alarm. "If the CIA finds out I gave up REGAL SPIRE, that'll be the end of my career! And unlike you, I'm a little young for early retirement!"

Pugliano glared at him.

"No offense," Strahm hastily added.

"None taken," he said icily. "Listen, you don't even need to mention me. Just tell your boss you came in for the Conrad crisis and pulled up REGAL SPIRE on a hunch. Tell him what you're seeing, and ask if you can share. He'll come up with a cover story to protect your program if he wants to play ball."

"And if he doesn't? Want to play ball, I mean?"

Pugliano gave him a sad smile as he reached for the door. "Like you said, kid, I get to try out early retirement."

FAVORS

MOUNT DIABLO, CALIFORNIA

Conrad called her team together, or what was left of it. She had factored two casualties into her plan; fifteen percent losses—standard military redundancy for high-risk operations like airborne assaults. She had taken more than twice that number of casualties, four dead and one wounded. She would still have enough manpower to cover the auction—as long as none of the parties tried anything. If they did, she no longer had enough operatives to assure success, especially if she was crossed by the French or the Russians, who still had both of their agents in play and inside her operation.

All she could do now was deploy her remaining assets in a way to minimize her risks, knowing whose loyalty was most likely to waver. She would make sure those she trusted would be kept close to the meet, and those she trusted less would be kept farther away. She would also team the suspect agents with an operative of another nationality, who would be quietly tipped off as to Conrad's doubts by the only people she still *really* trusted, Dieter and Meghan.

"Okay, listen up!" she said, kneeling to spread a large aerial photograph of the sawmill and the surrounding property on the floor. "The objective of this last stage is to provide security for your principals so we can conduct the auction and allow everyone to leave safely at its conclusion, no matter who wins. Since you will be depending on your principals for transport at the conclusion of the auction, it's in your own self-interest for this to go smoothly."

She pointed at the single road leading up the valley to the sawmill, ending at the front gate. "Nikolai and Javelin, you'll receive our guests here. They'll be limited to one sedan with no more than four occupants each. If there are any surprises, I suggest one of you station yourself far enough away from the gate to mount resistance and raise the alarm." *There, the two parties most likely to stab the rest of us in the back each have a representative at the entrance. Let's see how they get along.*

Nikolai and Javelin both nodded, stony-faced.

She pointed at the front of the warehouse. "Dragon, Bastille, you will direct our guests' parking so their vehicles and security teams don't rub on each other. Once they're parked, one of you will escort their negotiating team inside the warehouse and position them as I direct you. They'll be arriving five minutes apart, so you'll have plenty of time to get them situated before the next group arrives. Dragon, I know you took a round in the shoulder, but I need everybody to pull *more* than their weight tonight. Are you up to it?"

Dragon looked stoically insulted. "Of course."

"Very good, then. You four take your positions."

Nikolai looked confused. "But where will the rest of the team be positioned?"

"You don't need to know that," she countered. "Just watch the front gate and let me worry about the rest."

He wasn't happy with that answer, but left without further protest.

"Dieter and Tiger," she said once the first four were outside, "I want you two up on the ridges." She pointed to the valley walls that rose steeply on both sides of the sawmill. "You'll be the best defense we have against a double-cross. Meghan will set you up with sniper rifles." While Dieter was a crack shot, she knew Tiger was a demolitions specialist, not a sniper. But she also judged the Chinese group to be most likely to win the auction, therefore the least likely to pull something, which made Tiger a reliable asset.

After Gallagher pulled the pair away to procure new weapons for them, Shiva was the lone operative left with Conrad and Hendrix. She motioned him close.

"Shiva," she whispered, "You've been an incredibly useful asset, so I'd like to make you an offer. When this operation is concluded, we're going to need a ride out of here. We have ground transport, but a helicopter that's invisible to radar would also be handy."

"Of course."

"If you're willing to abandon your current principal and pilot me and my team to Mexico, we'll give you the share Ian had coming to him."

"Which was what?"

"One-tenth of tonight's proceeds. It might not be enough for someone your age to retire on, but it would certainly set you up handsomely as an independent operator. Interested?"

He laughed softly. "I'm already in. What do you want me to do?"

"Move the Huey offsite. A mile should do it in this terrain, just get it out of sight, but close enough to come a'runnin' if the shit hits the fan." She held up the map and pointed. "If that happens, I want you *here*."

He tilted his head, obviously not seeing what she did. "What's there?"

"My way out," she said proudly. She gestured to the warehouse walls. "I never walk into a box like this without an escape route."

"Understood. And thank you."

"Don't thank me yet. You still have to survive tonight."

* * *

Pugliano went straight from the SCIF to the command post's communications station. "Activate communications plan INFERNO," he told the technician. "I want every tactically trained agent we've got here and suited up within the hour."

"Got it," the young woman said, entering the appropriate command into her computer. All over the city, phones buzzed and flashed text message instructions to the agents who met Pugliano's criteria.

"And I want every helicopter you can get at the emergency staging area as fast as you can get them in the air. I don't care who you have to beg or borrow them from; the locals, Customs, Army, Navy, I don't care. But I need as much air transport as you can rustle up, and I need it *now*."

"I'll make it happen, sir," she replied.

He called the agent in San Jose in charge of wrangling the vehicles for the Nanovex operation that had been scheduled to take place later today. "Chad, I know the SJP vehicles are still tied up at Nanovex, but I want you to load up the FBI part of the convoy and get them moving northbound, ASAP. The destination is still fluid, but it's somewhere near Mount Diablo State Park. Get 'em started in that direction."

"You got it, sir."

"And hey, send a chopper to pick up Lyman and deliver him to my staging area downtown. He may not want to leave Nanovex right now, but lean on him as hard as you have to—just get him up here. If we recover that nanoagent from Conrad, he's probably the only person left who understands what we're really dealing with."

And once he had issued those instructions, there was very little else Pugliano could do. It was chilling to think that his career was in the hands of a twenty-something CIA paper-pusher behind the SCIF door. He had been mentally reviewing the shortcomings of his 401k for about five minutes when the desk phone rang.

"Pugliano!"

"Oh good, Agent Pugliano, glad I caught you. This is J. Laird Underwood III. I'm director of the CIA's West Coast field ops. I understand you need a lead on Angela Conrad."

"That would be an understatement."

"Well, I have good news! It appears she has some kind of meet in progress. We're lucky enough to have an agent inside one of her contacts' organizations. They're taking him right to her as we speak. Agent Strahm will give you the location and try to get you some imagery over the target."

He smiled at the cover story for Strahm's undiplomatic intelligence project. What the CIA sometimes lacked in competence, they always made up for with happy horseshit. "That *is* good news! I appreciate the information!"

He knocked on the SCIF door and waited for admittance. Strahm looked a lot more comfortable now that his backside was covered. He motioned Pugliano to an empty chair beside his terminal. The moving map with the REGAL SPIRE header had been replaced with the satellite photo of an isolated factory building.

"Looks like this is their destination," Strahm explained. "The first vehicle just pulled up. The others appear to be converging on the same location."

He squinted at the image. "That looks like a daylight photo."

"It is. We won't have a bird overhead for another four hours. That's the most recent archived photo from—" he checked the timestamp "—a day and a half ago." He handed over a folder labeled SECRET—merely SECRET, a huge step down from the above TOP SECRET classification of REGAL SPIRE. "I printed out a lower-resolution copy and a topographic map of the surrounding square mile you can use for your tactical planning."

Pugliano slapped him on the shoulder with the folder. "Nice work, Agent Strahm. Thanks a lot." He rose to leave.

"Don't forget about that favor you owe me," Strahm called to his back.

He looked over his shoulder. "I won't. Trust me."

THE AUCTION

MOUNT DIABLO, CALIFORNIA

Vasily and Manning sat on a crate in a darkened corner of the warehouse. Vasily had a pistol pointed at him, mostly for Conrad's benefit. Manning was long past any thoughts of resistance, or even escape. The survival of his family trumped all personal concerns.

Conrad and Hendrix stood nearby, waiting. She checked her watch frequently. Overhead Gallagher had surrounded the ladder leading to the roof with camouflage netting. Near the darkened ceiling, it was impossible to tell whether she was outside covering the approaches to the building, or inside covering the occupants.

"Not to look a gift horse in the mouth," he whispered to Vasily, "but do you have any idea why I'm not dead yet?"

The Russian looked concerned. "Frankly, no."

"And that bothers you?"

"Uncertainty always bothers me," he murmured, not wanting Conrad to overhear.

Conrad's radio squawked. "Headlights." It was Javelin.

"Acknowledged. That should be LaCroix," she replied.

She took a deep breath. "Here we go."

* * *

Pugliano reported to the armory and suited up, choosing a light flak vest over a black Nomex jumpsuit and an M4 carbine. And a .45-caliber pistol. That weapon was as much a part of his everyday wardrobe as underwear.

Agents rushed half-awake into the locker room, startled to see their agent-in-charge already dressed and ready for action. “What’s the word, sir?” one of them asked.

“The word is Angela Conrad, dead or alive. Dead would be more satisfying.”

A hulking agent nearby tugged on his heavy tactical vest, making his barrel chest even more imposing. “Hooah. Don’t have to tell *me* twice.”

Pugliano stepped out of the locker room when his cell phone buzzed. It was Director Fitzmaurice.

“Perry, are you *sure* Conrad is planning on selling that nanoagent to a foreign power?”

“Sir, we’ve got three known intelligence agents operating under diplomatic cover in the same place outside of town on the same night that Conrad stole the nanoagent. I don’t believe in coincidences like that.”

The guttural noise he heard in the phone told him his superior agreed, but didn’t like it. “Okay, you put your task force in the air, but *do not* move on Conrad without clearance from me, got it?”

“Received and understood, sir. I’ll be waiting for your call.”

A sigh. “Okay, I’ll wake the President.”

* * *

The Frenchman LaCroix stepped through the door into the warehouse, escorted by Dragon and two of his own bodyguards.

LaCroix beamed. “Ah, Angela! I was so pleased to receive your call! So your… *expedition* met with success?”

She motioned to two body bags nearby. “It was expensive, but yes, it was successful.”

His eyes widened. “No one *I* know, I hope.”

“You saw both of your men on the way in. They’re fine. I’m afraid I won’t have as good news for the Japanese. I also lost one of my own men and an Indian operative whose bodies we were not able to recover.”

“*Mon dieu,*” he breathed. “You have my sympathies.”

“No time to mourn, Renée. We have business to attend to. If you don’t mind, I have other guests to greet. Dragon will show you to your place.”

He nodded politely. “Of course.”

* * *

The communications technician in the emergency operations bunker had not disappointed Pugliano. The FBI's two Jet Ranger helicopters had been joined by two Army National Guard Black Hawks, each capable of carrying ten agents. He briefed the Guard pilots while waiting for his agents to suit up. All the pilots were former Air Assault drivers with the 101st Airborne and received his assignment with ill-concealed delight.

Lyman had arrived a few minutes ago. As Pugliano predicted, the Nanovex CEO was not happy to have been shanghaied as a bit player in the FBI operation. But in a way they were cleaning up *his* mess, so if he didn't like it that was his problem.

Pugliano checked his watch. Conrad's meeting was already underway and the flight to Mount Diablo would take fifteen minutes, even going balls out. He wasn't going to wait for all of his agents to arrive. As soon as he had eight agents for each Blackhawk, he was leaving. He met each agent as they arrived at the staging area, grouping them by specialty. Snipers, spotters, breachers, shooters. He made sure both Black Hawks had an even assortment of each, then called for their attention.

"All right, listen up!" he yelled. "We are not here to serve arrest warrants! We're about to engage a fleeting concentration of armed and extremely dangerous criminals! If they surrender, fine. But if they're holding a gun, shoot 'em! No warnings required."

He passed out aerial photographs. "This operation is about as shit simple as you can get. Here's the building we are about to assault, an abandoned lumber mill." He pointed at the photo. "We're going to put the helicopters down in the open spaces *here* and *here*. You will advance on the main building and eliminate all resistance. After that, secure the compound and hold it until relieved by the ground force, which is already on its way to your destination.

"One more thing," he held out his hand just below his nose. "If you see a slender woman about this tall with short blonde hair, don't take any chances. Just empty your magazine into her. She already has the scalps of a dozen federal agents under her belt, so don't hesitate. I won't. Any questions?"

There were no questions, just adrenaline-charged anticipation in the eyes of every agent. The helicopters' engines rose in pitch behind them.

"All right! *Load up!*"

1 "The shadow of official complicity and cover-up was unmistakable in Seal's [accused CIA drug smuggler Barry Seal] papers. In 1996, a former Seal associate would testify to congressional investigators how the operation had been provided CIA 'security' for flights in and out of the US, including a highly classified encoding device to evade air defense and surveillance measures." *Partners in Power* by Roger Morris, Henry Holt & Company, 1996

[2] In a previous chapter the CIA rendition aircraft N987SA and its crash on the Yucatan Peninsula with 3.2 tons of cocaine was mentioned. It is interesting to note that Mexican police now use infrared detection and tracking sensors for their aerial drug interdiction efforts as opposed to radar. Infrared sensors were used when N987SA was detected, chased, and forced down onto a jungle airstrip. Perhaps through experience the Mexicans have lost faith in American-made radar to detect "certain" aircraft invading their airspace.

CHAPTER 29

DEMONSTRATION

MOUNT DIABLO, CALIFORNIA

Hendrix ushered Manning and Vasily out of the warehouse when the bidders started to arrive. They watched Shiva load two boxes onto the Huey and lift off, disappearing over the ridge. The sound died off quickly, like he hadn't flown very far away.

In the silence that followed, they stood in the rural darkness and surveyed the cloudless night sky, emblazoned with more stars than the city-dwelling Manning remembered seeing before. "Kinda breathtaking, isn't it?" he offered.

"Indeed," the Russian agreed. "There are worse sights to contemplate before meeting one's maker. Are you at peace yet, my friend?"

No, actually I'm about to piss myself. "I just wish I could talk to my wife and kids one last time, to make sure they're okay."

"That is not likely. But she has given me her assurance that they will be fine," he lied.

Manning sighed. "Great. A promise from Angela Conrad. Not what I would have asked for as a last request."

They sat in silence as the vehicles of the bidders arrived and parked on the far side of the warehouse. Occasionally one of the security team members of the different countries would round the corner, give them a pointed stare, then walk away, convinced they posed no threat. A distant sound prodded Manning out of his anguished musings.

"Is Shiva coming back already?" he asked Vasily. "I hear a helicopter."

* * *

"Gentlemen! Shall we begin?" Conrad said, her commanding voice easily filling the empty warehouse.

"First of all, I present to you the weapon known as WICKER BASKET." She had Hendrix carry a vial of the nanoagent—carefully—around the warehouse to show each of the bidders that she had the goods. "WICKER BASKET is a radio-activated nanoagent, releasing its payload of VX nerve gas only when it receives a specific activation signal, and only over a tightly defined range, which can be specified by the user.

"Accompanying three vials of the nanoagent, the winning bidder tonight will also take delivery of the deployment and activation mechanism for WICKER BASKET, the complete technical records of the scientists who invented the system, and several pieces of equipment critical to fabrication of the nanoagent." That last part she had made up. She had no idea what had been in the second box they recovered at Nanovex, but if the trinkets had been important enough to evacuate along with the nanoagent and the technical data, she had no doubt they were worth selling.

"The merchandise is at a secure location and will be delivered to the winning bidder upon confirmation of funds transfer to my account."

She had arranged the five bidding parties strategically along the walls of the rectangular warehouse. She and Hendrix stood against one of the building's short sides, with the French directly across against the other. Out of easy pistol range, but an effortless shot for Gallagher in her sniper's nest over their heads. The Russians clockwise along the long wall, with the Chinese as a buffer between her and them. The Japanese and the Indians stood along the wall to her right.

She turned and bowed low to the Japanese delegate. "Out of respect for your courageous dead, Ozumi-*san*, I ask you to honor us with the opening bid."

The Japanese diplomat received the gesture well, bowing respectfully in return. He had indeed been livid over the deaths of his operatives, but her careful explanation of how Cosgrove had recovered their bodies only to fall himself and be left behind did much to dull the man's anger. The Japanese had an almost genetic preoccupation with honorable death in battle, which she had played to her advantage. "Japan bids two million dollars for the nanoagent," he said.

"Two and a half," India countered. She doubted they could raise even that amount and had thrown out the offer early only to be seen as a player before being safely outbid by other powers.

"Three million," the Chinese replied.

"Three and a half," bid Oleg Sabakov. She would be willing to bet that the Russians were in the same boat with the Indians and Sabakov couldn't have paid three and a half million to buy back his immortal soul.

"Four," LaCroix declared.

Silence.

"I hear four million," she announced. "Are there any other bids?"

"If we are to increase our bid beyond our initial offer," the Chinese delegate said. "We will require a *demonstration* that this nanoagent is everything you claim." He looked very proud of himself, as if he had already caught her in a lie.

"I second that motion," LaCroix chimed in.

She smiled back. "Very good, gentlemen, I'm actually glad you asked." She nodded to Hendrix, who exited by a side door.

* * *

On board the FBI Jet Ranger helicopter, Pugliano heard the communications technician's voice over his headphones. "Sir, I have Director Fitzmaurice for you."

"Ready. Put him on, please."

"Perry?" he heard through a scratchy connection. "This is Fitz, what's your status?"

Pugliano assumed the informality with which the Director addressed his subordinates was directly proportional to the distance their career stood from the crapper. So Fitzmaurice introducing himself with a nickname was a very good sign. "Sir, the strike team is assembled and enroute. Awaiting your authorization to engage."

"I just got off the phone with the President. He agrees that allowing Conrad to get away with the nanoagent is absolutely unacceptable. He has authorized you to use 'all necessary measures' to recover the nanoagent, or verify its destruction."

"None of these people are likely to surrender without a fight. How far can I take these 'necessary measures' before the President sees the body count and changes his mind after the fact?"

A growl. "Add the President's name to the long list of men who want to see Angela Conrad stone cold dead. I'd say short of using nuclear weapons, you're going to have a hard time exceeding your authority on this one."

He allowed himself a small smile. "Music to my ears, sir. Thank you very much."

* * *

The warehouse's side door opened and Hendrix joined Vasily and Manning in the darkness. "Manning, you're up," he said, motioning toward the open door.

For all the mental preparation he had made, now that the moment was here, he was frozen in place with terror, completely paralyzed.

Vasily took his arm. "Come, my friend. My promise remains true." He motioned to Hendrix for assistance. Together the two lifted him to his feet and steered him back toward the building. His legs were rubbery and his feet felt like they were on someone else's body.

"Courage, my friend," Vasily whispered in his ear, still walking him forward. "How we face death is at least as important as how we face life."

That pep talk worked for another ten steps, until it was time to cross the threshold into the building. His feet stopped cold again. Hendrix cursed and pushed him forward.

"Wait!" Vasily urged. "Michael," he said, using that name for the first time, "imagine your sons are watching you now. Wouldn't you want them to be proud of your composure at this moment?" He paused. "Wouldn't you?"

"Y-yes," he stammered.

"Then face this moment with courage," he said, squeezing Manning's arm, "And when your sons are old enough, I promise I will tell them of this day."

Hendrix yanked at his arm. "Enough of this bullshit! Move it!"

Manning willed his feet into motion, following Hendrix's lead.

DEATH CIRCLE

CHICAGO, ILLINOIS

Amanda Manning had watched their guard, Patchy Beard, all evening. Where there had been lust in his eyes before, now there was only death. But as the guard's night shift wore on, she also detected a slight flutter of sleepiness. Huddled under a blanket with her sons for warmth and emotional comfort, she nudged her eldest son Eric awake.

"Honey, it's time," she murmured in his ear. "As soon as I get up and go to the bathroom, wake up your brother and get ready to run. No matter what happens, run and don't look back."

"But Mom—"

"Do as I say!" she said in a harsh whisper, rising to her feet. She gave Eric a last stern look of motherly mind control before walking away—probably, she knew, for the last time.

* * *

MOUNT DIABLO, CALIFORNIA

They walked to join Conrad. She motioned toward the middle of the warehouse. "Vasily, put Manning in the center of the yellow circle and back away," she ordered.

Even Vasily looked worried at that command. His eyes met Manning's.

"Do it!" she shouted.

Vasily grasped Manning's right arm with both hands, urging him forward. "Whatever she has planned," he whispered, "my promise to you is unchanged. Have faith."

Manning swallowed hard and kept walking toward the yellow circle. He noticed a silver tube about a foot high sitting vertically in the center. He thought he recognized it from the chopper, one of the objects Conrad had stolen from Nanovex, but his mind was too panic-stricken to remember clearly.

He and Vasily entered the circle. The next sound he expected to hear was the Russian ordering him to his knees, but instead the silver tube beeped three times then hissed loudly like compressed air. Manning thought he saw a slight sparkle in the gas it shot forth, like infinitely fine glitter. Vasily immediately let him go and turned to flee.

"Right there, Vasily!" Conrad shouted, her gun leveled at his face.

"What is the meaning of this?" Vasily's superior Oleg Sabakov demanded.

"For this to be a proper demonstration," Conrad expounded, "there has to be an element of risk. Your man Vasily sat in the chopper while the rest of the operatives risked hostile fire and four of them died. Now it's his turn to take a risk. I have just released one gram of the nanoagent."

The delegates cried out in protest and fear. "What have you done? Are you mad?" they shouted.

Conrad raised her voice, holding up a binder. "According to the company's own data, the amount I released could only be harmful over a ten-foot radius, the circle I have marked on the floor. Only the two gentlemen before you have absorbed a potentially lethal dose. The rest of you can not possibly be harmed."

"Vasily!" she called. "Back slowly towards me and exit the circle, please."

The Russian exchanged a terrified look with Manning, but complied, retreating to a spot halfway between the death circle and Conrad.

"Stop there!" She held up the strange walkie-talkie Manning saw her handling on the helicopter. "Gentlemen, the genius behind the WICKER BASKET nanoagent is that it is completely harmless until triggered by a unique radio signal, such as from this device. But as an additional safety feature, only those within a specified range of the dispenser's transmitter will be harmed. In this case I have set the transmitter's range to ten feet. One subject remains inside the lethal circle, while Vasily is now safely out of range. I will now trigger the activation device, releasing a lethal flood of VX nerve agent into the expendable man standing in the circle, while Vasily will be left completely unharmed."

* * *

Javelin paced nervously at the front gate, while Nikolai crouched behind some barrels a short distance away. One man in the open to draw any hostile attention, the other hidden to return fire and sound the alarm.

"It goes well, don't you think?" Javelin asked when his patrol pattern took him close to Nikolai.

"It does," Nikolai responded, his voice seemingly disembodied in the darkness. "Very smoothly indeed."

"It will only be a few minutes now," Javelin said on his next pass. "What do you plan to do with your bonus when this is completed?"

Before Nikolai could respond, Javelin cocked his head. "Do you hear that helicopter? It doesn't sound like ours and it's rather close. Perhaps I should call it in."

"I wouldn't," Nikolai countered. "And to answer your previous question, I plan to spend some of it on flowers for your widow."

The flesh between Javelin's eyes bunched in confusion, only to be punctured by a bullet. The single silenced round lodged in his skull and he collapsed quietly to the ground.

Nikolai emerged from his hide, returning his pistol to its holster. With his night vision goggles he could see that one of the guards Conrad had placed in front of the building was looking steadfastly this way, but had not raised an alarm yet. He wrestled Javelin's assault rifle loose from its sling, dropped to the ground and pulled a radio from his vest.

"This is Nikolai!" he called to the inbound helicopter. "Snipers on both overlooking hilltops! Take them out first!" He leveled his gun on the other guards and flicked off the rifle's safety.

* * *

Over the sound of his own ragged breathing and his heart pounding in his ears, the helicopter Manning had heard earlier was now quite close, and it wasn't Shiva's Huey. Then he heard gunfire from behind Conrad, outside the building. One bullet punctured the thin corrugated metal wall and whizzed past his head. He flattened himself on the floor.

"We're taking fire from the main gate!" Bastille's voice crackled over Conrad's radio. Any more radio chatter was drowned out by the roar of the helicopter just outside the building and automatic weapons fire. Bullets tore through the wall to his left, cutting down two of the gangsters present for Conrad's auction. The bodyguards grabbed their principals and pulled them to the opposite side of the warehouse. Manning didn't know who they were, and didn't much care. He used the confusion to crawl out of the circle. He felt a hand grab the back of his shirt, lifting him to his feet.

"You must run!" Vasily urged. He pointed to a door on the far end of the building. "Go!"

* * *

Nikolai watched with satisfaction as the helicopter carrying his companions popped over the hilltop to his left, catching the Chinese operative Conrad had placed there by surprise. He was cut down instantly. The aircraft then yawed hard to his right, rocketing across the valley to rake the opposite hilltop with bullets where Conrad's German agent was hiding. No fire was returned.

Nikolai took this as his signal to shoot. He fired a three-round burst at both of Conrad's nearest guards, knocking one of them down. The other shot back, but he would be preoccupied shortly.

The helicopter circled down, three men with machine guns leaning out the doors on each side to blast the delegates' security teams. The men on the ground fought back skillfully, using their vehicles for cover. Nikolai saw one of the chopper's door gunners go limp, dropping his weapon and hanging from the open door by his safety harness. But the other five continued pouring a hail of fire from their superior position. The helicopter swooped and spun around the building, using speed as its primary protection. The door gunners had extensive training in high-speed engagements and cut down the exposed men on the ground until none remained, including Conrad's French and Chinese agents at the front door.

The helicopter plunged and tilted back, decelerating aggressively before settling onto its skids. The five remaining gunmen leapt to the ground and advanced in a wedge toward the building, pouring fire on the wounded to eliminate any possible threat.

"Visual contact with the team," Nikolai transmitted. "Advancing to join you." He slapped a fresh magazine into his rifle.

"Time to cut the head off the snake," he muttered to himself.

* * *

Manning staggered to his feet, running for the exit Vasily had indicated. He was not alone. One of the criminal gangs had the same idea and had already rushed through the door, disappearing into the darkness beyond. Vasily was close on their heels and also made it out. The gang led by the man with the French accent tried to follow them through, only to be cut down by gunfire. Bullets tore their bodies, jerking them like puppets before they fell.

Sparks danced off the concrete at the threshold. Manning skidded wildly in his dress shoes as he reversed course to run *away* from the door instead of toward it. He dove behind a post and the fire from outside died down. The gangs that had been neatly grouped about the warehouse were now scattered in ones and twos behind whatever cover they could find.

He was concerned for Vasily. Had he been cut down, his body just outside the door? *Probably*, he realized with a sinking sensation. He looked for Conrad. She was nowhere in sight.

* * *

Conrad dropped to the floor when the bullets started flying. She was startled, but had almost expected this double-cross and had confidence that her agents combined with the delegates' security operatives outside could respond to any threat. But she still didn't know who had stabbed her in the back. The Russians answered her question seconds later by dashing out the door and mowing down the French delegation when they tried to follow. Bastards.

Her confidence evaporated when she heard the helicopter swoop down outside, mowing down the exterior guards. She could hear Meghan firing from her rooftop perch, then watched two strings of bullets tear through the roof and converge on Gallagher's position. She heard a cry and watched Gallagher tumble like a load of laundry down the ladder and crumple on the concrete a dozen feet away.

"*NO!*" Conrad screamed. Meghan was one of the few friends she had admitted into her solitary world. Watching her die caused the nearest thing to grief her sociopath's heart could probably experience.

The return fire outside died off. She could hear the helicopter landing. In seconds a Russian commando team would storm the building and kill all inside. It was time to go.

* * *

"Two minutes to target," the pilot of the Jet Ranger informed Pugliano.

He sat in the left hand pilot's seat of the helicopter. A single sniper sat in the back with Lyman. They had removed the left side back door to provide the gunner with a clear field of fire. Pugliano's helicopter led the two Black Hawks around Mount Diablo to the target, using their night vision goggles to hug the terrain and mask the sound of their approach. It was unnerving to have the trees whiz by close enough to touch at a hundred miles an hour, but he had to trust the skills of his pilot.

"Done this before, I take it?" he asked hopefully.

He could hear the delight in the pilot's voice. "Oh yeah, just like old times!"

Pugliano felt his cheeks clench the seat cushion when the pilot pulled up at the very last instant to clear a ridge. Maybe he *was* getting too old for this. Lyman made no protests from the back. Pugliano assumed Lyman's recent experience in Afghanistan had hardened him to the joys of mountain flights in helicopters.

"Better issue last instructions, sir," the pilot warned a minute later. "The target is just over this next rise. You're patched in and transmitting…now."

"Attention all units, this is Pugliano. You are now weapons free. Assume everyone on the ground is hostile. Don't wait for them to shoot first. Good luck, and good hunting. Out."

They cleared the last hill with a drop that left his stomach somewhere above them. The familiar buildings from the satellite photo were now in view, along with several burning vehicles that were new additions. He thought he saw rotor blades turning as they screamed overhead, but the compound was now behind them.

"Was that a helicopter on the ground?" he asked the pilot. Before he could get a response, he heard the unmistakable sound of bullets hitting aluminum.

"We're taking fire!" Lyman called out.

The pilot was already evading. "Lumberjack flight!" he called. "Lumberjack One is taking ground fire, request suppression!" He pulled up into near-vertical climb that reminded Pugliano of the Batman roller coaster a mischievous nephew had once conned him into riding. He looked over his shoulder to see the Black Hawks pass over the landed helicopter. The National Guard door gunners blasted down on it with their six-barreled cannons, bracketing it from both sides with a continuous shelling resembling laser beams more than gunfire. The helicopter exploded like a movie prop, throwing rotor blades and burning chunks of metal over the landscape.

"Lumberjacks Two and Three, landing," he heard in his headphones.

UNDERGROUND RAILROAD

MOUNT DIABLO, CALIFORNIA

Manning cowered behind the support post, frozen in place. He was out of the death circle and Conrad was nowhere to be seen, but was he out of danger, or was danger just pausing to reload?

The answer came a few seconds later when two hand grenades came through the open door on the far end of the building. Screams of the wounded and dying followed the explosions. Bullets then blasted through the doorway, singing all around him. Two rounds smacked into the post directly opposite his head and chest.

Whoever was shooting must have made their entrance, because the Chinese agents a short distance away opened up, trapping him in a crossfire. He dropped to his belly and scuttled like a crab to the nearest wall. He chanced a glance behind him and saw four men with machine guns advancing from cover to cover toward him, cutting down anyone in their paths. Staying put wasn't an option. He kept crawling past the Chinese combatants, whose number had already shrunk to two. One of those had his shooting arm severed as if by an invisible chainsaw as Manning watched. The arm landed in his path, still clutching its gun. He pushed it aside and kept crawling, hugging the shadows.

He had almost reached the far end of the warehouse where Conrad had once stood when more helicopters passed overhead, followed by an enormous explosion. The world was coming apart around him. In the near darkness, his hand ran across the rough edge of a grate sticking slightly above the floor. He hadn't noticed this before. He stuck his fingers though and pulled. The cover came up easily, without noise, like it had already been worked loose.

Manning looked toward the nearest door, perforated with bullets from the initial volley. It didn't look like the way out to him. He lifted the grate carefully to the side, trying not to give away his position. He couldn't tell how deep the hole was, but it looked deep enough to conceal him. He slipped in feet first, disappointed to hit bottom almost immediately. The pit was barely three feet deep, but was much better than staying in the open. The last thing he saw above ground level was one of the death squad finishing off the final Chinese gunman with a burst to the head, barely twenty feet away. He lowered the grate carefully into place, flattened himself against the bottom of the dusty pit, and tried his best to be invisible.

* * *

After Pugliano's pilot determined the helicopter was still flyable, he resumed circling so the sniper in back could provide fire support for the troops on the ground. The sniper only fired twice, but both shots were followed with a satisfied call of, "Tango down!"

The National Guard helicopters touched down with the swiftness of hawks. Pugliano's agents surged toward the warehouse, but none found targets for their weapons. Bodies already littered the ground.

"I don't know who started the shooting," the team leader on the ground reported, "but these guys tore the shit out of each other before we even got here."

"Looks like we've got whoever's left bottled up inside," the sniper reported.

"Do we breach, sir?" the team leader below asked.

"Are you taking any fire?" Pugliano asked.

"Negative. There's an open door in the back my guys are staying well clear of, but it's all quiet for the moment."

"Then have your snipers cover the exits and give 'em the bullhorn. See if anybody inside wants to give up."

* * *

Early in the twentieth century when the Caldwell Brothers' sawmill had been in its prime, runoff from the mountain had been channeled down a sluice to power the debarking and planking saws. That same water carried away the waste to a holding pond, which was skimmed for any useful wood byproducts. The sluice fell into disuse in the fifties, when electricity became available even at remote rural locations like Mount Diablo, making water power obsolete. A smaller, more efficient electric sawmill was constructed, and the old sawmill building was converted into a warehouse. But the sluice remained, a forgotten concrete channel from the old building to the nearly dry holding pond.

Manning heard footsteps getting closer and men calling to each other in Russian. Did Vasily know his own side had been preparing an ambush? He didn't act like it. Maybe they had cut him out of the loop for security. Manning hoped so, or else Vasily would be just another back-stabbing criminal like Conrad.

He felt forward in the darkness, trying to find the far end of the pit to squeeze up against. To his surprise, there didn't seem to be any. The walls on either side were an easy reach, but ahead of him, nothing. He scooted forward carefully and felt again. Nothing. He crept forward a little more, the pit becoming a concrete tube. Had he found a storm drain? One big enough to crawl in?

At first he couldn't believe his good luck, but then realized this had been Conrad's escape route, her underground railroad if she needed to get the heck out of Dodge. Which meant if he kept crawling, he would eventually run into her. The Russian voices behind him got louder, seemingly right above him. Manning kept crawling.

ESCAPE

CHICAGO, ILLINOIS

Amanda signaled her captor, Patchy Beard. "I need to use the restroom."

He looked up from his cell phone game and waved her lazily toward the facilities.

Seating herself on the toilet, she left the door ajar, hoping he would move closer to spy on her again. She waited. An electronic noise outside indicated he had returned to his game. She let out a quivering sigh, as if she was pleasuring herself. Still no Patchy Beard, although she heard no more game noises either. She raised her sigh to a blissful groan, then repeated it, little louder.

She heard footsteps.

Patchy Beard leaned cautiously around the doorway with a concerned look. She moved her hand lower and rubbed, opening her mouth to pant softly as she raised her eyes to meet his. She gave him the slightest of smiles before closing her eyes and tilting back her head in faux ecstasy, her body rocking.

She fluttered her eyes at him. He had moved no closer, but a swelling in the front of his jeans telegraphed his excitement. Time to step it up. She reached under her sweater and unhooked her bra, pulling up her top. She bit her lip, gasping in delight, opening her eyes wide to make contact with his. He was breathing hard and fast.

She pulled the door fully open, then spread her legs. She opened her lips into a sensuous pout and held out a beckoning hand.

She watched his sexual instincts wrestle against his better judgment. His instincts won. He shuffled toward her as if being dragged against his will, his eyes burning with desire. She unbuckled his belt and pulled down his jeans. He didn't protest when she pulled them all the way around his ankles rather than just enough to reach his genitals.

Fighting her revulsion, she took him into her hands and stroked him to full rigidity. She looked up at him and smiled. He was panting like a dog now, exposing his crooked teeth and bathing her in his bad breath. She fought the urge to vomit.

She pointed to him, touched her mouth, then pointed to her crotch. She pulled him to his knees and scooted forward on the seat. He eagerly complied, lowering his head and sticking out his tongue in anticipation of tasting her tender flesh.

She smashed his eardrums with the bottom of her fists, then locked her thighs around his head, squeezing with all her might. He flailed with his arms trying to strike her, but was unable to reach higher than her chest. He grabbed at one of her breasts, scratching and twisting it. She responded by digging her thumbnails into his eye sockets. He screamed like an animal, pulling her off the toilet in his attempt to struggle free. She brought her weight down on him, wrapping her calf around his throat and tumbling in the confined space, trying to break his neck with a primal ferocity she had never experienced.

"*NOW,* ERIC!" she screamed. "*RUN!*"

* * *

MOUNT DIABLO, CALIFORNIA

"Nikolai, what have you *done*?" Vasily growled. They watched Colonel Sabakov examine the binder Conrad left behind, along with the dispersal tube recovered from the death circle.

"Me?" Nikolai snapped, careful to keep his voice low. "I followed orders, just like you."

"Did that include keeping me in the dark about *this*?" He surveyed the slaughter around them with disgust.

"As a matter of fact, *yes*," he hissed. "You kept Conrad occupied with her intricate planning so I could slip away and make contact. The fact that she kept me at her elbow during the raid and stuck you babysitting that fool Manning prevented me from warning you. My *apologies*," he said with pretended regret.

"Where is the transmitter Conrad showed us?" Sabakov demanded, his eyes frantic.

"She must have taken it with her," Vasily said.

Sabakov gestured frantically around them. "Taken it *where*? Was she not as trapped as we are now?"

"Attention occupants of the building," a bullhorn outside announced. "You are surrounded by FBI tactical units. If you do not surrender immediately, we will storm the building and kill everyone who resists." The demand was repeated in Spanish and French.

"So much for 'come out with your hands up,'" Nikolai snarled.

Sabakov clapped his hands. "*Pridúroki! Fools!* Focus! How do we get out of here?"

Vasily paced, scanning the walls with his flashlight, looking for the hidden portal Conrad must have used when he heard the sound of his footsteps change. He swiveled the flashlight downward until its beam illuminated the drainage grate he stood on.

"I think I found something," he called.

* * *

Conrad reached the end of the tunnel just in time to hear Shiva landing with the Huey. She and Hendrix cautiously emerged to find Dieter covering the landing zone. She charged through the blinding dust cloud as soon as she heard the skids scrape, finding the side door by feel and wrenching it open.

"Talk about timing!" she shouted. "Shiva, you are golden!" Hendrix and Dieter barreled in right behind her. She slammed the door shut. "Go, go, go!" she screamed.

The Huey lifted off and disappeared into the night.

* * *

Manning crawled for what seemed like an eternity. He paused frequently and listened for the sounds of anyone in the tunnel with him. It seemed like he was quite alone, and that suited him just fine. He realized this was the first time in days he hadn't had a gun pointed at him. He still dismissed the notion that his flight was doing anything but delaying his demise and buying a few more minutes of terrified existence, but the thought of permanent escape *did* cross his mind.

The tunnel turned and sloped perceptibly downward. The air in the tube slowly changed from dry and musty to moist and moldy. Somehow that seemed like a good thing and he found himself crawling faster.

* * *

Of the six gunmen who had helicoptered in, Sabakov was now down to three. He motioned one aside and gave final instructions to the other two.

"All you have to do is delay them long enough for us to escape. Offer no resistance. Call to them and make some kind of useless request like for a first aid kit. And speak only in Russian. Maybe they will waste time finding a translator. By then we will be gone. And I promise to look after your families *personally* until I can buy your freedom." He looked both of them in the eyes. "My word."

They nodded.

"Go then. Best of luck to us all. *Udachi.*"

Vasily led the way down the tunnel, followed by Nikolai and Sabakov. The last gunman brought up the rear and pulled the grate into place behind him. They could hear the decoys calling out to the FBI as they crawled away.

* * *

"They're doing *what*?" Pugliano demanded.

"It took a few minutes to find somebody who spoke Russian, but she believes the guy inside the building is asking for a first aid kit."

"Tell him he'll get the best medical care on the planet the minute he surrenders."

"She tried that. No dice. Do we play along?"

"Hell no! Conrad's probably trying to figure out how to deploy that nanoagent against us as we speak. You go in sixty seconds—shoot everything that moves. I don't give a shit about prisoners, I just want that nanoagent secured."

"You got it," the team leader assured him.

* * *

Manning thought the night outside had been dark, but that was before crawling hundreds of feet inside a concrete tube. To him, the moonless night at the end of the tunnel looked like Times Square on New Year's Eve. Despite his worries about Conrad, he felt drawn to the less-dark opening like a moth. Especially when he thought he heard voices behind him.

He stopped short of the tunnel mouth and listened carefully. He was *sure* he heard someone behind him now, but the outside was quiet except for the sound of a helicopter in the distance, and not Conrad's Huey.

Manning crept from the tunnel like a rat emerging from its burrow, ever vigilant for the snake lurking outside. The night air had never smelled as wonderful to him, even if it was mixed with the rot from a stagnant pond a short distance from the tunnel mouth. He cautiously poked his head above the culvert, seeing nothing but tall grass. A helicopter circled on the far side of a hill behind him.

He didn't think the helicopter could see him at this distance, but he waited until it flew to the far side of its orbit before dashing a short way and lying down in the tall grass. When it passed again he repeated the procedure. The grass started to thin out. He had reached the edge of a clearing. He heard voices speaking in Russian behind him. He lay very still.

* * *

"Ready to breach, sir," Pugliano heard in his headphones.

"Do it!" he ordered.

He watched the troopers storm every entrance to the building simultaneously. Flash-bang grenades flared through gaps in the building's roof. While waiting anxiously for the results, another voice intruded in his headphones.

"Lumberjack One, this is Hay Wagon. Are you still missing that Huey? We're five minutes out and one just overflew us."

"Position!" Pugliano demanded. He checked his watch. The convoy from San Jose was right on time, they just seemed early because he had lost track of time during the action.

"Three miles southeast."

He ordered the pilot to stop the turn and he focused in that direction, willing the night vision goggles to pierce the darkness far beyond their intended range. To his amazement, he saw the unmistakable profile of a UH-1 top above a ridge then disappear on the far side.

"Come thirty degrees right!" he almost shouted. "How fast can this thing go?"

"One-forty, flat-out," the pilot responded.

"Get me one-forty-five and I'll buy you a case of whatever you're drinking when we land."

The engine over their heads rose to a high-pitched roar. "Deal!"

* * *

"Conrad is out here somewhere," Sabakov whispered. "She could not have gotten far. Find her!"

The four Russians edged out of the culvert, Nikolai and Sabakov working their way to the right, Vasily and the last helicopter gunman to the left.

* * *

The Russian voices went quiet, then Manning heard steps advancing toward him. He froze in place, barely daring to breathe. The steps grew close enough for him to hear tall grass swishing against fabric.

A boot contacted his shoulder. The man jumped back.

"*Rooki za galavu!*" he shouted. The voice became more threatening. "*Rooki za galavu!*"

A flashlight blazed in his face. "He wants you to put your hands on your head," he heard a voice say in English. It was Vasily.

Manning complied. He couldn't see anything past the flashlight beam, but he heard two more men hastily approach. One made a demand in Russian.

"He wants to know where Conrad is," Vasily translated.

"I don't know," he said truthfully. "I think she went through the tunnel before me, but she was long gone when I came out. She probably left on the Huey."

Vasily relayed Manning's answer, but the man asking the questions obviously wasn't satisfied. He barked again in Russian.

"How long ago did she leave?" Vasily asked.

"That Huey makes a hell of a racket, and I didn't hear anything when I came out but *that* helicopter," he motioned with his head without moving his hands, "so my guess is she left at least five minutes ago."

* * *

"Do you believe he is telling the truth?" Sabakov asked in Russian.

Vasily was incredulous. "You just watched Conrad try to *kill* this man, why on earth would he lie for her? He just wants to survive. Leave him be and let us make our escape while we can."

Sabakov leveled his pistol at Manning. "He's seen our faces, we have to kill him."

"I have a flashlight pointed directly at his face! He sees nothing!" Vasily pleaded.

"He's certainly seen *your* face," Sabakov countered, "as well as Nikolai's. We can't take the chance." He raised his pistol again.

"No!" Vasily challenged, dousing the flashlight to prevent Sabakov from shooting. "I made this man a promise if it came to this, that I would do the deed myself." He held up his pistol for emphasis.

"Quickly," Sabakov allowed.

CORNERED

CHICAGO, ILLINOIS

Patchy Beard twisted and punched at Amanda but was unable to free himself. One of his hands flew down to his belt, struggling with something under his jacket instead of with her. The motion caught her eye just in time as he produced a gun and swung it toward her head. She ducked and grabbed his hand with both of hers. The gun went off with a deafening blast that made her scream. He started to wriggle free of her leglock, but she kept both hands wrapped around the gun. She pulled the gun hand toward her and sunk her teeth into his wrist.

He screamed and the weapon fell free. She tried to grab it, but was forced to push it out the bathroom door to keep him from recovering it. She might have thighs of steel, but his arm strength easily exceeded hers. He wrested one of his hands free of hers and grabbed at his ankle. Preoccupied with maintaining her choke hold with her legs and blocking his remaining hand from punching her, she only saw the flash of silver when it sank into her leg. He pulled out the knife and stabbed her again.

She shrieked in pain and released her hold. He rolled away, his movements hindered by the pants around his ankles. He lunged out the door for the gun, his pants still down.

She jumped after him, but he kicked her in the face with both encumbered feet and came up with the pistol. He rolled into a sitting position and leveled the gun at her face. "*Qu si chou samba!*" he hissed at her, rising to his feet and pulling up his pants with his free hand. "You die now, bitch!" he repeated in English.

* * *

MOUNT DIABLO, CALIFORNIA

The flashlight went out, leaving Manning completely blind. He felt a hand on his shoulder.

"I have pleaded for your life with my superior to no avail. I am sorry, Michael. It is time for me to fulfill my promise. If you will lower you head slightly and remain still it will make my aim sure. Again, I am so sorry."

Manning complied, his heart pounding. He realized it wasn't pounding as hard as when trapped in Conrad's death circle. Death at the hand of a friend *did* make things easier, although not much. He heard Vasily cock his pistol. He closed his eyes and thought of Amanda and his sons, praying to a god he had never really believed in that only his life would be forfeit, not theirs.

He opened his eyes again when he heard a scream to his left. Out of the corner of his eye, he watched the gunman who had first stumbled upon him explode like a hand grenade. Pieces of the Russian fell around him like meat-filled rain.

A blue spotlight illuminated Nikolai, who was already screaming. But instead of exploding, he melted like a wax figure. First his chest caved in from the weight of his head pressing down on his shoulders. Then his legs bowed like a grotesque exaggeration of a cowboy before his entire body collapsed into a fleshy pile, his scream fading to a high-pitched whine of air escaping from his misshapen mouth.

"*Chërt voz'mí!*" Vasily's superior shouted just before the blue beam lit him up next. His screams dissolved into a frightened schoolgirl squeal as the beam neither detonated nor dissolved, but instead lifted him from the ground. Manning followed the motion upward toward the source of the blue beam—three white lights directly overhead, so bright they burned his eyes. He couldn't be sure, but there seemed to be a solid triangular structure behind them.

As the beam pulled the man higher, another white light appeared in the center of the triangle, growing larger until it surrounded the blue beam suspending the Russian. For a second the white light silhouetted his flailing form, his shriek of terror still audible from the ground. Then the beam and the white light went out and his scream silenced. The night fell completely still again, except for a generator-like hum from the triangle and the sound of the second helicopter racing off into the distance.

Vasily exclaimed something in Russian, but then the blue beam returned for him. He rose over Manning's head, kicking and shouting, more in anger than fear, until the white light ingested him.

Manning had just started to congratulate himself at his deliverance when the blue beam pierced his body like a shock. Electric ants crawled all over his body, jerking him skyward. The out-of-body sensation was so profound he wondered for several seconds who was screaming until he recognized his own voice. Then the white light surrounded and swallowed him up as well.

CHAPTER 30

INTERVENTION

MOUNT DIABLO, CALIFORNIA

"Do you see it?" the pilot asked.

Willing the night vision goggles to find the Huey was apparently a trick Pugliano could only use once. "They were flying out on this bearing," he urged, "just keep the throttle pegged and we'll spot them eventually." It didn't sound convincing even to him.

"We only have a five-to-ten knot speed advantage—it may take awhile" the pilot warned. "And what did you plan to do once we catch 'em? They've already shot down one helicopter that got too close."

"We'll act as a spotter for the F-16s and they'll blow her out of the sky, at visual range if they have to."

"Works for me," the pilot deadpanned.

That reminded Pugliano to make the call to get the F-16s back in the air and homing on his position, which he did. Another voice intruded in his headphones.

"Lumberjack One, this is Groundhog. We've completed our sweep of the main building. No resistance or casualties. Two live Tangos and a dozen deads inside. No Conrad, no nanoagent."

"Understood," Pugliano replied. "Continue your search of the compound. We're in pursuit of a helicopter that may have her on board, but then again she could be fifty feet from you hiding in a shed or a cellar. Same story with the nanoagent. Watch yourself."

"Always. Good hunting, Lumberjack."

"Copy, Lumberjack One out."

"Holy cow, what's *that*?" the pilot exclaimed.

Pugliano had his head down tracing their progress on a map, checking to make sure there were no population centers on their current heading that would preclude a shoot-down. There weren't. Scanning the sky to find what had sparked the pilot's outburst, he spotted a bright white cone on the horizon. Lifting his night vision goggles for a moment, he realized the cone only appeared white because of the goggles' monochromatic circuitry. In reality the cone was a ghostly electric blue. The hairs on the back of his neck stood up. *Was that damned silver ball back?*

"I've got the Huey!" the pilot called.

"Where?"

"Under that spotlight! Have we got help up here?"

"Not that I know of," he murmured. After several seconds of willing his vision to focus on what the pilot's younger eyes had already seen, he finally spotted the Huey, at the bottom limit of the mysterious spotlight and descending rapidly.

* * *

“What the hell is going on, Shiva?” Conrad yelled from the Huey’s left-hand pilot seat. A blue light filled the cockpit. She could hear the turbine engine winding down.

“Complete systems’ failure!” he yelled back—even the intercom system stopped working. “All I have left is mechanical controls! Attempting an emergency landing!”

Conrad wrenched off her failed night vision goggles and tried to help Shiva scout a suitable landing spot, but the blue spotlight shining down on them blanked everything outside with an opaque glow. *This is gonna be bad*, she acknowledged to herself. *Dammit, I thought that silver ball was on my side!*

* * *

“It’s landing!” Pugliano said triumphantly. *Quarry on the ground in the middle of nowhere with a sniper ready in my back seat. Checkmate.*

“Huh-uh, that’s an autorotation descent!” the pilot’s experienced voice pronounced. “It ain’t landin’, it’s crashin’!”

In his mind’s eye he was already watching the Huey cartwheel in flames across the landscape. “Even better,” he whispered.

* * *

The only sounds in the Huey were the air whistling past the plummeting fuselage and the repetitive *whump-whump-whump* of the windmilling rotor blades, kept moving only by the vertical speed of their descent. Conrad knew that once they reached the ground Shiva would have one chance to trade the blades’ momentum for a few seconds of lift to slow their plunge.

The altimeter still worked, but they had only a general idea of the height of the hilly terrain below. If Shiva flared too late they would slam into the ground, and if he flared too soon they would stall the rotor blades—and *then* slam into the ground. But with that damned blue beam locked onto them they couldn’t see a thing outside the cockpit, which meant they were probably going to slam into the ground, hard. With all the power that damned silver ball packed, she mused, surely there was a more elegant way of killing them than by blunt trauma.

The beam switched off.

"Can you see the ground?" Shiva called.

She craned her neck, but the glare from the beam had ruined her eyes' night adaptation. She couldn't see jack. Then she realized the intercoms were working again. She grabbed her night vision goggles and slapped them against her face. They worked also.

"*Ground!*" she screamed. "Flare, flare, *flare!*"

The blades groaned as they bit into the air, putting up their last gallant fight against gravity's relentless pull. She could make out individual rocks rushing up from below.

"Impact! *Brace!*" she yelled.

Shiva's efforts almost saved them, but their speed was still too high. They hit with the screech of yielding metal and the right skid gave way. The Huey lurched sideways. Still-whirling rotors bit into the ground with a sound like a rapid-fire meat cleaver. She heard Hendrix scream in terror right before he hit the windshield and landed in their laps. *Guess who forgot to buckle up*, she mused, pushing his tangled limbs aside.

"Everybody out!" she ordered. The old bird could burst into flames any second.

* * *

"That's it, she's down! Ouch!" the Jet Ranger pilot announced.

"Was that survivable?" Pugliano asked.

"I've seen worse."

"Then take us in." He paused. "Mitch, you still awake back there?"

"You bet, boss," his sniper answered.

"Then look sharp on the left side, I got business for you. If it moves, *shoot it!*"

* * *

CHICAGO, ILLINOIS

Patchy Beard sneered at her over the pistol he had reclaimed. He glanced quickly about the basement. "Where boys?" he snarled.

Amanda looked toward the darkened stairwell. There was no sign of Eric or Kevin. "They're gone, you bastard!" she said triumphantly. Let him do what he wished with her now. Her sons had escaped.

He lunged and viciously pistol-whipped her across the mouth. She fell back against the shelves lining the basement wall, yelping in pain and anger. She fell limp to the floor, throwing an arm over her head. Maybe if he thought her unconscious he would try to rape her. That would give her one last whack at him at close range. It was better than standing with her hands up and waiting to be shot.

"*Mom?*" she heard Kevin wail from the stairwell. Her heart stopped in mid-beat.

When Patchy Beard saw her eyes open he thrust the pistol at her again. "Call back!" he shouted, gesticulating toward the stairwell. "Call back *now!*"

"I told you to run!" she cried out.

"The door's locked, Mom," Eric announced.

Her body sagged, her adrenaline spent. "All right boys, we tried. Come back down."

* * *

MOUNT DIABLO

Conrad had to twist in her seat and kick the left side pilot's door open. She scrambled to the ground and helped Dieter, who fought with the jammed left side door from inside. With her assistance it finally popped back into its track and slid to the rear. Dieter hopped down, sniper rifle in hand. Shiva still struggled to free himself from his harness and Hendrix's bulk. She jumped back inside.

"Come on!" she said, pulling on Hendrix's torso, eliciting a groan from what she had assumed was a corpse. "We gotta get clear!"

Shiva wriggled free of the pilot's seat. "What about Hendrix?" he asked, glancing over when the CIA turncoat moaned again.

She jerked her head toward the door. "Maybe we'll get lucky and the helicopter will blow. Let's go."

* * *

CHICAGO

Amanda motioned the boys to her for what she knew would be their last embrace.

"Mom, you're bleeding!" Eric protested.

She pulled them close. "I know, it's okay. It'll all be okay soon."

Even independent Eric buried his head in his mother's shoulder, knowing the words were meant to comfort, but not much more.

Patchy Beard used the lull to make a call on his cellphone. He spoke briefly in rapid-fire Chinese. He leered at her when he ended the call.

"Boss says you die now," he said with great pleasure. He held up the hand she had bitten. Blood ran freely down his arm. "For this you see boys die *first!*"

She pulled them behind her. "NO!" she shouted.

* * *

MOUNT DIABLO

Conrad called to Dieter. "See that damned silver ball anywhere?"

His eyes searched the darkness. "No, but don't you think if it wanted us dead it would have just blown us out of the sky?"

She hunched in the grass back-to-back with the German so they could scan the sky in two directions. "Beats me, I never psychoanalyzed a murdering silver ball before."

"I just meant—"

"Shh! You hear a helicopter?"

"Bell Jet Ranger," Shiva offered. "Two miles and closing. Fast."

"Shit!" She looked around the gently sloping hillside they had crashed on. Nothing but scattered scrub brush for the few hundred yards her night vision goggles could pierce. They'd never make it to cover in time. "Shiva! Is this thing gonna blow?"

He sniffed the air. "The transmission oil is cooking off but I don't smell fuel, so I think the tanks are intact. We're safe for the moment."

"Everybody under the helicopter! Maybe they don't have thermal sensors." They wedged themselves against the slanted underbelly of the Huey and lay motionless as the other helicopter approached.

* * *

The Jet Ranger came up on the right side of the crippled Huey. Thin wisps of smoke roiled from the engine compartment, but no fire was visible. Neither were the Huey's occupants.

"Mitch, you see anyone inside?" Pugliano asked his sniper.

"Uh, I think there's a body in the front seat, but no motion."

"See anybody on the ground from your side?" he asked the pilot.

"Negative. There's not much cover out here, I don't see where the hell they went."

"Circle around. Look sharp, Mitch!"

The helicopter orbited counterclockwise around the nose of the Huey. Suddenly the sniper's rifle barked three times.

"Gun sighted!" the sniper reported. "Tango down!"

Pugliano caught the fleeting target the sniper had engaged just before they passed behind the helicopter and the Huey's fuselage blocked them again. "Nice work! Anybody else under there?"

"I think so, sir. Can you give me another pass?"

"You bet!" He made a circling gesture to the pilot, who nodded. "Just remember, there's nobody innocent down there. If it looks like a target, put some rounds into it. Bullets are cheap."

"So are body bags," the sniper agreed.

* * *

Conrad watched the distinctive profile of the Jet Ranger helicopter round the nose of the Huey. She didn't even know who was flying it. Russians? The FBI? It could even be some local sheriff who saw the crash and came to investigate. They may even be the reason the silver ball didn't stick around to finish them off.

"Dieter, don't shoot!" she cautioned. "Not till we can ID them!"

"Acknowledged, weapons hold."

"Miss Conrad," Shiva whispered, "that helicopter has an upgraded engine used only by American federal agencies."

"At least it's not more Russians," she murmured back. "They'd probably just hose the Huey and—"

At that instant she saw a flash from the back of the Jet Ranger, followed by the thud of a round impacting behind her.

"Shit!" Another flash.

"Permission to—" Dieter began.

The second thud was followed by a gasp from Dieter, the third by the sound of air whistling from a punctured lung. He tried to speak, but only a gurgling sound escaped.

"Dammit! Dieter!"

No reply.

Maybe it was the Russians after all. But no matter who was doing the shooting, two moving targets had a better chance than one sitting duck. She picked the route she thought was most conducive to survival, then pointed in another direction.

"Shiva! We gotta run! You go that way!"

He stared at her in terror.

She pointed at Dieter. "You want to end up like that? Then *run!*" She took off without waiting to see if Shiva complied or not. She heard the helicopter change course toward her. *So this is how it ends*, a surprisingly calm dialogue in her head pondered, *running like a cornered rabbit until a bullet catches you in the back. You knew your luck had to run out eventually. Really, Angela, you should have been in a box years ago.*

She stumbled on a rock just in time to hear a bullet crack past her ear, followed by the gunshot half a second later. They were directly behind her. She cut hard right and ran in a zigzag. No sense making it easy for them.

She had seen enough nature shows to know that a glance over the shoulder was usually the last move the prey made before the predator sank its teeth in, but she couldn't help herself. *It's instinct, my dear*, the voice lectured her, *because now you're the prey.*

She watched the helicopter make a slight turn to the right, giving the sniper in back of the helicopter a better angle for the *coup de grace*. She kept running and waiting. Maybe the sniper was toying with her, like a cat with a mouse. Then she noticed the sound of the helicopter's engine had changed. Changed as in stopped. The Jet Ranger was making the same dying helicopter noises the Huey had made.

She chanced another look and saw the Jet Ranger caught in a spotlight that instantly fried her night vision goggles, turning everything a uniform gray. She stumbled again, ripped off the goggles and threw them aside.

The next look over her shoulder almost made her stop running. The source of the blue beam was not the silver ball but a triangular craft the size of a 737, with a bright white light at each corner. Unlike with the Huey, the craft kept the blue beam on the Jet Ranger all the way to the ground. The helicopter hit hard, collapsing both skids and breaking off the tail boom. With the tail rotor gone and the main rotor still turning, the now-lightened Jet Ranger hopped a few feet in the air, the fuselage spinning like a top. She saw the sniper fly out the door to the limit of his safety harness. His rifle kept going.

The helicopter slammed back to earth, rolling twice before coming to rest on its right side. Pieces of rotor blades flew in every direction. The triangle moved lower, coming to a stop over the wrecked Jet Ranger. Conrad kept running, not waiting to see what the triangle had in store for her pursuers.

* * *

CHICAGO

Amanda tensed to make a final lunge at Patchy Beard. Maybe she could make him expend all his bullets into her if she fought hard enough.

A blue beam pierced the ceiling and lit up Patchy Beard like a spotlight. He froze in confusion, not realizing his doom until he had sunk up to his knees. The beam liquefied the concrete at his feet, swallowing him like quicksand. He cried out in terror as he sank to his waist in the suddenly fluid floor.

He flailed with his hands trying to stop his descent. When the beam went out, Patchy Beard was submerged up to his neck. The hand with the gun was now locked above the surface, but only three fingers of the other wiggled in the now rigid concrete. He gasped for breath, his lungs locked in an unyielding vise of cement and earth. After two minutes of anguished convulsions, his head lolled and his eyes rolled back.

"What the hell was that?" Eric breathed. Kevin started crying.

Amanda stepped forward and twisted the gun from Patchy Beard's grasp. She had an almost uncontrollable need to urinate. "Watch your mouth, little man!" she scolded. "Anybody else here need a potty break before we go?"

GOING UP FIGHTING

MOUNT DIABLO

When Pugliano first came to he didn't even remember where he was, but the pain reminded him soon enough. A throbbing ache in his head played a duet with a shooting spasm up his back. He had to wipe blood out of his eyes before he could take stock of his surroundings. He peeled off the headphones, one side of which was smashed to dangling electronics. The moans he heard let him know he wasn't the only survivor.

"Who can hear me? Call out!"

"I'm here," Lyman said. "I think the gunner's gone though. Looks like a broken neck."

He tried to turn in his seat to see the sniper's condition but couldn't. "Pilot, you still with me?"

"Barely," he groaned. "I'm pretty sure my arm's broke—I think my leg too."

"Better than your neck," Pugliano countered. "Can you wiggle your toes?"

A pause. "Yeah, but—oh shit—it hurts! My leg is definitely fucked up."

"Lyman, if you can move, help us get out."

"Will do. What the hell was that blue light before we crashed?"

"You don't wanna know! Just get us out of here!"

He heard the executive unhook his seat belt and clamber out the open left side of the Jet Ranger. After some grunting and cursing, the door next to Pugliano popped open.

Pugliano unlatched his lap belt and moved his feet so he could push himself up and out the door. It hurt like hell. "Make a hole, I'm coming out," he said. Lyman moved aside and Pugliano lifted himself painfully out to a sitting position on what once had been the left side of the helicopter.

“Do we try to move the pilot or just wait for the rescue crew?” Lyman asked.

“You’re assuming that anyone is even *coming* to rescue us. We didn’t even have time for a distress call. I hope air traffic control saw us go down.”

Before Lyman could reply, a brilliant blue beam illuminated them.

* * *

Conrad topped the nearest ridge and dropped behind a low shrub. Seeing no signs of the triangle and hearing no sounds of pursuit, she crawled back just far enough to see over the rise. At least two men had survived the crash and were trying to climb out of the overturned Jet Ranger.

Suddenly the triangle appeared over the helicopter. It made no sound and gave no warning of its approach. It just seemed to materialize. When it flashed its blue beam at the Jet Ranger, she expected to see the chopper explode. Instead, both men flew up the beam toward the triangle. One kicked and clawed at the air like a fish trying to swim upstream. She couldn’t tell if the cry that reached her was of fear or just exertion from trying to escape.

The second man had just emerged from the left-hand pilot’s seat. Instead of fighting, she saw him draw his weapon and hold it up over his head with both hands, like he was a high diver and the triangle was the pool. He was going up fighting, whoever he was. She admired the poor doomed bastard—at least he had balls.

If there were more survivors in the helicopter, whoever drove the triangle didn’t care about them. The blue beam blinked out and the triangle shot upward too fast to follow. In a second it was gone.

“Well, I guess we *both* know who’s boss now, don’t we, fellas?” she muttered to the men who had just been taken. She waited several minutes for any sign of the triangle’s return, or of any other helicopters coming to the Jet Ranger’s aid. Just crickets.

* * *

CHICAGO

Amanda led the boys to the head of the stairs. Like they had said, it was locked.

“Stand back,” she ordered. She had no idea how to shoot out a lock, other than what she had seen on those stupid cop shows she had half-watched with Mike after the boys went to bed. She made sure they were shielded by her body before she aimed the gun.

The lock turned and the door suddenly opened. Mr. Wu's biggest guard stared down at them, a look of surprised fury in his eyes.

Amanda raised the pistol and fired wildly. Somewhere between the fourth and fifth shot she hit something important and the guard toppled backwards.

"Stay back!" she shouted to the boys, moving up the stairs and stepping through the doorway. She edged onto the landing, which opened left and right into a hallway. She glanced both ways. To the right was a shop of some kind, with Chinese signage over glass cases. She smelled herbs, strange and pungent. Mr. Wu, his son, and another goon stood frozen in surprise. They had just entered the shop, still wearing their coats. Her mind suddenly processed what she had glanced to the left. A door marked EXIT.

She fired three quick shots at the men, forcing them to dive for cover. She heard glass shatter and one man cry in pain.

"BOYS!" she screamed. "*RUN!*"

* * *

MOUNT DIABLO

Conrad ran in a crouch on the back side of the ridge until she was opposite the wreck of the Huey. She needed the loot from the Nanovex raid, or at the very least the box containing the technical records and the remaining nanoagent. If she could get out of the country she could go straight to the Chinese and offer the nanoagent at a discount for their trouble. Maybe a couple million and asylum inside China would be the best she could hope for. But without the loot from Nanovex she was a walking corpse.

She crept a few feet downhill and waited for any kind of reaction. Nothing stirred. Then she thought she heard another helicopter in the distance. *Reinforcements, gotta move.* She broke into a run, making a dash for the Huey. She jumped up into the cabin and found the first box. It was the gadgets. She was sure they were valuable, but she couldn't carry both boxes, they were too big. She found the other box wedged under the rear bench seat and yanked it free. She retrieved the nanoagent activation radio from the pilot's stowage pouch between the seats and stuck it in the box, then cut a piece of nylon webbing from the seats to make a carry strap. She leapt down and started running.

"Miss Conrad?" a small voice said from under the Huey. It was Shiva, still cowering under the helicopter.

“Shiva! Am I glad to see you!” She really was. Her chances of survival with a partner were much better, especially one who could fly any helicopter she could steal for him. “Come on, grab that other box in the chopper! We gotta go!”

He complied without argument, which was another reason she was glad to have him as a partner. She helped him make a carrying strap for his box as well. She could hear choppers approaching quite clearly now. “What kind and how far?” she asked Shiva, his expertise in such matters already established.

“Two UH-60 Black Hawks, three miles.”

“Shit, that’s just a couple of minutes! Let’s go!”

They broke into a run toward the ridge top she had just left. If they could get some terrain between them and the approaching helicopters they might make a clean getaway.

Her first clue of disaster was a vertical rush of air she felt against her head. Then the hair on her arms stood on end as if she had been charged with static electricity. When the blue beam flashed around them she knew they were screwed. For some reason they took Shiva first.

“Miss Conrad!” he screamed, as if she had some power to save him. He dropped the box, but the beam carried both him and the box up toward the triangle until they disappeared.

* * *

CHICAGO

The boys obeyed and rushed behind her. She heard the rear exit door bang open. So did Mr. Wu and his men. She saw one of them move behind the counter, angling for a shot. She fired again. It was a wild miss, but it broke more glass and kept her captors’ heads down. She ran.

The door opened onto a narrow alley. The boys had cut left and kept running, looking back to see if she followed.

She waved them on. “Keep running! Don’t stop!” She heard the door slam shut behind her.

She had only run twenty feet or so when she heard the back door open again. She turned, almost losing her footing. A guard burst through the exit, bringing up his gun when he saw her. She fired three shots before the pistol clicked on an empty chamber. She didn’t think she had hit him, but the bullets sparking against the steel door and the brick wall forced him to pull back inside. She heard him shout something in Chinese. She dropped the empty pistol and kept running.

Fifty feet further the alley intersected a narrow street. For a panicked moment she thought she had lost the boys, but they had turned left, running up the street. They wisely got out of the alley at their first opportunity, a street being a better chance to be spotted and rescued, although this one looked quite deserted.

She turned left and ran after them, although she would have turned right. This direction would lead them back to the street that fronted Mr. Wu's store. Maybe Eric hadn't realized that. She saw a street cleaner turn the corner onto the narrow street, almost hitting Kevin and Eric as they ran. She cried out in alarm, but Eric saw their peril and swerved, pulling Kevin out of the way. The street cleaner gave them a belated honk.

She had almost caught up with them when she saw them stop. She continued running until she reached them.

Mr. Wu and his son were waiting at the corner. He was already holding the boys at gunpoint. She kept running until she could place herself between her boys and the Chinese mobster.

"You will return with me to the shop," Mr. Wu ordered. Blood trickled down one side of his face from a cut on his forehead.

"Why?" she snapped. "Your guard already told us you gave the word to kill us." She glanced up at the windows along the street. Only a few were lit, but a gunshot would bring witnesses to those windows, and Mr. Wu would have to shoot at least three times. Maybe even the street cleaner would hear it and investigate. "Do it here—if you've got the guts. We're not going anywhere."

His eyes showed uncertainty for a moment, then his expression hardened. "As you wish," he said, aiming carefully at her head.

* * *

MOUNT DIABLO

Conrad didn't even try to run this time. Whoever the hell these people were—she assumed they *were* people and not aliens from another planet—they had a level of power beyond her comprehension. Fighting them was pointless and running was a waste of breath. Besides, the pistol in her waistband and the other one on her ankle would be more effective at close range—like inside the triangle. She raised her hands in mock surrender.

She almost cried out when an electric shock passed through her body and lifted her from the ground. Almost. She steeled herself to keep her wits about her and mind clear, constantly weighing her tactical options, as if she had any. She examined the bottom of the craft as she got closer. She could make out seams in the black metal and hear an almost turbine-like whine of rapidly spinning machinery coming from the bright corners of the triangle. She approached a circle of white light. Upon closer approach it became obvious it was an opening into the ship.

Suddenly she was inside and the blue beam flashed off. She was temporarily blinded, having gone from the nearly moonless night to the triangle's brightly lit interior. The instant the beam stopped she felt herself in free fall, landing gracelessly on a solid surface. The hole underneath her had closed, creating a solid deck.

She looked around the circular compartment, blinking against the sudden illumination. An older and younger man faced her, the latter leveling a futuristic-looking weapon at her chest. Shiva's box and the dispersal tube she had left at the warehouse were at their feet, along with several guns.

"Miss Conrad," the elder man said with a silver tongue, "if you would be so kind as to relieve yourself of your pistols." A knowing smile. "*Both* of them. And the nonmetallic throwing knife up your left sleeve as well. I took the liberty of scanning you when you passed through the portal."

With a sigh of consternation, she complied. *Well, they look human enough.*

"Just leave them there and move back against the wall, please," he said.

Again she obeyed, as if she had a choice. To her astonishment, she saw Oleg Sabakov and Vasily sitting on the floor on the left side of the circle. From her research she recognized Douglas Lyman sitting on the right side of the chamber. Next to him was an angry-looking man with a bulldog face. That had to be Perry Pugliano, the FBI chief for San Francisco. She was even more surprised upon reaching the wall when Shiva and Mike Manning scooted aside to make room for her. She pressed her back against the wall, seeking assurance that this bizarre scene was solid reality and not the ethereal result of accumulated head trauma.

The older man cleared his throat. "Now that Miss Conrad has joined us, we can finally begin. My name is Simon Crane. I'm sure you're all wondering why I've called this meeting."

CHAPTER 31

SAVIOR

CHICAGO, ILLINOIS

Amanda knelt down, covering her boy's eyes. Maybe she could shorten their horror by a few seconds. They were too shocked to even cry at the moment. But she locked eyes with her executioner.

"Murdering women and children," she spat, "I hope you're proud of yourself. And your son. What a *fine* father you are."

Mr. Wu looked pained. "I take no pride in my actions. But some orders I dare not disobey."

She saw motion behind his head, dismissing it as a helium balloon. But it kept coming, stopping directly overhead and emitting a blinding blue flash. Mr. Wu and his son collapsed like rag dolls to the pavement, convulsing like someone had shot them with a Taser.

She glanced up at the silver balloon over their heads. It moved a short distance down the street they had just left, then halted and flashed a blue glow twice. They remained frozen in their pre-execution crouch, too stunned to move. A few seconds later the balloon repeated the maneuver.

Eric was the first to decode the balloon's motions. "Mom! I think it wants us to follow!"

Frozen by indecision for a moment, Amanda quickly realized she was in no position to be choosy about her savior, even if it was filled with helium.

"Boys! Go!" she ordered. "Follow it!"

The boys chased the balloon, and she ran after the boys. They didn't stop for three blocks until they reached a four-lane street. She thought she was in good physical shape, but was breathless when she finally caught up with them. She looked overhead. The balloon was gone. She looked behind. No one followed them, yet.

"What just happened, Mom?" Kevin asked tearfully, on the verge of a melt-down. She didn't blame him a bit.

"I don't know, baby," she wheezed. She needed to catch her breath before they started running again.

"Was that silver ball an angel?" Eric asked.

"I don't know honey, anything's possible."

"You were awesome with that gun, Mom!"

"No, what was *awesome* was you sticking with your brother to get him out of danger." She pulled Eric close and kissed his forehead. "Nicely done, little man."

He didn't squirm away as his usual habit. "Thanks, Mom. What do we do now? Aren't they still after us?"

A car coming down the street caught her eye. "Boys, hold my hands and stay close." Together they stepped out onto the road, directly into its path. Maintaining her hold on Kevin's hand, she released Eric's and waved the vehicle down.

The Chicago Police cruiser braked to a stop and switched on its emergency flashers. The officer emerged cautiously, squeezing the mike on his left shoulder and sending a short message to his dispatcher. He then called out to Amanda.

"Ma'am, can I help you?"

PROPOSITIONS

PRESENT DAY – ABOVE CALIFORNIA

"Before we proceed with today's business," Crane intoned casually, as if presiding over a routine executive meeting, "I must bring all of you up to date, so you will understand why I have brought you together. Over forty years ago, my father was summoned to a meeting with the most powerful men in the world. They referred to themselves simply as the Group."

Nothing grandiose there, Pugliano thought wryly.

"They had a breathtaking proposal for my father," he continued. "After the proliferation of atomic weapons, the invention of nuclear weapons, and the arms race which produced such madness as the policy of Mutually Assured Destruction, these men realized it was only a matter of time before mankind let an even worse genie out of the bottle. But instead of obliterating entire cities, the next genie might destroy the whole planet on its first use. They decided to pool their resources to prevent that from happening. It was from that meeting the Kammler Organization was born."

"The Kammler Organization?" Pugliano challenged. "Never heard of it."

Crane raised an eyebrow. "And therefore it doesn't exist?" he opened his hands. "Allow me to present this ship as evidence."

Careful, Perry. "Perhaps I should have said I've never heard of your *father*."

"My father was a Nazi war criminal. He was also a great man. And in a way, my hero—although I did not truly appreciate his achievements until after he was gone."

Holy shit, Hendrix was right. Nazis. Nazis in flying saucers.

"The charter of the Kammler Organization was simple," Crane continued. "In expression, if not in execution. His charge was to monitor the development of technology worldwide, and if it posed a risk to mankind, the Kammlerorg was to take that technology out of circulation, permanently."

Oh what the hell, Pugliano thought. *Everybody in here is dead anyway.* "Is that what all the mayhem at Nanovex was about? Taking their technology off the table?"

Crane looked pleased. "Exactly. You would have to agree, an invention that would make the deployment and use of chemical weapons *more* likely rather than less would hardly be a stabilizing element in world politics. Especially after the technology proliferated and fell into the hands of third world dictators."

The thought had crossed my mind, Pugliano admitted to himself, upon reflection of the briefings he had received at Nanovex. He nodded at Seth Graves, the supposed DARPA representative at Nanovex, who now held them all at bay with some kind of ray gun. "Is that what *he* was doing," he said critically, "scouting ahead for *you*?"

Crane seemed amused. "*Really*, Agent Pugliano? Are you saying you've never run an undercover agent? Or are you just irritated at one being used on *you*? Mr. Graves' mission at Nanovex was threefold. First he attempted to dissuade Mr. Lyman from developing the nanoagent upon its first presentation to DARPA. When Mr. Lyman proceeded with the research using his own funds, I arranged for DARPA to finance the project, simply to have Mr. Graves there to monitor their progress. And once the Group decided that the nanoagent was to be taken off the table, Mr. Graves served as my executioner, implementing final security to assure that WICKER BASKET never reached operational status. Ever."

Pugliano locked eyes with Graves. "So *you* murdered all those scientists? I assume you also killed the CIA and Mossad agents at San Jose City Hall?" Graves regarded him with eyes of stone, but said nothing.

Crane held up a finger. "Ah, ah, Agent Pugliano! Mr. Graves acted strictly under my orders. He is no more guilty of murder than you were as a Marine Corps officer or as an FBI agent when you took a life in the line of duty."

"Those scientists were innocent American citizens under *my* protection," he said in a low growl. If they were going to kill him anyway, which was more of a certainty the longer the old man monologued, he might as well speak his piece.

"You are completely justified in your indignation, Agent Pugliano. However, there are larger interests at play here, which is why you were invited to this meeting, rather than summarily executed when you interfered with my plans."

"Huh?" he grunted.

* * *

I wish that FBI guy would shut the hell up, Conrad thought. *He's gonna get us all killed, if we're not dead already.*

"If you would allow me to continue, Agent Pugliano, all will be made clear," Crane said patiently.

Pugliano nodded.

"As I said, the role of the Kammlerorg is to prevent technology from becoming a threat to mankind itself. If you consider the fact that no more 'genies' like the atomic or hydrogen bomb have manifested during our tenure, I would say we have been quite successful, especially against the backdrop of the remarkable technological advancements of the last forty years. We have allowed mankind to expand into all manner of productive endeavors, without allowing the development of weapons that would inevitably spawn another world war."

"Like that damned silver ball," Pugliano said.

"Exactly. Imagine whole squadrons of those orbs laying waste to vast tracts of the planet. And it wouldn't just be on the *other* side of the planet, as Americans are fond of fantasizing. They would make events like September 11th a commonplace occurrence."

Pugliano made a face. "But as long as it's just *you* laying waste with your little silver ball, all is right with the world, huh?"

Would you please shut the fuck up? Conrad wanted to scream at the FBI agent.

If Pugliano's challenges angered Crane, it didn't show. "Indeed, we *do* use the advanced technologies collected by the Kammler Organization to forward our goals. For instance, to protect our investment in Miss Conrad."

Blinking, she felt every eye in the room bore into her. "*Excuse* me?" she protested.

Crane chuckled. "First of all, Miss Conrad, my gratitude for delivering the nanoagent and its delivery device. While Mr. Graves did package the WICKER BASKET materials for you, your operation made it unnecessary for us to assault a heavily armed federal convoy and steal it away. Agent Pugliano should probably thank you for the lives of the federal agents you saved."

Pugliano glared at her.

"Anything for world peace," Conrad offered.

Crane laughed out loud. From the strained sound it made, he obviously did not do so often. "Miss Conrad, monitoring your progress has been a rare pleasure in what is usually a very unpleasant business."

Now he had her curiosity. "How's that?"

He waved the question aside. "First, I need to backtrack to the beginning of Mr. Graves' operations at Nanovex. Once it became obvious that final security would need to be imposed, I saw a unique opportunity. I leaked the existence of the nanoagent to the underground arms trafficking community, and watched to see who responded. Of those, three truly stood out."

He motioned to his right. "I'm sure all of you know Mr. Sabakov. While you have just witnessed the brutality of his methods, I had to admire his ability to deal with adverse circumstances and paltry funding that would make most covert operators walk away in disgust. I was quite impressed."

When his name was mentioned, Sabakov demanded Vasily translate, which he performed quietly.

"Next was Renée LaCroix, who I believe you just killed, Mr. Sabakov, isn't that correct? In a way he was Sabakov's polar opposite—careful, calculating, and cultured. He may have been outmatched in a toe-to-toe slugging match with Sabakov's organization, but there's no doubt with whom I would rather share a bottle of wine."

He gave Conrad a knowing look. "Finally there was your mentor, Meir Eitan. A mixture of culture and ruthlessness, he was my personal favorite." He paused. "That is, of course, until you double-crossed and killed him."

I am so screwed, she thought. He was just toying with her before he used his ray gun to turn her into god-knows-what.

He shook a paternal finger. "Of course, I *had* heard of your cell wiping out the team the Saudis sent to stop you from carrying out the theft at Nanovex for Eitan's gang of thieves. I was impressed. But it was when you reversed Meir Eitan's ambush at Hunter's Point *and* escaped through an FBI cordon that you truly came on my radar. I had no intention of allowing you near the nanoagent, of course, but the audacity with which you took over Eitan's role and made Sabakov, LaCroix, *and* the others submit to your agenda—well, I just had to see how it would play out. That's why I intervened at San Jose City Hall."

Christ, I'm his entertainment! "So that was you." A statement rather than a question. He obviously had the technical horsepower.

"Actually, Mr. Graves piloted the orb during that operation. But he did so under my orders. Partly because I thought you might prove useful—to distract the FBI if nothing else—and partly because…well, I'll get to that in a moment."

"I thought you said everything was going to be made clear," Pugliano said. "Why didn't you just make a deal with the government to shelve that project and reassign the people? Sounds like a waste of lives, unless you get off on that."

Again, Crane gave the FBI agent no emotional reaction at all. "An excellent point, Agent Pugliano! Why indeed?" He let the question hang. The chamber was so quiet Conrad could hear the generator hum of the engines, or at least she assumed that's what it was.

"The answer is that I have been lied to so many times by the American government in their search for the *next* ultimate weapon that I had lost faith in *any* of their promises of self-restraint, and my father had firmly established the Kammlerorg's philosophy of operation—dangerous technical knowledge must be treated like a cancer and eradicated. No other approach provides satisfactory results."

Pugliano's face screwed up with rage. "Who gave your…*organization* the power over life and death anyway?"

"The same power that makes the American military the most feared force since the armies of the Third Reich. The same power that makes the FBI the preeminent law enforcement organization on the planet. *Money*. Without my superiors' wealth, the United States and most of the industrialized world would wither like a leaf in the drought. *That* is what gives us the right to deny you the opportunity to destroy yourselves, by force if necessary. We simply have too much invested in the system to allow it to fail."

Pugliano fumed in silence.

"So, Miss Conrad, when I realized that you might actually pull off your plan to steal the nanoagent, I was happy to clear away some of your obstacles, such as having Mr. Graves packaging the nanoagent for easy pick up. The termination of the Nanovex scientists also distracted the government and gave you some room to maneuver. But in the end, it was *your* skills and resilience that would carry the day, or not, although I was ready to come to your aid if your failure meant losing the nanoagent. To my astonishment, you succeeded without the slightest help from me."

His eyebrows lifted. "I was so impressed that I allowed Mr. Sabakov to stage his ambush at the auction, mostly to eliminate the criminals surrounding you at that point. I also viewed it as a final exam of sorts. Once you survived the best-laid traps of Mr. Sabakov *and* Mr. Pugliano, and I decided to call an end to the evaluation."

It angered her that she was some sort of plaything for him. "An evaluation for *what*?" she demanded.

He regarded her with amazement, as if the truth were obvious. "Why, to succeed me, of course."

They all contemplated the sound of the engines for several seconds.

"I-I'm sorry," she stammered. "I must have misunderstood."

Crane smiled. "No misunderstanding, my dear. After considering Messieurs LaCroix, Eitan, and Sabakov to replace me in the Kammler Organization, I have decided—partly through process of elimination, of course—that you are the obvious choice. You have the perfect mixture of brilliance, audacity, and ruthlessness to fill my shoes."

She drew back reflexively, only to bump her head against the chamber wall. "Replace you? Why?" To her, the idea that anyone would voluntarily walk away from this kind of power was inconceivable. He looked in his early sixties. Meir Eitan had been over seventy and never breathed a word about retirement. Most of the truly dedicated old intelligence warhorses only left involuntarily, when pushed out from above or below.

He crossed his arms and looked down. "I must confess, Miss Conrad, I am not as great a man as my father. He could sign a person's death warrant, or even perform the execution himself, then retire to sleep like a baby. I admit I am made from weaker steel. Too much of my mother's influence, I'm afraid. For while I gladly accepted this trust from my father and have never failed to faithfully discharge my duties, the burden has not rested as easily on my shoulders as it did on his."

"I think it's called a conscience," Pugliano interrupted.

Crane nodded, granting his point. "Nevertheless, it is a weakness Miss Conrad does not share. She has the perfect sociopathy for this position. She knows precisely the proper parameters of human behavior for any given situation, but is not the slightest bit constrained by that knowledge. In a way, my dear, I envy you."

At that point Sabakov could hold his peace no longer. He burst forth in a stream of Russian, which Vasily interpreted.

"Surely sir," Vasily implored, "you can not be serious about trusting such power to a...*madwoman* like Conrad." Vasily glanced nervously between her and his boss. She was pretty sure Vasily had substituted *madwoman* for a stronger term used by Sabakov.

Crane's demure manner dissolved. "I have no problem with killing," he snapped, "as long as it is focused on the mission at hand. Your ambush on the auction was nothing of the sort. It was wanton slaughter by a poor loser, and you *still* failed to achieve your objective. Unforgivable."

Crane pulled a small device from his pocket. It resembled a car's keyless entry fob, except it was silver. He pointed it at the portal on the floor, which opened. He then pointed it at the Russian.

"Mr. Sabakov, please stand, and walk to the portal."

Like a marionette lifted by its strings, Sabakov rose and stepped haltingly to the edge of the abyss, his eyes wide with terror. His mouth moved as if trying to emit a cry of alarm, but no sound came out.

Crane didn't even have to speak in Russian, Conrad observed. *Sabakov's mind knew what Crane wanted, and was powerless to refuse him. Amazing.*

"I'm ashamed to have even considered you as my replacement, Mr. Sabakov. Please leave us."

Shaking with the effort to stop himself, Sabakov took two more steps and fell toward earth. *The device must have a line of sight limitation*, she theorized. *He started screaming as soon as Crane's key fob wasn't pointed directly at him*. The screams continued for several seconds then abruptly stopped.

With another flick of his device, the portal closed. Crane took a deep breath. "Ah, I feel better about present company already. Mr. Sabakov was a blessed subtraction."

I like this guy, Conrad decided. *He's got style.*

Crane smiled at her. "Now, let's talk about your new position, shall we?"

"You're assuming I'm interested in taking your place," she countered. Actually, she had an almost sexual fascination with the offer he dangled, but she wasn't about to weaken her bargaining position by showing it. "You've just taken the fruits of an operation I've invested *everything* into and it doesn't look like you're going to pay me a dime for it."

Crane's eyes narrowed with a sly glint. "You're not in it for the money, Miss Conrad. You're in it for the *power*. You hold the power of life and death, and you like it. I'm offering you Power unlike anything you've ever dreamt of. I fear no man. I fear no government. I fear only what's inside the vaults of the Kammlerorg. And you'll wield this Power for the good of mankind, not for your own selfish motives or for some mobster boss on the other side of the planet."

"You still haven't told me how much it pays."

He closed his eyes and shook his head, as if disappointed with a slow student. "Miss Conrad, you misunderstand. You won't be paid a salary, as such. I will simply hand you the checkbook of the Kammlerorg. If you wish to pay off whatever debts you've accumulated, you will simply write a check. If you wish to buy a new house, you will write a check. If you decide you need a new executive jet to perform your duties, again, a *check*. Your checks will never bounce, and the account will never run dry. Of that you have my word."

Wow, this guy has been out of the loop for a while—who writes checks anymore? "You've just met me, and you're handing me your checkbook? No offense, but you don't strike me as the trusting type."

Crane laughed so hard he had a coughing fit. "My dear," he gasped, "you are a breath of fresh air! No one has dared address me with such candor in years. To your point, there may be an occasional *audit* to assure that the Group's funds are being spent prudently, but as far as your personal fiduciary desires, you will soon find yourself so busy that you won't be able to spend the money you have. But the money is not the true reward of this position—it is the work itself, as you will soon find out."

* * *

Pugliano was trapped in an insane dream. Or a nightmare. Crane was taunting him with the coronation of this psychopath Conrad, and he was tired of it.

"Excuse me," he scathed, "but if you're going to hand *her* the keys to your organization, I think I'd rather follow Oleg Sabakov to the ground. So if that's what you have in mind for the rest of us, I'd appreciate it if you'd just get on with it."

"Agent Pugliano," he said in astonishment, "if you would *prefer* to leave us, I'll be happy to open the door. But wouldn't you rather be Director of the FBI?"

The question hit him so unexpectedly he merely blinked. "What does that have to do with anything?" he finally managed.

"Everything, actually. Now that you know how the system *really* works, and the FBI's *true* place in the food chain, you are in a unique position to keep your organization out of trouble when our purposes cross. If you can live with that, I see no problem with you rising to Director five years or so from now. I can even see you presiding over the FBI for many years like J. Edgar Hoover, watching presidents come and go, while your power remains unchallenged for as long as you wish to hold it."

"And *you* can make that happen?" He realized the stupidity of the question even as he asked it.

Crane knew it as well, and ignored him. "I'm not asking you to *approve* of my appointment of Miss Conrad, merely to tolerate it and continue doing your job, with the understanding that someday Miss Conrad *will* call, and when she does she will speak with *my* authority. And please don't concern yourself over her trying to take over the world with her new found power. Like myself, she will have oversight, and they guard their supremacy quite jealously."

As far as offers you can't refuse, it could be a hell of a lot worse. "Better than following Oleg to the ground, I suppose."

"Splendid! I'll take that as a yes." He raised an eyebrow at Conrad. "And I would like *you* to resist any temptation to taunt Mr. Pugliano in the future, my dear. He was vectoring fighter jets to your position when I intervened. Had I not done so, you would be quite dead by now. Is that understood?"

"Yes sir," she said, casting down her gaze in feigned submission.

The way Conrad had the old man wrapped around her finger made him want to vomit. *Director Pugliano, Director Pugliano*, he kept repeating to himself.

* * *

Crane turned to Vasily. "Vasily Ivanovitch Orlov," he said formally. "To you I make the same offer as Mr. Pugliano. Now that Mr. Sabakov is dead, there is an opening to head Russia's covert US operations. I would very much like to see you fill that vacancy."

Vasily nodded respectfully. "I would be honored, sir."

"Excellent. Then in a few years I expect Russia's entire Foreign Intelligence Service will be in more capable and knowledgeable hands than it is at present."

Conrad watched Crane's eyes bore into her again. "And now it is time for your first assignment, Miss Conrad." He pushed a pistol toward her with his foot. "Mr. Lyman here is an honorable man, but he is also the last person with firsthand knowledge of the WICKER BASKET project. I need you to exercise final security on my behalf."

If he viewed this as another test, she certainly did not. She scooped up the pistol, chambered a round, and leveled it at Lyman. Then she *did* hesitate. "I'm concerned about pass through," she cautioned. "God knows where the bullet will end up."

"Not your concern. Complete the assignment."

Okay, I warned you. She aimed the gun at Lyman's sternum to maximize the bullet-stopping mass and pulled the trigger.

Click.

Crane smiled. "I'm sorry my dear, another test—of loyalty this time. I had to know what you would do with a loaded, albeit non-functional, weapon." He reached inside his coat and withdrew a small silver pistol. "Here, take mine," he said, tossing it to her.

The diminutive gun was the size of a Walther PPK, but made of featureless silver. No slide, no safety, no markings. It looked much more fake than the gun that had just failed to fire. "How does *this* work?" she demanded.

"Just aim and pull the trigger." He turned to Lyman. "Nothing personal sir, you have served your country well. But your secrets must die with you." Lyman swallowed hard, but to his credit showed no other emotion.

Conrad did as she was told, aiming the gun at Lyman's chest and pulling the trigger. The gun made no sound and gave no indication of having fired, but a blue lightning bolt arced from Lyman's back to the wall. He let out a single groan and fell to the side, limp.

She wondered whether to fire again. "Is he…?"

"Dead? Yes, quite." He motioned to Shiva and Manning, sitting to either side of her. "Now, about your companions—"

* * *

Manning watched in horror as the whole scene played out. He almost cried out in protest when Crane ordered Lyman shot. He had felt guilty enough spying on the man for Conrad. Watching her kill him in cold blood was almost unbearable. He kept silent, hoping that silence might buy him a reprieve, but knowing that if this high-tech madman had selected Conrad as his successor, he was as good as dead already.

Conrad rose to her feet, nodding toward Shiva. "This one is useful. I'd like to keep him on my team." She pointed the gun at Manning. "This one is not. Shall I kill him now?"

Manning had died so many times over the last few hours he finally had become philosophical about it, achieving the peace in death for which Vasily had urged him to strive. He gave Conrad his best death stare, hoping that the lightning gun was as quick and painless as it appeared to be.

Crane made a clucking sound with his tongue. "Now, now," he soothed, "you should be more careful about wasting your resources. This man is a trained cleanup agent. I think you will find him very useful."

Alive but working for Angela Conrad. "I think I'd rather be shot," he heard himself say. The conviction with which he made the statement shocked his own ears.

"No, you wouldn't," Crane answered firmly. "You've done well enough cleaning up the messes of corporations for no better excuse than money. *Now* you'll be serving mankind, and you'll get the money too. You may even develop a taste for the power, I know I have. It's quite addictive. But my time is passed, and I need to confer this power to a new generation while I'm still able to do so. The secrets I possess are too potent to leave in any but the most capable hands. Will you join me, sir?"

Manning was too stunned to answer.

"Oh!" Crane exclaimed, reaching inside his jacket and extracting a small silver plate. "I almost forgot. I have another reason for you to consider my offer." He walked over and handed it to Manning. It was a small video screen, but unlike any smartphone he had seen. The video quality was so sharp it was disorienting, like the plate was a window into the real world. The screen showed a police cruiser with its lights flashing on a darkened street. The camera zoomed in and showed a woman gesticulating wildly to the policeman emerging from his patrol car. The camera zoomed in further.

It was Amanda.

He sucked in a startled breath. The officer hurriedly motioned her and the boys into the back seat of the vehicle. He jumped back into the cruiser and sped away. The camera must have been mounted on a helicopter, because it followed the patrol car from above and behind without wavering.

"Your wife and children are safe, rescued by my agents in Chicago. They are almost to the nearest police station, where they will wait to be reunited with you. You can talk with them shortly. But first, I need your answer. I know your history with Miss Conrad has been, *strained.* But can you move past that and work together in the future? Consider it the repayment of your debt for the rescue of your family."

Manning felt his muscles go slack with relief. *Amanda and the boys safe.* Considering that he had been all too willing to die to buy them even a *chance* of survival....

"I'll do it," he heard himself say, again surprising his ears when he uttered the statement without conscious thought.

Crane took back the video plate. "Excellent, I am so pleased." He looked about the chamber at all present. "This has been an exceptional meeting, thank you all for your kind attention. Mr. Pugliano, I will drop you off first. I think you will find a traitorous CIA agent in the front seat of Miss Conrad's helicopter in need of hospitalization and incarceration. Would you see to that for me, please?"

Pugliano managed to work up a smile. "My pleasure."

He turned to Vasily. "Mr. Orlov, I can drop you off in the country of your choice. Please consider your cover story of how you were the sole survivor of Mr. Sabakov's party and how you made your escape from American soil. I will do my best to assist you."

Vasily bowed his head to Crane. "I am in your debt."

A few minutes later Crane waved the portal open again. This time grass was visible a few inches below the opening. He waved Pugliano toward it.

"This is where we say our good-byes, Agent Pugliano. It was a pleasure making your acquaintance."

Pugliano stepped down onto the ground. "Likewise," he said uneasily.

With a wave of Crane's hand the ship rose. Pugliano appeared to drop through and disappear. The portal closed.

Crane waved his key fob toward what Manning guessed was the front of the craft. "There, we are now on our way to Chicago. Mr. Manning, I will drop you off and my agents will drive you to meet your wife and family."

* * *

After what only seemed like a few minutes, Conrad watched Manning step to the ground and disappear just like Pugliano. *God, I can't wait to see the cockpit of this bird*, she thought. She imagined Shiva was even more excited at the prospect.

"I thought you might continue to find Mr. Wu's organization in Chicago useful," Crane explained, "so I spared as many of them as I could, with the exception of one particularly loathsome brute, whom I could not abide."

"I appreciate the gesture. They've proven quite reliable."

"And after we drop off Mr. Orlov, I would like you and Shiva to accompany me to my headquarters in Zurich. Would that be agreeable?"

Ah, Zurich, she thought. *Good food. Great spas. I need a massage, followed by about a three-day sleep*. "That sounds wonderful."

He waved his device, setting the ship once again in motion. "So one more stop, then back to work for both of us. I must say, my spirits are quite buoyed by the prospect."

Back to work. Her head still swam with the enormity of it all. Her premonition that Fate was about to deal her an unexpected hand had been dead on, especially the unexpected part. She wasn't naïve enough to believe that *all* her problems had just been solved, but like Crane, her spirits were certainly buoyed by the prospects.

"Yes, back to work," she agreed.

EPILOGUE

THREE MONTHS LATER – CHICAGO, ILLINOIS

Manning turned in his chair and looked out over Lake Michigan from the Kammlerorg's palatial offices in the Willis Tower. He had to admit, his thoughts were almost as serene as the sailboats gently plying the sun-sparkled waters below him. It was a frame of mind he never thought he would experience again, and certainly not while working for Angela Conrad.

But here he was. The money certainly helped, as did the stability of knowing he had a job for life as long as he didn't monumentally screw up. And with Conrad looking over his shoulder, sloppiness was not likely. But deeper than the pay and permanence his position offered, the biggest change from his ordeal at Nanovex had been between his own two ears. After being forced to choose between his life and those of his wife and children, he was suddenly much less likely to ignore them as he rushed about his business. Amanda seemed changed by her trial as well, although they would *all* be seeing a Kammlerorg-provided therapist for the foreseeable future, both individually and as a family. A phone call startled him out of his reverie. It was Amanda.

"Hi hon, what's up?"

"How did she *know?*" Amanda bubbled. "Did *you* tell her?"

He was clueless. "About what?"

"About the shoes! Angela just sent me a pair of Christian Louboutin shoes I've been lusting after! How did she *know*? I just saw them in the store and they're all I've been thinking about for a week and here they are! They're even the right size! Angela is the right name for her—she *is* an angel!"

"Wow, that's great," he said absently.

"Mike, what's wrong?"

He quickly corrected himself. "Nothing! That's wonderful—I'll be sure and let her know you liked them."

"Mike," she whispered, "those are *two thousand dollar* shoes! Does she *really* have money to throw around like that?"

He laughed. "Have you seen the Lamborghini she drives?"

Amanda sighed contentedly. "Fair enough. Mike, don't you even *think* of leaving to work anywhere else! Promise me!"

Manning thought of the fate that awaited him at Conrad's hands should he ever be stupid enough to express a desire to leave the Kammlerorg. "That's a promise. Uh-oh, here's the boss, gotta go. Love ya!"

Conrad stood at his office door. "Okay, I'm on my way to Hong Kong."

"How was your meeting with the President?"

She shook her head. "I thought the poor man was going to wet himself when Crane introduced me. He didn't even use an alias—he just blurted out my real name, right there in the Oval Office."

"I guess your reputation precedes you. But why the hell did he do that?" The Kammlerorg took the protection of their real identities very seriously.

She shrugged. "I think he was just rubbing it in. The Old Man has quite the sense of irony."

Manning made a sweeping gesture at his surroundings. "Irony? No!"

She chuckled. "Point taken."

"Oh, by the way, please stop reading my wife's mind, or at least give me one of those remote control thingees so I can do it too."

She made a face. "Don't be such a *mensch*, I was just practicing! Wouldn't want me to make a mistake in the field and tell the wrong guy to blow his own head off, would you? And your wife gets a new pair of shoes in the bargain." She handed over a folder. "Speaking of field work, you're about to go visit an inventor in California. He's nibbling a little too close to zero point energy. You need to ask him to invent something else."

He thumbed through the file, which was breathtaking in its scope and depth, as usual. "Incentives?" he asked.

"Standard package. One million or his picture on the back of a milk carton. Go as high as five if you have to, my people are really busy cleaning up the Nanovex mess. Oh, and if he starts babbling about the good of humanity *yada yada*, just show him the pictures in the back."

He kept thumbing until he reached several perfectly focused color photos of a woman *in flagrante delicto* with two men. His eyebrows rose.

"My, she's certainly…*limber*," he observed. "Where did you get these?"

"Never you mind that. Just tell him we can make her go away and arrange for uncontested custody of his three kids. I've met some men who couldn't be bought, but not one who wouldn't sell his soul to see his ex-wife's head on a stick."

He whistled. "Remind me to never cross you."

Shiva stepped to the door. "Miss Conrad? Mr. Manning? My helicopter is ready to take you to the airport. Both of your jets are standing by."

She smiled. "Thanks, Shiva. Hey, how are your lessons coming in Mr. Crane's triangle?"

He beamed. "Oh, *so* much easier to fly than a helicopter! And the speed—incredible!"

"Wish he would let *me* travel in that thing," she grumbled. "I could be to Hong Kong and be back in time for dinner tonight. Oh, and Mike, about crossing me…." She pulled a small silver device from her jacket.

Manning's hand flew up and slapped himself in the face, hard enough to sting.

"Consider yourself reminded," she said with a smirk. "Let's go, we've got work to do."

THE END

CPSIA information can be obtained at www.ICGtesting.com
Printed in the USA
LVOW081327160712

290227LV00002B/1/P